Praise for the novels of Kate Forsyth

The Tower of Ravens

"By the time you've finished, I guarantee you will say that this is one of the best fantasy reads ever. . . . A fantasy novel that will transport us into the realms of imagination."
—*Armidale Express* (Australia)

"A rich, enthralling ride across the pages of fantasy."
—FreshFiction.com

The Witches of Eileanan series

"A trilogy like the kind that made me fall in love with fantasy in the first place."
—SF Site

"An entertaining, old-fashioned adventure."
—*Locus*

"In the tradition of Anne McCaffrey and Marion Zimmer Bradley . . . a satisfying read."
—*Bundaberg NewsMail* (Australia)

"Kate Forsyth has woven a stirring epic fantasy, a marvelously rambling tale of outlawed witches, ruling-class conspiracy, blossoming occult talent, and strange and wonderful creatures. . . . A worthy first novel from a writer with a sound streak of both imagination and talent."
—*dB Magazine* (Australia)

"Superb! A rich, vividly described world peopled with such complex characters."
—*Australian SF News*

"A rich fantasy novel with a great cast of characters."
—*New Englander-Armidale* (Australia)

"A remarkable fantasy debut...it sings with quality."
—*The West Australian*

"Forsyth . . . writes with aplomb and style."
—*The Examiner* (Australia)

ALSO BY KATE FORSYTH

RHIANNON'S RIDE

The Tower of Ravens

THE WITCHES OF EILEANAN SERIES

The Witches of Eileanan
The Pool of Two Moons
The Cursed Towers
The Forbidden Land
The Skull of the World
The Fathomless Caves

THE SHINING CITY

BOOK TWO OF RHIANNON'S RIDE

Kate Forsyth

A ROC BOOK

ROC
Published by New American Library, a division of
Penguin Group (USA) Inc., 375 Hudson Street,
New York, New York 10014, USA
Penguin Group (Canada), 90 Eglinton Avenue East, Suite 700, Toronto,
Ontario M4P 2Y3, Canada (a division of Pearson Penguin Canada Inc.)
Penguin Books Ltd., 80 Strand, London WC2R 0RL, England
Penguin Ireland, 25 St. Stephen's Green, Dublin 2,
Ireland (a division of Penguin Books Ltd.)
Penguin Group (Australia), 250 Camberwell Road, Camberwell, Victoria 3124,
Australia (a division of Pearson Australia Group Pty. Ltd.)
Penguin Books India Pvt. Ltd., 11 Community Centre, Panchsheel Park,
New Delhi - 110 017, India
Penguin Group (NZ), cnr Airborne and Rosedale Roads, Albany,
Auckland 1310, New Zealand (a division of Pearson New Zealand Ltd.)
Penguin Books (South Africa) (Pty.) Ltd., 24 Sturdee Avenue,
Rosebank, Johannesburg 2196, South Africa

Penguin Books Ltd., Registered Offices:
80 Strand, London WC2R 0RL, England

First published by Roc, an imprint of New American Library,
a division of Penguin Group (USA) Inc.

First Printing, April 2006
10 9 8 7 6 5 4 3 2 1

Copyright © Kate Forsyth, 2006
All rights reserved

 REGISTERED TRADEMARK—MARCA REGISTRADA

Printed in the United States of America

To my three beautiful children,
Benjamin, Timothy and Eleanor

VISIONS OF THE NIGHT

"In thoughts from the visions of the night, when deep sleep falleth on men, fear came upon me, and trembling, which made all my bones to shake."

—JOB,
chapter 4, verses 13–14

Dark Wings

Olwynne sat up in her bed, choking back a scream. For a moment her nightmare beat around her head with dark, suffocating wings. Then the dream dissolved away, leaving her with little more than an impression of overwhelming grief and horror.

The air was cold on her damp skin, and she pulled her eiderdown up around her, grasping reluctantly at the tattered remains of the nightmare. Her aunt Isabeau said she should pay attention to her dreams, for they were often messages sent to warn or illuminate. All Olwynne could remember, though, was her father falling away from her into some deep pit, his black wings bent over his face, and then hundreds of ravens, an unkindness of ravens, plummeting from the sky to peck out her eyes.

She shuddered and curled her knees to her chest. The wind was keening around her windows, rattling the old leaded glass in its frames, and sighing through the trees outside. It sounded like banshees wailing. Olwynne told herself it was only the wind, but still all the hairs on her body stood erect and quivering, and her pulse rate accelerated. Such a feeling of morbid foreboding came over her that she almost cried out again, but she bit her lip and wrapped her arms about her knees, her face pressed into her pillow. Still the strange, high wailing went on. As it grew louder, Olwynne realized that it was not the wind making that unearthly keening cry but something else. Something living.

Shivering uncontrollably, Olwynne crept out of bed and went to stand by her window, pulling the curtain back a crack so she could peer out. It was a clear, starry night, with both the moons at the full. The sky was full of flying things, a whirling hurricane of bat-winged creatures that seemed to beat against the bright coins of the moons like moths against the glass of a lantern. Tall as the tallest of men, their limbs were like twigs and their tempestuous hair flowed and swirled like wind made visible. As they hurled themselves through the night sky, they screamed and sobbed, tearing at their wild manes of hair, beating themselves on their heads and breasts.

Olwynne stood transfixed. She had seen the nyx fly before, on nights when the moons were full, but never before had she seen so many, and never had she heard them sing. It was a lament of such wild grief that Olwynne felt tears start to her own eyes and her breath catch in her throat. Though she did not know why the nyx sorrowed, Olwynne slowly slid down to the floor and wept with them.

By the time the night had drained away, the grey walls and flying buttresses of the Tower of Two Moons rising from the darkness, the nyx had all gone. Olwynne released her clutch on the curtains and stood up stiffly.

She was very cold. She dressed herself in the long black gown of an apprentice-witch, then splashed her face vigorously with water. She combed back her sleep-tossed hair into its usual long, severe plait and wrapped her plaid tightly about her body. Still she felt cold and stiff and weary, but she had been taught to ignore the demands of her body. She opened the door to her little cell of a room and stepped out onto the balcony that ran the length of the building. Everything was deathly quiet. It was too early for the bell to have sounded to wake up the students. Only the occasional bird called out.

Olwynne went swiftly along the balcony and through a doorway into the Theurgia. She negotiated a number of stairs and corridors, coming at last to the northernmost tower, the building assigned to the Circle of Sorcerers. A magnificent spiral staircase wound up the center of the tower, its stonework carved with the crescent shape of two moons and a single star, set amidst intricate knot-work. Olwynne climbed the staircase all the way to the top floor, her feet settling into deep hollows worn in the center of each step. Her aunt Isabeau had her rooms up here, far away from the noise and bustle of the Theurgia.

Olwynne stood for a while outside her aunt's door, listening. Although she was sure Isabeau would be awake, she hesitated to interrupt her. It was very early. Just as she raised her hand to knock, the door opened and Isabeau stood in the doorway, smiling at her.

"Morning, Olwynne," she said. "Come in. The kettle is just boiling. Would ye like some tea?"

Olwynne nodded and came in shyly. She looked about her with pleasure as Isabeau went and swung the steaming kettle off the fire. She loved the Keybearer's room. Shaped like a crescent moon, it took up half the top floor of the tower. There was a fireplace at either end, one to warm the bed with its soft white counterpane and pillows, the other warming Isabeau's desk and chair where she worked. Comfortable chairs with deep blue cushions were drawn up before both fires. A spinning wheel was set up near one, with a little loom pushed up against the wall. A tapestry was half-woven upon it. Olwynne could see the pointed towers of Rhyssmadill overlooking a stormy sea and wondered what Isabeau was weaving. Olwynne knew her aunt loved to spin and weave the old tales and songs, but had little time for it with all her other duties as Keybearer of the Coven.

At the other end of the room, where Isabeau was busy making the peppermint tea, her desk was piled with papers and books. An old globe, so stained with age the lands upon it could hardly be seen, stood upon a wooden stand nearby. A crystal ball glowed softly to one side, set upon clawed feet. More books filled the bookshelves that rose from floor to ceiling all around the curve of the room. Set at regular intervals between the bookshelves were tall windows that looked out across the gardens to the golden domes of the palace, gleaming softly through the morning mist.

The Keybearer was dressed in her long white gown trimmed with silver, and her hair was neatly combed and bound away from her face. Once Isabeau's hair would have been the same fiery red as Olwynne's, but its color had faded to a soft strawberry blond, with grey at the temples. Her eyes were as vivid a blue as ever, however, and her figure was slim and upright.

Isabeau poured the tea into two delicate bone china cups and beckoned to Olwynne to sit by the fire. Olwynne obeyed with alacrity, for she was still cold and shaken. She held the cup between both her hands and sipped the hot liquid, feeling some of her tension drain away.

"Ye heard the nyx fly?" Isabeau said tranquilly.

Olwynne nodded.

"Aye, it was uncanny, was it no'? I have never heard such a lament. It made all my skin come up in goose bumps."

"Me too," Olwynne said eagerly. "Auntie Beau . . . what was wrong? Why did they sing like that?"

"Ceit Anna is dead," Isabeau said after a moment, her face shadowing.

Olwynne lowered her cup. Although she knew of the oldest and most powerful of the nyx, who had lived in a cave deep under the sewers of the palace, she herself had never seen the ancient faery. Stories were always told of her, though. Ceit Anna had woven the cloak of illusions that had kept Olwynne's father, Lachlan the Winged, hidden in the shape of a hunchback for so many years. She had woven the cloak from her own hair, as she had woven a pair of gloves to conceal the magical hands of Tòmas the Healer, and as she had woven the choker that kept Maya the Ensorcellor mute and powerless. Ceit Anna appeared in many of the MacCuinn clan's stories, and Olwynne knew she would be greatly missed.

"The nyx live very long lives," Isabeau said. "I certainly have never heard the death flight afore, and I ken none who have. I was just reading about it in *The Book o' Shadows*." She indicated the old and enormously thick book that lay open on her desk nearby. "The last time one was recorded was during the time o' Feargus the Terrible, when Aldus the Dreamy was Keybearer. O' course, we ken many nyx died during the Burning, but if the death flight was flown, there was certainly no one around to record it."

Olwynne was silent.

Isabeau looked at her intently, then bent forward to lay her right hand on Olwynne's knee. The other hand, her crippled one, was kept tucked in her lap. "What is troubling ye so much, my dear? Is it just the funeral song o' the nyx or is there more?"

Olwynne shrugged and looked away, embarrassed her aunt could read her so clearly.

"Are ye still having those nightmares?" Isabeau asked.

Olwynne nodded, fiddling with her cup. "Last night I was attacked by a flock o' ravens, hundreds o' them, beating all around my head and trying to peck out my eyes."

"Ravens," Isabeau repeated, her brows drawing together.

Olwynne nodded. "I thought at first, when I saw the nyx flying last night, that it was their wings I had dreamed, all those black wings against the moon. And it seemed I had dreamed that too, only . . . it is so hard to remember. For there are other wings in my dreams. My father's wings. And Donncan's too, turning all black like *Dai-dein*'s. A dark shadow falling on him, like the shadow o' wings . . . or happen a black cloak . . . or a shroud. Sometimes I'm being suffocated by feathers. Or maybe I'm buried alive, in a tomb. Or Donncan is—I canna always tell. It doesna make sense. And I wake with this horrible sense o' foreboding, like something awful is going to happen, and happen soon. . . ." Her voice trailed away.

"Can ye remember anything else?"

"*Dai-dein* falling into a dark pit . . . just falling . . . though sometimes it is me falling . . . or Bronwen. I dream o' Bronwen too." Olwynne's voice quickened. "I dreamed o' her diving off a high cliff and falling too, falling hundreds o' feet. And she was crying, I'm sure o' it. A waterfall o' tears. And I dream o' her and Donncan drowning in a great pool o' blackness, like ink spreading in water."

Isabeau's frown deepened. "I have dreamed o' ravens also," she said at last. "Though I ken o' disturbing news from Raven-shaw, which could well have fed into my dreams, while ye have no'. I think your dreams may be prophetic, though I fear what they foretell."

"What news from Ravenshaw?" Olwynne asked. Her voice rose. "News o' Lewen? Is all well?"

Isabeau smoothed the snowy folds of her gown over her knee. "Lewen is well. He is on his way back to Lucescere. I expect him any day now."

"But he is connected to your dreams o' ravens somehow, is he no'?" Olwynne demanded. "What is wrong?"

Isabeau smiled ruefully. "Ye have guessed it. Lewen is very

much involved in these happenings in Ravenshaw, and he has been much on my mind as a consequence. I may as well tell ye. The tattlemongers will have the news soon enough anyway."

"Tell me what?"

"Lewen was to travel back to Lucescere with Nina and her caravan, as ye ken. On their journey they somehow stumbled on a plot to raise the ghost o' the dead laird o' Fettercairn, which you may remember is the castle that guards the way to the Tower o' Ravens. Some necromancers were using the Heart o' Stars at the tower to open a gate between this world and the world o' spirits, and it seems they have raised a stronger spirit than they meant to. Nina scryed to me a few days ago, to tell me when they would be arriving, but although she was able to tell me most of the story, I am naturally eager to question Lewen and this lass who actually saw the necromancers—"

"Lass?"

Isabeau glanced at Olwynne. "Aye, some lass from the Broken Ring o' Dubhslain. She is named Rhiannon, I believe, and she rides a black winged horse."

"More black wings," Olwynne said hollowly. "Is it her coming that I foretell?" She pressed the heels of her hands into her eyes.

"I do no' ken," Isabeau said, sounding troubled. "Olwynne, how long have these nightmares been haunting ye?"

She shrugged irritably. "I dinna ken. It feels like forever."

"Ye first spoke to me about a dark dream on the night o' the spring equinox. Was that the first such dream?"

Olwynne moved jerkily. "I dinna remember. Happen so."

"Your floor mistress tells me ye have woken several times screaming in your sleep since then. How often do the dreams come, Olwynne?"

"Every night," Olwynne answered wearily. "I have tried no' to sleep, but I'm always too tired and fall asleep anyway. I've tried taking powdered valerian roots and drinking chamomile tea to help me sleep more deeply, but it doesna work. It just makes things worse, for I canna wake myself when the dream gets too bad, and when I finally do wake, I'm groggy and sick."

"I can close your third eye for ye," Isabeau said gently. "At least for a night or two, to help ye rest. Ye look exhausted, Olwynne, and they tell me your schoolwork is suffering."

Olwynne gazed at her aunt in dumb wonder. She could not believe her aunt knew so much about her when Isabeau was so busy with the work of the Coven. Olwynne's own mother did not know about the nightmares. She thought about what the Keybearer had offered and, after a moment, reluctantly shook her head. "Ye say such dreams are sent as warnings, or messages. Should I no' listen and try to understand?"

Isabeau nodded. "Aye, under normal circumstances. But ye are still only an apprentice-witch, Olwynne, and ye have had a month o' it now. I worry about your health and your schooling. Ye have been doing so well, I do no' want ye to fall behind."

"It comes soon," Olwynne said. "Whatever it is will happen soon."

There was a long silence. Then Isabeau stood up, her hand going up to grip the Key that hung on a ribbon around her neck. "Then happen we should try to find out more while we can," she said forcefully. "When Ghislaine Dream-Walker returns from Aslinn, I will ask her to see if she can travel the dream-road with ye. I'm sorry, I should have thought to check on you weeks ago. It is just we have been so very busy."

Olwynne knew everyone was preoccupied with her older brother Donncan's upcoming wedding to their cousin Bronwen, daughter of Maya the Ensorcellor. Olwynne had not thought she had minded their distraction, but at Isabeau's words she felt the knot of tension behind her breastbone loosen. She muttered thanks, hoping Isabeau's witch-senses would understand just how grateful she was.

"Now I think ye should go back to bed for a while. I'll write a pass for ye, excusing ye from the morning's classes. Then a walk in the fresh air and a proper lunch will do ye the most good, I think. Come, I'll walk ye back to your room."

"Och, there's no need. I'm fine, really," Olwynne gabbled, ashamed that she was trespassing on her aunt's good nature.

"It's no trouble. I wish to walk through the library anyway, and it's on the way. I'll be glad o' your company."

Olwynne smiled shyly and stood up, putting her cup down on the little table. Isabeau went to her desk and shut *The Book of Shadows* reverently, then called to her familiar, the elf-owl Buba, who slept on the back of the chair with her head sunk down into her wings. *Comehooh with me-hooh?* Isabeau said in owl language. Buba opened her eyes sleepily, stared at Isabeau a moment, then flew to perch on her shoulder. She was tiny, no bigger than a sparrow, and white as snow.

Why-hooh you-hooh frown-hooh? Buba said, rotating her head around so she could stare unnervingly at Olwynne.

I fear-hooh, but what-hooh, I know not-hooh, Isabeau answered.

She did look troubled, Olwynne thought, as she followed Isabeau out of her room and down the stairs. The Keybearer's face was pale and strained, and the frown between her brows had not smoothed away. She kept her right hand cupped around the talisman she wore at her neck, almost as if drawing strength from it. As they approached the library, which took up all of the great building between the northern and eastern towers, her pace quickened noticeably.

They went into the long, dark room together. The lanterns sprang into life at once, and the kindling laid ready in the fireplaces at either end blazed up into dancing warmth. Olwynne glanced at her aunt enviously, wishing she had such a ready facility with flame. Her strengths were in the elements of water and earth, not fire, and she had to concentrate hard to light a candle or bring witch-light. Isabeau had not even flickered an eyelid, let alone waved a finger, all her attention focused on the glass cabinets lined up against the walls in little alcoves surrounded by towering bookshelves.

These cabinets were used to display old relics and artifacts that might interest the students or help them in their lessons. There were ancient scrolls, fragile as skin, old maps of other lands and other worlds, suits of armour, famous weapons and jewels, a clàrsach that was said to have belonged to Seinneadair the Singer, even the cast-off skin of a harlequin hydra, its scaly coils glittering in the light, its hundreds of heads pinned up against the wall.

Isabeau strode straight to a glass cabinet on the far side of the room. She stood there in silence for a long time. Olwynne stood beside her. As far as she could see, the cabinet contained nothing but an old stick. It had not been cleaned for a long time, for the floor of the cabinet was thick with dust.

"What is it? What's wrong?" Olwynne asked at last, conscious of the tension in her aunt's slim body.

"This cabinet had your father's cloak o' illusions hanging in it," Isabeau said tersely. "That is his crutch. When I first met him, he had naught but the cloak and an auld stick to lean on. no' a stitch o' clothing, nor a knife or bowl—nothing. I gave him my spare pair o' breeches to wear, and much too tight they were for him too."

Olwynne was puzzled. "So where's the cloak now?"

"Gone," Isabeau said. She waved one hand before the cabinet's lock, and a symbol of blue fire flared up for a moment. Olwynne recognized a ward of protection. "No one could have stolen it, for the lock has not been tampered with."

"Where's it gone then?" Olwynne simply could not understand her aunt's tension. Although she knew it had some historical interest, as a relic from the days when her father had been a rebel fighting to overthrow the Ensorcellor, it was nothing but a hairy old cloak that probably smelled horrible. Her father had worn it day in, day out, for years to conceal the wings and claws he had been left with after being transformed from a blackbird back into a man. He had not been able to discard it until he had at last won the throne back from the Ensorcellor, and by that time, Olwynne guessed, he had probably never wanted to see it again.

Isabeau pointed to the pile of black dust on the cabinet floor. "I imagine that's the remains o' the cloak there."

"All that dust? Why, what happened to it?"

"Ceit Anna wove that cloak for your father, Olwynne, from her own hair," Isabeau said impatiently. "It took her seven days and seven nights, and he wore it for seven long years. It was a weaving o' great power. All this time it has hung here, so people could remember the time when one o' the MacCuinn clan had to hide himself beneath a cloak o' illusions to avoid being hunted down and killed. All this time, and now it is dust. Why? Why now?"

Olwynne shrugged. "It's been a long time. It must be twenty-four years or more, for *Dai-dein* won the throne no' long before Donncan was born."

Isabeau turned and pointed to a tiny pink silk dress and cap in another cabinet nearby. "That dress belonged to Meghan o' the Beasts as a child. It is much more than four hundred years auld. Why has it no' dissolved too, then?"

Olwynne's cheeks heated. "I dinna ken."

"Olwynne, have ye forgotten? Ceit Anna died last night. The cloak was hanging there yesterday, yet now it is gone."

"What a shame," Olwynne said. "I suppose ye'll have to find something else for the cabinet now."

Isabeau clicked her tongue in exasperation, and Buba swiveled her head to stare at Olwynne out of her round golden eyes. "Ye have no' considered, lassie. Think! What else did Ceit Anna weave for us that we may regret dissolving?"

Olwynne's eyes widened in horror. "The Ensorcellor's ribbon that binds her throat!"

"Aye! If Maya's powers are returned to her just now, when Bronwen and Donncan are no' yet married, and there is still so much controversy over who truly has the right to rule . . ."

Olwynne felt a cold clutch of fear. Although she saw Maya the Ensorcellor nearly every day—a thin, scarred, middle-aged woman who could communicate only by sign language and the writing of messages on a little slate—Olwynne did not underestimate the power of the onetime ruler of the land. She had been told many dreadful stories of the days of the Burning, when the Coven had been thrown down, its towers destroyed, and witches hunted mercilessly to death all over the country. She knew Maya's powers were so strong and so subtle she had ensorcelled many into doing her bidding and had been able to sway crowds of thousands to her will. Maya had only been controlled by the binding of her tongue to silence. Olwynne could not begin to imagine what might happen if she found that Ensorcellor's tongue again.

Olwynne's father, Lachlan the Winged, had won the throne from Maya after the death of his brother, Maya's husband, Jaspar. The land had been rent by civil war, and everyone had been relieved to have a strong leader occupying the throne. Those who had argued that Jaspar's baby daughter, Bronwen, was by birthright the true heir to the throne had been pacified by her betrothal a few years later to her cousin Donncan, Olwynne's elder brother. If Bronwen had been a meek and biddable girl, the matter might well have ended there.

However, the Ensorcellor's daughter had inherited her mother's imperious will and mysterious charm as well as her wild, fey beauty. In the six months since she had turned twenty-four, the age she would have assumed the throne in her own right, Bronwen had turned the court upside down with her antics. There had been much speculation that the betrothal between the two rival heirs to the throne might fail. Olwynne knew that her parents were angry and concerned, and Donncan furious and miserable, but the implications were far more serious than mere unhappiness within the family. There were those who envied the MacCuinn clan's power, or hated the witches, or passionately believed that Bronwen was the true heir. If the cousins failed to marry, there was a strong chance that civil unrest might again trouble the land. Olwynne could only shudder at the thought of the turmoil that Maya, unbound and vindictive, could cause.

"We had best go and see Maya at once," Isabeau said. "Happen she is still sleeping."

Olwynne nodded. She hurried after Isabeau as the Keybearer strode through the library and across the garth to the servants' wing. Though the other wings remained shuttered and quiet, the clanging of pots and pans, the gurgling of water, and the sound of voices and laughter did not bode well. The witches' servants were used to waking early, for many rites took place at dawn and the witches were always keen for their breakfast afterwards.

Maya had a dark closet of a room on the second story, tucked in behind the stairwell. Olwynne felt no pity for her. Her own room in the southern wing was not much bigger, and she was the Rìgh's daughter. Many doors along the corridor stood open, as serving girls bustled in and out with jugs of hot water or stood in the doorways, gossiping, as they combed back their hair. They all fell silent as Isabeau came past, dropping curtsies and murmuring respectful greetings. Isabeau nodded and smiled at them but hurried on, Olwynne trailing close behind. Behind them rose a hum of curiosity.

Maya's door was shut. Isabeau rapped on it smartly. There was a short silence, then the former Banrìgh opened the door a crack and looked out.

She was dressed, as usual, in a plain black gown, very like the apprentice's robe Olwynne wore, only Maya's was covered with a long white apron. Her greying hair was pinned back under a plain white cap. One side of her face was badly scarred, while the prominent knuckles of the webbed hand holding the door were red and swollen with hard work. She looked old and tired and sad.

"Maya, I'm glad ye're awake," Isabeau said. "I need to speak with ye. May I come in?"

Maya raised an eyebrow.

"I wish to examine your nyx-hair ribbon," Isabeau said bluntly.

With an eloquent gesture, Maya lifted one hand towards the black ribbon bound about her throat.

"I do no' wish to do it standing in the corridor," Isabeau said impatiently. "Why will ye no' let me in?"

Maya shrugged and stood back, allowing Isabeau and Olwynne to step into her room.

"Perhaps because she wishes to retain some illusion o' privacy," a lilting, musical voice said very sweetly.

Bronwen was sitting on the edge of the dressing table, swinging one foot. She was dressed in a short-sleeved linen gown that exactly matched the soft blue of her eyes. She had dispensed with the usual collar of lace, the neckline cut square to show off her white throat and breast. It was not just her flawless skin that Bronwen was revealing. Long fins curved from elbow to wrist, and gills fluttered gently just under her jaw on either side of her neck. Her skin gleamed with subtle silvery scales, as silky as a snake's throat, and her nose was long and highly arched, with flexible nostrils that could clamp tightly shut or flare wide in temper.

Her hair was secured back from her brow with a comb of silver-edged seashells and hung to her knees like a glossy black curtain. One white lock of hair sprang from her brow and wound its way down to the end, startling against the blackness. She was like a column of ice, so cool and sharp was her beauty, and so adamantine her composure.

"Bronwen!" Isabeau exclaimed. "What are ye doing here?"

"Visiting my mother. Or is that no' allowed?"

"At the crack o' dawn?"

"My mother works from sunup to midnight and is rarely allowed any breaks. When else am I to see her?"

"Oh, Bronwen, dinna exaggerate! She is no' a slave! She has

plenty o' free time, like anyone else who works in the service o' the Coven."

"A few hours a week. I happen to wish to see my mother more often than that, and preferably when she is no' exhausted by her work."

"Bronwen, ye ken ye can see your mother whenever ye want," Isabeau said in exasperation. "I would've thought midday a far more civilized time to come calling. Maya has a lunch break, just like anyone else does, and ye could have gone into the gardens and eaten together."

"Och, aye, the gardens at lunchtime. Very private, with five hundred squalling brats running around."

"I'm sure ye o' all people would know where to find a quiet corner," Olwynne said.

Isabeau glanced at her with a slight frown, and she subsided. Bronwen shot Olwynne a sharp-edged look, then smiled, as if deciding to accept the remark as a compliment.

"Maya, I need to look at your ribbon," Isabeau said, turning to Bronwen's mother, who had been standing silently by the wall, her hands folded together, her face impassive.

"Why?" Bronwen cried at once. "What has my poor mother done to warrant this . . . this intrusion?"

"Oh, Bronny, pipe down," Isabeau said. "I just need to make sure all is well. There's no need for these histrionics. It'll only take a moment."

Maya inclined her head, allowing her hands to fall down beside her body. Isabeau led her to sit in the only chair, flame uncurling from the wick of every candle in the room. Even the candlelight failed to alleviate all the shadows in the gloomy little room. With an impatient gesture, Isabeau conjured a ball of light to hang above the mute woman's head, casting a strong steady light upon her. Maya kept her face lowered as Isabeau carefully felt right around the black braid of ribbon bound about her throat. Isabeau was frowning, and Olwynne felt a sudden rise in tension. She glanced at Bronwen, who grimaced at her and stretched out one elegant hand to examine her nails.

Isabeau stood back. "Maya, did aught untoward happen last night?"

Maya looked up at her and shrugged. She lifted the little

slate that hung from her belt and rapidly wrote, "Heard nyx fly
over" with a piece of chalk she carried in her apron pocket.

"The sound woke ye?"

Maya put one hand behind her ear, then folded both hands
and rested her head upon them, closing her eyes.

"But then ye went back to sleep?"

Maya nodded.

"Naught else?"

Maya shook her head.

"Very well. Thank ye. I'm sorry to have intruded upon your
privacy." Isabeau cast a smiling glance at Bronwen, who gave
another expressive grimace and jumped to her feet.

"Let me show ye out," she said sweetly.

"Och, thanks, but I think we can find our way," Isabeau answered. "Come on, Olwynne, ye'll be late to breakfast if ye do
no' hurry. See ye soon," she said to both Maya and Bronwen
with a nod and a little smile, and led the way out of the narrow,
cheerless room, the witch-light winking out behind her.

The corridor was empty now, all the other servants gone to
their work. Olwynne was able to ask, "So the ribbon is intact?"

"The ribbon is very much intact, and I felt a tingle o' magic,
as I should," Isabeau said slowly.

"So everything's all right? No need to fear?"

"I'm no' sure," Isabeau answered. "Things did no' feel right.
It was a powerful spell Ceit Anna wrought for us, and nyx
magic is strange and unknowable, I had always thought. Yet . . .
the magic I felt seemed simple enough—spells o' binding and
silence. And though there was magic enough that my fingertips
still tingle, somehow . . ."

"What?"

The Keybearer shrugged. "I dinna ken. It is a very long time
since I last touched the ribbon. I do no' remember how it should
feel."

"As long as it's still intact, and the magic holds," Olwynne
said.

"Aye," Isabeau agreed, her frown deepening. "So long as the
magic holds."

SORROWGATE

"As for escaping, no man can look for that. The prison
is large and has many prisoners in it . . . some bound to
a post, some wandering abroad, some in the dungeon,
some in the upper ward, some building themselves
bowers and making palaces in the prison, some
weeping, some laughing, some laboring, some playing,
some singing, some chiding, some fighting. No man,
almost, remembers in what case he stands until,
suddenly, with nothing much looked for, young, old,
poor and rich, merry and sad, prince, page, pope, and
poor-soul priest . . . all . . . are put to death in different
ways in some corner of the same prison, are thrown
there in a hole, and are eaten either by worms under
the ground or by crows above. Now come forth, you
proud prisoner, for I know . . . all your pride is because
you forget that [this world] is a prison."

—THOMAS MORE,
Lord Chancellor of England,
executed on the order of Henry VIII in 1535

Lucescere

Built on a narrow tongue of land between two turbulent waterfalls, Lucescere had been named the Shining City for good reason. Where the two rivers met and fell over the edge of the cliff, a great haze of spray was flung up and, on a fine day, irradiated with sunlight so a double rainbow arched over the city. Tall towers topped with gilded domes and spires soared into the air behind high walls of warm sandstone. A bridge with many great arches spanned the river, which was lined on either bank with tall pillars of golden-leaved trees that rustled continually. Beyond the bridge, the sparkling waters seemed to simply dissolve into arching prisms of light.

That warm spring evening, with the sun balancing delicately on the peak of the distant mountains and flooding the whole landscape with vivid glowing color, Lucescere seemed like a city out of a faery tale. Rhiannon sat very still on the stallion's back, staring, her arms wound tight around Lewen's waist, her breath caught in her throat.

Her companions were exclaiming aloud with wonder and amazement, but Rhiannon could not utter a sound. She had never seen anything so beautiful.

"The river falls over the cliff just beyond the bridge," Lewen said, twisting in the saddle so he could see her face. "The waterfall is even bigger than the one we passed at Ravenscraig. It falls more than two hundred feet down into the valley. Ye're lucky it is such a bonny day, for ye can see the rainbows the falls are famous for. It makes the city look quite magical, doesn't it?"

Rhiannon nodded. Everywhere she looked were towers and

domes and pointed roofs and minarets, all gleaming with gold
or flying with flags or glittering with glass. Up until now, the
biggest town Rhiannon had ever seen was Linlithgorn in
Ravenshaw, and that had had no building taller than three stories and no more than a few hundred houses. Many of the towers in Lucescere soared seven stories high, and there were far
too many of them to count. Rhiannon could not begin to imagine how many people lived there.

Lewen clicked his tongue, and his big grey stallion, Argent,
began to make his way down the hill. Rhiannon settled back
with a sigh. Even after all these weeks on the road, it irked her
to have to ride pillion behind Lewen. If only she could ride her
winged mare, Blackthorn! They could have soared above the
city, seeing it as only an eagle could, instead of trudging their
way along the dusty road.

Rhiannon looked back at the forest behind them. She could
see Blackthorn, cantering along through the trees, her long
black wings folded along her sides. It was a great comfort to
Rhiannon, knowing her flying horse followed her still. Blackthorn could easily have disappeared back into the mountains.
She was not constrained by chains, like Rhiannon was, nor
even by a bridle and rein. Only love and loyalty kept her trotting along behind the caravans, for, as Rhiannon had discovered, these were bonds as strong as any manacle, in their way.

The thought made her stomach clench with anxiety and fear.
Soon they would ride into the Shining City, and Rhiannon
would at last discover her fate. She had been accused of murdering one of the Rìgh's most trusted lieutenants and, if found
guilty, would most likely be hanged for her crime. Lewen was
sure this would not happen, assuring her the Rìgh could never
execute one so young and fair. Rhiannon did not trust his judgment, however, for Lewen was her lover as well as her captor,
and she thought his passion for her must surely cloud his rea-
soning.

It had certainly clouded hers, she thought sourly. Lewen had
made her give her word of honor that she would not try to escape, and foolishly Rhiannon had promised. Despite her word,
the Rìgh's courier Iven had insisted she and Lewen be chained
together, and so a short length of clanking iron chain fettered

them, giving them neither the freedom to be apart nor the freedom to truly grow closer together.

Six weeks they had been chained together, night and day, unable to eat or sleep or scratch or squat without the other one witness to the act. At times the chain had made their lovemaking more intense, even inflaming their desire. At other times the enforced intimacy had been unbearable.

Rhiannon returned her gaze to the Shining City. Somewhere within those glowing walls lived the Rìgh, Lachlan the Winged, who ruled all of Eileanan and the Far Islands and had the power of life and death over her. Would she be executed for murder and treason, or would she be pardoned? If the order of execution was stayed, as Lewen promised it would be, what other punishment would be devised for her? Rhiannon had learned enough about the man she had killed to know that he had been greatly loved by the Rìgh. Surely he would demand retribution?

Rhiannon had heard tales of a man being branded with a T for "traitor" and condemned to wander as an outcast, begging for food and mercy. Others had been condemned to work in the mines, deprived of sunlight and fresh air. This seemed a terrible punishment to Rhiannon, who had grown up with only the sky as her roof and the moss as her mattress. She prayed mutely to whatever god might exist that she would escape such a sentence.

They reached the Bridge of Sorrows in the early evening, when only the very tallest towers were still gilded with light. Everything else was sunk into violet dusk, the river glimmering softly under the shadowy arches. The bridge was crowded with people hurrying in and out, for the gates would be shut at sunset, at the sound of the vesper bell.

Nina drew her gaudily painted caravan up on the side of the road before the bridge, her husband, Iven, coming to a halt beside her. Although they were dressed in the bright, shabby clothes of jongleurs, both were more than they seemed. Iven had once been one of the Rìgh's own elite force of soldiers, the Blue Guards, until he had married. Now he was a courier and emissary for the MacCuinn, gathering and disseminating news as he drove around the countryside, and singing the songs and telling the tales the Rìgh wanted to be told. Nina was a sorceress and journeywitch in service to the Coven of Witches. As well as teaching the lore of the witches as she traveled the roads of Eileanan, it was her task to find children of magical talent and bring them back to the Theurgia, to be taught the ways of the witches. She had six young apprentices traveling with her this time, three boys and three girls, ranging in age from sixteen to eighteen.

"Well, here we are, my bairns, at Lucescere at last," she said to them, as they all drew their weary horses close around her. "I just want to warn ye to keep close to the caravans once we are inside. Lucescere is no' the place to get lost in. It's a veritable maze o' streets and alleys, and it is hard to keep one's bearings, for the buildings are so tall ye canna see out once ye are in. So keep close, and keep a sharp eye out. Though the town watch do their best to keep things in order, there are many thieves and cutthroats here, as there are in any big city."

The apprentices murmured their understanding.

"Rhiannon, I do no' ken what to do with your mare. We canna let her just follow us into Lucescere. She'll be spooked, for sure, by all the noise and smells. I'm sorry, but I'm afraid she shall have to be bridled and put on a lead rein. Can ye call her for us?"

Rhiannon scowled, shaking her head instinctively.

Nina leaned forward persuasively. "If she's no' kept on a close lead, she'll hurt herself. She may bolt, and then she'll be lost in the back streets and ye'll never see her again. Someone would catch her for sure, and sell her to the highest bidder, or keep her for their own. Winged horses are highly prized—ye ken that."

"Canna I ride her?" Rhiannon pleaded. "She'll be much calmer if I'm on her back."

Iven frowned. "We canna allow ye to do that, Rhiannon. Ye ken that."

"But I promised no' to escape," Rhiannon said angrily. "Why do ye no' trust me? If I was going to run away, I would've done so by now!"

Nina and Iven exchanged a quick glance. "Very well," Iven said at last. "But Lewen will have to lead her, and ye will have to be tied on to her back, to make sure ye do no' slip off and try to escape in the crowd. I'll walk beside ye too, just to make sure."

"I wouldna leave Blackthorn," she protested. "She's mine!"

"Aye, I ken, but it is my task to deliver ye safely to the Rìgh's constables, and that means taking no chances."

Rhiannon jerked her shoulder, her face mutinous. "Blackthorn does no' like to be bridled," she said sulkily.

"And ye do no' like to be tied up. We ken, we ken. It canna be helped though," Iven said, swinging his legs around so he could jump down to the ground, leaving his cart horse to tear placidly at the grass with his big yellow teeth. "Will ye call her, Rhiannon, and put the bridle on her?"

Rhiannon obeyed reluctantly. Blackthorn came cantering up willingly enough but put her ears back at the sight of the bridle and danced away.

"At least ye dinna have to wear a chain and manacles like me," Rhiannon snapped. "Come on, it's only for a wee while. That city in there is big and noisy and dangerous, and we do no' want someone nabbing ye."

Blackthorn snorted and frisked away, shaking her mane, but Rhiannon followed inexorably, bridle in hand. "Come on, lassie," she said. "Settle down now."

The mare's lip curled back in distaste as the cold iron of the bit slid into her mouth, then she flung back her head, rearing in displeasure. Rhiannon clamped her hand over the fine bone of the mare's nose, forcing her head down. Blackthorn submitted with ill grace.

It was hard to do up the buckles with her hands hampered by the handcuffs and swinging chain, but Rhiannon managed at last. She then flung her little saddle—no more than a pad of soft leather and a girth—over the mare's back and buckled it tightly, digging the mare in the ribs with her elbow to stop her holding her breath. Nobody in their right mind would ride a flying horse without making sure the saddle was secure first.

Rhiannon leaped lightly up into the saddle and allowed Iven to lash her hands to the pommel. She kept her chin up, staring straight ahead, aware of the eyes watching her. The six apprentice-witches found Blackthorn utterly fascinating, even after all these weeks. There was more than a touch of envy in their gazes, for who had not dreamed of taming a flying horse?

With an apologetic glance, Lewen took Blackthorn's reins and turned Argent's head towards the city. Iven flung another rope about the mare's neck and held on to it firmly as he walked along beside them, his young son, Roden, picking up the caravan's reins and slapping them on the cart horse's broad back.

It was an odd procession that clattered over the long bridge and into Lucescere. Certainly it caused the heads of everyone they passed to turn and stare, and the people of Lucescere were used to strange sights.

First rode Lewen on his grey stallion, leading the dainty black winged mare and her defiant rider, her hands securely bound. Beside them strode a gaily dressed jongleur with a long fair beard forked into two, with a pair of garishly painted caravans trundling behind. Riding close about the caravans were six young men and women, some dressed in rich fabrics of fashionable cut, others in rough homespuns and clogs.

A little way behind came two huge, old-fashioned carriages of black enameled wood, bearing a coat of arms upon their doors and each guarded by four stout outriders. The first carriage was drawn by four perfectly matched black geldings, and its roof and back were piled high with luggage. Looking with weary interest out of the window was an old man, his grey hair cropped short, his thick brows drawn down towards his eagle nose. A big raven perched on his shoulder. This was Lord Malvern MacFerris of Fettercairn who, like Rhiannon, had been brought to Lucescere to face charges of murder and treason. Unlike Rhiannon, he had brought his groom, his valet, his harper, his piper, his librarian, his stableboy and his healer with him. The valet traveled with his master. The others jostled each other to see out the windows of the second coach.

Although Lord Malvern and his servants and guards had accompanied the jongleurs on the long journey through Ravenshaw and into Rionnagan, Rhiannon and the others had seen very little of him. On the rare occasions when no inn or farmhouse could be found in which to sleep, the lord's servants set up their own camp and the lord slept at ease in his big, well-cushioned carriage.

Relations between the jongleurs and Lord Malvern were tense, for the lord and his minions had tried to kidnap Nina and Iven's son, Roden, for their own nefarious purposes. With Rhiannon's help, Roden had been rescued, and the lord and his minions had all been placed under arrest, with eight soldiers from the town of Linlithgorn set to guard them.

It was not just the kidnapping of six-year-old Roden that had led to Lord Malvern's arrest. The lord of Fettercairn was also suspected of being responsible for dozens of mysterious deaths in the countryside surrounding his castle, as well as for dabbling in the forbidden art of necromancy.

If it had not been for Iven's badge of authority, the reeve of Linlithgorn would most likely have dismissed all these accusations out of hand, for the MacFerris clan had ruled in their part of the world for many centuries and were very rich and powerful. Like Rhiannon, Lord Malvern faced the death penalty if found guilty. Rhiannon wondered if he felt the same anxiety that she did, now that they were here at Lucescere at last. She did not think so. No doubt he expected the Rìgh would think twice before condemning a man of his ancient and noble lineage to death. Rhiannon could only hope the Rìgh would extend the same courtesy to a nameless nobody from a wild satyricorn herd.

It was dim inside the city walls, for the buildings leaned over the street like angry adults over a child. The air felt damp and cool, and everyone unrolled their riding cloaks and flung them about their shoulders. Rhiannon was too proud to ask Iven to do the same for her, but he saw her shiver and wrapped her cloak about her without a word.

The streets were lined with shops that opened directly onto the street, their wares spilling out onto the cobblestones and obstructing the passage of the hundreds of carts and carriages and riders and pedestrians hurrying along. Copper merchants brandished kettles and ladles, tanners thrust soft leather gloves and intricately worked belts under their noses, cobblers bemoaned the poor state of the travelers' worn boots and tried to convince them to buy new ones, and cursehags hissed at them from black-hung stalls. Brilliantly colored silks billowed in the breeze, and great loops of crimson and blue and yellow wool hung across the street on poles so they had to duck their heads.

Strong odors assaulted Rhiannon's sensitive nose. Some were foul, like rotting fish and sewage and half-tanned leather and horse manure. Others were delicious, like hot meat pies, dried herbs and powdered spices, and sweet perfumes from the scent merchants. The noise battered Rhiannon's ears too. She had never heard such a cacophony. One woman was trying to catch a squealing piglet that had escaped its cage; another harangued a fishmonger; yet another danced on a street corner in a swirl of orange skirts to the sound of a small boy bashing a tambourine.

A curtained litter carried by four enormous corrigans swayed through the streets, a cluricaun wielding a whip clearing the way before it. A Celestine in a pale green dress bent to speak with a filthy, ragged cursehag crouched inside a makeshift tent. Rhiannon had never seen a Celestine before, and craned her neck to watch. The faery seemed to glimmer with a frosty light like starshine, and her eyes were as bright and colorless as water. The cursehag cringed away from her and made some rude gesture, and at once the two men who guarded the Celestine stepped forward threateningly. The Celestine drew them back, her face very gentle.

The caravans made slow progress through the teeming streets, so Rhiannon had plenty of time to stare and marvel. She was not the only one awestruck and amazed. None of the six young apprentices had ever been to Lucescere before either, and they pointed and exclaimed at every sight.

At last they came to a big square before a tall pair of iron gates. Beyond were lawns and trees and, in the distance, a great building with many golden domes that gleamed in the last burnished light. After the rush and bustle of the city, it was a relief to rest her eyes on the green gardens, and Rhiannon paid little attention to the conversation between Iven and the guards on the gate. All her attention was focused on the palace. There lived Lachlan MacCuinn, the winged Rìgh of Eileanan and the ultimate arbitrator of justice in the land. Although Rhiannon would be tried before a jury, her fate ultimately rested in his hands. She wondered again what sort of man he was. Most of the stories told of him were tales of war and rebellion and great acts of sorcery. They were not reassuring.

Rhiannon was roused from her abstraction by a sudden splat of moisture on her cheek. She looked around, surprised, and realized one of the guards on the gate had spat at her. She flushed in rage and humiliation, unable to lift her bound hands to wipe the phlegm away. The guards were staring at her in overt anger and hostility. At first she was bewildered but then she realized, with a sudden sinking of her heart, that they all wore the same long blue cloak and tam-o'-shanter that she did. Rhiannon's cloak and hat had belonged to Connor the Just, the soldier she had killed. Rhiannon wore them still because she had no other clothes to wear, apart from the old shirt and breeches Lewen's mother Lilanthe had given her. From the looks on their faces, the guards knew she was the one who had killed Connor, and hated her for it. Rhiannon lifted her arm to wipe her face on her sleeve and looked straight ahead, her cheeks burning.

Iven was frowning as he came back to her side. "Sorry about that," he said stiffly. "The soldier responsible will be severely disciplined."

Rhiannon did not respond. Iven took her lead rein and nodded to Lewen, who rode on down the tree-lined avenue, looking tense and unhappy. The caravans rattled after them.

Under normal circumstances, Rhiannon would have been as excited and fascinated as the apprentices riding behind her. She could only think about what lay before her, however, and the winged mare sensed her fear and distrust and danced uneasily, causing Iven to put one hand upon her bridle.

The road brought them through a pretty little gatehouse and into a large courtyard. The bulk of the palace rose beyond another wall, protected by two round turrets topped with gilded domes. On either side of the courtyard were the stables and the mews and the kennels, and various tall stone buildings from which came the sound of hammering and sawing, and the smell of the forge. The courtyard was full of people. Most were dressed in rough brown breeches and smocks, belted with heavy leather hung with the tools of their trade. Some, however, were dressed in the blue cloaks of the palace guard. These men stiffened to attention as the cavalcade drew up before the gatehouse. Rhiannon was aware of their eyes upon her. She raised her chin a little higher in the air, fixing her gaze on the stone shield above the gate. It was carved with the shape of a rearing stag, a crown between its antlers.

Again Iven stepped forward to speak with the soldiers. The one in charge nodded and beckoned to the grooms waiting nearby. They came forward respectfully and helped down the weary apprentices, then took the reins of their horses and led

them into the stables. The caravans were deftly backed into the
carriage house, and the cart horses unharnessed, while the soldiers guarding the two black carriages dismounted and waited
for their turn to report.

Within minutes, only Rhiannon was left mounted, with six
hard-faced soldiers taking up positions all around her. She
looked at them warily, not liking the way they stood with their
hands on their sword hilts and their eyes fixed upon her. Blackthorn shied nervously, and Lewen moved quickly to put a calm-
ing hand on her bridle. He glanced up at Rhiannon reassuringly,
but she hardly noticed, all her attention focused on the soldiers.

A sudden bustle of activity caused her to raise her head
sharply. The gate swung open, and a tall, broad-shouldered man
came through. At once all the soldiers jerked upright, saluting
him. He acknowledged them curtly, his frowning gaze fixed on
Rhiannon. She stared back at him, concealing her fear beneath
a look of haughty defiance.

Dillon of the Joyous Sword, Captain of the Yeomen of the
Guard, was a stern-faced man, his brown hair clipped back severely. At some point his nose had been broken so badly a chip
of bone had been lost at the bridge. A thin white line slashed its
way across his cheek under his left eye, and his mouth was set
in a humorless line. He looked like a man who expected, and
got, instant obedience.

He was immacutely dressed in a white shirt, a blue kilt criss-
crossed with white and black, and a long blue cloak. His breastplate shone bright as a mirror, and his long black boots had
been polished to a glossy sheen. A long, beautifully crafted
sword hung at his waist. He caressed its hilt constantly, a nervy
mannerism so out of keeping with his frowning face and stiff
back that it made Rhiannon tense with trepidation. Blackthorn
sensed her fear and at once wheeled and reared, lashing out at
one of the soldiers with her front hooves. Lewen had trouble
bringing her back under control and, bound as she was, it was
all Rhiannon could do to keep her seat.

The thick dark brows drew even closer together over that
strong, crooked nose. He paid no attention to the soldiers from
Linlithgorn and their aristocratic charge. All his focus was upon
Rhiannon and her winged horse.

"Clip the mare's wings at once," the captain commanded. "And bring the prisoner here."

"No!" Rhiannon cried in horror. "Ye canna clip her wings!"

The soldier ignored her. Rhiannon saw a groom come running with a large pair of shears, and rage welled up in her.

"No, ye shallna clip her wings. How dare ye!" she cried.

"Subdue the prisoner," Captain Dillon ordered.

At once the soldiers converged upon her, drawing their weapons. Rhiannon leaned her weight upon her bound hands, swinging her legs up and around and smashing her boots into the face of one of the soldiers. He fell back with a cry, blood spurting from his nose. Rhiannon brought one knee up to balance on the saddle pad, using her other foot to kick away another soldier, then brought her knee back to balance herself. A mere nudge with her foot, and Blackthorn wheeled and kicked back her hind hooves, knocking the soldier behind her flying. Lewen was knocked off his feet, but he would not let go of the rein, bringing Blackthorn's head around with a jerk. Rhiannon could hear him yelling at her to stop, and Nina and Iven too, but she was too busy lashing out with foot and elbow and fist to listen.

Then a soldier seized Blackthorn's bridle, close to the bit. She reared, dragging him off his feet, then leaped into the air, her wings flashing out. After a moment he let go with a scream and crashed down onto the cobbles. Lewen tried to hold her down, but she was too strong for him and he was sent tumbling head over heels. As the winged mare rose into the air, a flushed and breathless Rhiannon clinging to her back, the captain strode forward and seized a rope from one of the grooms. A few quick gestures, and he had tied it into a lasso that he sent whizzing up around his head. To Rhiannon's utter consternation, the loop rose high into the air and dropped over her head, jerking tight about her shoulders. As he yanked at the rope, she was half dragged off Blackthorn's back. Only the bonds tying her to the pommel kept her on, and they hurt her wrists cruelly.

"Seize the bridle," the captain ordered his men. "Pull that horse down!"

As they ran to obey him, Rhiannon reached down with numb, clumsy fingers and wrenched at the girth strap's buckle. Once, twice, three times, then at last the buckle slipped free.

She fell to the ground with a crash, and Blackthorn soared away, the ropes and reins dangling.

Fly! Fly! Rhiannon willed her. *Fly far from here, my love!*

As she watched the black mare tilt her wings and obey, a sudden rush of tears confounded her. She had only time to raise her arm and wipe them away before hard, angry hands seized her and dragged her to her feet.

"Take the prisoner to the cells," the captain ordered. "And make sure she does no' try to escape again!"

She heard Lewen protesting desperately but to no avail. Dazed and sick from her fall, Rhiannon was marched swiftly away. She glanced back over her shoulder and saw his agonized face, calling words to her that she could not hear. Then cold shadows fell over her, as she was forced under the portcullis and into the guardhouse.

The Prisoner

Rhiannon's head was ringing from the blow to her ear. She staggered and they jerked her upright again. "Take her to Sorrowgate," Captain Dillon ordered without even a glance in Rhiannon's direction. "Put her in thumbscrews and toss her in the Murderers' Gallery. That should keep her quiet enough."

"Aye, sir," one of the guards responded smartly. Then they snapped manacles on her wrists and ankles so quickly she did not even have time to protest. They weighed heavily on her limbs, clanking every time she moved. She was taken through the building and out to another small courtyard, where she was put in a cart, her guards climbing up beside her. Rhiannon strained her head, trying to see past them, looking for some chance to escape.

The cart jerked forward and Rhiannon was flung to her knees. No one helped her, and she struggled up again, determined not to lie in the filthy straw at their feet.

The cart rattled through the narrow city streets, attracting a lot of attention from the crowd. A few young boys came running along beside it, hurling apple cores and laughing. Rhiannon evaded them easily, shooting the boys looks of fury. They only laughed and ran off.

They passed under the shadow of a huge gatehouse and into another dank, grimy courtyard. Rhiannon tried to cover her nose. The smell that rose from the slimy cobblestones was truly awful. The soldiers jerked on her chain to keep her hands low. She kept her head raised proudly as she was hustled out of the cart and into the prison. Inside was a crowded antechamber where Rhiannon's name was taken, the charges against her recorded, and where she had to make her mark on a scroll of paper. Rhiannon had been taught to write her name on her journey with Nina and the apprentice-witches, but her hand was trembling so much she barely managed to make the R. The rest was just a squiggle punctuated with blotches and smears.

As soon as Rhiannon laid down the quill, she was dragged out of the room, down a sweeping staircase, and through a maze of long gloomy corridors and halls. Three more times they descended steps, and each time the staircase was narrower, darker, and dirtier. The last flight was very steep, and her guards were so rough with her that Rhiannon slipped and fell. The soldiers hauled her up again, dragging painfully on the manacles about her wrists. She would have liked to strike out at them in retaliation, but she resisted the temptation, remembering Lewen's oft-repeated advice on controlling her more violent impulses.

At the bottom of the stairs was a small antechamber with a wall of iron bars, barred and padlocked on the inside with a thick rusty chain. The only furniture was a stool on which a burly guard sat, his back resting against the wall. He did not speak, just grunted, let the legs of his stool drop back to the ground, and got up to unlock a small gate in the bars for Rhiannon and her escort. It shut behind them with a hollow groan, and the guard locked it again.

The turn of the key was like a fetter on her soul. Rhiannon had never been locked up before. Until she had fled her herd on the back of the black winged horse, she had never even spent a night within four walls. She hated the feel of being enclosed in stone. It felt as if she had been buried alive.

Beyond was a long, low corridor set with heavy iron doors. The walls wept with moisture and every now and again were stained with green runnels of slime. The only sound was the tramp of their feet and the harsh rhythm of their breath. The air was dead and smelled unpleasant, so that Rhiannon's nostrils wrinkled in distaste. She tried to count the doors, but there were more than the fingers on both her hands and she soon lost count.

Every ten paces a lantern was bolted securely to the wall, its wick turned low so that it cast only a dim and fitful luminance. Between each circle of light was a well of darkness, as cold and numbing as black water. Rhiannon was not the only one to unconsciously quicken her pace as they plunged through these gaps in the light.

At last they came to a set of iron doors at the very end of the corridor. Two of the guards lifted the great bolt and hauled the doors open. Within was another small antechamber where a woman dressed in a grey uniform sat at a counter. She rose as the guards came in and fixed Rhiannon with a frowning glare. She was a massive mountain of a woman, at least as tall as Rhiannon and weighing four times as much. Her fingers were like overstuffed sausages, her hands like red cushions, her arms like bolsters. Her iron-grey dress was as large as a tent and threatened to split along every seam. Her face was as round as a white cheese and about as amiable as a bulldog's. Her mouth was so thin-lipped it was almost invisible, while her jowls were huge and heavy and wobbled when she moved. Around her waist was clasped a leather belt as wide as a horse's surcingle, with a hoop laden with huge old keys dangling on one side and a leather-wrapped cudgel on the other. She looked as if she would take great pleasure in using it.

"So what do we have here?" she demanded in a deep, slightly hoarse voice.

"Prisoner for ye, Mistress Octavia," the guard said, in the same deferential tone that he had used for the captain.

"I can see that, balls-for-brains. Who is she, and why isn't she on my list?"

"Just come in. Captain Dillon said to bring her to ye. She's to be put in the thumbscrews, he said, for trying to escape." As the guard spoke, he was unfastening the manacles about Rhiannon's wrists and ankles. She winced and rubbed her bruises, looking about her in apprehension.

Octavia looked displeased. "I don't want her," she grumbled. "Gallery's full. Cap'n kens that. Take her away."

"She's a hanging case."

The tiny eyes seemed to brighten. "Gallows apples, is she? What for?"

"Murder."

Octavia looked Rhiannon up and down, then yawned. "Knifed her lover, did she? Fool. No man's worth hanging for."

"Nay, she killed a Yeoman. Connor the Just."

The puffy lids widened enough to show more than just a glint of eye. "Really?" she drawled. "Now that's something I haven't had afore. Treason, isn't it? Would she be hanged, drawn, and quartered for that?"

The guard shrugged. "Should be. Bitch." He spat at Rhiannon to show whom he was speaking of. Rhiannon ignored him, which was not as difficult as it had been earlier. All her energy was going into hiding just how apprehensive she was. She had never seen such a grossly obese woman before, nor anyone with such mean little eyes.

Octavia was rubbing her fat red hands together. "Goody. I love a hanging. Been a while, stupid soft-bellied judges. Should hang this one, if it's true she killed a Blue Guard. She'll draw a big crowd too."

"Aye, and if I ken ye, Mistress Octavia, ye'll be conducting tours through the gallery for a very nice personal profit," the guard said with a twist of his lips that was half-amused, half-disgusted. "No' to mention selling her hands."

"Nowadays they give the hanged bodies to the healers' college, for them to cut up, Eà kens why. Bet ye the healers cut the hands off and sell them. Ye can get a pretty penny for a murderer's hand, if ye ken where to flog them. But these stupid new laws o' theirs have cut my profit in half, I reckon, if no' more. Soft-bellied and soft-headed, those judges are. If ye don't hang them, they just keep coming back, don't they?"

She winked at one of the guards, who looked revolted, for the contrast between the coyness of her voice and the grotesquery of her body was truly macabre. "But if they hang, draw, and quarter her, well, then I'll get her hands and any other bits I want, 'cause no one's going to notice, are they, once the city dogs have torn her to bits?" Octavia endeavored to push out the leaden weight of her jowls into a smile. Rhiannon felt the soldiers behind her shift uneasily.

"So, welcome to Sorrowgate," she said then to Rhiannon. "Got any money?"

One of the guards lifted Rhiannon's pack and dumped it on the table. "It'll be in here if she does," he said. "We havena had time to look through. We've only just apprehended her."

"No' your job to go pawing through a prisoner's belongings," Octavia said reprovingly. A sudden paroxysm seized her.

Her jowls shook and her breath wheezed in her throat. Rhiannon stared at her in alarm. Octavia bent over, placed both fists on what must have been her knees, hidden under the voluminous dress, and wheezed heartily. After a moment or two, Rhiannon realized she was laughing. "No' your job," she repeated. "Mine! Ha ha ha!"

The guards laughed politely.

Octavia dug through Rhiannon's pack. Rhiannon must have made some small sound of protest, for she lifted her gargoyle face and said menacingly, "Ye say something?"

Rhiannon shook her head. The guards sniggered. Octavia drew out the thin leather pouch in which Rhiannon kept the few coins she had managed to win gambling on their journey. The woman felt it disapprovingly, then emptied them out into her palm. "Well, I can see ye willna be trying to bribe me to help ye escape," she said with no attempt to conceal her disappointment. "Ye've got enough to eat tonight, though, and I'll let ye have a blanket." She tossed the empty purse back into the pack and shoved the coins away into a pocket.

"Ye canna just steal my money!" Rhiannon blurted out furiously.

"I havena stolen anything!" Octavia yelled. She surged forward, thrusting her face into Rhiannon's so that it seemed to fill the entire universe. Her skin had turned a nasty mottled color, and her eyes were completely lost in the slits of fat. Rhiannon fixed her attention on the tuft of hairs that stuck out of a wart on the woman's chin, willing herself to stand her ground. "How dare ye accuse me, ye filthy murdering sow! I just told ye that ye had enough money for a meal tonight and a blanket. How is that stealing?"

"There was enough money there to pay for two weeks' lodging!" Rhiannon yelled back.

That terrible wheezing paroxysm overcame Octavia again. Rhiannon shrank back, unable to help herself. The soldiers shifted from foot to foot, their boots squeaking.

Octavia managed to catch her breath. "Two weeks' lodging," she repeated, wiping her eyes. "Och, it's a clown, this one. Two weeks' lodging! No' at the Sorrowgate Inn, my love. Finest inn in town, we are, and that handful o' coppers only pays for supper and a bed for one night. Tomorrow ye'll be

sleeping on the ground and gnawing dead rats' bones, if ye
canna get me any more coins afore then."

Rhiannon said nothing.

The pendulous jowls slowly stopped their wobbling, and all
her flesh thickened and drew down until her mouth had once
again disappeared. Octavia pushed her bulldog's face very
close to Rhiannon's. Her breath was foul. "And if ye ever
smart-mouth me again, my girl, I'll smash your teeth in for ye,
do ye understand? Or hang ye up for the rats to gnaw on."

Rhiannon nodded, trying not to lean away.

"Ye say, 'Aye, ma'am,' and ye say it right quickly."

"Aye, ma'am," Rhiannon said, and Octavia at last stepped
away. Rhiannon took a deep breath. To her dismay she realized
she was trembling. She hoped no one else had noticed.

Methodically Octavia went through the pack, noting all of
Rhiannon's belongings and laboriously writing them down in a
thick ledger attached to her counter with a chain. When she
wrote, she stuck her tongue out one corner of her mouth.

"One longbow; one quiver; one dozen arrows, green
fletched," she said. "One dagger, silver; one boot knife, with
black hilt. One blowpipe, one bag o' barbs, standard Yeoman
issue." Octavia looked up and stared at Rhiannon expression-
lessly, then returned her attention to the ledger, her pale tongue
once more protruding. "One water pouch, one whetting stone,
one tinderbox, one large flint. One embroidered shawl. One
gold brooch, running horse design."

She took out a little painted box, lifted the lid, and listened
for a moment as it tinkled a pretty tune. "One music box," she
intoned, the quill scratching against the paper. "One silver goblet, crystal in stem. Mmmm, very nice. One silver badge, charging stag design. One gold medal . . ." She paused as she turned
it in her hand, then raised her gimlet eyes to stare accusingly at
Rhiannon. ". . . with haloed hand design."

"The League o' the Healing Hand!" one guard hissed.

"Dinna tell me she stole his medal," another said reproach-
fully.

"And his Yeoman badge!"

"Bitch," said the one who had spat at her before, and spat
again.

Rhiannon said nothing.

When everything in her bag had been documented, including "one purse, empty," Octavia laid down her ink-stained quill and said brusquely, "Right, then, time to strip."

Rhiannon just stared at her.

"Strip off!" she repeated impatiently, with an expansive gesture.

"Ye mean . . ."

"Och, aye, the lassie's shy," Octavia mocked. "Look at her, blushing and sighing, like a lassie whose lips are still wet with her mama's milk."

The soldiers guffawed.

"Take it all off!" Octavia barked. "Now!

Rhiannon set her jaw and obeyed. Naked and shivering, she passed her clothes over to Octavia, who duly noted them down in her ledger, then shoved them into the bag, did up the straps and stowed the bag away in a crowded cupboard that she then locked with a key. Rhiannon stood with her back ramrod straight, her arms crossed over her breasts, enduring the guards' grinning regard. Octavia then stood and looked her over with the same overt lasciviousness, her arms akimbo, the tip of her fat tongue protruding. "Bonny lass, isn't she? Skin like a babe. Mmm-mmm. Better get your tongues off the floor, lads."

Rhiannon stared straight ahead.

"Nice flat arse too. No' like mine, hey? Hey?"

The guards did not dare agree.

Octavia gave her hoarse wheezy laugh and tossed Rhiannon a coarse linen smock, which she hurriedly pulled on over her head. It was rough and itchy, and stank. Rhiannon wrinkled her nose in disgust.

The smell of her smock was nothing to that which assaulted her sensitive satyricorn senses when Octavia unlocked and hauled open the other door, however. The air that flowed over them was so foul that Rhiannon wrenched her wrist free of the guard's grasp so she could clamp her hand over her nose and mouth. The guard did not protest because he wanted to mask his own nose.

Octavia reached forward and seized Rhiannon's hands in her own hot, unpleasantly damp hands, dragging them away from her face. Rhiannon gagged. In that moment of weakness, Octavia grabbed her thumbs and forced them both into a metal clamp that she tightened cruelly and then locked. Rhiannon shrieked and jerked her hands away, but it was too late. Her thumbs throbbed painfully.

"Well, in ye go, girlie. I hope ye enjoy your stay," Octavia said, wheezing with pleasure at her own wit.

Rhiannon did not move, staring into the room beyond in horror. The room was dim and smoky, lit only by the sullen glare of a single lantern. Vague hunched shapes moved in the gloom, staring back at her with eyes that gleamed white and glassy.

Octavia unhitched her cudgel and slapped it into her palm.

"Get in there, girl," she said.

Still Rhiannon did not move. Her legs felt weak and trembly. One of the soldiers gave her a shove in the back and she lurched forward. Octavia grabbed her by the neck, lifted her, and flung her through the door, tossing a blanket and a wooden bowl after her. As Rhiannon landed on her knees on the filthy, freezing floor, she heard the door slam shut behind her and the key grate in the rusty lock.

Under the Portcullis

Lewen sighed in impatience and frustration. Lady Fèlice de Valonis of Stratheden turned and smiled at him in sympathy. Of all the apprentices who had ridden to Lucescere from Ravenshaw, she was the one who had grown closest to Rhiannon. A small, slim girl of sixteen, Fèlice managed to look fresh and pretty even with her crimson velvet riding habit crushed and travel stained, and her long brown curls ruffled.

Beside her Cameron MacHamish rolled his shoulders and cracked his knuckles, needing some kind of physical outlet for his emotions. Flanking Fèlice on the other side was Rafferty MacKillop, the brown-haired son of a clockmaker. These two young men were always vying for Fèlice's attention, as much now by habit as by inclination. So when the young lady had declared her intention of accompanying Lewen to the prison to seek news of Rhiannon, they had both naturally decided she needed their protection, even though Fèlice said she felt quite safe with Lewen as her escort, with a laughing glance at his strong, tall figure.

The other apprentice-witches had gone on to the Theurgia as planned, though it was clear Landon would have much preferred to accompany Lewen and Fèlice than escort the other two girls, Lady Edithe NicAven of Avebury and Maisie, the shy, plump daughter of a village cunning man. Edithe had been most annoyed to have been abandoned by the other boys, however, and had insisted that Landon at least stay with her and Maisie. So, looking back over his shoulder wistfully, Landon had obediently trailed off after the haughty young blonde. Edithe had made no attempt to wait for Maisie, who was still limping badly after being attacked by wild dogs on their journey.

It had taken Lewen some time to find his way to Sorrowgate Prison, for it was not a place he had ever had to visit before. A great dark hulking building built beside the gatehouse that guarded the Bridge of Sorrows, it was protected by a tall iron portcullis with prongs as sharp as spears. Although the portcullis was drawn up, they had to pass right underneath it, and no one was able to help glancing up uneasily. It was all too easy to imagine it rattling down at high speed and impaling them upon its prongs.

Within was a small dark courtyard, busy with people coming and going. The smell was strong enough to make Fèlice lift her handkerchief to her nose and for Cameron to make some lame joke to cover his unease.

Now the four apprentice-witches stood waiting in a vast chamber, along with a host of other people, some carrying baskets of food and wine, parcels of clothes, or bundles of blankets. Some were obviously prisoners, manacled and flanked by guards dressed in stern grey garb. Most looked resigned. One or two wept, and one man tried to resist and was belted across the back with a heavy cudgel for his pains.

At the far end of the room was an enormous desk, where a man sat half-hidden behind towers of papers. Every now and again, he looked up and jerked his head. Another person would rush forward to plead with him to allow them to visit a prisoner or to give him their parcel and a covert coin, or the guards would drag forward their captive, who would be efficiently processed, then marched through the huge iron doors behind the clerk by two big, hard-faced prison guards.

Slowly the queue inched forward. Lewen and his friends had been waiting now for more than twenty minutes, and their anxiety for Rhiannon made the wait very hard.

There was a stir at the great iron doors that led to the outside. Lewen turned to look, as did most people in the room.

Lord Malvern entered the room, carrying his raven on his gauntleted wrist. He was dressed in a black velvet jacket over a grey and black kilt, with a plaid of the same pattern thrown over his shoulder and secured with a heavy silver badge. Before him walked a young man with a curiously colorless and impassive face, dressed all in black and imperiously clearing the way with a long white stick. Following a few paces behind the lord were his valet, carrying one small carved box; his librarian, staggering under a great pile of books and scrolls; his harper and piper, both carrying their musical instruments on their backs; and a cheery-faced woman dressed in a brown skirt and a white apron, who was carrying an enormous basket. Behind them came six porters struggling with various trunks and cases, and two rough-clad men that Lewen knew had been grooms at Fettercairn Castle. Behind them, looking harassed, were the eight soldiers appointed by the reeve of Linlithgorn to guard the lord and his retinue. They looked more like bodyguards set to serve the lord than soldiers set to hold him prisoner.

Lewen wondered where the lord of Fettercairn had got his new seneschal. Irving, his last seneschal, had died at Rhiannon's hand, throwing himself before an arrow that had been aimed for Lord Malvern. This new man had the same stiff, white, unpleasant look about him as Irving had had, only he seemed about twenty years younger. Lewen wondered if it was Irving's son, knowing that most of a great lord's servants inherited their positions.

The seneschal ignored the long straggling queue and walked straight up to the desk, prodding a fat woman with his stick so she moved out of the way. He rapped on the desk to get the clerk's attention, then dropped a heavy purse of coins in front of him.

"My laird, the MacFerris o' Fettercairn, has been wrongly accused o' treason," the seneschal said in a bored tone. "He has submitted to the Crown until such a time as the charges are dismissed. He will require lodgings in Sorrowgate Tower for himself and his servants. Please ensure the quarters are clean."

The man at the desk stared up at him with dropped jaw, then shrugged and took the purse. "Very well," he answered and jerked his head. A guard came forward and opened the doors. The lord of Fettercairn walked forward and into the prison, disappearing from view. His retinue followed along behind him, all except Dedrie the castle healer, who paused at the table.

"I must attend upon his lairdship at once," she said. "He is sorely tired after his journey. I will need to organize the delivery o' some medicines from the College o' Healers first, however. I will need a pass out to ensure that all is in order for his lairdship. Will ye please write one for me now, so that his lairdship does no' have to wait too long?"

The man frowned, and at once another plump purse plopped on the table in front of him.

"O' course," he said. He scribbled on a piece of paper and pushed it towards Dedrie.

She thanked him, then turned and walked back towards the city. As she passed Lewen, their eyes met. Dedrie smiled sweetly and then stepped out through the doors and out of sight.

Seeing the lord of Fettercairn and his poisonous skeelie bribe their way into comfort and freedom made Lewen grind his teeth in fury. He seethed about it the whole time he had to wait, and when at last he was able to step up to the desk, said furiously, "Why did ye let the laird o' Fettercairn's skeelie just walk out the door? She's been accused o' murder, ye ken, and necromancy too!"

The man raised his eyebrows, and said, "Pass outs allowed in time o' need."

"What need?" Lewen demanded.

"A prisoner who has been granted liberty o' the tower is permitted to send servants on errands for him," the clerk said.

"Even if she stands accused o' murder herself?"

"I have no record o' such charges."

"But—"

The clerk tapped his quill against his ink pot impatiently. "Is there something else I can do for ye?"

Lewen swallowed his aggravation. "Aye. I'm here to see Rhiannon o' Dubhslain. She was brought in an hour or so ago."

The clerk shuffled some papers, then said, "Och, aye. Accused o' murder. Sorry. No visitors allowed."

"But why no'? Ye let the laird o' Fettercairn's skeelie just go wandering off into the city. Why will ye no' let me—"

"The girl has no' been granted liberty o' the tower. She's in the Murderers' Gallery. No privileges allowed."

"But I must see her! Please, canna I—"

"Sorry. I canna help ye. Next!"

"But please . . . canna I just—"

"Move along, please, sir." A prison guard suddenly materialized at Lewen's elbow, and he was politely but inexorably moved away from the clerk's desk. Fèlice and the other boys trailed after him, all looking upset and angry.

"What do we do now?" Fèlice asked.

"I suppose we had better just go to the Theurgia, like we're supposed to," Cameron said. "Nina said she was going to seek audience with the Rìgh just as soon as she could. I guess we leave it up to her."

"We'd better tell her about Dedrie," Lewen said through his teeth.

"I hope Rhiannon is all right," Fèlice said, looking about her with a theatrical shudder. "This is truly a most blaygird place."

"Did ye see the laird o' Fettercairn? It was like a royal progress," Rafferty said.

"They just let that auld nursemaid go wandering off," Fèlice said. "How can that have happened?"

Cameron rubbed two fingers together. "Filthy lucre always lubricates the way," he said.

"Rhiannon has no money," Lewen said. "Och, if only I'd thought! I could have given her some."

"She has some money," Cameron said feelingly, "because she kept winning all o' mine. She'd bet on a snail race, that girl."

They pushed their way through the crowd and out into the fresh air, Fèlice taking great gulps, her hand pressed dramatically to her chest. "The smell o' that place!" She shuddered. "I declare I feel quite ill!"

"I have to see Rhiannon!" Lewen cried. "I canna bear to think o' her locked up in there."

"But how?" Rafferty asked. "Ye heard that man. No visitors allowed."

"I must see the Rìgh," Lewen said. "I must beg him to grant her liberty o' the tower, whatever that is."

"And ye think ye can just charge in there and ask him?" Cameron said skeptically.

"Nay, o' course no'. Though I am one o' his squires, ye ken, and he is quite friendly to us, most o' the time. I canna just go

in and demand audience with him whenever I want, though.
But I ken someone who can!"

"Who?" Fèlice demanded.

"His daughter," Lewen answered.

Olwynne leaned her head upon her hand, finding it hard to concentrate on the book before her. She was tired yet she could not rest. She felt unsettled and fidgety, like a horse in a rising wind. She felt she was waiting for something to happen, even though she knew all the other students were in class, and the witches busy about their own concerns.

Suddenly her door crashed open. Olwynne jerked upright. She had not heard anyone walking down the corridor. In an instant she saw why. Her twin brother, Owein, hovered in the doorway. Like her, he was red haired and brown eyed, with the white lock of the MacCuinn clan curling at his left temple. Unlike her, he was blessed with a pair of glossy, red-feathered wings as long as he was himself. Ever since he had first learned to manage his wings, Owein had never walked if he could fly. He was as restless as a dragonfly, always in motion, always talking and laughing and fighting.

Olwynne had wondered once or twice if that was why she was so quiet and self-contained, so absorbed in her books and her studies. It was the only place where she could outshine her twin. Owein did not have much interest in studying and only tolerated his classes at the Theurgia because he knew he had to graduate before he was permitted to try out for the Yeomen of the Guard. Like many young men his age, he dreamed of joining that most elite company of soldiers. Few made the grade, however, and Owein had been told many times that being the son of the Rìgh was no guarantee of acceptance.

"Olwynne, guess what!"

"Ye've been kicked out o' school for missing so many classes," Olwynne replied promptly, eyeing her brother's clothes. Instead of being soberly attired in the black robe of an apprentice, as she was, he was wearing breeches, shabby boots, and an old, stained tunic rent from the shoulder.

He grinned and fluttered down to perch on her bed. "Nay, though I must admit auld Jock threatened to throw me out if I missed any more o' his classes. I told him he'd have to catch me first."

"Owein!"

"Och, he's all right, auld Jock. It's no' that I dinna like him; it's just that agricultural studies drives me crazy. So boring! And no one can convince me I need to ken aught about farming to be a Blue Guard."

Olwynne sighed. She could have tried but she knew it would be a waste of breath.

"So why are ye no' in class now?" she demanded.

Owein pulled a face. "Alchemy. So boring! Alasdair and I thought we'd go hawking. Much too nice a day to hang around in class. I ken Cailean wouldna give us away."

Olwynne frowned. Hawking, hunting, and other blood sports were forbidden to apprentices, as the Coven of Witches believed passionately that all living creatures were sacred. Witches did not eat the flesh of any animal, nor cheese that had been fermented with the juices of an animal's digestive system, nor eggs that had been fertilized. Skipping class would be frowned upon, but doing so in order to go hawking would be punished by suspension and perhaps even expulsion.

Owein rolled his eyes at her. "Dinna be such a muffin-faced prig, Olwynne. I've been good all winter. Ye canna expect me to stay at school and work when the weather's finally warming up!"

Olwynne wondered fleetingly how her brother could say he had been good all winter so sincerely when she knew for a certainty that he had regularly skipped school to go tobogganing, ice skating, and hunting with his hounds, not to mention he'd smuggled a greased pig into the dining room one day and released all the pigeons from the loft another day. She also harbored a very strong suspicion that it had been her brother who had strung Fat Drusa's drawers up the flagpole on Hogmanay. Luckily the very large sorceress was also very good-humored, else Owein might have found himself expelled.

"Anyway, dinna ye want to hear my news? Guess what we saw when we were in the mews. Go on, Olwynne, guess!"

"A falcon," Olwynne said sourly.

"Go on, muffin face! Try, at least. Some witch ye are, if ye canna even read your own brother's mind."

Olwynne looked at him in exasperation. She knew very well that, despite all Owein's madcap tricks and tomfoolery, he had had some of the Craft hammered into his head and was quite capable of shielding his mind from her.

"*Dai-dein?*" she said hopefully. Her father had little patience with Owein's wildness and would have sent him back to school with a flea in his ear.

"No! We saw a winged horse, a black one, and a real beauty. A girl was riding it, a prisoner o' some sort. Her hands were bound and she was on a lead rein. They tried to bring her in and she fought them off. Ye should've seen her! She broke Lyndon's nose, and her horse kicked Kenneth in the chest and stove all his ribs in. It was grand! Then the captain threw a rope around her shoulders and brought her down, and the mare took off up into the sky. Ye should've seen it go! What I wouldna give for a horse like that!"

"A black winged horse," Olwynne echoed. A peculiar hollowness in her stomach made her voice come out too high.

Owein did not notice.

"Aye, with two long blue horns. Reynard had his face opened by one o' them. He was lucky no' to lose his eye. It was great sport, seeing the Blue Guards routed by a skinny slip o' a girl and a horse! Though I tell ye what." His voice sobered. "Captain Dillon was no' at all pleased. I feel sorry for the girl. Lewen says—"

"Lewen?"

"Och, aye, didna I say? It was Lewen who brought her in."

"Lewen's here?" Olwynne jumped to her feet.

"Aye, he's in his room. I've just come from there. That's why I'm here: he wants to see ye."

"Me?" Olwynne felt her cheeks heating and put up a distracted hand to her hair, which was braided back tightly. She gave it a jerk and wished she dared loosen it from its ribbon. She knew it was her only real beauty, but if she shook it out, Owein would jeer at her and wonder aloud what she was doing, and she would be reprimanded by any witch who saw her.

"Aye, he's in a real state. Seems he's fallen head over heels for this girl, and he's afraid—"

Olwynne spun around to face her brother. "He's what?"

"Fallen for this girl," Owein said impatiently. "Hard, by the looks o' it. Poor auld fellow. Anyway, he needs our help. He wants to appeal to *Dai-dein*, try to have her freed. The auld man's got a soft spot for Lewen, ye ken, 'cause o' his *dai*, but things look pretty black for her. I'm no' sure if I got the story straight or no', but apparently she killed a Yeoman." Owein's voice hardened with indignation. "By all rights she should hang, and by the look o' the captain, he intends to make sure she will. Lewen is just sick about it all."

"We'd better go and hear what he has to say then," Olwynne said.

With his legs still crossed, Owein flung open his wings and shot up into the air. As he stretched out his long legs, reaching out his hand to open the door, he knocked over some of her books and sent her papers flying. He did not seem to notice. In one smooth motion he was soaring out the door and over the balcony rail. Olwynne picked up her books and papers with a long-suffering sigh and followed more sedately.

The boys' dormitories were on the far side of the garth and, in general, were out of bounds to the girls. However, rules were much more relaxed for the older apprentices, and as long as everyone was back in their own rooms by lights out, no one much cared. As Olwynne crossed the garth, she heard the bell ring, then the sound of several hundred students packing up their books and closing their desks. She quickened her pace, having no desire to run into any of her friends, who would want to stop her for a gossip.

Both Owein and Lewen had recently been promoted to senior students and so their rooms were up on the top floor. Owein, of course, simply flew up and over the balcony, calling mockingly over his shoulder, "Come on, slow coach!" Olwynne had to go up by the stairs.

Lewen's door stood ajar, and she knocked on it tentatively before going in. Lewen was lying on his bed, his arm flung up over his face. As Olwynne came in he dashed his hand over his eyes and sat up. He was white and haggard, his eyes red-rimmed. Shocked at the sight of him, Olwynne went swiftly to his side and put her arms about him. He gave a great sigh and slumped against her.

Lewen MacNiall of Kingarth was the twins' greatest friend. He had first come to the Theurgia at the age of sixteen and, being only a few months younger than they were, had been put in their class. Owein and Olwynne had been at the Theurgia since the age of eight and knew everyone and everything. Lewen had never left his parents' farm before and had been stricken by acute homesickness, which he had done his best to hide. At first it was his misery and the gameness with which he sought to conceal it that touched Olwynne's tender heart, but soon his skill at games had won Owein over completely too. The three had been inseparable ever since, particularly once Lewen was appointed squire to the Rìgh in honor of his father, who had once been one of Lachlan MacCuinn's most trusted officers.

"What in Eà's name is the matter?" Olwynne asked.

Lewen seized her hands. "Ye've got to help me, Olwynne. The captain's got Rhiannon locked up in prison and they willna let me in to see her! I've got to see her, Olwynne!"

"But why? Who's Rhiannon?"

Lewen got up and went to the window. After a moment, he said, "She's from Dubhglais. She's half satyricorn. She was raised in the mountains by her mother's herd, but they despised her for being so human-looking. When her horns didna grow, she thought they'd kill her and so she tamed a winged horse and flew it down out of the mountains. I found her and the poor exhausted mare and took them back to Kingarth. We thought . . . Mam and *Dai-dein* and I . . . that she had best come back with me to Lucescere. She has Talent, ye see. Strong Talent."

"But Owein says she was a prisoner . . . that she was bound and tied to the horse."

Lewen nodded, not turning around.

"But why? What has she done?"

"She killed Connor the Just," Lewen said, very low.

Owein had been floating up near the ceiling, but at this he exclaimed aloud and dropped down lightly to his feet. "Connor the Just! No' our Connor? Johanna's brother?"

Lewen nodded and leaned his head against the windowframe.

"Eà's green blood!" Owein exclaimed.

Olwynne was distressed. "But why? How?"

"No wonder the captain was so grim," Owein said, marveling. "Damn! He'll be out for her blood. And *Dai-dein* too. Och, she's gallows apples for sure."

"Owein!" Olwynne said softly. Obligingly he shut up and she went over to Lewen, tentatively putting her hand on his shoulder. "Tell me what happened," she said.

He would not look at her. "Connor was captured by the herd, riding through their territory. Rhiannon helped him escape, but he was captured again by Rhiannon's mother, who is First-Horn o' the herd. He tried to fight free. Rhiannon shot him to save her mother."

"Did they no' ken he rode in the Rìgh's service?" Owein demanded, scandalized.

"Dubhglais is deep in the mountains, a million miles from anywhere," Lewen said wearily. "The satyricorns are wild there. They ken naught."

"Ignorance is no defense," Owein said. "The satyricorns have signed the Pact o' Peace. They had no right to hinder a Yeoman, let alone murder him!"

"I doubt these satyricorns have even heard o' the Pact o' Peace," Lewen said. He shrugged off Olwynne's hand and went to sit on his bed again, his face in his hands. "Anyway, none o' it should matter," he said in a muffled tone. "Rhiannon is naught but a lass, and she shot him to save her mother's life. Besides, she's shown herself brave and true. She rescued Roden on the way here and saved his life. That has to count for something."

"Ye mean Nina's little boy?" Olwynne asked. "The heir to Caerlaverock?"

"Aye. He was kidnapped, and Rhiannon rescued him. Nina and Iven promised they would speak up for her, tell the Rìgh what happened. And now she's rotting in some foul dungeon and Laird Malvern is being waited on hand and foot in one o' the tower's best rooms!"

"Who?" Owein and Olwynne asked together.

"The laird o' Fettercairn," Lewen said impatiently. "He was the one who kidnapped Roden. He's a murderer and a traitor and a foul necromancer, and if it wasna for Rhiannon, we'd all probably be dead!"

Even Olwynne was beginning to be bewildered by the complexity of Lewen's tale. "I'm sure it willna be for long," she said hesitantly. "*Dai-dein* will get to the bottom o' it all, I'm sure."

"But she hates being confined," Lewen said miserably. "When I first found her, she'd never even seen a house afore. It'll send her half-mad, being locked up in a dungeon."

"I'm sure it's no' that bad," Olwynne said.

"Ye didna see the captain's face," Lewen retorted.

"He was pretty angry," Owein agreed.

"I've got to get in to see her!" Lewen cried, lifting his face to look at his friends. "I've got to reassure her. Please, ye've got to help me."

"O' course we'll help ye," Owein cried. "I'll bang the guard on the head and we'll steal his keys and then—"

"Dinna be such a gawk!" Olwynne said crossly. "We canna do that."

"At least I'm no' a namby-pamby muffin-faced prig," Owein retorted, firing up.

"Ye'll get yourself and Lewen into dreadful trouble and only make things worse for this Rhiannon girl," Olwynne said.

"Aye, happen we'd be best slipping something into his wine," Owein said thoughtfully. "Then he'll just think he dozed off."

"And the captain will order him put to the lash," Olwynne snapped back. "That hardly seems fair."

"Well, got any better ideas?" her twin jeered.

"Aye, I do, as a matter o' fact."

"O' course ye do, Miss Perfect," Owein muttered.

"Let's just go and see *Dai*," Olwynne said. "Surely if we just explain to him how important it is that Lewen gets in to see her . . ." Her voice faltered. She could not look at Lewen as she asked, "Just *why* is it so important, Lewen? I mean, *Dai-dein* will be in conference. . . ."

Lewen raised his face from his hands and gazed at Olwynne imploringly. If anyone could intercede with the Rìgh, it was Olwynne, for Lachlan adored his only daughter and often declared she was the only one with any sense in the whole family.

"I'm in love with her," he said haltingly, a hot rush of color burning his cheeks. "Wait till ye meet her, Olwynne. There's never been a girl like her. She can ride like a thigearn and fight like a man, and she's clever as a bag full o' elven cats. I . . . I want to jump the fire with her. One day, I mean."

Olwynne looked away, biting back angry words.

Owein grinned. "Lewen's in lo-o-ove," he sang.

Lewen flushed again. "Well, I am," he said doggedly. "And she loves me. And I promised I'd look out for her and make sure all was well. I canna let her be hanged."

"But how can ye stop it? If she's found guilty, I mean?" Olwynne asked.

Lewen looked stubborn, an expression Olwynne knew only too well. "I dinna ken how, but I will if I have to, I swear it. Ye've got to help me, Olwynne. Ye'll love her too, when ye meet her. I ken ye will."

Somehow Olwynne doubted that.

The Lord of
Fettercairn's Skeelie

Johanna the Mild sat listlessly in the cushioned window seat of her room. Outside she could hear the students talking and giggling, and the gruff voice of the sorcerer Jock Crofter as he ordered them in to their supper. It was growing late and, as head of the Royal College of Healers, Johanna should have been doing her rounds at the hospital and preparing for the evening lectures. But today she could not even find the energy to rise and put on her long green healer's robe, let alone face a room full of rowdy students.

Her brother was dead. She had heard of his death more than a month ago, after Lewen had used the Scrying Pool at the haunted Tower of Ravens to contact the Rìgh, but the news that his murderer had been brought to Lucescere to face trial had torn the wounds wide open again.

Johanna had no one else. Connor had been her only family. Orphaned when they were very small, they had spent their childhood begging on the streets of Lucescere, scrounging through rubbish and stealing whatever they could lay their hands on, just to stay alive. Then they had met the blind seer Jorge and his apprentice Tòmas the Healer, a little boy with the miraculous ability to heal any wound or illness with the mere touch of his hands. Johanna and Connor had helped them escape the witch-sniffers and had had to flee Lucescere to avoid being captured themselves. Along with the rest of their gang of street kids, they had formed the famous League of the Healing

Hand, sworn to help and protect Tòmas and to help bring back the Coven of Witches so all with magical powers would be safe.

Tòmas and Connor had been only seven years old. Johanna had been sister and mother to them both. For the next few years, the League of the Healing Hand had worked to help Lachlan the Winged overthrow Maya and her Anti-Witchcraft League, then beat back the Bright Soldiers of Tìrsoilleir, then win the war against the Fairgean so that Eileanan was finally at peace. Along the way, most of the League of the Healing Hand had lost their lives, including Tòmas himself. He had then been just twelve years old, and Johanna had been heartbroken with grief. It had seemed so cruel, so unfair, that the little boy who had saved so many thousands of lives, including that of the Rìgh, should not live to see the peace he had helped bring about.

Twenty years of peace and prosperity had numbed Johanna's grief. She still thought of Tòmas often, but her own busy, happy life as the head of the Royal College of Healers had filled the void his death had left, and she had still had her brother, tall, handsome, accomplished Connor, who had risen through the ranks of the Yeomen of the Guard to be one of Lachlan the Winged's most trusted lieutenants.

But now Connor was dead.

Her grief was a barbed and spiky creature with bloody jaws, chewing ravenously away at her entrails. She did not think she could survive the pain. Nothing helped her. Even drinking a vial of poppy syrup did nothing except plunge her into swelteringly hot, garishly colored nightmares where she saw Connor's grey decaying body rise up out of filthy foam, holding up beseeching crippled hands, his beautiful mouth a bloody and empty ruin where that satyricorn had hacked out his teeth, his eye sockets gaping where fish had fed on his laughing blue eyes, a crimson and black hole plunging through to his heart. It was better not to sleep.

Johanna had forced herself to keep working, filling her days and nights by easing the pain of others. This at least meant that her body was so weary that when she laid herself down on her bed at night, sometimes she did manage to sleep, for a few hours at least.

But today her brother's murderer had ridden into the city. Johanna had heard the news almost straightaway, for Captain

Dillon had been the one to form the League of the Healing Hand so many years ago. He was one of her oldest friends and her occasional lover, and he had come to tell her the moment the prison doors had clanged shut behind the satyricorn. Like Johanna, he was filled with a bitter corrosive hatred of the girl who had snuffed out Connor's bright life so heedlessly. All the while Johanna wept, he had stood still, caressing the hilt of his sword with obsessive tenderness, his eyes fixed on nothing. He had made no attempt to comfort Johanna. He knew there was no consolation, except perhaps the justice of seeing the satyricorn hang. That might ease Johanna's pain.

Johanna pressed her fingers against her throbbing eyes. She was filled with a heavy lassitude that weighed down her bones and made every movement an effort. Her head ached.

There was a knock on the door. Johanna sighed. When it came again, she said wearily, "Yes?"

"May I come in?" asked an unfamiliar voice.

"Who is it?"

"I'm a visitor here to the tower, ma'am. I'm interested indeed in herbs and healing and was told ye were the one who kens more than any other living soul. May I come in and introduce myself?"

"It is no' a good time," Johanna said with an effort.

"I ken, ma'am. I ken all about your trouble. I am so sorry. I think perhaps I can help."

Johanna covered her eyes with her hand, saying nothing.

"I come from Ravenshaw," the voice went on. It was the voice of an older woman, brisk and warm. "I ken this girl, the one who shot your brother."

Johanna sat up as abruptly as if a thorn had been driven in under her fingernails. "What?"

"Aye. I met her at Fettercairn Castle. I may be able to help ye, ma'am."

Johanna hesitated, then stood and went to the door, unlocking it.

The woman on the other side smiled at her sympathetically. She was at least fifty years of age, with rosy cheeks all withered like a winter apple and brown eyes. Her figure was plump and soft, and her eyes and skin glowed with health.

"I am sorry to disturb ye, ma'am," she said. "I was told I could find ye here."

"Who told ye? What do ye want?" Johanna was too distressed to be polite.

The woman smiled at her and stepped inside so that Johanna was forced to take a step back. Putting down her basket on the table, the visitor shut the door behind her and ushered Johanna back to her chair with one broad hand, saying warmly, "I am so sorry to intrude upon ye like this. I do feel for ye so much. Please, sit down again. Ye must be worn to pieces. Let me get ye a cushion. Your poor head must be aching so much."

Rather dazed, Johanna let the stranger put a soft cushion behind her head, which was indeed aching most unpleasantly. The woman then went to her basket and pulled out a bottle, dampening her handkerchief with lavender water and bringing it back to press against Johanna's brow. Johanna shut her eyes, tears stinging her lids.

"There now, that'll help a little. Let me put your feet up. Ye look worn out."

"Who are ye?" Johanna asked, even as she submitted to being made comfortable.

The woman clicked her tongue. "There now, how rude o' me. I forgot to introduce myself. My name is Dedrie and I'm the laird o' Fettercairn's skeelie."

Johanna's eyes flew open, and she tried to sit up.

Gently Dedrie pressed her back down again. "I see ye've heard o' my master, and naught good, I'd warrant. Indeed, that satyricorn girl has done naught but evil, as far as I can see. She murdered your brother in cold blood, and blackened my poor master's name, and had him thrown in prison, and all because he wouldna be taken in by her tricks. All he did was try to stop her from escaping."

"Really?" Johanna gripped her hands together.

Dedrie dabbed at Johanna's forehead with the cool, damp cloth. "Aye, indeed. It makes my blood boil just thinking about her. Och, she's a wicked one, cold-blooded and cruel. Just look at the way she murdered your brother! And pulled out all his teeth to make a necklace for herself, I heard."

Johanna caught her breath in a sob.

"Och, I'm so sorry, I've upset ye again. Come now, do no'

weep. Here, let me dampen that cloth again for ye. It must be
hot by now." Dedrie rose and uncorked the bottle of lavender
water again, bathing Johanna's temples and then laying the
cloth over her eyes. "Lay your poor head back now; there ye
are. Is that better? Now let me make ye some tea. Chamomile
and orange blossoms, I think, and perhaps some rose hips to
give ye strength to bear it all."

"Ye've kent the laird for long?" Johanna asked, pressing the
cloth over her eyes with one hand.

She heard the rustle of Dedrie's dress as she went to the fire
and swung the kettle back over the flames.

"Och, aye, I've worked at Fettercairn Castle since I was a
lass. At first I was nurserymaid to the young heir, Laird
Malvern's nephew, but after he died I stayed on at the castle,
nursing his mother and anyone else in the Fetterness Valley
who needed help. I dinna ken much, but I learned what I could
from those who still had skill and managed as best I could. The
witch hunts were cruel hard in Ravenshaw in those days, ye
ken, and all the old skeelies and cunning men were burned on
the fires, so there was no one left to teach me." Her words were
punctuated by the whistle of the kettle and the clink of glass
and china.

"Aye, they were bad times," Johanna said, her eyes still shut.
"Much knowledge was lost."

"And they were no' the days to be seeking after such skills,"
Dedrie said, unscrewing a lid. "I was lucky to be under the protection o' the laird and no' accused o' witchcraft myself, as anyone who grew herbs and plants for healing often were."

Johanna opened her eyes, glancing over at Dedrie with
warm sympathy. The skeelie was pouring boiling water into the
teapot. "Aye, it was brave o' ye. The people o' Fetterness were
lucky."

"Och, nay! Indeed, I was no' much o' a healer at first. Over
time, though, I learned more and I think I helped a wee. I wish
I could do more. Which is why I am here, ye see." She hesitated, fumbling with the teapot, then turned and straightened
up, squaring her shoulders. "The thing is, ma'am, I'm wishing
to be learning more. The sorceress Nina, the one they call the
nightingale, she says ye ken more about the arts o' healing than
anyone. . . ."

"Och, I dinna think that is true, though it is kind o' her to say so. I learned most o' my craft from the Keybearer, Isabeau, who learned it from Meghan o' the Beasts. I often consult the Keybearer when I am no' sure o' the best remedy."

"But I canna be going and bothering the Keybearer, an auld skeelie like me!" Dedrie cried. "Och, I walked the corridor outside your room for close on half an hour afore I got up the courage to knock, and my knees are trembling still. If I had no' thought I could help ye . . . if I had no' thought it was my beholden duty to tell ye what I ken, well, then . . ."

"What ye ken?" Johanna said sharply. "Ye ken something about this girl . . . this satyricorn who killed my brother?"

Dedrie nodded, pressing her hands together. "Only they willna listen to anything I have to say. I'm just a poor auld skeelie, and they all believe those dreadful, dreadful lies that horrible girl told them about my laird. Just because she's so young and pretty and looks so guileless. They'll let her off the hook for sure, while my poor master—"

"What do ye ken?"

"Ye only have to look at her to see she's as slippery as an eel. Why, I met her at the castle, and the playacting that lass put on, it puts me to the blush. She pretended to see ghosts and screamed and threw herself around in fainting fits, which a healer like ye would have kent straightaway were fake but deceived everyone else, and then said she had seen murderers and evil sorceries, and all the time she was trying to deflect attention away from the fact that she was the one who had murdered in cold blood. Aye, and mutilated the body too, and threw it in the river to rot."

Johanna tried to suppress an involuntary sob, but it burst out of her. She covered her face with her hands.

"I'm so sorry!" Dedrie cried, seizing one of Johanna's hands in her own. "I dinna mean to upset ye. What was I thinking, coming at a time like this? Please forgive me."

"I'm sorry," Johanna said, wiping her eyes with the handkerchief. "I just canna believe it. Connor . . . everyone loved Connor! He was so bonny and brave and true—a favorite with the Rìgh and the whole court. The Rìgh leaned on him heavily, ye ken—he was always sending him out to settle one disagreement or another, or to take messages o' grave import to the other prionnsachan. I just canna believe he's dead!"

"And in such a way! It just doesna seem right." Dedrie swirled the water in the teapot.

Johanna began to cry again.

"And to let his murderess off the hook, just because they havena any eyewitnesses. It's a crying shame! She should be hung out o' hand."

"Do they really think she will be released?" Johanna said, scrubbing at her eyes. "It just doesna seem right!"

"That it does no'!" Dedrie said emphatically, pouring out the tea and stirring honey into the cup. "But without any witnesses to stand against her . . . They say she has ensorcelled all those young ladies and gentlemen who traveled with her, and the witch too. She must be very crafty and cunning indeed."

Johanna sighed, her throat thick with grief.

Dedrie brought the steaming cup over to Johanna and pressed it into her hand. "There ye are. Get this inside ye."

Johanna gratefully took the cup Dedrie passed to her and sipped at it. The tea was sweet and hot. She felt her muscles relax.

"And all those dreadful things she's been saying about my laird," the skeelie went on, bustling around and packing away her tins of herbs. "All lies, every one o' them, but mud sticks, ye ken; mud sticks. My poor laird has to cool his heels in that blaygird prison now too for months, until his name can be cleared, and there will always be those that say there's no smoke without fire, and all because o' that sly girl and her lies."

"But are ye sure she is lying?"

"Sure as the sky is blue!" Dedrie cried. She sat down heavily and mopped her eyes with the corner of her apron. "It just breaks my heart to see my laird so disgraced and downhearted. And did ye ken she drove my lady to her death? Lady Evaline, who was the widow o' my laird's brother? Lady Evaline believed her dreadful tales and threw herself out her window."

"How terrible!" Johanna cried.

"Aye, it is. That family has kent such tragedy. And this satyricorn girl out o' the mountains cares naught for any o' that, but only sees how she can turn it to her own advantage. I just wish there was something I could do."

"But if ye were to stand witness," Johanna cried. "At her trial! If ye were to give testimony against her."

"But I'm naught but a poor auld skeelie and caught up in the slander against my laird, like all his faithful servants. They willna listen to me."

"They will! O' course they will."

"Happen if I was here, at the College o' Healers, attending ye," Dedrie said thoughtfully. "Learning what I could o' the art o' healing, maybe then they would . . . but no. As long as they think I am one o' the laird o' Fettercairn's party, they will never believe me. Her lies have blackened us all."

Johanna sat back, deflated. Her headache was gone, but in its place she felt a strange light-headedness, while all her limbs felt weighed down with stones.

The skeelie came and poured her more tea and rearranged her cushion more comfortably. Johanna drank the tea down, allowing herself to be comforted.

"If only there was someone to stand sponsor for me and give testimony to my character," Dedrie said slowly. "Then the judges would believe me. But with that creature's lies blackening my good name as well as my laird's, they'll think I lie to protect my laird, o' course they will, as long as he is my patron." She sighed heavily.

"What if ye were here, at the College o' Healers, under my protection?" Johanna demanded. "Would they believe ye then?"

Dedrie clasped her hands together. "O' course they would! How could they no' believe me? Och, that would be wonderful! And I could stay here, at the college, and study with ye, ma'am? Och, please!"

"I'll organize a room for ye now," Johanna said, looking around for the bell. Dedrie brought it to her hand, and she rang it emphatically. Johanna's assistant came, and she gave orders for a room near hers to be prepared and a letter to be sent to the prison warden, giving him her assurances on Dedrie's behalf. The skeelie made a few shy suggestions as to how the letter could be worded, which the assistant duly noted before withdrawing.

"I do thank ye, ma'am," Dedrie said, her round face pink with pleasure. "All my life I've dreamed o' doing all I can to help and heal those in need. And to think I can work to serve ye, and help ye, the head o' the Royal College o' Healers. Och, ye will no' regret it, I promise ye."

"It is ye who helps me," Johanna said, gazing up at Dedrie with heartfelt gratitude. "It is I who should thank ye."

"Och, nay. What have I done but my duty? It would've been very wrong o' me to let that terrible murdering creature escape justice without trying at least to make sure someone stood witness against her. Here, ma'am, let me rub lavender and peppermint oil into your forehead. It will make ye feel much better."

"I am in your debt," Johanna said, closing her eyes as Dedrie gently massaged her temples.

"No' at all," said the lord of Fettercairn's skeelie.

Murderers' Gallery

Rhiannon lifted her hot, throbbing hands and pressed them against her face, trying to block out the foul smell. As her eyes grew accustomed to the gloom, she looked about her anxiously, all her muscles ready for quick and violent action.

The Murderers' Gallery was a long, low, windowless room, with walls of weeping stone. Rank, moldy straw was scattered on the rock floor, and a bucket in one corner was overflowing with excrement. Rhiannon could see a dead rat lying not far from her knee, the stink of its rotting body adding to the stench.

There were more than twenty women crowded about the room. Some sat on the ground with their backs against the wall; others lay on rough stone shelves chipped into it. A few were confined by manacles or thumbscrews, as Rhiannon was, and one sat with her head and hands thrust through holes in a large wooden block. Another prisoner was confined in a cage of wood built under the overhang of rock in the far corner. All Rhiannon could see of her was her hands, gripping the bars with white knuckles, and a great mass of hair through which two eyes glared.

Most of the prisoners looked up at Rhiannon dully, then returned their gaze to the floor without any sign of interest, but one woman gave a snort of bitter laughter. "Welcome to Sorrowgate, sweetheart," she sneered. "Ye're a pretty one, ye are. I bet Octavia drooled over ye. Did she stick her hand up your skirt? I bet she wanted to. I bet she—"

"Leave the lass alone, Clarice," someone else said wearily. Rhiannon glanced at her. She was young and had a shawl huddled about her thin shoulders. "Look at her; she's frightened out o' her wits as it is," the girl went on, sympathy in her eyes.

Rhiannon wanted to deny this, but her throat was so dry and rigid with fear she could not force the words out. She gritted her teeth and tried to slow her uneven pants of breath.

Clarice got to her feet and came towards Rhiannon, her thin face twisted into a cruel leer. "How ye going to make me?" she mocked. "Come on, lassiekin, make me stop."

She bent over Rhiannon, grinning, and reached one hand down to stroke her long black hair. Rhiannon jerked her hands up, smashing her thumbscrews into Clarice's face. The woman reeled backwards with a scream, then rushed at Rhiannon with raking fingernails, blood streaming from her nose. Rhiannon came up off her knees in a rush, fending the woman off with her confined hands, then kicking her back to the floor. Clarice shrieked.

"Sssh!" the girl said urgently. "Ye'll bring Octavia down on us! Leave her alone, for Eà's sake!"

Clarice wiped away the blood with the back of her hand, staring at Rhiannon with cold, angry eyes. With her hair tossed back from her face, Rhiannon could see she was missing one ear, an ugly stump all that remained.

"Leave me alone and I'll leave ye alone," Rhiannon said as threateningly as she could, hoping no one noticed how her knees threatened to buckle beneath her.

Unexpectedly Clarice laughed. It was a cold, hollow sound. "Fair enough," she said and stood up, dusting off her bottom with one hand. She went over and sat down on an old sack, wrapping her arms about her legs to keep warm. She kept her cynical gaze on Rhiannon's face, her creased and weathered face twisted in a habitual mocking leer.

Rhiannon looked about her warily, clutching her blanket to her chest. The blanket smelled even worse than the smock, but it was thick and warm and acted in some way like a shield.

The girl who had defended her made a beckoning motion with her head and shifted over so there was a gap against the wall. Rhiannon went across to it and sat down, feeling a telltale prickle in her eyes. *I will no' cry, I will no' cry*, she told herself fiercely, but the hot tears forced their way through her lids anyway. Rhiannon gulped a breath and lifted her hands, weighed down with the cruel thumbscrews, to defiantly wipe them away.

"Dinna greet, lassie," the girl beside her whispered. "If ye greet, they'll just mock ye more."

Rhiannon glared angrily at the girl sitting next to her. She had an anxious, crooked face. It looked as if her jaw had once been broken and had not healed properly. Although dressed in the same loose smock as Rhiannon, she wore thick woolen stockings and boots and had a crocheted shawl wrapped around her shoulders and a red woolen cap on her head. Her long brown hair was neatly plaited, and she held in her lap a small basket from which she withdrew a clean white handkerchief. She offered this to Rhiannon who, after a moment's hesitation, took it and did her best to scrub her face dry. Her clamped thumbs were beginning to swell, and the movement hurt them. The girl saw this and gently took the handkerchief and dried Rhiannon's face for her, then matter-of-factly helped her blow her nose, as if Rhiannon was a small child.

"What's your name?" the girl asked, tucking the soiled handkerchief away.

"Rhiannon."

"No family name?"

Rhiannon shook her head.

"I'm Bess Balfour. What ye in for?"

Rhiannon had to swallow before she could answer. "Murder."

"Me too," Bess said sympathetically. "Who did ye murder?"

"A soldier," Rhiannon said shortly. "He was trying to kill my mother," she added after a moment.

"I killed my father," Bess said. "He was beating my poor auld ma almost to death, and so I grabbed the bedpan and whacked him across the head. He fell and hit his head on the hearthstone. Cracked his skull."

"And they locked ye up for that?" Rhiannon said indignantly.

Bess nodded. "I have a lawyer, though," she said with quiet pride. "He's costing my ma every penny she's managed to squirrel away over the years but she says he's worth it. I just have to wait till the next quarter sessions, when my case will go afore the magistrates, and then he'll argue my case for me. My ma and my sisters bring me food and coins to give Octavia, so she'll let me have an extra blanket and my shawl. I'm lucky. If ye havena any family to bring ye money, ye'll starve to death in here."

"I havena anyone to bring me money," Rhiannon said somberly.

"What about your ma? Won't she help ye out?"

"My ma's no' here," Rhiannon answered curtly. She wondered if this girl would be so friendly if she knew Rhiannon's mother was a satyricorn.

"Ye must've had some money since Octavia gave ye a blanket," Bess said. "Would ye like me to tuck it around ye? Ye canna do it yourself with the thumbscrews on."

Rhiannon nodded, and Bess reached over and took her blanket and tucked it around her. Rhiannon hung her head, blinking back another rush of tears.

There was a sudden howl from the woman in the cage, and she rattled the bars, thrusting a wild-eyed face against them. Rhiannon flinched back.

"Poor mad thing," Bess said. "I wonder what they'll do to her after her trial."

"What did she do?"

"Strangled her nurse," Bess said with a little shiver. "She was in the madhouse, has been there all her life, I was told. They always thought her gentle. But one day she just grabbed her nurse and choked the life out o' her. They said it took three men to break her grasp."

"What about her?" Rhiannon asked, jerking her head at Clarice, who had finally stopped staring at her and was digging gunk out from under her toenails with her fingernails. "Who did she kill?"

"Och, she didna kill anyone. She's a thief. She's already lost an ear, dinna ye see? If ye get caught again after losing an ear, ye hang for it. Or at least, ye used to. They do no' hang so many these days. Sometimes they send ye to work in the mines or summat like that."

"I thought this was the Murderers' Gallery?"

"It is. I mean, that's what they call it, but no' everyone in here has killed someone. There are other crimes they'll hang ye for, like poaching or stealing horses or hawks."

"Like me. I'm a prigger o' prancers," the woman on the other side of Rhiannon said, scratching absentmindedly at her armpit. She was an older woman with a branded face and scraggy arms marked with vague blue tattoos. At Rhiannon's blank look she grinned, showing crooked, discolored teeth. "Horses," she explained. "Me and my brother steal horses for a living."

"What about her?" Rhiannon asked, looking across at a young woman sitting on the far side of the room who had been intriguing her for some time. She was rocking a rolled-up blanket in her arms, swaying back and forth and singing to it under her breath.

"She drowned her baby," Bess said. "Her father's a rich merchant. He sells cloth, I think. No one kent she was pregnant. I dinna ken how she managed to hide it. They found the baby in the privy. She drowned it in her washbasin and tried to throw it out. I think they'll hang her for that too, though happen they'll just send her to the madhouse. She's as crazy as a loon, poor thing."

Rhiannon could not help shuddering. Bess saw and gave her a sympathetic look.

"What does hanged, drawn, and quartered mean?" Rhiannon asked suddenly.

"Do ye no' ken?" Bess asked in surprise. "Och, it's what they do for traitors. They hang ye till ye're almost dead, then they gut ye while ye're still alive, and then they cut ye up into quarters and throw the parts o' ye to the four corners o' the city, for the dogs to fight over. I havena heard o' it being done for years and years. No' since afore I was born, at least."

Rhiannon pressed her face down into her knees, within the circle of her imprisoned hands. Bess touched her arm in quick sympathy, but Rhiannon did not respond. She was afraid she might weep, or laugh, or throw up, or shriek, if she moved. Hanged, drawn, and quartered. No one had ever told her that was the fate she might have to face.

"Are ye all right?" Bess whispered. "What's wrong? Do ye feel sick? The smell from that bucket is enough to make anyone throw up!"

Rhiannon managed to nod her head.

"Here, hold this to your nose," Bess said, taking a little bottle from her basket. "It's lavender. It'll help."

Rhiannon reached out to take it but could not manage with her hands locked together with the thumbscrews. Bess held it to her nose for her.

"Thank ye," Rhiannon managed to say.

"Och, that's fine," the girl said awkwardly and put the bottle away.

They were silent after that, Bess sensing that Rhiannon did not want to talk. The hours crawled past. Rhiannon found herself getting more and more uncomfortable. The ground was bitterly cold, damp, and very hard, and no matter how she sat or lay down, her imprisoned hands tortured her. Her thumbs were now red and swollen and throbbed incessantly. She was hungry and thirsty too, and tormented by a constant crawling sensation on her skin, an itch that she could not scratch.

"Lice," Bess told her. "The smocks and blankets are full o' them. That's what I have the lavender oil for, to put on the bites."

Knowing the cause of the itchiness was no consolation. Rhiannon scratched wherever she could reach until her fingernails were bloody, but it did no good. The lice feasted upon her in high good humor.

Clarice the thief was one of the few prisoners not confined in some way. It did not take long for her to grow bored of exploring her toenails, and she began to prowl the room. First she tormented the madwoman in the cage, reaching through the bars to poke and pinch her. The madwoman began to wail, rocking back and forth, back and forth, until Rhiannon wanted to screech at her to stop. She was not the only one. Waves of unease rolled around the room. The woman in the stocks raised her head to look, but lacked the strength to crane it up for long and let it loll limply again. One woman hid her face in her hands and began to rock too, murmuring, "Make her shut up, make her shut up." Yet another tried to plug her ears with her fingers. Bess drew her shawl up around her ears and buried her face in her arms.

Clarice grinned and reached through the bars to tug at the madwoman's matted hair. At once she shrieked like a banshee and leaped up, one hand clawing out through the bars and raking Clarice's face. The thief was sent sprawling, her cheek bleeding. The madwoman laughed and laughed. Her high-pitched, hysterical giggle was weirdly infectious. Rhiannon had to cram her throbbing hands against her mouth to stop an answering chortle, and she heard a muffled snicker from somewhere on the other side of the room.

Clarice heard it too, and got up, her leathery face twisted with malice and hatred. "Who was that?" she demanded. "Who just laughed?" She prowled the room, prodding and kicking the chained women. "Ye think it funny, do ye?"

No one said anything. Rhiannon herself hardly dared glance that way, in case Clarice turned her mean eyes upon her. She was in so much pain from her engorged thumbs now that even shifting her weight sent dizzying waves of pain through her, and she had no desire to try to fight the thief off again.

The merchant's daughter was still rocking her bundle and humming a lullaby. She did not look up when Clarice stopped in front of her. Rhiannon felt Bess stiffen beside her.

"Look at ye, ye loon," Clarice sneered. "Ye should be caged up too. Baby killer."

The girl did not look up, though her humming rose a little in pitch and volume.

Clarice bent and seized the bundled blanket and flung it away across the room. It unrolled and fell on the filthy floor. The golden-haired girl started to her feet, her hands flying to her cheeks, and screamed. It went on and on and on. Bess scrambled up and ran across the room, seeking to comfort her. "It's all right, it's all right, do no' scream so, I'll get it back for ye." Hastily she grabbed the blanket and rolled it up for her again, trying to thrust the bundle into the girl's arms. The scream stopped, but the girl was only gathering breath to scream again, even higher and louder than before. Desperately Bess tried to calm her, but to no avail. Rhiannon covered her ears.

Then the door crashed open. Octavia loomed up in the doorway. Everyone shrank back, all except the merchant's daughter, who was sobbing now and tearing at her face with her nails, and the madwoman in the cage, who rocked back and forth on her haunches, muttering and giggling.

"What is going on?" Octavia demanded.

"She took the girl's baby." Clarice pointed at Bess. "I told her to leave the poor mad thing alone, but she's a nasty piece, that girl, for all that she looks so sweet."

Bess pressed back against the wall, her eyes dilated. "It's no' true," she stammered. "She did it, no' me. I was just—"

Octavia stumped forward, cuffed Bess hard across the ear, seized her by the hair, and dragged her towards the center of the room, where a thick wooden pole ran from floor to ceiling. Bess began to scream and plead, dragging back against the grip on her hair as hard as she could, but Octavia was too strong. Despite all of Bess's protestations, she was manacled and hung from a hook halfway up the pole, so that she could only stand on tiptoe. With tears pouring down her face, Bess tried once more to explain, but Octavia shrugged her massive shoulders and said curtly, "Ye interrupted my supper, girl. Ye've been here long enough to ken how much I hate that." She then shuffled back through the doorway, kicking aside the dead rat on the way.

Once the door was locked shut again, Clarice began to dance about, cackling in glee and singing, "Rat bait, rat bait."

Rhiannon took a deep breath and lifted her ironbound hands menacingly, saying in a low hiss, "Leave her alone, ogre breath, else I'll smash your face in."

Clarice stopped dancing and stared at her. "Octavia'll come back in," she taunted.

"Happen so, but by then ye'll have no face left. Octavia canna give ye your face back." Rhiannon had grown up the runt in a herd of satyricorns. She knew how to look and sound cruel.

"Happen no', but she'll kill ye for it."

"Nay, she won't. She's looking forward too much to seeing me being hanged, drawn, and quartered."

Clarice thought about this for a moment, then sneered at Rhiannon, pretending she was not afraid. She gave one last halfhearted jibe at Bess, then went to sit back down again, all the while shooting Rhiannon looks of hatred through the strings of her lank, grey hair.

Rhiannon went over to Bess. "Ye all right?"

"My arms . . ." Bess whimpered.

Rhiannon saw that the strain of her weight was almost pulling the girl's arms out of their sockets. She did her best to roll up her blanket, so Bess could step up onto it. Although it did not relieve the strain entirely, it did help a little and Bess murmured a miserable thanks.

"I'm sorry," Rhiannon said awkwardly. "It all happened so fast."

"What could ye have done?" Bess answered. "If ye'd tried to help, we both would be strung up here. It's Octavia's favorite punishment. I should've kent better than to interfere."

"I suppose so," Rhiannon answered, "but still . . ."

"If ye could try to drive the rats away when they come, that'd help," Bess said urgently. "Please?"

"Rats?"

Bess nodded, her eyes black with fear. She looked up the length of her arms to the top of the pole. "They come in there."

Rhiannon followed her gaze and saw a ragged hole at the top of the pole. Her heart sank. She returned her gaze to Bess's pleading eyes and nodded. "Me do what me can," she said.

About half an hour later, Rhiannon was dozing at the foot of the pole, her head resting on her bent arms, when she was jerked awake by a high-pitched squealing and rustling. She raised her head and looked around her. There was a general sigh and groan as all the women chained to the walls shifted unhappily. Those who could stand struggled to their feet, while those who could not pressed themselves back against the stone.

"The rats are coming," Bess said in terror, straining away from the pole. "They ken it's suppertime. Get up, Rhiannon."

The horse thief also got to her feet, hauling herself up by her chain. She called to Rhiannon. "I'd get away from there, lassie. Those rats are savage beasties. They'll gnaw off your face if they can."

Now Rhiannon could hear the clatter of hundreds of small claws on stone. The squeaking became louder. Bess gripped her chain and twisted, leaning as far away from the pole as possible. Her face was drawn back in a grimace of terror and disgust.

Then, like a stinking torrent of sewer filth, rats poured out the hole and down the pole. There were hundreds of them, big black brutes with red beady eyes and twitching noses.

Rhiannon tried to swipe them away with her manacled hands, but there were too many and they were too fierce. Bess pressed her face into her shoulder, trying not to shudder too violently, as they used her head and back as a bridge to the floor.

The rats rustled through the straw, seizing any crumbs or old bones or cheese rinds they could find. They swarmed around the feet of the prisoners, who shrieked and kicked out at them, sending the rats tumbling. The horse thief seized one by the tail and swung it against the wall, smashing its brains out and tossing it to the pack to be torn apart.

Still the rats kept coming, a heaving river of mangy fur and gaudy eyes. One stopped to smell Bess's ear, and Rhiannon saw the flesh there had torn where Octavia had cuffed her. Bess shrieked and writhed, trying to shake it off. Rhiannon tried in vain to help her, but she was handicapped by the thumbscrews.

"It's no good. She shouldna screech and jump around like that," the horse thief said. She shook her head in regret, expertly kicking away a rat that ran too close to her leg. "It'll bite her—and once they smell blood . . ."

Just then Bess screamed in agony as the rat sank its filthy fangs into her ear. The rats went into a frenzy. They all leaped at Bess, tearing at her flesh. Though she tried to fight them off, there were too many, and soon her face and arms and hands were streaming with blood.

"We've got to do something. We've got to help her!" Rhiannon cried, her face white with horror.

"They'll only attack ye too," the horse thief said. "I'm sorry for the lass but there's no helping it. She should never have crossed Octavia."

Rhiannon could not bear to watch. She turned her back, tears streaming down her face as Bess's screams grew shriller and more desperate.

"A few months back there was a prisoner who tried to escape," the horse thief said. "She grabbed Octavia and tried to choke her with her chains. . . . Octavia tied her up to that pole and smeared goose fat all over her belly. The rats chewed their way straight through her entrails. It took a long while for her to die."

Rhiannon pressed the back of her hands to her face. She had thought the satyricorns nasty and brutish, but none she knew of had ever done anything so cruel. Inside her she felt something shriveling and knew some last remnant of naïveté or hope was withering away.

One prisoner was rocking and weeping. "I want to go home. I want to go home."

"Who doesna?" the horse thief said.

Just then the door slammed open. Light streamed in, dazzling their eyes, then abruptly the massive shape of Octavia blotted out the light. She was carrying a bucket and a ladle. At once the tide of rats turned and converged on her. She tossed them a ladle full of slops and they scrabbled over one another to reach it, biting and snarling.

Everyone pressed themselves against the wall, wary and silent. She went over to Bess, hanging limply in her chains, moaning, her face and arms and breast ravaged with rodent bites. A few rats still huddled about her feet, feeding greedily on the hunks of her flesh they had torn away.

Octavia regarded her thoughtfully, then stuck the ladle in the bucket so she could unhook Bess's chains with her other hand. The rats lifted their pointy snouts to sniff at the aroma of soup so close above their heads, then went back to their feast. Octavia dragged Bess over to the wall and dropped her on a pile of damp, filthy straw.

"Tsk-tsk," she said. "How very dreadful. I must write to the prison governor and let him ken our rat problem is as bad as ever."

No one said a word.

"I do hope she doesna die o' her bites," Octavia said in a voice of mock concern. "The hangman's a good friend o' mine and he's no' paid unless they hang. If he's no' paid, he has no money to gamble with and that means I lose out too. Oh well. They probably wouldna have hung her anyway, stupid soft-bellied judges. All this talk about prison reform and the problem o' crime, and they never think to ask *me*. I could tell them, the only way to stop thieving, murdering scum like ye is to hang ye. No repeat offenders then, is there?'

She gave her hoarse, wheezing laugh and went around the room, kicking aside any rat brave enough to sniff at her, ladling soup into each woman's wooden bowl. Everyone slurped it down greedily.

Rhiannon's thumbs were now so swollen she could barely

grip her bowl. She was so hungry, though, that she endured the thudding pain, holding up the bowl to Octavia pleadingly. The jailer grunted and splashed some soup into it, and Rhiannon lowered her face to it. The soup was thin and cold and greasy, and tasted like old dishwater, but Rhiannon managed to swallow some down.

Octavia dumped the dregs of the bucket in the straw for the rats to squabble over, turned the lantern down low, and waddled out, locking the door behind her. Rhiannon's heart sank. The mouthful of soup had done nothing to quench her hunger, and she had hoped the jailer would remove her thumbscrews for the night. Her thumbs felt like fried sausages, about to burst in a splatter of sizzling fat.

She rested her throbbing hands upon her knees and laid her head back against the wall, shutting her eyes. She could hear Bess moaning in the straw. Rhiannon crawled towards her, one corner of the blanket clenched between her fingers, and tried as best she could to cover the wounded girl. Her hands were now so painful she could do no more. Bess was shivering violently, and Rhiannon managed to lie down beside her, her hands held awkwardly in front of her.

In her cage the madwoman rocked back and forth, laughing and muttering and occasionally rattling her bars. The rats scuffled the straw about, squealing in greedy outrage. The merchant's daughter rocked her cloth baby, humming a low tuneless lullaby, while someone else muttered, "Shut up, shut up, shut up, shut up."

Rhiannon closed her eyes, every now and again pressing her face into her sleeve to blot away her tears.

Liberty of the Tower

The ironbound door crashed open. Rhiannon startled awake. Octavia stood in the doorway, a lantern in her hand. She shone it this way and that, irradiating one ghastly, filthy face after another, their startled eyes wide and staring through the tangle of their hair. Then the light found Rhiannon's face and settled there.

Rhiannon shrank back, lifting her hands in their cruel metal contraption to shield her face. Her eyes felt gritty, her swollen thumbs pulsated horribly, and her skin was cold and clammy and crawled with lice. Worse than the hollowness of her empty stomach was the dreadful fear that the sight of Octavia provoked.

"Got friends in high places, do we?" the jailer cooed. "Should o' told me, dear. If I'd had any idea . . . Hope there's no hard feelings . . . Come, let's get ye out o' those." She bent and unlocked the clamp, releasing Rhiannon's thumbs. The sudden roar of pain was so intense Rhiannon almost fainted. Sick and giddy, she was lifted from the ground and a blanket wrapped around her shoulders. "Let's get ye cleaned up and some hot food in your belly," Octavia said, in the same treacle-sweet voice. "There are guards waiting for ye, to take ye to the Tower. I'll get ye your things. Come now, can ye walk?"

"Why? What's happened?" Rhiannon stammered.

"Ye've been given liberty o' the tower," Octavia said. "Seeing as how ye've got powerful friends. And rich too. Rooms in the tower dinna come cheap."

As she spoke, she half carried Rhiannon from the Murderers' Gallery. Rhiannon cast one dazed look back at Bess's motionless body before the door slammed shut behind her. Octavia took her down the hall and into a small stone cell where, amazingly, a fire cast out warmth and comfort. A big tin hip bath stood before the fire, with a ewer of water and a hunk of coarse yellow soap. Octavia dumped Rhiannon in the bath, dragged off the lice-ridden smock, and poured the water over her head.

"Sit," Octavia said and pushed on Rhiannon's shoulder till her legs buckled and she sat down with a plop. The water was lukewarm and came only halfway up the bath, so Rhiannon wrapped her arms about her shivering body and hunched there as Octavia scrubbed her head and back with the soap and a harsh-bristled brush. Suds poured down Rhiannon's face and she shut her eyes, totally dumbfounded by this sudden change in her situation.

Octavia dropped the brush in the bath. "Scrub yourself well if ye want to get rid o' the lice. I'll get ye some soup." She went out of the room and there was a sharp click as the key was turned in the lock. Although her thumbs were still swollen and ringed with dark bruises where the clamps had bitten into her skin, Rhiannon was able to use her fingers quite well and so, gripping the brush with both hands, she did as she was told, scrubbing herself till her skin was red and sore.

A thin, rough towel, a chemise, and a loose grey dress were draped over the chair, and so, when she was finally clean, Rhiannon rubbed herself dry and dressed herself as well as she was able, unwilling to have Octavia come back and find her still naked. There was something unnerving in the fat woman's lascivious little eyes. Rhiannon could not manage the buttons with her sore thumbs, so she held her bodice together with both hands and sat quietly waiting on the chair, her spirits soaring as she wondered who had paid for her release. Lewen? Nina and Iven? Much of her despair and misery had been caused by the fear that her friends had abandoned her. It was heartening to know they had not.

Octavia came in with a tureen of soup in her ham-sized hands. Amazingly, the soup steamed. She put it down on the table and looked Rhiannon up and down.

"I canna let ye go to the tower looking like that," she cooed, trying her best to smile. "Let me button ye up and comb your hair for ye, my dear, and then I'll get ye your boots and shawl."

Rhiannon submitted unwillingly, feeling revolted at the touch of those pudgy fingers at her bodice and then in her hair. She could not help remembering how Lewen liked to brush out her hair for her too.

"Eat up your soup then, dear," the jailer said tenderly. Rhiannon felt her hand lingering on the nape of her neck and could not help shuddering.

"Ye're cold. I'll stoke up the fire," Octavia said and thankfully removed her massive presence from behind Rhiannon's chair.

Rhiannon sipped at the soup. It was still thin and greasy, but hot and with soft lumps of potato and meat in it—far more palatable than what she had drunk before.

When she had finished and her long hair had been plaited away from her face, Octavia brought her pack, still bulging with all her belongings. She would not let Rhiannon check all was there but unpacked her boots, helping her draw them on, and wrapped her beautiful embroidered shawl about her, with all sorts of obsequious comments and attentions that made Rhiannon feel most uncomfortable. Then she was led out through the dark, dank corridors and given into the care of four heavily armed soldiers. They spoke not one word to her but did not hurry her along or push her, like the other guards had done.

She was taken out through a gate into a courtyard. It was dark, but she could see no stars in the sky, for the lights from the city reflected a red haze from the vault of the heavens that obliterated all starlight. The touch of the cold night wind on her face was wonderful, however, and she lingered for a moment, lifting her face. The soldiers gave her that moment, then silently urged her on. Cold stone closed over her again.

Led by a guard carrying a lantern, they passed through countless cold, cavernous halls and chambers, Rhiannon huddling her shawl about her. She wondered what time it was. It felt very late.

They passed through a large hall and into a room where other guards sat alertly, holding long, cumbersome weapons that Rhiannon had never seen before. Papers were checked and stamped with a red wax seal, and a big door was unlocked to allow Rhiannon and her escort through.

They climbed a narrow twisting staircase up three floors,

and then Rhiannon was ushered into a small dark cell. She looked around quickly. The bare walls were made from large blocks of stone, mercifully free from green slime. One wall was taken up by a heavy iron bed softened by a thin mattress and a clean sheet and pillow. A grey eiderdown was folded over the end. Under the bed was a chamber pot with a lid. A small table was set in the corner, with a heavy bench pushed beneath it. All the furniture was so solidly made Rhiannon would have difficulty shifting it, let alone throwing it or breaking it to make a weapon.

The guards were withdrawing, taking the lantern with them. Greedily the shadows swooped down upon Rhiannon's head.

"Wait!" She flung out one hand to halt them. At once the guards stiffened, hands flying to their weapons.

"Wait! Please," Rhiannon said with some difficulty. "Where am I?"

"Sorrowgate Tower," one replied tersely, not looking at her.

"What does that mean? Am I . . . ?" She stopped, unable to frame the question that meant so much to her. The four guards waited stolidly, and at last she managed to utter some more words. "Am I still . . . ?"

They did not answer for a moment. Then the youngest, a broad-shouldered, fresh-faced man of about twenty, said gruffly, "Ye've been granted liberty o' the tower, which means ye're out o' the public prison and into a room o' your own, with visitors allowed, and pen and paper if ye want it, and ye're allowed to walk in the warden's garden. Ye'll stay here until your trial or until the money dries up, whatever happens first."

"But I'm no' allowed out? Outside the tower, I mean."

He shook his head.

"Who's paying for it?" she demanded.

They all looked at each other and shrugged. Rhiannon bit her thumbnail.

As they once again began to withdraw, Rhiannon called out, "Wait! I'm sorry, I'm just wondering . . ."

They waited politely.

"What time is it?"

"After midnight, lass," another soldier said kindly. "I'd get some shut-eye if I were ye."

Rhiannon clenched her sore, throbbing hands together. "It's

too dark," she said, hearing the ragged edge of hysteria in her voice. "Please, canna ye leave the lantern?"

"Sorry, lass," the guard said. "Against the rules."

"Please. I dinna like the dark. Please."

The guard shared a glance with his companions, then said gruffly, "Each prisoner is allowed one candle after supper. I guess it willna matter if we let ye have one now. It only lasts a couple o' hours, though, I warn ye."

"Thank ye. Oh, thank ye," Rhiannon gabbled.

"Do no' think o' trying any tricks with it now," the guard warned. "It's hung high so ye canna reach it, see?"

He demonstrated to Rhiannon, showing her how he swung down the iron lantern hanging in the center of the ceiling with a long-handled hook, lit it with a taper from the lantern he carried, and then deftly hung it up again. It swung slightly, sending shadows swooping around the room. Rhiannon stared up at it. Even if she stood on her bed, she would not be able to reach it.

"It'll no' burn long," the older guard said. "Best get used to the dark, lass. We do no' get much sunshine here at Sorrowgate Tower."

Rhiannon nodded to show she understood, and the guards withdrew, locking and bolting the door behind them. Rhiannon sat gingerly upon her bed, looking about her. The single candle did not shed much light. The corners were full of shadows. After a while, she lay down, pulling the eiderdown over her. She did not sleep.

Dawn came slowly and with no fanfare of birds trilling or cocks crowing. As soon as it was light enough to see, Rhiannon got up and paced her room. It was five paces long and four paces wide. There was one tiny window, very high up in the wall. Even if Rhiannon was able to scale the smooth stone wall, the window was too small for her to do more than thrust her head out of it. The door was made of iron, with a slit through which an eye regularly appeared to check on her movements. After an hour or so of her pacing they brought her breakfast.

Rhiannon eyed the guards speculatively as they brought her tray in, wondering if she could somehow knock them out and escape that way. Both were tall, strong men, though, and well-armed. The first came in with his sword drawn and instructed her, gently but firmly, to sit on the bed while his companion set down the tray. The second soldier deftly unpacked the tray, then took it away with him, the guard with the sword backing out and quickly locking and bolting the door behind him. The whole operation took only a few moments.

Breakfast consisted of a wooden bowl filled with porridge, a trencher of black bread, a bruised apple, and a small jug of water. Nothing that Rhiannon could use as a weapon or tool. So she ate the lukewarm porridge, drank a cup of water, and lay down to rest on her bed again. She was, in fact, sick with weariness and misery, and sore and bruised all over. The thudding in her thumbs had settled down to a persistent ache, and the bruises had spread so that both swollen digits bloomed in varying hues of purple, blue, red, and yellow like ugly exotic flowers.

After a while the guards came and removed the remains of her meal. They left her the apple, the cup, and the jug of water. Rhiannon had nothing to do but watch a small tetragon of light move slowly down the wall, stretching longer and thinner as the morning passed. At some point she shut her eyes to keep back the tears, and slowly, strangely, she drifted away into sleep.

The sound of the bolts being dragged back jerked her awake. She swung her legs around to sit up, all her nerves jangling.

The door swung open. The guard stood with his sword drawn in the doorway. "Visitor for ye," he said, then stood back.

Lewen came in. He was dressed in a long blue tunic edged with silver braid over white satin breeches. On his shoulder was embroidered a badge with a golden stag rearing up on its hind hooves. A ceremonial cape was slung over one shoulder and secured with a silver badge. On his head was a soft blue cockaded cap, very like the one worn by the Yeomen. Rhiannon had never seen him so grandly dressed and it made her shy and awkward. He did not notice, though, coming forward eagerly and pulling her to her feet so he could embrace her. She cried out in pain, and at once he stepped back and exclaimed at the sight of her bruised and swollen thumbs.

She saw over his shoulder a tall redheaded girl hesitating in the doorway. Her thin red brows were drawn together in a frown.

"Who that?" Rhiannon demanded at the same time as the redhead asked in a cool voice, "Are you going to introduce me, Lewen?"

Lewen looked from one to the other, a little dismayed.

"Rhiannon, this is Her Royal Highness, the Banprionnsa Olwynne NicCuinn. If it was not for her, I would no' be allowed in to see ye. She . . . her father the Rìgh has granted ye liberty o' the tower. Olwynne, this . . . this is Rhiannon."

Olwynne inclined her head graciously, but Rhiannon only glared. She did not like the tone that came into Lewen's voice when he addressed the Banprionnsa, nor the way Olwynne looked at her.

She was a tall young woman, though not as tall as Rhiannon, and very straight-backed with dark, challenging eyes and a mass of fiery ringlets that hung down her back from under a forest green silk hood. Her gown was green too, of fluid silk that shimmered as the Banprionnsa moved and embroidered with tiny jewels at cuff and neckline. She wore no other jewelry except for a moonstone on her left hand, a twin to the ring Lewen wore on his left hand. Although Rhiannon knew all apprentices of the Coven wore moonstone rings, it infuriated her to see this link between Lewen and Olwynne, symbol of a world they shared and from which she was excluded.

"Tell her to go away," Rhiannon said. "Why is she here?"

Lewen was mortified. "But she . . . I wanted . . . Rhiannon!"

"I think it is best I go then," Olwynne said. She smiled ruefully at Lewen and shook her head as he apologized and entreated her to stay. As she gathered up the rustling folds of her skirt and turned to leave, Rhiannon came forward in a rush, saying fiercely, "Who was that girl?"

"Ye're no' jealous, are ye?" Lewen asked incredulously. "O' Olwynne? Oh, Rhiannon!" He reached for her, drawing her close. "Don't be so silly," he murmured and bent his head to kiss her. As Rhiannon melted into his embrace, her eyes closing, the door shut behind Olwynne with a click.

"Oh, Rhiannon, Rhiannon," Lewen whispered, raising his head at last. "Oh Eà, I have missed ye."

She leaned against his shoulder. "It's been only a night," she said shakily.

He lifted her face and kissed her again. "Too long," he said. "Far too long."

She wrested her mouth away, saying sulkily, "Long enough for ye to get all prettied up for some other lass."

Lewen glanced down at himself in surprise, then grinned. "I'm in court gear. I had to report to His Majesty and beg leave to come and see ye. I couldna go to court in all my dirt!"

He flung aside the cape and hat and sat on the bed, pulling her down beside him. Eagerly he kissed her again, one hand sliding under her skirt.

"So why she come, that Olwynne? Why ye bring her?" she demanded.

"Och, Olwynne! She's one o' my very best friends, she and her twin brother, Owein. The Rìgh is their father. If it had no' been for them I might no' have got in to see ye." He sat up, bringing his hand from under her shirt so he could stroke back her hair. "She's promised to help me petition the Rìgh on your behalf. I canna believe ye were locked up like a common criminal! Olwynne begged His Majesty to grant ye liberty o' the tower, which means at least ye can walk in the gardens and have visitors. Nina petitioned him too, and has offered to pay all the costs, which is good because, believe me, I almost fainted when I heard how much a dark little cell like this costs!" He looked around him in disgust. "Still, it's better than the public galleries."

"Indeed it is," Rhiannon said.

She searched for words to describe the Murderers' Gallery, but it seemed so far removed from Lewen. Everything about him was clean and fine. He washed and changed his linen every day, and though his clothes were not usually so grand, they were always clean and brushed. He smelled pleasantly of horses and fresh air and the rosemary soap he washed with and the mint leaves he chewed after eating, unlike so many men who smelled rankly of beer and tobacco and unwashed armpits and decaying teeth. Rhiannon had always appreciated this about him, since her sense of smell was very acute and easily offended.

And, ever since Rhiannon had first met Lewen, he had epitomized gentleness, kindness, and courtesy. He was a horse whisperer who had the ability to soothe just about any frightened animal or child. He listened to all that was said to him carefully and did not seek to impress by sneering at others. He had taught her to trust him, an investment of faith that Rhiannon had never expected to be able to make. She did not know how to tell him of all that was cruel, dark, pitiless, and foul. As she searched for words, he began speaking again and it was too late, the moment had passed.

"We tried to convince the Rìgh that ye did no' need to be kept in the tower even," Lewen was saying, "but he would no' agree, saying the charges are too serious. Which, I suppose, is fair enough. It was just such a shock, seeing them drag ye away like that."

He bent his head and kissed her lovingly, and she lost herself in the sweetness of it for a while. He had her pressed down onto her back, her bodice unlaced, before she stopped him again, reluctantly.

"How long?" she whispered. "How long must I stay here? For I shall go mad, Lewen. I swear I shall."

He raised his head. His eyes were black with passion. "I dinna ken, dearling," he said huskily. "I wish . . . och, how I wish . . . I canna bear to think o' ye locked up in here."

"Try being the one who's locked up," she said dryly.

He kissed her chin, and then the pulse at the base of her throat. "It shouldna be long, dearling." He pulled back her bodice so he could kiss the hollow of her shoulder. His hand had found her breast again, but she gently pushed him away.

"When? When?"

He sighed. "They hear serious cases, like murder or horse stealing, once every quarter. That means the end o' June. I tried to convince the Rìgh that your case should be heard straightaway, but he said they need that much time to gather their evidence and hear the witnesses."

Rhiannon did not know the names or meanings of months. Her idea of time was much more fluid and imprecise than that of these humans, who had a word for everything. Lewen understood her frown and said, sympathy warming his deep voice, "By midsummer, dearling."

"Midsummer," she said blankly. It was only early spring

now. That meant days and days, more days than Rhiannon could count. Two moons at least.

"They'll probably bring it forward a few days," Lewen said consolingly. "The Rìgh will want it all over afore the wedding."

"The wedding?"

"Aye, Donncan and Bronwen's wedding. The royal heirs. Ye remember. It's set for Midsummer's Day."

"How many moons?" Rhiannon demanded.

He lifted his shoulders and said reluctantly, "The moon is in its last quarter now. We'll see it wax and wane twice afore then."

"Two moons," Rhiannon said flatly.

"More," he answered.

She turned her face away.

He turned it back to him with both hands, kissing her passionately. "I ken it's a long time," he whispered. "But the Rìgh says I may visit ye. . . ."

"So kind o' him."

"And I'll bring ye books and paper. . . ."

"If only I could read."

"Ye'll be able to practice your lessons."

"What's the point?" she said sullenly.

"Dearling, dinna say that. I canna bear to see ye so unhappy. Banprionnsa Olwynne and I will do all we can to ease things for ye."

"That redhead? Why would she want to help?"

"She's my friend. She feels sorry for ye," Lewen said awkwardly.

"How sweet o' her," Rhiannon said acidly.

"She can do heaps to help. Her father adores her and will listen to her, I ken."

"Can she help another too?" Rhiannon demanded. "Lewen, there was a lass in the Murderers' Gallery. . . . She was sore hurt, Lewen. The warden there is a cruel, mean woman. She should be the one locked up! Lewen, can ye ask her?"

"Ask Her Highness? To help some other lass?"

"Aye! She was strung up for the rats, Lewen. It was awful, just awful! Please, canna ye find out how she is? Her name is Bess . . . Bess Balfour."

"I'm no' sure how. . . . I can ask someone, though. I canna

see how Her Highness can help. She kens naught about prisons and so on. But I'll ask one o' the guards on the way out."

"Ye should be telling your Rìgh about it," Rhiannon said. "Ye talk about how good and just he is, and yet he allows such things to happen. It isn't right!"

Lewen looked troubled. "I dinna ken who. . . . Happen I'll ask my mentor. He'll ken what to do."

"What about that girl? Why ye no' tell her, if she the Rìgh's daughter?"

"I do no' want to presume," Lewen said unhappily. "If I can, I will, I promise. But in the meantime, Rhiannon, ye must be thinking about yourself. I canna help but worry. . . . I mean, the Yeomen are a close-knit unit, and Connor was well-liked. I'm afraid. . . ."

"Aye, me too," Rhiannon said dully.

Once again he turned her face to his, kissing her ardently on the mouth. "Oh, Rhiannon, do no' be afraid. I swear I will do all I can to get ye free. And I'll come whenever I can, I promise." He bared her breast so he could kiss it, cradling it in both hands. Despite herself she arched her back. Lewen groaned and slid his hand under her bottom. She slipped her own hands around to cup his buttocks, pressing him closer to her.

"Every day," she demanded. "Promise me. Every day."

"Whenever I can," he said hoarsely. "I do no' think I can keep away. Rhiannon, Rhiannon, what spell have ye cast on me? I swear, I think I shall die with wanting ye. Please, please, we have so little time. The guards will come back soon. . . ."

"Then why waste time talking?" she asked.

"Good question," he said, and dragged his tunic over his head.

HAUNTED

"Rest, rest, perturbed spirit."

—SHAKESPEARE,
Hamlet, Act I, scene 5 (1601)

The Ghost

Rhiannon lay and watched the candle flame slowly splutter out. Then darkness descended like a hood. Her eyes were stretched wide, but she could see nothing at all. All she could hear was the rising thunder of blood in her ears.

She took one deep shaking breath, and then another. Her fingers dug deep into the stiff linen of her sheets. She longed for her horse with every fiber of her being. She wished she could reach out her hand and seize Blackthorn's flowing mane and swing herself up onto the mare's back. She wished she could feel the powerful surge of muscles below her as the mare flung out her wings and sprang into the air. She wished they were flying free under the stars.

Rhiannon's longing was so intense it was like grief or thwarted desire. It wove through the coldness and darkness pressing against her eyelids until she imagined she really did feel Blackthorn's silky mane under her fingers. Rhiannon imagined the swift easy swing as she vaulted onto the mare's back, and leaned forward, urging the mare into a canter. Air rushed through the canals of her ears. She was dizzy. She clung to Blackthorn's mane and urged her on. They soared into the darkness.

Hollowness and dislocation. A sense of the world falling away. Shapes loomed up out of the shadows. A long corridor, a room lit dimly by a lantern. Two men playing cards. As the horse and rider flew silently, invisibly past, the light flickered. One of the guards glanced up, then rubbed the back of his neck uneasily. Rhiannon looked back at him. He did not see her.

A wall sprang towards them. Horse and rider flew through

as if stone was water. Rows of beds with men sleeping. As the shadow-horse passed over them, they stirred and frowned. One cried out. Another turned and huddled his blankets up around his ears. Another wall flowed over them, then another. Rhiannon tried to remember to breathe.

In a dark cell. A window in the far wall glimmered frostily. A man lay on a narrow bed, moving his head and limbs restlessly, muttering and sighing. He cried out. Rhiannon looked down at him as she and the shadow-horse flew over him, towards the window. It was Lord Malvern. Even in the darkness she knew him at once.

Rhiannon felt a sudden spur of terror. Something floated above the sleeping man. In the darkness it was just a pale frosty shimmer, like breath on an icy morning, like starlight on water, like crumpled chiffon. There was the mere suggestion of a woman's shape hovering over the sleeping man. He was shrinking away from the cold blast of her presence. "No! No!" he cried out.

Rhiannon heard a low murmur.

"What use are ye to me, locked up here like a trussed chicken?" the ghost said. "We do no' have much time. There is much to be done if we are to have all ready by Midsummer's Eve. Do ye no' want your revenge? Do ye no' want your dear brother to live again? We made a pact, ye and I. I expect ye to honor it, else I shall haunt your every moment, waking and asleep. I will make ye sorry ye ever sought to cross me."

"No, no," he murmured. "Let me be!"

"Never," the ghost hissed. "There is no way to escape me, no' even through death, for I stand at the very threshold o' life and there is no way to sneak past me, I warn ye. Ye must uphold your promise. Ye must bring me back to life again!"

Her words were like a torrent of icy water, unrelenting. Rhiannon cowered as much as the man lying blasted in the ghost's icy presence.

"But how? What am I to do?" Lord Malvern asked, and he was awake now, his eyes wide and terrified, pressing his body back into his pillows, as far as he could get from the cold diaphanous spirit hovering so close above him.

"Get yourself out o' this cell," she jeered. "What use are ye to me in here? Find the spell, as I bade ye, and a warm living body, young and strong and filled with power. Like her! She will do! Bring me the girl who dares spy on me in the darkness!"

To Rhiannon's horror the ghost turned her head and pinned her with terrible eyes. Rhiannon took a breath to shriek, but the air was so bitterly cold, it pierced her lungs. She felt a rushing, an unraveling. The darkness spun about her. Rhiannon felt she was spinning in a vast, cold, windy abyss, falling thousands of feet into space. Then, strangely, she felt herself crash back into her own bed. She put out her hand and felt between her fingers the stiff linen of her sheets, pressed her hand against the hard mattress. She was lying on her back. She took in a great breath of relief and felt cold strike down into her lungs. She could not shriek. A massive icy weight was pressing her down. Wintry hands dug into her shoulders. A blast of arctic breath in her face. She struggled to breathe. Cold lips pressed against her ear. "Ye dare spy on me?" the ghost hissed. "I ken ye now. Do no' dare cross me. Ye'll learn ye canna thwart me without pain!"

Tears started from Rhiannon's eyes and at once froze on her cheeks. Her face was numb, her hands heavy and nerveless as lead. She made a great effort and heaved at the thing weighing on her chest, throwing it away. She heard a thin wailing, which could have been laughter or tears, then all was quiet. Rhiannon huddled her arms about her, shivering with cold, her chest heaving. Slowly her breath steadied and the humming of the darkness eased. At last she must have slept.

In the morning they brought her cold porridge and lukewarm tea, and then she was again left by herself. As the hours crept past, lethargy fell upon her. She sat and watched the bar of sunlight move across the stone. She felt tired and gloomy. Her eyes were gritty, and her chest hurt. At noon they brought her dark bread and cheese. Rhiannon was not hungry, but she forced herself to eat. She needed to keep her strength up if she was to escape. It was like eating ashes.

When the guards came to take away her plate, she demanded angrily when they planned to let her out, to walk in the garden at least. They did not answer or even look her way. Quickly, efficiently, they gathered up her leftovers and backed away, locking the door securely behind them. Rhiannon kicked her chair furiously but only bruised her foot. Silence descended again. The walls were so thick Rhiannon could not even hear birds twittering. All was quiet and chill and lonely.

The bar of sunlight reached the far wall and began to climb. The higher it climbed, the more orange it grew. Despite herself she began to pace again.

When she heard the bars grating open, she spun round on her heel, her heart thumping. It was not Lewen that the guard was showing in, however, but Nina the Nightingale. She was no longer dressed in the bright, shabby clothes of a jongleur, having changed into flowing white robes edged with silver. Her unruly chestnut hair had been bound back into a severe plait, and her necklaces of amber and gold were gone. A silver cord about her waist was hung with the heavy pouch in which she kept her witch's paraphernalia. It was the only familiar thing about her.

"Rhiannon, my dear, how are ye yourself?" the sorceress asked, coming forward with a quick, light step to kiss her cheek.

Rhiannon's hands were balled into fists. She searched for a way to tell Nina about all that had happened to her, about the Murderers' Gallery and the rats, and about her dream that seemed more real than any nightmare could be. But what could she say? *I feel sick and cold with dread, for I saw a ghost last night that says she wants my body for her own*? She could not say the words. Nina would think her mad. So she said through stiff lips, "Me? Och, I'm just dandy."

Nina looked hurt at the sarcastic tone. "I'm sorry I couldna come afore. We've been busy indeed reporting to the Rìgh and settling ourselves back into our rooms at the palace. The place is like a hive o' bees! I dinna ken how Lachlan—I mean, His Majesty—can stand it."

Rhiannon did not reply. She was afraid that if she spoke, she would begin to cry, and that she could not bear. Rhiannon despised such weak indulgences as tears.

Nina went and sat down at the table, putting down the basket she carried. "How are they treating ye, Rhiannon?" she asked anxiously.

"Just dandy," Rhiannon said again, with the same heavy intonation of sarcasm. She felt lumpish and awkward but did not know how else to behave. All the easy camaraderie that had grown up between her and this silver-tongued sorceress seemed out of place now. It was one thing to be friends when they traveled the roads together, eating out of the same stew pot, singing songs around the campfire at night, their clothes as shabby and dusty as each other's. It was quite another story when that scruffy jongleur was transformed into a cool, white sorceress who called the Rìgh by his first name.

Nina seemed to understand, for she took no offense at Rhiannon's gruff tone, saying, "Och, good, I'm so pleased. I was worried they might treat ye roughly. Are they feeding ye well?"

"I wouldna say 'well,'" Rhiannon answered, feeling herself relax a little. "A nice haunch o' roast venison wouldna go astray."

"Well, I canna do aught to help ye there, but I have brought ye some food," Nina said. She pulled a few jars and muslin bags out of her basket. "Some honey to sweeten your tea, and some cheese, and a bag o' dried bellfruit, and a pot o' quince jam, and look, a bottle o' goldensloe wine. I ken how much ye hate being confined. I thought it might help."

Tears prickled Rhiannon's eyes. She stared at the ground and did not speak for fear her voice would give her away.

After a moment, Nina went on cheerfully, "I've brought ye some books too, to help while away the time. There's an illustrated bestiary I am sure ye will like, and an alphabet book, and a book o' rhymes and songs that Roden always loved. I ken ye canna read it yet, but ye can look at the pictures and I will sing some to ye, if ye like, and ye can then try and puzzle out the words."

Rhiannon nodded. "Thanks," she said gruffly, knowing she sounded ungracious.

"No' a problem," Nina said, piling the books neatly on the table. She hesitated, then said, "Rhiannon, we have told the Rìgh the whole story."

"Did ye tell him about Roden?" Rhiannon asked.

Nina nodded and dropped her eyes, looking discomfited. "He was shocked indeed at the tale and pleased that we were able to wrest Roden back from Laird Malvern."

"But it'll make no difference to me," Rhiannon said, her heart sinking. "He will no' pardon me for saving him."

Nina shook her head. "No' out o' hand, just like that. He is deeply grieved at the news o' Connor's death, as we kent he must be. There . . . there is much anger . . . at the way Connor died, I mean . . . and I think ye should ken the Rìgh shares it. He is a just man, though, Rhiannon. He says there must be an inquiry, and a fair trial."

"Och, aye, so ye've told me afore," Rhiannon said.

"It will be fair, Rhiannon," Nina said reprovingly. "All will be debated openly, and proof demanded. It is one thing His Majesty has done well, reforming the law courts. It is no' so long ago that the courts were naught but a mockery in this country, and innocent men and women condemned out o' hand—"

"What about accused murderers being allowed to walk out the gates and into the city as they please?" Rhiannon demanded.

"Pardon?"

"They let Dedrie out the very first day. She said she needed to go buy some medicines for the laird. I thought she was meant to be in prison too."

"So did I," Nina said, puzzled. "It seems very odd. Are ye sure?"

"Lewen said he saw her walk out the gates himself. He says she smiled at him ever so sweetly."

"There must be some misunderstanding," Nina said. "I'll ask the prison warden."

"While ye're there, ask him what happened to a poor lass by the name o' Bess Balfour, who was hung up alive for the rats to feast on, in the Murderers' Gallery," Rhiannon said in a flat, hard voice. She could not help it. Whenever she thought of what had happened to Bess, she felt sick and helpless and, worst of all, vulnerable.

"What? What did ye say happened?"

Rhiannon told her, her voice cracking once or twice as she fought to suppress her emotions. Nina was as shocked and horrified as Rhiannon could have hoped for. She promised to find out how Bess was and then said unhappily, "I had no idea conditions were still so bad in the prison. I ken His Majesty has launched any number o' investigations and was assured things were improving."

Rhiannon snorted.

"I will speak to him," Nina said.

"Aye, we've seen how much good that can do," Rhiannon answered.

"I'm sorry," Nina said, sounding hurt.

Rhiannon sent her a heavy-browed look of misery and resentment, then stared down at her hands. There was a lump in her throat as big as a bite of apple.

Nina got to her feet. "I'm sorry, I have to go."

"A party at the palace tonight, is there?"

"Actually, yes," Nina answered, caught between irritation and compunction. "I am to sing to the court."

"Have fun."

"I'm sorry I could no' do more," Nina said unhappily.

Rhiannon opened her mouth to say something cutting, and then shut it, remembering that Nina had paid the gold that had got her the small comfort of this cell. She took a deep breath and muttered thanks.

Nina nodded. "It's the least I could do for the lass who saved my lad. I dinna want to think o' ye in there with a lot o' common murderers."

Rhiannon thought of Bess and her imploring eyes. "Thank ye. I am grateful," she managed to say. "I just wish . . ."

"Aye. I ken. I'm sorry." Nina hesitated, then bent and picked up her basket. "I will come again when I can," she said. "It may no' be for a few days. I have a lot to do."

Rhiannon tried to smile.

"I'm sorry, but they would no' let Lewen in as well as me," Nina said. "He came, but they turned him away."

Rhiannon shrugged one shoulder, trying hard not to show how disappointed she was. Nina came and laid her hand on her shoulder. "Be o' good heart," she said. "Ye ken ye have friends. We will do what we can to set ye free."

Rhiannon was not heartened.

The next day passed as slowly. Rhiannon was weary, for she had had another disturbed and restless night, and so she rested on her bed, looking through the books Nina had brought her, and dozing. When she was not lying flat on her bed, she paced back and forth, tearing at her fingernails with her teeth. The square of light stretched up to the ceiling and dimmed to a soft orange color, and her pacing grew more frantic, and the silence unendurable. She missed Lewen with an ache like a dislocated joint.

The key squealed in the lock, and she leaped to her feet, looking eagerly towards the door. The guard looked in, gesturing to her to keep back, his sword at the ready. He was a tall, gangly young man with blue eyes and very fair skin marred with an angry outcrop of pimples on his forehead. Rhiannon sat obediently on the bed as he stepped back, allowing the two people behind him to come in hesitantly.

Landon came in first. He was a thin boy around sixteen years of age, with lank fair hair and the beginnings of a scholar's stoop. Loose black robes hung off his shoulders. A dog-eared notebook protruded from one pocket, and his fingers were stained with ink.

Behind him came Fèlice. Her long dark hair was drawn back from her face and secured with a clasp set with seashells, the rest of it hanging in a shining sheet down her back. She was dressed in the same long black robe as Landon, but it had been altered to fit her slim figure becomingly. She carried a bunch of spring flowers, which filled the air with their delicate scent. As she passed the guard, she smiled at him warmly and said, "Thank ye for letting us both come in. We do appreciate it!"

The guard blushed and nodded, shutting the door behind her.

"Landon! Fèlice!" Rhiannon cried. "Ye look so different!"

"We're students o' the Theurgia now," Fèlice said, swinging around so her gown billowed out. "Do we no' look frighteningly stern? I swear, I hardly recognized myself in the mirror this morning. I look so dreadfully grown up."

"Your hair is all different too," Rhiannon said. The last time she had seen Fèlice, her hair had hung in thick, unnaturally regular ringlets. She had had to tie her hair up in hard little knobs every night to make the ringlets but had declared the pain and discomfort was well worth the result.

Fèlice smoothed back her glossy brown hair complacently.

"Straight hair is all the rage now," she said. "The Banprionnsa Bronwen's hair is straight, ye ken, and black as night. Edithe is cross as cats, for she's quite out of fashion now with her blond curls. Even if she irons it in the morning, it's all frizzy again by lunchtime, while look at mine, still dead straight by evensong."

"How do ye iron hair?" Rhiannon said, feeling both bemused and amused, which was the effect Fèlice usually had on her.

"Same as ironing a skirt," Fèlice said. "Ye canna do your own, o' course. I ironed Edithe's and she ironed mine this morning. I swear she almost scorched it! All the lassies in our dorm iron their hair. Unless, o' course, ye're a real curly mop like all the NicCuinn girls. They havena a hope o' ironing out their curls. Happen that's why the Banprionnsa Olwynne wears it back in such a tight plait, to hide her ringlets."

"I doubt she cares," Landon said dryly.

Fèlice opened her eyes wide, as if to say how could she not, but she said nothing more for Landon had turned to Rhiannon and was asking her awkwardly how she was. Rhiannon wished he had not. She had almost forgotten her prison cell, listening to Fèlice chatter away, but now her situation rushed back upon her, and she felt her gloom and fear and frustration with greater force than ever.

"Och, I'm grand," she said lightly.

"How's the food?" Fèlice asked. "It canna be any worse than the slops they serve us up at school. I've had naught but porridge and stew since I've arrived."

"We must share the same cook," Rhiannon responded.

"At least ye get a room to yourself. I'm sharing a room with six other girls and I swear they all snore. I havena had a wink o' sleep."

Rhiannon stared at her. She looked fresh enough. "I'm sure ye slept better than me," Rhiannon said coolly.

"Better than I," Fèlice corrected her.

Rhiannon scowled.

"That's the right way to say it. 'Better then I,' no' 'better than me.'"

"Me, I, me, I—who cares?"

Fèlice said defensively, "Ye said ye wanted me to teach ye to speak properly."

Rhiannon's scowl deepened.

Landon said quickly, "Rafferty and Cameron would've come to visit ye too, Rhiannon, but ye're really only meant to have one visitor at a time. They'll come another day, they said."

"I'm surprised no' to have seen Edithe," Rhiannon said sarcastically.

Fèlice giggled. "Edithe has her nose completely out o' joint. She's a country clodhopper compared to all the lairds and ladies all over the place here, no' to mention the prionnsachan and banprionnsachan. And after the last few days o' school, well, she's realized she's not the powerful sorceress she thought she was."

"But what happened to her nose?" Rhiannon asked, puzzled. "Did someone punch her?"

Fèlice pealed with laughter. "Nay, ye gawk! I mean she's disgruntled."

"She's grunting?" Rhiannon was more puzzled than ever.

"Nay, nay! She's peeved. Cross. Miserable. Because no one pays her any attention."

"But what about her nose?"

"It's just an expression," Landon said. "It doesn't mean her nose is really dislocated."

Rhiannon frowned. It was a constant struggle for her to decipher the language of these apprentices. They had so many odd phrases and figures of speech. She wondered if she would ever come to know them all.

"I wouldn't be surprised if someone did end up punching her in the face," Fèlice continued. "The airs and graces that girl gives herself! Just because she's a NicAven o' Avebury. Just about everyone here has some famous witch in their background, and half o' them are related to the Rìgh somehow. And the way she licks the boots o' anyone she thinks is important—"

"Does she really lick their boots or is that just another expression?" Rhiannon demanded.

Fèlice giggled. "Och, ye are a clown. O' course she doesna really lick their boots."

"Then why did ye say . . . ?" Rhiannon gave up.

"I think it's going to be an awful lot o' fun, being here at the Theurgia. Did ye ken the students are given passes to go out into the city at night? I've never been allowed to go into town by myself afore. I've always had to go with my maid and groom. And we share classes with the boys! And eat with them! I've already had three very nice-looking lads stop and welcome me to the school, and one has asked me to go to one o' the city inns later tonight to hear this new singer they say is really something special."

"Ye aren't going, are ye?" Landon was scandalized.

Fèlice pouted. "I do no' see why no'. I willna go by myself, o' course. I thought I'd see if Maisie wants to go, or maybe one o' the other girls in my dorm. They all seem awfully nice." She recollected herself and turned to Rhiannon with all the warm impulsiveness that was so endearing and yet so exasperating. "I wish ye were in our dorm too, Rhiannon, and could come with us. I'd feel totally safe if ye were there."

"Are ye no' afraid I'd say something to embarrass ye?" Rhiannon said, trying to speak lightly but not entirely succeeding.

"O' course no'," Fèlice answered. "I like the things ye say, I think they're awfully funny. I'm no' easily shocked, ye ken."

Rhiannon said nothing.

Luckily Fèlice did not require too much encouragement to keep a conversational ball rolling. "Besides, I do no' reckon anyone here would be too badly shocked by ye," she went on cheerfully. "They're all frightfully sophisticated, ye ken. There are all sorts o' faeries here, even a Celestine! She's the daughter o' the Stargazer, which makes her a kind o' banprionnsa too, I suppose. And there are corrigans and tree-changers and cluricauns everywhere, and someone told me there's a company o' satyricorn soldiers among the Greycloaks, so really ye would no' be so odd. And the witches are much less stuck-up than normal people. Even the Banprionnsa Olwynne is no' allowed a maid or any ladies-in-waiting while she's at the Theurgia; she has to look after herself like we all do. It'll take some getting used to, I tell ye what! I keep looking around for someone to frown at me and tell me to sit up straight and mind my manners and what degree of curtsy to make, but there's no one!"

She laughed in glee. "And I tell you what else! During class everyone seems absolutely deadly serious. My heart quite sank. We had mathematics, alchemy, history, and basic spell-work,

all on our first day! Ye'd think they'd have given us a chance to
settle in. And everyone with these long serious faces, scribbling
down every word the teachers say. I was quite dismayed. But
then, once school was over, well! We had some fun then. After
dinner everyone played games, and there was an impromptu
dance in the hall, and some o' those lads and lassies can sing!
We had a ball."

Rhiannon thought about what she had been doing while
Fèlice danced and flirted, and felt rage rise in her like nausea.
She gritted her teeth and clenched her fists and said nothing,
though it hurt her badly to think Fèlice could have been so carefree while she was caged up in Sorrowgate Tower.

Fèlice did not notice her silence, though Landon regarded
her with keen, anxious eyes and a deepening look of trouble.
After a while, he said, "Have ye heard any news, Rhiannon?
About your trial, I mean."

"No' much," she said just as abruptly. "I have to wait two
moons or more afore they even have it. Two moons, locked up
in here!"

"Och, that's terrible," Fèlice said, sobering hurriedly. "Two
whole months! I thought it'd be a day or two, and then ye'd be
coming to join us at the Theurgia."

"Unless I'm hanged, drawn, and quartered," Rhiannon said
coldly.

"What? I mean, ye're joking, aren't ye?"

Rhiannon shook her head, feeling an easing of her unhappiness at the obvious shock and horror on Fèlice's pretty face.

"That's the penalty for treason, I'm told, and apparently
killing a Yeoman is treasonous."

"But it was self-defense, or something, wasn't it?"

"No' exactly," Rhiannon answered, then, mindful that Fèlice
might well be called as a witness, said with a show of deep regret, "He was going to kill my mother. If I had no' shot him,
she'd be dead now."

"Och, well, that has to mean something, hasn't it?" Fèlice
said, quite innocent of the fact that Rhiannon had always hated
her mother.

"But why do ye have to wait so long?" Landon said. "Two
months is a long time to be kept locked up without a trial."

"They do all the trials together, once every quarter," Rhiannon said. "The high courts sit only four times a year."

"Och, ye poor thing," Fèlice said. "Didna Nina tell the Rìgh how ye saved Roden?"

"It made no difference," Rhiannon said, and was suddenly overwhelmed by tears. She stopped, cleared her throat, and went on rather unsteadily, "I do no' think he cared, really. He insists the courts have to hear all the evidence and decide what is to be done with me."

"I'm sure they'll find ye innocent and let ye go," Fèlice said uneasily.

"Are ye?" Rhiannon answered.

"I'm writing a ballad about ye," Landon said suddenly. "I'm calling it 'Rhiannon's Ride.' I'll print it up, and then everyone will ken about how brave ye were."

Rhiannon did not know what to say. She had already seen just how little everyone thought of Landon's poetry. The girls had laughed about him behind his back, and the other boys, Rafferty and Cameron, had done so to his face. Even Iven, who loved to sing and tell jokes and stories, had rolled his eyes at some of Landon's efforts. The young poet was looking at her with such earnest and worshipping eyes, however, that she managed to say some kind of thanks.

"Once they ken the whole story, everyone will say ye must be freed," Landon said solemnly. "I'm sure o' it."

"Well, that would be grand," Rhiannon said and found herself wishing they would go and leave her alone again. She felt sick and weary and perilously frail.

Landon understood her sigh. He stood up, saying unhappily, "We've upset ye. I'm sorry. Fèlice, we should go."

"But why? I havena finished cheering Rhiannon up," Fèlice said indignantly. "I wanted to tell her all about Maisie and what the healers said about her face, and I ken she'll want to hear all the gossip about the Banprionnsa Bronwen—"

"Another day," Landon said and rapped on the door.

The young guard opened it.

Fèlice gave Rhiannon a warm, sweetly scented hug and kiss, and told her to keep her chin up, an odd piece of advice that puzzled Rhiannon but was accepted without comment by everyone else. Fèlice then turned to the guard and asked him, very sweetly, what his name was.

"Corey, miss . . . I mean, my lady," he answered bashfully.

"Well, Corey, ye'll take good care o' my friend here, won't ye, and no' let her mope too much?"

Corey glanced at Rhiannon and looked away, scarlet mounting his cheeks.

"Sure," he answered after a moment.

"Thank ye so much. I'll see ye again soon, Rhiannon, dinna ye fear!" And Fèlice went smiling out of the room, leaving her bunch of flowers on the table to spread its faint sweetness into the air.

Landon nodded his head at the guard and went out, looking awkward and unhappy.

The guard hesitated at the door for a moment, then said curtly, "I have a message for ye. Lewen MacNiall came to see ye, but the captain wouldna let him in, seeing how ye had so many visitors already. He . . . Lewen . . . he said he would come again tomorrow, if he could."

Rhiannon jerked her head in response, determined not to let him see how disappointed she was.

The guard glanced at her shyly. "He was very sorry," he said, then suddenly flushed, as if ashamed to have shown her any kindness. He clanged the door shut, and Rhiannon heard the bolts shot home.

She sat back on her bed, looking up at the window. Already the light was beginning to sink low. Rhiannon dreaded the coming of darkness. Even though she told herself they had only been dreams, the strange hallucinatory flights through the darkness she had taken each night, she could not forget the terrible icy glow of the ghost's eyes, the feeling of freezing hands clutching at her.

She got to her feet and paced up and down the room, her arms wrapped over her chest. Then she sat at the table and drew Nina's books towards her. She opened the biggest. It was sumptuously illustrated with paintings of beasts and faeries, all surrounded by margins of leaves and flowers and butterflies, and edged in gilt, with great swirling letters in crimson followed by neat flowing script in black. Rhiannon turned the pages, absorbed. Then she came to a page with a great black horse leaping into an azure sky, its violet-tipped wings unfurling behind it. Rhiannon's breath caught. She stared down at it in longing, then was suddenly overwhelmed with scorching-hot tears. She put her head down on her arms and sobbed aloud, the sound harsh in the silence. She was still weeping when the last of the light faded away into darkness.

On the Garth

Lewen leaned his head on his elbows and tried to concentrate on what his teacher was saying. Normally he enjoyed Cailean of the Shadowswathe's class. Like Lewen, the young sorcerer had a strong affinity with animals and could speak fluently with most beasts. His most profound connection was with dogs, however, and he had as his familiar a great shadow-hound named Dobhailen. The dog stood waist high to most men and moved as silently and sinuously as smoke, his eyes glowing softly green. Although Cailean was a thin, gentle-mannered man, with Dobhailen by his side he commanded the unswerving respect and attention of all his students.

But not Lewen. Not these past few weeks.

Lewen had found it very hard to adjust to being back at school after his adventures in Ravenshaw. Nothing had changed at the Tower of Two Moons. Apprentices still spent the days studying with their various teachers, practising ahdayeh every morning and meditation every evening, filling in their rare spare time with games of chess or trictrac or dice if their habits were sedentary, or football, archery and wrestling if they were of a sporting nature. Lewen still spent most of his evenings at the palace with the Rìgh's other squires, running messages, serving His Majesty at the high table, or cooling his heels and playing cards as they waited for the MacCuinn in one antechamber or another.

Last year Lewen had enjoyed his life very much. He had looked forward to another four years of it, until the day he would graduate from school and join the ranks of the Blue Guards. Now everything had changed.

It was Rhiannon who had changed it all. Since the first time he had laid eyes on her, his world had been tipped topsy-turvy. He had not realized just how much until he was back here, in the familiar halls and corridors of the Theurgia. In the weeks since he had arrived back in Lucescere, Lewen had not been able to interest himself in his lessons nor in any of the silly, childish games the other students wanted to play. Everyone knew that he had got himself entangled with a satyricorn girl, and many eyed him askance. He had always been very friendly with the palace guards, since all knew his father had been one of the Rìgh's general staff during the Bright Wars. Now, however, they were cold and distant. No one joked with him, or asked after his parents, or teased him about his dream to be a Blue Guard. They stared over his head as he passed them, answered his greetings with nothing more than a jerk of the head, and if forced to respond to a direct query, were curt in their answer.

Only his closest friends treated him the same, and he could tell it was an effort for them. Connor the Just, the Yeoman Rhiannon had killed, had been a favorite of everyone's. He had served the Rìgh from a very young age, rising from his page to his squire to one of the officers of his general staff, a path Lewen had hoped to follow. He had been a handsome man, fair haired and blue eyed, and well liked by the ladies of the court. Known for his fairness and integrity, Connor the Just had gained a reputation as an excellent arbitrator and had been sent many times by his Rìgh to settle arguments between lairds or merchants.

His untimely death had been a shock and, once details of the manner of his death had begun to circulate, an outrage. The satyricorn girl had shot Connor in the back, it was said, and then hacked off his finger and wrenched out all his teeth for trophies. She had stolen all his clothes and weapons and then tossed his naked, mutilated body into the river.

If Lewen had been able to deny these rumors angrily, his life would have been much easier. He knew they were true, however, and he was unable to explain to anyone's satisfaction how Rhiannon could do such a thing, nor how he could overcome his horror and revulsion for her acts and abide by his declared love for her. They all knew he was in love with her, everyone

at the Theurgia and the whole court. Some thought he must
have been ensorcelled into love, like Jaspar, the previous Rìgh.
Others thought it was mere bestial lust and were variously repulsed, scandalized, or amused.

Certainly lust for Rhiannon was a driving force in Lewen's
emotions. He found he could think of little else, day or night.
He was tormented by his desire for her, and the difficulties in
acquiring ease and fulfilment. Although he had managed to
snatch the time to go and see her every day, he was not always
allowed in, and when he was, he could never stay for very long.
The guards were vigilant too, and did not give them much time
unobserved. Only twice had Lewen and Rhiannon been able to
couple, and the last time had been in desperation, fully clad, up
against the stone wall. It had been over in moments and had
done nothing but fuel his hunger for her.

Sometimes Lewen feared he had been ensorcelled, so overwhelming were his feelings for her. Sometimes he wished he
could be free of this mad passion and go back to his pleasant
life as a student and squire, the whole of his life mapped out
neatly for him. Mostly, though, he longed for Rhiannon, fretted
and feared for her safety, dreamed of a life entwined with hers,
and spent long hours remembering every detail of every encounter with her and imagining doing it all again.

Lewen shifted in his hard chair and wondered how long
until the bell rang and freed him from the classroom. He was
not on duty at the palace that evening and thought he might try
to bribe the guard to let him stay a little longer with Rhiannon,
long enough perhaps to remove all their clothes and feel her
soft skin against his. He sighed. He had not had time to whittle
any arrows or do anything else to earn any extra coins, and
bribing the guards every day had quickly depleted his earnings
as a squire. His pocket was sadly empty.

At last the bell rang. Chair legs scraped against the floor,
and a hum of conversation rose as the students stood up gladly
and stretched, beginning to make their way out. Lewen gathered up his books and rose too. He knew he should go to the library and work on the assignment he had due, but writing a
paper on the *Historia de Gentibus Septentrionalibus* seemed
impossible when the woman he loved was in prison facing a
death sentence.

As he walked towards the door, Cailean raised his head and beckoned him over. Lewen went to stand by his desk.

"Lewen, ye ken that lass ye told me about? The one ye thought had been hurt in prison?"

"Aye. Bess, her name was, I think. Bess Balfour."

"There are no records o' any girl o' that name, or any similar name, being admitted to the prison. I asked him to check again, and he said he had. So then I checked to see if anyone had been injured. There were a number o' knifings, and quite a few cases of jail fever, but no reports o' any rat bites. I'm sorry, Lewen. I'm no' sure what else I can do."

Lewen was puzzled, but he thanked Cailean and apologized for wasting his time, and then went out into the garth, feeling heavyhearted.

Outside the sun was shining and the sky was blue. The tall spires of the ancient witches' tower were etched sharply against its perfection, their symmetry pleasing to the eye. Black-clad students strolled across the garth or lay in the sunshine, talking. Lewen stared at them. He felt so dislocated, as if he was looking at them through a spyglass from another dimension altogether. He could not fit the ragged edges of his world together, the world in which he loved Rhiannon and the everyday world of school and books and dormitories.

"Lewen!"

He turned around.

Fèlice and Maisie were coming towards him, smiling broadly. As always, Fèlice looked fresh and pretty. Her black robe fit her perfectly, and she wore a posy of flowers at her belt. Beside her, Maisie looked chubbier and plainer than ever. Since being attacked by wild dogs on their journey through Ravenshaw, her round face was marred by a nasty red scar that ran down from a torn and crooked ear. She tried unsuccessfully to hide the scar by wearing her hair looped over her ears, a style that did not suit her. She limped painfully as well, leaning heavily on a walking stick Lewen had carved for her. The scars upon Maisie's face always made him feel guilty and uncomfortable, and he had to resist the urge to avoid her, even though he knew it was not his fault that she had been so badly mauled. In fact, if Lewen had not faced the dogs down, talking to them in their own language, the country girl might not have escaped at all.

"Hey, Lewen!" Fèlice called. "How are ye yourself?"

Lewen grimaced.

"No news on Rhiannon?"

"Nay, she's still stuck in that blaygird prison. They willna let her out until after her trial, and the trial is set for midsummer. Naught Nina can say will make the Rìgh bring it forward. They need time to gather evidence."

"Poor thing," Fèlice said and made a face.

"I went to see her the other day," Maisie said. "She seems very low. She hardly said a word. I dinna ken what to say to her."

"That was nice o' ye. I'm glad ye went. She finds it very hard, being locked up between four walls like that. She's used to running free."

"Aye," Maisie said uncertainly.

Lewen could see she did not like being reminded that Rhiannon was half satyricorn. He changed the subject. "How are ye finding the Theurgia?"

"It's grand!" Fèlice said exuberantly. "I wish we didna have to study so much, but apart from that, I'm having a marvelous time!"

"They've let me take up extra classes at the Royal College o' Healers," Maisie said. "I want to be a healer, ye ken. They have scholarships I can apply for. They've all been so kind."

"I'm glad," Lewen said. "What about the others? Have they settled in well?"

"Och, sure," Fèlice answered. "Cameron's in heaven, being so close to the palace and all those Yeomen. He goes to watch their weapons training every morning, and as far as I can tell the only classes he pays attention to are wrestling and archery."

"He has to pass if he wants to get into the Yeomen," Lewen warned. "Being good at the arts o' war is no' enough."

As they talked, the three students had been walking across the garth towards the dormitory wing. At the sound of their names being called out, they paused and turned. Landon came hurrying towards them, looking like a stork with his long gangly legs and stooped shoulders.

"Fèlice, have ye checked the notice board?" he cried as soon as he reached them, out of breath and flustered.

"No' yet. I was just about to. Why?"

"We've been granted a pass out. We can go tonight. Oh, Fèlice, do ye think I should? I dinna ken. It's too soon."

Fèlice clasped her hands together. "We've been given leave? Oh, wonderful! Oh, marvelous! O' course ye have to do it, Landon! We've talked about naught else all week."

She turned to Lewen. "Have ye had town leave yet? I went last week and it was so exciting. I've never had such fun. We got all dressed up, a crowd o' us, and went to the theater and then on to some inn in the faery quarter. All sorts o' people were there: goblins, tree-changers, cursehags. There was even an ogre—can ye believe it! They had the most amazing food and drink there. I've never tasted anything like it. I danced with a seelie. He was the most gorgeous thing I've ever clapped eyes upon. They say seelies can make a woman swoon just by smiling at them . . ."

"I saw a Fairge," Maisie said dreamily. "I've always wanted to."

"I must admit, I did feel quite giddy after I'd danced with him, but that might have been the foul stuff I was drinking. They called it bog ale, and indeed, it did taste like swamp water! I willna touch that stuff tonight, I'll try something different. Maybe the fuzzle gin. That looked like fun."

"I wouldna touch the fuzzle gin," Lewen said.

"But it's so pretty and pink!"

"Aye, but the effects are no' so pretty," he answered.

"Really? I guess ye may be right. Katrin, this girl in my dorm, well, she was drinking it and we had to practically carry her home and then she was sick all over Cameron's shoes, and then the next day, she was so sick she had to stay in bed all day and the healer said she couldna have town leave for a whole month if she was going to abuse the privilege. Fancy! No town leave for a *month*!"

"So will ye come out with us tonight?" Maisie asked, looking up at Lewen with a shy glow in her eyes. "Please do!"

He shook his head. "I canna. I'm sorry."

"Oh, please?" Fèlice pleaded, clasping both her hands together. She gave him her most bewitching smile. "I promise no' to drink too much fuzzle gin and vomit on ye."

"There's an offer that's hard to refuse," another voice cried, laughing.

Lewen turned and smiled as Owein and Olwynne came up behind him.

Landon, Fèlice, and Maisie were thrown into confusion. They knew at once who the twins were, of course, for the younger children of the Rìgh of Eileanan were very striking with their red-gold hair and tall, slim figures, while Owein's magnificent red wings marked him out in the biggest crowd. Fèlice was passionately interested in everything to do with the royal family and could probably have told Owein a few things about himself that he thought no one but a few of his closest friends knew. She had known that Lewen was friends with the royal twins and had hoped she would get to meet them through him. So, while Maisie blushed and gaped and tried to think of something to say, Fèlice recovered her composure quickly and smiled up at the winged Prionnsa.

"Well, ye are welcome to join us if ye wish, Your Highness," she said, dimpling. "We have town leave and are just trying to convince Lewen he should come too. We have the whole night planned, and it should be such fun!"

"Why, we'd love to, wouldna we, Olwynne?" Owein responded at once, smiling down at Fèlice with a great deal of warm admiration in his eyes. "We havena had a chance to go into town for weeks. It's all work, work, work for us fourth years."

"That's too bad," Fèlice said sympathetically. "Surely it canna be good for ye, all work and no play?"

"A lass after my own heart," Owein cried. "I couldna agree more. Lewen and Olwynne, though, they're no' such fun. Always worrying about school and studying. Auld afore their time, they are."

"*Responsible* is the word ye are looking for, I feel," Olwynne said. She looked Fèlice up and down, and the dark-haired girl blushed, dropped her eyes, and curtsied gracefully.

"Olwynne, Owein, this is Lady Fèlice, daughter o' the Earl o' Stratheden, and this is Maisie, granddaughter o' the cunning man o' Berkeley, a village near Ravenscraig, and this is Landon MacPhillip, from Magpie Wood. We call him the poet, for he's always scribbling away."

Owein and Olwynne both inclined their heads, and Owein glanced again at Fèlice, who was looking prettier than ever with her cheeks flushed and her eyes sparkling. "Do we no' ken your father? Is he no' one of the MacBrann's men?"

"Och, aye, I was raised at court, at Ravenscraig. It is no' at all like Lucescere, though. The MacBrann—the auld one, I mean—he was sick for so long, and there were no' many parties or balls, and then he died, which was very sad, o' course, but—"

"But rather boring for ye, with the whole court in mourning," Owein said sympathetically.

Fèlice flushed rosier than ever, and her dimple flashed briefly. "We were all very sorry. The MacBrann—Malcolm MacBrann—he was our laird for ever so long. I ken my father misses him very much. But the new laird, he's a good man and canny too, they say, and when the mourning period is over, I'm sure the court will be gayer. But no' like Lucescere! Never like Lucescere!"

"It sounds like ye've been enjoying our city," Owein said.

"Och, aye! Indeed I have. We all have, havena we, Maisie? I canna wait for tonight. There's a new play on at the Mandrake Theater that's meant to be very good. We were thinking o' seeing that first, and then going on to the Nisse and Nixie. We were there last week and had an absolute ball. I danced with a seelie! And there were ogres there! One got so drunk he tried to dance on a table and it broke underneath him. It was hilarious!"

"The Nisse and Nixie is always good value," Owein said, "though ye should be careful, ye ken. No' all faeries are friendly."

"And I am naught but a country lass, and no' at all accustomed to such a place," Fèlice said sadly, causing Maisie and Landon to look at her in surprise. "That is why I need someone aulder, and more sophisticated, to accompany me and make sure I do nothing harebrained."

"Like drink fuzzle gin," Owein said, smiling.

"Exactly."

"Well, I really feel it is my duty to accompany ye young things then," Owein said. "Since I am so much aulder and so much more sophisticated."

"Och, that is so kind o' ye," Fèlice said, flashing him a look from under her eyelashes. "I do declare, I shall feel much safer with ye there."

Landon was still staring at her in bafflement, but Maisie's expression was half-scandalized, half-amused, while Olwynne was looking Fèlice over very closely.

"Will ye come too, Olwynne?" Owein said. "Come on! It'll be fun. How long is it since ye've seen an ogre trying to dance on a table?"

"Far too long," Olwynne said dryly. She glanced at Lewen. "Are ye going, Lewen?"

"I dinna think so," he answered. "I'd better no'."

"Oh, come on! We've hardly seen ye since ye came back from Ravenshaw," Owein protested. "And look at ye! Ye're as wound up as a fob watch. Come on! A night on the town will do ye good."

Lewen hesitated.

Olwynne laid her hand on his arm. "Please? We've hardly seen ye."

"I canna," he said. "Really I canna."

"But ye're not on duty tonight, are ye?" Owein asked, puzzled. "I thought Fymbar and Hearne were."

"It's no' that," Lewen said. "It's just . . . Rhiannon . . ."

"Surely she can do without you for just one night," Owein said, exasperated. "I dinna ken how ye can spend so much time at Sorrowgate. It's such a blaygird place."

Fèlice gave a theatrical shudder. "Horrid, isn't it?" she asked. "Poor Rhiannon. I'm glad it's no' me shut up in there."

"That's why I really have to go and see her," Lewen said. "She canna stand being enclosed in such a small space. She's no' used to it, and her spirits have been very low. She needs me."

"Well, we need ye too," Olwynne said. "Ye've been away for months and months, and then when we finally get ye back again, ye spend all your time at the prison. Did it never occur to ye that we may want to see your bonny face occasionally too?"

"I'm sorry," Lewen said miserably. "I ken I'm no' much fun at the moment. I canna abandon her, though. She has no one else. Canna ye see that?"

Owein rolled his eyes and said with exaggerated emphasis, "I suppose so."

"Ye do no' have to spend all evening with her, though, do

ye?" Olwynne asked. "How about ye go and see her after dinner, and then come out and meet us later? Ye're in the city anyway, at Sorrowgate. It'll only take ye another few minutes, if ye grab a corrigan cart."

"Go on!" Fèlice pleaded. "Ye canna waste a city pass! Besides, this inn we've been telling ye about, the Nisse and Nixie, it's all the rage now. Anyone can get up and sing a song, or tell a joke or a story, or perform a trick, and Landon's going to read his ballad, ye ken, the one he's been writing about Rhiannon. Ye canna miss it! I swear, he's going to take the town by storm. He read it to me and Maisie and the boys last night, and it brought tears to my eyes. Ye have to be there for its first public performance. If the crowd likes it, we're going to have it printed up, aren't we, Landon, and sell it on the streets a penny apiece."

"I dinna ken," Landon said gloomily. "I'm sure it's no' any good. I'll probably get booed and hissed off the stage."

"Rubbish! It's marvelous. It'll be a sensation."

"I dinna think it's a good idea to read it in public. No one here seems to like Rhiannon."

"That's why it's so important that ye set them straight on what really happened," Fèlice said. "Tell him, Lewen! His ballad is the best way o' changing public opinion. Everyone here believes the sort o' rubbish Edithe's been spreading around, because they havena heard the whole story. We could talk till we were blue in the face, and it wouldna have anywhere near the effect o' hearing your ballad. Besides, it'll make your name as a poet! Is that no' what ye dream o'?"

"I'll probably get sued for slander," Landon said, "once the Laird o' Fettercairn hears what I've written."

"It's no' slander if it's true," Fèlice said, "and we can all attest to that. We were there! Oh, come on, Lewen, ye've got to come. Landon'll never get up on stage if we are no' all there, encouraging him."

"All work and no play makes Lewen a very dull dog," Owein said.

"Oh, all right," Lewen said. "I must admit a few ales would go down well."

"That's the lad," Owein said, slapping him on the shoulder.

"Where is this inn?" Olwynne asked, her eyes still on Fèlice.

"It's down in the faery quarter, on the corner o' Avalon and Cormoran streets," Landon said diffidently.

"Och, aye, I ken," Owein said. "We'll meet ye there, what, about nine? We have to be back afore the palace gates shut at midnight, remember."

"Remember last summer, when we all got locked out, because Lewen had to try to stop that bearbaiting?" Olwynne said.

"Och, aye, and we snuck in through the secret way, the auld drain? And Lewen got stuck, being too broad across the shoulders?" Owein said.

"And we thought we'd be stuck there all night, and expelled for sure, for being out past curfew?" Olwynne said.

"And ye lot slathered me all with the stinkiest mud ye could find. . . ." Lewen smiled at the memory.

"At least we managed to get ye out eventually. And we were all filthy by the end o' it," Olwynne said.

"No' to mention stinky." Owein grinned.

"There's a secret way into the palace grounds?" Fèlice asked.

Owein and Olwynne exchanged glances. "Sorry! Canna tell. It's a family secret."

"But it might come in useful one night," Fèlice pleaded. "Go on! Canna ye tell us where? Ye showed Lewen."

Owein grinned. "Aye, but Lewen's practically family himself. No, no. No use begging. We willna tell ye, even if ye tied us up and tortured us with feathers."

"That doesna sound like torture to me," Fèlice said with a flirtatious glance at Owein from under her long lashes.

Owein grinned and was about to respond in kind, but Olwynne slipped her hand in the crook of his arm and said, "Well then. The Nisse and Nixie at nine. See ye there! Dinna fail us, Lewen!"

"I willna," he answered and watched as Olwynne drew Owein away, the Prionnsa shooting a quick rueful smile at Fèlice over his shoulder.

"Ye really are the most shocking flirt," Lewen said to Fèlice.

She laughed. "Am I? Really? Oh well. How much trouble can I get into with ye and Landon and Maisie all frowning at me every time I open my mouth? And Cameron and Rafferty will come, no doubt, and Edithe too, I bet, once she hears who else is coming."

"Do no' tell her, please," Lewen begged. "I willna come if that sourpuss does."

"Mmmm, hard choice," Fèlice said. "Ye or her? Mmmm, what shall I do?"

"Cheeky arak," Lewen said. "All right, I'll meet ye tonight at the Nisse and Nixie. Try no' to get into any trouble afore then."

"I'll try, but I canna make any promises," she said, smiling over her shoulder as she left him, flanked on either side by Maisie and Landon, both grinning despite themselves.

Lewen was smiling too as he went back to his room and shed his black robes, which always irked him with their confining folds. Dressed in his usual breeches, boots, and soft white shirt, he made his now-familiar way through the gardens, past the palace, and into the maze of dark, crowded streets that led him to the grim stone gateposts of the Sorrowgate Tower, so named for all those heads that had hung upon its lintel.

Lewen knew the guards in the entry foyer well enough to nod and smile at now. They did not ask his business, just jerked their heads to indicate he might pass.

He made his way unerringly through the labyrinthine corridors and up the stairs to Rhiannon's room, at the very top of the tower. Corey, the youngest of the prison guards, was on duty, along with Henry, one of the oldest. They grunted at the sight of Lewen and laid down their cards. Corey unlocked the door and let him in to Rhiannon's room with a sympathetic moue of the mouth to indicate that all was not well.

Rhiannon was lying on her bed, her fists clenched under her chin.

As soon as Lewen came in, she came to her feet in one fluid movement and flew across the room to fling herself into his arms. Lewen held her close. Her hair smelled sharp, like an animal's fur. She drove her head hard into his shoulder, shaking with tears. He felt stiff and unhappy and woefully ill-equipped to deal with her distress.

"Why ye take so long?" Rhiannon accused. "Where ye been?"

"At school," he answered. "Ye ken I have a late class on Friday. I came as soon as I could."

"It's nearly suppertime," she said, pointing at the long lozenges of light on the wall, red and faint. "The guards will bring it soon, and ye'll have to go."

"I'm sorry. I couldna come any earlier. Really, I couldna."

She put her head on his shoulder. "The day goes past so slowly. I thought ye were no' coming."

He put his hand up under the midnight fall of her hair. Her nape felt soft and vulnerable. "I wouldna fail ye," he said. He felt like he was suffocating. It was an effort to draw a breath.

Rhiannon dashed the tears away from her eyes. "No one cares," she said pitifully.

"I do. Ye ken I do," Lewen answered as he had many times before.

She stared at him with shadow-haunted blue eyes. She had lost a lot of weight since being imprisoned. Her bones were hard under her skin. Her hands looked frail, and her eyes were red-rimmed.

"Have ye been eating?"

She shrugged one angular shoulder. "The food is horrible."

"Ye need to keep your strength up."

"Why? What's the point?"

"Ye canna lose faith now. I ken it's hard—"

"Do ye just?"

"Aye—"

"Ever faced being *hanged*, *drawn*, and *quartered*?" She spoke the words with a peculiar intensity, as if she had rolled the words over her tongue so many times they had gained a certain sweetness, a poetic rhythm.

"Nay, but—"

"Ye canna even begin to ken what it feels like. Do no' speak to me o' *hard*."

"I'm sorry. I just—"

"Do no' talk! Stop talking!"

"What do ye want me to do?" Lewen raised his hands in helplessness.

"Dinna talk!" She took his hand and put it to her breast. "Dinna waste time!"

He let her kiss him, his love for her and his feeling of utter helplessness and failure meeting each other, like stags locked antler to antler and unable to step either way. Even allowing his hand to close upon her breast was almost too hard, and for the first time ever he felt no instant rush of desire. He roused himself with an effort, kissing her neck, brushing his hand across her nipple, and was rewarded with a sigh and a rush of tears. He let her draw him down on the bed and strip away his shirt. She was frantic with need. She could scarce draw breath, and her face was wet when she pressed it into his bare shoulder. He stared across her head to the stones of the wall, so damp and grey and drear. He could smell the chamber pot under the bed. He pressed his face into her bare shoulder and closed his eyes.

She caught her breath in a sob. When she kissed him, she tasted of salt and mucus. He could feel her heart pounding under her ribs, and his heart accelerated to match the rapid beat of hers, the uneven jerk of her breath arousing him at last. He would have liked to have taken the time to calm her, and bring her to pleasure slowly, but he was as aware of the guards outside as Rhiannon was, and kept listening for the rusty squeal of the grille in the door that meant they were being watched. So it was another hasty coupling, the prison blanket harsh under his shoulder blades and Rhiannon's face above him tense and white with misery.

Although it eased him physically, Lewen felt an almost unbearable oppression of his spirits as he sat up and pulled his shirt back on. There was no joy in this loving, none of the blissful abandonment of self that he had felt in their first few couplings.

He had found Rhiannon infinitely desirable from the first time he had seen her, a filthy, scratched creature who had tied herself to the back of a wild winged horse, so desperate was she to escape her herd. He had had to tame her as he might an unbroken foal or a wild bird from the forest. He had coaxed her with gentleness and kindness, listening to the emotions behind her rough words, her fierce gestures. He had been rewarded with a gorgeous flowering of her personality, a spreading of gaily colored wings, a sweet-throated song. Yet all along he had loved the wildness in her, the fierceness, the refusal to be tamed. To find her now so humbled by her incarceration troubled and distressed him. It was like finding a canary mute in its cage when once he had seen it flying free and singing. He did not know how to help her.

The squeak of the bolts being pulled back galvanized them both to action. Lewen buttoned himself up in haste, and Rhiannon dragged her grey prison dress together and scrubbed her wet face with her hand. By the time the guards came in with a tray for her, the length of the room was between them and they were each studiously avoiding each other's gaze. Although neither had ever articulated it, Lewen knew they both feared that Rhiannon's warmness towards him would make her vulnerable to unwanted attention from her guards. She was so vulnerable, locked up in this small stone cell with nowhere to flee to and no weapon with which to defend herself.

"Time to go," Henry said, jerking his head towards the door.

Lewen always hated this moment. Each time he had to go, Rhiannon grew more and more distressed, and he had not yet had a chance to give her the news about her friend Bess.

"Just one more moment. Please?" he asked.

"Make it quick," Henry said, dumping the tray on the table. He and Corey withdrew, the younger guard trying his best to hide his sympathy for the satyricorn girl.

Lewen braced himself. "Rhiannon, I just wanted to tell ye . . . Cailean made inquiries o' that friend o' yours, the one ye say was attacked by rats . . ."

"Aye?" Rhiannon stared at him with her hands clasped tight together.

"There's no record o' her anywhere. It's as if she never existed."

"She did exist! She real!" There was a raw edge of hysteria in Rhiannon's voice.

Lewen tried to speak soothingly. "O' course she really existed, I'm no' saying—"

"Ye dinna believe me! She real!"

"I do believe ye, Rhiannon, I do. It's just—"

"What happened to her? She canna just disappear! What they do to her?"

"I do no' ken. . . . I'll try to find out, I promise."

"Will I just disappear too?" Rhiannon spoke wonderingly, staring at Lewen with very wide eyes.

Lewen felt sick. "No, no, o' course no'."

The door to the cell opened.

"Time to go," the guard said stolidly.

"Don't go," Rhiannon said. "Please, don't go."

"I have to," Lewen answered. He tried to summon a reassuring smile.

"Please."

"Ye ken I canna stay. They willna let me. I'm lucky they let me visit ye as often as I do."

"Please don't go."

"Rhiannon, I'm sorry, but I have to go. Ye ken I do."

"I canna stand it, Lewen, truly I canna. Ye canna leave me here!" Her voice rose.

"Time's up," the guard said with a note of impatience in his voice.

Rhiannon seized Lewen's hands. "The ghost . . . Bess . . . I canna stand it anymore. Please, Lewen. Please!"

"I'm sorry. I have to go." He embraced her awkwardly and kissed her cheek. She would not let go of his hands. He tried to wrest them away from her, but she clung to them frantically, tears pouring down her cheeks.

"Lewen, ye canna leave me here. Lewen!"

He managed to free his hands and put her away from him, moving swiftly to the door. She threw herself after him, but the guards caught her and quickly wrestled her back.

"I'm sorry!" he cried and went out quickly, his eyes smarting, his whole body hot. All the time she wept and called out to him, her voice rising high into a shriek. Then the door slammed shut.

The Nisse and Nixie

Lewen went quickly down the stairs and through the gloomy corridors until at last he was out in the fresh air, breathing great gulps to rid his nose of the prison stink. He was blind and deaf to all around him, seeing only Rhiannon's pale, gaunt face, hearing only her pleas to him to stay. His heart was beating so fast he felt it would choke him.

It felt good to walk the city streets. He strode out, arms swinging. After a while his heartbeat steadied, though he still felt an awful hollowness within. He tried to think of other things, concentrating on the dramas and spectacles of those around him. It was dark, and the streets were all lit with lanterns strung high overhead. Light spilled out from doors and windows, and the streets thronged with people. The inns were all doing good business with the weather fine and warm. Through the windows he could hear music and see people dancing. His step slowed, and he glanced in through one door, his mouth lifting at the sight of the laughing faces and swinging skirts. A young man was sitting in a chair by the window, a mug of ale on the table before him, a smiling girl sitting on his lap. She bent her head and kissed him on the mouth, twining her arms about his neck. Lewen stared at them and felt a shameful hotness in his eyes.

After a moment, he went on again, wishing with all his heart that Rhiannon strolled along beside him, in a blue dress, with a flower in her hair. He would take her to the theater. He knew she had never been. He imagined her face all lit up with wonder and amusement, turning to him to demand an explanation, scowling in disbelief at his answer. He would buy her a bracelet of blue moonstones at the markets to match her glowing eyes, and they would share a paper cone of hot chestnuts as they stood and watched the jongleurs walk on stilts and do one back-flip after another. They would go on to the inn together, and drink wine and dance until they were tipsy with laughter. Then he would walk her home, stopping to kiss in the velvety shad-ows between the pools of lantern light, perhaps lying with her in the gardens that encircled the Tower of Two Moons, seeing how the moonlight through leaves patterned her pale skin.

It was such an enticing fantasy Lewen felt his eyes grow hot again. He pressed the back of his hand against his mouth, swal-lowing his misery. *Soon*, he promised himself. *When she is free . . .*

He came to the Nisse and Nixie and went inside. The com-mon room was large, with lots of alcoves hung with gold-fringed green velvet curtains. It was crowded with people and faeries, all drinking and talking and smoking so that the room was hazed with blue. Lewen looked around for his friends but saw no sign of them. He followed the sound of music through to an inner room. This was even darker and smokier. A lantern was hung right above the door so that he had to pass under its light to enter the room. It dazzled his eyes for a moment so that he could not see. He stepped quickly through and paused for his eyes to adjust.

In the center of the room, couples were dancing to the music of a small band of faery musicians: a cluricaun with a flute, a corrigan with a double bass, two willow-haired tree-shifters playing fiddles, and a hobgoblin banging a drum that was big-ger than he was. The room was so crowded the dancers were barely able to do more than sway in each other's arms. Lewen jumped back to avoid a lurching pair of drunken bogfaeries and stepped on the gnarled rootlike foot of an enormous tree-changer. He shouted an apology and squeezed his way through the crowd to get himself a mug of ale. The barmaid was a del-icate, green-eyed seelie dressed in a clinging gown cut to look like forest leaves. A massive ogre stood guard behind her, arms folded on his granite chest. He scowled at Lewen, glaring at him as if daring him to admire the frail beauty of the seelie too much. Lewen averted his eyes, paid for the ale, and then gulped down a mouthful. It was very good.

The song came to an end, and everyone clapped. Lewen used his shoulder to push his way through the crowd, looking for the others. There was a stir of interest before the stage, and he turned to see. A woman had come out from behind the curtains and was sitting on a tall stool at the front of the stage. She wore a long red velvet dress, buttoned high to her throat, with clinging sleeves that widened at her wrist to fall in long points down her sides. Her blue-black hair was unfashionably short, cut in a straight line above her brows and again level with her ears. It gave her an exotic air, enhanced by the black silk mask she wore over her eyes. Lewen stared at her, troubled by a feeling that he had seen her somewhere before.

He could not remember where. She was not young. Lewen could see silver glinting in her hair and deep lines on either side of her thin-lipped mouth. As he racked his brains, trying to place her, the musicians began to play a slow, melancholy tune and the woman began to sing.

Her voice was smoky and deep and quavered with an intensity of feeling that struck Lewen deep in the heart. He was ashamed to feel the sting of tears in his eyes for the third time that night. It felt as if she sang only for him, as if she knew his deepest, innermost longings and gave them voice. The smoky, crowded room faded away. She seemed to look straight at him, and he looked back, riveted, lost.

The song came to an end. The room erupted with applause. Lewen came back to himself with a start. He shook his head and rubbed his hand over his eyes, ashamed of his tears. He realized he was not the only one in the crowd weeping.

The singer smiled and inclined her head. "Thank ye," she said huskily. "I sang to ye then o' love. Now I shall sing o' sorrow."

She began then to sing a song Lewen had never heard before. At first he thought it told a made-up story, a tale from other times or other lands. After a while he realized, with a growing sense of incredulity, that she was singing of the death of Jaspar the Ensorcelled. She sang of the Rìgh's bitter grief that he must die so soon after the birth of his beloved daughter, Bronwen. She told how he named his daughter heir before he died, and how she, a mere babe in arms, was then declared Banrìgh of Eileanan. She sang of how Lachlan the Winged stormed the palace and wrested the crown away from the baby Banrìgh, and how he sought to keep Bronwen from bonding with the Lodestar, as was the right of all those born of MacCuinn blood. An old cook, she sang, who loved the child dearly, braved his wrath to make sure the Rìgh's daughter had her chance to lay her hand upon Aedan's Inheritance, and the Lodestar had kindled at the touch of her baby hand.

It was always said whoever holds the Lodestar shall hold the land, the woman sang, and so Lachlan's heart was filled with rage. He had fought the Banrìgh for the singing sphere, and he was a man and she but a babe. She could not hold it and so she lost: the throne, the crown, the Lodestar.

"But now she is a woman grown," the singer sang, "Bronwen the Bonny they call her. Now she is a woman grown, the Banrìgh she should be."

Lewen looked around him, amazed. He saw the whole crowd was as riveted as he was. A few had tears in their eyes. It was a most beautiful and sorrowful song. More than that, it had the ring of utter truth. Lewen had always known Bronwen was the daughter of Jaspar the Ensorcelled, but it had never occurred to him to wonder how her uncle Lachlan came to rule after his brother's death. He saw now how it had happened, and his heart swelled with anger and sympathy for Bronwen. No wonder she was so wild and intractable, flaunting her disobedience in Lachlan's face. No wonder she submerged herself in frivolous pleasures, having no other place for herself at court. So many things seemed clear now.

There was the sound of a group of people coming in. He heard a laugh he recognized and turned his head. Owein and Olwynne stood together in the doorway, the lantern shining on their bright curls. Owein's wings flamed out of the darkness like wildfire.

The royal twins were recognized at once. A stir and mutter ran over the crowd. Everyone gaped and fell back, and the twins came forward, smiling, supremely confident, unaware of any ill will.

Lewen wanted to stand up, to shout at them and warn them. He glanced back at the stage. The masked woman was gone as if she had never been. Lewen shook his head, trying to clear it of the fumes of smoke and ale. He felt dazed. Suddenly he was not so sure of what he had just heard. Surely no one would dare sing such a song, right here in Lucescere, the capital of Rionnagan? Surely the twins could not be in danger?

The crowd eased back, clearing the way for the twins. Owein smiled around, oblivious to the tense atmosphere, but Lewen saw Olwynne frown and draw herself up. She glanced at their bodyguards, who followed close behind. The Khan'-cohban warriors both had their hands close to their weapons belt, their thick brows drawn together as they scanned the crowd. Tall strong men with long pale hair bound back from their faces and sharp curving horns, their dark skin was marked with three slashes on either cheek, showing they were warriors of high distinction. One wore a cloak of spotted sabre leopard skin, and the other of white snow lion fur, the snarling heads still intact.

Accompanying the twins were their usual entourage, chief among them Alasdair and Heloïse MacFaghan, the younger children of Ishbel the Winged and Khan'gharad the Scarred Warrior. Having recently turned nineteen, Alasdair and Heloïse were fifteen months younger than their nephew Owein and niece Olwynne. They had been born twenty-two years after their famous sisters Isabeau and Iseult, and had come, like all the other young prionnsachan of Eileanan, to study at the Theurgia.

As the elder twin, Heloïse was heir to the throne of Tìrlethan, and so spent much of her time reluctantly studying politics, history, law, economics, and land management. Alasdair occupied his time with riding, drinking, flirting, and getting up to mischief with the other squires. Like Lewen and Owein, Alasdair was one of the Rìgh's six squires. He was accompanied by his great friend and fellow squire, a thin, intense, dark-haired boy called Barney, the youngest son of the MacRuraich.

Accompanying the MacFaghan twins were their own bodyguards, also fierce Khan'cohban warriors. Among the lively party was Cailean of the Shadowswathe, with his enormous shadow-hound, Dobhailen, and the old and rather portly cluri-caun Brun.

Their entrance caused such a stir that the subtle dissonance created by the masked singer's song seemed to evaporate like ale fumes. Lewen was left with nothing more than a vague sense of disquiet. He stood up and waved at Owein, who grinned at him and veered his way. A table of corrigans rose and bowed and offered them their table, and they were all able to squeeze in together, their attendants taking the table Lewen had vacated. The bodyguards took up positions against the wall, their eyes moving constantly and suspiciously over the seething crowd, while Brun found himself a comfortable chair by the fire with an equally stout and elderly hobgoblin who was evidently an old friend.

"I've never been to an inn yet where Brun didna meet someone he kens," Owein said, signaling to the seelie waitress. She came at once, smiling, the ogre looming behind her.

"I havena seen Brun leave the palace in a while," Lewen said. "I'll have some more ale, thanks."

"Fuzzle gin for me," Heloïse said.

"Are ye sure?" Owein teased. "I've heard it has the most unfortunate effect on young ladies."

"I may look like a young lady but I have the stomach o' a man," Heloïse replied serenely.

"Fuzzle gin it is then," Owein said.

"Make it two," Olwynne said.

Lewen raised an eyebrow at her, for Olwynne rarely drank. She made a face at him and shrugged one shoulder sharply. She was, he noticed suddenly, looking very pale and tired.

"If ye two are drinking fuzzle gin, I'll be damned if I drink ale," Owein said. "What else do ye have?"

"Apart from ordinary ale, there's scurvy ale, and plague ale, or whiskey," the seelie said. "Or if that's no' what ye be wanting, there's moonflower ruin, or weasel fizzle, or oak-apple wine, or—"

"What in Eà's name is weasel fizzle?"

"The cursehags like it, and the goblins too."

"Reason enough to keep away from it," Owein said. "What about moonflower ruin?"

"Ye willna be wanting that, sir," the ogre said suddenly, startling them. He was a great hulking creature, with scaly limbs, coarse dark hair, and a tusked and warty face. His eyes glowed red. "May I suggest blue ruin instead?"

They stared at him in fascination, ogres still being rare enough, and brute enough, to be seldom seen in the city.

Owein recovered first. "What's that?"

"Gin," the ogre answered. His voice sounded like he shouted through a funnel in a vast, windy canyon. It caused the girls' hair to fly back from their faces.

"Seems rather tame," Owein replied. "What do ogres drink?"

"Ye willna be wanting that either, sir," the ogre said firmly. "If ye willna stick to gin or whiskey or ale, how about clamber skull?"

"Never heard o' it."

"It's green, it's evil, and it does the job," the ogre said. "It's called clamber skull because it climbs up into your skull and knocks out any thoughts ye might have rattling around up there."

"Sounds good. Bring it on."

"Me too," Lewen said.

The seelie bowed and smiled her triangular smile that was half-sweet, half-sly, and moved away, her hips swaying under the fall of her rich golden hair. Despite himself, Lewen found himself staring after her, as did every man in the room. He wrenched his gaze away, recalling how some Lucescere matrons had tried, unsuccessfully, to convince the Rìgh to sign and seal an act forbidding female seelies from walking the streets unveiled. Their beauty was simply too intoxicating and their morality too lax. Seelies believed the act of love to be as natural as breathing and would lie with anyone who smiled at them, or offered them a flower, or a bright pebble, or a song. They were said to be careless lovers, whose own lack of jealousy made them indifferent to another's agonies. Since they were forest faeries, who dwelled far from the filth and noise of human inhabitation, this had never been too much of a problem before. But since the Pact of Peace, more and more had come to the towns and cities, apparently driven by curiosity and a desire for the bright, useless things that humans made. In recent years, they had caused a great deal of trouble.

"So what is Brun doing here?" Lewen asked, forcing his gaze back to Owein's face. "It's no' like him to move far from the tower."

"I dinna ken. Happen he has friends here," Owein said. "Look at the place. It's swarming with faeries."

"He said he's heard rumors o' a new singer here who is stirring up all sorts o' trouble," Olwynne said. "He thought he'd come and have a listen."

"If she's who I think she is, ye've just missed her," Lewen replied.

"Really? Any good?"

"Extraordinary," Lewen replied. "And verging on treasonable, I think."

"Indeed!" Owein swung round to look at him. "How so?"

Lewen shrugged. He was already wondering if he had misconstrued or overstated the power and intent of the song. "A different version o' history," he answered.

Owein lost interest, glancing back at the door. "Boring! I'm glad we missed her. I'd much rather see those dancing ogres."

"I'd have liked to have seen her," Heloïse said. "The whole school is buzzing with talk o' her. Apparently she's been singing every night the last few weeks and drawing such a crowd they've been turning them away in droves. I hope she comes back on. We would've been here sooner, but Owein insisted on going to see some play at the Mandrake that I'd already seen, and really had no interest in seeing again."

"Did ye see the others there?" Lewen asked.

"Nay," Owein answered, rather shortly.

Their drinks arrived. The girls' fuzzle gin was pink and frothy, and after only a few sips Olwynne and Heloïse were both giggling. The boys' clamber skull was the color and texture of slime and made their eyes water. After three glasses, swallowed at first with difficulty, it tasted marvelous and the world seemed a sweeter, more melodious place.

Alasdair staggered away after the seelie, his bodyguard moving unobtrusively after him. Heloïse found someone to dance with. Cailean was deep in conversation with a tree-changer, while Dobhailen menaced a group of goblins with a stare and lifted lip. The room grew so crowded it was like a thick bean soup, steaming and bubbling. The musicians played at a great rate, the tree-shifters tossing their manes of long hanging twigs about, the hobgoblin tapping one enormous broad foot.

Lewen drank down his poison-green drink, his head spinning, and ordered yet another. Owein matched him drink for drink, growing more morose with every mouthful, his gaze continually straying towards the door. Suddenly, though, his eyes brightened and he sat up straighter. Lewen squinted through the smoke.

The young apprentices who had traveled through Ravenshaw with him crowded in through the doorway, along with a collection of other young students, all talking and laughing. Fèlice was at the center of it all and, Lewen hazarded, the cause of Owein's sudden attention. She was dressed, he was pleased to see, in a very pretty and demure dress of dusky pink with a narrow edging of white lace at hem and sleeve. He had been worried, after her boldness in the garth that afternoon, that she would try to impress Owein by following the new fashion in the court of wearing very clingy and revealing gowns. Owein had been raised by Iseult of the Snows, however, who always dressed with great simplicity, almost to the point of austerity. Although Lewen had never heard the young Prionnsa express much opinion on fashion, except to mock it in general, he was sure he would have thought less of Fèlice if she had dressed, like some of her companions, in a diaphanous gown with fluttering sleeves sewn to mimic the fins of the Fairgean.

Fèlice saw them crammed into their narrow booth and raised a hand to them, but made no move to come over.

She had no need to. Owein rose at once and tried to make his way towards her, but found his way blocked by a line of dancers. Always impatient, the Prionnsa did not wait for the dance to end, but spread his wings and flew over their heads, causing a general outcry of amazement and laughter. He landed lightly next to Fèlice, who smiled and curtsied, her eyelashes lowered.

"So ye've come at last," Owein said to Fèlice. "I'd almost given ye up."

She looked up. "Really? Are we so late?"

"Nay, I s'pose no' . . . though I'd thought to see ye at the Mandrake."

"Och, I heard the play was no' so good after all, so we went to see a puppet show at the Astral. It was most amusing!"

"I wish I had been there," Owein said in a voice devoid of any expression.

Fèlice dimpled at him. "I wish ye had too. If I'd kent ye'd

go to the Mandrake, I would've sent ye a message, but indeed, Your Highness, I did no' expect to see ye there."

"Didn't ye?" Owein said.

They were interrupted by Edithe NicAven, dressed in a dashing gown much the same color as the clamber skull, with fake fins and a plunging neckline. "Your Highness!" she cried and dipped into a deep curtsy that gave him an excellent view down her cleavage. Owein took an involuntary step back and saw Fèlice hide a quick smile that made him shoot her a wry glance.

"I am so very pleased to meet Your Highness at last," Edithe cooed. "I have heard so much about ye from our mutual friend, Lewen o' Kingarth. We all grew to be very close, ye ken, on our journey here from Ravenshaw. I do declare, I have hardly seen him since we arrived here at Lucescere! It's been such a mad whirl, hasn't it, Fèlice? Parties one night, balls another, and then, o' course, I have been very busy with my studies—I am taking Advanced Magic, ye ken. My father will be *so* pleased! Though I suppose it is no' surprising considering I am descended from Aven the Mysterious, who was one o' Brann's foremost acolytes."

She paused to take a breath. Owein at once bowed and murmured, "I am glad ye are enjoying the Theurgia, my lady. If ye would excuse me, I must just—"

"Oh, I always kent I would blossom once I came to the Tower o' Two Moons," Edithe went on, glancing away modestly and so missing Owein's mute appeal to Fèlice for help. "It has been my burning ambition to be a sorceress since I was a mere lassiekin and first began to demonstrate such striking powers. I remember my grandmother saying that I was a born witch, and she should ken. Her mother had been First Sorceress at the Tower o' Ravens for many years, ye see. I was only three when I first—"

"Ladies and gentlemen, faeries and *uile-bheistean*, may I have your attention!" The ogre's voice boomed through the crowded, smoky chamber, drowning out even Edithe's high-pitched nasal drone. Thankfully Owein turned to the stage.

"Every Friday evening we present the Song and Dance Night, an opportunity for us to showcase the talents o' our patrons. If ye can tell a joke, or juggle, dance a jig, or walk on your hands, if you can sing a song or tell a story, swallow a sword or turn a somersault, then this is the place and this is the time for ye! The prize for the best act is six gold royals!"

A cheer went up from the crowd, and Owein's eyes widened. It was a rich prize indeed. No wonder it was such a popular event.

"Just remember, it costs three coppers to enter, and no professional singers, dancers, or jongleurs allowed. The penalty is to be stomped on by me." To illustrate his point the ogre raised one enormous boot and slammed it back down on to the wooden stage. The whole room shook. Dust drifted down from the rafters, making the air even hazier. There was another roar of laughter, and the ogre grinned, showing a cavernous mouth filled with crooked, discolored fangs. He then tramped off the stage, and the show began.

"Come on, Landon, let's pay our fee and get ye on the list," Fèlice said.

Landon hung back. "I canna do it, Fèlice! Have ye seen how many people there are here?"

"All the better for getting your point across. Come on, Landon, dinna be shy. This is why we're here, remember?"

Landon glanced up at the stage, where two portly young cluricauns were juggling battered pots and pans, then around at the swaying crowd. He shook his head and clutched the sheaf of papers to his breast.

"Och, give them to me!" Fèlice seized the papers. "I'll read it for ye, Landon! It's too good an opportunity to miss. If anyone is going to be sympathetic towards Rhiannon, it's the Nisse and Nixie crowd. Most o' them are faeries, or faery friends, and most do no' have much liking for authority. They willna think it such a crime that she shot down a Yeoman, when they ken she did it to save her mother!"

She shot Owein a challenging, defiant glance, then marched off to the side of the stage, where the ogre was taking down names and accepting money.

The juggling cluricauns were followed by a hilarious ballet by four hobgoblins, and then a series of jokes by a nervous young corrigan, which fell rather flat. Then it was Fèlice's turn. She was swung up onto the stage by the ogre, and dimpled at the crowd, saying in her clear, high voice, " 'Rhiannon's Ride,' or 'The Prisoner o' Sorrowgate Tower,' a ballad in three parts written by the brilliant young poet Landon MacPhillip from Magpie Wood."

There was a round of applause, and then Fèlice began to read the poem with great gusto. She was a natural actress with a flair for the dramatic and absolutely no self-consciousness. At the scary moments, she lowered her voice and made it toll, her whole body twisting and shrinking in on itself; then the very next moment, her voice would soar up into a shrill falsetto that made the audience laugh. With no more than her face and hands and voice, she was able to bring the various characters alive— the wicked laird of the castle, his mad sister-in-law, the malevolent chamberlain, the smiling castle seelie with her basket of poisons, the sad ghost of the little boy who wandered the castle corridors moaning, "So cold, so cold." Through it all strode Rhiannon, the only one able to see clearly.

When at last Fèlice finished on a ringing note, pleading for mercy for the wrongfully accused Prisoner of Sorrowgate Tower, there was a resounding storm of applause. Fèlice tossed out handfuls of broadsheets of the ballad, which Rafferty and Cameron had printed up on the Theurgia's printing press, and then told the crowd that more would be on sale tomorrow, in the streets, a penny apiece. Only then did she climb down, flushed with her success.

"I do think the freedom o' the Theurgia must have gone to her head," Edithe confided to Owein. "Would her father no' be shocked to see her performing like that in a common inn, afore a crowd o' rough faeries? Really! I hardly kent where to look."

But Owein did not respond, surging forward with the rest of the students to congratulate Fèlice and Landon, who was speechless with joy at seeing his poem brought so vividly to life and by its uproarious reception.

"Fèlice, ye were marvelous!" Maisie cried. "I swear I almost wept!"

"Landon, I take it all back! That was jolly good," Cameron said.

"Ye were wonderful, the best act o' the night by far!" Rafferty said. "I bet ye win the purse."

"Do ye think we've helped Rhiannon at all?" Fèlice asked

anxiously. "I mean, I ken they liked the poem but do they understand that it's all true?"

Owein, finding himself jostled and ignored, went back to his table, looking disgruntled.

Lewen had found the performance of Landon's poem very affecting. It felt as if he carried a boulder in his chest, which squeezed his lungs so he could not breathe. Olwynne had seen his distress and taken both his hands, and that small touch of sympathy saw words come spilling out of Lewen.

"It's just that I dinna ken what to do, how to make things right for her. Sorrowgate Prison is an absolute hellhole. I should never have persuaded her to come to Lucescere. She could've escaped, but I made her promise no' to. I told her it'd be all right, that we'd talk to the Rìgh on her behalf. I never expected she'd be shut up for months on end without a trial."

"It's only a couple o' months," Olwynne said. "Just till midsummer."

"She's no' used to being confined, Olwynne. Each day is a year to her. She canna eat or sleep. She says the prison is full o' ghosts that mock her at night . . ."

"Satyricorns are very superstitious," Olwynne said. "I've heard about how she mutilates herself in fear o' ghosts or demons, or something."

"Dark walkers," Lewen said defensively. "And she's no' doing that anymore."

"Only because they do no' let her have a knife or aught else sharp," Owein said, his eyes on the crowd of talking, laughing apprentice-witches.

"No, she doesna believe in dark walkers anymore. Nina and I convinced her they do no' exist."

"Yet she still lies awake imagining ghosts," Olwynne said.

"She's no' imagining them!" Lewen cried. "Sorrowgate Tower has been a prison for close on a thousand years. Hundreds o' people must've died there, many o' them horribly. Why, we've all heard the stories o' all the poor men and women who were tortured and burned to death there during Maya's reign, when the witch-sniffers were in charge. I am no' near as sensitive as Rhiannon to such things, and the place makes my flesh creep on my bones, I swear."

"Is she really so sensitive?" Owein asked curiously. "I've heard it was all an act, to divert suspicion from herself."

"Fettercairn Castle was as blaygird a place as I've ever been," Lewen said. "I was glad to get out o' there alive. Ye heard Landon's ballad. It was indeed just as dark and grim as he described it."

"I thought much o' it was poetic license," Olwynne said.

"Nay, it was all true!" Lewen cried. "And they call Rhiannon a murderer! Laird Malvern is a murderer a hundred times more foul!" He drained his cup of clamber skull.

"Well, I'm sure the courts will establish the truth o' it all," Owein said, beckoning to their waitress.

"Aye, but there's been so much talk, how can she have a fair trial, really? And despite the Pact o' Peace, there's still a lot o' bad feeling about her being a satyricorn." Lewen was having trouble framing his thoughts. "Everyone thinks they're stupid and brutal. . . ."

"O' course they do no'," Olwynne said soothingly, and gulped down her fuzzle gin.

"They do, they do. And it's no' fair. Rhiannon's no' like that. She's the sweetest, dearest . . ." Lewen felt the tissues of his throat growing thick.

"Evidently," Owein muttered, then, at Lewen's look, put up his hands. "I'm sure she is . . . apart from being a wee bit too quick to draw back her bow."

"What do ye expect? She was raised by satyricorns, by *wild* satyricorns, satyricorns who've never heard o' the Pact o' Peace, satyricorns who had to fight and hunt to stay alive, satyricorns—"

"He's getting rather stuck on the whole satyricorn thing," Owein said to Olwynne.

Lewen tried not to mind.

"Do no' worry so much," Olwynne said. "I'm sure the courts will find it was no' murder with malice aforethought. They willna hang her then."

Lewen thought of seeing Rhiannon with her head in a noose, the executioner drawing it tight, the horses whipped up to drag the cart away. His whole world seemed to splinter. He grasped his glass very hard and managed to bring it to his mouth.

"Never," he pronounced. "I never. I blow up Sorrowgate first. I blow it up. I blow it all up."

"I'm sure that's no' necessary," Olwynne tried to say. It came out, "I ssshaw tha' na neshassary."

Lewen found this very amusing. "No' neshassary, no' neshassary," he repeated.

He and Olwynne laughed together, heads bent over their empty glasses.

Impatiently, Owein signaled again for more clamber skull. The seelie materialized at their elbows, smiling sweetly upon them, bending close to Lewen to pour out more of the sickly green alcohol. Lewen was suddenly, violently, aroused. He hid his face in his glass. More than ever, he longed for Rhiannon, and yet, perversely, he wished he could just be here, at the Nisse and Nixie, drinking and laughing with his friends, enjoying himself without guilt or despair.

"I missed ye lads and lassies," he managed to say.

"Us too," Olwynne said, squeezing his hand.

"I wish I'd never met her," Lewen said into his cup.

Olwynne leaned closer to him. "I beg your pardon?"

"I wish I'd never met her," he repeated, and laid his head on Olwynne's arm, tears suddenly choking him.

The Keybearer

Rhiannon lay on her bed. There was a mottled stone high on the far wall that, when the light began to sink at the end of the day, looked a little like the silhouette of a black flying horse. Rhiannon liked to stare at it, longing for Blackthorn, imagining herself flying high in the sky, free as a bird.

She had had no visitors for three days. Rhiannon had walked the length of her room so many times she thought the stones should be showing the track of her feet. She had pounded on the door in her frustration and snarled at the guards when they finally came. She had demanded and then begged them to let her out, then had sunk into an apathy from which it was hard to rouse herself. It seemed to be the only way to keep the panic at bay. Whenever Rhiannon thought about the situation she found herself in, she had to bite her lips bloody to stop herself from screaming.

At the sound of the key in the lock, she turned and looked towards the door, her lips clamped together to hide her misery, her eyes hot.

But it was not Lewen whom the guard showed in through the heavy oak door. It was a tall woman dressed all in white.

At first, seeing the long plait of ruddy hair, Rhiannon thought it was Lewen's sanctimonious friend Olwynne and stiffened instinctively. Olwynne had come once, a few days ago, and had brought her a child's picture book and a wooden puzzle, as if Rhiannon were four years old. It had been clear to Rhiannon how much Olwynne feared and disliked her, and she knew with utter certainty why. Olwynne had spoken of Lewen as if they spent every minute of every day together, as if they had been born sharing the same heart, lungs, and stomach, like the freak babies she and the other apprentices had seen at the fair in Linlithgorn.

After Olwynne had left, with fake smiles and offers of friendship, Rhiannon had lain awake for hours torturing herself with imaginings of Olwynne and Lewen studying together, riding together, dancing together, laughing together. It was a small step to imagining Olwynne's arms sliding up around his neck, pulling Lewen's head down to hers, pressing her mouth against his. She could easily imagine Olwynne whispering in his ear, "Ye ken she's no good for ye. She canna love ye the way I love ye. I'm the only one who can make ye happy. . . ."

Again and again Rhiannon had replayed the scene in her mind. Although she sometimes imagined Lewen flinging Olwynne's arms away and declaring his love for her, more often than not she saw him succumb, that skinny red-haired witch driving all thought of Rhiannon out of his head. After all, why would he want a wild satyricorn girl when he could have a banprionnsa dressed all in rustling silks?

So she glared at her visitor with great suspicion and dislike. It was not Olwynne who stood in the door, however, but a woman entering the middle years of her life. She was very like Olwynne, with the same red-gold hair and the same tall, slim figure. She carried a staff with a large crystal set at its head, and a tiny owl was perched on her shoulder. She came in with great authority, drew her brows together at the dimness, and waved one hand nonchalantly. At once the lantern hanging overhead burst into light.

"Who are ye?" Rhiannon demanded, rolling over and getting to her feet defensively.

The woman raised one thin, red brow. "I am Isabeau NicFaghan, the Keybearer o' the Coven. May I sit down?"

Rhiannon jerked her head in agreement and watched as the Keybearer sat down at the table, arranging her silver-edged robes about her feet. Rhiannon's attention was caught by the sight of a beautifully wrought dagger hanging at the sorceress's waist. Rhiannon glanced away at once. Pretending insouciance, she sat down on her bed, even as her brain got busy with schemes for wresting the dagger away.

"I would no' try, Rhiannon," the Keybearer said. "I ken ye

are quick and strong, but no' quick or strong enough, I'm afraid. And I have no wish to hurt ye."

Rhiannon secretly jeered at her words, for was she not twenty years younger and a satyricorn to boot? She said nothing, however, just pretended incomprehension and waited for her chance.

"I am sorry I have no' come to see ye afore," Isabeau said. "I have been much tied up with affairs o' state. I do hope ye will forgive me. I feel some responsibility for ye, since Lilanthe sent ye into my care, and so I—"

"Have ye come to release me?" Rhiannon interrupted.

Isabeau shook her head. "It is no' my place to interfere with the workings o' the court. Even if ye were a witch and my own apprentice, I could no' have ye released. Those o' the Coven are subject to the laws o' the land, as is anyone else."

Rhiannon drooped. "Then why are ye here?"

"I came to see if there is aught I can do for ye," Isabeau said. "I have heard ye are no' used to being confined within four walls. I can understand that."

"Then why will ye no' let me out!" Rhiannon cried. "It's like being buried alive. I hate it, I hate it, I hate it!"

Isabeau regarded her gravely. "Ye are allowed to walk in the prison garden."

"Och, aye, that's a treat. It is twelve paces long and six paces wide, and surrounded by such high walls all I can see is grey stone and a wee patch o' sky. And they watch me all the time!"

"O' course they do. Ye are a prisoner o' the Crown, and the captain o' the guards considers ye an escape risk. The garden is open to the air. Ye are known to have a winged horse as a familiar. They dare no' allow ye any greater freedom in case ye call your horse and fly away."

"Blackthorn is gone," Rhiannon said in bitter misery.

"I'd be surprised if that were true," Isabeau answered. "Familiars are bound tight to their witches, even after death. My guardian, Meghan, had a little donbeag as her familiar, and after she died, the donbeag stayed on her grave for three years before it at last died. Naught we could do would coax it away."

"I am no witch."

"Again, I do no' believe that is true. One does no' have to be trained in the craft and cunning o' the Coven to be a witch. It is

clear to us all that ye have Talent in abundance. I have heard o'
your antics. Ye called a flying horse to ye and bound it to your
will, ye can see and hear ghosts, ye can listen through walls, ye
can pull iron bars out o' solid rock with naught more than your
will, ye can talk to any horse and, if I am no' greatly mistaken,
ye can bend others to your will without them even realizing. A
forbidden skill, I should add, and one that ye would have to
learn to control if ye were ever to be admitted to the Coven.
Witches believe all people must have the freedom to choose
their own path."

Rhiannon was startled. She scowled at the Keybearer and
said waspishly, "I see ye've been listening to tittle-tattle about
me."

"O' course," Isabeau answered. "I am troubled and intrigued
by your case, and so is the Rìgh. Quite apart from my natural
interest in your witch talents, I am most concerned with the effect ye have had on Lewen, who is the son o' my dearest friend.
He is no longer permitted to visit ye, Rhiannon. I do no' believe
ye intended to ensorcell him but—"

"What gives ye the right?" Rhiannon flared, jumping to her
feet. "How dare ye? Ye canna take him away from me. He's
mine!"

"He is his own self," Isabeau said. "People do no' own each
other."

Rhiannon made an emphatic gesture of dismissal. "Ye no'
understand. Owning naught to do with it! He mine, I his. We
swore to each other!"

Isabeau shook her head. "I'm sorry, Rhiannon, but I canna
allow him to—"

To Rhiannon's utter chagrin, tears were flooding down her
face. "Ye canna take him away from me," she sobbed. "He's
mine! He's all I have!"

"I see," Isabeau said quietly. "I do no' think I understood."

She was silent for long moments while Rhiannon struggled
to bring her face back under control. Then she said, "Rhiannon,
I do no' wish to hurt ye more than ye have already been hurt. I
can sense deep wounds in ye. I understand that ye love
Lewen—"

"And he loves me!"

"—but I canna allow ye to see him alone. I do no' think it is good for either o' ye when the future is so uncertain. More important, I am afraid ye may compel him to acts that he will regret bitterly hereafter. Ye are half satyricorn, Rhiannon, and ye have been raised by different rules than Lewen. His honor is most important to him. If ye were to compel him to betray all he holds dear—his family, his Rìgh, his allegiance to Eà and the Coven—I fear he would never recover."

Rhiannon stared at her. "Do ye have some reason to fear he may do so?" she asked at last.

Isabeau regarded her gravely. "My niece, the Banprionnsa Olwynne, fears so. She says he has been in great distress, making wild plans to break ye out o' prison and run away with ye. It would ruin him—ye must see that. She says he seems quite mad with despair. I have been to see him, and although I do no' fear he has lost his reason, it is quite clear to me that he is acting under strong compulsion."

Rhiannon was incapable of hiding her pleasure and triumph. She did her best until Isabeau's last words; then her feelings got the better of her. "Ye and your compulsion," she said scornfully. "Have ye never been in love, that ye think what Lewen feels is some sort o' ensorcellment? He loves me, I tell ye, and I love him!"

There was a long pause; then Isabeau said, "I am no' such a stranger to love as you suppose. It is true it can seem like madness sometimes, to those who watch from beyond."

She was quiet a moment longer. Rhiannon forced herself to be silent.

At last the Keybearer looked up, her eyes very blue and luminous in her pale face. "I do no' wish to forbid ye seeing each other altogether. I ken how ardent, how impatient young love can be. Yet I have a responsibility to Lewen too. His studies are suffering badly, and his whole life has been turned upside down and inside out. If he is no' careful, he will lose all he has worked so hard to gain. I canna allow that."

Under the cover of her heavy prison gown Rhiannon's foot beat an impatient tattoo. She stared at the Keybearer defiantly, not allowing her desperate hope to show on her face.

"I will allow Lewen to see ye once a week, on his rest day, and then ye must no' be alone. Either I or another sorcerer must be with ye at all times. If ye are accompanied by a sorcerer and guards, ye and Lewen may walk in the witches' gardens, but ye must no' call to your horse. If ye do, I shall ken it, I tell ye now, and this privilege will be revoked."

"I tell ye, Blackthorn is gone," Rhiannon said, her sullenness more of a ruse to hide her elation than true truculence.

Isabeau and the owl on her shoulder both regarded her steadily. "A black winged horse has been seen most days, flying about in the early morn."

Rhiannon clasped her hands together. "Blackthorn has been seen? Here?"

"I have given orders none are to try to catch her and no one at the Tower o' Two Moons would dare disobey. I canna speak for the city, though. There is much curiosity about ye and the horse, and there are many who would be glad to capture her. Ye would do well to send her news o' that and warn her to keep away from the city."

"She'll be able to hear me? Even from in here?"

"Maybe, maybe no'. It is hard to mind-speak over water or through stone, even for accomplished witches. I would try from the gardens. If I can, I will walk with ye and Lewen at the week's end, and afterwards, I will come back here and set ye some lessons. I understand that ye are bored, cooped up here all day with naught to do. I feel ye will be happier if ye had something to occupy your hands and mind."

"I doubt it," Rhiannon muttered, but she could not hide the lifting of spirits she felt at Isabeau's words.

"I want ye to work hard at your lessons, Rhiannon. It is important that ye show your judges that ye have submitted to the will o' the court and await their judgment. I will tell ye now what I told Lewen last night. I do no' think they will hang ye for Connor's death, if you have been telling the truth about why and how it happened. It is more likely that ye will be asked to make restitution to the Crown and to Connor's family through some kind o' bond o' service. A lass with your talents and abilities would be wasted swinging at the end o' a hangman's noose, and Lachlan . . . the Rìgh kens it. If ye wish, at the end o' your bond service, ye may come to the Theurgia and we will test ye and see if ye have any potential as a witch. The Coven needs all the Talent it can find, and so, I might add, does the Rìgh. However, ye must learn our ways and abide by them. Ye have rejected your satyricorn past. Now it is time to embrace your future among those of humankind."

Isabeau ended on a ringing note, and Rhiannon found it hard not to be swept up in her enthusiasm. Only a lingering distrust enabled her to scowl and say gruffly, "Aye, fine words, but happen I should wait for the verdict afore I make too many plans for the future."

Isabeau looked disappointed, but she nodded and got up, one hand going up absentmindedly to pet the little owl who had sat so quietly on her shoulder all this time. The owl hooted softly and Isabeau hooted back.

Rhiannon said in a rush, surprising herself, "Ye asked if ye could do aught for me . . ."

"Yes?" Isabeau queried, turning back.

"I want my things. In my pack."

Isabeau frowned. "I'm sorry, Rhiannon, but I canna allow that. They have been submitted for evidence in your trial."

"I do no' want my daggers," she said. "I mean, I do, but I can wait for those if I must. And I ken ye'll take away my bonny blue cloak—I've been told so often enough! It's not those I want now. . . ."

"What is it then?" Isabeau asked gently.

"Lewen whittled me a wee charm the night we spent at the Tower o' Ravens," Rhiannon said. "For me to wear around my neck. Please, I want it."

"I will ask the captain o' the guards," Isabeau said after a moment. "I canna see any harm, but it is no' my decision to make. And Captain Dillon is suspicious o' things o' magic. If Lewen whittled it for ye, it will have some virtue o' enchantment. It is impossible for it no' to. I will ask Dillon this evening and let ye ken tomorrow."

She made a move towards the door but Rhiannon once again detained her with a quick, impulsive gesture. "Can ye teach me how ye did that, then?" She pointed up at the lantern. "Lit the lantern, I mean, just like that."

Again she suffered under that cool, searching glance. After a moment the Keybearer asked, "Why?"

Rhiannon could not meet her gaze. She turned away, mumbling, "They willna leave it on for me. I canna sleep with it so dark. There's no light at all. No starlight, no moonlight . . . and I can hear things . . . hanging over me in the dark . . ."

"Dark walkers?" Isabeau asked with sudden keen interest.

"Nay . . . maybe . . . Fèlice said they do no' exist and indeed, none o' ye seem to fear them. I have no' been able to cut myself since I've been here and they have no' come to drink my blood so happen it is true and they are no' real. I do no' ken. It is no' them I fear, anyway, but . . ."

"What?"

"Ghosts," Rhiannon whispered. She did not look at Isabeau.

Isabeau did not laugh. "These cells are auld, and many cruel things have happened here in the past. If ye are very sensitive, the memories o' those events will press upon ye, no doubt o' that. But ghosts strong enough to disturb your sleep . . ." She hesitated, then said very slowly, "The ghosts I feel are all very auld and faint, mere whispers. They are no more than shivers o' sadness and fear. . . ."

Rhiannon looked up, startled, meeting Isabeau's gaze for the first time. "Ye see ghosts too?"

Isabeau nodded. "Aye, I can. We call it the gift o' clear-seeing. If there was a ghost haunting this room, I would expect to be able to feel it too. But all I can feel is shadows, whispers, unhappiness. . . ."

"Nay! This ghost is strong! And angry! She mocks me. She is like ice in my blood, like . . . lightning. She seizes me in her hands and shakes me."

Isabeau leaned forward intently. "Is that so? Can ye feel her or hear her now?"

Rhiannon shook her head vehemently. "Nay! She no' here. She comes at night. Is gone by day."

Isabeau put up her hand and stroked her owl thoughtfully. "Are ye sure she is a ghost?"

"She says she wants life again. Says she wants *my* life."

"What else does she say?"

Rhiannon hesitated and looked away. "She says to free her."

Isabeau chewed her thumbnail, the first sign of indecision Rhiannon had seen in her. "Who is she, this ghost?" she asked.

Rhiannon shook her head. "I dinna ken. But I have seen her afore, at the Tower o' Ravens. The laird o' Fettercairn raised her by mistake, and it is him that she haunts."

"She haunts another too?"

"The laird o' Fettercairn. It is him she comes to see, really. She hangs over him and steals his breath away so he wakes choking and afraid. She tells him he will never be free o' her."

"And ye fear her too, this ghost?"

Rhiannon hesitated, for it was difficult for her to ever admit any fear, but when Isabeau raised one eyebrow, she jerked her head angrily.

The sorceress sat still for a long moment, her brows drawn together in thought, her hands folded on her staff. Rhiannon had never met anyone with so much composure. It made her acutely aware of her own restless hands, which she stilled with an effort. Isabeau did not seem to notice the silence, which drew out until it was painful.

At last she glanced up. "I canna help ye learn to conjure flame. I am sorry. I am sure Captain Dillon would no' approve o' me teaching a prisoner the secrets o' summoning fire or any other skills that ye may be able to use to help ye escape." She smiled a little at Rhiannon's scowl and went on, "I am concerned about this ghost, however. The spirits o' the dead are usually confined to haunting the place of their death or some other place to which they are tied by intense emotion. To say ye have seen a ghost at the Tower o' Ravens and then again here, so many miles away, that puzzles me. It is no' unknown for a ghost to choose to haunt a person, particularly their murderer, but ye say ye do no' ken her and that she haunts the laird o' Fettercairn as well. Why does she haunt him, do ye ken?"

This time it was Rhiannon's turn to sit silent, though she twisted her skirt in her fingers and kicked her foot back and forth until she remembered and stilled her limbs. The sorceress waited patiently, and at last, with a furtive glance about her, Rhiannon muttered, "She comes to him at night and reminds him o' the pact they made."

"What pact was that?"

"She told him she would show him the spell to bring the dead back to life, but that he must promise to raise her first."

"And how do ye ken this?"

"I was there when they made the pact, at the Tower o' Ravens. I was hiding and watching. The laird has been trying to find out how to raise the dead for years and years. That is why he murdered all those people, all those little boys. He wants to raise his brother and his brother's son. Who were killed, oh, many years ago. When she . . . when the ghost told him about the spell, he was eager to agree. He was glad to! But now he's in prison, and the ghost is angry. He canna raise her from the dead while he is here. So she comes and torments him. She says, 'Free me or I'll haunt your sleep forever.'"

"How do ye ken what she says to him?"

Again Rhiannon hesitated, twisting her body about, jamming her hands between her knees. "I go there," she said at last. "I dinna ken how. I go and I listen. Maybe I dreaming. But it dinna feel like dreaming."

"Tell me exactly what it felt like," Isabeau said very softly. "Tell me everything."

Rhiannon took a deep breath, and then the words came tumbling out. She told the Keybearer as much as she could remember of the night she had first seen the ghost, here in Sorrowgate. It was hard to find the words to express so many things outside the usual realm of her experience, but the Keybearer was quick to understand and help her.

"So this ghost . . . she comes to haunt ye often?"

"Aye. She says she kens me now. She comes every night, to mock me. She tells me to enjoy my life while I have it. She says it will be over soon enough."

"And this feeling o' being out o' your body . . . it's happened more than just this once?"

Rhiannon's eyes flashed up to Isabeau's face and then dropped again. "Aye," she admitted. "Every night since. I imagine I am riding Blackthorn. Sometimes we fly far, far away, but it is always dark and I start feeling . . . dizzy, as if I'm about to fall into space. Or I think o' Lewen, and then I . . . come back."

"It is a good thing ye do," Isabeau said. "I thought at first ye were dream-walking, but it sounds more as if ye were skimming the stars, which is a very dangerous thing to do if no' properly trained. Ye can get lost and no' be able to find your way back to your body, and then ye would die."

She put up one hand and fondled the little white owl, who gave a long mournful cry. "Have ye seen this ghost again? Have ye eavesdropped on her again?"

"Eavesdropped?" Rhiannon asked, puzzled.

"Watched and listened without her knowing."

Rhiannon gave a little, reluctant nod. "I go sometimes, quiet as a wee mouse, trying no' to let her ken. I want to ken who she is. I want to kill her! But she's already dead."

"There are ways to rid oneself o' a ghost, dinna ye worry! But tell me first everything she has said. I need to ken it all."

Rhiannon tried to remember. "She says he must escape, and bring the sacrifice to her grave, and a healer, for if she was to be brought again to life, they must have . . . something . . . the anti-something . . ."

"Antidote?"

Rhiannon shrugged. "Maybe. I dinna ken. They needed it, anyway, to heal her. The laird was awake; he was sitting up in bed. He said he had a healer. She said the healer must find the anti-whatever-it-is, and the spell, and bring it to her grave by . . . I dinna remember when."

"I wonder where her grave is?"

Rhiannon shrugged. "She said he would need a fast ship and fair winds, and he said that he could manage both o' those, once he is free."

"This is getting stranger and stranger," Isabeau said. "I must admit I am sorely puzzled. Did she say anything else?"

"Aye. She said she wanted the sacrifice to be a young woman, a beautiful young woman, just coming into her powers. And then . . . and then she said . . ."

"What?"

"She said I would do perfectly."

"Ye?"

"Aye. She calls me the satyricorn girl with the dark hair and the ruthless heart. Only I'm no', truly I'm no'." To Rhiannon's surprise and chagrin, tears were suddenly burning her eyes. She rubbed them away angrily.

"So she kens who ye are."

"Aye." Rhiannon took a few deep breaths, trying to control her tears. Isabeau was frowning. Rhiannon risked a look at her face, then went on. "She has come nearly every night since then. I tell her I'll never submit, but she says it is no' up to me. She says she will live again, and if I must die to give her life, so be it. That is why I want my charm. Lewen whittled it for

me, to keep me safe from ghosts. I . . . I'm afraid o' the night.
I'm afraid to sleep."

Isabeau twisted her staff around and around, staring into the
crystal embedded at its crown. "A powerful sorceress, poisoned
to death, who longs for life again, who longs for revenge. Someone whose grave lies a long way away, across the sea. Someone
powerful enough to cling to this world and seek another body to
inhabit, a beautiful dark-haired body, with a ruthless heart—"

"I'm no' ruthless!" Rhiannon cried, but Isabeau was not listening. She looked sick and white.

"Surely it canna be?" she whispered. "I must think on this."

She got to her feet abruptly. "I will stay with ye tonight," she
said curtly. "I must see this ghost for myself. I will go now, and
bathe, and change, and make my excuses to Lachlan and Iseult,
and then I will come back."

Rhiannon gaped at her, startled out of words.

Isabeau smiled at her. "Surely having me here is better than
leaving the light on all night?"

Rhiannon felt so pathetically grateful, she scowled more
fiercely than ever and said ungraciously, "I suppose so."

To her surprise Isabeau smiled and said, "I'm glad. I will see
ye again soon."

At her commanding rap on the door, the guards opened it at
once and she went out, the owl swiveling its head to keep its
golden eyes on Rhiannon until the very last moment.

Then the door shut, the lantern winked out, and Rhiannon
was left alone in her dark cell. She felt oddly exalted. Unable to
sit still, she leaped up and paced her room again. Rhiannon
wanted so much to believe in the Keybearer. Firmly she
stamped down upon the little tendril of hope springing up in her
mind, grinding it into the ground. It was a tenacious plant, however, fed and watered by the lightning charge the Keybearer
seemed to emanate. Rhiannon had never met anyone quite like
her. The Keybearer had seemed to fill the damp little cell with
life and warmth and energy. It was as if she was a crucible filled
to the brim with molten metal, blazing with white fire, all im-
purities dissolved into ash, leaving behind only power, truth,
beauty. She was a newly forged sword, still smoking. Rhiannon
could no more disbelieve her than raise a foolhardy hand
against her. She knew, with absolute certainty, that she would

never dare try to wrest away the Keybearer's dagger. Understanding that, it was only a small step towards believing Isabeau might indeed be able to save her.

By the time Isabeau came back, Rhiannon was weary indeed with all her pacing and thinking and wondering. It was late, and the Keybearer had a soft white plaid flung around her shoulders against the night chill. Rhiannon had taken refuge in her bed and was trying her best to stay awake. She jerked around when the Keybearer came in, haloed with the light of a single candle. She would have sat up and spoken, but Isabeau smiled and lifted her finger to her lips.

"Sleep, lass. I'll stand watch over ye."

The owl on her shoulder hooted softly, as if in agreement. Rhiannon lay down again, facing the room, watching as Isabeau set down the candle on the table. The Keybearer began to unpack the basket she had carried over one arm. Even though Rhiannon's eyelids felt irresistibly heavy, she fought to keep them open, fascinated by what she saw. First the Keybearer took out an immensely thick old book covered in worn red leather, then a bundle of candles, small crystal bottles filled with various powders and potions, a silver saltshaker, and a squat, dark statue of a woman with three faces. Then the sorceress looked around and saw Rhiannon still watching. She came silently to her side.

"Sleep, lass," the sorceress said gently and touched her finger to Rhiannon's brow. She felt herself sinking away into unconsciousness, as if into a warm dark cocoon of feathers. She slept.

It was bright morning when Rhiannon woke again. Light splashed through the grille high in the wall, casting bright lozenges against the stone. Rhiannon stretched and yawned, her eyes thick with sleep-sand. She rubbed them clear and saw Isabeau sitting quietly in the chair, reading a page in the old, red-covered book. She looked up as Rhiannon moved and smiled.

"Did ye sleep well, my bairn?"

"Aye. I did. Have ye been here all night?"

"Indeed I have. Did I no' say I would watch over ye?"

"Did . . . did the ghost come?"

The Keybearer shook her head and turned the corners of her mouth down ruefully. "No' a sigh or a murmur o' a ghost, I'm pleased to say."

"The ghost is real, I swear it!" Rhiannon cried.

The Keybearer raised her brows. "Did I say I disbelieved ye? I did no' really expect her to come while I was here. I fancy it would no' suit her to have me banish her back to the realm o' the dead forever, which is what I planned to do if she came. Whoever she once was, she sounds like a most unpleasant ghost to have haunting ye. And I can see only evil coming o' a spirit that kens the secret o' necromancy and is willing to trade her knowledge for life. Necromancy is a forbidden art, ye must ken, one o' the few the Coven prohibits. One should no' meddle with Gearradh."

Rhiannon was confused. Although she felt she had heard the name before, she did not know where or to whom it referred.

"She who cuts the thread," Isabeau explained. "Our name for the last o' the Three Spinners."

Still Rhiannon did not understand.

"It is the way we describe birth, life, and death, the inescapable fates o' all," Isabeau said with a tired sigh. "Come, I am weary. I have no wish to discuss metaphysics with ye now." She shut the great thick book she had been reading and began packing away her wand and dagger and the silver cruets of salt and herbs and powdered dragon's blood. "I will tell ye tales o' the Three Spinners another time, and tell ye o' Eà, the three-faced goddess we worship, who contains these powers within her—maiden, matron, crone, as some see it, or child, mother, father. All ye need worry about now is that your ghost feared me enough no' to come, and ye have a good night's sleep behind ye, which I promise ye will make the future seem immeasurably brighter. I must go and catch some rest myself now, for I have a busy day ahead o' me, but I will send a message to Lewen and tell him he may come and see ye at the end o' the week. I willna be able to chaperone ye myself, I think, but I will send someone else, I promise. Oh, and by the way, I brought ye your charm."

She gestured with her hand to the table, where lay a small talisman whittled from silvery rowan wood. Rhiannon sat up eagerly, and the Keybearer tossed it to her. Rhiannon snatched it out of the air and clutched it to her breast.

Isabeau smiled, one eyebrow raised at the speed of Rhiannon's response, then rapped sharply on the door. Once it had been swiftly opened by the guard, the Keybearer nodded and smiled at Rhiannon and went out, the guard bowing low to her and then slamming the door shut again. Rhiannon did not mind so much this time. It was true that the future did seem immeasurably brighter.

The Bluebird

Five days later, a sorcerer came. He came when the lengthening oblong of light on Rhiannon's wall was growing dim
and red, and Rhiannon had given up hope of seeing anyone that
day. He was a dour, gruff man with a sardonic look to him,
dressed in brown with a tall staff made from an old knobbly
stick. His name was Jock.

"Do no' try and ensorcell me, lassie," he said curtly. "I have
no liking for those o' your sex and will ken if ye try any o' your
pretty tricks."

Rhiannon lifted her chin. "I have no tricks."

"Och, aye, o' course no'," he answered mockingly. "No lass
o' your age does. Which is why I have one o' my best students
mooning about and wasting my time in class instead o' listening as he should. He'll be waiting for ye in the garden, if ye're
interested."

"Lewen?"

"Nay, Lachlan the Winged himself," he answered sarcastically.

Rhiannon stared at him, and he snorted. "O' course Lewen.
Who else? The Keybearer tells me ye two are to have some
time together to hang on each other's necks. Ridiculous le-
niency, if ye ask me. The lad should be packed home for his
part in this sorry business, and ye kept locked up until after
your trial like any other prisoner. No wonder Dillon the Bold is
fuming. Well, aren't ye coming?"

Rhiannon took a deep breath and marched out the door. In
the corridor four prison guards waited with impassive faces.
One carried a long bow and quiver of arrows, another a great

sword strapped to his back, another a long-handled double ax, the fourth a strange-looking weapon bristling with knobs and levers and a long pipe with a large round mouth. The sorcerer stalked off down the corridor with his staff tap-tapping loudly, and as Rhiannon followed meekly behind, the guards fell into formation around her.

The dimly lit corridor was lined with ironbound doors identical to Rhiannon's. At the end of the corridor was a set of stairs that they descended, their bootheels echoing hollowly. They came out into a big empty hall, then wound their way through to the back of the building.

Rhiannon looked around her with keen interest, glad to fill her eyes with something other than the four walls of her cell. She was led past a busy guardroom filled with men polishing weapons, cleaning boots, playing cards or trictrac, or crowding around a table where two men arm-wrestled, panting and laughing. They all looked up as she walked past the open door, and silence fell. Rhiannon gritted her jaw and walked on, her heavy skirts swishing around her legs and hampering her stride.

The sorcerer glanced over his shoulder. "Remember, no tricks now," he warned. "Ye may think yourself very clever, bamboozling the Keybearer into allowing this folly, but I'm no' as soft as she is and willna hesitate to strike ye down if ye should try to escape. Neither, I might add, will your guards, though their weapons are far more crude than mine."

But ye have no weapons, Rhiannon thought.

The sorcerer grinned, showing bad teeth. "I am a sorcerer o' four rings, my dear. I have no need o' swords or pistols. I can stop your heart with a thought if I have a mind to."

Rhiannon did not know whether to believe him or not. They walked through the city streets, the guards keeping close. Rhiannon looked about her greedily, her eyes soaking up as many details of the bustling streets as she could. The sorcerer strode ahead of her, scowling at anyone who dared look too closely.

Then they came to the palace gates, which stood open, guarded by a row of blue-clad soldiers. They turned to stare at Rhiannon, who clenched her hands in her skirts and walked on, following the sorcerer through the massive iron gates. Beyond lay a long drive lined with trees dressed all in the fresh green of springtime. On either side smooth verdant lawns stretched

away, bordered with neat hedges. In the center of each lawn
was a marble fountain splashing with water, white graceful statues dancing amidst the rainbow spray. Tall yew trees were
neatly clipped into identical cone shapes. The eye was led irresistibly to the palace, a tall wide building capped with great
golden domes that gleamed in the warm reddish rays of the sun.

Rhiannon was disappointed. Although the garden was very
beautiful, in a stiff, formal way, it was not what she had been
expecting from Lewen's rhapsodic descriptions. In silence she
followed the sorcerer along the avenue to the palace. He did not
go into the magnificent building but led her and her guards
round to the left. A paved road led around the back of the
palace, lined with a tall yew hedge and pretty formal gardens
filled with newly budding roses and starlike narcissus within
low hedges grown in diamonds and circles.

Through an arched gate, Rhiannon saw a massive kitchen
garden, with rows and rows of herbs and vegetables and trel-
lised vines and espaliered fruit trees. To her surprise the sorcerer turned to her and said, "All the students o' the Theurgia
must work in there, ye ken. There are nigh on a thousand
mouths to be fed in this place, and it is backbreaking work
keeping them all from going hungry. Lewen is one o' my best
students; he has a gift with growing things, did ye ken? I shall
be sorry indeed if he does no' sit his Tests as we all expected.
He's a wood witch in the making; indeed he is."

Then the sorcerer shut his mouth into a hard line, and Rhiannon realized that he was angry with her. She looked back at
the beautifully tended garden and saw hot-looking students in
grubby black robes resting on their spades and hoes to stare at
her until another brown-robed man ordered them peremptorily
back to work.

The palace was now behind them, and Rhiannon's step faltered as she looked ahead of her with growing wonder and delight. Beyond spread a green, shady forest broken by long
stretches of velvety lawn and great banks of flowering shrubs.
Mossy flagstoned paths curved away into little dells of spring
bulbs or led through into sunlit gardens where statues or ponds
filled with waterlilies or great urns of flowers stood in just the
perfect place to entice the eye. On one side the avenue led down
the side of a great wall, several hundred feet high and smooth

as glass. Beyond, Rhiannon could hear the roar of a turbulent river. The brown-clad sorcerer led her down this avenue, and Rhiannon followed slowly, her eyes fixed on the garden rolling away to her right. She longed to explore the many paths and steps that ran away through arches of blossoms or deep green tunnels of leaves, but dared not disobey the emphatic tap-tapping of that staff.

Then she saw, buried deep in the verdant gardens, another small golden dome surrounded by row upon row of high green hedges. Rhiannon craned her neck to see more, realizing that this was the maze she had been told grew in the heart of the gardens. There was a magical pool there, Nina had told her, and an observatory where the witches watched the movements of the stars and planets.

Rhiannon gazed back over her shoulder at the dome, wishing she could find her way to it through the maze, when, unexpectedly, she felt the air grow thin and cold about her. The sound of battle smote her ears. Shouts, screams of pain, the clang of metal on metal, the whine of arrows, the howling of a wolf. The peaceful sunlit garden faded away, and she saw instead a wild tangle of neglected trees and vines wreathed in dank mist. Men fought everywhere she looked, their faces twisted with effort. Everywhere men died. Rhiannon cringed back, ducking a sword swipe. She felt hands seize her shoulders, and she screamed, falling to her hands and knees. Looking up, she felt every hair on her body stand erect as an icy shudder of fear swept over her. Ghosts shrieked through the mist, wielding cold shining swords. Rhiannon cowered down, arms over her head.

"Lass, what is it? What's wrong?"

At last the voice penetrated her brain. She looked up, dazed, and saw the sorcerer in brown leaning over her. The sun shone warm and red on his head. Beside him the soldiers had all their weapons drawn, not sure whether to menace her or some unseen threat in the garden. Rhiannon looked around her, bewildered.

"But . . . there was a battle . . . Ghosts . . . ghosts o' dead soldiers . . . and a wolf . . . It was dark, misty. . . ."

One of the soldiers made a sharp sound of disbelief and

sheathed his sword. The others lowered their weapons, their faces hardening. One looked at her in open scorn.

"Is this what ye saw?" the sorcerer asked.

Rhiannon nodded, rubbing her aching forehead with her hand. She felt like weeping. All she could do was hang her head and try not to let the soldiers see. The sorcerer put down one broad, callused hand. After a moment she took it and let him pull her to her feet. Shamefaced, she busied herself dusting the leaves off her skirt.

"There was a famous battle here, many years ago. The horn o' the MacRuraich clan was blown, calling up the ghosts o' clansmen past. Tabithas Wolf-Runner fought in that battle too, in the shape o' a wolf."

Rhiannon looked up. "A black wolf?"

"Aye, a black wolf."

Rhiannon nodded. "And soldiers in red cloaks."

"Maya the Ensorcellor's Red Guards," the sorcerer concurred. "It was a decisive battle in Lachlan the Winged's bid to regain the throne." He glanced at the soldiers. "I didna think it happened so long ago that the Blue Guards would've forgotten. Why, your own captain was here that night. He was given his sword Joyeux for the part he played that Samhain Eve."

It was the soldiers' turn now to look shamefaced. The sorcerer motioned to Rhiannon to step forward and walk with him, and she obeyed, casting her four guards a disdainful glance.

"That is a rare Talent ye have, lass," the sorcerer said. "Few can see the past so clearly. Does it come to ye unbidden?"

Rhiannon nodded, unable to control a shudder that rattled her teeth together.

"Uncomfortable," the sorcerer said. "I would brace yourself then, lass, for there are many ghosts here at the Tower o' Two Moons. Most o' the students barely notice them, for the halls are filled with noise and laughter now, but we sorcerers see them often. Do no' be afraid. They are just the memories o' the stones. They willna harm ye."

Rhiannon cast him a quick look. She did not believe him. He frowned at her, as if sorry for the moment of connection, then said brusquely, "There's your mooncalf lover. Let us hope he finds it easier to listen in class tomorrow after seeing ye, for he sure as apples could no' be any worse!"

Rhiannon barely registered his words. Her gaze had flown up eagerly, seeking Lewen's tall familiar shape. He had been sitting under a big oak tree, whittling at a piece of wood with his knife, but at the sight of her he dropped them both and stood up, looking awkward and unhappy. Rhiannon's step faltered too. He was dressed in the austere black robe of an apprentice, and his unruly brown curls were swept back and tied severely at the nape of his neck with a black riband. It made him look very different.

They stood and looked at each other and said not a word. The sorcerer made a noise of disgust. "The Keybearer said ye were to walk in the garden, so walk, for Eà's sake!"

Rhiannon gritted her teeth together, inclined her head to Lewen, and began to walk along the lawn. He picked up his knife and sheathed it, dropping the bird he had been carving into his pocket, then came to walk by her side. Still they said nothing.

Rhiannon's heart was sore. After several more minutes of that painful, unhappy silence, she said stiffly, "Ye have no' been to see me."

"I'm sorry. They wouldna let me."

"Ye should've made them."

"How?"

"I dinna ken! Begged them. Paid them money. Knocked them down."

"I tried to bribe them," Lewen said unhappily, "but it was that auld guard, Henry. He willna take bribes. I've tried afore. He says I havena enough money to compensate him for losing his job. Most o' the other guards will gladly let me grease their palm for a wee bit more time with ye, but he never does."

Knowing Lewen had at least tried to see her made Rhiannon feel a little better. She glanced sideways at him. He was looking tired.

"She said I could only see ye once a week," Rhiannon said. "Canna ye beg her to let ye come more often? A week is such an awful long time."

"I canna go importuning the Keybearer!" Lewen said. "I'm just grateful she hasna vetoed my visits completely."

"Why canna ye?" she demanded.

"Well . . . she's the Keybearer," Lewen tried to explain.

"So?"

"She . . . Ye're lucky she's taken the interest she already has. The Keybearer is the head o' the whole Coven, and o' the Theurgia too. . . . She's very busy."

Rhiannon brooded over this for a while. "She like First-Horn?"

Lewen nodded. "Aye. Ye must treat her with respect."

"She dangerous?"

"She can shapechange into a dragon," Lewen said.

Rhiannon was impressed indeed. "A dragon! No wonder she told me I was no' quick enough or strong enough to grab her dagger."

"Ye did no' try to grab her witch-dagger, did ye?"

Rhiannon was affronted by the overt horror and dismay in Lewen's voice. "Nay, I didna, but I could've if I'd wanted to."

He snorted.

They walked on in a stiff, angry silence.

The grassy path led under a tall maple tree. As the shadow of its leaves fell on their faces, Lewen suddenly turned and seized her hands. "Don't be angry," he said. "I couldna come. I'm sorry, but they forbade me. I got drunk, I suppose I said some wild things. Olwynne was worried; that's the only reason she told—"

At the sound of Olwynne's name, Rhiannon stiffened.

Lewen noticed and went on quickly. "I ken how much ye hate that prison. I wish I . . ." He struggled for words, then took something out of his pocket and thrust it into her hands. "I made it for ye," he said. "I hope ye like it."

It was a small bird, carved from wood, its wings unfurling for flight.

"It's a bluebird," Lewen said. "A mountain bluebird. I saw many o' them up in the highlands o' Rionnagan. They fly in great flocks, as fast as swifts, and sing so beautifully. Do ye ken the ones I mean?"

"Och, aye," Rhiannon said blankly. If Lewen was to think of her as a bird, she would have preferred something grand and fierce, like a golden eagle or goshawk. She turned the bird in her hands and only then saw how graceful was the line of the turned head and throat, how shapely the long pointed wings. She remembered lying in the highland meadows as a child, watching the bluebirds soaring and diving, the sun flashing upon their iridescent wings, and her throat suddenly closed over. "It's bonny. Thank ye," she choked.

"I'm glad ye like it. . . . I only wish—"

What Lewen wished for, Rhiannon would never know, for she heard the sudden, unexpected whinny of a horse, high overhead.

"Blackthorn!" she screamed.

She ran out from under the shade of the maple and saw, with a wild leaping of her pulse, the beautiful familiar shape of her flying horse high in the sky above, wings spread, forefeet tucked under her breast. Blackthorn whinnied again.

Rhiannon called her name, and the winged horse began to circle down.

Then Rhiannon saw the four guards running out into the open, the archer raising high his bow, arrow cocked. The soldier with the long metal pipe had it lifted to his shoulder, squinting along the barrel. The other soldiers had their weapons hefted and ready to use.

"Rhiannon!" Lewen cried. "Tell her to go! They'll shoot her!"

Tears surged to her eyes. *Go!* she cried soundlessly. *Fly free!*

The winged horse spread her wings and hovered, her ringing neigh echoing through the trees.

Go, beloved! Rhiannon thought. *I will call ye when I need ye!*

Blackthorn responded with another defiant call, then beat her great wings, rising high into the sky once more. They watched the mare disappear into the violet distance beyond the witches' tower, and then everyone turned to look at Rhiannon.

She was distraught, silent tears flooding down her face. Occasionally her breath caught, but she repressed her sobs valiantly, her hands clenched by her sides.

Lewen bent and picked up the little wooden bird, which had fallen into the grass. "I'm so sorry," he said helplessly.

She did not answer.

Lewen bent his head over the wooden bird cradled in his hands, his throat thick with longing. Rhiannon took a deep breath, rubbed her hand across her face, and held out her hand for it mechanically. It was warm from Lewen's hand. She glanced down at it, then gasped in surprise.

Azure was blooming across the satin-smooth wooden sides of the bird. Over its breast, down the length of its tail, along each feather of the out-flung wings, up its throat and over its cheeks, to the edge of the sharp little beak that turned as black as its claws. The head turned. One bright black eye regarded Rhiannon. Its soft throat swelled. A bubble of music filled the air. Rhiannon could feel its heart hammering away at her fingers.

"Eà's green blood!" Lewen breathed.

"Dark walkers, hunt me no'," Rhiannon swore.

They stared at the bird in silence. It warbled and sang, cocking its head to one side.

The sorcerer strode up, his face screwed up in an expression of anger. "Lucky that horse o' yours didna fly closer, else they'd have shot it down out o' the sky," he said.

Rhiannon did not answer. She was staring down at the bird with an expression of wonder.

"What do ye have there?" the sorcerer demanded.

She held it out for him mutely.

"A mountain bluebird. Strange. I've never seen one so low at this time o' year. Normally they are back in the highlands by spring. It looks tame. I wonder where it can have come from."

"Lewen carved it for me," Rhiannon said. "And then he brought it to life."

"What? Rubbish!"

"No' rubbish. True."

"But . . . Lewen, is this the truth?"

Lewen nodded.

"Heavens! But that's high sorcery! I've never heard o' it being done afore. Are ye sure? O' course ye're sure. Here, let me feel the bird."

Rhiannon would not let him take the bird, which nested happily in her hands still, but allowed him to feel its soft blue feathers, its rapidly beating heart. As he tried to run his hand down its back, it turned its head and pecked him, drawing up a bright bead of blood on his leathery skin.

"Gracious alive! Lewen, my boy, this is extraordinary. I must tell the Keybearer, show it to the Circle o' Sorcerers. I've never heard o' a creature carved o' wood being given life afore. Here, girl. Give me the bird. I'll take it now—"

"Nay," Rhiannon said. "Bird is mine." She clasped it close to her, within the circle of her hands, and the bird gave a little trill of contentment.

The sorcerer stared at her for a long time; then he nodded his head once, sharply. "Very well. Lewen made it for ye; Lewen brought it to life for ye. How, boy? How did ye do it?"

"I dinna ken," he said, the first words he had spoken.

"I'd think on it, boy. Try to do it again. The Keybearer will want to see. My heavens. Talk about ye being a wood witch!"

Rhiannon bent her head and stared at the little bird in amazement. It chirped at her, then, suddenly, spread its wings and launched itself into the sky. Rhiannon cried aloud in dismay, and the sorcerer cursed her for a fool. But the bird did not fly away. It darted through the sky, snapping at insects, then came back to rest on Rhiannon's shoulder, rubbing her cheek with its smooth beak. There it rode, all the way back to Sorrowgate Tower, up the narrow dark stairs and into Rhiannon's cell. That night, Rhiannon did not eat alone, staring at the blank wall. She shared her supper with the bluebird, listening to its liquid song with a painful swelling in her heart.

"He made ye for me," she whispered to it, holding out a seed for it to peck. "Ye're mine now."

NIGHTMARES

" 'Tis now the very witching time
of night."

—SHAKESPEARE,
Hamlet, Act III, scene 2 (1601)

Walking the Dream-Road

Olwynne followed Ghislaine Dream-Walker through the trees, her eyes downcast. Although she had seen the green-eyed sorceress many times before, she had never spoken to her and she could not help feeling nervous.

Ghislaine was a beautiful woman, with hair the color of corn hanging to her feet. Her face was pale and the skin under her eyes was faintly touched with purple, as if she slept uneasily. There was a faraway quality to her, as if she was touched only lightly by the demands of this existence. Olwynne had heard that she took many lovers, though she was so ethereal it was hard to imagine her feeling any earthly desires.

Ghislaine was dressed in a loose white gown fastened at the waist with a cord from which hung a black-handled silver dagger. Around her neck hung a small silver shield engraved with the shape of a flowering tree, and she wore three rings on each hand, green and white and blue. She was a powerful sorceress, descended directly from Aislinna the Dreamer herself, mother to daughter for a thousand years. Her cousin, Melisse Nic-Thanach, ruled Blèssem, and her elder sister, Gilliane, had inherited the throne of Aslinn only a few years earlier. Ghislaine herself had spent the winter in Aslinn, overlooking the rebuilding of the ruined Tower of Dreamers, and had returned to Lucescere only the day before. Soon she would go back to Aslinn, to head the new tower and begin her own school. But for now she had resumed her usual role at the Tower of Two Moons, teaching the senior students and walking the dream-road in service of the Coven. No wonder she was always so pale and bruised under the eyes.

Olwynne was feeling rather pale and bruised herself. She had hardly slept the last few weeks. Every night she replayed in her mind's eye the sight of Lewen holding his black-haired satyricorn girl in his arms. Olwynne saw again the moment that Lewen had run his hand down the curve of Rhiannon's waist, and the way the girl had flowed into his arms, mouth to mouth, breast to breast, groin to groin. She tortured herself with imaginings of what had gone on inside the cell. She had scolded herself silently. *They would no' dare*, she told herself. *They would no' have time. Surely they are only talking. . . .*

But Lewen had come out, flushed and heavy-eyed, his tunic askew, his curls rumpled, a smile playing on his lips. He had hardly acknowledged Olwynne, lost in his own thoughts. It was clear to Olwynne that Lewen and the satyricorn were lovers, and that she had lost any chance of winning him for herself. Every time she thought of it, Olwynne was scalded with a bewildering mix of scorn, dismay, jealousy, and humiliation. Here she was, a brilliant scholar, learned and literate, able to match Lewen word for word in battles of wit, able to read the old languages, sing and play the clàrsach, quote from the old masters, navigate a ship by the stars, and work out difficult mathematical equations; a banprionnsa, descended on both sides from the First Coven of Witches, daughter to the Rìgh, niece to the Keybearer, and ready and willing to lay all her wit, wisdom, and worldly goods at the unnoticing feet of Lewen the Whittler, son of a woodcutter's son and a tree-shifter.

Every night she went through the same cycle of emotion. First she would burn with indignation and anger, declaring her indifference to Lewen, her hope that he would be happy with his wild girl of the mountains, her utter scorn for men who could be wooed by a shapely figure and a pair of blue eyes. Then she would sink into a morass of utter mortification, only able to hope that no one had guessed how much deeper than friendship were her feelings for Lewen. She had miscalculated, she had to admit, telling Isabeau about Lewen's wild ramblings on the night at the Nisse and Nixie. Not only had Lewen felt hurt and betrayed, and had drawn away from her, but Olwynne felt sure she had betrayed herself to her aunt. Isabeau had turned a very keen look on her, and Olwynne had often felt the Keybearer's gaze upon her since.

At times Olwynne hated herself, both for loving a man who did not love her in return and for the degree of antipathy and spite she felt towards her rival. It shocked her, that she could hate so intensely. At such times, black misery and despair overwhelmed her, and Olwynne would turn her face into her hot pillow to blot away the tears she could not control.

It did not help that, when she did finally fall asleep, her dreams were still haunted by black-winged horrors. Night after night, Olwynne jerked awake, unable to breathe, her heart pounding, oppressed by the utter certainty that evil crouched around the next corner. Often she lay awake the rest of the night.

Racked with misery and exhaustion, Olwynne moved through her days like a revenant, trying hard to retain her usual composure so no one would realize just how overwrought was her nervous system.

Isabeau must have guessed something of her state of mind, though, for she called Olwynne to her the moment Ghislaine returned to Lucescere.

"I want Ghislaine to walk the dream-road with ye and find the source o' all these nightmares," Isabeau said kindly. "I do no' like to see ye look so pale and wan."

Olwynne was not at all sure she wanted to do this. Her dreams frightened her dreadfully. But she nodded her head and agreed, obedient and respectful as always.

So now, in the warm dusk of an early summer day, she followed the Dream-Walker through the shadowy forest to the sacred glade in the heart of the Tower of Two Moon's garden. The glade had been planted a thousand years earlier, by Martha the Wise. Seven enormous old trees grew in a circle, their branches knotted together. Ash, hazel, oak, blackthorn, fir, rowan, and yew, the seven trees sacred to the Coven. Beneath the trees grew soft grass and flowers—clover and angelica and heartsease—and a spring burbled nearby. The shape of a star within a circle was scored heavily into the soil.

Ghislaine led Olwynne into the circle and silently gestured to her to lie down. Olwynne obeyed, looking up at the intermingling leaves above. The sky was fading from blue to green. She could see the round uneven shape of the smaller moon through the leaves, looking almost transparent. It was very quiet and peaceful here in the glade. Olwynne took a deep breath, feeling some of her tension leave her.

Quietly the sorceress set tall white candles at the six points of the star and anointed them with oil from little crystal bottles. Olwynne could smell rosemary, angelica, hawthorn, and gillyflowers, for healing, consecration, an increase of psychic powers, and protection against evil. Then she smelled lemon verbena, which she knew from her studies aided clear-seeing and clear-dreaming. The aromatic oils worked on her senses, making her feel both more peaceful and more alert.

Then Ghislaine drew her knife and traced the shape of the circle and star, chanting:

> *"I consecrate and conjure thee,*
> *O circle o' magic, ring o' power,*
> *Keep us safe from harm, keep us safe from evil,*
> *Guard us against treachery, keep us safe in your*
> *eyes,*
> *Eà o' the moons.*
> *I consecrate and conjure thee,*
> *O star o' spirit, pentacle o' power,*
> *Fill us with your dark fire, your fiery darkness,*
> *Make o' us your vessels, fill us with light,*
> *Eà o' the starry skies."*

She sprinkled the deeply scored lines with water and salt and ashes, each time chanting: "Keep us safe from harm, keep us safe from evil, open our eyes, open the door, draw aside the veils, keep our bodies safe, keep our spirits safe, I beg o' ye, O Eà o' the mysteries."

Ghislaine then sat down cross-legged at the apex of the star, lifting Olwynne's head so it was cradled in her lap. She placed her fingers lightly on Olwynne's forehead, at the point between her brows where her third eye was meant to be.

"First we must sit the Ordeal," she said. "From sunset to midnight, ye must no' move or speak. Have ye fasted today?"

Olwynne nodded.

"Good. Make yourself as comfortable as ye can. Close your eyes. Listen now to the wind as it moves among the trees. Let it move through ye. Breathe deeply o' the good air, let it fill your body, let your body empty. Feel the earth beneath ye, feel it spin as it moves about the sun. Feel at one with the earth, feel at one with the darkness as it slowly falls upon the world, feel at one with the great trees reaching down deep into the soil, feel at one with the sun as it sinks away into night, feel at one with the moons as they fill the sky with radiance, feel at one with the wind, breathe now with the wind, breathe now with the earth, breathe now with the universe, breathe now . . ."

Olwynne was very tired. Within moments she felt herself spiraling away from the soft insistent voice. Meditation was part of Olwynne's daily routine, but never before had she felt such a quick or powerful response. She felt like she was falling. Some time passed, she did not know how long, before she became aware of Ghislaine's fingers tracing a spiral shape on her forehead as she began again to chant.

Around and around the chant went, spiraling with the touch of Ghislaine's voice. Only her voice and her touch kept Olwynne anchored. Otherwise she could have been floating in darkest space, untethered to any world. Then the circular motion stopped and Ghislaine pressed her fingertip hard against Olwynne's third eye.

"Ye are standing afore a door," she whispered. "Reach out your hand and open the door."

Olwynne saw with surprise that she was indeed standing before a door. It was green and had a knocker in the shape of a gargoyle's face. She lifted her hand and pushed it open. Beyond was a wild, desolate landscape. A pale road led away under low grey skies, through wind-blasted thorn trees. Perched on one of the thorn trees was a great black raven, as big as a gyrfalcon. Olwynne shrank back at the sight of it, but she felt someone take her hand reassuringly. Ghislaine stood there beside her.

"Do no' be afraid, Olwynne," she said. "I am here. I shall walk the road with ye."

The raven regarded them with a mocking yellow eye and gave its melancholy cry. Olwynne shook her head, leaning back against Ghislaine's hand. She remembered her dream, when a storm of ravens had whirled about her head, pecking at her eyes with their sharp beaks. At once she and Ghislaine were engulfed with frantically beating black wings and the scream of raven voices. Olwynne shrieked and tried to protect her head

with her hands. One hand was held in a viselike grip. She tried
to drag it away, but Ghislaine would not let her go.

"Do no' let go o' my hand," she said in Olwynne's ear.
"Hold on to me tightly. Remember, ye walk the dream-road. All
this is only a dream."

Olwynne could hardly hear her over the raucous screech of
the ravens. She felt beaks and sharp claws slashing at her face
and arms, tearing her skin.

"It is only a dream," Ghislaine repeated. "Walk with me."

Her hand was so insistent that Olwynne had no choice. She
stumbled forward a few steps, and the cloud of black birds rose
and swirled away, and she was once again standing on the
chalky road, a cold wind tugging at her hair. She lifted her hand
to her face and was surprised to find herself unscratched. The
raven still watched them with an unblinking eye. Olwynne
stared back suspiciously.

"The raven may be the gatekeeper o' your door," Ghislaine
said. "If so, it is here to guard and guide ye. It is a powerful
symbol, the raven, the bringer o' truth."

Olwynne shook her head instinctively. She knew the raven
meant her ill.

"Ye may speak here; I shall hear," Ghislaine said.

Olwynne tried to speak but her throat was dry and sore. She
cleared it and tried again. "The raven . . . it brings only nightmares."

Ghislaine frowned and regarded the raven. It cawed mockingly and rose into the air with lazy beats of its wings, circling
the thorn tree once, twice, thrice, before soaring away. Ghislaine stood still, holding Olwynne fast when she would have
stepped forward.

"Look about ye," she said. "Do no' let the raven distract ye.
Can ye see anything?"

Olwynne glanced about, seeing nothing but a vast undulating landscape, empty of all life. Suddenly Ghislaine bent,
beckoning to Olwynne to do the same.

"Look, a spider," she whispered. "Spinning her web."

A tiny spider, no bigger than Olwynne's smallest fingernail,
was busy constructing a delicate cobweb between thistles.

"Is that my gatekeeper?" Olwynne asked, disappointed.

"Perhaps," Ghislaine answered. "If so, it is a great omen,

Olwynne. The web a spider spins represents the web that holds all worlds and all creatures together. She is a creature o' the Three Spinners and thus o' Eà herself. If she is your guide and guard, then I feel ye are blessed indeed."

"Ye said that about the raven," Olwynne muttered.

Ghislaine's face was stern. "Ye are in the dream world now. No' all is as it seems." She indicated the spider. "Pick her up. Greet her. She is here to help."

Reluctantly Olwynne bent and laid her finger across the spider silk, breaking it. The spider dangled below. Olwynne lifted her hand so the spider hung level with her eyes. She stared, surprised to find it was a pretty creature, soft and grey. Not knowing what else to say, she muttered the ritual greeting, "How are ye yourself?" and felt silly and uncomfortable. The spider hung there a few seconds longer, then rapidly descended on her fragile line of silk and swung back into the thistle.

"Let us walk," Ghislaine said.

Hand in hand they walked down the road. "Where are we going?" Olwynne asked. "Where does the road lead?"

"I dinna ken," Ghislaine answered. "This is your dream. Take me where ye will."

Olwynne dragged her feet. "I do no' ken where we go."

"What do ye wish to see?" Ghislaine asked. "Or more important, what are ye afraid to see?"

At once another door stood before them, slightly ajar. It was made of heavy oak and barred with iron. Olwynne did not want to open it, but Ghislaine raised her hand and Olwynne's with it, and pushed the door open.

Lewen stood inside, Rhiannon in his arms, his mouth on her neck. Rhiannon looked over his shoulder at Olwynne and smiled triumphantly, gloatingly. Lewen pushed Rhiannon onto the bed. Olwynne watched, half-repelled, half-fascinated, as he slid his hand up her bare leg, pushing her dress up around her waist. Olwynne slammed the door shut. Tears stung her eyes.

"Open the door, if ye wish to see," Ghislaine said implacably.

After a moment, hating her, Olwynne opened the door again. Rhiannon was astride a black winged horse. It was evening. Lightning flashed and thunder muttered. Lewen clung to her hand, drawing her down to kiss her. Their mouths fit together, then at last drew reluctantly away. The horse leaped up and away into the dark stormy sky, black disappearing into black. Lewen turned away. At the sight of his face, Olwynne stepped forward, hand outstretched, longing to comfort him. He brushed past her as if she did not exist. Tears poured down her face, and then the whole world was awash with rain. It battered Olwynne's face and body, soaked her hair and clothes, swirled up around her knees till she could barely stand. She fell to her knees and wept and wept.

"Walk on," Ghislaine's voice whispered. Olwynne became aware the sorceress kneeled beside her in the rising water. "Come. Walk on."

Wiping her face with her free arm, Olwynne struggled to her feet and took a faltering step forward. The rain pelting her face softened and warmed. She realized feathers were now whirling against her, black feathers. They tickled her nose and throat and made her cough. Faster and faster they whirled against her, like black snowflakes. She began to fear they would engulf her, suffocate her. She flailed wildly, coughing.

"Walk on," Ghislaine urged. "Walk on."

"I canna!" Olwynne cried, choking on feathers. "Which way, which way?"

"Follow the girl," Ghislaine whispered. "She may be the key."

Olwynne looked up wildly. Somewhere far above her, the moon was breaking out of clouds, and silhouetted against it was the shape of a black flying horse and rider. Olwynne leaped to the silvery break, and found herself flying. Olwynne had always longed to fly, all her life, the only child without wings in her family. She had always imagined it to be a glorious feeling. It was not. Helter-skelter she flew through the air, wind dragging at her, endless space yawning about her, blind and deaf and terrified.

"I am here," Ghislaine said in her ear. "Fly on."

They burst out of the storm into a deep, calm, silvery place somewhere between the clouds and the moon. The girl Rhiannon lay sleeping, curled into tendrils of mist as if it were an eiderdown. Her hair writhed out among the softness like sleepy black snakes. She opened her eyes and said in a deep, gruff voice, "There are ghosts gathering close all about. I see them. He must beware."

"Who?" Olwynne demanded.

Rhiannon shook her head and shrugged, bewildered. "Him. The one with the singing staff." She pointed away into the darkness. Olwynne turned and saw a man standing with his back to her, a long way away. He was draped in some long black cloak. She took a step towards him, then another. Each step seemed to take her leagues across the sky. Now he was standing just before her. She saw his cloak was made of feathers. He held a tall staff between his hands. Crowning the staff was a round white orb. Light twisted in its heart. Faint music of indescribable beauty lilted and fell.

"Dai?" she whispered. *"Dai-dein?"*

He turned to her gravely, looking at her with hollow eyes. Horror crept over her. Olwynne knew without a doubt that her father was dead. She tried to seize him but Ghislaine was still there beside her, holding her fast. She struggled to be free, but the sorceress would not let her go. All she could manage was to reach out one despairing hand. It brushed through him, touching only icy-cold air.

"No!" she cried. He seemed to shiver and dissolve like ice crystals before her, leaving only a plume of snow that trailed away in the wind. Olwynne leaped after him, jerking Ghislaine after her.

Spider Silk

Down they fell, plummeting through freezing darkness. Ghislaine was clutching her hand so hard it was numb with pain. Olwynne tumbled head over heels helplessly. She had never been so afraid. Suddenly she saw, shining faintly in the abyss, a delicate thread. Again she flung out her free hand. Somehow she caught it.

They swung gently back and forth in the darkness, buffeted by needle-sharp winds. Distance howled in their ears. Then slowly, almost imperceptibly, they began to rise, the line of spider silk drawing them ever higher.

"Thank ye, thank ye," Olwynne whispered.

They came again to clouds and water. It was hard to tell if it was rain, or river, or sea. There was ground beneath their feet, boggy and unstable. Olwynne could hardly see through the mist or rain or sea spray. She tried to say, "My father," but her grief choked her.

"Walk on," Ghislaine urged. "We must find out how, when, why. Walk on."

Olwynne walked on. She came through a door into the palace banquet hall. Couples danced, minstrels played their instruments, candles shone among flowers. Olwynne's father sat at the high table beside her mother, his black head bent over her curly red one. They shone with happiness.

Donncan was dancing with Bronwen, who wore a wreath of flowers on her head. Her dress belled out around her as she spun, shimmering like moonlight. People jostled everywhere, drinking, eating, gossiping, all dressed in gorgeous silks and satins and glittering jewels. Everywhere Olwynne looked she saw laughing faces. She grew frantic, seeing nothing to help her.

"Walk on," Ghislaine whispered.

So Olwynne moved forward into the crowd. Through the twirling mass of people she saw someone in the shadows, a woman. Where all else was bright and gay, she was grey and still, watching. Olwynne walked slowly towards her, dread rising up in her throat like vomit. She realized mist was swirling up from the floor, dragging at her feet. She and Ghislaine struggled on, the mist now breast high and smelling like an open grave.

At last they came up close to the woman, who stood in shadow. The candlelit banquet hall seemed very far away, and the sounds came distorted, as if through water. With a jerk of her heart Olwynne saw two faces, two spirits, one inside the other like water inside a glass jug. With eyes inside eyes, mouth inside mouth, hand inside hand, intent inside intent, it was hard to see who she was. Just as Olwynne felt she almost knew her, the other face pressed out and took over, and the insight was lost.

She saw the hand lift to the mouth, saw something dark and fierce fly out, straight across the dance floor and into Lachlan's throat. He jerked and slapped at his skin, as if at a stinging fly. His face grew livid. He stood and swayed and tried to cry out. Then he fell. The floor beneath him dissolved into darkness, and he fell away into it, his wings folding up about his face. Away he fell, into the abyss, and all that was left was one small black feather, floating in an eddy of air.

Olwynne felt tears on her face, or rain. The scene slipped away from her, as if she stood on a boat on a slowly moving river. Mist surrounded her. Her whole body was numb with cold. The arm that Ghislaine hung on to ached fiercely. She would have liked to slip her hand free, to be released from that heavy weight, but she was too tired, too miserable. She began to long to wake up, to leave this dreadful nightmare behind her.

"No' yet," Ghislaine said. "We may walk each dream-road only once. We must walk on."

Olwynne shook her head. Her arms and legs were stiff and heavy as logs.

"Walk on," Ghislaine urged.

Olwynne tried, but her body would not obey her. She
wanted to lie down in the boat and let it take her down the river
into sleep.

"Ye must no' fall asleep in your dreams," Ghislaine commanded. "Olwynne! Rouse yourself! Walk on."

Olwynne tried. After a moment her foot moved, just a frac-
tion of an inch. Her next step was a little larger. She felt excru-
ciatingly painful pins and needles creeping up her muscles, and
froze still, pressing her feet hard against the ground.

"Walk on!" Ghislaine cried, and Olwynne did. She was
stumbling through icy mud and water, matted with reeds, obscured with mist, but she was walking.

"Good lass," Ghislaine said, heartfelt relief in her voice.
"Just keep on walking."

"Where to?" Olwynne asked, hearing the despair in her
voice.

Ghislaine hesitated. "I dinna ken," she answered at last, very
low. "This is a dark road ye walk, lass. I canna see my way."

"Which way am I meant to go?" Olwynne cried out loud.
"Help me! Which way?"

"What do ye wish to see?" Ghislaine asked. Her voice
sounded strange, as if she spoke in a windy ravine. Her hand
was icy cold. "Or, more important, what are ye afraid to see?"

At once there was another door before them. It was the color
of blood and had a knocker in the shape of a skull, with eyes
that glowed. Olwynne dared not raise her hand to push it open.
Her limbs were trembling. She looked at Ghislaine, wanting re-
assurance. To her horror she did not hold hands with the sorceress anymore but with a small skeleton dressed in a long
white nightgown. The skeleton turned hollow eye sockets to
her, saying in that thin, echoing voice, "So cold. So cold."

Olwynne screamed and tried desperately to wrench her hand
away. The skeleton clung on with unnatural strength. Olwynne
felt as if it was crushing all the bones of her hand. "Help me,"
it whispered. "Help me."

"Ghislaine!" Olwynne screamed.

At once the sorceress was beside her, looking at her with
startled eyes. "What is it? What's wrong?"

"Dead . . . ye were dead," Olwynne panted.

"It is only a dream," Ghislaine said. "Do no' fear. I am alive. I guard ye still."

"Ye were dead!"

"Walk on, lass," the sorceress said. "Trust me. Walk on."

So once again Olwynne stepped forward, through the red door, the muscles of her legs screaming in protest. They came out of the mist onto the white chalky road again. The raven circled in the leaden sky above them, calling, calling. Olwynne raised her eyes to it. *The bringer of truth*, she thought. *A harbinger of death. What truth does it seek to bring me?*

She followed it down the road. They came to a crossroad. Ahead the road rolled on through grey moors, as far as the eye could see. To the left the road led to a dark wood, and to the right it wound into a valley where water ran. The raven came down to rest in the fork of a tree.

"Which way?" Ghislaine asked.

Olwynne hesitated. She remembered the maze in the palace garden that led to the Pool of Two Moons. To find one's way through the maze, one must always turn left. It was her instinct to turn that way now, but the wood looked forbidding indeed, thick with thorns and hanging with long veils of grey moss. Ghislaine waited patiently, and Olwynne took a deep breath and turned towards the wood. The raven spread its wings and flew ahead of them.

A few steps, and they were within the wood. Moss brushed their faces, thorns tore their clothes and skin, tree roots caught their feet, mist swirled up about their waists. Olwynne began to feel afraid. The mist took on human shapes, flowing around them, whispering in their ears. "Open the door for us," they pleaded. "Set us free."

"What do ye do here?" Ghislaine said sternly. "Ye must go on. The world o' the living is no' for ye anymore."

The ghosts began to weep. "The door has been opened for some. Why no' for us? Why no' for us?"

"The door must be closed," Ghislaine said resolutely. "It is time for ye to go on. Let go o' this world, go on in your journey. Go!"

A wind rose and swept away the mist, and the ghosts with it. They saw before them, hunched in the gloom of the moss-hung trees, a small cottage. The path led through a gate into a garden where many dark and deadly plants grew—yew and black elder and deadly nightshade and mandrake and stinging nettles and angel's-trumpet and mistletoe and wormwood. They pushed open the gate and a bell tolled, making Olwynne flinch. Reluctantly they walked up the path, their feet crushing plants underneath and releasing a foul odour. Olwynne lifted her free hand to cover her nose and mouth. The raven was perched on the porch roof, watching them derisively. They passed under its gaze and came to a small door hanging open on its hinges. They ducked their heads and walked inside, Olwynne dragging back on Ghislaine's hand.

Inside the cottage all was dark. After a moment their eyes adjusted to the gloom. They saw a small room with many sorts of strange things hanging from the rafters—dead bats, shriveled lizards, mummified salamanders, bunches of dead flowers and leaves, great hanks of wool. Cobwebs drooped everywhere. The ground was thick with dust and dry leaves.

In the center of the room was a round hearth where a fitful fire glowed. Smoke from the fire found its way through a hole in the round, peaked roof. Hunched beside the fire was an old hag, a spinning wheel before her. *Whizz, whiz* went the spinning wheel, as it spun around and around, impossibly fast. From it flowed a long, smooth thread of crimson wool.

Squinting her eyes against the smoke and the gloom, Olwynne could just make out another old hag working a loom on the other side of the fire. *Clack, clack* went the loom, impossibly fast. A scene grew on the warp and weft of thread, a moving picture. Olwynne could see dancing figures, minstrels playing, servants carrying laden platters of food and brimming jugs of wine. She saw a girl in a silver dress, spinning. Her breath caught.

"Time to cut the thread?" a wheezy old voice asked. "Now, at last, is it time to cut the thread?"

Another old and ugly woman shuffled out of the shadows, dressed all in black, an enormous pair of silver shears in her hands. *Whizz, whiz* went the spinning wheel. *Clack, clack* went the loom. *Click, click* went the shears.

"No!" Olwynne cried. But the thread had been cut. It unspooled across the floor, red and liquid as blood.

The old woman with the shears turned towards her. She

grew taller and taller, stretching up until her face was lost in shadows. Or maybe Olwynne was shrinking—she could not tell. The whole house seemed to be growing, the death-hung rafters as high as the night sky, the spinning wheel as huge as a mill wheel.

Then the woman bent low to look Olwynne in the face. She was no longer a hideous, wizened old hag, gap toothed and crook nosed, but cold and beautiful and terrible. She wore a hood white as bone.

"All threads must be cut," she said softly. "In the end, all threads must be cut, even yours. There is naught to be afraid of in that."

Olwynne huddled against the floor.

The woman smiled. "Do not fear. Your time is not yet."

"My father," Olwynne croaked.

"It is not his time yet either," she answered. "Not yet. Not yet."

"But soon," Olwynne said.

The Cutter of Thread nodded. "Yes. Soon. Though I have slid his thread through my scissors many times before and yet not cut."

"So he may be saved?" Olwynne asked desperately.

The woman turned back to her, lifting one eyebrow. "Perhaps. Though if I do not snip one thread, I must snip another. My blades must have blood."

"How? How can I save him?"

"You ask me?" she said and laughed as she moved back into the shadows.

Olwynne stretched out her hand to the Spinner. She was a hag no longer but a beautiful young woman, with pale hair fine as dandelion seeds. "Please," Olwynne begged. "Tell me how I can save my father."

"Forewarned is forearmed," the Spinner said, not looking up from her wheel.

"Please, can ye no' help me?"

The Spinner looked up. "I already have," she answered. "Walk on."

Without volition, Olwynne's feet dragged her forward. Cottage and garden were lost at once. She found herself following a billowing rope of red silk, hurrying along through smoke and mist. Ghislaine hurried beside her, their hands still glued together.

"Where now?" Olwynne cried. "Is it time to wake? Can I wake now?"

"Walk on," Ghislaine panted. "We will never walk this road again. Walk on as long as ye can."

"I canna, I canna," Olwynne cried.

"The Spinner said to walk on," Ghislaine said. "Ye must do as she said."

So Olwynne stumbled on. The silk rope led them through great barriers of thorn and thistle and strangling snakes of vines and veils of moss. They heard the raven cry and saw the black of its wings as it soared ahead of them. The fog grew so thick they could not see their own hands. The silk unraveled and disappeared. Hand in hand, they fell to their knees in the mud.

"Where now?" Ghislaine muttered. Her hair was snarled and tousled and filled with burrs. Her face was scratched and bleeding. "There is no road. We're lost."

Olwynne peered through her damp tangles of hair. Against the formless grey of the mist, with trunks and branches and vines all looming through, she could see only one moving thing. "The raven," she whispered. Then she repeated what Ghislaine had said to her earlier. "What do ye wish to see? Or, more important, what are ye afraid to see?"

"The raven," Ghislaine said, lifting her face.

Olwynne struggled to her feet, helping the weary sorceress stand. Fixing their eyes on the black bird, they followed it helter-skelter through the forest. It led them out into a vast clearing. An avenue of yew trees led to a dark hulking building surrounded by tall evergreen trees. A long pool of water stretched out before it, lined by yews and ghostly white statues. Involuntarily Olwynne and Ghislaine's footsteps slowed. Horror and dread weighed down their limbs. They crept forward, following the raven. It hopped up the wide steps, cocking its head to look back at them. Then it disappeared inside a yawning black door. Slowly, clinging together, they followed it.

Inside was a mausoleum. Tombs lined the walls on either side, each topped with a stone figure lying with arms crossed on their breast. Iron gates barred the way into vaults on either side. Carved atop every pillar were stone ravens, only the white of their marble distinguishing them from the living raven perched on the breast of a sepulchre lying on a raised platform at the far end of the mausoleum. Together Olwynne and Ghislaine walked up the long shadowy hall and paused at the foot of the steps.

The raven suddenly took flight in an explosion of black wings. Olwynne cried out, all her nerves jumping.

A man leaned out from the shadows. He had a strong, ruthless face, and his dark hair and beard were streaked with grey. He leaned on a tall staff, and his fingers were laden with rings. Then he came slowly down the stairs, and they saw with shrinking hearts that he was clad in a trailing white shroud. They could see the stone steps behind him, as if seen through dark glass, and a dank, horrible smell swept over them.

"What do ye do here, dream-walkers? It is no' in dreams that ye can rouse me. I must have blood—hot, living blood. Go back and come again in daylight."

There was such menace and power in his voice that both Ghislaine and Olwynne shrank back, their fingers clutching tightly at each other.

"Begone! The dream world is o' no use to me, no more use than the world o' spirits. Come again in daylight, with a living soul and a knife, and then ye shall see me walk again. What? Have ye no' read the spell aright? What ails ye, dream-walkers?"

Ghislaine tried to speak, but her voice failed her.

The ghost made an impatient gesture with his hand. "I say to ye, begone!"

At once they were seized with a rushing wind. It whirled them away, hair and skirts and limbs spun around and around them like a corpse's winding-sheet. They could only cling together desperately, choking on their own hair, buffeted by sleet-laden winds. They had no idea which way was up or down; they were lost once more in a storm, an abyss, a star-whirling darkness.

"Help us!" Olwynne called. "Please, please, help us."

Her reaching hand felt the brush of a sticky silken thread. She managed to seize it between her forefinger and thumb. Again they swung back and forth for a moment, joints screaming as gravity sought to rip them apart. Then, spinning more smoothly, they were brought up out of the pit. Silken threads spun them all around, a soothing cocoon that swiftly muffled their eyes, their ears, their mouths, their limbs. For a moment Olwynne was cradled like a child; then, very gently, she was lowered to the ground.

"Olwynne, wake up!" a hoarse, insistent voice cried in her ear. "Olwynne, ye must wake. Ye must no' sleep in your dreams."

She ached all over. Her eyes were sore and gritty. Tentatively Olwynne raised one hand to rub them. Pain lanced through her temples.

"Olwynne, wake up!" the voice commanded.

Reluctantly she opened her eyes. She saw Ghislaine leaning over her. The sorceress's hair and clothes were wildly tossed, but there was no sign of any scratches on her face and arms. She looked white and sick. It was dawn. The dim light hurt Olwynne's eyes cruelly. She shut them again, but Ghislaine shook her and called in her ear until she opened her sticky eyelids again, murmuring fretfully. Suddenly nausea overwhelmed her. She rolled over and retched into the grass.

"Do no' sleep again," Ghislaine said. "The dream-road is still too close. Let it unravel, else ye may be drawn back into the dream and never escape. We came close to death this night, ye and me. I do no' wish to tempt the Spinners by returning to their realm."

Olwynne wiped her mouth, feeling sick and dazed. Her head ached so fiercely she had to press both hands to her temples.

"Come," Ghislaine said. "Can ye walk? We must go back and tell Isabeau what we saw. They were terrible visions indeed. And there were crossroads in your dream, roads we did no' travel. This does no' augur well at all. We shall have to travel together again, when we can, ye and I."

"I hope no'," Olwynne said. "Never again."

"That would be a shame," Ghislaine said. "Ye have talent indeed. I would like to take ye on as an apprentice, when ye are auld enough. Though I hope no' all your dreams are so dangerous."

"Was it really all just a dream?" Olwynne felt so dazed and disorientated she could barely look Ghislaine in the face. "It felt so real."

"Aye, a dream," Ghislaine answered. "And, like all dreams, unknowable." She sighed and shuddered. "Indeed, ye have been traveling a dark road," she said. "Come, can ye get up? We must try and pin the dream down while we can. It will fade all too soon. And ye will be sick enough to swoon. Both o' us will."

Olwynne rubbed her aching forehead. Just moments before, the dream had been all too vivid and real. Already it was dissolving like ink in water.

"What does it all mean?" she wondered aloud, pain needling her temples. "Eà's bright eyes, what does it mean?"

"Dark times ahead," Ghislaine said. "That much I can tell ye. Dark times ahead."

Squiring Lessons

Lewen stepped forward and poured his Rìgh another cup of the dark, bitter brew called dancey that Lachlan liked to drink first thing in the morning. He said it sharpened the mind and gave a warm glow to the day, but Lewen had never been able to acquire a taste for it himself. Neither had the Banrìgh, Iseult of the Snows, who was drinking rose-hip tea sweetened with honey.

The Rìgh and Banrìgh always ate breakfast alone in their private suite. For the rest of the day they would be mobbed by servants, guards, courtiers, guild masters, foreign ambassadors, and visitors to the court. Each day was too short for all that must be done, and often Lachlan and Iseult did not see each other again until the evening meal, which was usually eaten in the great hall with the rest of the court. This small time in the morning was therefore precious to them both, a time to share the intimate conversation of husband and wife.

Usually, the meal was brought to them in their blue-and-gilt sitting room by a train of servants, under the stern eye of the palace chamberlain, Roy Steward, whose family had served the MacCuinns for generations. After the trays had been unloaded, Roy and the other servants would withdraw, leaving only the royal couple's squires to wait on them. This morning Lewen was sharing the duty with Owein, who was waiting upon his mother. Both boys were neatly attired in their court livery, Owein's cut to accommodate his long red-feathered wings.

"Is that a letter from Donncan I spy beside your plate?" the Rìgh said to his wife, spreading griddle cakes with bellfruit jam.

Iseult looked up and smiled. "Aye, it is. I'm almost afraid to open it, in case he says he canna make it home for Beltane. Twice now he's postponed his return! I dinna ken what entertainment Elfrida is putting on for him, but it must be something special, he has stayed there so long."

"Hunting, I'd say," Lachlan said tolerantly. "He does no' need to fear his teachers' displeasure now he's finished with school, and I hear the sport is good in Arran in the wintertime."

Owein rolled his eyes at Lewen and mouthed silently, *Lucky duck!*

Lewen shook his head slightly. Squires were meant to be deaf, dumb, and invisible.

"I'm glad he's enjoying himself," Iseult said, "but I do wish he'd come home. He's been gone since Hogmanay! He has a wedding to prepare for."

"Happen that's why he's reluctant to come home," Lachlan said.

"But why? I thought he was eager to be married. The way he looks at Bronwen, I thought he could hardly wait to jump the fire with her."

"I think he can hardly wait to jump into bed with her," Lachlan said dryly, causing Owein to grin and wink at Lewen, who stared stolidly ahead, willing himself not to smile. "Whether he's as keen to commit himself to a lifetime with her, well, that I canna tell. He's only young."

"Twenty-four now, and a man grown," Iseult said tartly. "Ye were his age when we jumped the fire together."

"Aye, but things were different for me. By the time I became a man, I had been exiled from home and family for years, and lived six o' them in the shape o' a blackbird. I had been ensorcelled, betrayed, and hunted almost to my death. All I dreamed o' was a family o' my own. I longed so much for someone to love. Donncan has had a different life. He's been so cosseted and confined, I do no' wonder he wants to run wild for a while."

Lewen could not help glancing at the Rìgh in surprise. Despite being his squire for four years, he had never heard him speak so openly about his time as a rebel and outcast. Lewen had only ever known Lachlan the Winged as the strong Rìgh he was now, a tall, dark, broad man with burly shoulders and a full beard clawed with white. White streaked upwards from his left temple too, and wound itself through his thick, dark curls to the end of his ponytail. Lewen knew this blaze of white in the Rìgh's hair was no sign of approaching decrepitude. It was the mark of the Lodestar, and the sign of a true MacCuinn. It only made him seem more regal. Hearing his Rìgh reveal such vulnerabilities made Lewen feel suddenly uncomfortable.

Owein was gazing at his father with his mouth open, looking dumbfounded. Lewen mimicked his expression in exaggerated form, then lifted one hand and tapped under his own chin, closing his mouth. Owein grimaced at him, then stood up straighter, his mouth shut, his eyes gazing ahead. Lewen did the same.

"Och, aye, I suppose that's true," Iseult was saying. "But it's been almost three months. Surely he should come home?"

"I wonder if he's heard all the gossip about his wife-to-be," Lachlan said. "Certainly, Bronwen seems to have been amusing herself in his absence. Happen he's heard o' all her antics and is staying away because he's hurt or angry."

"Surely he's no' such a fool," Iseult said impatiently. "What has the lass done, apart from hold a few noisy parties and dress like a whore? The problem is, the court has naught to do but gossip. We should send them out to fight a sea serpent or two or to hunt down renegade ogres. Then they'd ken they're alive."

"That'd be something to see," Lachlan said mildly. "The Dowager Duchess o' Rammermuir, out on an ogre hunt."

Lewen stifled a smile. The Dowager Duchess of Rammermuir was a very stout woman with three immense chins and an equally fat lapdog who smelled horrible and had to be carried everywhere by her maid. Although she had a pretty estate of her own, in the lowlands of Rionnagan, the dowager duchess was rarely to be found away from court, enjoying stirring the ever-boiling broth of scandal and adding various tasty tidbits of her own imagining. Her son, the Duke of Rammermuir, was one of Lachlan's councillors and a very sound adviser, so Lachlan tended to forgive him his mother and think her gossipmongering amusing. Iseult, however, had no patience for the ladies of the court and found the Dowager Duchess of Rammermuir more repulsive than most.

So she did not smile at Lachlan's comment. This was not unusual, however. In general, the Banrìgh was stern and straight-backed, more prone to sharp flashes of temper or scorn than merriment. Lewen was not alone in finding her intimidating. Her face was marked on either cheek with long white slashes where she had been scarred as a young woman in the custom of her people, the Khan'cohbans of the snowy heights. Her red-gold hair was smoothed back and coiled tightly at the nape of her neck, and she wore little jewelry, just a ring on either hand and the brooch that pinned her white tartan plaid around her shoulders.

Since she was in charge of overseeing the training of the Yeomen, the Banrìgh was often dressed in leather breeches and boots, with her heavy weapons belt about her trim waist. Today, though, she was receiving deputations from the Far Isles in the great hall and so was dressed more conservatively in a simple gown of blue linen, slashed to show a white underdress. The skirt had been designed to allow her freedom of movement, however, and she wore, as always, a sharp dagger and an eight-pointed, star-shaped weapon called a *reil* hanging from her embroidered girdle.

"If Donncan is going to let the stupid fools o' this court disrupt this wedding, I shall be so angry," she said, tearing a soft bread roll to pieces. "He should ken better than to listen to gossip!"

"Why do ye no' open the letter and see what he has to say?" Lachlan asked, draining his cup. Lewen stepped forward and would have poured him more, but the Rìgh waved his hand and smiled, and he stepped back into his place behind the Rìgh's chair.

"Och, aye, then I will," Iseult said.

She picked up the letter and Owein at once stepped forward and offered her his knife, hilt first. She took it with a smile and a nod, and cut open the envelope. There was silence for a few moments as she read the letter, then the Banrìgh looked up with a smile.

"He's on his way home. He's written this from Dùn Eidean. Neil's with him, and so are Iain and Elfrida. They should be here by the end o' the month."

"Excellent!" Lachlan said, wiping his mouth and laying down his napkin. "I havena seen Iain in close on a year. I'll be glad to speak with him and Elfrida about these reports I've been getting from Tìrsoilleir. I've written to her three times already and have had naught but sweet platitudes in response."

"That's Elfrida for ye," Iseult said caustically. She laid down her knife and fork on her plate and made a slight motion as if to rise. At once Owein pulled out her chair for her. She rose, her skirt gathered up in one hand, and smiled at him.

"Nicely done, dearling. I think we'll make a courtier out o' ye after all."

"Ye dinna see all the faces he was pulling," Lachlan said dryly. "And I thought he would choke on his own tongue when ye said Bronwen dressed like a whore."

"Well, she does," Iseult said. "Though, mind ye, the ladies o' the court used to say the same thing about me."

"Actually I think they said ye dressed like a stable lad, which is a far more cutting insult in their minds," Lachlan said. "O' course, they are used to your breeches now, and it is hardly uncommon nowadays for women to wear them riding or learning to fight. I do no' think anyone would raise an eyebrow if Bronwen wore them all day long. I think it's rather her *lack* o' clothing the ladies o' the court object to."

"She's just showing off," Iseult said. "The Fairgean do no' feel the cold, so she can swan around all winter in chiffon if she wants without raising a single goose bump. The rest o' the court is no' so lucky. If they could wear silver sandals in the snow, they would too, no doubt about that!"

Lachlan smiled and nodded in agreement.

"And o' course, all those lamb-brained lassies copy her and just look ridiculous, blue and shivering with cold, with their bare arms looking like a newly plucked chicken's. Thank the White Gods Olwynne is no' such a fool!"

"Speaking o' Olwynne, I wonder how she went last night," Lachlan said, with a frown.

Both Owein and Lewen looked at him in sudden quick interest, but he had moved across to the tall window and was staring out at the day.

Iseult looked to the door, frowning. "We're about to find out," she said.

Lachlan turned at once.

There was a sharp rap on the door. Lewen went quietly to open it. Roy Steward stood outside, flanked by the two guards standing sentinel. Behind him stood Isabeau, looking anxious. Her hair, falling from its rough plait, twisted about her face like hissing red adders. Her elf-owl was huddled on her shoulder, staring with huge golden eyes.

Lewen had not seen the Keybearer since she had called him to her room after the bluebird he had carved for Rhiannon had come to life. She had been most interested in this miraculous giving of life, and had questioned him closely about how it had happened, and asked him to try to do it again. Lewen had tried, carving a little dormouse, and then a donbeag, and then another bird. They all stayed obstinately wood, no matter how hard he tried to channel power into them. Lewen had been both sorry and pleased, for it was a frightening thing to give life to an inanimate object he had carved from an old bit of wood. It seemed too close to the realm of Eà. Lewen knew that one must never forget the dark face of the triple goddess. If Eà could give life, she could also take it away.

Isabeau had not been surprised by his failure to replicate the miracle of the bluebird. "That is how it goes," she sighed. "That is why the great acts o' sorcery are always so hard to do. Your desire, your longing, have to be strong indeed. Do no' try again, Lewen, and do no' draw on the One Power for a while. I do no' want ye coming down with sorcery sickness, like so many other apprentices who have overreached themselves. Ye may feel sick and dizzy for a day or two. Stay quiet, and give your books a miss. We will see how your little bird goes. Who is to say it will no' turn back into wood in a day or so?"

But the bluebird had not returned to wood, and Lewen had not succumbed to sorcery sickness, though he had indeed felt low and weary ever since. This may have been due to the after-effects of the clamber skull, though, which had made both him and Owein feel very sick indeed, or it may have been due to his loneliness and unhappiness. Lewen had been badly hurt by Olwynne telling her aunt what he had said about Rhiannon. Even telling himself Olwynne must have been worried indeed about him did not stop it feeling like a betrayal of his confidence. So Lewen had kept away from her, a task made easier by the Keybearer's directive to him to have a few days away from his books.

Without his usual companions, Lewen had sought out his

younger friends, the apprentice-witches he had traveled with
from Ravenshaw. But they too were busy and distracted to the
point that Lewen felt quite rebuffed. Only Fèlice and Landon
were their normal selves with him, though he could tell it was
an effort. One afternoon, after Cameron and Rafferty had made
a lame excuse not to catch up with him, he had asked Fèlice
what was wrong.

She had hesitated for a moment and then reluctantly said,
"Ye ken the boys both want to be Blue Guards when they graduate?" Lewen had nodded, and she had gone on, "They've both
been warned that it'll no' do their cause any good by being seen
to be too close to Rhiannon, or to ye." At the sight of Lewen's
expression, she hurried on, "It makes no difference, o' course.
We are all still very much your friend, and Rhiannon's. It's
just . . . well, Maisie has been told the very same thing by the
head healer Johanna. Maisie wants to be a healer, ye ken. And
although I really have no intention in joining the Coven after I
finish at school, I do no' want a bad report o' me being sent
home to my father, else he may call me home again. We've all
just decided to keep our heads down awhile, and work hard,
and wait for Rhiannon's trial."

Lewen had nodded and tried to smile. He did understand.
The apprentice-witches were only sixteen or seventeen, and in
their first year at the Theurgia. They all must feel unwilling to
start off on the wrong foot. It did not help Lewen, however,
who felt even lonelier than ever. If it had not been for Owein
and his fellow squires, all of them staunch in their friendship
and loyalty, he would have felt wretched indeed.

Lewen bowed to the Keybearer, and she came past him
quickly, not even noticing him. It was clear she was very distressed. She reached out her hands to Iseult, who stepped forward quickly to meet her. Standing together, face to face, their
likeness was startling, even though one was so contained, and
the other disheveled and upset.

"What's wrong?" Iseult demanded. "Olwynne?"

"Ye ken she walked the dream-road last night with Ghislaine?"

Iseult jerked her head in acknowledgment.

"They traveled too far, perhaps . . . or what they saw was
too . . . I dinna ken. It's hit them hard, though, both o' them."

"She's all right, though?" Lachlan demanded. "She's no'—"

"Nay, nay. She'll be fine . . . in a week or so. It's just sorcery sickness. I've had it myself, from doing too much too soon."

You-hooh fool-hooh too-hooh, Buba hooted.

"Ye said she was ready! Ye said she was strong enough!" Iseult cried.

"I'm sorry. I thought . . . Ghislaine was walking the dream-road with her, and ye ken how strong she is . . . but Ghislaine is sick too. I've never kent Ghislaine to succumb to sorcery sickness."

Iseult moved towards the door. "I must go to her."

Isabeau stopped her with a hand on her arm. "Wait! There's naught ye can do for her now. . . . She's sleeping. She needs to be kept very quiet. Any noise or sudden movement . . . and I need to tell ye about the dream."

At the tone in her voice both Iseult and Lachlan stared at her in sudden alarm. Then Iseult turned to Owein, who was containing himself only with great difficulty.

"Would ye be so good as to order us some fresh tea?" she asked with immense composure.

Owein was distressed. "But Mama! Olwynne! Canna I—"

"Ye heard your aunt. Olwynne needs to be kept quiet. And your father and I need to hear Isabeau's news. We may as well be comfortable. Will ye ask Roy to send for more tea?"

"O' course. But, Mam, please, canna I go . . .?"

She shook her head, though her face softened. "Nay, dearling. No' without Isabeau's clearance. I ken how anxious ye must be about your sister but we canna risk hurting her by rushing in on her." She turned back to Isabeau. "Can the lads stay and hear the news, Beau, or would it be better if they left?"

Isabeau hesitated. "I'm no' sure. . . ."

Owein fired up quickly. "We're no' lads anymore! Olwynne's my twin. I want to ken aught that concerns her. Please! Dinna send us away like bairns. I want to ken what's going on."

Still Isabeau hesitated; then she nodded her head, saying, "Very well. It concerns ye both, I suppose. Ye canna talk about it to anyone else, though. Ye do understand that?"

"O' course," Owein said, insulted.

Lewen nodded. The muscles under his chest had tightened into such a tight band of fear it was all he could do to take a breath. He had barely spoken to Olwynne since she had betrayed his trust; he never would have thought she could be so disloyal. Lewen knew, though, how very dangerous sorcery sickness could be. At worst, a young witch could die, or be reduced to a gibbering idiot, or have her powers burned out and cauterized. The idea of Olwynne in such danger made his hurt and anger evaporate, leaving only sudden sharp concern.

"Ye ken Olwynne has been having nightmares? Every night, since the spring equinox?" Isabeau sank down on one of the gilt couches. "I have been worried indeed about her, for dreams so vivid, so overpowering . . . well, often they mean naught but ill for the dreamer."

Iseult sat down beside her and put her hands over Isabeau's. The touch helped calm her. She took a deep breath and went on more steadily.

"I have been sleeping badly too. Faces and voices and deeds from the past have come back to haunt me, long after I thought I had laid those ghosts to rest. I've woken weeping more than once, or woken unable to breathe, as if a dark thing crouched upon my chest, its hands about my throat. . . . I feared a psychic attack and cast circles o' protection about my bed, and the dreams lessened. But still I have slept badly."

Gloom-hooh, Buba said miserably, her ear tufts sinking.

"I have no' been sleeping well either," the Banrìgh said, glancing at her husband, who was still standing, his hands bunched into fists. "Though I dinna ken why. I canna remember much about the dreams. I dreamed Lachlan was cursed again, lying in that unnatural sleep, and I was unable to wake him. That was distressing. And I dreamed Donncan was lost to me too. I was no' remembering the time when he was kidnapped by Margrit o' Arran . . . at least, I do no' think so. It was Donncan as he is now, Donncan as a young man. I thought they were just dreams—" She stopped and said no more, never comfortable about revealing her innermost feelings.

Isabeau ran her hands through her hair, causing her curls to spring out even more wildly. "Aye, I ken. I should've thought to ask if ye were dreaming too. It did no' occur to me that . . ." She paused and took a deep breath, looking around with eyes that were bluer than ever against their reddened rims. "I didna realize the dreams were more than just dreams. I've been so busy . . . so preoccupied . . ."

"Me too," Iseult said.

"So what does all this mean?" Lachlan demanded impatiently. His black wings were raised high and lifted back, as if ready for flight. Lewen knew that this was a sign of anxiety or anger in Lachlan, as if those six years trapped in the body of a blackbird had somehow entered the Rìgh's blood and given him the instincts of a bird. Owein stood in the same poised stance, balancing on the balls of his feet, his firebird wings slightly spread. Despite the difference in stature and coloring, he looked very like his father. He had forgotten his mother's command, all his attention focused on the conversation between his mother and aunt.

So Lewen moved softly across to the door and opened it, asking the guard outside to send someone for more tea and some fresh dancey and to ask Roy to cancel the Rìgh's and Banrìgh's first meeting of the day. He knew the two guards but they barely acknowledged him, Ferrand the Grey jerking his head and setting off to find Roy, and Mathias Bright-Eyed, so named because of his vivid blue eyes, staring straight ahead as if Lewen did not exist. This was not the first time Lewen had been snubbed by the Rìgh's bodyguards since he had returned to Ravenshaw, but it hurt all the more because Mat was generally good-natured and friendly.

When he stepped back into the sitting room, Isabeau was speaking again.

"I have tried to walk the dream-road. Ye ken it is no' my Talent, though I have walked it afore. But now all the doors stayed closed for me. Ghislaine said this may mean it is no' my dream, that I am . . . *hearing* Olwynne's dream. Or else someone has closed the doors against me. I didna think this was possible. Who is there strong enough?" She spoke with neither false modesty nor arrogance, and both Iseult and Lachlan nodded, frowning, accepting the truth of her words.

"So I thought it best if Ghislaine and Olwynne walked the dream-road together. I'm sorry if I was wrong. . . . I swear it'll do no harm in the long run. Sorcery sickness is dangerous— there's no doubt about that. But I've seen witches struck much harder and recover their wits in the end—"

"What did she dream?" Iseult's voice cut through Isabeau's like a knife. Isabeau stopped, flushing suddenly and biting her lip.

"Sorry," she said. "I just feel terrible about it. What did she dream? I canna tell ye all o' it. She was no' very coherent, and Ghislaine no' much better. She dreamed o' a raven again, though—"

"A raven?" Lewen said sharply, startled out of his role as squire.

Isabeau glanced at him. "Aye, a raven. A messenger in dreams, no' always o' bad news. Olwynne saw it as a bad omen, though, a portent o' death."

Gloom-hooh, the owl said again, solemnly.

"Something to do with the laird o' Fettercairn?" Lewen said, quite forgetting he was addressing his Rìgh and Banrìgh and the Keybearer of the Coven.

They did not seem to mind his lack of courtesy.

"Perhaps," Isabeau said. "Though Olwynne kens naught about the laird o' Fettercairn. Certainly no' that he carries a tame raven on his shoulder."

"A raven," Lachlan said pensively. "That jogs a memory, a very faint memory."

"Ye think o' Jorge and his familiar," Isabeau said, her expressive mouth twisting in sorrow.

Lachlan shook his head. "Nay. Something to do with a raven and Fettercairn Castle . . . Nay, I canna remember."

"The laird told us a story about ravens while we were there," Lewen said. As everyone turned to look at him, he gulped and rubbed his damp hands down his breeches.

"Go on, lad," Lachlan said impatiently. "What story?"

Lewen, trying not to fidget, went on. "About how his ancestor saved Brann's raven from being killed by gravenings, Your Majesty. He drove them away with stones, and Brann had the stones gathered together into a cairn and ordered a castle to be built there, to guard the pass up to the Tower o' Ravens. He said as long as ravens lived at Fettercairn, the tower would never fall. But it did, o' course, on the Day o' Betrayal."

"The tower did no' fall, just the witches who lived there," Isabeau said. "O' all the Thirteen Towers, it is the one least damaged. If it was no' so cruelly haunted by the ghosts o' all who died there, we would have tried to reestablish it. Nobody wants to go there, though. The stories are too frightening. So we've concentrated on rebuilding other towers. One day, happen, witches will live there again."

Lachlan had listened to Lewen's tale with close attention, but now he said decisively, "I had no' heard that tale afore. It's interesting, but it's no' what's teasing my memory. Go on, Isabeau. Olwynne must've dreamed more than a raven for ye to look so grave."

Isabeau nodded. "O' course." She took a deep breath. "Olwynne dreamed o' your death, Lachlan. She dreamed ye were murdered."

Who-Hooh?

I seult jerked upright, the blood draining from her face. Owein gave an inarticulate cry, and the owl hooted miserably. Lewen felt as if he had been punched just below his breastbone.

Lachlan stared at Isabeau. "I see," he said. "So am I to believe I'm soon to die?" Isabeau shrugged, her mouth twisting. Lachlan sat down heavily.

"Isabeau, is it no' true that one canna see the future for sure, that it's only ever future possibilities that one sees?" Iseult demanded.

Isabeau nodded. "Aye, Iseult, the future is no' fixed. The smallest thing can change it."

As Iseult nodded and relaxed a little in relief, Isabeau continued, "However, I do no' think we can just dismiss this dream out o' hand. I think Olwynne has a strong Talent, and dreams o' foretelling often presage an event that is very hard to avert."

There was a moment's silence.

"So what exactly did she dream?" Lachlan asked.

Isabeau hesitated. "I dinna ken. Olwynne fainted soon after her awakening. Ghislaine has collapsed too. All they managed to tell me was that ye were in danger, that ye must beware. They said someone wants to kill ye."

"Who?" Iseult asked sharply.

Who-hooh? Buba echoed, swiveling her head around so she could look at each of them in turn. *Who-hooh?*

"She dinna ken. A woman. Ghislaine felt she should ken them; she got quite distressed about it. She said something odd. . . ." Isabeau paused.

"What?" Lachlan asked impatiently.

"She said it was two women in one."

There was a long pause.

"Twins?" Iseult said.

"But surely then it would be two people *as like as* one? Or even one person in two," Isabeau answered. "Besides, Ghislaine kens many twins. She can hardly help it, the way our family keeps popping them out. I dinna think she would describe them that way."

"Two people in one," Lachlan said thoughtfully. "Maybe . . . a pregnant woman?"

"Maybe," Isabeau said. "I canna tell. We must wait for Ghislaine to wake and tell us what she means. My fear is that she will have forgotten most o' the dream by then. Ye all ken how hard it is to remember a dream once ye are awake. Dreamwalkers normally try to record their dreams as soon as they can, to capture as many details as possible."

"When do ye think she will wake?" Lachlan asked.

Isabeau sighed and shrugged. The owl blinked its eyes sleepily and rotated its head around to stare at him. Lachlan looked away uneasily, rubbing at his beard.

"But surely, now that we ken . . . I mean, there must be something we can do!" Iseult's voice shook, and she crushed the pristine linen of her skirt between her hands.

Lewen had never seen the Banrìgh so distressed. He had thought her incapable of strong emotion, yet here she was with unshed tears glittering in her eyes and her skin blanched of all color.

"O' course there is," Lachlan said, touching her gently on the arm. "Forewarned is forearmed, is that no' so, Isabeau?"

Isabeau clicked her tongue against her teeth. "Happen so," she answered. "I must admit I'm worried, though. I think we must double your guard and do what we can to root out any insurgents. Lachlan, tell me, have ye any enemies that may be wishing to assassinate ye?"

Lachlan twisted his mouth, flinging himself back in his chair. "Any new ones, do ye mean? For all rìghean have enemies. Ye ken that. In every court there are those hungry for power and riches, or those who believe they have some grudge."

"But any that hate ye enough to plan your death? For that is a desperate enterprise, the killing o' a king."

Lachlan nodded. "Aye, that it is. No matter how greedy one may be, regicide is surely the last resort. The whole country would be plunged into chaos, and happen even civil war. No one prospers then, except perhaps the undertakers."

He paused and rubbed his temples wearily. "Unless, o' course, it was no' just me ye wished to remove but the whole edifice o' power. It would have to be someone who wished to knock down all that I have built, happen someone who rues the day the Coven o' Witches were returned to power, even though twenty-odd years have passed. The Coven has its enemies. Ye ken that better than I, Isabeau."

The Keybearer nodded, her face somber. She glanced at Iseult, who was struggling to bring herself back under control.

"I distrust this new Fealde in Tìrsoilleir," the Rìgh continued. "My spies tell me she is preaching a return to the days o' the Bright Soldiers. . . . Och, no' overtly. She would no' be such a fool! But softly and slyly, and more dangerously because o' it. If she had uttered a single word o' treason I could have her arrested and put on trial, or at the very least suggest strongly that she be replaced. But, nay, it is all hints and innuendoes, and I canna arrest her for those."

Iseult took a deep breath and smoothed out her crushed skirt. "Tìrsoilleir is a thorn in our side," she said in a voice that shook only slightly. "Their tithes are always late and too small, and the soldiers they send to join the Greycloaks are sullen and unwilling."

"They send us few acolytes for the Theurgia either," Isabeau said, frowning, "and journeywitches there are always reporting difficulties. None has faced anything worse than curses and insults, and perhaps a few rotten apples, but no one likes to be chosen to travel there. It does no' take much for rotten fruit to become stones."

"So do ye think it is the Fealde that wants ye dead, *Daidein*?" Owein demanded. "Surely she would no' dare!"

"We are a long way from Tìrsoilleir," Isabeau said, massaging her tired eyes with her fingers. "Would her arm reach so far?"

"There is trouble closer to home too," Iseult said dryly.

"That wool-witted bairn o' yours causes waves wherever she goes. I swear she delights in vexing us and making Donncan look a fool!"

Isabeau looked troubled. "Bronwen is no' as wool-witted as ye seem to think," she said defensively. "But I take your point. There must be those who think she would be easier to sway than ye, Lachlan, particularly if she felt herself beholden to them for winning her the throne."

"So ye think she wants it?" Lachlan said indifferently, toying with the brooch that pinned his plaid together.

Isabeau was not deceived. She bit her lip, then said frankly, "I do no' think so. I hope no'. For it could only be won with a great deal o' bloodshed and misery, and to what avail? She will sit on the throne in time anyway, when she and Donncan wed. Ye may think her shallow and frivolous, Iseult, and indeed I do no' blame ye, but she is no' malicious or cruel. Why incite civil war to gain a crown she will wear anyway?"

"Only as Donncan's wife, though, no' as the true heir," Lachlan said softly. "And she willna carry the Lodestar."

"True enough," Isabeau admitted. "Do ye think she wants to?"

Lachlan put out one lazy hand and caressed the glowing white sphere that stood in a special stand near his chair. At the touch of his fingers, it glowed more brightly and a delicate strain of music wafted through the room.

"O' course she does," he said, quirking one side of his mouth in a sardonic expression so characteristic it had driven a line deep into his lean cheek.

True-hooh, the owl said softly, opening its eyes wide and then shutting them again.

Isabeau sighed.

Made by Lachlan's ancestor Aedan Whitelock, the first Rìgh, the Lodestar responded only to the hand of a MacCuinn, killing anyone else who touched it. It had taken the current Rìgh many years to master its powers, but in the end he had succeeded, vanquishing the Fairgean, faeries of the sea, who had sought to drown the land and all who lived upon it. Lachlan had almost died in the attempt, and the Lodestar would have been lost if Bronwen had not dived down through the raging waters and seized it. Together she and Donncan had managed to raise it high, the two children together calling upon its magical powers.

The cousins had been betrothed soon after, their proposed wedding sealing the peace treaty between human and Fairgean. When Lachlan died, they would sit the throne and rule the land together. Only one could wield the Lodestar, though. Isabeau had no doubt that Lachlan was right and Bronwen wished it was to be her.

"I canna see that assassinating ye would secure Bronwen the Lodestar, anyway," Isabeau said tartly. "Ye have named Donncan as heir. If someone wanted Bronwen to rule alone, they would have to kill him too."

Iseult's whole body went rigid. "Do we have cause to fear this?" she said in a very low, dangerous voice.

"I dinna think so," Lachlan reassured her. "They would have to kill Owein and Olwynne too, surely, if that was their plan. They are next in line to the throne after Donncan, no' Bronwen."

Owein looked from his father's face to his mother's, looking suddenly white and frightened. Lewen wondered if this was the first time he had ever realized that being a MacCuinn had its dangers and responsibilities as well as its privileges. The Rìgh saw his son's glance and smiled at him reassuringly.

"Unless, o' course, these mysterious assassins believe that Bronwen is the true heir, being the daughter o' your elder brother," Isabeau argued. "Ever since she turned twenty-four last September, there have been more reports o' people recalling those auld stories, o' how she was named Banrìgh for just one day—"

"It was no' a day," Lachlan said in exasperation. "A matter o' hours only. And she was naught but a newborn babe. How could she have ruled?"

"She could no' have, o' course," Isabeau answered. "But the point is, ye did no' name her Banrìgh-in-waiting and appoint yourself as the Regent until she was auld enough to rule. Ye took the throne for yourself and named your children heirs—"

Lachlan leaped to his feet, shoving his chair back so hard it crashed over to the floor. "She was the Ensorcellor's get!" he roared. "A Fairgean half-breed!"

"She's only one-quarter Fairgean," Isabeau pointed out reasonably. "And the sea faeries are our friends and allies now, remember."

"Her mother cold-bloodedly seduced my brother and married him just so she could break the back o' our power," Lachlan cried, his wings flaring open. "She murdered hundreds and thousands o' innocent men, women, and children. Her daughter was only conceived with the help o' a Spell o' Begetting, and even then Maya sought the most evil time for her conception and birth—"

"Except Bronwen was premature, thanks to me," Isabeau said.

"The point is she's the Ensorcellor's daughter!"

"The point is she's Jaspar's daughter," Isabeau said softly. "Do no' glare at me like that, Lachlan. I am simply reminding ye what people are saying. I had no' heard those auld tales for many a long year, but since Bronwen has turned twenty-four, I've been hearing them again, from all over the country. Nina and Iven heard them in Ravenshaw only a few weeks ago. There are some that call ye the Auld Pretender, I've heard."

"What!"

"Dinna tease him, Isabeau! Lachlan, ye ken none o' this is news. Sit down and stop shouting at Beau. Do ye want the whole court to hear ye?"

Lachlan took a deep breath. Slowly his wings sank down, and the yellow glare went out of his eyes. He picked up his chair and sat down, his arms crossed over his burly chest, his brows knotted. He looked at Isabeau angrily.

"What I'm trying to say is Bronwen has no need to have ye killed," Isabeau said gently. "She will rule in time anyway, hand in hand with Donncan, who adores her. Ye say she would like to wield the Lodestar. Well, happen that is true. Who is to say that she and Donncan canna raise the Lodestar together, like they did at the Battle o' Bonnyblair? Either way, I do no' believe Bronwen wishes to inherit a land soaked in blood."

"Happen no'," Lachlan said heavily. "But what o' those who seek to find power for themselves through her? It is hard to challenge an established order. I have been Rìgh now for twenty-four years; I have proved myself worthy o' the crown. But if I was dead, and the court in chaos—well, it would be easier then to challenge the legitimacy o' Donncan's claim and to set Bronwen up as rival."

"It would have to be done soon then," Iseult said. "Afore she and Donncan were married."

Just then, there was a knock on the door. Mathias Bright-Eyed opened it with a bow, and Roy Steward came in, carrying a tray. He bowed to the Rìgh, gave the Banrìgh a smaller genuflection, inclined his head to the Keybearer, laid the tray down quietly on the table, and then withdrew.

Lewen went and poured the twin sisters each a cup of hot rose-hip tea with a swirl of honey. They accepted it with thanks, and he went back to the table to make the dancey for the Rìgh. Once it was brewed, he poured the seething black liquid into a small cup for Lachlan, adding a dash of mare's milk.

"I'll have a drop o' the water o' life too, I think," the Rìgh said with a wry twist of his mouth. "It's no' every day ye hear death's bells."

"Aye, my laird," Lewen said, and poured in a generous measure of whiskey from the crystal decanter on the sideboard.

"Give Owein some as well," the Rìgh instructed. "It's been a shock for him too."

Owein accepted the cup of whiskey-laced dancey with thanks and tossed it back with a grimace. Lewen poured him another cup, glad to see some color returning to his friend's face.

"Sit down, lad," Iseult said, sipping her tea with a grateful sigh. "I think the squiring lessons are over for the day. Ye too, Lewen. Get yourself a cup o' something if ye like."

Lewen shook his head shyly and sat down on a chair against the wall, grateful to take his weight off his feet but uncomfortable to be on such terms of intimacy with the Rìgh and Banrìgh. Although he knew Lachlan counted his father as a good friend, Lewen was still very much in awe of the royal couple.

There was a long moment of frowning silence; then Isabeau said, "Let us no' get too hung up on the idea that any assassination threat must be linked to Bronwen. Ye have other enemies, surely?"

Lachlan shot her a rueful glance. "Who, me?"

Who, you-hooh? the owl asked.

Isabeau managed a smile.

"Ye spoke afore o' Ravenshaw," Iseult said. "Could this dream o' Olwynne's be linked to the news Iven and Nina brought us about all the murders there? I mean, Olwynne did dream o' ravens."

Isabeau nodded. "That thought has been very much in my mind."

"It surely is no coincidence that I have two hanging charges on my hands at once," Lachlan said. "There is the satyricorn girl who killed Connor, and the laird o' Fettercairn, charged with necromancy, o' all things."

"Could it be one o' them who seeks to kill ye?" Iseult asked. "Perhaps to stop the death penalty from being passed?"

"Do no' forget that Connor was on his way to us with news when he was killed," Lachlan said. "He would no' have tried to cross the Razor's Edge without sore need. Nina and Iven have pleaded for clemency on the satyricorn's behalf, but I canna help but wonder if she kent the news Connor was carrying and killed him so the news could no' reach us."

Lewen's cheeks burned, and he had to bite back a sudden rush of angry words. Isabeau glanced his way, and he turned his gaze to his boots.

"What news could he have had?" Iseult wondered.

"Connor was with my uncle when he died," Lachlan said. "Malcolm was often called mad, but though he was certainly eccentric, he was no fool. Perhaps he knew something o' this nest o' necromancers? If what Nina and Iven suspect is true, the laird o' Fettercairn is responsible for countless kidnappings and murders as well as grave robbing and the calling up o' the spirits o' the dead."

Lewen could keep quiet no longer. "It is true," he said indignantly. "I was there!"

Lachlan looked at him with interest. "Aye, I ken ye were, lad. But ye did no' see the necromancy yourself, did ye?"

"Nay," Lewen admitted. "But I saw them try to kill Rhiannon, to stop her talking o' it. And I was there when they kidnapped Roden."

"And ye'll be called to testify at Lord Malvern's trial, no doubt," Iseult said coolly, "but, for now, do ye ken aught about the news Connor was carrying from Ravenscraig?"

It was a snub. Lewen colored hotly and muttered, "Nay, my lady."

"Well, then," Iseult said and turned back to Lachlan, who scratched his beard ruminatively.

"I have to wonder why, if Malcolm did ken about the necromancy and so on, he did naught about it? Apparently it's been going on for years."

Lewen could have told them why, but he stared at his boots and said nothing.

"Nina says everyone who lives in the Fetterness Valley is too afraid and too much in awe o' the laird to say a thing," Isabeau said, as if reading his mind.

"And if that was the news Connor carried, why would he feel it was o' such urgency that he risked coming through the Whitelock Mountains? As far as I ken, the last time anyone came safely over the Razor's Edge was when Duncan Ironheart and I fled the Red Guards in Ravenshaw. That was no' long afore I first met ye, Isabeau." He turned his brooding yellow gaze to Isabeau's face.

Isabeau nodded. Her gaze dropped down to her fingers entwined in her lap.

Lewen's eyes followed hers involuntarily. She felt his gaze and twisted her hands so that her left hand, the crippled one, was hidden in a fold of her skirt.

Lewen had heard the story of Isabeau and Lachlan's first meeting, although it was not a tale the jongleurs told in the city inns. As far as he knew, few had heard the whole tale. Lewen's mother, Lilanthe, was one of those few.

Lachlan had been a prisoner of the Anti-Witchcraft League, bound hand and foot, bruised and bloodied, and naked beneath his filthy cloak of nyx hair. In a moment of despair he had called out in the language most natural to him, the language of birds, and, hidden in a tree above the witch-sniffers' camp, Isabeau had heard him and determined to rescue him.

Thanks to her magic she had succeeded, but the next night Lachlan had stolen all her food and her knife and disappeared. Isabeau had found herself hunted by the Anti-Witchcraft League. She had been captured and tortured, and the fingers of one hand had been pulped in a cruel machine called the pilliwinkes.

Although her remaining two fingers and thumb were now adorned with her three sorceress rings—a golden dragoneye stone; a glowing emerald that had once belonged to her guardian, Meghan of the Beasts; and a heavy square-cut ruby—Isabeau still instinctively hid her crippled hand from view. Her other hand was laden with rings, five in all, showing that she was a sorceress of eight rings, the most powerful witch since the time of Morgause the Bright. Isabeau had been heard to say that it was just as well she had not the power to win another sorceress ring as she had no more fingers to wear a ring upon.

"Ye ken what's interesting," Lachlan was saying. "Duncan and I and the other Blue Guards—we crossed the Razor's Edge to flee the laird o' Fettercairn. He had legions o' soldiers scouring the land for us. It was our chance to escape him."

"Och, aye," Lewen said, again forgetting himself in his eagerness. "We heard the tale in Ravenshaw. Ye'd tricked your way into Fettercairn Castle—"

"That's right," Lachlan said with a sudden grin of amusement. He turned to Iseult and Isabeau. "It was back in the days when we were all rebels, fighting to undermine Maya and running around rescuing witches and faeries from the Burning. We sneaked into Fettercairn Castle to rescue Oonagh the White, who become sorceress o' Dùn Gorm—do ye remember her?"

Isabeau nodded.

"She was only a lass then, and we kent she'd be tortured cruelly afore they killed her. We couldna take the castle by force—it is far too strong, and there was only a handful o' us. So we came in hidden in the dung cart. Foul, but effective." He grinned, remembering.

"Anyway, we got in all right but we couldna get out. They had a witch-sniffer there at the castle, a strong one, and a great many soldiers. We had a hard fight o' it but managed to subdue them in the end, I canna quite remember how. I think some o' the castle folk helped us. I remember we put the witch-sniffer on trial. It was something we liked to do back then, I think in some kind o' protest at the sham they had made o' the justice system."

"Aye, so we heard, my laird," Lewen said. "It was one o' the auld potboys who told us. They did help ye. They locked all the soldiers up."

"Good on them," Lachlan said. "That certainly would have helped."

"So what happened?" Owein asked in lively curiosity. His color had come back and he was listening with great interest, always enjoying the stories of his parents' wild adventures.

"The witch-sniffer—whose name I forget . . ."

"It's Laird Malvern," Lewen said impatiently. "He's the one ye have locked up for necromancy. It's the same man."

"Is it now? I had no' realized. . . . So how does he come to be laird o' Fettercairn now?"

"It was his brother whom ye killed, my laird," Lewen said. "Malvern inherited the title after that."

"Ye killed the laird o' Fettercairn's brother?" Iseult exclaimed. "Surely that's reason to want ye dead."

"Except it was twenty-four years ago," Lachlan said. "Surely if he wanted revenge for his brother's death, he would have sought it a long time since."

"He said revenge was a dish best eaten cold," Lewen said.

"The laird o' Fettercairn said that?" Iseult demanded.

"Aye, my lady."

"But was there no' a son?" Lachlan asked. "I'm sure the laird I kent had a son."

"He died too," Lewen said. "The laird hid his wife and the little boy in a secret room, for safekeeping, ye ken, but then ye killed him, and no one kent where they were hidden. They were there for days. The lad died o' hunger and cold, and his mother was driven mad with grief."

Isabeau sighed. "How very sad."

"And all the more reason to hate ye, Lachlan," Iseult said grimly.

Lachlan was perturbed. "Aye, true indeed. What a tale! I had no idea."

"Surely ye could no' have kent!" Isabeau said, her eyes sparkling with tears. "Ye could never have left them there to die, surely!"

"We had to flee for our lives," Lachlan said defensively. "How was I to ken the laird had hidden away his wife and son? I never meant to kill him. He attacked me!"

"How in the name o' the White Gods did ye manage to kill

him?" Iseult said dryly. "If I remember rightly, ye were no' much o' a fighter till I took ye in hand."

"A lucky stroke," Lachlan replied, looking peeved. "Or should I say an unlucky stroke?"

"Very unlucky for the poor wee lad," Isabeau said.

"His ghost haunts the castle," Lewen said. "Rhiannon saw him, and I think I did too."

Owein gave a superstitious shiver.

"We really did no' ken that the wife and son were missing," Lachlan said, half-pleading, half-angry. "We thought they'd escaped with the witch-sniffer. He'd slipped away in the fighting—we didna ken how or where. A week or so later he came back with an army. We had to bolt in the night. The only safe way out o' Ravenshaw was over the Razor's Edge and no' all o' us made it, I can tell ye! There are ogres up there, and hordes o' goblins—"

"And satyricorns," Iseult reminded him, with a glance at Lewen.

"Aye, indeed, as poor Connor found out," Lachlan said. He rubbed the Lodestar thoughtfully, and a low hum of music rose, almost as if the silver orb was purring. Then, suddenly, the Rìgh exclaimed, "That's right! I remember now. The raven."

He looked around the circle of intently listening faces. "A raven followed us for days. Right over the Razor's Edge and into Lucescere. It was soon after that I was caught by the Awl, which was when you took it into your wool-witted head to rescue me, Isabeau."

"More fool me," Isabeau said mildly.

He grinned at her, suddenly looking much younger. "Aye, I've always said so."

"So ye think the raven that followed ye was Laird Malvern's raven?" Iseult said. "Spying on ye?"

"Could be," Lachlan answered. "What a shame I did no' have my bonny Stormwing back then. He would soon have got rid o' the blaygird birdie for me." He sighed, his face darkening as he thought of his beloved gyrfalcon who had died the previous winter at a very venerable age.

"I wonder if the raven with Laird Malvern is the same bird," Owein said. "Surely no'!"

"Familiars can live unnaturally long," Isabeau said, putting up one hand to caress the elf-owl perched on her shoulder. Buba had been asleep, her head sunk down deep into her snowy feathers, but at the touch of the Keybearer's hand her round face popped up and her golden eyes snapped open indignantly.

Who-hooh? What-hooh?

"Naught, naught, go back to sleep," Isabeau crooned affectionately.

"So the laird o' Fettercairn blames ye for his brother's death, and his nephew's too," Iseult said. "I think we should keep a close eye on him."

"He's safe in prison and can do me no harm," Lachlan said reassuringly. "Besides, did Olwynne no' dream o' a woman?"

"Well, all we can do is keep a sharp watch and try to keep ye safe," Isabeau said. "I will set my spies to gathering what information they can, and when Ghislaine is well enough, I will walk the dream-road with her again. Owein, Lewen, I want ye to watch and listen too. Nobody notices squires. Happen ye will hear something that I or your parents would no'."

Owein and Lewen both nodded.

Isabeau got to her feet, gathering up her skirts in one hand. "I will go back now and check on Olwynne."

Iseult was leaning her head on her hand, looking pale and unhappy. She rose with a sigh, saying, "I'll come too. I feel so bad that my poor Olwynne has been suffering these nightmares and I never kent. I've been too busy...." Her voice trailed away, and then she turned suddenly to her husband. "Stay close to the palace, Lachlan," she said urgently. "Do no' go anywhere without your bodyguard, do ye hear me?"

"Do no' fear, *leannan*," Lachlan said, putting his arm about her. "I'm a tough auld rooster and hard to kill."

"I hope so," she whispered, then straightened her back as Lewen opened the door for her, sweeping out with her face set in its usual stern, proud lines. One by one the others followed her, all trying to conceal their perturbation at the news Isabeau had brought.

Bronwen's Boudoir

Outside the door, Mathias stood rigidly, staring straight ahead. He hoped none of his anger and resentment could be seen on his face. How dare the Banrìgh say the divine Bronwen dressed like a whore!

Mathias had never liked the Banrìgh. She had criticized his swordsmanship in front of the whole company and then shamed him by knocking him flat on his back with a single blow. "The job o' a Yeoman o' the Guard is to protect his Rìgh, no' merely to look good on horseback and on the dance floor," she had said to the assembled soldiers. "Just because we are at peace does no' mean we should allow ourselves to get slack and soft. I would like to see less partying and more sword and bow practice."

Just the memory was enough to make Mathias burn with humiliation. For weeks, it had been thought a great joke for fellow Yeomen to thrust a finger into his belly as hard as they could, while shaking their heads and saying, "Aye, soft he is indeed." Other jokes had been lewder and more difficult to shrug off with a laugh. Even his captain had exclaimed once in aggravation, "Are ye as soft in the head as ye are in the belly, Mat?" much to his companions' amusement.

It did not help to tell himself they were just jealous of his popularity among the court ladies or suspicious of his Fairgean ancestry. Mathias knew the Banrìgh had been right in her estimation of him. He could swim faster than any other Yeoman, and dance the galliard with greater grace and agility, and sing love songs as sweetly as any minstrel. All of these gifts were extremely useful in the true life of the court and had brought him to the attention of the Banprionnsa Bronwen and her circle, the most beautiful and fashionable of all the sets at court. They were not likely to endear him to the Banrìgh, though, for she scorned the more frivolous of the court's entertainments.

Mathias had not been appointed a Yeoman of the Guard for nothing. He was a strong wrestler, an excellent rider, a skilled sailor, a clever swordsman, and a very pretty shot with the longbow, the harquebus, and the new matchlock pistol now gaining popularity among the guards. It was just that there was little need for these arts of war nowadays, when all was peaceful and prosperous. Most of the work of the Yeomen was really quite boring, standing about in full ceremonial dress and trying not to yawn at yet another long-winded speech from some pompous bore. It was far more pleasant to dance the night away, and show off his swimming and diving skills to the flocks of fluttering ladies, and ride to hounds, than it was to slog his way around the practice field with his fellow Yeomen.

So his swordsmanship had grown a little rusty, and perhaps he was not such a keen shot as he had been when he had first joined the Yeomen. There was no need for the Banrìgh to single him out. Unless, of course, she had heard how favored he was by the divine Bronwen.

Thinking about Bronwen made Mathias grow hot and uncomfortable. Often he could not sleep at night for thinking about her, all his sheets getting twisted about his legs and body as he writhed about, pressing his pillow into his aching groin. There was no other girl like her—with hair like black silk, and eyes like the sea at dawn, and a figure of such sinuous grace it could haunt a man. Wherever she went, heads turned. No one could be indifferent to her. And brave! The Banrìgh sneered at the way her daughter-in-law-to-be dressed yet did not have the wit to realize how much courage and pride it took for a girl like Bronwen to reveal her gills and fins in a court that had not forgotten the last Fairgean War.

Mathias stared straight ahead, hoping his fellow guard did not notice how hot his cheeks were. He admired this bravery of the Banprionnsa as much as he admired her beauty. He himself was the son of a half-Fairgean woman. She had always worn her sleeves long and her collars high, and had dreaded anyone noticing the strange silvery shimmer of her skin in certain lights. Mathias had inherited her vivid sea-colored eyes and her singing voice, but not her gills and fins. He had spent most of his childhood hoping no one would ever find out about his mother's ancestry.

The Banprionnsa had recognized the strangeness in him at once. Or so Mathias believed. Perhaps it was just because no one could dance the lavolta as well as he. It was a bold, lithe dance, the lavolta, with plenty of room for a man to show off his leaps and twirls. Often when he and the Banprionnsa danced together, other couples would move to the side of the room to watch and applaud and to murmur behind their fans.

At first Mathias had been afraid to dance with the Banprionnsa. She was affianced to the Rìgh's son and heir, and was the daughter of Maya the Mute, whose role as a servant at the Tower of Two Moons in no way detracted from her dangerous aura of barely contained power. He had been aware of Bronwen watching him once or twice, however, and had exerted himself to impress her. A smile had curled her lips, but he had not had the audacity to go up to her. Indeed, to do so would have been to court the eye of every gossip at the court, for Bronwen was watched closely and not always kindly.

One evening she had boldly beckoned him over, asking him sweetly if he found her ugly.

"Nay, my lady," he had stammered.

"Ye find me awkward, then? Ungainly?"

"O' course no', my lady," he had protested.

"Ye have a lover? A lady bonnier than me?"

"Nay, my lady," he had answered, growing brave enough to look her in the eye.

"And I can see with my own eyes that it is no' men ye desire."

He had been scandalized. "O' course no'!"

"Then why do ye no' ask me to dance, Mathias o' the Bright Eyes?"

He had not known how to reply. After a few awkward phrases, in which he had tried to frame his respect for her and for her betrothed, she had grown bored and dismissed him with a wave of her hand. "Well, then, if ye are so easily frightened away, do no' worry," she had said. "I am never short o' dancing partners."

Which was all too true. Bronwen was the most sought-after lady of the court. After a week of watching her dance with other men, Mathias had found the courage to solicit her hand, and since then they had often danced, Bronwen laughing and glowing with pleasure at his skill, and sometimes deigning to flirt with him a little too.

His stomach clenched at the memory. He could not wait to see the Banprionnsa again that night. She was holding a private party in her suite, and only a select few were invited—maybe twenty or thirty, no more. It was an honor indeed to have been asked. Mathias wondered if she knew that her bridegroom was on his way back to Lucescere, and if his return would mean the end of these intimate parties. He hoped not, since this party would be his first.

Mathias knew, of course, that he was not meant to have heard the news of Donncan's return, let alone the Banrìgh's comment about the way Bronwen dressed. Mathias had exceptionally good hearing, however, which meant that he often heard things not meant for his ears. In general, he did not repeat what he had heard, unless he had had a few too many drinks and it was too tasty a tidbit to keep to himself, in which case he always exacted a solemn vow of honor that his confidants would not tell.

In general, he did not bother listening to the private conversation between the Rìgh and the Banrìgh. It was only hearing Bronwen's name that had caught his attention today. Even then, with his ears straining, he managed to catch only snatches of the conversation. He had heard enough to feel a bitter resentment against the Rìgh and Banrìgh, though. He did not know which comment troubled him the most, the Banrìgh's spiteful remark about Bronwen, or the Rìgh declaring that she was nothing but a Fairgean half-breed.

Although Mathias had done his best to conceal his own Fairgean blood, it made his jaw clench with anger hearing Lachlan speak that way. For all their assertions of equality, the Rìgh and Banrìgh were as racist and intolerant as any of the old Red Guard, Mathias thought. To think Bronwen had to marry into such a family! No doubt Donncan felt the same way as his

parents. Once they were married, he would frown at her and tell
her to cover up her arms and throat, and stop swimming in public, just like the ladies of the court always did. Bronwen the
Bonny deserved better. He went off into a daydream, imagining
the Banprionnsa turning to him in distress when she heard what
her betrothed's parents really thought of her. The daydream was
so sweet that Mathias tingled all over, and barely heard a word
grey-haired Ferrand said to him. He could not wait for the party
that night!

Hung with curtains of sea-green gauze that swirled and swayed
in the breeze, and painted with the undulating forms of nixies
diving through waterweed, Bronwen's suite was unlike anything Mathias had ever seen before. He felt as if he had fallen
through the ocean into another world.

The three long rooms were filled with the sound of splashing water, for they opened out onto a narrow terrace that overlooked the fountains in the formal gardens before the palace.
Lit only by the dancing flames of candles, the room was filled
with flickering shadows that played over the pointed faces of
the faeries painted on the walls so that they seemed to smile and
wink.

All three rooms, including the Banprionnsa's boudoir, were
thronged with people, standing and chatting with glasses in
their hands, or sitting on the low couches pushed against the
walls. One daring couple reclined on the bed, which was hung
with curtains of the palest green gauze. Other couples twirled
about the sitting room, while a trio of musicians played out on
the terrace. In the center of the boudoir was a sunken pool filled
with water, faintly tinged green with the mineral salts and seaweed extract the Banprionnsa added to make it as much like the
sea as she could. Flower-shaped candles floated on the water,
the bright reflections of their flames shimmering and dissolving.

Bronwen and her ladies had once scandalized the court by
swimming an aquatic ballet in this pool during one of her parties. Although the ladies-in-waiting had been dressed in cun-
ningly designed swimming suits, a lot of bare skin had
nonetheless been seen, and Bronwen had of course transformed

into her sea shape, which Mathias privately thought was the true cause of the scandal. Although everyone knew she could grow a tail like a fish, no one really wanted to be reminded of it, he thought.

Tonight the Banprionnsa looked ravishing in a clinging satin gown the color of mother-of-pearl, with a low neckline and short cap sleeves that barely skimmed her shoulders. The fins that curved down her arms were almost the same color as the dress so that they looked like part of its design. Many of the ladies at the party had similar frills of silk or organza tied to their arms with ribbons. To think a Fairge's fins were now fashionable! Mathias wished his mother was alive to appreciate the irony.

As Bronwen danced the dress swirled up around her slim ankles, showing a pair of silver sandals that were little more than a few glittery straps. Her toenails were painted silver, and she wore an anklet of silver bells that chimed softly.

Mathias's blood quickened at the sight of her, and he was not the only one, he realized. Many of the men thronging the room were watching her. Mathias grabbed a glass off a tray carried by a suave manservant dressed all in black, and tossed it back. The liquor burned its way down into his gullet like acid, and he choked.

"What . . . in blazes . . . was that?" he cried, trying to catch his breath.

"Seasquill wine, sir," the manservant said. "The Fairgean ambassador gave Her Highness a barrel o' it, as Her Highness was curious to taste the favored drink o' the sea faeries. I fear it is rather strong."

"That's an understatement," Mathias said but grabbed another glass, conscious of a warm glow spreading all through his body.

He drank this more carefully, his eyes resting on Bronwen's lithe form. She was dancing with Aindrew MacRuraich, who was trying, with limited success, to draw Bronwen closer. She was leaning back on his arm, laughing. Mathias tried to repress the surge of jealousy that rose in him like black bile. He swallowed another mouthful of the seasquill wine, gasped and coughed, and leaned his shoulder against the wall, glaring at the heir to the throne of Rurach, who, he decided, he had never liked.

The Fairgean ambassador, Alta, an arrogant man with ice-blue eyes, was standing on the far side of the room, his form draped in a magnificent cloak of white sealskin. Diamonds flashed on his breast and in his ears, and he wore a small black pearl suspended at the pulse in his throat. He was a sinuous creature, all lean muscle and sinew, and his skin gleamed with close-knit, silken scales. Tusks curved up from either side of his narrow mouth. His eyes, eerily pale, followed Bronwen as she skipped up the center of the room, through the archway of up-raised arms.

Beside him stood another Fairgean lord, named Frey, a glass of seasquill wine in his webbed hand. The look in his eyes as he watched Bronwen was very close to that of his superior, a mingling of speculation, amusement, and blatant desire. It made Mathias want to punch them both to the ground.

There were other Fairgean among the crowd, all men, as the sea faeries did not allow their womenfolk the same freedom as humans did. They did not dance but busied themselves gambling and drinking at various small gilded tables drawn up around the walls. All of the young prionnsachan currently studying at the Theurgia were also there, dressed in their best silks and velvets. Hearne MacAhern was flirting with Heloïse NicFaghan, while her twin brother Alasdair gambled recklessly with the towheaded Fymbar MacThanach of Blèssem, who was losing steadily, being unable to wrest his eyes away from Bronwen.

The attendance of so many of Eileanan's young nobility was no surprise, Mathias thought drunkenly. What added so much piquancy to Bronwen's gatherings was the unexpected. Bronwen had gathered around her many of the faery kind, some of whom rarely joined in the royal court's revelries. Mathias saw a couple of corrigans, big hulking creatures with only one eye in the center of their foreheads, and a tree-shifter with sweeping twiggy hair. There was even a seelie, the rarest and most beautiful of all faery kind, sitting on a chair with his knees drawn up to his pointed chin, watching the eddying crowd with slanted green eyes. A nisse was cuddled up under his golden hair, chattering away in her own shrill language.

Maura, the little bogfaery who had once been Bronwen's nursemaid, was busy carrying around a tray of tasty delicacies and making sure everyone's glass was full. When she was satisfied that all were comfortable, she sat down on a low couch against the wall, where a plump and elderly cluricaun also sat, a snuffbox in one hand, and gold-rimmed spectacles perched on his nose. The bogfaery and the cluricaun seemed like old friends, for they spoke together comfortably, neither of their feet reaching the floor.

Dancing with Prionnsa Owein was a snow-haired Celestine girl, daughter of the Stargazer herself, dressed in a superb silken gown of palest shimmering yellow. Mathias had never spoken a word to her and found her crystalline gaze very hard to meet. It seemed to him that she saw straight into his heart, and saw all the fears and resentment and jealousy he hid there. She and Bronwen seemed very good friends, though, for after the Banprionnsa had extracted herself from Aindrew MacRuraich's arms, she went and seized the Celestine by the hand. They embraced warmly and sat close together on a couch by the wall, holding each other's hands and staring intently into each other's eyes. No matter how hard Mathias tried, he could hear nothing of what they said to each other. Indeed, their mouths were not moving. It made Mathias extremely uncomfortable. He tossed back another glass of seasquill wine and watched covertly, a maggot of jealousy and spite worming its way into his heart.

My dearest Thunderlily! I'm so glad ye came. I ken ye've been studying hard. No' long now, and ye'll be finished with school and able to come dancing with me every night!

I do no' think so, the Celestine answered. *My mother hopes to come and see ye wed at midsummer, and I know she will say it is time I went home. I have not seen the garden of my family for three years now.*

Bronwen frowned. *But surely your mother willna demand ye go back right away?*

I am sure she will, Thunderlily answered. *I am, as you know, the first of my kind to study side by side with those of humankind. My mother was happy to allow me to do so, but I am and shall always be a Celestine, and my place is among those of my own kind.*

But ye will come and visit us often, won't ye?

The Celestine shrugged again. *I would like to, you know that, but the Auld Ways are growing dangerous again, my mother says, and they are restricting passage upon them. That is why I have not gone home in so long: my mother does not wish me to walk the ways by myself. This midsummer, they will sing the summerbourne again, and that will, I hope, drive away the malevolent spirits that haunt the roads, for a time at least, so that my mother can come to your wedding. It will be safe for me to walk the ways home, then, with my people.*

Bronwen looked unhappy. *I do not wish ye to go. Everything is changing.*

That is the nature of life, the Celestine answered tranquilly. *All must change.*

Well, I do no' want it to!

You are to be married, sea-child. Surely that is the greatest change of all. You will be a wife and, in time, a mother. Although I cannot see both ways along the thread of time, as the dragons do, I am sure this lies ahead for you. Why does this make you unhappy? It is my fate also, and my fate then to kill my beloved. At least this is a cruelty you will be spared.

Bronwen moved restlessly and for the first time dropped her gaze from the Celestine's star-bright eyes.

Do you not wish to marry him? Why, sea-child?

Bronwen tossed her head, and hunched one shoulder. *We are too different. He is a creature o' the sky and the air, and I am a creature o' the sea. Ye ken that; ye are the one to call me sea-child. What do ye call Donncan?*

The winged one.

Ye see?

Yet he loves you, and you, I thought, loved him. Are you not unhappy because he has spent so much time away this past year?

What do I care?

You know you cannot lie to a Celestine, Thunderlily said.

Bronwen pleated her dress with her fingers.

You have never before tried to hide your feelings from me. I am troubled that you do so now. I can see that you are restless and unhappy. Will you let me touch you, sea-child, and see you clear?

Bronwen shook her head. *I canna*, she said silently, a touch of pleading in her mind-voice. *Come, be no' so grave, Thunderlily. We're at a party!*

I do not know any other way to be, Thunderlily said.

"I will teach ye," Bronwen said aloud. She seized Thunderlily's hands and pulled her up, laughing at her. "Come and taste the seasquill wine. I tell ye, it's wicked stuff! One glass and ye'll feel quite giddy, I swear. Then let us dance. I'll be the man and show ye the steps. Come on!"

She seized a glass from the tray and held it to Thunderlily's lips. The Celestine smiled and took a sip. Her bright eyes, as clear as water, opened very wide and she made a hoarse rasping sound deep in her throat.

"Horrid, isn't it?" Bronwen laughed. "That's one custom o' the Fairgean I think I'll pass up. Here, have some goldensloe wine! Much more to your taste, I imagine. Maura!"

The bogfaery got up and brought the Celestine a glass of the rich, sweet-scented wine, which she sipped gratefully. Then Bronwen pulled Thunderlily on to the floor, holding both her hands and swinging her about so that the Celestine's yellow skirts billowed about her like a twirling buttercup.

The Yeoman gulped another glassful of the seasquill wine. He could not understand why Bronwen wanted to dance with that strange-looking Celestine girl instead of with him. The Banprionnsa had hardly noticed he was here, tossing him a quick smile when she had met his brooding gaze but otherwise ignoring him. He propped his shoulders against the wall, watching the two girls dancing in the center of the room, smiling at each other warmly. He saw Aindrew MacRuraich was watching too, looking rather put out, and the Fairgean ambassador was frowning, his lips pressed firmly together.

The music changed to a slower promenade, and several of Bronwen's ladies-in-waiting got up and came, giggling, to dance, so that the floor was full of swirling skirts, like a meadow full of flowers. It was not usual for two women to dance together, but Bronwen always took great pleasure in thwarting convention, and her ladies-in-waiting enjoyed copying her. After a moment, the dance floor cleared of other dancers, everyone standing around and watching as the women danced as close as lovers.

The music stopped, and the servants circulated with more wine and food. Mathias drained another glassful, then came forward with a surge, ready to beg Bronwen for the next dance. He collided with Aindrew MacRuraich, who had leaped forward with the same intention. By the time they had disentangled themselves, both rigid with fury, the Fairgean ambassador was bowing over Bronwen's hand.

"Ye seem heated, Your Highness," the Fairgean murmured. "May I suggest we retreat to the terrace for some fresh air? And perhaps a glass o' something cool?"

"Thank ye," Bronwen replied. "How kind."

At once the ambassador straightened and snapped his fingers at Frey, then offered Bronwen his arm, escorting her out to the terrace, which was strung with garlands of tiny filigree lanterns. Frey took them out a tray of sea-grape juice in tall glasses clinking with ice, as well as another pewter decanter of seasquill wine.

Aindrew straightened his velvet doublet and went over to talk to Owein and Alasdair, but Mathias went to stand by the tall glass doors leading out to the terrace. He told himself he did not trust the ambassador, and he wanted to be nearby in case the Banprionnsa needed him. As Maura trotted past with a laden tray, he grabbed another of the tiny glasses of seasquill wine. It was making his head swim, but it was not an unpleasant sensation.

"Tell me more about the sea serpents," Bronwen was saying. "I saw some once, ye ken, when I was a wee girl. They were so beautiful, and so big. How can ye possibly tame them?"

The ambassador spread his hands. "They are raised from the egg to respond only to the secret words o' the jaka, who are the most elite o' all warriors," he answered. "Wild sea serpents are very dangerous indeed. There is no point trying to ride one. They will only plunge under the ocean and drown ye, or crush ye in their coils."

"I would so love to ride a sea serpent one day," she said.

"Perhaps I will come and visit ye in the Fathomless Caves, so ye could take me out on one."

She said this in a voice of gentle raillery and was obviously taken aback when the ambassador straightened his back and said abruptly, "I'm afraid that would be impossible. No woman is permitted to ride a sea serpent. They are only for warriors."

"Oh, but I'm sure ye could make an exception for me," she said.

Alta bowed curtly. "I am sorry, Your Highness. Sea serpents are dangerous creatures. It would no' be suitable."

She sighed. "Ye ken, sir, ye do no' encourage me to want to visit ye, as ye are always urging I do."

He bent his head over hers. "Indeed I do urge it, Your Highness. The blood o' the people o' Jor runs in your veins; it is there in the sheen o' your skin and the frill o' your fins. Ye should no' have grown to womanhood knowing naught o' your people. There are many things I wish to show ye. Though ye may no' ride upon the back o' a sea serpent yourself, ye can watch the warriors in their races and jousts, and it is permitted for women to ride on porpoise-back, which they seem to enjoy. Then ye could play with the sea otters as they slide down the icebergs into the ocean, or ye could bathe in the hot pools o' the Fathomless Caves. The water there is rich and strong, Your Highness, and fills ye with such strength and vitality. Then, at night, the sky is filled with a thousand stars and with curtains o' colored light we call Ryza's Veils, after the god o' dreams and visions. It is very beautiful."

Bronwen looked up at him, fascinated. "I would like to see it," she sighed.

"Then why do ye no' come to the Isle o' the Gods to see for yourself? I believe those o' humankind often go on a tour after they are married. Why do ye and your husband no' come to see the Fathomless Caves? Your husband should know about your ancestry as much as ye should."

"It is so far," she stammered, looking down again, discomposed to find him so close. "I dinna think Donncan—"

"But are ye no' to be his wife and his Banrìgh? Use those feminine wiles on him, as I have seen ye use them on every other man whose path ye cross."

She drew away from him. "I beg your pardon?"

He smiled down at her, taking her hand. "Do no' think I do no' understand ye, Your Highness. O' course ye are bored, incarcerated here so far from the sea. That tiny little pool is no' enough for a princess o' the royal Fairgean family. Ye need to swim in the fathomless sea, ye need to feel the drag o' the tides in your blood, ye need to fight the waves and the icebergs and dive so deep your blood drums in your ears."

"Och, aye," she whispered. "I do. Ye're right."

His voice dropped so low Mathias could hardly hear it. "Ye need to stand at the lip o' the Fiery Womb and know the names o' your own gods, the true gods. Ye are one o' those anointed by Jor, and ye do no' even ken his name or the name o' his brothers."

She stared at him, shaken and confused. For a moment he loomed over her, his ice-pale eyes glittering; then he let go of her hand, moving away to pour her a tiny glass of the pungent seasquill wine. "So ye see, ye really must come to visit your family home," he said lightly. "I know King Nila is eager indeed to see ye again."

"I will try," she said, her voice for once unsure.

"I do hope ye will no' take this amiss, Your Highness, when I express my fervent hope that your very understandable restlessness and boredom does no' tempt ye to behave unwisely. Your uncle, my king, is very eager to see relations between the Fairgean and the humans continue in their current pleasing route. Any imprudence that may cause a coolness to grow between ye and your betrothed would be seen with great sadness by both your uncles, I fear."

She stared at him, flags of color flying in her cheeks.

"When is your betrothed due back from his travels?" Alta asked. "Soon, I hope."

"Very soon, I am sure," she answered coolly.

"Excellent," he answered. "I am looking forward to your wedding very much, and so, I may assure ye, are King Nila and Queen Fand, who are already making preparations for the journey."

"I look forward to seeing them here," she said, looking down into her glass.

"Slàinte mhath," he said, raising his glass.

She inclined her head and sipped at her glass.

Mathias could hardly hear for the roaring in his ears. He could not have explained why he was so angry, though he knew the ambassador's comment about Bronwen's feminine wiles had cut him on the raw. He stepped onto the terrace, determined to demand a dance from the Banprionnsa. She raised her head at the sight of him and smiled mechanically. He bowed at the ambassador, then bent his head to press a passionate kiss into her hand. "Your Highness," he said urgently.

She pulled her hand away.

Mathias was mortified. He glared at the Fairgean ambassador, who looked aside, smiling, he thought, mockingly. Mathias grabbed for a glass of seasquill wine and knocked it over, spilling the potent liquor onto the tray. He crossly seized another one and drained it dry, rocking back on his heels.

"I thought ye wanted to dance," he said to Bronwen sulkily.

"I think I may withdraw now," the ambassador said. "Thank ye for a most amusing evening, Your Highness."

She bent her head, murmuring a polite response.

"Your devoted servant," the Fairgean said mockingly to Mathias, with a slight inclination of his head. He then bowed low over Bronwen's hand. "And yours, as always, Your Highness."

"Good night, Alta," Bronwen said, looking troubled. He bowed again and then left with a dramatic swirl of his sealskin furs.

Mathias scowled. Bronwen did not notice. She seemed preoccupied.

"I had best go back in," she said, looking back through the doors at the party within.

"Nay, do no' go in. Please stay out here. Ye look so lovely in the moonlight, Your Highness," Mathias said.

"No, I am growing rather cool," she replied, putting her glass down on the tray and gathering up her skirt in her hand.

He sprang towards her. "Let me keep ye warm, Your Highness!"

As soon as the words were out of his mouth, he wished he could bite them back, but it was too late. She turned an affronted face towards him. "I beg your pardon?"

His head swimming, his whole body aching with longing, he seized her hand. "Ye must ken, I live for your smile. . . . My days are filled with thoughts o' ye. . . . Ye canna be so cruel as to deny me—"

"Ye're drunk," she said incredulously. "How dare ye? Let me go!"

He had seized her waist, the feel of her skin beneath the sinuous satin inflaming him beyond all reason. "Please . . . Bronwen . . ." He dragged her against him, bending his head to kiss her lips.

She fought free. "Are ye mad? Let me go!"

"Ye canna pretend the way I feel is a surprise to ye," he managed to say, though his tongue felt thick and his brain foggy.

"Just because I like dancing with ye does no' mean I want ye to manhandle me," she retorted, trying to smooth her crushed dress. "I like dancing with many people!"

"Aye, so I've seen," Mathias said angrily. "The Banrìgh was right about ye: ye are naught but a whore!"

"What did ye say?"

Mathias was conscious of having spoken unwisely, but the fumes from the seasquill wine were clouding all thought. He swayed on his feet. "That's what she said. This morning. I heard her."

"The Banrìgh said I was a whore!"

"That's why Prionnsa Donncan willna come home," he said spitefully.

Bronwen's cheeks were scarlet, her breast heaving with angry breaths. "How dare she!"

Mathias took an unsteady step towards her, reaching out one hand. "Bronwen . . ."

"Do no' dare call me by my name," she hissed. "Get out o' here now! I never want to see ye again."

"But my lady . . . Your Highness . . ."

"Go now, else I'll call my men to throw ye out."

He tried to marshal his thoughts, but she had spun on one foot and gone back into the ballroom. He saw her seek refuge by Thunderlily's side, the Celestine turning at once to embrace her, bright eyes flying up to stare through the door and straight into Mathias's heart. The wrinkled eyelid of her third eye rolled back and he saw the dark liquid well of her secret orb stripping him of all pretences. He shrank back, trembling, aghast.

After a few moments, he hurried back through the ballroom and out into the corridor, knocking over a table with his hip. All the way he was conscious of the Celestine's terrifying three-eyed gaze.

MERRY MAY PUNCH

"So when you or I are made
A fable, a song, or fleeting shade;
All love, all liking, all delight
Lies drowned with us in endless night.
Then while time serves, and we are but decaying;
Come, my Corinna, come, let's go a-Maying."

—ROBERT HERRICK,
"Corinna's Going a-Maying" (1648)

Dabbling in the Dew

Olwynne drifted up from the dark dreamless void of her slumber, slowly becoming aware of herself again. Outside her window some bird was going crazy with joy at the prospect of another day. Olwynne wished it would shut up.

Another bird joined in, and then another. With her eyes still closed, Olwynne wondered idly if the birds' dawn chorus was some kind of rite demanded by their religion. Was the sun a god to them, a deity to be worshipped and placated? Did its sinking every night herald a time of terror and despair, a period of darkness and silence stalked by owl and cat and rat? Did they fear, huddling in their flimsy nests, that the sun would never rise again? This hosanna of rejoicing could be, then, a desperate plea for the sun not to abandon them as much as a shout of relief at the first paling of the night. Perhaps the birds believed that if they failed in their duty to sing the sun to life, it would be dreadful night forever.

Today was the first of May. Today the Coven would ring bells and blow whistles to welcome the dawn, and light a chain of bonfires across the land. All the people would dance and sing and feast, welcoming the coming of summer and the passing of winter, celebrating Eà of the green mantle, Eà the mother. There was as much fear as joy in these celebrations, Olwynne realized for the first time. Did they all not dread the cold and the darkness, the barren and the bleak? Did not every living creature— man or woman, beast or bird—did they not all long for love and happiness and warmth and health?

Olwynne's eyes filled with tears. She flung her arm over her eyes and turned her face into the pillow, castigating herself once again for this dreary misery that dogged her every waking moment. More than a week had passed since she had walked the dream-road, yet Olwynne had not been able to throw off the effects of the sorcery sickness. A blackness lay over her spirits, a blight that drained her of all will and energy. She could find no desire to get up out of her bed, to rejoin her classes, to see her friends. *What's the point?* she thought to herself. So she stayed in bed for most of the day, picking listlessly at her food, waking in the darkest hour of the night in sudden bouts of inexplicable terror, to pace her floor or stand staring out at the moonlit garden, twisting her hair in her fingers.

It was not nightmares that disturbed her repose. Olwynne's sleep was devoid of any dreams at all. Isabeau had placed a ward on her third eye. Every time Olwynne fell asleep, it was into a sensory void, a long period of blankness from which she woke feeling strangely dislocated. At first it had been a blessed relief, for Olwynne's fever had brought all sorts of terrible hallucinations and fancies to haunt her. But now, after so many days, the emptiness of her sleep was as ghastly as any of her dreams had ever been. Olwynne felt as if her waking life had been leached of all color and purpose and marvel. She did not wish to sleep; she did not wish to be awake. She seemed to hang in a no-man's-land between worlds, lacking the desire or the ability to cross back into her own world or to move forward into the land of dreams.

Isabeau was worried about her and kept the healers busy making bitter-tasting potions for her, and nettle tea, and soup rich with herbs and mushrooms. Iseult stroked her hair back from her brow and told her not to fear for her father's life, that she was watching over him as she had always done. Her father suggested a good meal of roast lamb and mulled ale, a solution Olwynne regarded with horror, while Owein tried to coax her out to visit the city inns or to attend a ball at the court. Nothing helped. The rest of Olwynne's life stretched out before her, grey and flat and featureless.

Not even to herself would Olwynne admit that Lewen was the primary cause of her depression. *I'm just tired*, she told herself. *I'm worried about* Dai-dein. *I'm having trouble recovering from the sorcery sickness. The fever has taken it out o' me. I'll feel better soon.*

Yet often, as she lay in her bed, drifting in and out of sleep, her thoughts turned back to the previous summer, when she and Owein and Lewen had been the best of friends, and the days had been bright and golden and filled with laughter. They had ridden out and picnicked in the green woods together, Lewen whittling a lump of wood into something magical and beautiful while Olwynne made clover chains and Owein floated on his back, his freckled face turned up to the sun. They had read books together and argued over the laws of nature and the universe; they had danced together at balls, attended concerts and plays, and drunk ale together. If only she had known it was their last summer together. If only she had realized Lewen would be so stupid as to fall in love with a half-breed satyricorn girl whose hands reeked of murder. If only, if only, if only . . .

It seemed a lifetime ago. Now Olwynne hardly saw Lewen. If he was not at school or squiring at the royal court, he was at the prison, visiting his paramour. When he did come to see her, he was preoccupied or wanting to ask her advice on lawyers and court procedure, as if Olwynne knew anything about a murder case. Rhiannon, Rhiannon, Rhiannon—it was the only word she ever heard him say anymore. She was heartily sick of hearing it.

Olwynne threw back her bedclothes and got up, pacing the floor in her bare feet, heedless of the chill striking up from the stone floor. It was dark still. The birds singing their desperate chorale had not yet dragged the sun out of its night shell. She went and looked at her face in the mirror. All she could see was a pale blob surrounded by a wild riot of hair. Using flint and tinder, as magic had been forbidden to her since the sorcery sickness, Olwynne lit her candles and placed them on either side of her mirror. They illuminated her long face, her skin marred with reddish freckles, her eyes very dark between their red lashes and hollowed underneath with violet shadows that began in the corner of her eye like the bruise of a thumbprint. Her nose was long and thin and had an arch in the center like a crag of stone. Her mouth was nicely shaped—she had to admit that—but it was pale and bloodless. And her hair! Orange as carrots, frizzy and wild, dry to the touch. Black, straight hair was all the rage now. If the satyricorn girl had been at court, she would have been feted for her beauty, her dreamy blue eyes, her milk-white skin, her night-black hair. No one would ever call Olwynne the Bonny or the Fair. She was called clever, quick, bright, and sometimes the Red, like her aunt had been.

Olwynne sighed. On an impulse she caught up her plaid and wrapped it about her shoulders and went out barefoot into the dim morning. All was quiet, though soon the witches would be rousing, ready to begin the Beltane rites. As soon as the sun rose over the horizon, the bonfire would be lit, and the chosen Green Man would carry his blazing torch out into the city, to light the hearth fires of the townsfolk. But for now, the only sound was the ridiculous clamor of the birds. No one would see Olwynne NicCuinn, daughter of the Rìgh, gathering the May dew like a common goose girl.

Of course, Olwynne did not truly believe that washing one's face in the May dew caused freckles and other blemishes to fade, or gave one that baffling glow of beauty that some girls had so effortlessly. Olwynne would have been mortified if anyone had seen her. Such country superstitions were not the lot of banprionnsachan. If anyone had suggested she was capable of doing such a thing, she would have poured scorn on their head. Yet here she was, out dabbling in the May dew, and all for the love of a man who was in love with another. Olwynne felt angry, resentful tears in her eyes, but she did not turn back, slipping under the cover of the trees before bending her hand to sweep it through the icy, dew-silvered grass.

She rubbed the dew into her face, half laughing at herself, half-angry. Her skin tingled. She stood then, lifting her face to the silver sky, watching the stars fade away.

From deeper in the woods, a woman's voice rose in song.

> *"By a bank as I lay*
> *Myself alone did muse, Hey ho!*
> *Methinks I ken that lovely voice,*
> *She sang before the day.*
> *She sang, the winter's past, Hey ho!*
>
> *Down, derry down,*
> *Down derry, down derry,*
> *Down, derry down, derry down,*
> *Derry down, down!'*

Olwynne turned, utterly smitten. She had never heard such a gorgeous golden voice, filled with such joyous abandon. The sound of it raised all the hairs on her arms, and sent chills down her spine.

> *"The laird o' spring's sweet music,*
> *The timid nightingale, Hey ho!*
> *Full merrily and secretly*
> *She sings in the thicket*
> *Within her breast a thorn doth prick*
> *To keep her off from sleep, Hey ho!*
>
> *Down, derry down,*
> *Down derry, down derry,*
> *Down, derry down, derry down,*
> *Derry down, down!*
>
> *Waken therefore, young men,*
> *All ye that lovers be, Hey ho!*
> *This month of May, so fresh, so gay,*
> *So fair by field and fen,*
> *Hath flowered over each leafy den;*
> *Great joy it is to see, Hey ho!*
>
> *Down, derry down,*
> *Down derry, down derry . . .'*

Olwynne went running through the trees, ducking under branches and pulling aside leaves, eager to see who it was who sang so beautifully. She had heard that song sung many times before, but never with such warmth and joy. The woman's voice was unusually deep and rich, but as she sang the chorus her voice flowed up into the higher registers with an ease few could ever hope to match. Olwynne came from a family of singers. Her father had the same golden quality to his voice, and so did her eldest brother. She herself was counted a very pretty singer, and certainly music was one of the few indulgences Olwynne allowed herself. She was overcome by an urgent desire to hear more, and to know the woman who could sing with such technical purity and yet also with such heartfelt emotion.

Through the dark tangle of leaves and twigs, she saw a woman dressed all in black sitting on a fallen log, her face a pale oval lifted to the sky. As Olwynne hurried towards her, a twig cracked under her foot. At once the singer broke off mid-note, leaped up, and fled away into the garden. Olwynne hurried after her, but it was no use, she had disappeared. Olwynne stood alone in the clearing, feeling acute disappointment. There were no clues as to who the singer had been, no footstep in the mud, no scrap of black cloth hanging from a stick. She could have been a figment of Olwynne's imagination. Yet, as Olwynne slowly turned and retraced her steps, she was humming *"Down, derry down, derry down"* under her breath.

Whistles sounded shrilly.

Black-clad students ran through the trees, blasting away the tranquillity of the dawn. A procession of witches, sorcerers, and faeries followed Isabeau the Keybearer along the avenue towards the palace, all wearing crowns of leaves and early spring flowers. The Keybearer carried a bouquet made up of the seven sacred woods in her hand, her owl blinking sleepily from her shoulder. A flock of nisses flew about her head, shrieking in excitement, while two tall tree-changers walked at her shoulders.

Olwynne stood under the trees and watched them walk past. Whether it was the freshness of the dew, the pleasure on the faces of the crowd, or an echo of that joyous voice she had heard singing in the dawn, Olwynne could not tell, but she was filled with a new sense of hope and happiness. Her lips curved upward in a smile for the first time in weeks. One of the crowd turned and smiled in response, then held out a narrow, long-fingered hand to her. Olwynne's smile deepened. She stepped forward and took the Celestine's hand, joining the procession.

You have been dwelling in a dark place, Thunderlily said.

Aye, Olwynne answered.

The shadow of it is still there, behind you.

Olwynne felt her spirits dip and made an effort to hold on to her newfound gladness.

But there is light breaking upon your face. That is good.

Once you follow a road down into darkness, it can be difficult to find your way out again.

Thunderlily, do the Celestines travel the dream-roads?

The Celestine bowed her snow-white head. *We may travel all roads. They are not always safe though. Darkness overwhelms them. I cannot reach my mother even in dreams. I have been sorely troubled, for it is not our nature to walk in silence and darkness, alone. I cannot see what lies ahead of me, and my heart is uneasy.*

Mine too, Olwynne whispered.

I know. Yet when I saw you there, coming out of the forest, you were gilded with gladness. It was like an enchantment laid upon you. It made the darkness behind you larger. My heart troubles me. Who did you see, to cast this spell upon you?

A spell? Olwynne was surprised. *It was no spell. I heard someone singing, that's all. It was a lovely song. And such a lovely morning.*

It is a lovely morning, the Celestine agreed. *And beauty is its own spell. Perhaps that is all it was.*

I'm sure it was, Olwynne said, but she felt troubled. She glanced at the Celestine with something approaching resentment. The Celestine knew, of course. She returned a look of regret and apology.

If it was true, it should not pass so quickly, she said. *Who was this singer, that you saw in the dawn?*

I do no' ken, Olwynne answered sulkily. *She ran off afore I saw her face. It could've been a student. She was dressed all in black.*

There are many here that have magic in their voices, the Celestine agreed. *There is so much magic here, at the Tower of Two Moons, that it clouds my sight and makes it hard for me to trace its sources. The air itself sings with it, and the earth thrums.*

Olwynne glanced sideways at the Celestine again. Although Thunderlily had been at the Tower of Two Moons for almost eight years, she was several years older than Olwynne, and so they had not often conversed. She was indeed fascinating. Olwynne could understand how her brother Donncan and her cousin Bronwen could be so enamored of her. Thunderlily was their great friend, as Lewen was hers and Owein's. The Celes-

tine had made a foursome with Donncan and Bronwen and Neil
MacFóghnan of Arran, whom they all called Cuckoo. Olwynne
wondered if she missed them, now the other three had all turned
twenty-four and left the Theurgia. Donncan had been away,
traveling with Neil, ever since he graduated five months earlier,
while Bronwen had thrown herself into life at the court since
her graduation.

I do indeed miss my friends, the Celestine said, a tone of
wistfulness in her mind-voice. *Soon I too shall celebrate the
anniversary of my twenty-fourth year in this life, and my days
at the Theurgia will come to an end. I must return then to the
garden of my ancestors, deep in the forest, far from the cities
and towns of those of humankind. Then I will see my friends
rarely indeed.*

I am sorry, Olwynne said awkwardly.

So it must be, the Celestine answered.

They had reached the great square before the palace, and
many of the courtiers and servants were thronging out the doors
to join them. Everyone was shouting and cheering, throwing up
handfuls of petals and waving long colored streamers, while the
sound of the whistles was deafening. The Celestine turned her
face towards the palace, her eyes, which seemed so full of light
yet also so blind, looking with a strange, intense expression at
the crowded steps. *My days here are not yet finished, though*,
she said, so softly her voice was little more than a murmur in
Olwynne's mind, *and look, they are all here now. If there is one
thing I have learned from your kind, it is how to live lightly, in
the here and now. . . .*

Olwynne gazed at her curiously, then turned to look where
she looked.

Standing on the steps, smiling around at the roaring crowd,
stood Olwynne's eldest brother, Donncan Feargus MacCuinn,
heir to the throne of Eileanan.

He was a tall, slim young man, with thick wavy hair the
color of ripe corn and great golden wings that sprang out from
his shoulders and brushed the ground behind him. They seemed
to attract the light so that, even in the grey dimness of the fading night, he seemed haloed in sunshine. He was dressed in the
forest-green kilt of the MacCuinn clan, with a crimson sash
across his breast.

Olwynne caught her breath in surprise, then waved at him enthusiastically. There was no chance to speak to him. He was separated from her by a thronging crowd, all blowing whistles and cheering. She saw Bronwen beside him, dressed in a scandalous gown of silvery-green gauze that clung to her as if it had been dampened, which it probably had. Neil of Arran stood on her other side, gazing down at her with admiring eyes. They did not see her wave, but Owein and Lewen did and plunged through to her side.

"When did Donn get in?" Owein demanded.

Olwynne shrugged. "I dinna ken. Listen to the crowd! They're going mad."

"They love him," Owein said. "He always looks so damn princely!"

Lewen was carrying a pretty nosegay of spring flowers, the dew still on the petals. He offered it to her shyly. "I picked these for ye," he said softly. "I'm glad to see ye up and about. Are ye feeling better?"

"Och, sure," she answered lightly, taking the flowers with a smile but moving away from him, not wanting him to see her eyes had filled with tears. "I couldna miss May Day!"

The sky had been growing steadily paler, and light gilded the top of the palace's golden domes. Trumpets sounded, and the crowd quietened, turning as one to look at the Keybearer, who was standing before a massive pyramid of wood, her hands resting on her staff.

"The sun has arisen," she said into the sudden silence. "Let us light the Beltane fires and celebrate the return o' summer and the green months. Let us rejoice, for winter has gone and the time o' quickening is upon us."

Sunlight fell upon the top of the bonfire. Isabeau flung up both hands, her staff standing upright on its own.

The bonfire roared with flame. Everyone cheered and the whistles blew again, maddeningly loud. Olwynne covered her ears, laughing, and saw many in the crowd were doing the same.

Bells rang out, peal after peal filling the air. Men and women came and thrust long torches into the fire, forming a long procession that would wind around the palace towards the city.

Donncan had been seized by a group of laughing girls, all clad in green, who were trying to tie leafy twigs to his arms and legs.

"All hail the Green Man!" they cried to the crowd.

Donncan was protesting, but no one listened, the crowd roaring their approval. One girl had a wreath of leaves and would have crowned him with it, but Bronwen, laughing, seized the wreath and put it on his head herself, kissing him on the mouth. The cheers were deafening. Donncan came down into the crowd, shaking hands with the men and allowing himself to be kissed by the girls.

Owein applauded loudly, laughing. Donncan saw them and waved, smiling wryly. Owein put his hands to his mouth and called, "When did ye get in?" but his brother could not hear him over the crowd. He smiled, shrugged, and let himself be borne away by the crowd. Then they heard his warm golden voice raised in song.

"I wonder who was meant to be Green Man today?" Owein whispered in Olwynne's ear. She shrugged.

"I hope whoever it is doesna mind too much," she whispered back. She saw one of the palace guards standing on the steps, dressed all in green, looking disgruntled. She pointed him out to the others, who both grimaced.

"That's Mat," Lewen said. "He's one o' Bronwen's crowd. He doesna look happy at all, does he?"

"He'll get over it," Owein said. "Mat's always getting in a huff over something."

Donncan's voice was receding as he ran at the head of the procession, leaping and twirling, a flaming torch held high in his hand.

"Come on!" Owein cried. "Let's go watch the chain o' fires being kindled. We'll get a good view from the bell tower."

Olwynne shook her head. "Nay. I'm rather weary still. I think I'll go back to bed."

"Ye'll come to the feast tonight, won't ye?" Lewen asked anxiously. "Ye canna miss the party."

"Why, ye could be crowned May Queen," Owein said teasingly.

"I doubt it," Olwynne answered, her voice coming out more bitterly than she had intended. She tried for a lighter tone.

"With Donncan as the Green Man, the May Queen will have to be Bronwen. There can be no other choice!"

"I'd say she was always first choice," Lewen said.

"Aye, that's why Mat's looking so put out," Owein agreed. "All right, then, I'll see ye tonight, will I?"

"Aye, I'll come tonight, if only to reassure Auntie Beau that I'm feeling better. I do no' think I can stand any more o' her medicines!"

"Fair enough. See ye tonight then," Owein said. "Come on, Lewen!"

"Have a good rest," Lewen said. "See ye tonight!"

She raised a hand in farewell.

"I'm glad to see ye looking so much better," he called over his shoulder as he ran to join the others.

Olwynne turned to walk back to the Tower of Two Moons, bending her head to smell her flowers to hide the pleasure his concern had given her. The Celestine was still standing at the edge of the gardens, half-hidden beneath the drooping branches of a weeping greenberry tree. Their eyes met. With a start, Olwynne realized that Thunderlily was also trying to conceal some strong emotion that threatened to crack the composure Olwynne had thought effortless. Recognition leaped between them. If they had been able to phrase the thought, it would have said: *You too love and are not loved in return?*

After that moment of recognition and empathy, Olwynne and Thunderlily looked away, the apprentice-witch making her way slowly back down the avenue towards the tower and the Celestine disappearing into the trees. Neither wished to name her pain.

A Sweet Nosegay

Olwynne slept that afternoon, and for the first time in days woke refreshed. She had gone to her aunt before the midday meal break and asked her to remove the ward Isabeau had placed on her third eye, to protect her after her attack of sorcery sickness. After a long, searching glance the Keybearer had done as she asked. Although she had done no more than touch her lips lightly to Olwynne's brow, it had felt like a sharp blow that the Banprionnsa fell back from, reeling. She had gone back to her room slowly, feeling odd, as if her arms and legs were too long and loosely jointed. She had been afraid to lie down, afraid of what her dreams might show her, but although she had dreamed, it had been the usual vague inconsequence and had left no residue of terror.

Olwynne lay for a while in the green dimness, looking out into the trees, then she yawned, stretched, and rose. She stripped off her clothes, heated water on the fire, and filled a hip bath with jug after jug of warm water. She washed her body and her hair with rose soap, then anointed herself with precious oils scented with rose and jasmine and lovage, all of them herbs used in love spells. Drawing upon the One Power, she dried her hair gently between her hands so it sprang up in thick, glossy ringlets the color of the Beltane fires.

Naked, Olwynne looked at herself in the mirror for a long time. She thought of Lewen's last look at her, his face lighting up with a smile. *He canna want to love that satyricorn girl*, she thought. *It's for his own good.*

Lying before the mirror, casting a delicate fragrance upon the air, was the little nosegay of flowers Lewen had given her—tiny pink roses, lavender, jasmine, violets, and lovage, hemmed with bright new leaves from the hazel tree. Olwynne picked it up and smelled it, then, wincing in anticipation, plucked one long, red, wiry hair from her head and wound it about the stems.

She went to her spell-box and drew out two tall pink candles, candleholders made from rose quartz, a long pink ribbon, and a tiny vial of precious dragon's blood. When Olwynne uncorked the vial, the rich, cloying smell almost made her gag. Holding it away from her, she quickly corked it again; then she set up the candles on either side of the mirror, anointing them with the aphrodisiacal oils.

Lit only by the dancing flames of the candles, in the cooling dusk of the day, Olwynne looked herself in the eyes. She knew what she was doing was forbidden by the Coven. If anyone found out, she could be expelled from the Theurgia. All her dreams of being a sorceress would be ashes.

But in the warm candlelight, she was beautiful. It hurt her that no man would ever get to touch her skin, to breathe her breath. She had loved Lewen so long and so secretly. All her dreams of desire were tied up in him, and she felt she could never recover. It was wrong that he had given himself to some other girl. It was cruel. Olwynne could not bear that all her sweet imaginings should bear no seed, no blossom, no fruit. It was unnatural.

So, gazing into her own eyes, she took the dragon's blood upon her fingertip and drove it into the deep, hot, wet absence of her. She felt an immediate dilation, an opening of the hard closed petals. Her breath came in a quick pant. She pulled her hand away and, furtively, lifted it to her nose.

Finding it hard still to catch her breath, Olwynne dipped her fingers again in the sweet-scented oils and touched, ritualistically, her third eye, her left breast, her right shoulder, her left shoulder, her right breast and then her third eye again. As she drew the pentagram of protection, she said in a shaky voice, "By the powers o' the five directions, above me, below me, within and without, may I be protected from all harm."

She then took the ribbon and ran it through her warm, oily fingers, chanting softly: "Flowers and ribbon, make him love me, flowers and ribbon, make him need me, flowers and ribbon, bind him to me, as long as our hearts should beat."

Three times she chanted the spell; then Olwynne bound the ribbon about the flowers five times, knotting it each time and saying, "By one this spell is done, by two it will come true, by three so let it be, by four for the good o' all, by five so shall love thrive."

Olwynne was frightened but also exhilarated. She lifted the nosegay and breathed in the sweet fragrance deeply, then laid it down and began to dress. It had taken her a good part of the morning to decide what to wear. She had discarded outfit after outfit until, at last, she had settled on the dress she had worn to her first ever ball. She had loved the dress then but had rarely worn it since, thinking it too pretty for a woman who wished to be a sorceress.

A skirt of white satin, embroidered all over with tiny flowers, was worn under a kirtle of pale spring green. The bodice was of the same color and was usually worn with a lace collar, which Olwynne now discarded. She tucked the nosegay of flowers into her cleavage, aware that it drew attention to the curve of her pale breasts above the deep-cut square neckline. She then carefully crowned herself with a wreath of roses, jasmine, lovage, and violets, woven together with a silken ribbon the same color as her kirtle. From beneath her wreath, her heavy red-gold curls hung down her back to her knees. Olwynne looked at herself in the mirror critically, pinched her cheeks, and smiled. She truly did not think she had ever looked so well.

The central garth was filled with excited students, all dressed in their best. The predominant color was green, as befitted the celebration of the first day of summer. A few of the music students were playing flutes, fiddles, and guitars, and couples were dancing. Olwynne walked through the crowd, smiling and nodding to those she knew. Fèlice was dancing with a tall medical student and waved at her enthusiastically. Landon was seated on a step, writing in his notebook, occasionally splattering passersby with ink as he finished a word with a flourish. Then Olwynne saw Edithe, who called to her and tried to speak to her. Olwynne deftly sidestepped and went on. She only wanted to see Lewen.

She found him and Owein together in the square before the palace, drinking Merry May punch and watching the dancers. They rose to their feet at the sight of her.

"Look at ye, ye've scrubbed up well," Owein said. "Ye must be feeling better."

"I feel grand," she answered.

"Ye look grand," Lewen said quietly, staring as if he had never seen her before.

"Grand as a goat's turd stuck with buttercups," Owein said.

She ignored him, smiling at Lewen and holding out her hand. "Care to dance?"

"I'm no' much o' a dancer—ye ken that," he said, but took her hand and led her on to the dance floor.

Olwynne smiled and let him turn her, his hand on her waist. It was a warm night and the air smelled of woodsmoke and flowers. Paper lanterns hung from tree to tree in the garden, and from window to window all along the palace walls. Grey-clad servants moved unobtrusively here and there, carrying glasses of wine punch and plates of little honey cakes. In the center of the square, the Beltane bonfire still glowed, casting a warm light on the gaily dressed couples twirling all around it. Jongleurs amused the crowd with their stilt walking and fire eating, and a troupe of cluricauns showed off their tumbling tricks. A maypole had been erected near the high table, its colored ribbons still hanging loose.

Olwynne and Lewen did not speak, though it was a slow dance and they should have had breath enough. Olwynne let herself fall into a sweet trance, her head very close to Lewen's shoulder, the feel of his fingers burning through the fabric of her dress. She felt him heave a breath and glanced up at him.

"I'm glad ye're feeling better," Lewen said. He spoke awkwardly, and his arm on her waist was stiff.

Olwynne smiled at him. She felt she knew him better than even his own mother. He did not find words easy. The slick compliments that other men found so easy to say would never slide off Lewen's tongue. He was better with horses and falcons and dogs, creatures that understood slow, quiet movements and a strong hand. The deep connection he felt with the creatures of the field and the forest found their way out through his fingers as he whittled a scrap of wood into something so beautiful it as-

tounded all who saw it. A shapeless lump of wood became a
running horse, a dancing girl, a charging stag. Arrows flew true,
javelins always found their mark, and his bowls and cups were
perfectly balanced, a pleasure to hold and use. Plants under his
care flourished, maltreated animals grew sleek and tame, and
people in general felt comfortable and at ease without realizing
why. All this Lewen did without words, for he spoke seldom
and never without thought, and never ever with the honeyed
ease of the courtiers with their long ringlets, their feathered hats
and velvet doublets, their oiled and perfumed beards.

He did not dance with their graceful ease either, his back
stiff and his brow furrowed as if he was mentally counting his
steps. Olwynne thought, with a little upturn of her lips, that if
he was ever admitted to the ranks of the Yeomen of the Guard,
it would be for his strength and steadiness, his skill with the
sword and the bow, not for his ability to dance a graceful set,
like the green-clad guard now holding Bronwen so close on the
other side of the dance floor. She recognized the guard as the
soldier who should have been the Green Man. He was glaring
down at Bronwen as if he wished to strangle her, while she spun
and twirled about him as easily as a flower on a long green
stem, her gauzy skirts gleaming silver in the moonlight.

The sight of Bronwen dancing stirred a deep unease in Olwynne. A shudder ran over her. She pressed closer to Lewen,
who bent his brown head over hers. "Is all well?" he asked. "Ye
shivered."

She looked up into his eyes, which were dark and intent, and
for a moment could not breathe. She nodded dumbly, and his
mouth relaxed, his eyes crinkling.

"I'm sorry about your toes," he said. "I'm a terrible dancer."

"Nay, ye're fine, really," she said, and cursed herself for her
own inept tongue.

"It must be all the sword practice," he answered.

There was a long moment of silence.

"So do ye like my dress?" she asked, spreading her skirts
and giving a little twirl before coming back into the curve of his
arm.

"Aye, indeed. Ye look very bonny," he answered quietly.

The music came to an end, and he gave a grave bow and
said, "Thank ye for the dance."

"Ye will no' go another round with me?" Olwynne said, masking her disappointment with a smile.

He shook his head. "I do no' feel much like dancing, I'm sorry. I'm sure ye'll have no shortage o' partners, though, so pretty ye are looking tonight."

"I'd rather dance with ye," she said, moving closer to him.

He smiled, rather wistfully, and moved away. "It feels all wrong, me being here, dancing under the stars, when Rhiannon is locked away where she canna even see them."

Olwynne wanted to shriek in vexation and jealousy; she wanted to cry, *Never say that name to me again!* But she smiled in sympathy and said, "O' course, I'm sorry, it was thoughtless o' me. It's just that I'm feeling so much better and it is such a beautiful night . . ."

"It is bonny," Lewen replied, looking up at the two moons that wheeled together close to the soaring spires of the Tower of Two Moons. One moon was red, one moon was blue, but the light they cast on the intricate mosaic of twigs and leaves was silver-bright.

"Would ye rather walk in the gardens?" Olwynne asked.

Lewen looked back at her in surprise, then nodded. "Aye, I would. . . . But would ye no' rather dance?"

"The night is young. I can dance again later," she said. "Come and tell me how Rhiannon is doing."

Eagerly he led Olwynne away from the dance floor. She stopped one of the lackeys and seized a decanter of the Merry May punch and two glasses from his tray. Made from goldensloe wine, strawberries, honey, fermented lime, and woodruff blossoms, the punch was an intoxicating brew and often blamed for any babies born nine months after the lighting of the Beltane fires. Olwynne was certainly hoping it would work its usual magic, but to make sure, she had an extra ingredient to add.

Shielding the decanter from view with her body, she hurriedly uncorked a vial she carried in her reticule and let one, two, three drops slide down its long translucent throat, dripping down to dissolve into the heady wine punch within. It was the honey of the golden goddess flower, a powerful aphrodisiac from the fens of Arran, that she had purchased at great cost on the black market only that afternoon. They said it could not fail.

Lewen turned and glanced back at her, and her heart swelled with longing for him. She tried to keep the intensity of her desire from showing in her face, and she must have been successful, for Lewen took the decanter and glasses from her with his usual quiet courtesy and directed her down one of the paths, his fingers just touching the small of her back.

The paths were lined with tiny candles in paper hoods, with more paper lanterns hanging in long chains from tree to tree. They wandered along the paths for some time and came at last to a small grove where a fountain softly tinkled, and there was a bench where they could sit and talk. Lewen spread out his cloak for Olwynne to sit on, so her skirts would not be stained with moss, and then sat beside her, the scent of the night jasmine climbing the arbor adding to the enchanting smell of Olwynne's nosegay.

The splashing of the fountain, the tiny glow of the candles, and the warm play of the breeze in Olwynne's hair was all very pleasing and romantic. Olwynne could only wish Lewen would not keep worrying about his wild satyricorn girl and talk about something else instead. As long as she was prepared to listen, he was prepared to talk, though, and she realized with a pang of guilt that Lewen had been feeling very alone in his loyal defense of his lover. He was questioning her now about the procedure of the courts, and Olwynne, who, like all the prionnsachan and banprionnsachan, had been made to study law at the Courts of the Inns, did her best to answer him. Whenever she could she refilled their glasses, until her heart and loins ached with the warm glow of the wine, and the decanter was empty.

At last Lewen said, with an effort, "I'm sorry, I must be boring ye to death. Would ye like me to take ye back to the square now?"

"Nay, I'm fine," Olwynne said. "I'm enjoying the peace o' the gardens. Listen! Can ye hear that nightingale? It feels like an age since I last heard one."

"Me too," Lewen said, and they listened for a while in silence. The leaves murmured quietly, and they could hear the distant sound of the fiddles and flutes.

Olwynne sighed in pure happiness.

"Ye've no' been well," Lewen said with contrition, "and I have no' once asked ye how ye are feeling. I'm sorry."

"Hopefully ye feel no need to ask because ye can see with your own eyes that I am well," Olwynne said, wishing she was better practiced at the arts of flirtation.

The candlelight slanted warmly across his cheekbone, and she saw his cheek curve as he smiled down at her. "Indeed, ye do look well. I've never seen ye look so . . . so glowing."

Olwynne felt her cheeks grow warm with pleasure. She looked up into his intent eyes, then dropped her gaze at once. She could smell the scent of the flowers, rising heady and warm from her body, and taste the sweetness of the wine on her tongue. *Kiss me*, she begged him silently. *Kiss me now. Please* . . .

But Lewen turned his head away and said awkwardly, "Which is why ye should no' be sitting out here in the gardens with me, but enjoying yourself at the party. So fine ye are tonight, ye'd be the belle o' the ball, if ye just tried."

"With Bronwen the Bonny sharing the dance floor? I think no'." Olwynne was icy in her disappointment.

"No' everyone is drawn to the Banprionnsa Bronwen like a moth to the flame," Lewen said impatiently. "I am sure there are many young lairds and courtiers there tonight who have no wish to be burned by that fire."

"Happen so, but I am no' interested in any o' those silken fools," Olwynne said.

"No, I suppose that's true," Lewen said, grinning down at her. "All ye've ever wanted is to learn the Craft, is that no' right?"

He spoke affectionately, but the words caught Olwynne on the raw. "That's no' *all* I've ever wanted," she cried. She reached out and seized his hand, meeting his startled gaze with a fierce intent gaze of her own. She saw the sudden comprehension in his eyes and felt him instinctively retreat, but she would not let him go. Holding him fast, she leaned forward and kissed him on the mouth. For a moment he sat still, frozen with surprise, then he wrenched his mouth away.

"Olwynne!"

She would not let him speak. She kissed him again and, her

heart hammering, fearfully touched his tongue with hers. At
once he leaped back. "Olwynne, what . . . I canna . . ."

She seized his hand and slid it within her bodice, crushing
the flowers so their scent sprang up in a heavy, dizzying wave.
His other hand, trying to hold her off at the waist, flexed instinctively but he would not succumb, pushing her away,
wrenching his hand free. The flimsy material tore, and she
heard his breath founder. Her bare breast felt cold at the absence of his hand.

"What do ye do? Olwynne, ye ken I canna . . . Rhiannon . . ."

She stopped the hated word with her mouth, almost swoon-
ing as emotion flooded through her. Still he resisted, holding
her away with both hands. His eyes were heavy-lidded, his
mouth swollen. Again she bent to kiss him, holding his dear
face with both her hands, her bare breasts pressed against the
warm skin of his throat and chest.

"Nay, Olwynne," he murmured against her mouth. "I
canna . . . really, I canna . . ."

She hung heavy against him, not allowing him room to
breathe or protest. She felt him harden against her, and put
down her hand to touch him, very briefly. "Olwynne," he
sighed. "Nay . . ."

But his legs spread involuntarily, and she rubbed her hand
against him more boldly so that he moaned. "Olwynne . . ."

Still she would not speak, all her will and desire focused on
him. He could not retreat far, the vine-entangled wall of the
arbor holding him fast. She kissed his mouth, his jaw, his
throat, the soft skin under his ear. Whenever he tried to murmur
a protest, she stopped his mouth with her own. Meanwhile her
hand was busy at his laces, fumbling and tearing, trying to un-
knot them. She could feel his body's response to her clumsi-
ness, and pressed her own body more closely against him.

"Olwynne, ye smell . . . ye feel so good," he murmured.
"Oh, but I canna . . . I must no' . . ."

"Ye can," she whispered. "Ye must. Please. Ye ken she's no
good for ye. She canna love ye the way I love ye. Please,
please. I'll make ye happy, I promise."

She lifted her skirts and mounted him, and he slid his hands
up her legs to grasp her bottom. She was naked beneath her

skirt, and his breath caught. "Oh Eà!" he breathed. His fingers digging into her bare flesh, he lifted her and brought her down sharply upon him. They both cried out. Tears burst from Olwynne's eyes. She bent and hid her face in his shoulder, and he grasped her tighter, pounding up into her, his breath gasping. Olwynne was laughing and crying together, shaken and torn and slippery with need. He groaned, and she seized his hair and rode him harder. Suddenly she felt a rush of blood to her head so fierce her ears roared. She cried out and froze in surprise, but he was bucking and twisting beneath her, bruising her hips and buttocks with his hands. Her pelvic bone was sore, the muscles of her legs screaming. Then Lewen arched his back and cried out in joy and surprise.

They crouched together in silence, breathing hard. Slowly Lewen let go of Olwynne's buttocks and drew away from her with a soft sucking sound that made Olwynne catch her breath in a little embarrassed laugh. He did not laugh. He was so grave and silent she grew worried and drew closer so she could see his face in the soft erratic glow of the swinging candles. His dark eyes were somber, but there was a glow in them that made a dark flower of triumph and malice bloom deep in Olwynne's heart.

"What have we done?" he whispered. "I must be mad . . . or drunk. Rhiannon . . . your father . . . Oh Eà!"

"We've made love," Olwynne said fiercely. "I wanted ye, ye wanted me. What's wrong with that?"

"Rhiannon . . ."

"Eà curse her!" Olwynne said. "She was never meant for ye. Ye're mine and have always been mine. Ye just needed to see that."

"I must've been blind," he cried. Then he drew his breath in on a long hiss. "Or ensorcelled!"

Olwynne felt a bitter jab of shame but thrust it away. Lewen had bent his head to kiss her hands. Burning tears fell on her skin. She drew him close to her again, and wiped his eyes with her fingers, and kissed his mouth. "Come back with me to my room," she whispered.

He nodded, and when she drew down to kiss him again, he kissed her back with sore and desperate need.

The Lovelock

Bronwen laughed and tossed back her hair, spinning away from Neil and then swiftly back. He caught her in his arm and almost stumbled, so sudden was her weight, but recovered himself quickly. The music came to an end and she smiled and curtsied, and he bowed.

"Another?" he begged.

She gave her quick flashing smile. "I wish I could, Cuckoo, but I'm already promised to another. I'm sorry. Happen again later?"

"But I have no' seen ye in months. Surely that counts for something?"

"Aye, o' course, but the thing is, I didna ken ye were coming back in time for the feast, and my dance card has been full for weeks. I'm sorry!" She smiled brilliantly over her shoulder as she took the proffered arm of the Earl of Kintallian, a brilliantly polished young man with a small pointed beard and so many slashes on his sleeve he looked as if he had barely escaped with his life from some frantic duel.

The music began again, and she swirled away on his arm. Neil scowled, well aware the earl was a far more graceful dancer than he could ever be. Moodily he made his way back to his table, jerking his head to the page for some more Merry May punch and watching Bronwen as she spun down the center of the dance floor. His scowl only deepened when the Earl of Kintallian was replaced with Alta, the Fairgean ambassador, and then with Aindrew MacRuraich.

His mother, Elfrida NicHilde, the Banprionnsa of Tìrsoilleir, bent closer to ask him a question, laying her hand caressingly on his arm. He hardly noticed.

Neil had just decided he would demand the very next dance when he saw a young man with brilliantly blue eyes under heavy, scowling eyebrows cut in, interrupting the lavolta. Bronwen seemed at first to protest, but when the young man, dressed all in green from head to toe, insisted, Aindrew relinquished her with a graceful bow and away she whirled again. Neil sank back into his chair and signaled for his glass to be refilled. His mother uttered a gentle admonishment, which he ignored. Elfrida pursed her lips and began to lecture him, in the mildest way possible, on the evils of alcohol and fast women.

To Neil's chagrin, the green-clad man was the most accomplished dancer he had ever seen. He leaped like a deer, spun on his toes and then on his knees and, worst of all, sent Bronwen twirling about with the merest touch and gesture. Together, they danced so beautifully the floor cleared for them, and an audience gathered, cheering and clapping.

Neil, tossing back another cup of honeyed wine, saw Donncan was standing at the edge of the dance floor, watching with much the same black, sullen, brooding look that Neil imagined was on his own face. Their eyes met. Donncan's expression darkened even further, and Neil felt his throat close over.

"Neil . . ." Elfrida said.

"Just leave me alone!" Neil said and lurched to his feet.

Mathias drew Bronwen close and bent her backwards over his arm as the music came to an end.

He said, pleadingly, "Ye canna pretend ye do no' enjoy dancing with me, my lady."

She straightened up and took a step away, raising her brows. "Why would I pretend any such thing? I have always said ye were a very pretty dancer."

"Is that all I am to ye?" he demanded.

"But o' course," she answered, drawing up the fragile folds of her silvery-green skirt. "What else?"

He flushed dark red, and she gave him a little ironic curtsy and moved away. Mathias caught her arm.

"Unhand me at once!" she hissed through her teeth. "Do ye seek to make a scene?"

"I must speak with ye," he said unsteadily. "Please, my lady . . . Your Highness. I wish . . . I wish to apologize . . . to explain . . ."

"Surely no' here and now, in the middle o' the dance floor, with every eye upon us?" the Banprionnsa answered haughtily.

"Then when?"

She disengaged her arm and yawned behind her fan of bhanias feathers. "I am sure I shall tire o' dancing soon and shall seek to cool myself with an iced bellfruit juice in the garden, away from the heat o' the fire. Happen I shall see ye there. Though, really, there is no need for ye to explain. Ye are no' the first man to drink too much seasquill wine and make a fool o' himself."

He colored angrily and bowed with a click of his heels that made her roll her eyes impatiently as she moved away. The crowd parted to let her through, the men bowing their heads, the women curtsying gracefully. More than one set of eyes followed her, both men and women. Bronwen knew the women were eyeing her dress, and the men the long-limbed, supple body underneath. She had designed her dress herself for maximum effect. Made of pale green gauze, the gown tied over her shoulders with nothing more than a narrow satin ribbon, leaving her arms and shoulders bare. Beneath the gauze, Bronwen wore a tight satin sheath that had been carefully matched to the hue of her skin so that it looked as if she was naked beneath. A few sprays of appliquéd beading helped preserve her modesty. She wore her hair loose, like a young girl, under the crown of flowers that declared her May Queen, the most beautiful girl at the court.

Bronwen had moved only three steps when she was accosted by one of her uncle's squires, young Fymbar MacThanach of Blèssem, a plump boy with a shock of tow-colored hair and an unfortunate tendency to blush. Bronwen smiled, waved her fan languidly, and begged him to find her something to drink. Fymbar turned scarlet, stammered his willingness to serve her, and went plunging off to find a waiter. Another few steps, and Aindrew MacRuraich was bowing over her hand and begging her for the next dance.

"But I have already danced with ye three times tonight, my laird," she said, smiling demurely at him from behind her fan. "Any more and we'll cause a scandal."

"I thought ye delighted in scandalizing the court," he said with a grin. "And ye ken I am always willing to assist ye in putting firecrackers under those auld biddies' tails."

"Indeed, ye are a fine companion in any game, but I feel I should, perhaps, play a more sober and respectable charade tonight," she said. "Given that my beloved betrothed has seen fit to return to my side, after these long months o' absence."

"And looking very sour too, I should add," Aindrew said. "Surely ye do no' really want to marry that sobersides?"

Bronwen looked thoughtfully across the floor at Donncan, who was watching her with a very unhappy expression on his face. "Donncan does no' dance," she said regretfully. "He finds his wings can be rather a nuisance on a crowded dance floor."

"But surely he does no' forbid ye from dancing?" Aindrew cried. "When ye are the bonniest dancer in the whole court?"

"Nay," Bronwen answered. "He does no' forbid me."

"But he doesna like it, does he?"

Bronwen returned her gaze to Aindrew's handsome, laughing countenance. "Would ye?" she answered.

He sobered. "Nay, I would no'," he answered.

"So we can hardly blame him, can we?" she said and, smiling, left him.

Donncan watched her approach with no lightening of his expression.

"Ye are failing in your duties as Green Man," she chided him. "The Green Man is meant to lead the festivities, drinking and dancing till dawn."

"Happen your cavalier would have been a better choice then," he said stiffly.

"Ye mean Mathias Bright-Eyed? Well, he certainly is a keen dancer and an even keener drinker. I'll warrant he is still here, drinking and dancing at dawn, long after ye've sought your bed."

He flushed. "I'll warrant ye're right. The question is, where will ye be?"

She drew away from him. "What kind o' question is that?"

"A fair enough one, by all accounts."

"So ye listen to the gossipmongers now, do ye?"

"It's rather hard no' to, when there is so much to listen to."

"It's all malicious and untrue," Bronwen cried, then recollected herself, remembering the many curious eyes upon them. For a moment she stood still, trying to regain her composure, and then she said lightly, "Come, Donncan, I have no' seen ye in months. Is this the way ye greet me? It is no' like ye to believe the false tales o' those who delight in spite and mischief. Ye ken what the court is like after the long winter. Everyone is restless and out o' sorts, me among them. I ken ye willna dance with me, with the floor so crowded, but can we no' walk in the gardens together? I have no' had a chance to hear a single thing about your stay in Arran these past months. How was the Tower o' Mists?"

Donncan frowned. "Strange," he answered after a while. "It is very isolated, ye ken, hidden at the heart o' the fens as it is, and so often covered in mist. There was no' much to do there, really. We boated on the lake, and when the marsh was iced over we had some good hunting. But once the thaw came, it all grew rather flat. I didna sleep so well while I was there. . . . They say the air is bad, ye ken, and certainly I had some strange dreams."

"Really?" Bronwen asked. "What kind o' dreams?"

Donncan shrugged, looking uncomfortable. "Just run-o'-the-mill nightmares, I guess. Darkness, and no' being able to breathe. A heavy stone on my chest. Wings beating around my head. Birds, or bats, or something. Naught I could really remember the next day."

"So did ye no' dream about me?" Bronwen asked provocatively as they stepped away from the glare of the torches and into the soft breathing dark of the gardens.

At once he turned and seized her wrist, drawing her close to him. "Ye ken I did," he said angrily. "I was tormented with dreams o' ye, as is every man who crosses your path."

She was surprised to find it hard to catch her breath. "Och, I think ye exaggerate."

"I wish I did," he answered and let go of her wrist.

She rubbed it, torn between feeling flattered and angered. He stood, staring moodily into the candlelit trees, sipping at his wine. She decided to be flattered.

"I'm glad ye thought o' me," she said softly. "Ye were gone a long time."

He glanced at her, surprised into a smile. "Did ye miss me?"

"Maybe just a little," she said.

"Well, I'm glad to hear it. By all accounts, ye were having too much fun to even notice I was gone."

"Did ye expect me to just sit in my rooms and mope?" Bronwen's voice sharpened.

"Some moping would have been nice."

"Moping is just no' my style," Bronwen said with a sweet smile and drank down her punch recklessly.

"So I heard."

"Ye seem to have heard a great deal o' me while ye were gone. Am I to infer ye had spies watching my every movement and reporting back to ye?"

"I had no need o' spies," Donncan said. "Every traveling tinker had a new tale to tell o' Bronwen the Bonny. There's no' a village inn in the land where ye are no' the favored topic o' conversation."

"Wonderful!" Bronwen retorted. "I'm glad I've given so many people something new to talk about. Their lives are so very drab and boring, it is my pleasure to bring them some poor form o' excitement."

"Well, I canna say I'm glad," Donncan said, his voice under tight control. "It gave me no pleasure at all to hear my wife-to-be has been entertaining other men in her boudoir by swimming naked in the pool."

Bronwen bit her lip. She was rather sorry for that particular escapade, which had been prompted by Iseult quietly advising her that perhaps she should not make such an exhibition of her Fairgean ancestry. Bronwen was not fond of her betrothed's mother, who always seemed to view her with disfavor. She grew weary of everyone expecting her to be the model of prudence and discretion, just because she was a banprionnsa and betrothed to the heir to the throne. A throne that she should have inherited, she reminded herself. Her uncle might think that he had sidestepped the issue by promising Bronwen to his own son when they were mere bairns, but Bronwen had not forgotten she had been named heir by her own father, and certainly others had not forgotten either. The Rìgh and Banrìgh liked to think they had her trapped in a silken net, bound to a future not of her own devising, but Bronwen enjoyed reminding them that she was not entirely without power, even if the only way she could express her defiance was in wearing unsuitable gowns and spending her time in expensive frivolities.

Bronwen had no real desire to escape her fate. She certainly wanted to be Banrìgh one day, and if she had to marry anyone it might as well be Donncan, who was as handsome as any man she had ever seen, and kind, courteous, and generally good-natured as well. She certainly did not want to accept everyone else's plans for her meekly, however. As far as she was concerned, it was good for Donncan to worry occasionally, and as for her uncle Lachlan, she had never forgiven him for loading her mother with chains and keeping her captive, or for rendering her mute, a cruel and imaginative punishment that saw the former Banrìgh a mere servant to the witches she had once persecuted.

Her lips lifted in a secret smile. "I was no' entirely naked," she protested with a little look of mischief at Donncan. "I had quite a few artfully placed frills, I assure ye. And it was quite dark. I had Maura snuff a few candles first."

"I think that only made it worse," Donncan said, responding to her roguish smile despite himself.

She shrugged one bare shoulder. "I swear the tattlemongers would whisper if all I did was sit in my boudoir and sew a fine seam. I may as well do something worth gossiping about."

Donncan turned and seized her by the arm, looking down into her eyes. "Bronwen, ye ken I do no' care what the court gossips about, as long as there is no truth in it. . . ."

She looked away. "Well, my ladies and I did swim in the pool, though we were no' really naked . . . no' entirely."

"I do no' care about ye swimming, naked or no'," he said impatiently. "It is the other things they say."

"What other things?" she said, although she knew.

He took a deep breath. "That ye take lover after lover, discarding them when they no longer amuse ye."

"And whom am I meant to have taken as my lover?" she said scornfully. "That poor boy ye scowled at so fiercely afore? Am I meant to have taken him to my bed?"

"O' course I do no' think ye've taken Fymbar o' Blèssem to

bed! He's little more than a lad, though it's clear he's smitten with ye."

"Then who? Who are these so-called lovers o' mine?"

Donncan's grip tightened. "I have heard Alta, the Fairgean ambassador, is often seen in and out o' your rooms, and has brought ye many fine gifts."

"On behalf o' my uncle Nila," she answered furiously. "Except for a barrel o' seasquill wine and a platter o' raw fish which he brought me after I expressed curiosity about the cuisine o' my mother's people. *I* thought it was very kind o' him."

"So he has no' . . ." Donncan hesitated, finding it hard to put what he wanted to know into words.

"Nay, he has no'," Bronwen replied icily. "He has three wives and half a dozen concubines o' his own, and far too much sense to try to seduce his king's niece. I do enjoy speaking with him, however. He has told me many fascinating things about the Fairgean and about my mother's family."

"So all ye do is talk?"

"Aye, all we do is talk. I would like to gamble with him too, as he is said to be clever at cards and dice, but he, being very stuffy and proper, does no' think it would be seemly."

Donncan's breath came out in a sigh. "What about your cavalier, then?" he asked, in a slightly mollified tone. "Ye certainly seemed to be enjoying dancing with him earlier."

"He's a very pretty dancer," Bronwen replied.

Donncan snorted. "A bit o' a show-off."

"That's all the rage now," Bronwen replied, nose in the air. "The young bloods compete with each other to show the highest kicks and leaps, the fastest spins. If ye had spent more time at court, ye would ken this."

"He certainly seemed to wish to do more than *speak* with ye."

"Maybe so, but that does no' mean I wish the same," she answered angrily. "When did it become a crime to enjoy dancing?"

He drew her close. "Bronwen, can ye no' understand how I feel? It is less than two months until we are to be married. Do ye think I like hearing such tales about ye?"

"Do ye think I like having such tales told about me?" she countered.

"But ye seem to positively delight in stirring the scandal broth! Look at what ye are wearing!"

She gave a little twirl. "Do ye no' like it? I designed it myself."

"It's quite scandalous," Donncan said. "It looks as if ye wear naught beneath it."

"That was the effect I was trying to achieve."

"But why! No wonder they . . ." He stopped and took a breath, making a visible effort to control his tongue.

"Call me a whore?" Bronwen said pleasantly. "I thought if my own mother-in-law was to name me such, I may as well look the part."

Donncan was taken aback. "I beg your pardon?"

"Your mother," Bronwen clarified. "Said I looked like a whore. Ye ken how much I wish to please your mother. I would no' like the court to think she exaggerated."

"My mother said that to ye?"

"No' to me," Bronwen answered, smiling still, though her fingers were clenched hard on the stem of her glass. "O' course no'! Nay, she said it behind my back, o' course. I have it on the best o' authorities. I made a special effort today to make sure I looked the part."

"I'm sure my mother said no such thing," Donncan said angrily.

"She has said as much, though in slightly more moderate language, to my face," Bronwen replied. "Why should I doubt she would say so behind my back? Though I suppose ye are right. I should no' believe all I hear, should I?"

"Nay," Donncan said. "Perhaps ye should have gone to speak to her, and ask her, no matter how difficult that might be, as I am here asking ye."

For the first time, color rose in Bronwen's cheeks. She looked up at Donncan, then looked away. After a moment she said lightly, "I assure ye, I have done naught to cause ye any shame, my laird."

His grip on her wrist relaxed, and he ran his hand up her bare arm. "I'm glad to hear that," he said softly. "As I am sorry to hear ye were bored without me. I will do my best to remedy that."

He bent his head and kissed her.

Bronwen's breath caught. His kiss deepened, his thumbs tracing small circles on her arms. When at last he lifted his head to brush a kiss across her temple, she looked up at him with heavy-lidded eyes. "I would be most grateful," she murmured. "Ye ken I am very easily bored."

He grinned. "Ye witch," he said admiringly. "What am I to do with ye?"

She slipped her arms up about his neck. "Kiss me again?"

He obliged, sliding his hand up under the heavy fall of hair to find the soft nape of her neck. Suddenly his fingers stiffened, and he drew away from her.

Bronwen opened her eyes. "Donncan?"

He was frowning, his mouth grim. "What is this?" he demanded.

"What?" She twisted, but could see nothing, for his hand was gripping her by the back of her hair.

"Ye have cut off a lock o' your hair, here at the back, where none can see. Why?"

For a moment her poise deserted her. "What? My hair?"

"Ye have cut some off, here at the back. I can feel the tuft where it is shorn. Who did ye give it to? Some paramour o' yours?"

She drew away angrily. "Nay! O' course no'!"

"Who? Who did ye give it to?"

"That is none o' your business," she retorted, then tried to recover. "Indeed, ye are being foolish. Ye think I would cut off a lock o' hair to give as some kind o' love token? O' course I have no'. I had a knot there, that is all, that I was too impatient to comb out."

"Ye expect me to believe that? Ye have a bevy o' handmaidens who would gladly spend all day combing out your hair for ye. Ye think I do no' ken your hair has never afore been touched by scissors? Ye would no more chop out a knot than ye would hack off a finger because o' a hangnail. Nay, ye had some other reason for cutting off a lock o' your hair. Who? Who did ye give it to?" He shook her.

Bronwen took a deep breath and put up her hand to ease the strain of his furious grip on her hair. "Nay, nay, ye wrong me. I was cross, impatient. I could no' bear them tugging at my hair, so I cut it out, that's all. . . . Please let me go!"

Suddenly someone came leaping out of the darkness towards them, fist swinging.

"Unhand my lady!" he cried. "Bronwen, my darling, are ye hurt?"

Instinctively Donncan spun on his foot, releasing Bronwen's hair and swinging her behind him. It all happened so fast Bronwen tripped and almost fell. She grabbed at Donncan's arm to save herself, accidentally inhibiting him as he tried to block the blow that smashed into his jaw. The Prionnsa staggered, his wings flying up to save him from falling, and then leaped at his attacker furiously.

Bronwen's hands flew to her mouth as they crashed over the little table. Donncan's arm came back, then punched viciously, his fist connecting with a sickening thump. She saw a glimpse of green silken breeches and doublet and knew at once who their attacker was.

"Mat, ye fool, stop it!" she cried. "Ye canna hit the Prionnsa! Ye'll be discharged at best. Donn, stop it! Please!"

They did not listen. Over they went in a grunting tangle of flying fists and knees. Bronwen yelled at them again, then seized the jug of Merry May punch and threw it over them. The shock made them pause for a moment. Mathias was straddling Donncan, one hand pressing his head into the ground, the other drawn back to strike. He glanced at Bronwen wildly, his face dripping with wine, soggy woodruff blossoms snagged in his hair. "Stop!" she cried. "Ye must stop this nonsense!"

But in that instant of hesitation, Donncan threw Mathias off and got him in a headlock, grinding his face into the dirt. Mathias heaved wildly until he managed to throw the Prionnsa off, then he rolled and got to his feet, spitting out grass and dirt and blood. Donncan came at him again, and Bronwen saw a sudden flash of silver as the Yeoman drew the little dagger he wore at his waist. It was only a short knife, used for carving meat off the roast and spearing food to bring to the mouth, but like all blades worn by a trained soldier, it was wickedly sharp.

Bronwen screamed. "Donn! Look out!"

Donncan seized the swinging knife hand and somersaulted over it, twisting Mathias's arm. As he landed, his foot slipped in the sticky puddle of punch, and he staggered. The knife was wrenched sideways, plunging deep into the Yeoman's stomach.

Mathias choked and staggered, then turned a look of such bewilderment upon Bronwen that tears sprang into her eyes. He dropped to his knees, both hands going to cradle the knife hilt protruding from his abdomen.

"Nay! Stop! Do no' pull it out!" Donncan gasped, reaching out one hand to him.

But it was too late. Mathias had dragged out the knife. It slid free with a great gush of blood. Mathias looked down at his bloody hands, his red-soaked shirt, looked up once more at Bronwen, then pitched forward on to his face. When she and Donncan together tried to lift him up, it was too late. He was dead.

The High Table

Lachlan raised an eyebrow at his page, who came forward and kneeled, pouring more wine punch into his jewel-encrusted goblet.

"Thank ye," the Rìgh said.

His page nodded and rose, stepping back to his place behind the Rìgh's chair. "No sign o' any trouble yet," Iseult said softly, leaning her head close to her husband's.

"Nay, everyone seems as merry as they should be on May Night. I am glad we didna cancel the feast, as Dillon thought we should."

"It would have caused a lot o' talk," Iseult said. "I think ye are right: we have a better chance o' discovering any plot to assassinate ye if we do no' scare the killer away by showing we suspect anything. If he thinks we ken naught, he will be less cautious and more likely to show his hand."

"She," Lachlan said.

"Aye, that's right. She."

"It may be nothing — ye ken that," Lachlan said very softly. "It is but a dream, and one that Olwynne can barely remember anyway."

Iseult sighed. "I do no' like this . . . this *fear* that has come into our lives, with this dream o' Olwynne's. I do no' like looking at all our friends and servants and wondering who it is that seeks to kill ye. I *hate* worrying that I might lose ye!"

"We never ken the time or means o' our own death," Lachlan said somberly. "Ye may die tomorrow, struck down by lightning, or —"

"Hit by a runaway carriage —"

"Or ye could worry yourself to death."

They looked at each other and smiled ruefully.

"What long faces!" a merry voice called. "Who's died?"

Lachlan's face lit up. "Dide!" he cried. "Welcome!"

Didier Laverock, the Earl of Caerlaverock, came up smiling. He was dressed in old worsted breeches, rather worn at the knees and seat, and had a battered old guitar slung over his shoulder. His dark, curly hair was pulled back into a messy ponytail beneath a rakish crimson cap with a long green feather stuck in the brim. His long coat was shabby indeed.

Lachlan leaped to his feet and pulled Dide in for a close embrace, slapping his back in delight. "When did ye ride in?" he demanded.

"Just now," Dide replied. "Forgive me my courtly attire. If I'd taken the time to change, I'd have missed the feast altogether."

"Ye'd be welcome in your nightgown and cap," Lachlan exclaimed. "Come, have a drink, man, and join us. Tell us all your news!"

"Gladly," the earl replied. He unslung his guitar, propping it against his chair as he sat down. He looked about him with interest as the Rìgh's page poured him a cup of ale. Dide quaffed it and held out his cup for another. "Where's Beau?" he asked.

"She'll be at the witches' feast," Iseult said. "I expect she'll walk up later to have a cup o' wine with us. Nina will be here soon too, to sing to us as usual. What are ye doing here? I thought ye were in Tìrsoilleir still."

"I was, but thought I should come home and report to ye myself. I dinna trust my mail to come to ye untampered. Quite a few o' my missives seem to have gone astray, and I wanted to make sure all was well with ye. I've been hearing rumors . . ."

"What?" Lachlan demanded.

Dide had been scanning the crowd about them as he spoke. His keen eyes had noted the blue-clad guards standing at attention behind the high table and patrolling the perimeters of the square, and he had lifted a hand in greeting to Dillon, who, as always, wore his cursed sword at his belt.

"It looks as if ye may have been hearing some o' them yourself," Dide said softly. "Prepared for trouble, are we?"

"Always," Iseult said.

Dide smiled at her. "I ken ye are," he answered, "but Lachlan is no' usually so well-guarded in his own garden. What's up?"

"Why do ye no' tell us your news first?" Lachlan suggested. "Yours may have bearing on ours, though I hope no'."

"Tìrsoilleir is in turmoil," Dide said bluntly. "The new Fealde has the common people all stirred up with religious fervor, and Elfrida has done naught to rein her in. She has no' been to Bride at all this year, staying in Arran the whole time, so it is as if they do no' have a ruler at all."

Iseult raised her brows. "That is no' like Elfrida. She does no' like Arran much, and is always trying to make Iain stay with her in Bride."

"While Iain loves the marshes and is never happy for long away from them," Lachlan said ruefully. He was very close to the Prionnsa of Arran, counting him as one of his closest friends and advisers. Both were glad their sons had grown up to be such good friends, and had taken turns to foster Donncan and Neil, so that the centuries-long feud between the MacCuinn and the MacFóghnan clans could finally be laid to rest.

"Elfrida has never been a very confident ruler, particularly when it meant standing up to the Fealde. I guess her early indoctrination by the Bright Soldiers in the Black Tower was no' so easily shaken off," Dide said. "Although she paid lip service to the Pact o' Peace and the doctrine o' free worship, I do no' think she ever actually enforced it. This past year, though . . . I have heard o' persecution o' witches again, and I myself have listened to the Fealde preach against us from the pulpit. The Parliament does as it pleases, and all o' them now are the Fealde's men and her puppets."

"Is that so?" Lachlan frowned.

"That is no' the worst o' it. The Fealde is hinting at another holy war. She refutes the tale that ye are the warrior angel as heresy and sacrilege, and exhorts the people o' Tìrsoilleir to rise up and overthrow ye."

"What!" Lachlan slammed his cup down on the table, spilling his wine. "She dares preach treason?"

Faces all along the high table and on the dance floor turned to stare at him, including Elfrida and Iain, who were seated a little farther along the table, with their son Neil beside them, picking unhappily at his roast swan. Iain smiled at the sight of Dide and rose at once to come to greet him. Elfrida rose too, pausing to speak quietly to her son before following her husband.

Dide lowered his voice and said quickly, "Ye should ken also that Elfrida has taken one o' the Fealde's closest supporters as her personal spiritual adviser. I believe he travels with her everywhere."

Lachlan had time only to raise his eyebrow and glance at the black-clad man following a few steps behind Elfrida before Iain was upon them, greeting Dide warmly. In repose, the Prionnsa of Arran's face was thoughtful, even melancholy, but when he was animated, as he was now, deep lines about his mouth and eyes crinkled charmingly. He had a rueful, self-deprecating way of speaking and a habit of pausing before he spoke, as if to consider his words carefully.

"We have no' seen ye in an age," he was saying now. "Good it is indeed to see ye!"

Elfrida came up behind him and added her greetings to the jongleur-turned-earl, her eyes assessing him swiftly even as she smiled and inquired after his health. Elfrida had once been a pretty, fair woman, but her looks had faded. She was very thin, so that all her features had sharpened, and there were blue hollows under her eyes and a deep line between her fair, almost nonexistent brows. As usual, she was dressed in a heavy gown of some dark stuff, made up high to her chin and covering her arms to the wrists.

Dide was an accomplished dissembler, after spending most of his life in the secret service of the Rìgh, and he gave no hint that he had just that moment been discussing her affairs. By inquiring after her son, he was soon hearing an eager account of Neil's activities and accomplishments.

All the while, the black-clad pastor stood behind Elfrida's elbow, his hands folded before him in a pious attitude. He was all angles, with sharp elbows and knees jutting against the heavy fabric of his robe, and a chin like a spear point. His nose was pointed too, and he had oddly long nails for a man, very clean and white and carefully polished. His hair was pale and cut as close to his scalp as scissors could reach, while his pointed chin positively gleamed, it had so recently been shaved.

"And no plans for matrimony as yet?" Dide asked Elfrida at last. "Or do ye plan to look for a bride for Neil while here at the royal court? Most o' the first families will be here for Donncan and Bronwen's wedding, I imagine."

A shadow fell over Elfrida's face. "Nay, no plans as yet. Neil is still only young."

"He's twenty-four, a man grown," Lachlan said, drawing his brows together. Having married young himself, Lachlan was an enthusiastic advocate for early weddings. "He'll be getting into mischief if ye do no' marry him off soon."

"Neil does no' wish to marry," Elfrida said coolly.

"What, no' ever? We canna allow that! He's the sole heir to both Arran and Tìrsoilleir. Imagine the trouble there'd be if he doesna breed up at least one heir. Nay, nay, ye canna allow that, Elfrida! Iain?"

Iain cast a glance at his wife. "Och, he just hasna met the right girl yet, has he, dearling?"

Some note of strain in his voice made Dide look at him more closely, then glance over at Neil. He had risen and was pacing the dance floor, clearly looking for someone. The others followed his gaze and there was a moment's silence; then Iseult said in her forthright way, "I hope Cuckoo's no' still carrying a torch for Bronwen, Elfrida. That would be very foolish, since she and Donncan will be jumping the fire together in a matter o' months."

"Neil and Bronwen have always been very close," Elfrida answered defensively.

"Aye, maybe so, but yearning after another man's wife has never brought anything but trouble," Iseult answered sternly. "Lachlan is right. He is twenty-four now and it is high time he was married and thinking o' setting up a family. We must give some thought as to a suitable wife for him."

Elfrida's lips shut into a tight line. She did not answer. Behind her the pastor clasped and unclasped his hands.

"I do no' think Neil is ready for marriage just yet," Iain said placatingly. "These childhood crushes sometimes take a while to cool. I'm sure, given time . . ."

"There's no harm in introducing the lad to a few pretty lasses," Lachlan said. "Particularly ones with a pretty dowry and a few strategic connections as well. Ye must remember the lad will one day have to rule both Arran and Tìrsoilleir. He'll need a girl who has been brought up to fill such a position. How old are Fymbar's sisters now, Iseult? One o' the banprionnsachan o' Blèssem would do very nicely, since their lands lie so close to Arran—"

"Neil is no' interested in those towheaded ninnies," Elfrida said flatly. "We stayed with them on our way here and he could no' have been more bored!"

Lachlan raised his brow. "Busty blondes no' to his taste? Well, what about that raven-haired lass from Carraig. What's her name, Iseult?"

"Nathalie NicSeinn, do ye mean?"

"Aye, that's the one. They say she is quite lovely, as well as clever and accomplished. I wonder if she plans to come to the wedding? Perhaps a subtle hint to the MacSeinn . . ."

"Thank ye, but I do no' think that will be necessary," Elfrida said, rising to her feet, two spots of color burning on her thin cheeks. "If ye will excuse me . . ." And she went swiftly away towards her son, who had given up searching the dance floor and was now standing by himself, staring off into the shadowy gardens. She took his arm and tried to lead him back to their seats, but he shook her off and went plunging off into the garden. Elfrida stood staring after him, her pastor behind her like an elongated shadow.

"I'm sorry," Iain was saying. "Ye've struck a sore spot, I'm afraid. Indeed, we're very worried about Neil. It's true what ye said, Iseult. He is still rather dazzled by Bronwen and steadfastly refuses to have anything to do with any other girl. Donncan kens, o' course. It's a wonder they are still such good friends. If Bronwen did no' keep treating Neil like a favorite younger brother, it would be a different story. Elfrida finds it upsetting, though. It has made Neil very unhappy these past few years, and she naturally feels for him. I'm sure once Bronwen and Donncan actually tie the knot . . ." His voice trailed away.

"Let us hope so," Iseult said neutrally. She laid her hand on Lachlan's arm, for the Rìgh was scowling and looked as if he might burst into intemperate speech.

Dide was just stepping in with a smooth question about the past hunting season in Arran when a sudden disturbance at the far side of the dance floor attracted all their attention. There were cries of alarm, then a shrill scream that sent waves of unease through the crowd. The music came to a jangling halt, and all the dancers stopped mid-step and drew back, whispering and pointing.

"What has happened?" Lachlan cried and strode forward. Dillon at once leaped up and moved to stand beside him, his hand on his sword hilt.

Iseult rose also, her face draining of color as she saw Donncan coming slowly in from the gardens, his face grey with shock, his hands and clothes heavily stained with blood. He held a dagger out before him as if it was a hissing snake.

Behind him stumbled Bronwen. Her gauzy skirt was marked with a dreadful wet black patch in front, and she walked with both her hands held out before her, staring with fascination at her bloodstained palms.

"He's dead," she said to the crowd, her eyes blackly dilated. "He's dead."

The Interrogation

"No' Neil!" Elfrida screamed. "No' my Cuckoo?"

Bronwen turned slowly and stared at her in bafflement. "No," she said. "No' Neil."

Neil came hurrying out of the garden, throwing an exasperated glance at his mother. "What is it? What has happened?" he demanded.

Bronwen saw him and her face crumpled. She ran to him and he enclosed her in his arms. She began to weep, stammering incoherently.

"What in Eà's green blood has happened?" Lachlan demanded also, striding forward, his wings spreading. Iseult was close behind him, her hand going automatically to the *reil* at her belt.

The Blue Guards had closed ranks about the dance floor, responding to the slightest jerk of Captain Dillon's head.

"It was an accident," Donncan said. His voice shook slightly. He looked towards his father with frowning eyes and lifted his bloody hands in what looked like a gesture of appeal. "Indeed, I didna mean to kill him."

"Who? Who's dead?" Lachlan demanded.

Donncan looked at Bronwen, shuddered, and looked away. "Mat."

"Mathias o' the guards?" Captain Dillon demanded. "Mathias Bright-Eyed?"

Donncan nodded. Captain Dillon sent some of the guards off at a run, seizing lanterns from the poles to light their way, then came to stand before Donncan, searching his face with hard eyes. "What happened, Your Highness?"

"He attacked me," Donncan said, outrage firming his voice. "Without any warning at all. He just came leaping out o' the darkness and punched me!" He indicated his bruised face with one hand.

"Is that so?" Captain Dillon responded with a quick glance at Bronwen. Even though his voice was carefully neutral, Donncan flushed vividly.

"Aye, that's so," he said furiously. "I do no' ken why! He pulled a knife on me!"

"Is that what happened, Your Highness?" Captain Dillon asked Bronwen.

She gave a great shudder but nodded.

Iseult had come flying forward and was examining her son frantically. "Are ye hurt?" she demanded. "He did no' stab ye, did he?"

"Nay," Donncan said. "He tried, but I used his own arm to swing over and away, like so."

He demonstrated, and Iseult nodded. "A good response," she said approvingly. "What happened then?"

"I slipped as I landed. There was wine or something spilled on the grass. He was trying to recover, maybe to try to stab me again. The knife just twisted when I fell. . . . It went straight in. I'm sorry! I never meant . . . it all just happened so fast."

Neil had drawn Bronwen to sit down and had wrapped his plaid about her shoulders. He passed the Banprionnsa a glass of wine, but Bronwen's hands were shaking so much she could not take it. Instead, Neil held it to her lips. Bronwen's chattering teeth rattled on the rim, but she managed to gulp a mouthful and her shivering eased a little.

"Can ye tell us what happened, Bronny?" Neil asked gently.

"It was just as Donncan said," she whispered.

"But what possible reason would Mathias Bright-Eyed have for attacking His Highness?" Captain Dillon asked coolly.

"He . . . he was jealous," Bronwen said, her voice catching. "He thought . . . he wanted . . ." She could not go on.

Iseult had gone to Donncan and drawn him to sit down too, giving him a glass of wine to drink as she quickly looked over his injuries, which consisted primarily of a rapidly swelling eye, a split lip, grazed knuckles, and a bruised jaw.

"Where is Johanna?" Iseult asked. "We need a healer here. Donncan is sore hurt. Should Johanna no' be here?"

"I must go and view the body," Captain Dillon said. "He was one o' my men. Your Majesty, I beg o' ye, retire to your chambers. It is just this sort o' confusion that an assassin may seize upon. I will order my men to keep close and will return just as soon as I have seen for myself that Mathias is dead."

Donncan looked up at his father. "We tried to rouse him. It was no good."

Lachlan looked around at the shocked and curious crowd, his jaw thrust forward angrily; then he said, "Come, let us go back to the palace. Ye must change out o' those bloodstained clothes and bathe, and let the healers look ye over and make sure all is well. Dillon, attend me as soon as ye can! Call the Privy Councillors. We must hear the whole story."

"It was an accident," Donncan said pleadingly. "I never meant to kill him."

"O' course no'," Lachlan answered. "Come, where are the Banprionnsa Bronwen's ladies? Roy! Send a message to the witches' tower. Tell Isabeau and Gwilym and Nina and bid them attend me."

Neil had been crouched beside Bronwen's chair, holding her hand between both of his. She was struggling with tears. He helped her to her feet, and she leaned on his arm, hiding her face in his shoulder.

Out of the crowd came Thunderlily, her hand outstretched. Bronwen let go of Neil's arm and seized Thunderlily's, her face crumpling. The Celestine passed her arm around Bronwen's waist and helped the drooping figure up the steps and into the palace. Neil watched them go, then opened his hand, looking down at the blood smears on his skin. His face was unreadable.

Elfrida was at once by his side, her face pale, her eyes glittering with something that could have been excitement, or fear, or distress. This time Neil did not shake her off but let his mother comfort him and guide him away. Behind them went the black shadow, his cold eyes raking the crowd with contempt.

*　　*　　*

Bronwen felt very odd.

It was not as if she had never seen men die before. She had been present at the bloodiest battlefield in living memory, the Battle of Bonnyblair, when the Fairgean had brought the power of tidal wave and volcano against their human enemies. Bodies had been tumbled in the surf like flotsam, and afterwards the decks of their ship had been lined with row after row of the bloody wounded. Her nursemaid had been cut down before her eyes, and she had seen her mother sing her enemies to death, including her own father, Bronwen's grandfather, the dreaded king of the Fairgean.

All that was a very long time ago, though. Bronwen could hardly remember it. It was like it had happened to some other girl, in a tale of long, long ago, far, far away.

Mathias, though, had died right there before her, staring up at her in unspeakable terror and bewilderment. She could smell his blood in her nostrils and feel its stickiness on her skin. Twenty minutes ago, his arm had been about her waist, his breath had been on her ear. She had mocked him, she had scorned him, and she had driven him to the reckless act that had seen him die at the hand of her betrothed. Bronwen could not see how she could wriggle away from self-blame this time, and by the cold, distant look on Donncan's face, the way he could not bear to look at her, she guessed he blamed her too.

Bronwen could not stop her legs from shaking. They trembled so violently the jeweled heels of her silver sandals beat out a quick tattoo on the ground. Her knees knocked. Her hands quivered. She clenched them tightly together, between her knees, and pressed her heels down hard. She tried not to see the strange, blank look in Mathias's eyes as he fell down to the ground. It kept repeating, though, before her eyes, and she felt hysteria rising like nausea in her throat.

The councillors talked and argued among themselves. Bronwen, who was normally quite interested in court politics, could barely understand a word. It seemed some thought Donncan should stand trial to show that even the Rìgh's son was not exempt from the new judicial processes the Rìgh had fought so hard to introduce. Others argued that there was no need, that it was clearly a dreadful accident, that Bronwen herself was witness to there being no malice aforethought. They questioned her again and again, but Bronwen could not answer.

Then Thunderlily was standing before her, facing the councillors, humming deep in her throat. They needed no translator. Thunderlily's meaning was evident in her blazing eyes. They let Bronwen go, and the Celestine helped her up the stairs to her boudoir, washed the sticky residue of blood from her body, and held her hand until she at last began to calm. The last thing Bronwen saw was the strange, crystalline eyes of the Celestine, bending down close over her, and the last thing she heard was the low, soft humming, deep in Thunderlily's throat, as comforting as a cat purring. Then she slept.

"He was in love with Bronwen—that's why he attacked me!" Donncan said, goaded into fury. "Ye were all there. I saw ye watch as he danced with her and whisper behind your hands. And ye saw how he tried to hold Bronwen back when she came to me. He must've been half-mad with jealousy, to attack me that way."

He saw the Lord Chancellor frown and tried to moderate his tone.

"I'm sorry for it," he said. "I wish it had no' happened."

"There can be no blame attached to the Prionnsa," the Master of Horse said. "Mathias Bright-Eyed was partial to a dram—we all ken that. He was drinking heavily tonight. I noted it myself."

Donncan felt tired and sore and melancholy. He could still remember feeling the tuft of shorn hair at the base of Bronwen's skull. It troubled him greatly that it was this that haunted him and not the easy way the dagger had slid into Mathias's body. He closed his mind to it. He had not told the Privy Council about the lovelock. He wanted no more talk about Bronwen.

The court would be seething with gossip, though. He knew that. He shut his eyes and pressed his fingertips into his aching temples. He heard his mother rise and suggest he be left in peace, to rest and recover, then the rustle of silken clothes and the click of jeweled heels on the parquetry floor as the courtiers all departed. Then he sensed rather than heard her, for Iseult always moved with the silent grace of a snow lion. She sat down beside him and took his hand.

"Were ye two quarreling?" she asked.

Donncan moved his wings restlessly. "We had words," he admitted.

"What about?"

He made a vague gesture with his hand. "I'm sure ye can guess."

"How could ye be so foolish!" Lachlan exploded. "To fight a duel over your betrothed with one o' the royal guard! At the May Day feast! How are we meant to smooth this over?"

"I wasna dueling!" Donncan protested. "Ye think I would fight a duel at a feast in your garden? With a Yeoman? O' course I wouldna do such a thing. I'm telling ye, Mat attacked me. I didna even ken who it was at first. He just came at me out o' the darkness."

"With his knife drawn?" Iseult asked.

Donncan shook his head. "Nay, he drew that later."

"He must've been mad!" Lachlan paced restlessly, his hands tucked behind him, under his wings. "Ye both must have been mad!"

Angrily Donncan looked up to find his father glaring at him, his golden eyes as fierce as a gyrfalcon's.

"It's a bad business," Lachlan said. "So close to your wedding too. It's bound to cause a lot o' talk." He began to pace again, and Donncan heaved an involuntary sigh of relief to be free of that raking stare. "If only ye hadna killed him!"

"I didna mean to!" Donncan protested. "I told ye, it was an accident."

"Every gossipmonger at the court will have noted that he and Bronwen were dancing just afore ye killed him," Lachlan said angrily. "And the way they danced! Why is that girl such a hoyden?"

Donncan's temper frayed. "That is my wife-to-be who ye are referring to in such terms," he said icily. "I'll thank ye to keep your comments to yourself."

Lachlan's temper, never sweet, flared as quickly. "I'll speak in whatever way I please, thank ye very much! I was no' the one who killed one o' my very own bodyguards, in my own garden, in a quarrel over a girl who's little better than a strumpet!"

Donncan leaped to his feet, feeling the giddy rush of anger through his blood as hot and exciting as a dram of whisky.

"Ye canna deny that your wife-to-be has behaved in a very reprehensible manner," Lachlan said, trying to control his own temper. "She is no witch, to take lovers where and when she pleases. She is a banprionnsa o' the royal house, and soon to be wed. The whole time ye have been away, we have had to watch and say naught as she caused one scandal after another."

"Say naught! When ye call her a strumpet and a whore! Aye, she told me o' that tonight and angry and upset she was indeed. . . ."

"I beg your pardon?"

"I heard how ye and Mam have called her a whore. What do ye think—"

"What in Eà's name are ye talking about?"

"Are ye saying Mam didna say so? For Bronwen certainly believes she did."

"I suppose I may have," Iseult admitted, casting her mind back. "But only ever in private conversation, and I didna mean . . . Who told ye I had done so?"

"Bronwen did. She said she had it on the best o' authorities."

"Only Owein and Lewen were there, serving your father and I. Ye canna mean one o' them repeated what I said to Bronwen? I do no' believe it!"

"Ye should never have said such a thing," Donncan said furiously.

"I'm sorry, but I never meant—"

"It is no' your place to tell your mother how she should speak or behave," Lachlan roared. "Bronwen deserves every raised eyebrow and every snigger she gets. She is too much her mother's daughter. Did ye see what she was wearing tonight? She might as well have been naked."

"She only decided to dress that way after hearing what Mam had said about her," Donncan said. "She said if that is what Mam thinks o' her, she may as well dress the part."

Lachlan's eyes blazed. "How dare she! She said that to ye?"

"I never meant to hurt her feelings," Iseult said, both troubled and defensive. "I canna remember what I said. I think I was just commenting on the way she likes to stir up the hornet's nest. I never intended what I said to be repeated to her."

"She does dress like a whore," Lachlan said angrily. "I was afraid that gown—if ye can call it a gown—would just slide off her tonight, the way she was dancing. Held up with little more than a bit o' string, for Eà's sake! I'm sorry now that I ever arranged this marriage!"

All the anger suddenly drained out of Donncan. "So am I," he said and turned to sit down, resting his head on his arms.

Both Lachlan and Iseult froze. They exchanged a charged look over his bowed head. Then Iseult came to sit down next to him, laying her hand on his arm. "Are ye saying ye wish to break the engagement? I thought ye wanted it."

"It'll be no easy task to break it," Lachlan warned. "It was the key component o' the Pact o' Peace, remember? That sly, sneaky Fairgean ambassador does nothing but remind me o' how important this marriage is to King Nila. If ye decide to break it, it could mean war again."

"No need to remind me o' that," Donncan said in a muffled voice.

"Ye canna break it," Iseult said. "It is too important."

"But, *leannan*, if he doesna love her—"

"Love! He's been besotted with that wool-witted lassie since he was no' much more than a toddler!"

"Aye, but calf love is no' the same as the love a man feels for a woman."

"It is a good foundation," Iseult said. She turned back to her son. "Ye canna break the engagement now, Donncan. It is too close. The Fairgean are proud. They would see it as an insult. We canna risk another war with the sea faeries. The last one cost us too dearly."

"I ken, I ken."

"What is wrong? Did ye two quarrel tonight? Did ye interrupt something between her and this Yeoman? Is that why ye killed him?"

"I told ye! He attacked me, out o' the darkness. Bronwen and I were together . . ." Donncan sat up and twisted to face his parents. His eyes were red-rimmed.

"Doing what?"

"Talking." His voice was sullen.

"Just talking?"

Donncan did not answer.

"We need to ken what happened, Donn. The whole court will be afire with speculation. We must nip it in the bud, and soon."

"We were just talking," Donncan said.

"What was there in that to cause Mathias to attack ye?"

"We might have kissed a bit too."

"Might have? Did ye or didna ye?"

"We did," Donncan answered. "A bit."

"Well, that must've been oil on the flames," Lachlan said. "If this soldier thought he had some claim on Bronwen's affections."

Donncan did not answer. He rested his head in his hand, and squeezed his eyes shut.

"Donn needs to get to bed," Iseult said. "It has been an ordeal, this whole evening."

Lachlan frowned. "I'm no' finished yet. I must get to the bottom o' this sorry affair. We canna leave it to the morning."

Donncan made a sharp movement. "I've told ye what happened. Canna I just go, please?"

"Nay, ye may no'. We must make sure none suspect ye o' murder. We'll need to find witnesses, to prove what ye say is true. People who saw ye leave with Bronwen. People who can attest to Mathias Bright-Eyed's state o' mind. And I must say, we must also do what we can to scotch rumors o' any affair between Bronwen and this gallant o' hers. From now until the wedding, Bronwen's behavior must be impeccable."

Donncan gave a bitter snort. "Good luck," he answered.

There was a short silence. "Are ye saying ye believe there was some relationship between them?" Iseult demanded. "I had no' thought so. I watched them together and thought Bronwen cared no more for him than for any other o' her admirers. Are ye saying there was more? Was he her lover?"

"I dinna ken," Donncan said in utter misery.

"We canna risk a barley-child," Lachlan said. "Any child o' this marriage must be legitimate, else we'll have endless trouble and intrigue. I have worked too hard to bring peace to this land to see it thrown away by a lamb-brained lassie. We must make sure there is no doubt o' Bronwen's faithfulness, else there is no point to the wedding at all."

Donncan felt unutterably weary. "No point at all," he echoed.

"It is no small thing, to kill a man," Iseult said after a moment. "And there is no denying that Bronwen brought this tragedy upon us with her coquettishness. If she had no' encouraged that soldier, he would never have dared raise a hand against ye. But what's done is done. We must salvage what we can from this calamity. Breaking your engagement now would be very foolish."

Donncan thrust out his jaw. "Do I have any say in the matter? What o' my wishes, my needs?"

"Ye are the Crown Prionnsa!" Lachlan shouted, slamming his fist down on the table. "Do ye wish to bring down war upon our heads? Ye have a duty and a responsibility to your people and to your crown!"

Donncan stood up. "Aye, o' course, Your Majesty," he said coldly and bowed.

Olwynne stirred in her sleep, and Lewen stretched his arm across her back to soothe her. Suddenly she sat up, jerking him into full wakefulness.

"My blades must have blood," she said. Her voice was very deep and strange.

"What?"

"My blades must have blood."

"Go back to sleep, *leannan*," Lewen soothed her. "All will be well. Go back to sleep."

But even as Olwynne muttered in response and lay back down to fall immediately asleep again, Lewen knew that he lied. All was not well.

The Rowan Charm

For the first week after Lewen carved the bird for her, Rhiannon was happy. She did as the Keybearer had suggested and threw herself into her studies, puzzling over the books and scrolls she had been brought until the marks on the paper began to make sense, becoming words, and then sentences, and then stories.

She forced herself to eat the food they brought her, sharing her bread and fruit with the bluebird and teaching it to take tidbits from between her lips. She tried to remember the ahdayeh she had been taught on her travels with the witches, stretching and strengthening her body, and finding peace in the rhythmic, repetitive movements. She slept dreamlessly, the rowan charm held between her hands.

She had no visitors. As the days passed, each exactly the same as the day before, her happiness began to seep away and in its place rose a bitter acidic anxiety. Rhiannon tried to press it down, concentrating on the routine she had built herself, but it ate away at her composure with slow corrosive inexorableness.

She knew there was to be a May Day feast at the palace that Lewen was expected to attend. She knew her other friends would also be celebrating the coming of summer and that they might not find time to come to see her for a few days. They had all explained and apologized to her in advance, and she had tried not to feel lonely and neglected. Yet as the day of the feast passed, Rhiannon's anxiety grew so sharp she found she could not calm herself. In her hands she jerked and twisted her linen handkerchief until it tore, and she flung it down in disgust, but then she had nothing to keep her hands busy but themselves, and soon her nails and cuticles were torn and bleeding. She tried to sit but rocked back and forth, back and forth on her chair until she forced herself to stop, then found her foot beating a rapid tattoo on the floor.

So May Day passed. Even the little bluebird fled the cell, soaring out through the bars and away, so that Rhiannon was in despair, thinking it would never return. When it did at last, in the dim twilight of that endless day, it carried a little spray of lily of the valley for her. Rhiannon was comforted and put the flowers in the cup by her bed so she could smell them in the dark, and pretend she was lying in the meadows and not in a hard prison bed.

Even with Lewen's rowan charm clutched between her hands, Rhiannon slept badly that night. She dreamed of a great wheel spinning before her eyes, light and dark flashing past her as the spokes whirled around. She dreamed she heard bells ringing out, filling her ears with doom, and saw she stood on a scaffold, the black-hooded hangman drawing a sack down over her head. Rhiannon looked out wildly into the crowd, screaming Lewen's name with all her strength, but he was not there and then all her senses were muffled and she knew it was too late, this was the end. She woke up screaming and opened her eyes into the darkness, whispering, "Lewen, Lewen, where are ye?" Then her eyes closed again and she fell back into sleep.

She saw Lewen. He was asleep. He lay sprawled on his back, his dark curls tousled, a sheet drawn up to his hips. He shifted in his sleep, turning on his side and curling around close to the white naked body of another woman. Rhiannon saw the mass of curls flaming down the woman's bare back and breast and knew it was her enemy, the redheaded Banprionnsa. She cried out in agony. Olwynne opened her eyes and looked at her but did not see her. "My blades must have blood," she said in a voice as deep and ringing as a bell. "My blades must have blood."

Rhiannon watched Lewen soothe her back to sleep and felt tears spring to her eyes. "No, no," she sobbed. She turned and fled, as far and fast as she could. The darkness streamed past her, and then she felt the cold wind turn sharp in her hand and realized she was astride Blackthorn once more, the mare's mane cutting her palm. She cried aloud in relief and joy, and the mare whinnied in response. Rhiannon looked back, and saw a delicate silver string winding away behind her. The farther she flew, the tauter the string grew till it was tuned as tightly as any harp string, dragging at her heart until she thought it must snap or pluck her very heart out of her body. Rhiannon leaned into the wind, urging the mare to go faster, wanting to escape or die in the attempt.

"My blades must have blood," she remembered, and saw, or imagined, a scythe slicing down through her heartstring, severing it. Rhiannon saw, with great clarity, that she would indeed die then, or be lost. She pulled back on Blackthorn's mane, leaning back all her weight, and the winged mare slowed her headlong flight and hovered there in the starless abyss. "I want to live," Rhiannon said aloud. "Dark walkers spare me, I want to live."

With a great twang, the silver thread snapped her back into her bed. Rhiannon cried out at the shock of it. "Blackthorn!" she called. "Blackthorn!"

But all was quiet.

Rhiannon's hands smarted. She opened and shut them, the cuts on her palm throbbing. When she pressed her hands over her eyes to blot away her tears, the salt water seeped into the cuts, stinging them.

The next morning, she could not eat the cold porridge the guards brought her. All the nervous energy that had driven her to pace her cell was gone. She could barely find the strength to move from her bed to the chair or to turn the pages of the bestiary she had come to love so much. The bluebird perched on the edge of the bowl and pecked at the oatmeal, then flew about singing. Rhiannon watched it but did not smile.

The morning plodded on. At noon, the door grated open. Rhiannon turned her eyes that way. Lewen stood in the doorway. Olwynne stood close behind him, dressed like a banprionnsa in shimmering yellow silk and gold embroidered brocade. Rhiannon saw that she had dressed to look her best. Her skin glowed, and her hair was like rippling lava. Rhiannon was all too aware of her own dull hair and skin, her shadowed eyes and stinking prison garb.

"Rhiannon . . ." Lewen faltered over her name.

"Go on," she said.

"I am sorry. I find I am mistaken . . . in my feelings for ye. I should never . . . It was wrong o' me . . ." He could not go on. He cast one beseeching glance at her, then turned his eyes away.

Olwynne stepped forward. A wave of perfume washed over Rhiannon, making her feel suddenly dizzy. She clutched at an iron bedpost to steady herself.

"I ken ye and Lewen are lovers, and that ye consider yourself . . . affianced in some way. I'm sorry to have to say that Lewen finds himself mistaken in his feelings for ye. He hopes ye will understand that his feelings have changed, and that there are no hard feelings."

Rhiannon looked past her to Lewen. He would not meet her eyes. She said his name. He glanced at her but only for a second, shaking his head and backing away.

"I'm sorry," Olwynne said again, her voice shaking. "We must go. It'll only make it worse if we stay."

Rhiannon did not know if Olwynne spoke to her or to Lewen, but she straightened her back and stared Olwynne in the eye. "He is mine," she warned. "Do no' think ye can have him."

Her defiance strengthened the Banprionnsa.

"But I can," she said and stepped backwards, not taking her eyes off Rhiannon.

Even so, she was unprepared for the speed of Rhiannon's attack. With one leap Rhiannon crashed them both to the floor. Sitting astride the Banprionnsa, she seized two handfuls of the red curls and slammed Olwynne's head hard into the floor, lifted and slammed again. Olwynne screamed. Rhiannon would have slammed her head down again, but Lewen and the two guards were on her, dragging her away. One guard cuffed her hard across the ear, but she ignored the blow, leaping for Olwynne again, raking her nails down one cheek. Only with great difficulty did they restrain her, for she kicked and squirmed and fought against their hold.

Olwynne's dress was crushed and torn, her face was scored red, and her careful coiffure was in wild disarray. When she gingerly felt the back of her skull, her fingers came back blotched with blood. Lewen looked dazed with shock, while both the guards were grim faced and abjectly apologetic.

"Get every single one o' my hairs out o' her hands," Olwynne said icily. "I do no' want her using them for her sorcery."

Rhiannon's fingers were forced open, and the great tufts of Olwynne's hair prised free. Rhiannon was pleased when she saw how much she had torn out of the Banprionnsa's head, though she did not understand what Olwynne meant with her comment about sorcery. She stared at Olwynne with burning hatred as the Banprionnsa straightened her dress and hair, Lewen supporting her with one arm about her waist. When he looked at Rhiannon, it was with horror and disgust. Olwynne was able to say, "See, she is quite wild! I told ye how it would be."

Rhiannon struggled once more to be free, her eyes burning with tears she refused to shed. The guards held her still, and Lewen led Olwynne out the door and away. Rhiannon was flung back on the bed, then the door was slammed shut and locked and bolted. She turned over, bringing her knees to her chest, trying hard to breathe, waves of pain beating through her.

That night, when the surly bad-tempered guards brought Rhiannon her supper, she could not eat a bite. The bluebird pecked at the bread, then flew to her shoulder with a questioning chirrup. She lifted it off and put it on the chair back, already deeply scored from its sharp claws and beak, and went and lay down on her bed. The candle flame devoured the time rings scored upon the wax until at last the flame flickered out and she was left alone in the darkness again. She rolled over to press her hot, wet face into her pillow, and her fingers found the rowan charm under the pillow. Rhiannon hurled it away from her.

That night the ghost came to her again.

She stood at the foot of Rhiannon's bed, a white-faced woman dressed all in darkness. "Ye sought to keep me away," she said in a low, intense voice, "but ye canna, can ye? I have penetrated all your defenses."

Rhiannon, caught between sleep and wakefulness, sought desperately under her pillow for the rowan charm but could not find it.

"He has betrayed ye, your love, hasn't he? What is there left for ye in life now? Nothing. Nothing."

Rhiannon turned her head back and forth on the pillow, her eyes smarting. Her limbs felt weighted down with chains.

"Why do ye suffer this incarceration? Ye might as well be buried alive. Why do ye no' claw your way out? I would. I would never let a man use me so." The ghost's voice dropped even lower, growing sweet and persuasive. "If ye escape, if ye find your way free, I can help ye find power. If ye help me live again, if ye bring me a sweet young body to sacrifice, I will repay ye, I swear. I will make ye rich beyond your wildest dreams, I will give ye the power o' life and death over your enemies. I will teach ye all I ken o' the craft and cunning these witches guard so jealously. Ye want to conjure fire? I can teach ye."

Suddenly the room was illuminated so brightly Rhiannon cried out and flung her arm over her eyes. Imprinted upon her retina was the shape of a grinning skull with gaping eye hollows, stuck upon a curving stick of bone. Even when she blinked, the sizzling impression did not fade.

The low whisper went on as slowly the light in the room faded away. "Aye, I am dead. I am naught but bones and dust in some grave over the seas. I was no' even buried in my own land, the land o' my clan. I want to live again! We could help each other, we two. We are o' a kind."

Rhiannon forced her wooden tongue to shape the word *no*.

"If ye will no' help me, then ye are my enemy, and believe me, ye do no' wish to be that. Come. I ken ye could escape from here if ye tried. It is no' in your nature to be so meek and feeble. Kill these stupid guards o' yours and get yourself free. I ken ye are afraid o' what would happen then, but if ye help me, then ye need no' fear pursuit or retribution. I would make sure ye grow so strong, so powerful, that none dare touch ye."

"How?" Rhiannon whispered.

"First ye must help me back to life. Without life, without blood, I am still naught but bones and spirit. Once I am alive again . . ."

"Ye dead," Rhiannon said brutally. "Ye canna live again. Accept it."

"Never!" the ghost cried. A wind sprang up from nowhere, blasting Rhiannon's face with icy-cold air. Turning her face away, lifting her arm to protect herself, Rhiannon saw the wind whipping the ghost's long black hair about her face and sending the darkness eddying about her like mist.

"Close on twenty years now I have clung to my powers, when the void o' death has sought to suck them away. I canna hold on much longer. I must have life again! And if ye will no' help me, I shall take your life, and so I warn ye. Defy me and ye shall die. Help me, and I shall help ye."

"Help me to what?"

"Whatever ye want," the ghost said impatiently. "Life, freedom, power, revenge . . ."

"Revenge?" Rhiannon wondered aloud.

"Aye, on all those who have betrayed ye and imprisoned ye. We will have our revenge together. All ye need do is escape, and I will show ye the way forward."

"Escape," Rhiannon repeated and pressed the tears back into her eyes with icy fingers.

The next morning Fèlice came, laden down with fruit and flowers and wine. Rhiannon knew at once that she had heard the news. She looked pale and distressed.

"Oh, Rhiannon, I'm so sorry. I canna believe . . . I never would've thought . . ."

"I will throttle her till she dead." Rhiannon paced the floor, her hands balled into fists. "I will chop her up for dog food. How dare she? He mine! Lewen mine! I'll hang her up for the rats to chew on, I will, I will!"

"Oh, Rhiannon, I am so very sorry. I really thought . . . It seems so unlike Lewen!"

"She has ensorcelled him," Rhiannon spat. "I'll flay her alive, the bitch!"

"Oh, surely no'? She canna have. It's no' allowed. The Coven says . . . That's compulsion, a spell like that. It's taking away free will. The Banprionnsa could never do such a thing."

"She could and she has," Rhiannon said with conviction. "Just wait until I get out o' here! I'll kill the skinny witch and rip her to bits. We'll see whose quarters are thrown to the city dogs!"

"Oh, Rhiannon, ye canna speak so! She's the daughter o' the Rìgh! They can hang, draw, and quarter ye just for speaking so. Ye must be still! Do no' be so angry."

"Do no' be so angry! What ye want me to do, cry? Weep like

a baby? I won't, I won't!" Rhiannon cried, even as the tears poured down her cheeks. She dashed them away and went on, almost incoherently. "I willna cry, I willna, no! I willna let her have him. He mine! He mine!"

Then the tears overwhelmed her and she flung herself down on the bed and sobbed wildly. Fèlice kneeled beside her and tried to comfort her, but it was no use. Rhiannon wept and pounded her pillow and tore at it with her teeth until the feathers flew. All Fèlice could do was try to shield her from the curious eye that appeared at the peephole in the door.

At last Rhiannon's sobs shuddered away. She sat up, thrusting Fèlice's hand away, and turned her hot, swollen face towards her with a grimace. "If ye ever tell anyone that I cried . . ."

"I ken, I ken, ye'll grind my bones for bread," Fèlice said, trying to joke. She got up and moved away to the table, pouring Rhiannon some water from the jug there and dampening the facecloth so she could press it to her tear-ravaged eyes. "I am so sorry, Rhiannon," she said again, speaking very gently. "I thought . . . I hoped ye would no' care so much. I never would've thought Lewen could be such a bastard. Ye're better off without him."

To her dismay, Rhiannon was crying again, swift silent tears that poured down her face. She licked them from her upper lip and covered her eyes with her hand.

"Nay, he mine," she muttered. "We promised. Me no' give him up."

Fèlice did not know what to say. She thought of the Lewen she had seen that morning, his arm about Olwynne's waist, their fingers entwined, their eyes fixed upon each other's faces. It was as if they could not bear to have even an inch of air between them. Then there was Donncan and Bronwen, due to be married in six weeks, standing as stiff and cold and polite as if they were strangers while all about them swirled rumour and speculation, visible as smoke. Between the two couples, the gossipmongers were having a field day.

"Ye will no' have heard the other big news," Fèlice said, seeking to distract Rhiannon. "There was a death last night, at the palace. His Highness, Prionnsa Donncan, accidentally killed one o' the Blue Guards. We were no' there, o' course—

we were at the Theurgia's party—but we heard all about it this morning. They say the soldier that was killed was a great admirer o' Her Highness, Banprionnsa Bronwen, and was quite mad with jealousy. Ye ken His Highness only returned from his travels yesterday? He's been away months apparently, and the Banprionnsa has been amusing herself in his absence with a dalliance or two. Prionnsa Owein says she is even more o' a flirt than I."

Fèlice giggled, then recollected herself, recounting the rest of the tale with greater sobriety. Rhiannon barely listened, so preoccupied was she with her own problems, until she caught the word "Yeoman" and it dawned on her that the Crown Prionnsa Donncan had apparently done exactly what she had done—killed one of the Rìgh's own guards.

"So why is he no' in prison too?" Rhiannon demanded.

Fèlice looked surprised. "Why . . . because it was self-defense, I suppose. Mathias attacked *him*."

"The Yeoman I killed attacked my mother," Rhiannon reminded her. "He would've killed her too. So why am I in prison for months and months, and this prionnsa o' yours walks free?"

Fèlice fidgeted with her sash. "I dinna ken," she admitted. "I mean, ye couldna put His Highness in jail!"

"Why no'? He killed a man too, a Blue Guard, just like me."

"Aye, but it was an accident."

"How do ye ken?"

"He said so, and Her Highness the Banprionnsa Bronwen too."

"How do ye ken they do no' lie?"

"He's the Crown Prionnsa. He wouldna lie," Fèlice argued, looking harassed. "We all ken him! He wouldna murder one o' his father's own guards."

"No' even if the guard was trying to steal his lover away?" Rhiannon demanded. "Ye told me the guard who attacked the Prionnsa was mad with jealousy. How do ye ken the Prionnsa was no' the one driven mad? If he thought the Blue Guard was mating with his woman, he would want to kill him, wouldn't he? Anyone would. I ken I would."

Fèlice looked troubled. For a moment there was silence, and then she said, "There is to be an inquiry. The Privy Council has set up a special group to investigate."

"I'll bet ye two gold royals that the Prionnsa does no' have to wait in prison while they do it," Rhiannon said bitterly.

"No," Fèlice said. "I don't want to lose my money."

The eyes of the two girls met.

"I have some good news that might cheer ye up," Fèlice said with an effort. "Ye ken Landon's ballad, the one he wrote about ye? It's all the rage in the faery quarter. We've been selling bundles o' it. Ye have a lot o' supporters among the faeries now."

"Wonderful," Rhiannon said. "I bet no' one o' them is a magistrate sitting on the quarter sessions."

"Well, no," Fèlice answered. "But at least we're making your case a cause célèbre. . . ."

"A what?"

"A much-talked-about event," Fèlice answered, stroking back the damp hair from Rhiannon's face. "If we can just get public opinion going your way, I'm sure it'll make a difference. It must!" Her eyes suddenly became thoughtful. "I wonder . . . surely it canna do any harm to just point out the difference in the way ye and His Highness are being treated? I wonder if they'd let us print up another broadsheet on the Theurgia's printing press?"

Rhiannon was feeling unutterably weary. She shrugged and put her head back down on her pillow. The bluebird flew back in through the bars of the window and came to alight on her knee. It tilted its head and regarded Fèlice with its bright black eyes, trilling sweetly.

Fèlice stared at it in amazement. "What a lovely little bird! Have ye tamed it?"

"Lewen made it for me," Rhiannon said.

"He *made* it for ye?"

"Aye. From wood. He whittled it, then touched it and it came to life."

Fèlice regarded Rhiannon with wide brown eyes. "But . . . that's extraordinary."

"I ken."

Fèlice was silent for a long moment; then she stood up, shaking out her skirts. "Now I truly do believe he has been ensorcelled! Lewen could not bring a bird to life for ye one day, and turn around and kiss and canoodle with another lassie the next."

Rhiannon lifted the bird on to her hand so she could sit up and face Fèlice. "Told ye so."

"Aye. But the thing is, what to do about it?"

"I can do naught in here," Rhiannon said, fire kindling in her eyes again. "But when I get out—"

"Aye, I ken, I ken. Ye'll carve her up for mincemeat and end straight back in here."

"Nay, I'll win Lewen back again," Rhiannon said fiercely. "He mine!"

"Well, it's still another month until your trial," Fèlice said, frowning, "and then it'll be bang on time for the wedding. I think I should talk to Lewen, try to talk sense into him."

"One whole moon still! Me want out now!"

"Well, ye canna," Fèlice said practically. "As far as I ken, there's only ever been one breakout from Sorrowgate Tower, and that was led by Tòmas o' the Healing Hand."

"How did he get out?" Rhiannon demanded.

"A nyx led him out through the sewers," Fèlice answered. "But unless ye happen to ken a nyx . . ."

Rhiannon scowled.

Fèlice bent and gave her a quick kiss, startling her. "I am so sorry, Rhiannon. I wish . . ."

"What?"

"I wish there was more I could do to help," Fèlice answered.

"Ye could get me out o' here."

Fèlice shook her head. "I'm sorry," she said helplessly. "But truly I canna."

Fèlice tried to talk to Lewen, but she could never find him alone. Day or night, he and Olwynne were together, brown head bent over red, brown eyes hooked into brown. Many times Fèlice tried to draw him apart for private conversation, but the Banprionnsa was always quick to return to his side or to call for his attention. Brought up from birth in the etiquette of a royal court, Fèlice could not interrupt or intrude upon a banprionnsa. She could only curtsy and withdraw obediently, despite her growing frustration and suspicion.

Then, almost a week after May Day, Fèlice was in the library studying at one of the little tables when she saw Lewen come in, arms linked with Owein and Olwynne. They were laughing. This made Fèlice feel quite cross, when she remembered Rhiannon's heart-wrenching grief and despair. She leaned over and whispered to Edithe, who was frowning over a massive tome at the table next to hers, "Look, Edithe! It's Lewen and the royal twins. Would it be presumptuous o' us to go and greet them?"

Edithe at once closed her book and stood up, smoothing down her hair and shaking out her skirt. "No' at all," she whispered back. "Why, after so many weeks in Lewen's company? O' course no'. I'm sure he shall be delighted to see us again." Then she picked up her book and, head bent in apparent concentration upon the page, stepped forward, right into the threesome's path.

"Oh, my gracious, I am so sorry," she cried, starting backwards. "Your Highnesses, please forgive me. I was so engrossed in my studies I did no' see ye. Lewen! Well met! How are ye yourself?"

Lewen and the twins were forced to stop and return her greeting, and soon, as Fèlice had expected, Edithe had cornered Owein and Olwynne, requesting their advice on which teacher of alchemy was considered the best. Owein, of course, had no interest in this subject and rolled an agonized eye at Fèlice, silently begging her to rescue him. Olwynne, however, replied gravely and in full, and Fèlice was able to seize Lewen's sleeve and draw him aside.

"Lewen, is it true what I have heard? Have ye and the Banprionnsa Olwynne . . ."

Lewen looked dazed but happy. "Aye, it's true indeed."

"I canna believe it!" Fèlice cried.

"Neither can I, really," Lewen said, smiling. "To think she would want me! I'm the happiest man alive."

"But what o' Rhiannon?" Fèlice demanded, having no time for diplomacy.

Lewen's expression darkened. "What o' her?"

"But she loves ye, and ye love her," Fèlice said, her throat closing over in distress.

"It was no' true love," Lewen replied. "She ensorcelled me."

"Nay, she didna. She canna have," Fèlice said softly and urgently, aware of the Banprionnsa's dark eyes upon them. "Ye ken she has no knowledge o' spells and suchlike. She has had no training in the Craft."

"Aye, happen so, but she's cunning indeed," Lewen said sharply. "Ye ken Nina believes she has a strong natural Talent. Why do ye no' believe she could have laid a compulsion upon me? It must be so, for I feel naught now."

"Then how could ye have fallen out o' love with her so swiftly, if she had compelled your will with such strength?" Fèlice argued. "Canna ye see that it is a spell o' love upon ye now that has turned your eyes away from her so suddenly?"

She became aware of Owein turning towards her, frowning, and lowered her voice. "Please, Lewen. Rhiannon is in such distress. Could ye no' go and see her?"

"Olwynne thinks it best if I do no' hurt her any further," Lewen said stubbornly, "and I think she is right. Olwynne says I must be careful she does no' ensorcell me again, which she would very likely do, I think, if she thinks I can help her escape justice. Olwynne says—"

"Olwynne says, Olwynne says," Fèlice cried. "What o' Rhiannon?"

Lewen drew back, looking angry; then Olwynne was there beside him again, sliding her fingers through his and turning a cool, haughty look upon Fèlice, who at once bowed her head and curtsied.

"Good day to ye, Lady Fèlice," the Banprionnsa said politely. "I hope ye are well."

"Very well, thank ye, Your Highness," Fèlice replied, and Olwynne nodded, gave a polite smile, and begged to be excused. Fèlice bent her head again and, arm in arm, Lewen and Olwynne went away down the library.

Owein disengaged from Edithe, much to her disappointment, and came up to Fèlice, asking her, with a look of most unusual gravity, if he could walk her back to the dormitory. She smiled and thanked him, but kept her spine stiff, knowing full well that Owein did not wish to flirt with her.

As soon as they had left the cool of the old building behind them, stepping out into the warmth of the spring sunshine, Owein began to speak. "What is wrong, Lady Fèlice? Why are ye angry with Lewen? Is it because o' the satyricorn?"

Fèlice nodded, blinking back tears.

"But why? I mean, I ken Lewen imagined he was in love with her, but it was a dreadful thing for him, to be enamoured o' some wild girl from the mountains with no name and no family, and one accused o' murder and treason to boot. It would've ruined him—canna ye see that? If she was found guilty and hanged, and he was her partisan—well, I canna see him being chosen as a Blue Guard, can ye?"

"No, I suppose no', Your Highness," Fèlice said.

"It is much better for him to have come to his senses now, afore the trial, afore he had to give testimony on her behalf. Connor the Just was a favorite here at the court, ye ken. Or maybe ye do no' ken. Certainly we were all rather surprised to hear ye performing that ballad about Rhiannon. I mean, I ken ye meant no harm, and certainly it was a lively story and one the faeries all seemed to enjoy, but still . . ."

Fèlice was silent. Owein tried to see her face, but she kept her eyes resolutely fixed on the ground.

"I dinna mean to upset ye," he said.

She said nothing.

"It was a most rousing performance ye gave," he said teasingly. "Ye deserved your bag o' gold."

"I gave the money to Rhiannon," Fèlice said. "Even prisoners who have been granted liberty o' the tower must pay for their food and bedding, Your Highness, and at a price far greater than they would fork out at the meanest inn!"

"That was nice o' ye," Owein said after a moment. When Fèlice still did not glance at him or smile, he said tentatively, "Ye are friends with her too, then? I had no' realized . . ."

"Aye, I am friends with her," Fèlice said shortly.

"Is that why ye're upset with Lewen? For I heard she didna take his change o' heart well."

Fèlice glared at him. "Why should she? They were lovers, Your Highness! He had sworn to jump the fire with her!"

"Really? I mean, I ken he said he wanted to, but I had no' realized he had made promises . . . but it can be o' no account. If she laid a spell o' love on him, it makes a difference, doesna it? He canna be held responsible—"

"It is your sister who has ensorcelled him, no' Rhiannon," Fèlice said gruffly. She drew her handkerchief out of her reticule and discreetly blew her nose.

Owein stopped short.

"Never!" he declared. "Olwynne would never do such a thing! She has trained all her life to be a sorceress. Do ye really think she would just throw it all away? Besides, why should she need to? She is a NicCuinn! Nay, it was that satyricorn girl who ensorcelled Lewen. I canna believe ye do no' see that. Lewen choose a wild girl from the mountains over Olwynne? That was what I could no' believe—no' that he's finally come to his senses and seen what was under his nose all the time."

Fèlice turned to look up at him. "Your Highness, I traveled with Lewen and Rhiannon for more than a month. I saw them falling in love. It looked real to me. Indeed it did, Your Highness."

"And ye ken so much about love," Owein teased.

Normally Fèlice would have sighed and admitted she knew nothing, that she needed someone to teach her, but for once she was in earnest and would not be swayed by dalliance. "Nay, truly, Your Highness," she said. "I swear Rhiannon kens naught about any spells o' love. She is very forthright. It is no' her way to be underhanded or secret in her dealings."

"And ye think that is my sister's way?" Owein said, offended.

Fèlice dropped her eyes. "I'm sorry, Your Highness. I do no' mean to offend ye." She glanced up at him under her lashes. "It's just . . . do ye no' think it all happened very fast? One minute he is in despair over Rhiannon, and the next, he has eyes only for your sister?"

"I daresay the satyricorn's spells wore off," Owein said stiffly. "Lewen and my sister have always been close. I was no' alone in wondering if they would make a match o' it. I was far more surprised to hear he had fallen head over heels for a satyricorn, especially one who he kent had killed a Yeoman."

"Rhiannon is only half a satyricorn," Fèlice said angrily. "And she killed the Yeoman to save her mother!"

"So she says," Owein said coldly. "We will find out the truth o' it all at the trial, I daresay. Here we are at your dormitory. If ye will please excuse me?"

Then, with a slight bow, the winged Prionnsa turned and strode away, his bronze-red wings held up stiffly behind him, his hands clenched by his sides. Fèlice watched him go, feeling miserable; then she fled into her room and buried her face in her pillow, blotching it with tears that she told herself were for Rhiannon.

IN THE DARK OF
THE MOON

"Let them bestow on every hearth a limb."

—JAMES GRAHAM,
Marquess of Montrose (1612–50),
"Lines Written on the Window
of His Gaol the Night Before
His Execution"

Jail Fever

Nina sat at her dressing table, hanging her antique amber pendant about her neck and looking at herself in the mirror. She looked well enough, in a gown of yellow silk with trailing sleeves slit to show crimson under-sleeves, and scalloped edging of the same color at hem and cuff and girdle. The dress suited her tawny coloring and was a good choice for a midsummer feast. Nina was not happy, however. She felt stifled in the heavy gown and wished she was barefoot in a forest somewhere, dabbling her feet in a stream and calling birds down to her hand.

She rose and, with a rueful twist of her mouth, asked the seamstress's assistant to help her disrobe. Nina hated not being able to dress and undress herself. It was one of the many things that she disliked about court life. A woman should be able to run and dance and pick up a child, she thought, not mince about in clothes so tight and heavy they made one faint and weary. Seven weeks they had been back at Lucescere, and it was seven weeks too long for Nina. She longed to be back on the road with her husband and son, their big old cart horses Sure and Steady pulling their caravans, able to go where they wished and do what they wanted.

Yet Nina had promised to stay in Lucescere for the royal wedding, still three weeks away. She could have gone to Caerlaverock, her brother's estate, which was only a few days' ride away, and returned in time for the wedding, but Nina felt a strong responsibility for Rhiannon, incarcerated in her bleak little cell in Sorrowgate Tower. Rhiannon had saved Nina's son, Roden, at great risk to herself, and Nina could never repay that debt. It was a small sacrifice to make, feeling stifled in the luxury and idleness of the royal court, when Rhiannon grew thin and sick and pale in the evil air of the prison.

Nina was feeling very troubled about Rhiannon. She was far too quiet and listless. The half satyricorn had always been a wild, fearless girl, quick with a blow or a curse, and ever unwilling to compromise. She would never have submitted to the restrictions of court dress just because it was fashionable. She would have scowled and demanded, "Why?"

"Ye ken, I've changed my mind," Nina said abruptly. "I will no' wear the dress to the wedding."

The seamstress paused in her task of unhitching the many hooks at the back of the dress. "But, my lady, ye look so fine in it! And it has taken us weeks to make."

"I'm sure ye will find another lady to wear it," Nina said. "I will wear something a little . . . lighter." She had to smile at the aghast expressions on the faces of the seamstress and all her assistants and said apologetically, "It will be very hot, ye ken." She rose and found her purse and pressed a few gold coins into the woman's willing hand. "If ye could design something more to my taste?"

"Aye, my lady, o' course," the seamstress said. "Ye would like something more like what the Banprionnsa Bronwen and her ladies wear. Tight and low cut? In gauze, perhaps? With artificial fins?"

Nina shook her head. "Silk," she answered. "With none o' these trailing sleeves. They only dangle in the soup and knock over one's cup. And no buttons up the back. And no petticoats." She took a long, deep breath and added firmly, "And no laces!"

"Ye wish to start a new fashion?" the seamstress said doubtfully, her look telling Nina that she was neither young enough nor pretty enough to be a leader of fashion.

"Nay," Nina replied, smiling. "I want to be comfortable."

The seamstress's assistants exchanged rolls of the eyes, but Nina felt much more cheerful. She watched the seamstress and her girls sadly gather up the billowing mass of the dress and carry it away, and then dressed herself again in one of her favorite old gowns, shabby but comfortable, and went out into the living room.

Roden was standing on his head, his boots making dirty

marks on the silk-hung walls. His constant companion, Lulu the arak, stood on her head next to him. They were sharing an apple, passing it back and forth between them. Nina smiled and bent her head down so she was face-to-face with her son.

"Ye quite comfortable there?"

Roden considered her question. "My head feels like it's blowing up like a balloon," he said. "It's rather strange. But it's been more than three minutes now, which is my best ever record. I'm trying to beat Lulu."

"Ye'll never manage that," Nina answered. "Ye're no' an arak, ye ken."

"Nay," Roden said regretfully. He was turning red in the face.

"Happen ye should come right way up now," Nina said.

"All right," Roden said and let his boots fall down to the floor with a clunk. He lay there for a while, breathing hard, then rolled over and took the apple from Lulu, who was still standing on her head.

"I'm going to the prison to visit Rhiannon," Nina said. "I'm worried about her."

"Canna I come too?" Roden demanded, sitting up. "I want to see her!"

Nina shook her head. "Nay, sweetie, I'm sorry. I really do no' want ye going to the prison. I ken ye love Rhiannon and want to see her, but it's truly a most blaygird place, Roden. Ye willna like it. And I think Rhiannon is unwell. I wouldna want ye to catch jail fever."

"What's that?" he asked through a mouthful of apple.

"A sickness ye get from the bad air in prison," Nina said.

"Why is the air bad?"

Nina considered her reply. "It's shut up all the time," she said after a moment. "The doors and windows are always locked up tight, so the fresh air canna get in."

"Why do they no' open them up?"

"Because then the prisoners would escape."

"Why do they want to keep them locked all the time?"

"Because they've done bad things and need to be punished for them."

"But Rhiannon hasn't done anything bad. Why is she locked up?"

Again Nina had to think about the best way to answer him. "She killed a man, remember," she said at last. "It's wrong to kill people, Roden."

"But she killed him because he was trying to kill her mam," Roden reminded her. "I'd kill someone if they were trying to kill ye."

"I'd probably kill someone too if he was hurting or threatening ye," Nina admitted.

"And would they lock ye up for it?"

"I'm afraid so. At least until the court was satisfied I had only done it to save ye."

"But would they—"

Nina shook her head at him and said, "I'm sorry, honey, I really need to go."

"Canna I go and see Uncle Dide? I havena heard all his adventures yet."

"All right," Nina said. "But if he's busy, I want ye to stay with the nursemaid and no' go anywhere. Deal?"

"Deal," Roden said, and they spat on their palms and shook hands.

"Come on then," Nina said, and Roden got up and held out his hand for Lulu, who rolled forward and on to her feet, cackling in her shrill voice. Nina took Roden's hat and jacket down from their hook behind the door. With her son swinging from her hand, his boots making a great clatter on the polished floors, they made their way to Dide's rooms, where the earl was enjoying a late, leisurely breakfast. Roden was perfectly happy to eat again, though his uncle protested at having a gravening come to pick his bones clean.

"That son o' yours should be as plump as a parson," he grumbled to Nina, "the way he eats. Do ye no' feed him?"

"Altogether too often," Nina replied. "Thanks for minding him, Dide. I willna be long. I just want to look in on Rhiannon. She was looking very peaky yesterday."

"Ye're visiting that prison rather often, aren't ye?" Dide said. "Need ye go every day?"

"I do no' go every day," Nina answered. "I wish I could! But I'm teaching a few classes at the Theurgia again, ye ken, and I have my apprentices to keep an eye on, as well as court duties,

Eà blast them! I do find it hard to find the time to go as much as I should."

"I ken ye feel ye owe this Rhiannon a lot," Dide said slowly, "but . . ."

Nina looked at her son's ruddy curls, bent in great concentration over an egg-and-bacon pie. "I owe her everything," Nina said simply. "Everything."

Dide nodded his understanding. "Feeling is high among the Yeomen," he said soberly. "They will no' like it if she is pardoned or found guilty only o' manslaughter. Connor was much liked."

"As long as they do no' . . . execute her," Nina said softly, trying to keep her voice low enough that Roden would not hear. "I do no' ken how I could explain that. . . ." She indicated Roden with her head.

"I'll speak to Lachlan," Dide said. "Hanging is rare enough these days that he may be able to issue a lesser sentence without too much o' an outcry. I ken he will be sympathetic to your feelings, no matter how angry he is over Connor's death."

"Thanks," Nina said and rose. "I willna be long. If Roden is too much trouble, take him to the Theurgia. Fat Drusa will be happy to keep him occupied for a few hours there."

"Won't be long before he'll be a student there himself," Dide said. "Look how tall he is. He must be eight by now, surely?"

Roden looked up and grinned. "Nay, silly, I'm six. Don't ye ken aught?"

"Don't be a cheeky arak, Roden," Nina said sternly and took her leave.

She knew the way to the prison well enough now to walk it with no conscious effort, her mind busy with many problems. Foremost was her worry over Rhiannon and the puzzlement caused by Lewen's sudden change of heart. She would never have thought of Lewen as fickle or capricious. She had thought him to be as sure and steady as her cart horses, faithful and unswerving in his loyalties. It troubled her that she had been so wrong in her reading of his character, and she was indignant on Rhiannon's behalf. What troubled her the most was the effect it had on Rhiannon, who had become bitter and sarcastic, and less likely to trust anyone than ever. This hurt Nina, who had grown to have a real affection for the wild satyricorn girl and had welcomed the warmth that had grown between them. She dreaded the coming trial, for she greatly feared that those who had not come to know Rhiannon would find it all too easy to misconstrue her motives and find her guilty.

At Sorrowgate, the young guard Corey clucked his tongue at the sight of Nina. "It's no' good," he said. "I think she's right poorly."

He opened the heavy iron door and Nina went swiftly in, drawing in her breath in dismay at the sight of Rhiannon, who lay restlessly on her pallet, breathing hoarsely. Her hair was wet with sweat, and hectic color burned in her hollow cheeks.

"How long has she been like this?" Nina demanded, putting down her basket and going to sit beside Rhiannon, smoothing back her damp, tangled hair. She was shocked at the heat radiating from Rhiannon's skin and the way her eyes worked beneath her half-closed eyelids. Her lips were dry and cracked, and she moaned as she moved her head from side to side, seeking a cool spot. Nina looked for some water to give her but saw that Rhiannon's cup was empty and cursed under her breath. It was clear she was very sick.

Hamish, the other guard on duty, shrugged. "She cried out a lot in her sleep, but then, she always does. We thought nothing o' it. It was no' until we brought her breakfast that we noticed she seemed sick."

"Why did ye no' send word to me?"

He looked sulky. "No' paid to run messages."

Nina drew her purse out of her belt and flung it at him. "Now ye are," she said tersely. "Now get me some fresh water, and be smart about it."

Hamish picked up the purse and stowed it away in his uniform and went out, looking shamefaced.

Nina remembered she had brought a little bottle of goldensloe wine in her basket and went to fetch it. She had to support Rhiannon's head with her hand as she brought the bottle to her lips. Suddenly Rhiannon flayed out with her hand and sent the bottle flying, spraying the potent liquor everywhere. Nina cursed again and wiped her face. Rhiannon was crying out, but her voice was so hoarse it was impossible to hear what she said. Nina remembered the last time she had tried to give Rhiannon medicine. Unwittingly she had been helping the lord of Fettercairn's skeelie to administer Rhiannon poison. No wonder Rhiannon was wary of accepting any cup offered to her in her fever.

Hamish brought water, and Nina bathed Rhiannon's face and neck and hands, and filled her cup and held it to her lips. To her relief, Rhiannon did swallow a few mouthfuls, though her head fell back on the pillow, exhausted, afterwards.

"Is there a healer here at the prison?" she asked the guards, who were watching from the doorway, their handkerchiefs over their mouths to stop themselves from breathing the tainted air.

Hamish snorted in derision.

Nina stood up. "I'm going back to the Tower o' Two Moons. I'll be back as soon as I can with a healer. Can ye keep her as cool as ye can while I am gone?"

"We're no' paid to be healers," Hamish said brusquely.

"I gave ye more money than ye would normally earn in a week," Nina said angrily.

"No' enough," Hamish said. "Dinna want to catch the fever."

Nina held out her hand. "Then give me back my purse."

Hamish snorted with laughter.

"I'll tend her," Corey said. He saw Hamish's look and added quickly, "If I have the time. We're right busy today."

Nina accepted this with a set jaw, not having time to argue.

"Better bring back a flock o' them," Hamish said. "There's fever all through the prison. Comes every summer. They call it the summer scythe, as it clears the decks right fast."

Nina nodded and went out hurriedly.

She went as quickly through the crowded city streets as she could, breaking into a run whenever there was a gap in the throng. The heat of the cobblestones struck up through the thin soles of her shoes, burning her feet, and perspiration prickled her skin. It was a relief to leave the stink and sweat of the streets behind her and reach the forest that separated the palace and the tower. For the first time she realized what a difference the trees made in regulating the temperature and wondered if the city folk begrudged the witches their cool green gardens.

Nina hurried to the eastern tower, where the Royal College of Healers was situated. She had a stitch in her side, and her breath came harshly, but she did not moderate her pace as she strode up the stairs, towards the top floor where Johanna had her quarters.

A door opened above her, and she heard a murmur of voices. Then someone came out on to the landing. Nina paused in surprise. It was Elfrida NicHilde, the Banprionnsa of Tìrsoilleir, followed closely by a tall fair man dressed all in black.

The NicHilde had turned to give her male companion a heavy pouch that clinked and a sheaf of papers. "Ye will need to hire a ship too," she said. "One that is fleet and strong, for the sea is rough beyond the—"

Just then the man saw Nina, and reached out a hand to stop Elfrida, indicating the sorceress with a slight inclination of his head.

Elfrida stopped short, then turned her head. At the sight of Nina she gave a little start but recovered herself at once.

"Lady Ninon," she said. "How are ye yourself?"

"Well indeed, Your Grace, and ye?" Nina said.

"Oh, very well, thank ye."

"I'm glad to hear that. Is it Neil, then, who is ill?"

"Neil?" Elfrida demanded. "No! What do ye mean?"

"I'm sorry. It's just . . . ye've been to see Johanna, Your Grace. I thought ye must be ill, or if no' ye, then happen your son, or Iain . . ."

"Oh." Elfrida relaxed. "No, no, we are all well. A little tired, perhaps, with all the bustle o' the court. In general we live very quietly, ye ken."

Nina scrutinized the Banprionnsa's face closely. She did not look well. Her skin was pasty, with a faint sheen of sweat on it, yet she wore her plaid clasped close about her. Her eyes were too bright and darted about nervously, and she kept licking her dry lips. Her whole manner was tense and uncomfortable, as if she was in a hurry and unwilling to admit it. Nina frowned. "Are ye sure it is only tiredness?" she asked. "There are some bad fevers about at this time o' year. Are ye sure ye are no' coming down with something, Your Grace?"

"Quite sure," Elfrida snapped. "I am just no' sleeping well. The heat . . . I am no' used to the heat."

Nina's puzzlement grew. Tìrsoilleir, where Elfrida had grown up, had the warmest climate of all of Eileanan and in summer was much hotter than Lucescere, which was built high on an escarpment and cooled by the constant breeze over the waterfall.

"Is that why ye came to see Johanna?" she probed. "For something to help ye sleep?"

"Yes, yes," Elfrida said. "That's right."

"She did no' check you first, to see that ye are no' sickening for something? For indeed—"

"I told ye, I am quite well!" Elfrida cried. As Nina took an involuntary step backwards in surprise, the Banprionnsa drew herself up. "I do beg your pardon," she said formally. "I did no' mean to shout. I . . . I am rather tired. I think I will go and rest."

"Good idea," Nina said, trying not to feel affronted.

Elfrida walked down the stairs past her, nodding her head in farewell. The man in black followed her, acknowledging Nina with a polite nod. He had a face like an elven cat's, with a pointed chin and narrow eyes that gleamed blue.

"I hope whatever Johanna gave ye helps," Nina said. The Banprionnsa's head snapped back around, her eyes wide and startled, color flaring under her skin. "To sleep," Nina said.

"Oh! Oh, yes. I'm sure it will." Then Elfrida went scurrying away down the stairs, leaving Nina feeling troubled.

She stood for a moment, remembering what Dide had told her about how uneasy Tìrsoilleir seemed under the righteous sermons of the new Fealde and how angry Lachlan was with Elfrida for not keeping the country's religious leader under stricter control. She remembered the way the tall man in black, who must be one of the Fealde's pastors, had stilled the Banprionnsa with a mere gesture of his hand, and frowned. Their intimacy did not bode well for the freedom of religion clause of the Pact of Peace, which stated that all must have the right to worship as they saw fit.

Nina remembered the Banprionnsa's edginess, the beads of sweat on her upper lip, her short temper and the nervous way she had clutched her plaid. She wondered why Elfrida wanted a ship and why she had given her pastor such a heavy bag of coins. *I smell an intrigue*, she thought. *I must tell Dide. . . .*

She went on up the stairs, still puzzling over the Banprionnsa of Tìrsoilleir's behavior. Then the door opened in answer to her knock, and all thoughts of Elfrida fled.

Rat Hunting

Dedrie had answered the door. Nina stared at her in stupefaction. "What . . . what are *ye* doing here?" she managed to say. For a moment the lord of Fettercairn's skeelie looked seriously discomposed. Her mouth gaped, her eyes grew wide, and her whole body stiffened. Nina saw her hands clench in her skirts, crushing them. The very next moment, all signs of discomfiture fled.

"My lady! Please, do come in. Are ye here to see Mistress Johanna? She is just finishing a letter; she will no' be a moment. Please, sit down. May I make ye some tea?"

"I do no' want tea!" Nina said angrily. "Tell me, what do ye do here? I thought ye were in prison, awaiting trial with all the rest o' the laird o' Fettercairn's henchmen."

"Oh, but I am no' a henchman, my lady," Dedrie protested, opening her brown eyes wide. "I am a healer, and where else should a healer be but at the Royal College o' Healers?"

"But ye were arrested! Brought here to Lucescere to face charges!"

"No charges were ever laid against me," Dedrie said in a hurt voice. "I'm naught but a poor auld skeelie. All I've ever done is try to help and heal, as a skeelie should."

Nina groped for a chair and sat down. Her head was whirling with so many questions and accusations she could frame none of them. It seemed impossible that the weeping, furious woman she had seen manacled and under guard in Fetterness should be here, plump, rosy, and smiling, in Johanna's comfortable suite of rooms in the Tower of Two Moons. Nina's dazed eyes took in the fact that Dedrie was dressed in the green robe of a healer, with the usual heavy pouch of powdered herbs and tools at her waist.

"But how?" she managed to say.

Dedrie smiled, and for a moment Nina saw a flash of malicious glee in her eyes. Then the moment was gone.

"Indeed I do no' ken why ye are so surprised to see me, my lady," Dedrie said, bustling about the room, swinging the kettle over the fire and laying out a tray with clean cups. "I have been here for more than a month now, helping Mistress Johanna with her work and attending lectures at the Theurgia." She laughed. "Och, I ken I'm auld for it. The bairns must think me a right auld biddy. It is interesting, though. The things I'm learning! I feel downright humble to be allowed in."

As she spoke, she made tea and brought it to Nina's hand. Nina took it and raised it to her lips, then suddenly put her cup down so roughly the tea spilled. She rose to her feet. "Where is Johanna?" she demanded. "I need to speak with her at once."

"Och, she'll be a while yet. Bide a wee, and drink your tea."

Nina shook her head. "Ye think I want to drink aught made by your hand?" she said coldly. "I am no' such a fool."

Dedrie's face suddenly turned ugly. She pressed her hands together before her, her chest rising and falling rapidly. Nina waited for the burst of words, but none came. Instead, after a moment, the skeelie gave her a pleasant smile, saying chidingly, "Och, there's naught in there but rose-hip syrup, chestnut flowers, and honey, my lady. Ye fear I'd try to poison ye? Here in Mistress Johanna's rooms? Why would I do such a thing?"

"Why indeed?" Nina answered.

"Exactly! I have no desire to hurt anyone. I'm right happy to be here. Come, my lady, sit down. Ye seem hot and ruffled. Would ye prefer something cool? I have bellfruit juice or fresh lemonade—"

"Nay. I want to see Johanna. I need to see her now!"

"Very well, I'll call her." Dedrie moved towards the inner door, then paused, looking back at Nina with a sharp, cold look. "Do try no' to upset her," she warned. "My poor mistress has suffered much grief these past few months. She needs kindness and sympathy in these hard times."

Nina opened her mouth to retort angrily, then closed it again, utterly dumbfounded. Dedrie smiled at her and rapped gently at the door.

"Mistress Johanna? I'm so sorry to disturb ye, ma'am, but ye have a visitor."

"Coming!" Johanna called back.

Nina heard rapid footsteps and then the door opened and Johanna came out. Nina was surprised at the sight of her. The last time she had seen Johanna she had been white and haggard, racked with grief over her brother's death. Now she looked calm and content, with a dreamy smile on her face.

"Nina," she said, and came forward, smiling. "Good to see ye!"

"And ye," Nina replied, allowing herself to be embraced.

Johanna led her to sit down, asking her how she was, and Roden, and Iven, and Dide.

"Fine, fine, they're all fine," Nina answered distractedly.

Johanna acknowledged her words with a vague nod, then turned her head and smiled at Dedrie, saying, "Och, ye dear, ye've made us tea already. What would I do without ye?"

"It's my pleasure," Dedrie answered, bringing Johanna a cup and then bending to arrange the cushions at her back more comfortably. "Are ye hungry? I have some little honey cakes here, or I could ring for some soup if ye like."

"Nay, I'm fine, thank ye," Johanna answered, sipping her tea.

Nina regarded her closely. Was it her imagination or were Johanna's pupils far too small? Certainly the healer had a dazed, dreamy expression on her face, as if she had just woken up. Nina pressed her hands together, a nagging worm of anxiety wriggling in her stomach.

"Now what can I do for ye?" Johanna asked, holding up her cup so Dedrie could refill it. "Ye are looking rather white, Nina. Is all well with ye?"

Nina looked from her to Dedrie, and back again. "No, it is no'," she said bluntly. "Johanna, do ye no' ken . . . do ye no' ken who this is? She's the laird o' Fettercairn's skeelie."

"Aye, o' course I ken," Johanna said comfortably, smiling at Dedrie. "And a fine skeelie she is too."

Nina tried to choose her words with care. "Ye do ken, do ye no', that she has been accused o' murder? And necromancy?"

"Aye, and stuff and rubbish it is too," Johanna replied. "As if Dedrie could possibly be guilty o' such dreadful deeds! Why, she is the kindest, most thoughtful—"

"Och, please, ma'am, ye'll put me to the blush!"

"How I ever managed without Dedrie is beyond me," Johanna continued. "I'm so glad she came to me for help. Why, if it were no' for her—"

"Now, ma'am, that's enough, please," Dedrie said firmly, bringing the plate of cakes and offering it to Johanna, who took one and ate it absentmindedly.

Nina was dismayed to find she was near tears. It had wearied her, rushing through the crowded city in the heat, only to find someone she thought of as an enemy where she had expected to get help. She took a deep breath and managed to swallow her distress.

"Aye, I need your help," she said to Johanna, who was gazing at her with a look of mild inquiry, her head lolling back against a cushion. "I need a healer."

"Why, what is wrong?"

Nina took a deep breath. "There's fever . . . in the prison. I am no' a healer, as ye ken. I do no' ken the best thing to do. . . ."

"Fever! In the prison! Och, my poor laird!" Dedrie stood stock-still, her hands clasped before her breast, then turned to look at Johanna pleadingly. "Oh, ma'am, may I go? My laird is elderly now and much weakened by his weeks imprisoned. A bout o' jail fever would kill him."

"O' course ye must go," Johanna said. "Take whatever ye need from the simples room. Ask Annie and Mirabelle to go with ye, to assist ye. And Dedrie, take a plague mask. I do no' want ye catching the fever." She smiled at the skeelie fondly.

Nina swallowed her distaste. "I do no' ken if the laird is ill too, or any o' his men, but it would be wise to check him," she said. She found she had difficulty framing her next words, knowing how Johanna must feel about Rhiannon, her brother's killer. She forced herself to speak. "It is Rhiannon o' Dubhslain who is ill, though, very ill. May I take one o' your healers to her? Perhaps this Annie . . . or Mirabelle?"

Johanna sat bolt upright, her cup tumbling from her hands to crash and break on the floor. "Ye dare . . . ye dare ask me . . ." she began, in a high shrill voice. "Ye want me to succor that . . .

murderess . . . that foul . . ." Her voice failed. She flung up her arm to cover her face, beginning to weep in great heaving breaths. "Get out!" she rasped. "Get out!"

"But Johanna . . ."

"Get out!"

"But she is ill, very ill. . . ."

"I hope she dies," Johanna spat, staring at Nina with blazing hatred in her eyes. "I hope she suffers terribly first." Then the healer turned and pressed her head into Dedrie's lap, the skeelie bending to embrace her.

Dedrie looked over Johanna's distraught form at Nina, and this time she made no attempt to hide the malice in her smile. "I would beg ye to leave now, my lady," she said in a treacle-sweet voice. "I do no' wish ye to upset Mistress Johanna any more. I mean no disrespect, but it was cruel o' ye, cruel and thoughtless, to ask her to do such a thing."

"Aye! Cruel!" Johanna cried out, her voice muffled by Dedrie's embrace.

Nina stood up. "I'm sorry, I did no' mean to distress ye," she said. "But ye are a healer, sworn to help and heal all those in need. I thought—"

"Get out!" Johanna screamed.

Nina bowed her head and left the room.

She stood for a long moment on the landing outside, staring out the tall windows at the green branches swaying in the breeze. She had to repress her own misery in order to think through what had just happened in the healer's room. Nina had not seen Johanna in such distress since the death of Tòmas some twenty years earlier. Johanna was renowned for her composure and strength in times of trouble. All through war and rebellion and plague, Johanna had alleviated pain and suffering and fear with her calm good sense and steadfast courage.

Nina tried to think how she would feel if it had been Dide shot in the back by a wild satyricorn. Would she have felt such savage hatred towards the archer? Would she have wished her brother's murderer dead, even without a trial to establish the truth of the shooting? Nina would like to think she would not, but in truth she could not tell. She sighed and went down the stairs, crossing the garth towards the Royal College of Sorcerers.

She found Isabeau at last in the library, reading a great heavy book with the title *Ghosts and Ghouls and Ghasts* picked out in gold. The Keybearer looked up as she came in and smiled warmly, putting her book down and coming forward to embrace her. "Nina! How lovely to see ye. But what is wrong?"

Nina told her about Rhiannon, and how Johanna had refused to send anyone to tend her.

"I'll come at once," Isabeau said. "I was only just worrying about Rhiannon. See this book I am reading? I've been brushing up on my knowledge o' ghosts and hauntings, and very troubling reading it makes too. It's sorry I am indeed that I have no' found the time to visit her again. Come, I just need to get my healer's bag from my rooms. Walk with me and tell me more. Ye say Johanna was very distressed?"

Nina told her everything, including how the lord of Fettercairn's skeelie had somehow wormed her way into Johanna's confidence. She described the healer's lassitude, her dreamy expression and her contracted pupils, and wondered aloud if Dedrie had somehow drugged Johanna, having had a bad experience with the skeelie's basket of potions and poisons before. This reminded her of Elfrida and her visit to the healer, and how edgy and nervous she had seemed. Isabeau listened to all she had to say with great interest, as she retrieved her healer's bag from her suite of rooms at the very top of the tower and sent one of her maids running to the stables to order horses.

As they made their way back to the prison, a passage through the crowds cleared for them by four tall guards, Nina told the Keybearer how troubled she was about the conditions at Sorrowgate Prison. She told Isabeau about the mysterious disappearance of Bess Balfour, after she had been strung up for the rats to gnaw on by the warder of Murderers' Gallery, and described, with some exasperation, how much it was costing her to keep Rhiannon in a cell of her own, with two meals a day and clean sheets and blankets once a week. By the time they rode under the cruel portcullis, Isabeau was frowning and Nina was feeling much easier in her heart.

"It must no' be allowed," Isabeau said tersely. "Lachlan must be told! Why have ye no' told him yourself?"

"I canna get near him," Nina said. "The court is like a hive o' hornets, all buzzing around. There's this new unrest in Tìr-

soilleir, and all the scandal over Bronwen and this Yeoman that
Prionnsa Donncan killed. No' to mention the upcoming wedding!"

"Aye, I must admit it's been mad," Isabeau said. "I have had
a lot on my plate too."

"Aye, I'm sorry. I didna ken who else to come to."

"Ye did right," Isabeau answered. "Lachlan will see me!"

"Once he would've seen me too, at any time," Nina said unsteadily. She dashed her hand across her eyes. "But I am no' in
favor right now, given that I keep importuning him on Rhiannon's behalf. "

"Och, well. He loved Connor dearly and misses his wise
counsel. We all do. He had an uncanny knack o' getting to the
truth o' a matter."

Having left their horses in the care of Isabeau's guards, they
climbed up the twisting stairs to Rhiannon's cell. The satyricorn
was gravely ill, Nina could tell at once. She lay in a tangle of
hot, damp sheets, her eyes unseeing, her face flushed as red as
if she had been eating scorch-spice. Isabeau wasted no time in
forcing her to drink a bitter cordial made of powdered willow-
bark, feverfew, wormwood, and borage, easily evading Rhiannon's wild struggles, then stripped her and bathed her in cool
water. She sent Corey running out into the city streets to pur-
chase a cup of snow from the icemongers, and squeezed lemon
over it and fed it to Rhiannon with a spoon. Hamish, the other
guard, rather sulkily brought soup that Isabeau sniffed suspiciously and then poured into the stinking chamber pot.

"Remove this at once," the Keybearer said coldly, "and
bring us a clean one, then have a messenger sent to the Tower
o' Two Moons, to Gwilym the Ugly. I want fresh cooked soup,
and nettle tea, and agrimony water, and an infusion of yarrow
and vervain. Tell him I want plenty o' it, and I want it now. Mistress Rhiannon will no' be the only one sick in this foul place.
Tell Master Gwilym I want a team o' maids too, to scrub out the
cells and strew them with fresh herbs. They had best wear
gloves and masks. Oh, and tell him I want another message sent
to the kennels. I want all the cairn terriers brought here and set
to catch the rats. Have him search out some ferrets too, to go
where the dogs canna. Is that understood?"

Hamish gaped at her.

The Keybearer clicked her teeth in exasperation and sat down to scribble a hasty note, which she then gave to Corey to carry, he being the younger and more willing.

"I wish to speak to the prison warder. Have him attend me here," she said then to Hamish, who did not dare deny her, even though it was clear he did not relish carrying that particular message.

Nina had been sitting quietly by Rhiannon's bedside, smoothing back her sweaty hair from her brow and smiling to see how the guards jumped at the Keybearer's orders.

Within a few hours, the whole prison was turned upside down with battalions of chambermaids armed with scrubbing brushes and pails of hot water working methodically through the labyrinthine building, flinging open shutters and throwing down piles of lice-infested bedding to be burned. Little brindled terriers with shaggy coats and sharply pricked ears rushed about everywhere, barking joyously and chasing the rats, who poured away from them in a dark, scrabbling flood that slowly reduced to a trickle. The long sinuous shapes of ferrets writhed through the drains and the chimneys, dragging out more rats until, by the end of the day, a tall, black, evil pyramid of dead rats was stacked in the courtyard.

Nina stayed by Rhiannon's side all night, giving her agrimony water to sip every time she moaned and stirred, and bathing her forehead with lavender water. Through the window slit she could see the dancing flames of the bonfire burning all the filth of the prison, and as the smoke rose high into the night sky, Nina felt her spirits rise also.

Three times Isabeau came back, to give Rhiannon another dose of the feverfew potion. By daybreak, Rhiannon knew who she was again, and was wearily allowing Nina to lift her up so she could sip at a cup of hot vegetable broth, and making faces over the bitter green nettle tea.

"Drink it up. It'll make ye well," Nina said.

"What has happened? What is wrong with me?" Rhiannon's voice was hoarse and faint.

"Just a touch o' jail fever," Nina said. "Do no' worry; ye are over the worst o' it."

Rhiannon wrinkled her nose. "What is that smell? What is burning?"

"That is just the Keybearer, cleansing this place with fire," Nina said, laying Rhiannon down again and tucking her up in a clean, sweet-smelling sheet. "I swear there is no' a rat or a louse left anywhere in Sorrowgate."

"Me glad," Rhiannon said and wearily closed her eyes.

None left except for the laird and his skeelie, Nina thought to herself. *And I will do what I can to sweep them into the dust pile too!*

The Cat and the Fiddler

Rhiannon was weak and listless after her bout of jail fever and often disinclined to leave her bed. Her only consolations were her growing pile of books, the little bluebird who delighted her with its song and joyous flight, and the visits of her friends, who tried to come at least once a week.

Nina and Iven had hired an attorney to represent Rhiannon at her trial, which was to take place at the dark of the moon, the day before Midsummer's Eve. The attorney had a stern eye, a beak of a nose, and deeply engraved lines between his heavy black brows. His eyes were black also, but his hair was silver, and he looked as if he rarely smiled.

He asked Rhiannon many questions, and all so superciliously that she wanted to grind his face into the rough stone of her walls. She managed to keep her temper, though, and was rewarded with a grunt and a muttered, "Very well. Ye'll do."

As the date of her trial came ever closer, he came more often, teaching her about the judicial system and coaching her in her responses.

Otherwise, Fèlice continued to be her most faithful visitor, bringing her flowers and wine and copies of the news broadsheets to read, and enlivening the dull hours with her chatter about the court and the Theurgia.

One day, a week before her trial, Rhiannon said rather idly, "What o' the other prionnsa, the younger one? I have no' heard ye speak o' him for a while."

A shadow crossed Fèlice's face, but she said lightly, "Och, it has all been such a whirl that I have scarce laid eyes on Prionnsa Owein! He spends most o' his time with Lew—with his

brother and sister, ye ken, and I do no' move in such exalted
circles."

Rhiannon, realizing only that Fèlice had sidestepped saying
Lewen's name, did not notice the trace of misery in Fèlice's
voice, being too busy bearing her own pain. Since Fèlice then
went on to discuss the much-remarked upon coolness that had
grown between the Crown Prionnsa and his betrothed, Rhiannon did not pursue the topic, and all mention of Owein was allowed to lapse.

The Keybearer came once also, her elf-owl perched sleepily
on her shoulder. She questioned Rhiannon again about the
ghost that haunted her sleep and about the night of the spring
equinox when Rhiannon had watched Lord Malvern and his
circle of necromancers. When she had extracted everything
Rhiannon could remember, she sat for a moment, thinking, and
then said gently, "Nina told me ye had a friend, a lass named
Bess Balfour, who was injured your first night in Sorrowgate."

"Aye, injured," Rhiannon said bitterly. "That's one word
for it."

"I've made inquiries," Isabeau said.

"Good o' ye," Rhiannon answered. "Let me guess. There is
no record o' a lass named Bess Balfour."

"No, there is no'," Isabeau answered, "though there is a
Mistress Balfour making a nuisance o' herself every day at the
front desk, demanding to ken what has happened to her daughter."

"Bess's mam?" Rhiannon sat upright, turning to stare at the
Keybearer.

"I would guess so."

"So I didna dream it all," Rhiannon said.

"Nay, I think your Bess was real enough, as real as the
thumbscrews that gave ye your scars." Isabeau indicated the
faint bloom of discoloration that still encircled Rhiannon's
thumbs and looked as if it would never fade.

"So where is Bess?"

Isabeau put up her hand to stroke the owl, who hooted softly,
almost as if seeking to comfort or reassure.

"The Royal College o' Healers has difficulty in finding
enough bodies for their research and teaching," she said. "Most
people do no' want their remains to be dissected once they die,

yet the healers and their students need to know as much about the human body as possible if they are to learn to heal it. So some years ago the Rìgh passed an act allowing the bodies o' murderers to be given to the college instead o' being buried, as usual."

"What has this to do with Bess?"

The Keybearer continued as if she had not spoken. "The corpses o' the destitute and homeless are meant to be buried at the city's expense, but, sad to say, many sheriffs do no' want to bear the cost, which often has to come out o' their own pocket. So, sometimes, if someone dies on the street and their body is no' claimed by their family, well, the sheriffs give the body to the College o' Healers."

Rhiannon waited.

"The body o' a young woman was brought in a few days after ye were imprisoned in Sorrowgate Tower," Isabeau said. "She fits your description o' Bess Balfour. I was particularly struck by what ye said about her crooked face. This girl had at one time broken her jaw."

"Or had it broken for her," Rhiannon said.

Isabeau nodded.

"The body was much gnawed by rats. There was some argument among the students as to whether this happened before or after death. No conclusive agreement was reached."

"So Bess was dumped on the street? Alive or dead?"

"Who is to ken?" Isabeau answered. "No autopsy was performed, just a dissection o' her major organs."

Rhiannon put her hands up to cover her face.

Isabeau said gently, "I am sorry. If it is any consolation, all bodies dissected by the College o' Healers are given the proper funeral rites afore being cremated."

"What do I care for your rites?" Rhiannon said, her voice muffled by her fingers. "It is the living that matter."

"Aye," Isabeau said. "I do agree. I can only say how very sorry I am. Ye must believe me when I say those responsible will no' go unpunished."

"It was Octavia." Rhiannon lifted her face from her hands. "She did it. She strung Bess up for the rats and then got rid o' her, afraid o' who I would tell."

"Aye, I think so. Do no' worry. The city guards have gone already to arrest her."

This gave Rhiannon some satisfaction, and she waited eagerly for news. Yet somehow Octavia escaped the net spread to capture her. When the city guards kicked down her door in the dingy guesthouse where the warder made her home, it was to find the room in disarray and Octavia gone. No one knew where. And although both Nina and Isabeau reassured Rhiannon she would be found and brought to justice, Rhiannon had little faith that this would be so. Lucescere was a labyrinth of lanes and alleys and dark, stinking passageways, of chimneys and drains and sewers, of cellars and caves and secret tunnels. Huge and heavy as Octavia was, she somehow managed to slip away into Lucescere's shadowy underworld and disappear.

The moons began to wane, and Rhiannon's anxiety grew sharper the closer her trial came. Her attorney was not an optimistic man, and all his grunts and exhortations to prepare herself for the worst preyed heavily on Rhiannon's peace of mind until the slightest noise or draft of cold air was enough to make her jump.

Then, the day before the quarter sessions were to be held, and all the capital cases tried, Nina came, white and edgy with news.

"The Cat and the Fiddler are here!" she burst out, as soon as she had stepped into Rhiannon's cell.

"Who?" Rhiannon asked, looking up from her book in surprise.

"The Cat and the Fiddler. Do ye no' ken? Finn the Cat and Jay the Fiddler. Finn NicRuraich is Head Sorceress o' the Tower o' Searchers in Rurach, and Jay is her husband. He is a sorcerer too, though all his music is bound up in his viola. Ye must have heard tell o' them."

Still Rhiannon looked blank.

"She is one o' the MacRuraich clan," Nina said impatiently. "They are Searchers. Their Talent is to search and find. The Rìgh employs them to find things he needs. He sent Finn and Jay to Ravenshaw to find what evidence they could against ye and Laird Malvern. I had hoped, when there was no sign o' them, that they had been unsuccessful or that they would no' be back in time. But I should have kent better. Finn always finds what she searches for."

"So what has she found?" Rhiannon asked anxiously.

"I dinna ken, no' yet. We willna ken until the trial, for sure. It's just . . . I'm afraid . . ."

"O' what?" Rhiannon demanded.

"Finn and Jay were both good friends o' Connor's," Nina said. "They were all in the League o' the Healing Hand together."

Rhiannon's heart sank. "So they hate me. They bring bad evidence against me."

"They have certainly been very thorough," Nina admitted. "That is why they have taken so long. They have brought back witnesses against ye, as well as many statements and reports about the laird o' Fettercairn. It was quite a procession!"

Nina and Iven had gone into the city as soon as they had heard the news that the Cat and the Fiddler were approaching. Nina knew both Finn and Jay well, but they had had no chance to greet them, for the city streets had been seething with people. Thousands had turned out to watch the sorceress ride in with her escort of Yeomen, followed by a long string of packhorses.

"I do no' ken if it is true, but I have heard the packhorses carry many dreadful things that Finn found at Fettercairn Castle," Nina said. "Boxes and boxes o' severed hands, and mummified heads, and the flayed skins o' faeries, and the skulls o' the murdered, and instruments o' torture stained with blood, and knives and black candles and all sorts o' poisons."

Rhiannon nodded her head. "They cleaned out his library then," she said. "I saw all those things there."

"Ye will have to testify to that," Nina said. "I am so pleased. I want that wicked laird found guilty, and all his henchmen too! That such evil walked abroad for so long! Ye ken, I have heard that one o' those packhorses carried naught but scrolls and scrolls o' statements by hundreds o' witnesses, all signed and sealed, giving testimony against him. They will have to find the laird guilty now!"

"But what o' me?" Rhiannon asked.

Nina hesitated, then said, "There is a lot o' support for ye, Rhiannon. Many in the city have taken Landon's ballad to heart. There have been many fights and scuffles, ye ken, between those who think ye guilty and those who think ye are no'."

"Are any o' them my judges?" Rhiannon said with heavy sarcasm. "I think no'. So what does it matter?"

"Public opinion can sway the Rìgh," Nina said.

"It is no' up to the Rìgh," Rhiannon said. "He does no' try my case. It is the judges who will find me innocent or guilty."

"Aye, but the Rìgh can call for a lighter sentence or issue a pardon," Nina said hopefully.

"Aye, he can, but he willna, will he? The Rìgh abides by the verdict o' the judges, and they judge me on the evidence offered at the trial. That sour-faced lawyer has told me that over and over again, so that I can say it in my sleep. So tell me, what evidence has this Cat o' yours found against me? What witnesses has she brought?"

"I dinna ken who they are," Nina said hesitantly. "There was one, a poor auld bent and scraggy man, all wild hair and beard. Apparently he has been held captive by the satyricorns for years."

Rhiannon could not believe what she had heard. "Reamon? They brought Reamon here? But why?"

"Who kens? If he is a friend o' yours, surely he will testify on your behalf?"

"I suppose so," Rhiannon said, though she felt sick in the stomach. Try as she might, she could not imagine how the Yeomen of the Guard had managed to capture Reamon. She could not imagine why they would have brought him and could not help feeling anxious about what he might say.

"At least ye do no' have so long to wait now, Rhiannon," the sorceress said consolingly. "One day more, and then it'll all be over."

"Aye, one day more," Rhiannon repeated and heard how the words echoed with grief between them.

That night Rhiannon found it hard to sleep. She lay in the darkness for a very long time, her mind churning over the past few months. Nina's words ran like a refrain through her mind. *One day more, and then it'll all be over. One day more, and then it'll all be over.* When she managed to force her mind away from this chain of words and what it meant, it was only to hear again another sequence of words that had haunted her for weeks. *Hanged, drawn, and quartered. Hanged, drawn, and quartered.*

She may have dozed for a while, drifting away into images that seemed to have no connection one to another. A winged horse carved from wood. Lightning striking down from the sky. A silver thread unspooling. A black knife slashing. Blood. A cry of triumph.

Rhiannon woke, or seemed to wake. She felt the familiar lumpiness of her pillow under her cheek, the scratchiness of her blanket on her legs. She was cold, but she could not reach down to drag her blanket higher. She could not move her arms or legs, or fret her head against her pillow. She felt as if she had been chained down. Her hair was wrapped tight about her throat, choking her, strangling her.

The ghost hovered above her, coating her in ice. "It's time," she whispered. "Are ye ready to die?"

Rhiannon screamed. Her eyes opened into darkness. She lay rigid, listening. All was quiet. She dragged one icy-cold breath into her lungs, and then another. Gradually her pulse stopped hammering in her ears, and her clenched fingers uncurled. Still she listened. Then she heard a furtive scrabbling at her door and sat up, staring towards it even though she could see nothing but blackness. Every nerve shrilled.

The door scraped open. She heard a soft footfall, then another. Rhiannon slipped off her bed and lay on the floor. Swiftly and silently she rolled underneath her bed. Her head clunked against the chamber pot. At once the footsteps paused. Rhiannon fought to soften her fear-quickened breath. She heard another soft step, then heard someone standing right next to the bed, breathing quietly. They bent and seized what lay in the bed, but found their arms full of only pillows. A curse was muttered, and Rhiannon heard the quick scrape, scrape, scrape of flint and saw the sudden flowering of light. At that very moment she struck out with the chamber pot. The man beside her bed fell with a thump, and Rhiannon rolled out and was astride him in a moment, hitting him as hard as she could over the head.

His lantern had fallen to the ground and rolled away. Just before the light guttered out, Rhiannon saw her attacker's face.

It was Shannley, the lord of Fettercairn's groom.

As Rhiannon stared at him, stupefied, she heard a quick flurry of footsteps and looked up to see the lord of Fettercairn himself, dressed all in black, and carrying another lantern. Behind him came his servants, all looking grim and intent in the flickering light of the candles they carried.

Rhiannon had no time to wonder how they came to be free of their own cells or opening the door to hers. She just knew they had come for her, to do the ghost's will. She screamed.

Rhiannon had a good set of lungs, and her scream was driven by an engine of terror. It was so shrill, so piercing, that the lord of Fettercairn was stopped, involuntarily, in his tracks.

"Shut her up!" he hissed. "She'll have the whole guardroom down upon us."

As that was Rhiannon's intention, she took a good, deep breath and screamed again. The sound was shut off abruptly by a rush of bodies, but Rhiannon had no intention of going meekly. She laid about her with the chamber pot, with satisfying thunks and umphhs, all the while calling, whenever she could draw enough breath, "Help! Help me!"

There came a cry and a clatter of boots. Rhiannon screamed again, as loudly as she could with so little breath left to her, and fought her attackers off fiercely.

"Leave her!" Lord Malvern cried. "We'll find ourselves another sacrifice! Let us go while we can!"

His servants drew back at once.

"She is the only one who saw us," a quavering voice said. Rhiannon recognized the voice of the lord's librarian and genealogist, Gerard.

"True," the lord said. "Best leave no threads dangling."

He stepped forward, his lined face grotesque in the wavering light of his lantern. Rhiannon saw he had a dagger in his hand and staggered back. He drew back his lips in a smile more grimace than grin and advanced upon her.

Just then a massive dark shape appeared in the doorway. "The guards!" a hoarse and all too familiar voice hissed.

Lord Malvern took another step towards Rhiannon, the point of his dagger glinting.

"No time!" Octavia whispered. "They come. Leave her to the hanging judges!"

Lord Malvern hesitated, then drew back. He turned away, taking the light with him. In the darkness, pressed hard against the rough stone wall, Rhiannon heard the thud of their feet as they ran down the stairs. She listened hard for a betraying breath, or scrape of shoe against the stone, or the whistle of a sharp knife blade against the air. Nothing, except the distant shout of voices. Then she heard feet running up the stairs towards her, and, as light once again bloomed up the stairwell, a harsh clamor of bells.

The prison guards came thundering into her cell with weapons drawn and lanterns raised high. Shannley, the lord of Fettercairn's groom, still lay unconscious on the floor. Rhiannon sat upon her bed, the chamber pot decorously hidden behind her feet under the bed, her hands folded on her lap.

"They've gone," she said. "Ye'll have to be fast to catch them."

But of course they were not fast enough. Lord Malvern and all his men were gone into the night, and Octavia with them, leaving only Shannley the groom to face the Court of Star Chamber in the morning.

The Court of Star Chamber

Lewen woke. He lay still, leaden with misery, wondering why his chest ached with such grief. Then he remembered. Today was the day of Rhiannon's trial. He turned on his side. He did not want to get up. He would have liked to pull his sheets over his head and stay in bed all day, pretending it was not happening. But he could not. With all that had happened between him and Rhiannon, the least he could do was stand up in court for her, as he had promised, even though the very thought of seeing her made him squirm with anxiety and dread.

The bed beside him was hollow with Olwynne's absence, though if he pressed his face into his pillow he could still smell her sweet lingering fragrance. It filled his nostrils and made his groin tighten with longing for her. The scent of roses, jasmine, and violets, with a hint of something else, something that was Olwynne's alone.

Lewen closed his eyes and groaned. He did not understand this fierce love for Olwynne that had seized him and shaken him like a terrier shakes a rat. Everyone kept saying how sudden it had been, yet it did not seem sudden to Lewen. It felt rather as if he had always loved her, without realizing it, as a man loves his own heart for beating and his own lungs for breathing, without any knowledge or effort or need. It hurt and grieved him that he had not understood any earlier. How Olwynne must have suffered while he stumbled, blindly and stupidly, into Rhiannon's sorcerous toils. How bravely Olwynne had borne her secret hurt and grief, and how nobly she had forgiven him. Lewen just wished he was worthy of her.

Sometimes, at night, when Olwynne had slipped from his

bed to creep back through the moonlit corridors to her own room, and Lewen rolled over and deeper into sleep, he found himself remembering Rhiannon again. Not with his mind but with his skin, his flesh, his nerves. When he woke the next morning, he would remember, in flashes, and feel sick with shame that he could betray Olwynne so. But his banprionnsa never blamed him. She questioned him often about his feelings for Rhiannon, and reassured him that the satyricorn's spell had been strong and subtle and would take time to completely overthrow.

Which was one reason Lewen dreaded seeing Rhiannon today, the first time he would have seen her since that last encounter in her cell. What if she worked her magic on him again? Lewen could not bear the idea that he might weaken and betray Olwynne's love, in thought and feeling, if not in deed.

Yet he must go. Apart from anything else, he was one of the key witnesses in Rhiannon's defense. Nina had begged him to stand for her, and Lewen had promised to do his best, putting aside his own revulsion at what she had done to him. It was not an easy thing for him to do. For now that Lewen was truly in love, he realized with fervent intensity what a terrible thing it was to enslave another's will and spirit with desire, to make them love where they would have loved not. He knew now why love spells were forbidden by the Coven, considered as heinous as necromancy. For where necromancy was a black art aimed at controlling the dead, eromancy was a black art to control the quick, and so arguably even more wicked.

Lewen still felt Rhiannon's chain upon his soul, no matter how hard he tried to dissolve it with the scent and flavor and bright goodness of Olwynne. When Olwynne was with him, it was easier, but too far away from her and he felt the slow drag of Rhiannon's hand upon the chain, drawing his thoughts and longings back to her. So Lewen tried never to be apart from his new love, his true love, and struggled to unclasp his body and his will from Rhiannon.

He groaned again in weariness and frustration, flung back his bedclothes, and forced his body to rise. He bent and splashed his face and body with lukewarm water from his jug, and flung open his window, leaning out in search of a breath of

fresh air. It was already very hot. The leaves of the oak tree outside his window hung listlessly.

He dressed slowly and carefully, in pale wool breeches and
a brown linen coat trimmed with velvet, with a blue sash across
his breast to show he worked for the Rìgh. He forced a comb
through his unruly thatch and tied it back neatly, then polished
his shoes and brushed his coat. Inside his pocket, over his heart,
he tucked the withered nosegay of flowers that Olwynne had
given him the morning after their first night together. Lewen
wore it in his inner pocket every day, even though the flowers
were all crushed and broken now and a faint whiff of rot wafted
up from their brown petals.

Lewen stared at himself in the mirror for a moment. He saw
the same face he always saw, broad and brown and smooth-
skinned, yet he felt he did not recognize himself. How did he
come to be here? He was about to give witness at the murder
trial of a woman he had thought he had loved as truly and as
deeply as it was possible to love, and when that was done, he
planned to jump the fire with another, a girl he had never even
dreamed of loving till a few scant weeks ago. None of it made
sense to him. It was as if he had lost his lodestone, the pull of
the true north that held him steady on his life's course. It made
north south and up down, made love hate and good evil. All
Lewen could do was hold fast to the knowledge of Olwynne
and hope that she could drag him free of this magnetic mael-
strom.

There was a soft tap on his door. Lewen huffed out his
breath, squared his shoulders, and went to open it. Fèlice stood
on the other side, her face grave. Lewen's heart sank at the sight
of her.

"It's all right, Lewen, I'm no' here to reprove ye," she said.
"I just want to make sure all is well with ye. I mean, for Rhiannon's trial today. Ye are coming?"

Lewen could only feel miserable that her opinion of him had
sunk so low. "Aye, o' course I'm coming."

Fèlice hesitated.

"There's no need to fear," Lewen said stiffly. "I would no'
perjure my soul by giving false witness, no' even to punish that
ensorcellor!"

Fèlice set her jaw. "She's no ensorcellor, Lewen. Ye o' all

people should ken that. How could she have learned to spin a love spell o' such power, high in the mountains by Dubhglais?"

"No doubt the satyricorns have their own magic."

"I hardly think love spells are their style," Fèlice answered angrily. "As far as I can tell, a satyricorn prefers to use a club!"

"Och, aye, happen so, but then Rhiannon is no' your usual run-o'-the-mill satyricorn, is she?"

"Nay, she is no'," Fèlice replied.

Lewen paused and glanced down at her, troubled, and Fèlice grasped his arm with both hands, saying in a low, urgent voice, "Oh, Lewen, canna ye see—"

Just then another voice called his name, a warm musical voice. At once Fèlice dropped her hands and stepped back, turning to curtsy demurely as Owein and Olwynne came up the stairs together.

The Banprionnsa was exquisitely dressed in a simple gown of dark yellow silk. The MacCuinn plaid was draped over her shoulder and pinned at her slim waist with an emerald pin. Owein too had made some effort to dress for the occasion, with his bronze-red curls neatly combed, and his chin freshly shaven. His clothes were neat, even if put together with very little thought for fashion, and his shoes had been polished, for a change. He paused a moment at the sight of Fèlice, then inclined his head politely, asking after her health.

"I am well, thank ye, Your Highness," Fèlice replied, just as coolly.

"Have ye come to escort Lewen to the Court o' Star Chamber?" Olwynne asked, a note of surprise in her voice. "How kind o' ye."

"I ken how difficult this day must be for him," Fèlice replied, lifting her chin a little.

Olwynne raised her brows. "Aye, indeed," she replied. "As it is for all o' us who kent Connor well. We miss him sorely."

Fèlice opened her mouth to retort, then thought better of it, merely bowing her head and drawing back so Olwynne could pass, her hand tucked into the crook of Lewen's arm.

Owein fell in beside Fèlice as they went back down the stairs. For once he walked like an ordinary man, his wings folded down his sides. Fèlice did not want to look at him, but

she was very conscious of his long, warm body beside her and
the occasional brush of his wingtip against her skirt.

"I imagine ye have heard o' the laird o' Fettercairn's dramatic escape, my lady," Owein said after a moment.

"Aye, I've heard, Your Highness," she answered. "Who hasna?"

"It looks as if he may have had a guilty conscience," Owein said.

"Aye, it does, doesna it?"

"They say Finn the Cat brought back a lot o' evidence against him, enough to hang him for sure."

Fèlice said nothing.

"I wonder why your satyricorn friend didna escape with him, when she could?"

"Rhiannon is no friend o' Laird Malvern's."

"Aye, but still . . ."

"She kens better than anyone what a dangerous man he is," Fèlice said. "Happen she thought she was safer in the hands o' your father's court. I hope she was right."

Owein glanced at her, troubled. Fèlice did not return his look but kept her gaze fixed on the ground ahead of her.

"I hope so too," he said after a moment. "I ken how much it would grieve ye to see your friend . . . found guilty. I do no' want that."

"Thank ye, Your Highness," she whispered, tears stinging her eyes.

They walked on in silence.

The Court of Star Chamber was crowded with people from all walks of life. Faeries, country folk in homespuns, lords and ladies in shimmering silks, merchants' wives with jeweled wrists and ears, witch-apprentices in their simple black robes, servants in demure grey, street roughs in rags and bruises. Hundreds had turned out to see the satyricorn who was accused of murder and treason, and the noise of their rustling and murmuring echoed through the great vaulted room. It had been a long time since the court had had to judge such a high-profile case, and the spectacular escape of the lord of Fettercairn had only focused more attention on Rhiannon.

Heads craned to stare at Lewen and Fèlice as they self-consciously went down to the front to sit with the other witnesses in the first rows. Nina and Iven were already there, both dressed formally as sorceress and Rìgh's emissary. They gave Lewen a tense, unnatural smile, and then turned their gaze away, leaving Lewen with a bitter residue of sadness and loneliness, even though he knew they did not mean to hurt him. He had just grown used to warmth and camaraderie from Nina and Iven, not this awkward coolness. Not for the first time, he cursed the day that Rhiannon of Dubhslain had flown into his life.

The other apprentice-witches who had traveled with them from Ravenshaw sat in a row beside them. Landon looked sick, Rafferty and Cameron were fidgety and uncomfortable in their suits, Maisie was overawed, and Edithe stared about her with a look of self-satisfied importance, smoothing down the plush velvet of a richly trimmed red gown.

Cameron had been minding a seat for Fèlice and after a moment shifted sullenly along so Lewen could sit too.

Lewen had not seen much of the former squire since they had arrived in Lucescere, but once Cameron had looked up to Lewen and admired him greatly as the son of a former war hero. It rubbed Lewen on the raw to see Cameron cast him a darkling look and mutter something to Rafferty, who sat on his far side. When they had first met, Lewen had been Rhiannon's champion and Cameron had been her enemy, after she had publicly repulsed his advances in her usual blunt way. Their journey together had changed all that. Now Cameron was as quick to defend Rhiannon as he had previously been to mock her. He was a straightforward lad, with a traditional and chivalrous attitude to human relationships, and it was clear he thought less of Lewen for his change of heart towards Rhiannon. Lewen sighed and glanced back over his shoulder at Olwynne's bright loving face.

Olwynne and Owein had caused a great deal of interest by choosing to sit right behind the witnesses instead of joining the other aristocrats up in the dress circle. Olwynne was making it as clear as she could that Lewen was the cause of her intense interest in the case by smiling at him constantly, leaning forward to lay her hand upon his arm, and ignoring the others to-

tally. Owein looked uncomfortable with this tactic, casting
Nina and Iven apologetic glances and trying to engage Fèlice in
conversation. She had evidently seen the battle lines drawn up,
however, for she was cool and unresponsive, saving her attention for her fellow apprentices. Owein gave up after several
tries and sat back, looking down at his boots and trying not to
fidget too much.

Cailean of the Shadowswathe came hurrying down the aisle,
dressed still in his white sorcerer's robe, and sat down beside
the twins. His huge black shadow-hound loomed beside him.
The faery dog's eyes glowed with an uncanny eldritch light, as
green as marsh gas, and it did not need to curl its black lip to
keep a wide circle clear about it. No matter how curious the
crowd, no one would risk a shadow-hound's ire.

Cailean's arrival distracted Olwynne for a moment, giving
Lewen a chance to look about him anxiously. There was no sign
of Rhiannon. The imposing wooden rostrum in the center of the
room was empty. Lewen wiped his damp palms on his breeches
and stared about the room, wondering when she would be
brought in. The walls soared high overhead, to a domed ceiling
of dark blue glass decorated with gilded stars. More stars were
set at the head of each of the great fluted columns all around the
room, while the familiar shape of two crescent moons marked
the apex of the dome. Great curtains of midnight blue velvet
fell from ceiling to floor at regular intervals, looped back with
golden ropes as thick as Olwynne's waist. It was stiflingly hot,
and livery-clad pages waved fans of colorful bhanias feathers
over the heads of the lords and ladies in the box seats high
above the common rabble on the main floor.

Bellfruit sellers wandered the aisles, offering cups of iced
juice, while cluricauns bounded everywhere, thrusting paper
twists of hot chestnuts or dried fruit under people's noses.
There was a scuffle at the door between an ogre in studded
leather and an ancient tree-changer with a great white beard
sprouting mushrooms. It was settled so quickly and smoothly
Lewen barely had time to register the combatants. What he did
notice was how many soldiers there were, many dressed in the
distinctive blue jacket of the Yeomen. Lewen's heart sank,
though he could not have explained why. It just seemed to bode
ill for Rhiannon.

Olwynne caressed his arm, and he turned back to her, just as there was a loud flourish of trumpets. Everyone stood and bowed as the Rìgh and Banrìgh were escorted in through one of the doors and led to their thrones high on the dais. Both were dressed formally for the occasion in long blue velvet robes edged with white ermine fur. Iseult's white NicFaghan plaid was pinned over her breast with her dragon brooch, while Lachlan wore the royal blue-and-green tartan plaid, pinned with the MacCuinn stag. Lachlan held the Lodestar in his right hand. It glowed white and cold.

As the six judges filed in behind the royal couple, a hubbub erupted. Most cheered but many, to Lewen's surprise, hissed and booed. He craned his head to see who had greeted the judges so disrespectfully and saw the street roughs of Lucescere, on their feet and waving crumpled copies of a broadsheet that he recognized as being Landon's ballad, "Rhiannon's Ride." Leading them on was the big ogre from the Nisse and Nixie, the beautiful seelie at his side. There were many other faeries among them, all chanting, "Rhee-anne-on! Rhee-anne-on!"

A ripple of shock and excitement ran along the witnesses' bench. Rafferty elbowed Landon in the side in obvious glee, while Fèlice leaned forward to grasp his hand, smiling broadly. Edithe lifted her nose in the air, as if smelling something foul, while Nina and Iven smiled at each other in astonishment and relief. Living in the palace as they did, they had been aware only of the strength of the feeling against Rhiannon.

The raucous protest of the faeries and the poor of Lucescere roused those who vilified Rhiannon for what she had done, so that they began to cheer more loudly. "Hang her!" some shouted, and the call was taken up by many of the courtiers and soldiers until the room rang with it. "Hang her! Hang her!"

Lewen's eyes smarted with hot, unexpected tears. He did not want Rhiannon hanged. No matter how much he hated and feared her, he did not want her to die like that. In his heart of hearts, he hoped that she would be banished, sent far away over the seas to some other land, a punishment that would remove her from his life and sphere of influence so that he never had to set eyes on her again. For secretly Lewen feared he would never be able to loosen the fetter she had placed upon him, not as long as she was anywhere near him.

The noise in the vast chamber mounted and mounted, until at last one of the court's officials came forward and pounded on the floor with a long golden staff topped with the blindfolded figure of justice. Gradually the noise subsided. The judges sat in a line at a red-draped table set below the Rìgh and Banrìgh. Their numbers had been drawn from the aristocracy, the merchant class, the guilds, the crofters, the army, and the Coven of Witches, but all had laid aside their usual clothes to wear the elaborate purple robe of the Court of Star Chamber, with its heavy double-sided mantle. If a death sentence was passed, Lewen knew, the judges would turn back their hood to show its crimson side, but if the accused was proven innocent, the white side stayed uppermost.

The judges did not share the febrile excitement of the crowd. They all looked grave. Lewen knew two of them by sight: the sorcerer Gwilym the Ugly, who was second in command of the Coven of Witches, and Aidan the Brave, one of the Yeomen's general staff. He was grim-faced indeed.

The heralds blew their trumpets again. At once the rustling and talking died away, until the room was almost silent. Everyone leaned forward, looking eagerly at the double doors at the far end of the room. Lewen stared too, though not with the same feverish anticipation. Despite the heat of the overcrowded room, he felt cold and shivery, and his hands were slick with perspiration that he wiped repeatedly on his crumpled breeches. His gut felt like it was twisted in an iron vise. He wished the day was over.

The Accused

The doors flung open. Rhiannon came in, flanked by four guards. Pale and composed, she was dressed in a simple grey gown, with her black hair severely braided down her back, hanging almost to her knees. She had lost so much weight her misty blue eyes seemed huge, and the strong bones of her face were sharp. She looked young and vulnerable, and there were sighs and murmurs of pity amidst the hisses and catcalls.

Lewen's heart moved sharply at the sight of her. Their eyes met, and he dropped his at once, his stomach churning with a weird collection of emotions. He could not have named them without admitting to regret, and guilt, and shame, and tenderness, none of them emotions he wished to feel.

The court herald read out the charges in long, convoluted phrases that, when deciphered, accused Rhiannon of wilfully murdering and mutilating a servant of the Rìgh while upon His Majesty's service, thus endangering the safety of his royal person and that of the whole country.

The head judge, the Duke of Ardblair, fixed Rhiannon with a frowning gaze and asked what she had to say in response to the charges.

Rhiannon said in a clear, firm voice, "It is true I shot Connor the Just, Your Worship, but I swear I did no' ken who or what he was, and I felt no hatred or malice for him or for His Majesty. He was trying to escape the herd and was struggling with my mother, who was trying to stop him. He would've killed her, my laird, if I had no' shot him. I did it only to save her life."

Such a roar of voices rose, the Duke of Ardblair had to bang his gavel on the table several times before the crowd quietened.

"But why was a Yeoman taken prisoner in the first place?" Aidan the Brave demanded. "That in itself is a treasonable act!"

She shrank back a little at the intensity of his voice. "He was a man, sir. Any man who rode into the herd's territory would've been taken prisoner. There are few males born to the satyricorns, ye ken, and they are keenly sought as mates."

The crowd reacted with sniggers and whispers. Aidan's face twisted with distaste. "So we are to add the charges o' abduction and unlawful imprisonment to your account? I shudder to think what else!"

"I didna capture him!" she cried. "I tried to help him escape."

"Is that so?" His voice dripped sarcasm.

"Aye," she said eagerly. "I undid the straps for him. He would never have got free if I had no' untied them."

"Yet ye shot him in the back only moments later."

"It wasna only moments, it was much later," she said indignantly. "The herd had to hunt him first, all the way down the river."

"And ye joined the hunt?" asked one of the other judges, a rough-spoken man with huge, work-hardened hands and a thick neck. A farmer by trade, he was called Craig of Glen Fernie, and he had been chosen by lot from a ledger of justices of the peace. He was far more used to settling disputes over stolen pigs or tavern brawls, and was clearly uncomfortable in his heavy robes.

She colored. "Aye."

"Why?"

"I had to! If I didna, they would've suspected . . ." She took a deep breath, trying to control her voice. "If the herd guessed I had helped him, they would've killed me," she said at last, her voice quivering only a little.

"Is that why ye *really* killed him? So your herd would no' realize ye had helped him escape?" Aidan the Brave asked.

She went red, then white. After a moment she replied steadily, "I told ye, he had my mother—he was going to kill her. He would've broken her neck like that!" She snapped her fingers. "No one could reach her in time, none o' the herd. I was up behind them, on the ridge. If I had no' shot him, he would've killed her."

"So ye say." Aidan sat back skeptically.

The crowd murmured.

"When the body o' Connor the Just was found some weeks later, he was found to be cruelly mutilated. The smallest finger o' his left hand had been hacked off, and all his teeth had been wrenched from his head. Were ye responsible for this also?" the Duke of Ardblair asked in arctic tones.

Rhiannon hesitated, then nodded unwillingly. "It's what satyricorns always do," she said defensively.

"So you admit that this is yours?" Aidan the Brave said, catching up a long necklace of teeth and bones that he brandished in his fist. The court hissed and sighed, and the duke had to call for order several times before it at last quietened. Rhiannon said nothing, her face drained of color, but when she was asked the question again, she nodded.

"Please answer 'aye' or 'nay' for the court records," the only woman judge said in a neutral voice. Named Glenwys, she was the head of the guilds in Lucescere, a clockmaker by trade. She wore, perched on her nose, a pair of spectacles that made her eyes look alarmingly large.

"Aye," Rhiannon said sullenly.

"Please note the prisoner answered in the affirmative to the question," the court herald called.

Aidan shook the necklace. "And these teeth, these *human* teeth, hanging on this string, they are Connor's teeth? And the bone is his finger bone?"

"Some o' them," Rhiannon muttered.

The Duke of Ardblair banged his gavel until the court at last quietened.

"I beg your pardon?" Aidan said over the noise. "Did ye admit these teeth and bones are his?"

"I said, some o' them are his. There are goblin teeth there too, and some coney paws. Other things I've killed." Rhiannon sounded sullen indeed, and Lewen clenched his fists between his knees. Silently he willed Rhiannon to look up, to speak respectfully, to be polite.

"Did ye say *other things* ye've killed?" Aidan spoke with heavy emphasis.

Rhiannon flushed. "Aye."

"I see. So ye always take trophies o' the creatures ye kill, to gloat over later?"

"It's what satyricorns do," she protested. "I didna do it to gloat. It made me sick to the stomach having to do it."

"Yet still ye did it, and wore your trophies about your neck, for all to see."

"Only while I was with the herd," she protested hotly. "They would've suspected me if I had no'. They would've fought me for blood-right."

"Blood-right? And what does that mean?"

"My right to his things," she said sulkily, dropping her eyes.

"So, by killing Connor the Just, ye were able to claim his belongings as your own?" Aidan the Brave asked silkily.

She nodded, then, after another prompting from the judges, said, "Aye," in a very low voice.

Aidan picked up one thing after another from the table. "His knife, his blowpipe and barbs, his *sgian dubh*, his uniform?" He raised the blue coat and cap reverently. "His silver brooch with the design o' the charging stag, ensign o' the Yeomen o' the Guard, given to him by the Rìgh himself and worn by Connor with justifiable pride? The medal o' the League o' the Healing Hand, the rarest o' all honors?"

As he held up the small golden medal, with its device of a child's hand radiating lines of light, a woman sobbed aloud. Turning his head, Lewen saw it was Johanna the Mild, sitting up in the witches' box. Her hands were clasped together and her face was harrowed with tears. Lewen saw she wore the same golden medal pinned to her long green robe. Finn the Cat was sitting next to her, looking almost as distressed, with Dillon, captain of the Yeomen, on her far side, his arm about Johanna's shoulders, his face grim. Jay the Fiddler sat next to his wife, holding her hand. They also wore the golden medal prominently, being the only other surviving members of the famous band of children who had helped Lachlan win his throne. Isabeau sat with them, listening intently, occasionally frowning and biting her lip.

Aidan the Brave had gone on inexorably. "And those few

precious belongings o' Connor that he carried with him always, the music box he was given by His Majesty as a reward for his help, the goblet that belonged to his dear friend Parlan . . ."

As Aidan held up the silver chalice with the crystal in its stem, Isabeau stifled an exclamation and leaned forward in interest. Lewen himself had to choke back a flood of memories evoked by the sight of the cup. Rhiannon, drinking thyme tea from it, firelight flickering over her bare shoulders. Himself, drinking cold water from it the next morning, trying to wash away the great lump of horror and misery in his throat that Rhiannon's confession of guilt had brought. He clenched his jaw and looked down at his fists pressed tightly between his knees. He felt Olwynne's hand rubbing up and down his arm and had to repress the urge to shake it off.

"Satyricorns do no' have such precious and beautiful things as these, do they? Ye would have coveted them, and by claiming them as yours, ye would have gained kudos in the eyes o' the herd, wouldna ye?"

"I'm sorry, I dinna understand," she faltered.

"Is it no' true that weapons such as these, forged o' true steel, are very rare among wild satyricorns and therefore precious? Is it no' true that ye had no such weapons o' your own?"

Rhiannon did not speak, and the Duke of Ardblair asked her, not unkindly, to answer the question.

"The herd had a few knives," she answered reluctantly. "No' many. Most o' the women made their own clubs, from stone and wood, or sharpened sticks into spears. I had my bow. It was my father's." There was a trace of defiance in her voice and Lewen drew his brows together, thinking she would do better to moderate her tone. She glanced at him, so that he wondered if she heard his unspoken thought. He looked away.

"Your father was human?" Glenwys asked.

"Yes, ma'am," Rhiannon replied. "I never kent him. He died when I was a bairn. I think they killed him when he tried to escape."

"So ye admit ye had no weapons like this?" Aidan cried, turning the silver dagger so it glittered in the light.

She turned back to him. "Nay, sir."

"But a sharp dagger like this would've been o' great use to

ye, wouldn't it?" he demanded. "And it would have greatly
raised your standing within the herd."

She shook her head sadly. "No' even a dagger could do that,
sir," she answered. "Without horns like the other satyricorns, I
was considered a nothing, a nobody."

Clever lass, Lewen thought, and again she glanced towards
him. She was deathly pale.

Aidan tried again. "But with weapons such as these, sharp,
steel weapons, even a nobody could hold her own with the
herd, is that no' so? With weapons like these, ye'd be one o' the
best hunters—"

"But I was already a good hunter with my bow," she
protested. "I had never used a dagger—I would no' ken how to
hunt with it. And I would never be as fast as the others without
hooves. I'd never get close enough to the prey to kill it with a
dagger."

For a moment Aidan seemed stymied, but then he laid down
the knife and picked up her bow. "So ye were a good hunter
with this bow?"

"Aye, sir," she said, lifting her chin.

"And a good killer," he said, and dropped the bow as if it
disgusted him.

There was a short silence. The crowd sighed.

"Perhaps we should hear from Berget, the First-Horn o' the
Royal Satyricorn Squad," the Duke of Ardblair said. "I feel we
really need to understand more o' the prisoner's background."

The First-Horn got up and strode to the witness stand. She
was very tall and wore a short blue kilt under a leather jerkin.
Her thick, muscular legs ended in cloven hooves, and a tufted
tail hung from beneath her kilt. Her face was broad and somehow bestial, with a squat nose and large mouth. Her head was
covered with short, stubby horns that had been filed to sharp-
ness. Around her neck hung many necklaces of teeth and bones.

"I see ye wear bone necklaces," Glenwys said. "So it is true
that this is the usual custom o' satyricorns?"

Berget jerked her head. "Aye. True." Her voice was deep
and guttural.

"The necklace is made from the teeth and bones o' the creatures ye have killed?"

"Aye."

"But does it have human teeth strung upon it?" Aidan cried.

She grinned at him. "Aye. Many. Enemy soldiers."

The Blue Guard frowned and sat back in his chair.

"Why? Why do the satyricorns make such necklaces?" Gwilym the Ugly asked.

Berget shrugged. "Warn away dark walkers. Tell them we strong, we brave. Dark walkers no like noise." She clattered the bones together.

"And dark walkers are evil spirits?" Gwilym asked.

The satyricorn shrugged. "Dark walkers live in shadows. In caves and cracks and in our footsteps. Want blood every day. Must have blood. Without blood will come to feed. May come anyway. Wear necklace, show how much blood ye've spilt, show how brave ye are." She shook her necklace and roared, causing many in the audience to scream and shrink back.

Listening to her, Lewen was reminded strongly of how Rhiannon had spoken when he first met her. There was little left of that curt, guttural accent in her voice now. He marveled at how quickly she had learned the formalities and intricacies of their language. Berget had grown up among humans and she still had a very strong accent. Perhaps it was because the satyricorns kept very much to themselves, even when at court. There were none at the Theurgia, even though many others of faery blood were there, and Lewen had only ever seen them in their ceremonial function as guards at the Rìgh's table. Towering over all the men and women, they stood stiffly against the wall, as solid and silent as statues. After his initial curiosity, when he had first been appointed as a squire, Lewen had barely noticed them. He wondered now what sort of life they led, when not away fighting on the Rìgh's behalf.

"Tell us, Berget, is it true the satyricorns o' the prisoner's herd would've killed her for aiding the Yeoman to escape?" asked Claude, the fat judge of the merchant class.

The satyricorn flashed Rhiannon a contemptuous glance. "Kill her anyway."

Everyone stirred and whispered, and Aidan sat up and turned his hawklike gaze back to the witness.

"Ye mean, the satyricorns would have killed the prisoner anyway? Why on earth?"

"Kill no-horns."

"Satyricorns kill those born without horns?"

"All born no horns. Horns come when woman. No horn come, useless. Kill then."

"So the prisoner would've been killed by her herd as soon as it was clear she was no' growing horns?"

"Aye."

"But she looks a woman grown now. Why was she no' killed?" Aidan ran his eyes over Rhiannon in such a way that Lewen felt himself grow hot. His nails cut into his palms.

Berget shrugged. "She escape in time?"

Aidan leaned forward, his gaze intent. "So if the prisoner had no' left the herd when she did, she would most likely have been killed?"

"Aye."

Aidan turned back to the other judges. "Surely then, Connor's things must've been o' import to her? She must've wanted them to aid her escape! His weapons, his clothes, his saddle and bridle, his horse—"

"The herd ate his horse," Rhiannon interrupted angrily. There was a shocked mutter from the crowd. Aidan shot her a look of intense dislike.

"Please only speak when ye are asked a direct question," the Duke of Ardblair said gently.

Rhiannon bowed her head. "Aye, Your Worship. I'm sorry." She cast a quick glance at her attorney, who was sitting behind his table, frowning at her and looking dour.

"It seems clear to me that the prisoner killed Connor to conceal her part in his escape and to get hold o' his belongings, to aid her in her escape from the herd," Aidan argued. "She shot him in the back, and then stole his saddlebags—"

"I didna steal them," Rhiannon said indignantly. "They were mine, by blood-right."

Lewen bit his lip, entreating her silently to be quiet. The duke told her the same, rather shortly, and again she apologized and bowed her head.

"It seems to me a question o' intent," Gwilym the Ugly said. "If she did indeed shoot Connor in order to save her mother's life, without kenning who he was or that he rode on the Rìgh's business, well, that is a far different matter to murdering him with malice aforethought."

The other judges nodded thoughtfully, all except Aidan, who cast up his eyes to the star-embossed ceiling as if unable to understand the sorcerer's gullibility.

The crowd's murmur was rent by a sudden scream from the gallery. Johanna had leaped to her feet, her face distorted in a howl of grief and rage.

"No! Hang her!" Johanna screamed. "She killed him—she admits it! She should die too. Hang her, I say!"

The cry was taken up by the crowd and, despite the loud banging of the gavel, the whole room rang with the chant. "Hang her!"

"She killed my brother—she admits it!" Johanna cried. "Let her swing for it!"

"Order in the court!" the duke bellowed until at last the room quietened, and all eyes turned back to Rhiannon, who was looking white and frightened.

Gwilym took a deep breath.

"Apart from Connor's death, we must also consider the question o' treason," the sorcerer went on. "Can it truly be possible that a herd o' wild satyricorns ken naught at all o' the Rìgh o' Eileanan and the Far Islands? The satyricorns signed the Pact o' Peace; they are vassals o' the Crown and owe allegiance and loyalty to it. And if they do ken naught o' the law, does that give them the right to flaunt it? To waylay and murder one o' the Rìgh's own officers, riding in His Majesty's service?"

Aidan nodded his head gravely and looked at Gwilym with new respect, as if he was a man who had at last spoken sense.

"These are weighty issues," Gwilym said. "The penalty for such crimes is death by hanging, drawing, and quartering, as we all ken."

"Aye! Hang her!" someone in the crowd shouted. "Hang, draw, and quarter her!"

Gwilym turned to look at the rows of upturned faces. "It is a cruel and pitiless punishment," he said. "Those so condemned are hung by the neck till near death, then cut down while still alive so that they can be disemboweled and torn into four. We must be sure o' the accused's guilt afore we inflict such a sentence upon her."

Lewen swallowed and pressed his hands together. He could

hear Fèlice's sharp indrawn breath beside him. He dared not look at Rhiannon.

"I think we should call upon Lewen MacNiall now," the Duke of Ardblair said.

White Mantles

Lewen wiped his sweaty palms down his breeches. His breath was like a sliver of glass in his throat. "He was the one who had first contact with her. Perhaps he can shed light upon the extent o' her ignorance and her true motivations," the Duke of Ardblair went on. "I think that is what we must try to grasp the truth o' here, what drove this young woman to raise her bow against the Yeoman Connor. Lewen MacNiall, will ye come to the witness stand?"

Lewen got up. He felt as if a thousand eyes were staring at him. He went up to the witness stand and swore by the Creed of the Coven of Witches to speak only what he knew to be true in his heart. He only wished he could be sure of this himself.

The judges began by asking him to explain to the court who he was and how he had found Rhiannon, tied to the back of the black winged horse, both exhausted and hurt, after her flight from the herd. Lewen responded awkwardly. He did not like to remember his first meeting with Rhiannon. It tugged too sharply on the chain strung between them.

After a while, describing Rhiannon as he had first known her, Lewen grew more fluent. "She had never even seen a house afore, she'd never slept anywhere but on the ground," he said. "We had to teach her how to use a knife and spoon—"

"By all accounts, she certainly kent how to use a knife," the Duke of Ardblair interjected dryly.

Lewen was thrown off his stride. He heard laughter from the crowd and a few hisses. After a moment he went on. "She didna even have a name. They all called her 'No-Horn,' which is a term o' contempt. My parents and I named her, for we could no' go on calling her 'lassie' all the time, which was the only other name she kent. . . ."

"That's something that has puzzled me all along," Glenwys said. "If this young woman is indeed born o' a wild satyricorn herd, how is it she speaks our language so well? Does she no' claim to have been brought up in the wilds o' Ravenshaw far from any human civilization? The First-Horn o' the Royal Satyricorn Squad, who was born and brought up here in Lucescere, does no' speak so fluently."

Lewen flushed. "She was no' so fluent when we first met her," he said. "Her language was quite broken. She's learned quickly."

"Amazingly quickly," Aidan said pointedly.

"But how was it she kent any o' our language at all?" Glenwys persisted, pushing her spectacles back up the bridge of her nose so she could look at Rhiannon, standing straight and still at her stand. Lewen could not answer. His cheeks burning, he tried to think of something to say.

Rhiannon answered for him. "My father was human, remember," she said coolly. "Although I do no' remember, he must've spoken to me as a bairn. And there was another human there, named Reamon."

Involuntarily Rhiannon looked towards the rows of witnesses, and Lewen followed her gaze. He saw an old man sitting nervously on the edge of his seat, dressed in what was obviously a borrowed suit. He was all lines and angles like a skinny plucked chicken, with a halo of straggly grey hair and beard, and great startled eyes. At the sound of his name he jerked wildly, then hunched down as if dreading the hundreds of eyes that stared at him.

Rhiannon turned her gaze back to the judges and went on steadily. "Reamon was the one who taught me how to use my bow. He always talked to me in his own language. He was the one who called me 'lassie.' It was the only soft word I ever kent."

The judges muttered among themselves for a while, then Glenwys directed another question at Rhiannon.

"And this man, Reamon, did he never tell ye about the Rìgh, or the Yeomen o' the Guard?"

Rhiannon dropped her gaze, fidgeting with her skirt. Then

she recollected herself, raising her head and saying, "Nay, no'
really. I mean, he might o'. He may have mentioned them
but . . . no' so I understood. It was all . . . like make-believe . . .
and we couldna talk much, ye ken, for they . . . my mother . . .
they didna like it when I acted like a human. I tried hard to be
as much like a Horned One as I could. So when he talked o'
such things, I didna really listen. . . ."

The judges nodded in understanding, and Lewen breathed a
little easier. He looked towards his seat, wondering if he would
be allowed to sit down now. They had not finished with him
yet, however. Gwilym the Ugly bent forward and picked up a
folded sheaf of papers from the table.

"Lewen, do ye recognize this handwriting?"

Lewen took the papers held up to him by the court herald.
"Aye," he said in surprise. "'Tis my mother's."

"Who is the letter addressed to?"

"To Auntie Beau . . . I mean, to Is—to the Keybearer."

"Your mother is an auld, dear friend o' the Keybearer's, is
she no'?"

"Aye," Lewen agreed.

"This letter was found in the pocket o' the coat the accused
was wearing when taken into custody. She claims your mother
gave it to her, to give to Isabeau upon arrival in Lucescere."

"Aye," Lewen answered, baffled. "Mam said she would
write."

"Would ye read aloud the marked paragraphs for the court?"

Lewen began to read aloud. "'I hope I have done the right
thing in sending this lass to ye. I am greatly troubled about her.
It seems clear to me she has been mistreated by her family, for
she flinches when one comes too close and looks at everyone
with suspicion. If that was all, I would have no hesitation in
sending her to ye, for I ken ye o' all people would be gentle and
loving with her. I fear there is more amiss, however. I canna
read her at all. She guards her thoughts very carefully, so carefully her mind is like a locked casket. This may be naught more
than a desire not to betray her feelings to those who are cruel to
her, but I fear she hides a darker secret. She wears the clothes
and weapons o' a Yeoman and I fear she may have killed him
for them. She says she did no', but I do no' trust her to tell the
truth. She is quite wild, and as far as I can see has no under-

standing o' the values we hold dear. She almost killed Niall at the breakfast table, and all because he told her she could no' keep Connor's things! Indeed, I'm afraid I've sent ye a lass as wild as a snow lion and quite as dangerous. I only hope ye can tame her.' "

Somehow Lewen got to the end of the letter and looked up, swallowing hard. The crowd was murmuring to each other, and the judges looked grave.

"A lass as wild as a snow lion, and quite as dangerous. One that canna be trusted to tell the truth. One that draws a knife on her host at the breakfast table," Aidan said. "A pretty house-guest indeed."

Lewen did not know what to say. He glanced apologetically at Rhiannon, and said, "She didna ken . . . she didna mean . . ."

"By all accounts, your mother is a woman o' great insight with an uncanny ability to read minds," Gwilym said gently. "The Keybearer Isabeau has always trusted her intuitions greatly."

"Aye, but—"

"Elsewhere in that same letter, your mother says the accused attacked your father with a pitchfork. Is that true?"

"Aye."

"And she bit ye till she drew blood."

"Well, aye."

"And fought so viciously it took both your father and ye to subdue her."

"Aye, but—"

"And she threatened some o' your mother's guests with violence, drawing her knife upon one?"

"She didna mean aught by it," Lewen stammered.

"Drew her knife upon some young lady at the dinner table and meant naught by it?" Aidan asked sarcastically.

Lewen went red. "Nay," he said stubbornly. He did not dare look at Rhiannon.

"I see," the fat merchant Claude said. "Very well then. Let us move on. Now, ye were present when the body o' Connor the Just was recovered at Barbreck-by-the-Bridge and so was the accused. Did she admit then that she was the one responsible for his death?"

Numbly Lewen shook his head.

"Ye must answer 'aye' or 'nay,' lad," the duke said impatiently.

"Nay," Lewen muttered.

"Can ye please answer so the court can hear ye?"

"Nay," Lewen shouted, and then blushed hotly.

"Did ye no' wonder if she had been involved, given that she was wearing the clothes o' a Yeoman, clothes that show the passage o' an arrow through back and breast?" Glenwys asked.

"Well, aye," he admitted.

"Did ye no' ask her?"

Lewen gritted his teeth.

"Please answer the question. Did ye, or did ye no', ask the accused whether she had been in any way involved in the death o' Connor the Just, whose clothes she wore and whose weapons she carried?"

"Aye," Lewen said stiffly.

"So ye did ask her?"

"Aye, I asked her.'

"And what did she answer?'

Lewen paused for a long time, then said unwillingly, "She said she had no'."

"So she lied?"

"I suppose so."

"This is an question that can only be answered with an 'aye' or a 'nay.' Did she lie?"

"Aye," Lewen said through stiff, white lips. He felt an insane desire to leap forward, to declaim on Rhiannon's behalf, to let his clamoring instincts run away with him. He fixed his eyes on Olwynne, leaning forward in her seat, and tried to keep his voice and manner cool and considered.

"So how did ye come to discover that the accused was, in fact, the one who so callously murdered our brother-in-arms?" Aidan asked coldly.

Lewen looked at him angrily, hating the way he spoke. "It wasna like that," he said.

"Oh, ye were there, were ye, and saw it all?"

"Nay, I was no', and neither were ye!"

Aidan gripped his lips together and stared at Lewen with such intense dislike he was dismayed. Aidan was a man Lewen had always admired and dreamed of being like one day. It hurt

him to realize how much of a pariah he now was to the Blue
Guards.

"Please just answer the question," the Duke of Ardblair said
wearily. "How did ye realize she had killed Connor, after she
told ye she had no'?"

"I found the necklace," Lewen said. "It was in her bag. As
soon as I saw it, I . . ."

"Ye what?"

"I realized what she had done."

"What did ye do?"

"I . . . I . . ."

The judges waited. Lewen made a big effort and said, "I left
her . . . I left her alone."

"Ye did no' call for the reeve or take her into custody? Ye
did no' tell anyone?" Aidan's voice expressed utter scorn and
amazement.

"It was wet, stormy. We'd taken shelter at the Tower o'
Ravens. It was night. Later, the next day, I told Nina, through
the Scrying Pool. Then I told His Majesty."

"Also through the Scrying Pool, I presume?" Gwilym said
with a faint smile.

Lewen could not smile back. He nodded his head, then muttered, "Aye."

"And where was the accused then?"

Lewen stared at the wooden stand before him. "She'd
gone."

"She had tried to escape?"

"I suppose so."

"Please answer—"

"Aye," he cried.

"The men o' Fettercairn Castle had to ride out and hunt her
down, did they no'? Afore she could be taken into custody."

"Aye," Lewen muttered.

"But ye did no' ride out with them, did ye?"

"Nay, I . . . I didna. I—"

"Thank ye, that will be all, I think," Aidan said. "Ye may
stand down now, sir."

"But I havena told ye . . . I need to tell ye—"

"I do no' think we have any more questions," Aidan said
coldly. "Ye may stand down now."

His cheeks hot, Lewen went to his seat and sat down. He could not look at Rhiannon. He was acutely conscious of the murmurs of the crowd and was certain every eye was upon him in mocking judgment. All the things he had planned to say in Rhiannon's defense had come to naught. He had failed dismally.

Reamon was then called to the stand. He did not want to go. He had to be encouraged and then, when that failed, coerced. He looked frail and pitiful hanging between the two burly bailiffs, his eyes bulging with terror.

Lewen leaned forward to stare at him in fascination. He could not imagine what it must be like to be dragged back to civilization after so many years as the captive of a wild satyricorn herd. By all accounts, Reamon had been used like a prize stallion, forced to sire as many young satyricorns as possible on the childbearing females of the herd. The crowd had evidently heard what his role had been, by their whispers and sniggers, and Lewen's cheeks heated in pity for him as Reamon cringed back in mortification.

Aidan the Brave spoke gently. "Tell me, Reamon, did ye ken Rhiannon well?"

Reamon squinted at Rhiannon, standing all alone in her caged stand. Rhiannon gazed back at him with unhappy eyes. "Aye, I kent her. No' that she was called that. The Horned Ones, they called her 'No-Horn,' to mock her."

"How long have ye kent her?"

He shrugged his skinny shoulders. "Who kens? A long time. Since she was but a bairn. Ten, fifteen years? I dinna ken anymore."

"Are ye the one who taught her to speak our language?"

"Sure I was."

"Tell me, Reamon, what sort o' lass was the accused? Was she a clever girl, or rather slow on the uptake?"

"Och, she was a clever lassie," Reamon answered fondly, relaxing under Aidan's gentle, courteous manner. "Sharp as a tack. Much smarter than the other Horned Ones. She was the only one to learn how to talk wi' me, and mostly I only had to tell her summat once or twice for her to remember."

"So she was an eager pupil?"

"Och, aye, indeed."

"And what else did ye teach her?"

"Och, how to shoot and how to ride. I was a gillie once, ye ken, long ago syne."

"Did ye talk to her much about your home?"

"Aye, she loved to hear my stories. She had no' kent there was another way o' life, ye ken, other than the herd."

"Did ye tell her any other stories?"

"Och, aye, all I could remember."

"Stories about the city and the court? About the Rìgh and his men?"

Reamon nodded his shaggy head, and sighed and smiled, murmuring, "Och, aye," again. Lewen felt his whole body tense.

"So the accused kent about Lachlan the Winged, Rìgh o' all Eileanan and the Far Islands? She understood all that ye told her, and kent it to be truth?"

Reamon gazed at Rhiannon fondly and murmured again, "Sharp as a tack, she was."

Aidan paused for a long moment, then continued in the same gentle, cajoling tone. "Tell me about the day Connor the Just was captured by the herd."

Reamon sighed. "A sad day that was, aye. He fought well, the young fellow, but it was no use. They tied him up tight as a lamb going to slaughter. He begged me for help, the poor lad, but what could I do? I was a prisoner myself."

"Did he say aught else?"

Reamon nodded earnestly. "He told me he rode on urgent business, with news for the Rìgh. He said it could mean the Rìgh's life, if he failed to get through."

A loud murmur rose. Lewen felt sick with trepidation. He looked at Rhiannon. She was looking down at her hands, her face noncommittal. So he looked to the judges. Aidan was trying hard not to gloat too obviously, Craig of Glen Fernie had his thick brows drawn together in troubled thought, and Glenwys was staring at Rhiannon with her huge, magnified eyes filled with disapproval. Gwilym the Ugly looked merely sad.

"Did ye tell this to the accused?"

"Aye, o' course. I begged her for help, but she wouldna. She said the Rìgh meant naught to her."

There was another even louder murmur. Rhiannon bit her lip. She looked pleadingly at Reamon, as if silently begging him to say no more.

Lewen's distress and confusion grew. He no longer knew if he believed in Rhiannon's innocence or not. Olwynne rested her hand on his shoulder, sensing his misery, and he leaned back against her, drawing strength from her.

"I told her it was treason to waylay him," Reamon's reedy voice went on. "I said it meant the hangman's noose, to hold a Yeoman against his will."

"Indeed it does," Aidan said with heavy emphasis. "Thank ye, Reamon. Ye can stand down now."

Rhiannon looked appealingly at her attorney, who sighed and shrugged. He was not permitted to address the witnesses in the court. Only the judges had that power, and unless one of them decided to interrogate Reamon further, there was nothing he could do.

Reamon shuffled back to his seat, with no idea of the damage he had done.

The rest of the hearing dragged on. Nina and Iven were called to testify and had to describe how they had seen Connor's water-bloated and mutilated body soon after it had been dragged from the river at Barbreck-by-the-Bridge. They were both asked if they had suspected Rhiannon might be involved in the Yeoman's death. Their reluctance to answer was palpable. Nina tried valiantly to tell the court how Rhiannon had risked her life to fly to Roden's rescue when he had been kidnapped by the lord of Fettercairn. Aidan the Brave would not allow her to continue, however, asking what possible relevance it had to the case against Rhiannon.

"The laird o' Fettercairn is no' on trial here," he said chillingly. "Whatever is the truth o' the accusations against Laird Malvern, that is a separate case entirely. Here and now, we deal only with the question o' Connor the Just's death, and whether Rhiannon the Satyricorn acted with malice aforethought or no'." His voice made it quite clear what he felt about her motivations, and to Lewen's dismay, the head judge seemed to agree, dismissing the whole of that wild ride and Rhiannon's part of it as beside the point.

The witch-apprentices who had traveled with them through Ravenshaw were all called as witnesses, confirming and amplifying what Lewen had said, and, willingly or unwillingly, adding many more tasty morsels to feed the crowd's salacious hunger. The court heard how Rhiannon had repeatedly slashed her own wrists to draw blood to feed the so-called dark walkers. They heard of fits of hysteria and fainting, of night terrors and sleepwalking and the constant talk of the sightings of ghosts. They heard of her pride and her temper and her quickness to draw her dagger.

Then Dedrie, the lord of Fettercairn's skeelie, was called to give evidence. Her appearance caused a great murmur and outcry among all who had known her at Fettercairn Castle. Lewen sank his head into his hands, dragging at the roots of his hair with his fingers and gritting his jaw together to stop himself from leaping to his feet and shouting at the judges.

Rhiannon was not so controlled. She cried out furiously, "She's a murderess, do ye no' ken! She tried to poison me! She should be on trial here herself! She does his will—canna ye see that? Only one night past he tried himself to take me, and when that failed, he tried to kill me! What does she do here, walking free? She should be—"

With each exclamation, the Duke of Ardblair's gavel came crashing down upon the table. When that failed to quiet her, he rose to his feet, shouting at Rhiannon to be quiet. Nina was on her feet too, yelling, trying to draw the judges' attention to her, protesting as loudly as Rhiannon herself.

"Why do ye call Dedrie?" Nina cried. "Ye said yourselves that what happened at Fettercairn Castle is o' no relevance! What does the laird o' Fettercairn's skeelie ken o' Connor's death?"

"She is a trained healer," the Duke of Ardblair said sternly, "and she had the opportunity to examine the accused closely during the period when the accused was still attempting to mislead those around her to her involvement in Connor the Just's death. Skeelie Dedrie believes she can help us understand the accused's intentions and motivations more clearly, for which we thank her."

"But, Your Honor—"

"Please sit down, my lady, else we shall have to have ye escorted from the courtroom."

Reluctantly Nina sat down, though her cheeks were flushed and her lips were compressed together in anger. She shot a furious glance up at the Rìgh, who was listening to the proceedings intently, his brows drawn together in a frown.

"But she kens naught!" Rhiannon cried. "She works the laird's will. They want me dead because I ken too much! Ye canna let her speak. She only seeks to blacken me—"

It did no good. Dedrie was escorted up to the witness stand, looking comfortable and sweet-faced in her soft green healer's robe. In contrast to her, Rhiannon was wild-eyed and distraught, her voice rising high in appeal. The Duke of Ardblair gestured impatiently, and the bailiffs mounted the podium and seized her by the arms, dragging her back. Still Rhiannon called to the judges, begging them not to listen to the skeelie. Dedrie shook her head in pity.

"If ye do no' quieten, we shall have ye gagged and bound!" the duke roared, his face purpling with anger.

Rhiannon dashed the tears from her face and was silent, though the whole chamber buzzed with excitement. The Duke of Ardblair sat down, adjusting his robes. "Proceed," he said to the skeelie.

Dedrie's testimony was damning. She seemed to sense every judge's private prejudice and speak straight to it, all the while pricking and poking at Rhiannon until the satyricorn was driven past reason and cried out against her every comment, demanding to be heard. By the end of Dedrie's testimony, Rhiannon seemed, at best, highly strung to the point of imbalance. If not, she was, it was inferred, sly, ruthless, and manipulative.

Nina could not contain herself, leaping to her feet. "This is all wrong!" she cried. "That woman should be on trial for murder, no' Rhiannon! How can ye call this justice?"

Iven sought to draw her down, but she was beside herself with anger. The Duke of Ardblair made a gesture, and the bailiffs seized Nina and wrestled her out of the courtroom, and then Iven too, when he sought to protest and prevent them.

Lewen, aghast, rose to his feet and then, when he felt Olwynne's hand on his arm, drawing him down again, shook her
off. All the other witch-apprentices were on their feet too.

"No' fair!" Fèlice cried.

"How come she's just walking free?" Landon asked. "She
was meant to be in prison!"

The Duke of Ardblair's gavel banged down again and again.
Dedrie, shaking her head mournfully at what her duty had
forced her to do, stepped down from the witness's stand. Lewen
saw her cast one quick, self-satisfied glance up into the gallery.
Her gaze was met by Johanna, sitting forward on her bench
seat, her hand clutched around her haloed-hand medal.

"Ye will all end up in prison yourselves if ye are no' quiet,"
the duke shouted, beside himself with anger. "I tell ye now, be
quiet!"

At last the noise died down. Fèlice hid her face in her arms,
and Lewen wished he could do likewise. He felt sick with trepidation. He raised his eyes to Rhiannon's but she refused to
meet anyone's gaze, keeping her face lowered to her inter-
locked hands.

The judges withdrew to consider their verdict. Rhiannon's
attorney was shaking his head and gathering together his papers. Up in the gallery, Dillon was looking as pleased as his
hard-set face would allow him, while Johanna was weeping in
relief.

The judges were gone a very long time. The crowd grew
restive. Some began to chant again, "Hang her! Hang her!"
while the Nisse and Nixie crowd jeered and shouted Rhiannon's name. Soldiers sought to keep the mob calm.

When at last the doors swung open to let the judges back in,
Lewen could not bear to look at them, so certain was he that
they would decide to condemn Rhiannon to death. He heard a
sharp collective intake of breath, then an outbreak of cheering
and clapping, drowned out by hissing and booing. Fèlice
sobbed out loud.

Lewen slowly raised his eyes.

The six judges stood in a row behind their table, their hands
clenched before them. They had turned their white mantles inside out, to red.

DEATH BELLS

"And therefore never send to know for whom the bell tolls; it tolls for thee."

—JOHN DONNE,
Meditation XVII (1624)

The Book of Shadows

Lewen stood on the lawn before the palace and watched as the midsummer bonfire was built higher and higher in the center of the square. It was almost dusk. Soon the Keybearer would come and chant the midsummer rites, and the bonfire would be lit. Laughing, dressed in yellow and gold, the revelers would come and thrust the torches into its great blazing heart and carry them in a noisy procession through the palace, rekindling the hearths with the balefire.

They would feast and dance the night away, and many, intoxicated with the sparkling rose-colored wine, the warmth of the sweet-scented wind, would take their lover's hand and leap the fire together, pledging their troth.

For a year and a day, they could lie together like man and wife, and take their pleasure, and explore their love. Then, on Midsummer's Day the next year, if both were still willing, they could come again to the embers of the fire and leap it again, their wrists bound together with cord. Once the marriage vows were sworn, and the wedding rites fulfilled, they would be man and wife, their lives entwined together forevermore. The thought of it dazzled and frightened him, and filled him with both joy and terror.

For Lewen and Olwynne planned to jump the Midsummer's Eve fire that night. No one else knew. Olwynne was sure her parents would put a stop to it if they realized, and Lewen knew she was right. He, the son of a soldier and a tree-shifter, was not at all the bridegroom the Rìgh and Banrìgh would have planned for their only daughter, and the shadow of Rhiannon hung over them, disturbing both their sleep with nightmares.

"Maybe we should wait," he had whispered to Olwynne the

night before, in the stuffy darkness of her bed. "I mean . . . Rhiannon . . ."

She had seized his face in both her hands. "I ken ye are shocked by the verdict, Lewen, and I ken ye blame yourself. But it was no' ye who shot Connor through the back, and no' ye who lied and gave false testimony! She has brought this evil fate down upon herself. Forget her! This is for the best, canna ye see?"

He was dismayed to feel tears stinging his eyes. Unable to answer, he turned from her and buried his face in his pillow. Olwynne had fitted her body all along his back, cradling him with her arm. "Trust me," she had whispered. "The sooner ye forget her the better. Jump the fire with me, Lewen! Let us tell the world how we feel for each other!"

He had said nothing and she had drawn away from him. "Do ye no' love me?" she demanded. "Do ye no' wish to be handfasted?"

He had shifted a little so he lay on his back, looking for her in the darkness. Her scent overwhelmed him. "Aye, o' course I love ye," he had whispered. "It's just I—"

"I ken," she answered and kissed him on the mouth. "Truly I do. But she is no good for ye, Lewen. It would have meant ruin for ye. I will be a good wife to ye, though. I'll love ye and help ye, and ye'll have all ye've ever wanted. Canna ye see how much better it is this way?"

He had nodded, and she had hung close over him so her breasts weighed on his chest. "If ye love me, jump the fire with me, Lewen. For I need ye to show the whole world that I'm the one ye love. If ye canna do that, ye canna really love me and I'm better off without ye."

The idea of being without her had plunged him into panic, and so he had promised. He had lain awake then, all the hot night, trying to banish the image of Rhiannon with a black hood being drawn down over her lovely face, of her body jerking as the boards opened beneath her . . .

He knew Olwynne slept badly too, for she whimpered in her sleep, and cried out, and some time before dawn got up to sit by the window, staring out into the garden. Lewen felt in his heart that it was not a good omen, to toss in nightmares the night before one planned to jump the fire, but he could not bear for Olwynne to doubt him and so he kept his resolve firm, refusing to think on Rhiannon at all.

Now the shadows of the cypress trees were lengthening over the pavement, and the golden domes of the palace were blazing in the last light of the sun. He heard singing and turned to watch a long procession of witches come along the road from the Tower of Two Moons, their heads crowned with flowers. His hands were damp with nervousness. He wiped them on his best handkerchief and straightened his jacket.

As the sun slowly sank behind the trees, the Keybearer spoke the midsummer rites; then, as dusk fell over the garden, she flung up her hands, so the bonfire lit with a great whoosh of flames.

Lewen stood quietly and watched as the revelers laughed and danced, and the last light of the day ebbed away into darkness, the red glowing eye of the bonfire seeming to burn brighter and brighter even though it too was dying. His whole body ached with grief. The more he tried not to think of Rhiannon, the more she occupied his thoughts, and he had to lift his hand and press it to his eyes. The flames of the fire were blurring and doubling, though Lewen had touched no wine or ale. He watched as one couple after another joined hands and jumped the fire, some giggling, some in awe and struck with shyness. For some reason, the sight affected Lewen powerfully. Grief, or envy, or longing struck him as sharp as a spear in the side. Blindly he turned aside and went to stumble away.

But Lewen felt a gentle touch on his hand and turned. Olwynne stood beside him, smiling shyly. She was dressed all in golden silk, with a circlet of roses and violets on her fiery hair. It hung unbound down her back like a river of molten lava. Lewen could not take his eyes off her. *I'm doing the right thing*, he told himself. *This is the beginning o' my new life. Olwynne is my true love. Forget Rhiannon, who tricked and lied to and ensorcelled me. . . .*

Olwynne met his eyes and smiled so radiantly the heavy ache of unshed tears in his breast suddenly melted away. He smiled back and stepped forward to take her hand. Then, to the accompaniment of cheers of surprise and encouragement, they ran hand in hand at the bonfire and leaped high over the glowing embers. Sparks flew up at their faces like attacking bees, and Lewen's eyes suddenly stung with the smoke, so that he had to raise his hand and scrub at his eyes, glad of the darkness that hid his face from view.

Rhiannon sat on her hard cot and stared at the brick with the dark blotch shaped like a flying horse. If mere will and desire could break down walls, the stones before her would be exploding into dust and she would be on Blackthorn's back, flying free into the night. She wished for it with every fiber of her being. But Sorrowgate Prison had been built to contain stronger and darker spirits than hers; spells of strength, binding, and containment had been spoken over every stone. The only thing breaking was Rhiannon's own heart. It was late. Outside, the sound of the Midsummer's Eve feast rose from the square— squeals of laughter, the hum of conversation, the lilt of fiddle and guitar, the beat of dancing feet.

Inside the royal suite all was subdued. Lachlan and Iseult were still shocked and dismayed by the sight of their only daughter leaping the fire with a boy they were not at all sure they approved. Lewen might well have been the son of one of Lachlan's most faithful lieutenants, but he had no money and very little land, and he had only recently broken free of the toils of a murderous satyricorn. The whole court was buzzing with the scandal, and the only redeeming factor was the glow of happiness on Olwynne's face.

Through the windows came the flickering orange light of the bonfire. Lachlan stood with his hand on the window clasp, watching the dancers twirling about the pyre.

"I am troubled, I must admit," the Rìgh said. "It goes against the grain to hang one so young and fair, and one championed by some o' my auldest and dearest friends. I am just glad they did no' find her guilty o' treason too. I could no' have stomached the drawing and quartering."

"They are rioting in the city," Iseult said, sitting very straight on her blue-and-gilt chair, her red brows drawn together. "The faery quarter is up in arms. Something about this satyricorn lass has captured their imagination."

"It is the tale that lass from Ravenshaw tells," Brun the cluricaun said. He was sitting comfortably on a low sofa, a foaming mug of ale resting on his broad paunch. "I seen her at the Nisse and Nixie—she sure can tell a tale! It fair creeps my blood when she talks about the dead laddie touching Rhiannon with his icy hand, and whispering how cold he is all the time. She's pulling bigger crowds now than the masked singer I was telling ye about, the one who insists on sitting all wreathed in smoke and disappears anytime I come near her."

"Is that the lass Owein is moping over?" Iseult said sharply. "The pretty one, keeping her chin in the air?"

"Aye, that's the one," Brun said and drank some of his ale, smacking his lips noisily. "She should be on the stage, that lass. Wasted as a duke's daughter."

"If only Donncan had no' gone and killed a Yeoman himself!" Lachlan said gloomily. "O' course it looks bad, him being cleared after a mere inquiry, and this Rhiannon girl being condemned to death."

"The inquiry was fair," Iseult said defensively.

"Was it? Ye canna tell me that any other young man would have been treated so well. Donncan was spared the indignity o' a public trial because he is my son, no other reason."

"Ye canna want Donncan to face a trial!"

"O' course I do no' want him to! Nor do I think he should. It was self-defense, clearly enough. It is just bad timing, this murder trial happening right on the heels o' the young guard's death. Ye must admit it doesna look good."

"Nay," Iseult agreed slowly, "but what can we do about it?"

"Do ye mean to pardon Rhiannon?" Isabeau asked. She was sitting in the window seat with Buba the owl nestled in her hands. Still dressed in her ceremonial robes, she had pulled off her crown of flowers and it lay on the cushion beside her, the flowers wilting.

"I dinna ken," Lachlan replied slowly. "Dillon and Johanna are howling for her blood, and even Finn and Jay seem convinced her motives in killing Connor were no' as pure as she makes out. They were the ones who found this wild man and brought him in, and certainly his testimony was damning. Yet . . ."

"Yet she saved Roden from the laird o' Fettercairn," Isabeau said.

"Aye," Lachlan agreed.

"Nina says she could've escaped then, if she had wanted to," Dide said. He was sitting sideways on a low stool, gently strumming his battered old guitar. "She risked her life to save him. Nina does no' ken how she is to explain to Roden that Rhiannon is to be hung."

Lachlan winced and gave a little groan. "No' a task I'd relish, I must admit," he said.

"It was a fair trial and the judges made their decision on the evidence presented," Iseult said impatiently. "Ye ken they willna like it if ye go meddling in what is really none o' your business."

Lachlan frowned. "I am the final arbitrator o' justice in this land. I have the right to issue a royal pardon," he reminded her.

"Aye, but that doesna mean the Inns o' Court will like it," she replied.

Lachlan shrugged his shoulders irritably.

"She has Talent," Isabeau said, returning her gaze again to the garden. "The strongest we've found in a while."

"So ye think I should pardon her? Because ye want her for your Theurgia?"

"I do want her, but I would no' ask ye to pardon a convicted murderess simply because I think she has Talent. No, there's more to it than that. I think the judges made a mistake."

"How so?" Iseult's voice was not encouraging.

"How many o' us can state with utter truth that our motives in this life are always pure and simple? I ken I canna."

Iseult's face relaxed. She shrugged ruefully, saying, "How true. Ye think perhaps they failed to understand that? In regards to this satyricorn girl, I mean?"

Isabeau nodded.

Lachlan brought the Lodestar to rest between his knees, staring down into its swirling white heart.

"It would be a bad omen, to have gallows fruit hanging on the gate the day Donncan and Bronwen finally jump the fire together," Dide said.

"Yet she admits she killed Connor," Lachlan said with a spurt of anger in his voice. "He was one o' my best, my most loyal men! I have too few o' ye, Dide. I canna afford to have them being shot in the back by a wayward satyricorn lass. If I pardon her, am I no' declaring the murder o' a Yeoman is o' no account?"

The room was silent. Dide's fingers were still on the guitar strings. Lachlan sighed heavily and rubbed his forehead. "So many o' them died in my service," he said. "Parlan, Artair, Anntoin . . . Tòmas . . ."

They all heard the dull grief in his voice. It had been a cruel death, that of Tòmas the Healer, who had spent his strength saving others and then died in the last moments of that desperate war. The Rìgh still smarted from the injustice of it, and they knew he felt for Johanna, who had mourned Tòmas so savagely and now mourned her brother as well.

Brun wiped away a foam moustache. "I have a riddle for ye," he said.

"And what may that be?" Lachlan answered with grave courtesy. He had learned many years before to listen well to the wise old cluricaun's riddles and jests.

Brun held up his hairy paw, the first finger and thumb touching to form a small circle. "What is no bigger than a plum, yet leads the Rìgh himself from town to town?"

"I canna tell ye," Lachlan replied, smiling a little.

"His eye," Brun replied and winked.

There was a short silence as they absorbed the cluricaun's possible meaning. Brun buried his mouth back in his ale.

"Aye," Lachlan said slowly. "A Rìgh must see clearly. A satyricorn should have the same justice as a prionnsa. I canna hang this girl and let Donncan walk free." He sighed heavily. "I will stay the hanging. She must serve us some other way. I will go now and explain to Johanna. I fear she will no' be happy. She has conceived a hatred for this lass that I must admit has surprised me." He got up, frowning. "I shall make the announcement tomorrow, at the wedding banquet. I shall pardon all the prisoners who have been condemned to hang, so we have no grief or horror to mar the wedding."

"Ye had best tell Dillon and Finn and Jay too," Iseult said.

Lachlan nodded. "But no one else. Let us keep it quiet till then."

"May I tell Nina?" Dide asked. "She is making herself sick with grief and self-recrimination."

"Aye, tell Nina," Lachlan said. "We want her in good voice for the wedding."

As he went towards the door, Isabeau stopped him with a hand on his arm.

"I'm glad," she said. "Thank ye, Lachlan!"

"I do it for Roden's sake," he said. "He is Dide's only heir." Isabeau said abruptly, "Lachlan, do ye remember the Samhain Night we won ye Owein's Bow?"

"O' course," he replied in surprise.

"Ye remember giving the League their choice o' gifts in the auld relic room? Finn took the MacRuraich horn and used it to call up the ghosts o' her clan."

"And she took the cloak o' nyx-hair too, on the sly," Lachlan said, nodding in remembrance. "O' course I remember."

"What did ye give the others? Do ye remember?"

"Dillon took the sword, o' course. Joyeux. Who could forget that? Jay took the viola d'amore, to replace his lost fiddle. Johanna took some bauble—a bangle, I think."

"She wears it still," Isabeau said. "It was the wedding bracelet o' Aedan's wife, Vernessa."

"What!"

"Aye. I looked it up in *The Book o' Shadows*. I was interested in those gifts, ye see. So many o' them proved to have power or history o' some kind."

"Johanna wears the wedding bracelet Aedan Whitelock gave his wife?" It was clear Lachlan felt such an heirloom should have stayed in the clan, and Isabeau had to remind him gently that he had offered the members of the League of the Healing Hand a gift of their own choice as a reward for their assistance in gaining the throne. Giving Johanna the bracelet was not the first action of generosity he had lived to regret.

"What were the other gifts, do ye remember?" she urged him.

"The other boys took swords too, I think."

"No' Connor. He took a music box, didna he?"

"Aye, that's right. It was a pretty trinket. It was like carrying an orchestra around in one's pocket. It played a hundred different tunes and needed no more than a turn of its key to wind it. I remember he loved it as a boy."

"I wonder who it belonged to, to end up in the relic room,"

Isabeau mused. "I have found no mention o' it in *The Book o' Shadows*."

"Why so interested, Beau?" Dide asked.

"I'm always interested in things o' power," she replied, smiling at him. "Just think on Dillon's sword. What a gift to give a small boy! A sword that will fight to the very death once it is unsheathed, even if the bearer o' the sword must die himself o' exhaustion. A cursed sword, that longs always for blood."

"I didna ken what it was when I let him have it," Lachlan interjected angrily.

"O' course no'. My point is ye kent what none o' it was. Yet they must all have been things o' power, for Meghan to seal them up like that on the Day o' Betrayal, hiding them from the Red Guards."

"Why ask me about them now, though?"

Isabeau hesitated. "Rhiannon had the music box among her things. I saw it in the courtroom today. Plus a very fine dagger, that Aidan made much o'."

"Aye, well, that showed she took all Connor's things," Iseult said impatiently. "What is your point?"

"There was a silver goblet there too," Isabeau said. "It strikes a dim chord in my mind. . . ."

"Parlan chose a goblet," Lachlan said. "I remember thinking it was an odd choice for a lad. I would've thought he would take a sword, like the others."

"What happened to the gifts ye gave the other Leaguers?" Isabeau asked. "After they died, I mean?"

Lachlan did not know. "Meghan had them, I think," he said vaguely. "She was angry with me for giving them away. I think she locked them up in her chest. Certainly she took Joyeux away from Dillon, but he went and took it back, afore he kent what it was."

Isabeau nodded. "That's what I thought. I wondered . . . I thought perhaps Connor may have been given their things once they died . . . or taken them."

"Highly possible," Lachlan agreed. "But what does it matter, Isabeau?"

"I just wondered," she said. "That goblet . . . it fairly

shrieked magic at me when I saw it. I'd like to know what it is. I think I'll consult *The Book o' Shadows* about it."

"Ye think it may have bearing upon the case?" Lachlan demanded.

She hesitated. "If it is what I think it is, well, perhaps it explains some behavior that has puzzled me."

"Like what?" Iseult asked.

"Like why Rhiannon confessed to Lewen in the first place. Her every instinct is for survival. Every time she was questioned about Connor's death, she lied. So why did she no' lie again, when Lewen asked her about the necklace o' teeth?"

"She saw the game was up?"

"But it wasna, no' at all. Lewen was in love with her; he would've believed her if she had made up some story, some excuse. There was no need for her to confess the way she did. It just does no' seem to ring true to me."

"So ye think this goblet o' Connor's is some kind o' confessing cup? A cup that compels truth telling?" Iseult asked, turning the idea over in her mind. "I can see how that would be useful."

"Me too," Isabeau replied.

"Ye seem to be putting two and two together and getting forty to me," Lachlan said dismissively. "So what if the lass confessed? She was in love with Lewen too, remember. Love makes ye do very stupid things sometimes." His voice was dour, and it was clear he was thinking of his daughter.

"True, but then remember what we all called Connor. Connor the Just, for his ability to find the truth o' a matter and sort out a solution. How much easier would his job be if he had a cup o' truth? And then think o' Lewen. He too was driven to confess the next day, telling first Nina what Rhiannon had said, and then ye, Lachlan. Lewen is loyal to a fault. He would never have betrayed her confidence so lightly."

"I always thought so too, but Lewen has surprised me a great deal in recent months," Lachlan said grimly. "Seducing my daughter, for one! He's lucky I do no' have *him* hanged, drawn, and quartered!"

"Well, I have my theories about that too," Isabeau said.

Iseult bristled up at once in defense of her daughter, but Isabeau said, in a flat, hard voice, "There is something wrong there, Iseult, and do no' try and tell me ye canna see it. Why else are ye so upset?"

"It was just so sudden, so unexpected," Iseult said.

"Exactly. It stinks o' compulsion, this sudden mad passion o' Lewen's. Olwynne is too strong and subtle a witch to reveal much o' her hand, but I'll lay ye three gold royals that she has worked a dark spell or two."

"Why would Olwynne do such a thing?" Lachlan cried angrily. "She is a royal banprionnsa, second in line to the throne. She could have anyone she wanted—"

"No' if the one she wanted was in love with someone else."

"If Lewen is too blind and stupid to see what she had to offer, she'd be better off without him."

"I agree, but tell that to a lass in love."

"I will no' believe my daughter has been casting love spells, like some half-witted village skeelie. . . ."

"Why no', when ye did it yourself?" Iseult said suddenly. "Och, there was no need for ye to do so, for I loved ye already and *ye* were just too blind and stupid to see it. But ye must admit ye tried. . . . Ye sang me the song o' love, remember, and seduced me in the wood."

Color rose under Lachlan's olive skin. "Aye, happen so, but that was different. . . ."

"Why?" Iseult asked.

Lachlan floundered, unable to explain.

"I am very angry with her," Isabeau said. "Olwynne has the potential to be a great sorceress. She shouldna be wasting her time on romance now!"

"No' everyone thinks romance is a waste o' time," Dide said, and she flashed him a quick look of apology.

"No," Lachlan agreed, "and besides, it is done now. They are handfasted and, if Olwynne is to have her way, will be married in a year and a day. I canna say I am altogether sorry. Lewen needed to be taken into hand, after all that folly with this satyricorn girl. Personally, I feel she is the far more likely candidate for spinning love spells!"

It was very late when Isabeau finally got back to the Tower of Two Moons, having wasted a fair amount of time with her own romance in Dide's clothes-strewn suite of rooms. Isabeau was used to managing without much sleep, however, and she was invigorated by her walk through the sleeping gardens, the two moons little more than frail slivers of light in the star-laden sky. The tower was quiet, and she climbed the stairs to her room with a little witch-light bobbing above her head to illuminate the way.

She laid her hand upon her doorknob and at once hesitated, sensing a fleeting trace of human contact there that was not her own. It was too insubstantial for her to identify the hand that had touched there, but her ward was still intact and so Isabeau, relieved, unlocked her door and entered her room, lit only by the faint moonlight filtering through the arched windows.

She stood silent, her witch-senses alert. It seemed some other presence had ruffled the atoms of her space, leaving behind a faint, disturbingly familiar suggestion of their presence, like a trail of scent notes. She could not identify the intruder, though she felt that she should know it.

Isabeau lit every candle in the room with a thought, the kindling in her hearth blazing up. She looked about her. All was as she had left it. Nothing seemed to have been touched. Isabeau walked slowly over to her desk, feeling a chill on her skin that made it rise up in goose pimples, smelling a faint metallic tang to the air like a storm rising over the sea. Magic had been done here, and not so long ago.

The Book of Shadows rested where it always did. An enormously thick old book bound in red leather and locked with an iron clasp, it held within it all the collected lore and history of the Coven of Witches. Each Keybearer recorded within its pages all that he or she had learned or discovered, so that their knowledge would not be lost to later generations. It was one of the great treasures of the Coven.

Isabeau rested her hands upon its worn red leather. She felt edgy, uneasy. Her hands tingled. She took a deep breath, drew upon the One Power, and opened her third eye.

An image came to her. A woman leaning over the book, unlocking its clasp, turning the pages, searching. Her lantern rested on the table, casting a ray of light upon her green robe but leaving her face in shadow. The hair that hung in a long plait was brown, with faint gleams of grey. Her search grew more desperate, and she spoke aloud, a curse, a command. The pages of the book began to riffle over by themselves, far faster than any hand could turn them. Then suddenly they stopped. The book rested wide open. The woman bent and read the page displayed.

All this Isabeau saw in a few scant moments. Then the vision faded, and she saw once again only her candlelit room, the white curtains swaying in the soft breeze, the red book under her hands as solid and unyielding as ever.

"Who?" Isabeau whispered to herself. "And why?"

She knew that it could only be someone who knew her well, for the key to *The Book of Shadows* was hidden in a secret compartment of a little box Lewen had carved for her some years before. Isabeau had been raised by Meghan of the Beasts to guard secrets carefully and so few knew where to find it.

She bit her thumb, then went softly across to the mantelpiece and took down a little wooden box that rested there. A rose set among thorns was carved upon its lid. If one pressed the rose firmly on its ruffled heart, it rose up out of the lid, revealing a hidden hollow. Within was a heavy iron key, as long as Isabeau's little finger.

Isabeau held the key between her hands, feeling and listening with her witch-sense for any subtle and elusive trace of personality anyone touching the key would have left behind. This time she recognized it at once. "Johanna," she whispered, and felt a sharp stab of betrayal.

She turned and looked at *The Book of Shadows*, wondering again *Why, why, why?*

Isabeau took the key to the desk and unlocked *The Book of Shadows*, laying her hands firmly upon it and saying, "Show me the last page read."

As soon as she lifted her hands away, the book opened with a great thud, lying open at a page very early on in its history. Isabeau was at once aware of the temperature dropping fast, as if she had opened a door into a snowstorm. She shivered and hesitated, feeling an unaccountable dread. She could discover nothing until she read the page, however, and so, after only a pause of a few heartbeats, Isabeau bent and looked at the first line of writing.

By the time Isabeau had read the first four words, she

wished to stop but she could not wrench her gaze away. The spell held her fast, searing through Isabeau's eyes and into her brain.

"To Raise the Dead," it said, "one needs a living soul, whether willing or unwilling, and a knife well-sharpened . . ."

The paper was old and stained, and the letters were written in a faint brown ink that looked horribly like blood. The handwriting was large and formal, with many embellishments and flourishes that made it hard to read. Isabeau could no more prevent her brain from puzzling out the words than she could stop her eyes from moving along the lines. It was as if a giant hand had reached inside her skull and seized the ends of her nerve strings, plucking them as it pleased, so that she danced and bowed at its will. Isabeau had never experienced such a strong compulsion before. Even worse, as she fought not to read the Spell of Resurrection and failed, she felt another spell, laid down in every bloody curlicue of writing, lay its dark compulsion upon her.

"I will live again," she whispered, in a deep, rasping voice, "and ye shall be the one to raise me."

Singing the Summerbourne

Bronwen lay in her ocean-green, gauze-hung bed and tried to tell herself that this was the happiest day of her life. *All brides feel anxious on their wedding day*, she told herself. *It's only wedding jitters. Nerves. That's all it is.* But Bronwen knew the leaden lump of misery in the pit of her stomach was not normal. A bride should not lie in her lonely bed on the morning of her wedding fighting back tears.

Bronwen tried to think of her husband-to-be objectively. He was heir to the throne of Eileanan, young, tall, strong, good-looking, and intelligent. Certainly every girl Bronwen knew would think her lucky indeed.

He would not dance, which was a major strike against him, and he was a weak swimmer, hampered as he was by his heavy golden wings. This made him a poor mate for one of Fairgean ancestry, she thought. Bronwen had to swim in salt water every day, for the health of both body and spirit.

He loved music as much as she did, though, and there was no one with whom she would rather play a duet, or go to the music halls and theater.

He was far too serious and would not dress up and act in masques or follies, nor would he write poetry extolling her eyes or her lips. Bronwen had begun to find that one love poem was much like another love poem, however, and Donncan at least could make her laugh out loud, which was something few could do.

She thought of him as one of her best and dearest friends. She had known him all her life. He was her cousin. They shared the white lock that bonding with the Lodestar had seared at their brow. It was the visible insignia of their lineage from Cuinn the Wise, the leader of the First Coven of Witches, who had commanded the amazing and perilous journey across time and space from the Other World, the true home of humans, to this world, a land of scattered islands floating in a boundless ocean.

Cuinn the Wise had died in the Crossing, but his son had survived to found this ancient city of Lucescere, and the Mac-Cuinn clan. In time one of his descendants, Aedan Whitelock, had been crowned Rìgh of all Eileanan. It was Aedan Mac-Cuinn who had created the Lodestar, using its magic to quell the warfaring faeries of the sea and bring peace to the human inhabitants of the island, at least. All those born into the Mac-Cuinn clan were given the Lodestar to hold as a babe, forging a bond that never corroded. Bronwen could hear the song of the Lodestar in her dreams. She always knew where it was, even when Lachlan was far away traveling the land. She remembered how it had responded to the touch of her hand, all those years ago when she had saved it from being lost in the waves at the Battle of Bonnyblair. She had never been permitted to touch it since, though Donncan and the twins had often been given it to play with as children. If it had been up to Lachlan to decide, she would never have been allowed to bond with it at all. It was her mother, Maya, who had brought Bronwen to the Lodestar, not her uncle, who had seized the magical sphere from her and, with it, the Crown.

This was an old resentment, though, like having to endure her mother being named the Ensorcellor, or having to watch her scrub floors at the witches' tower. It had not been easy being the Ensorcellor's daughter. It had not been easy being of Fairgean descent, either, no matter how many peace treaties were signed. Hardest of all had been having one's mother rendered mute during all the years of one's growing up, unable to comfort or advise her in times of trouble. Bronwen's mother could not sing her a lullaby, or share a joke, or tell her a story, or say that she loved her.

It had been such a relief, such a joy, to find the spell broken with the death of the old nyx, Ceit Anna. The morning after the nyx's death flight had been the happiest of Bronwen's life. She had been woken by the eerie wailing of the nyx's dirge but was slipping back towards sleep when she had heard, deep in her mind, her name called, and then a single exultant word. *Come!*

Bronwen had not heard her mother's voice since she was seven years old but she knew it at once. She had leaped out of her bed, scrambled into the first dress she could find, and then crept through the dark sleeping palace, avoiding the guards. It had been the night of the full moon. Bronwen had made her way through the silver and black garden with a thumping heart. She had not dared conjure a witch-light so close to the witches' tower, knowing they would sense magic being used, and so she had had to find her way like a blind girl, hands stretched out before her, feet feeling their way. It had been exhilarating.

At last she had come to the servants' quarters at the Tower of Two Moons, heart pounding so hard she thought it would choke her. Maya had been waiting for her, her door held open just a crack to show a thin sliver of warm light. She had drawn Bronwen in without a word, so that her heart had sunk with disappointment. But then, once the door was shut fast behind them, Maya had embraced her, whispering hoarsely, "Bronwen, my darling girl!"

Her voice, once so rich and sweet and warm, had been harsh and cracked after so many years of disuse, but it was still the most beautiful sound Bronwen had ever heard. She had wept and hugged her mother hard, and then at once begun to think of ways of keeping her mother's secret safe.

For no one must know that Maya was mute no longer. All of Maya's considerable power was contained in her voice—the power to charm, to compel, to sing and seduce and enthrall. If the Rìgh had known the ribbon Ceit Anna had woven to bind Maya's voice had dissolved upon her death, he would have ordered another made at once.

There had not been much time. Bronwen had known she could not be the only one to wake at the sound of the nyx's lament. Already it was growing light. Birds were beginning to sing. So Bronwen had stepped away from her mother's embrace and seized her scissors from the workbasket on the table. She had grasped a hank of her own hair in her hand and chopped it off, then swiftly twisted and plaited it into a long black ribbon, whispering as many spells as she could remember as she wove—spells of binding and containment, dark spells of negativity and silence, and bright spells to deflect suspicion. Bronwen had barely had time to knot the ribbon about her mother's throat before the Keybearer's imperious knock had sounded on Maya's door. While her mother had answered the door, Bronwen had thrust the scissors back in the basket and the basket under the table. She had then done her best to pretend all was as usual.

So far the deception had not failed. No one suspected Maya was no longer mute. She went about her work as silently and obediently as ever, speaking to Bronwen only when they were sure no one was listening. Deep in the witches' wood, at night or in the dawn when no one was about, Maya sang and shouted and laughed and declaimed spells as loudly and exultantly as she liked, reacquainting herself with the range and subtlety of her powers.

She had disguised herself in a glamourie and walked out into the city as freely as any other woman, pausing to chat with the fishwives and the flower sellers, to buy herself a cup of wine at the market and laugh with the crowd at the antics of the jongleurs. Bronwen knew of these forays and approved, having resented the bitter silence and loneliness of her mother's life, cut off forever from normal human communication.

When she had heard of a new singer at one of the inns in the faery quarter who was causing a sensation with her treasonous songs, however, Bronwen had known at once that it was her mother, and her heart had quailed. She would much have preferred her mother to keep herself safe. Although Bronwen felt a certain sour melancholy that she would only ever be Banrìgh in name, as the Rìgh's consort, she had grown resigned to that many years earlier. She had no desire to start another civil war. Bronwen had lived through one, and that was more than enough. She knew Donncan to be a gentle, loving, courteous man who valued her wit as much as her beauty. She would have power and influence in plenty, without having to enforce it with the slash of a sword.

Bronwen had begged Maya not to go to the Nisse and Nixie anymore. "There are cluricauns in that crowd, and witches, Mama. Ye ken they can see through any glamourie! They will recognize ye."

"If I see a cluricaun, I'll slip away, I promise."

"What about a witch, or anyone else with the gift o' clear-seeing?"

"Very well, then, I'll wear a mask. That'll only add to the air o' intrigue."

"But why, Mama? Why draw such attention to yourself? Ye canna really hope to throw Uncle Lachlan off the throne, can ye? I do no' want ye to, truly!"

Maya's mouth had set into the adamantine line Bronwen knew so well. "Ye would no' deny me the pleasure o' a small revenge, would ye?" she said. "I do no' want to throw him off the throne, just to make him uneasy on it. Slip a burr under the saddle, as it were."

"But if ye are discovered . . ."

"I will no' do it for long, I promise," Maya said. "In a few weeks' time I'll start singing somewhere else."

"But, Mama . . ."

Maya had smiled at her and said softly, "It is petty, I ken, but deeply satisfying nonetheless. And it will no' do ye any harm, my dear, for the court to remember ye are the true heir."

Bronwen knew this to be true and so did not try to dissuade her, though she remained anxious in case Maya's disguise was penetrated. If there had not been so much else for the court to gossip about that summer, an investigation into the perfidious singer would probably have been launched, but Maya's small rebellion had gone largely unremarked, to her disappointment, and so their secret had remained safe.

Bronwen's lip curled in scorn as she remembered how Donncan had assumed she had cut off a lock of her hair as some kind of love token, as if she was a frivolous country miss without sense or morals, and not a daughter fighting to keep her mother safe. The very next instant, though, tears smarted her eyes, for it hurt Bronwen that Donncan, her cousin and dear friend, could so underestimate her. And his suspicion, and her hurt pride, had erected a wall of coldness between them that Bronwen did not know how to dismantle.

The weeks between May Day and Midsummer's Day had only seen the wall grow higher, for an inquiry had been called into Mathias Bright-Eyed's death that had seen his relationship with Bronwen examined exhaustively. Every dance, every conversation, every flirtation Bronwen had enjoyed over the past year or so was scrutinized, and many of Bronwen's friends and servants were called to give evidence, much to her chagrin. Although the inquiry had eventually found Donncan innocent of any wrongdoing and established that the relationship between the guard and the Banprionnsa had been no more than occasional dance partners, still it had galled Bronwen badly to have her behavior inspected so closely.

During all this time Donncan had remained cool and distant, never seeking her out, and when forced into her company, giving her only the politest of exchanges. His parents, too, seemed to view her with disfavor, something Bronwen could not entirely blame them for since the list of her parties, masques, and escapades was long enough and silly enough to make her squirm with mortification. She could not explain even to herself why she had embarked on such an expensive and frivolous way of life after graduating from the Theurgia. It may have had something to do with the fact that she was not permitted to join the Coven and study to be a sorceress, despite her obvious Talents. It was always the custom to keep Crown and Coven independent of one another, and so any of the prionnsachan who wished to pursue their magical studies must, like Finn the Cat, abdicate any claim to their country's throne.

Or perhaps it was because Donncan, the acknowledged heir to the throne, had been sent away on a tour of the country he would one day be ruling, to learn what he could of its people, while Bronwen was kept kicking her heels at court. Perhaps it was just pique that Donncan was away from her for so long. She could not explain it, and so she just raised a brow to the inquiry and said languidly, "Well, any antidote to boredom."

Donncan had frowned and turned away from her, and Bronwen had tossed her head and pretended she did not care. She did, though. She cared very much. She had not been able to forget the horror of the May Day feast, when Mathias's dagger had sunk so inexorably into his own flesh and cut short his bright, careless life. Again and again Bronwen went over it, wishing she could have the time again. Why had she not realized how dangerous her lighthearted flirtation had been? She had not meant to cause any harm.

But harm she had caused, and now Mathias was dead. He

would never again dance the galliard, or bow over a pretty girl's hand, or wrestle with his friends.

And Donncan would never be able to forgive her. She saw that in his face every time he turned his eyes away from her. All of their lives, he had adored her and championed her. She could do no wrong in his eyes. But that was all over. Everything had changed.

Tears seeped out between Bronwen's lids and she put up a hand to wipe them away. At her movement Maura rose from her chair by the door and came trotting over. She was not much bigger than a child, though her plum-black skin was heavily wrinkled. Her eyes were huge and sad, and as lustrous as a pool of ink.

"What wrong?" she whispered. "Ye sad, Miss Bron?"

Bronwen tried to smile. "Och, nay! I'm grand! And hungry as a horse. Where is my breakfast?"

"I go get," Maura said. "Ye stay."

As the bogfaery went to call the maids, Bronwen rubbed away her tears ferociously, exhorting herself not to be a fool. She sat up and eagerly took the cup of hot dancey that Maura brought her and drank it down in three great gulps, burning her tongue but feeling at once its buzz in her blood.

"Is it dawn yet? Have I missed the singing o' the summerbourne?"

Maura shook her head. "No sing-sing yet. I no' let my miss sleep too long. No' good, on wedding day, to thumb Rìgh so."

No, it would not be wise to thumb her nose at the Rìgh today. It was a long-held tradition that the MacCuinn and his family all got together and joined the Celestines in singing the summerbourne to life every midsummer. Lachlan the Winged had powerful magic in his voice. Once, long ago, he had won the Celestines to his cause by joining them in this most blessed song, which helped the life-giving waters of the sacred springs run clear and strong. Nowadays his three children and his niece always joined him in this ritual, at the Pool of Two Moons in Lucescere, which had been built upon one of the Celestines' holy hills.

There were many of these holy hills all over Eileanan, each with its pool and spring of water, and each crowned with a ring of stones built long ago by the Celestines. They were called the

Hearts of Stars, and acted as a focal point for the magnetic forces of the earth and the universe. If one knew the secret, one could step through the stone doorway and on to the magical roads the Celestines called the Old Ways, enabling one to move swiftly and invisibly about the countryside.

The faery roads were dangerous to those who did not fully understand their secrets, however. One misstep could strand you in another land or another time, or leave you wandering between worlds, unable to find your way home. Ghosts and evil spirits were drawn to the energy of the ley lines and could attach themselves to any traveler or drive them mad with their malevolent hunger. When the Celestines sang their strange, unearthly song at every equinox and solstice, it cleansed the ley lines of their negative energies, making the faery roads safe to travel along again.

Generally Bronwen enjoyed the singing of the summer-bourne. She was fascinated by the Celestines and loved the chance to weave magic with her voice, something she was generally discouraged from doing.

But the dawn ceremony was the first in a long day that would be crammed with the various midsummer rites and rituals, culminating in the lighting of the bonfire at sunset. Once torches from the fire had been carried into the palace, lighting the hearth within, she and Donncan would jump the fire together and be married. The very thought was enough to make her stomach twist with anxiety. How could she spend the rest of her life with a man who treated her with cold courtesy? Bronwen thought she would rather die an old maid. She turned and pulled her pillow over her head.

Maura's wrinkled paw patted her shoulder. "Do no' be sad, Miss Bron," she said. "Happy day!"

Bronwen sat up and smiled gaily. "Aye, o' course," she said. "A very happy day."

But Maura's anxious face did not ease.

Dressed in a simple white robe, a crown of flowers on her black hair, Bronwen went downstairs to the great hall, where a crowd was already milling around, talking and laughing.

The Rìgh acknowledged her entrance with a nod. He looked

weary, she noted, and was surprised. Her uncle so rarely seemed to show any sign of the strain of his position. She wondered if it was worry over her marriage to Donncan that had kept him sleepless, or the sudden and rather scandalous liaison between Olwynne and one of his squires. Everyone had always thought Olwynne would be the one to join the Coven, but here she was, at the tender age of twenty, handfasted to a boy from the back of beyond. It was rather surprising. Witches rarely married, and although they were generally free and easy with their sexual favors, relationships between apprentices were very much frowned on, as it was thought to stunt the flowering of magical talent. No wonder the Keybearer was looking preoccupied, and the Rìgh and Banrìgh so troubled. Bronwen could only be grateful to Olwynne, though, for deflecting attention away from herself.

She went quietly up to the family group and nodded a greeting, wishing she did not feel such an outsider. Lachlan was standing before the fire, warming his hands and talking with Isabeau, who had dark shadows under her eyes.

"So tell me, did ye read what *The Book o' Shadows* had to say about the goblet?" he was asking in a low voice that no one but Bronwen could have heard.

"Nay," she answered shortly.

It was still dark outside, but a few birds began to trill. At the sound, there was a stir of anticipation through the crowd. Donncan had been sitting talking to his sister, but he rose then and came to Bronwen's side.

"Good morning," he said, as grave-faced as his father.

"Good morning," she answered and tried to rouse herself to lightheartedness, saying with a smile, "How are ye yourself, my husband-to-be?"

"Well, I thank ye," he said but did not smile.

"Is it no' unlucky for us to see each other this morn?" she asked with false gaiety. "Surely we are no' meant to see each other until we are to be wed?"

"Then I had best remove myself from your sight," he said and bowed and walked away.

She felt a surge of desperation and reached out to seize his sleeve, saying, "Donncan . . ."

But the Rìgh had moved forward, holding up his hand for silence. Bronwen let her hand fall.

"Let us go to the Pool o' Two Moons, to sing the summerbourne with our friends and allies the Celestines, and to watch the sun rise on Midsummer's Day," Lachlan announced in his deep, ringing voice.

Carrying a flaming torch in his hand, he led the way out into the dark garden and along the shadowy paths until they reached the maze that lay at the heart of the forest separating the palace and the witches' tower. Bronwen had always enjoyed this solemn procession through the dark gardens, the rim of the world etched in flaming red. The maze in particular was a place of rustling mystery at night, the tall yew hedges so high on either side, like a secret tunnel, and all sense of direction lost as they turned and turned again. She did not enjoy it today, though, seeing Donncan's tall form ahead of her, not once turning to look for her.

Lachlan knew the way through the maze well and led them unerringly to the Pool of Two Moons, set like a dark emerald in its small knot of garden, with the golden dome of the observatory rising beside it. The only clue to its origin as one of the Celestines' holy springs was the huge, ancient stones that surrounded it, etched with faint shapes and symbols. At some later date, the pillars had been crowned with stone arches decorated with the symbol of the Tower of Two Moons—a six-pointed star crowning two crescent moons.

At one end of the pool was a dais with huge bronze doors that led into the observatory, below a shield with the tower crest carved upon it. At the other end was a stone channel where water from the pool trickled out, leading into an aqueduct that flowed down to disappear under the maze. This had once been the summerbourne, a naturally flowing spring of crystal-clear water, but now it was all enclosed in stone.

Their orange torchlight shimmered on the Pool of Two Moons, making it seem dark and mysterious. Bronwen stared down at it in fascination. Her mother had escaped Lachlan once by diving into the pool. It was said to be bottomless. Bronwen could see it had sunk very low in the heat of the summer, the walls above it showing a brown stain.

The witches and courtiers stood back in the garden to watch, but Bronwen mounted the steps with her uncle and cousins and those witches who manifested their power in their voices. Thunderlily went with them, her grave expression belying the excitement and joy she felt at the prospect of seeing her mother for the first time in three years. Bronwen knew that the young Celestine felt sorrow also, for Midsummer's Day was her twenty-fourth birthday and marked the end of her carefree years at the Theurgia. Her mother, Cloudshadow, was coming to fetch her home, and Thunderlily would need to begin preparing for her role as the heir of the Stargazers.

Silently Donncan held out his hand to Bronwen and she took it, casting him a glance under her lashes. He was not looking at her but stared straight ahead. His grip was loose, as if he touched her only reluctantly. Bronwen felt a sudden upsurge of tears but blinked them back obstinately, holding out her other hand to Thunderlily, who at once felt her distress and squeezed her fingers gently.

She shut her eyes and waited, listening. She heard a deep, low hum that resonated up through her feet, reverberating inside her very bones. The small bones inside her skull seemed to grind one against the other. Slowly the humming rose, as if the earth itself was growling, and Bronwen knew the Celestines came. She drew a shaky breath and began to sing.

It was the melody that was important, the weaving of sound, rather than the words. Some time ago Lachlan had written a simple chorus that they all sang in rounds, welcoming the sun this day. Bronwen knew it well, but even so she had trouble concentrating on the tune. She felt off-key, off-kilter. It had been drummed into her from an early age how important it was not to break the melody once it had begun, and so she wrenched her mind away from the aching hollow of her heart and tried to focus on the song. It was difficult. None of them were singing well this day. Lachlan's voice, normally deep and strong, sounded weary, and Owein sounded as if he had a cold. Only Olwynne was singing with her usual verve and beauty, her glorious mezzo-soprano voice soaring high on the far side of the pool. Listening to her younger cousin sing, hearing the joy and hope of happiness in her voice, made Bronwen's throat suddenly close over. Her voice wavered and broke. Donncan gripped her hand in sudden warning, but she could not help herself. Her eyes were full of tears, her throat was thick. She could not sing.

Bronwen's failure discomposed all the others. She heard Donncan stop and take a ragged breath, then he gasped and tried to sing on. Beside her Owein was gamely keeping time, but there was no conviction in it, and on the far side of the pool the joyous refrain of Olwynne's voice had faltered. Bronwen tried to recover, but the tears were coming fast and she had to wrench her hand out of Donncan's to dash it across her eyes. She knew how wrong it was of her to break the circle but she could not help herself.

The song ground on to its broken and inconclusive end. Bronwen had her hands over her face, her pulse juddering. She could not bear to open her eyes or look anyone in the face, but the silence drew out until it was unbearable, and at last she dropped her hands and smoothed down her dress with trembling hands, finding the courage to look up.

The sun had risen. Six Celestines stood on the dais above the pool, the sun shining on their white ripples of hair and their pale, stern faces. They were all looking at her, their distress evident in their faces.

Bronwen looked down at the pool. Although there was a low bubbling in the center of the murky pool, it was not enough to raise the water high enough to spill over the lip of stone. They had failed in their singing. This year the summerbourne would not run.

Storm Rising

A cold shudder took hold of Isabeau, despite the sultry heat of the morning. The sun glared through a thin veil of cloud, burning the fair skin of her arms and making her robes feel almost unbearably heavy. Yet still Isabeau shivered, her skin rising up in goose pimples all over her body.

It was a very bad omen for the singing of the summerbourne to falter and break.

The Keybearer opened her eyes and looked towards the Pool of Two Moons, as did all the other witches standing in the circle. Bronwen stood with her hands over her face, obviously fighting back tears. Her uncle and cousins were staring at her.

Standing between the ancient blocks of stone were six Celestines. Isabeau recognized one as the Stargazer Cloudshadow, the faery who had healed her after her torture by amputating the two infected fingers on her left hand. The Stargazer was the title of the ruler of the Celestines, a role Cloudshadow had inherited at an unusually early age due to the death of her parents in Maya's faery hunts. Many, many Celestines had died during the Ensorcellor's reign and very few children were born to them, making Thunderlily, Cloudshadow's daughter, their great hope for the future.

Standing beside the Stargazer was a tall, slender young man, with a long, strong-boned face. Of all the Celestines, he looked the most shaken by the failure of the summerbourne to run. His third eye was open, dark as night, and his long-fingered hands were gripped into fists, a most unusual gesture among the gentle-natured faeries. Cloudshadow looked grave, but she

came down the stairs with her usual noiseless grace and bowed
to the Rìgh.

Lachlan moved forward to greet the Celestines formally,
bending his head so Cloudshadow could touch her fingers to his
brow. They stood in silent communion for some time, Lachlan
holding himself rigid so he did not break their connection. Then
Cloudshadow's fingers dropped and Lachlan straightened and
stood back, bowing to the other Celestines and touching his fingers to his own brow in the ritual greeting.

Cloudshadow turned to greet her daughter, humming softly
in her throat. They each touched each other's brows and then
Cloudshadow turned and indicated the young Celestine man,
who came to bow before Thunderlily. She bowed back, cool
and remote, and then stepped back to stand next to Bronwen,
who had been left alone, everyone drawing away from her as if
she had marred the singing of the summerbourne on purpose.
Bronwen shook back her hair and said something to Thunderlily in a teasing undertone, as if nothing had happened.
Thunderlily smiled and shook her head.

Isabeau could not help frowning at Bronwen as she walked
past her to greet the Celestines, and Bronwen looked away defiantly, pretending she did not care.

I am so sorry about the summerbourne, Isabeau said without words. *I have never known the song to falter before. What
does this mean for us all?*

*Already the Old Ways are too dangerous for us to walk eas-
ily,* Cloudshadow said. *Even I, the Stargazer, could barely find
my way. Now passage between the Hearts of Stars will be more
difficult than ever. I shall take my daughter and I shall return to
my garden, and we will wait for the lines of power to be
cleansed and protected another year, another time.*

But why are the Auld Ways so dangerous? Isabeau asked.
*We have sung the summerbourne strongly for years now. I had
thought we had cleansed the lines of power and made them
safe.*

The Old Ways are haunted. There is evil brewing.

Haunted? Ye mean by ghosts? Isabeau asked, her mind-
voice sharpening with interest.

*Haunted by the shades of the dead, those who have refused
to let the ethereal substance of their souls be dissolved into the*

*ethereal substance of the universe. The immoderate emotions
that so trouble you of humankind chain them to this world, and
so they are dragged along with its revolutions of seasons, unable to break free and move on, or come back and be what they
were. They are not one thing or another, not flesh nor spirit, not
quick nor dead. They are all hunger, all greed, all hatred, all
grief, all envy, all pride, all spite. They swarm along the Old
Ways, seeking a door into this world. They press against the
doorways. The fabric between their world and ours bulges with
their weight.*

Why? What has drawn them here?

*They are always drawn to the lines of power. They are lines
of connection, seams between space, time, and matter.*

But why are there so many now?

*A door has been opened. It was slammed shut again, but not
before at least one spirit of the dead found its way free. The others hope to find an open doorway too.*

Who opened the door? Where?

Not here. Far away.

Do you know where?

Isabeau received a mind-image of a tall crag of stone rising
high above a waterfall. A ruin of a great stone building crowned
the cliff, and ravens wheeled above it. "The Tower o' Ravens,"
she breathed, even though it was what she had been expecting.

That is not our name for the holy hill, Cloudshadow said
quietly. *Once it was a place of great power, a Heart of Stars
where the Celestines gathered to worship and celebrate the
powers of moon and sun and star. Now it is a place of evil. Men
have gathered there, using their dark magic to open the gate, to
call up the shades of the dead. They were not wary. They did not
hold the door fast. There is one, a spirit of great hunger and
greed, who felt the opening of the door and rushed through it.
Now she walks the Old Ways as she pleases and draws other
spirits with her, like the sun drawing moisture from the sea. She
leaves a dark trail of malice behind her like the slime trail of a
snail. It poisons the Auld Ways and leaves its residue on all of
us who must walk in her footsteps.*

Who is she?

*I do not know. She has not been dead long. Her spirit is
strong still and grips to the memory of life voraciously. She has*

*used this doorway often. She has drawn many, many ghosts
here. They press their bodies against the door and rend it with
their claws. It took much of my strength to close the door behind us when we came today. Only my determination to see my
daughter and bring her home again drove us through.*

Will it hold?

*I do not know. It takes a very sharp knife to rend the fabric
of space and time.*

Isabeau gave a little shudder.

What is wrong? Your soul shrinks away from my gaze.

Nothing is wrong.

*There is a dark imprint upon your mind, as if burning fin-
gertips have scorched you. May I touch you?*

Isabeau looked away. There was a long silence and then
slowly, reluctantly, she kneeled before the Stargazer and allowed Cloudshadow to press her finger between her brow.
There was a snapping sound, like a bridge of wood cracking;
then Isabeau fell back, her head swimming.

A finger from the grave, the Celestine said softly. *But
whose?*

It was very hot. The day passed in a whirl. There was a feast
laid out in the gardens, the tables decorated with lavender and
roses and vervain. Minstrels wandered the crowd, serenading
the merrymakers with love songs. Gaily painted puppet theaters
were set up on the lawn, entertaining the children with noisy
plays, while bizarrely dressed stilt walkers towered above the
flower-crowned heads of the dancers, stalking along with their
stilts hidden beneath immensely long striped trousers. A troupe
of musicians paused in their playing to wipe the perspiration
from their faces, and more than one reveler glanced at the sky
and said, "Looks like a storm's on its way."

Bronwen laughed and danced and gulped down glass after
glass of sparkling rose-colored wine. Although her blue gown
was as light as butterfly wings, she was so hot she thought she
might faint. She had not seen Donncan since the dawn meeting
at the Pool of Two Moons. It seemed everyone had heard how
she had torn free of his grasp and broken the circle. Bronwen
pretended it was all because of the heat. She fanned herself

frantically and said, "We Fairgean do no' like the heat, do we, Alta?"

"No, we do no'," the Fairgean ambassador replied and ordered the servants to bring her crushed ice flavored with lemon. "Though ye would no' feel the heat so badly if ye did no' dance so much."

"Happen so, but where's the fun in that?" she retorted and inclined her head to him in ironic farewell, leaving his side to find company that did not scold her so much. Aindrew MacRuraich was happy to oblige, and she whiled away a merry hour with him, watching a procession of fabulous beasts made of silk and wood and paint, playing a riotous game of croquet, and dancing a few of the sedate sets that the Master of Revels considered appropriate for midafternoon.

Aindrew would have been happy to while away another hour, but Finn the Cat, his elder sister, strolled over and linked her arm in his, saying affably that she had not seen him in an age and would he not come and tell her all his news. She was a tall, handsome woman with heavy chestnut hair that she wore pulled back in a simple plait in the fashion of the witches. Although born the heir to the throne of Rurach, Finn had given up her claim to her brother Aindrew so that she could pursue her dream of being a sorceress. She was rarely at the royal court, spending a good part of every year back in Rurach overlooking the rebuilding of the Tower of Searchers, a venture she funded by the lucrative business she ran with her husband, Jay, of searching for and finding anything or anyone that was lost, stolen, or otherwise misplaced. As a consequence, she and Jay traveled all over Eileanan, and Bronwen suspected she was the source of a great deal of secret information for the Rìgh.

Finn smiled and nodded at Bronwen agreeably enough as she adroitly maneuvered Aindrew away, but the tiny black cat that rode on her shoulder hissed and bared its fangs at her. Bronwen could not help feeling that the elven cat was expressing the sorceress's real feelings.

Looking about her with her usual air of cool arrogance, Bronwen saw that, as she had suspected, she was the subject of many stares and whispers. She cooled herself with her fan, accepted another glass of pink sparkling wine, and drank it down to the last drop with great deliberateness. She then strolled over to join a group of the youngest and most fashionable ladies, as if that had been her intention all along. She was received with squeals of delight and much banter, which she deflected with the lift of an eyebrow and a mocking jest that made them laugh.

A puppet show began at a small theater nearby, and they strolled over to watch it, the servants carrying over chairs for them to sit on and bringing parasols to shade their faces. The puppet show was a mocking rendition of a royal wedding, with the bride dashing from one suitor to another, all the while pretending to be madly in love with the dim-witted prince. The audience screamed with laughter at one ridiculous scene after another. It was an effort for Bronwen to keep the smile on her face, but she managed, waving her huge fan of white bhanias feathers to and fro. The other ladies eyed her fan covetously, for white bhanias birds were very rare, and Bronwen had ordered a long silver handle studded with pearls to keep the long tail feathers in place. It was a most unusual and magnificent fan, and it cast all the other ladies' fans, no matter how prettily painted, into the shade.

A large troupe of apprentice-witches came by in their long black robes, carrying baskets laden with herbs and flowers from the kitchen garden, for Midsummer's Day was the best day to gather herbs for spells and healing.

Bronwen recognized a few faces among them, particularly the little dark-haired girl from Ravenshaw who the gossips said Prionnsa Owein was courting. She trudged at the back of the group beside a plump girl with a limp and a tall blonde with a most disagreeable expression. The blonde was staring enviously at the party of court ladies in their flimsy gowns, sitting under the shade of their parasols and drinking the pink, fizzy wine that had been especially chilled in tubs of snow brought down from the mountains.

Bronwen could remember all too well how she used to slog past every midsummer, cursing the Coven and its philosophies and longing for the days when she would be free to join in the court festivities. Now she could not help feeling nostalgic for the days when she too had to get all hot and grubby, with dirt under her nails and bramble scratches on her cheek. They seemed impossibly carefree and halcyon. She smiled in sympathy at the apprentices, and the blonde girl whispered to her companions in excitement, then swept Bronwen a most elegant curtsy. The plump girl, who was already red in the heat, turned crimson and tried to imitate her, with clumsy results. The dark-haired girl barely seemed to notice, though, and Bronwen saw she was sunk in a deep and profound misery. Her eyes were red, as if she had been weeping, and her shoulders drooped.

Bronwen was just wondering if it was Owein who had caused her such distress, when a shadow darkened her eyes. She looked up and saw to her surprise that Elfrida NicHilde had come to join her. Unlike the other women all dressed in pale blossomy gowns, she was dressed severely in black, matching the pastor who was her constant companion. When she sat down, it was with a sigh of relief, as if her legs were about to give way beneath her. The pastor came to stand behind her chair, his hands folded before him in a pious attitude. Bronwen gave him a cold, unwelcoming look.

"I am surprised to see ye, my dear," Elfrida said. "I thought ye would be resting, ahead o' the ceremony tonight."

"But how boring," Bronwen said, fanning herself languidly. "I see no reason to miss the masques and games simply because I am to be married tonight. What should I do all day, sitting by myself in my room?" She took a sip of her wine and cast Elfrida a bright, challenging look. "Besides, why should I rest? I am no' weary."

"'Now it is high time to awake out of sleep: for now is our salvation nearer than when we believed,'" the man in black said in a deep, ringing voice that made the other ladies fidget and whisper.

Bronwen glanced at him, raised an eyebrow, then looked away, yawning delicately behind her feathery fan. Elfrida cast him a pleading look, and he bowed his long, narrow head, his hands folded one over the other in front of his chest.

What a prig, Bronwen thought and wished they would go away. She had never much liked Neil's mother, who had always seemed to disapprove of her.

"It is my wedding anniversary today," Elfrida said, leaning close and speaking softly so as not to disturb the other ladies. Bronwen noticed her hands were trembling and felt uncomfortable.

"Really?" She fixed her eyes on the puppet show, pretending to be enthralled.

"Yes. I married Iain o' Arran on Midsummer's Day, the same day that Lachlan and Iseult were married. It was the year ye were born, I think. Twenty-four years ago."

"I wish ye very happy."

"We have been happy, strangely enough. I never saw him until our wedding day. He was a complete stranger to me."

"Is that so?" Bronwen asked, growing interested despite herself.

"Yes. His mother arranged it." Elfrida gave a quick shudder but set her teeth together and forced her shoulders down again.

"It must've been hard, being forced to marry a man ye didna ken."

"It was very hard. I would no' recommend it."

"No." Bronwen spoke slowly, not sure what Elfrida was trying to tell her.

"I was lucky, very lucky, to find some measure o' happiness in my marriage," Elfrida said, speaking in very low tones so that only Bronwen and the man standing quietly behind her chair could have heard her. "Marry unwisely, and ye will find nothing but misery and unhappiness. Trust me in this, my dear. It is no' too late for ye to stop this foolishness. Do ye think I do no' ken when a man and a woman are in love? Find a man who truly loves ye, afore ye condemn yourself to a life of emptiness and sorrow—"

Bronwen stood up so abruptly her chair almost fell over. "I thank ye for your advice, Your Grace," she said sweetly. "I am sure we shall be very happy."

Then, lifting her parasol so it shaded her face, she went away towards the palace.

She heard footsteps hurrying up behind her and quickened her pace, but the footsteps broke into a run and a hand seized her elbow.

"Bronwen!"

"Neil."

"What did my mother say to ye?"

"She wished me well this evening."

"Really? Is that all?"

"What else would she have said?"

"I dinna ken. I thought perhaps . . ." He hesitated, his eyes searching her face. He saw how angry she looked and said unevenly, "She did say something. Oh, Bronny, I'm sorry. . . . My mother has no' been well lately. She's got this fancy into her head. . . . She thinks . . . she thinks . . ."

"She thinks ye are in love with me?"

"Yes."

"And are ye?"

"Yes." He said the word on a long sigh.

Bronwen tapped her foot impatiently. "Neil, in about two hours' time I am jumping the fire with your best friend. Do ye really think it is wise for ye, or your mother, to be telling me this?"

"So she *did* say something! What? What did she say?"

"She did no' mention ye."

Neil heaved a sigh. "I thought she had. . . . Ye looked so upset."

Bronwen looked down at the pointed toe of her slipper. "She thought fit to tell me that my husband-to-be does no' love me."

"He canna love ye as much as I do," Neil said simply. "Oh, Bronny, must ye really marry him? He doesna understand ye, truly he doesna. He is so angry still about Mat. He blames ye. But *I* ken it's no' your fault, Bronny."

She searched his face with her eyes. He was much the same height as she was, and he was standing very close. She could see nothing but sincerity in his face.

"Ye're alone in that," she said bitterly, and looked away.

He caught her hand in both of his and carried it to his lips, kissing her palm fervently.

She pulled her hand away but said with mild curiosity, "Ye and Donncan have been the best o' friends since ye were bairns. Does it no' trouble ye, flirting with me the very day o' our wedding?"

"I am no' flirting," Neil said, very low and intense. "I'm in love with ye, Bronwen. I have loved ye all my life and I will never love another. Ye and Donncan were betrothed as children. Ye have never been given the chance to ken your own hearts. It was no' fair to any o' us. If ye had been free, do ye no' think I would've told ye how I felt earlier? And if ye and Donncan

were happy, do ye think I would tell ye now? O' course I
wouldna. But I can see ye are no' happy."

Bronwen did not know what to say. Tears choked her. Neil
pressed her fingers in sympathy.

He said, "If ye do no' want to marry him, just let me ken. I'll
take ye away. I'll do whatever ye want. We can go to Arran, we
can go to the Fair Isles, wherever ye want. I can keep ye safe
from the MacCuinns, if ye are afraid they would be angry. I
would love ye and look after ye all our lives, I'd make ye
happy, I swear it. Just let me ken. . . ."

For a moment Bronwen almost reached towards him, almost
begged him to take her away. It was intoxicating to have a man
love her so deeply, so intensely, for her own sake and not
merely for some political gain. But then she took a step away,
shaking her head. "I am a banprionnsa and a NicCuinn," she
said. "If this wedding fails, so does the Pact o' Peace. We could
have war again. Do ye think I want that?"

His shoulders sagged. "No," he said.

Bronwen held out her hand to him. "I'm sorry, Neil."

He took her hand and bent to kiss it. Over his head Bronwen
saw Elfrida watching them and felt her spine stiffen. She pulled
her hand away.

"Time for me to go and make myself bonny," she said gaily.
"See ye again at sunset."

Neil's hand dropped to his side, his eyes widening in sudden
hurt. Bronwen smiled at Elfrida and made her escape. She went
straight to her room. The door had barely shut behind her before Bronwen had stripped off her hot, damp, clinging gown
and dived naked into her pool. She swam to the far side in three
swift strokes and cursed its smallness, turning and striking out
for the edge again. She would have liked to have swum so far
her lungs labored and her arms ached with exhaustion. She
would have liked to have dived so deep that light diminished
around her and strange bulbous eyes began to glow like weird
whiskered stars. She would have liked to fight the waves, surging up their foam-dappled sides and leaping beyond their sudden slap and hiss and crash. She would have liked to scream
and shout and smack someone very hard—Donncan preferably, for making her weep in public and show that she cared,
when he so clearly did not.

The water in the pool heaved and splashed as she swam, stroke, stroke, stroke, turn, stroke, stroke, stroke. At last she lay still, floating facedown, breathing noisily through her gills and watching hexagonal reflections of light break and coalesce on the tiled floor of the pool below her. Gradually the tumultuous water subsided. The hexagons steadied. Still Bronwen floated, arms and legs spread. The salt of her tears flowed into the salt of the pool, and no one saw or heard.

Sea-child . . .

Bronwen jerked upright, her tail slapping the water.

Thunderlily sat cross-legged on the side of the pool, regarding her with clear eyes. Her long mane of white hair hung down her back and pooled on the ground around her.

Why do you grieve? the Celestine said, in response to Bronwen's wordless demand. *I heard you far away. I came.*

Did ye really hear me?

Yes.

Were ye listening for me?

Yes.

Ye shouldna have. It was private. I wanted no one. . . .

I know, but I could not help but hear.

Bronwen swam to the side of the pool and climbed out, water streaming from her. She caught up a linen towel and wrapped it around herself.

Only because ye were listening, she thought crossly.

I am sorry.

Bronwen sighed. "Is it time already?" she asked aloud.

Yes, Thunderlily hummed. *It is time. The earth is turning, the sun moves towards the horizon, soon it will be dusk and your people's midsummer fire will be nothing but embers.*

It is time, Bronwen repeated, and the thought was both pleasure and pain to her.

I too am to be mated, Thunderlily said somberly. *His name is Stormstrider.*

I saw him at the Pool of Two Moons, Bronwen said. *Do ye no' like him?*

The Celestine stared down at her bare feet, very long and elegant. *It is not for me to like or not to like.*

But I thought that ye must love your beloved, if ye must sacrifice him for the Summer Tree. Does it work if ye do no' love him? Bronwen fumbled to express her thoughts, for no matter how fascinated she was by the Celestine's culture, part of her was still horrified by the blood sacrifice that was their most sacred ritual.

In time I am sure I will love him. I must. Thunderlily's mind-voice was miserable indeed.

It is your duty, Bronwen said with ironic seriousness.

Yes. As today is yours. But you truly do love the winged one, try as you might to deny it, Thunderlily said. *Do you think I do not know?*

"Celestines do not always see truly, believe it or not," Bronwen said.

I believe not.

"Arrogant creature," Bronwen said.

Thunderlily smiled.

"Have ye brought me my dress?"

Thunderlily hummed in pleasure and rose, crossing the room to where a dress hung from the doorknob. It was made of the silk the Celestines spun from the weaver-worm's cocoons, a heavy shimmering fabric of palest silver embroidered with silver flowers at hem and cuff. It was a dress spun of moonshine. There was a veil to match, delicate as cobweb, and a long train embroidered with silver roses, with tiny pearls stitched along its length.

"Glory be!" Bronwen whispered. "Well, if Donncan doesna like me in this dress, he isn't a man!"

He will like you, Thunderlily hummed.

"He is a man after all," Bronwen agreed. She rubbed herself dry and wrapped her long black hair up in the towel before slipping the dress on. Made without seam or button, it flowed along every curve of her body, sensuous as water. Bronwen twirled and pirouetted, unable to help smiling in delight. "Well, naught like a new dress to cheer ye up," she said ruefully. "Thank ye, Thunderlily."

The Celestine hummed and bowed her head, hands pressed together.

I will go now and prepare myself, she said. *I have never been to a human wedding before. I am honored indeed that you wished me, above all others, to be in attendance upon you. I will not fail you.*

It is an honor and a blessing that a child of the Stargazers has consented to cast their radiance upon my wedding, Bronwen replied formally, bowing low. *May it augur well for the future.*

May it be so, Thunderlily answered gravely.

Wedding Bells

The air was filled with a strange green light. Thunder rumbled. A hot wind was rising, pulling at Olwynne's hair and shaking the leaves of all the trees in the garden. It caught Bronwen's veil and dragged it sideways and almost tore the long rose-embroidered train out of Olwynne's hands. A few large drops of rain splattered the stone pathway.

Olwynne looked up at the low, dark clouds with foreboding. It was considered a very bad omen for rain to fall on Midsummer's Day, particularly if the fire that had burned all night and all day was doused before sunset.

She wondered if it was also a bad omen to have one's maid-of-honor fall ill so unexpectedly just before the wedding. Olwynne had certainly not expected she would have to carry her cousin's bridal train today. That honor had been reserved for Thunderlily, Bronwen's closest friend. Yet Thunderlily had not come with Olwynne, Heloïse, and all the other bridesmaids to help Bronwen finish dressing, to advise the maids on the styling of her hair and the placement of the wreath, and to exclaim over the magnificent ropes of pearls that had been a gift from her Uncle Nila.

Bronwen had looked for Thunderlily and asked for her often, as the maids had dressed her black hair with pearls and flowers, and attached the long train, and powdered her cheeks and rouged her lips. Olwynne had even sent one of the pages running to find the Celestine. He came panting back with a message from the College of Healers, saying she had been struck down with a sudden bout of sickness and could not possibly come.

Bronwen had been startled and upset. For a moment she had balked, so that Olwynne had wondered if she meant to refuse to go on with the wedding. She had composed herself, however, and allowed Olwynne and Heloïse to draw the long veil down over her face, which was so pale and impassive it looked as if she had been carved from ice.

Now Olwynne did her best to keep the heavy train from snagging on the thorns of the roses that bent their heavy heads over the aisle. She could hear the musicians striking up a stately refrain, and she raised her head, smiling as naturally as she could when her heart was so heavy in her chest it felt like a stone.

Roden led the bridal procession up the aisle, his chestnut curls combed back neatly. He was dressed in a white satin doublet and breeches tied under the knee with silver cord, and trimmed with seed pearls and knots of silver. It was clear he felt he looked ridiculous, for his lower lip was pushed out mutinously, and every now and again he lifted a hand to tug at his cravat. Since he was carrying a silver bell upon a silken cushion, this caused Olwynne some anxiety as every time he tugged, the cushion tipped, almost sending the bell crashing to the ground. Olwynne was sure that would be yet another inauspicious omen.

Behind Olwynne walked eleven handmaidens, chosen from all of the great families. Among them were two of Bronwen's Fairgean cousins, daughters of King Nila and Queen Fand. They were tall and silent, with pale silvery eyes and hair as black as night. Beside them, the four giddy daughters of the NicThanach of Blèssem looked plump and highly colored, though in general they were held to be very pretty girls. The twelve bridesmaids all carried posies of white moonflowers, roses, and vervain, matching the wreath on Bronwen's head.

Donncan was standing at the far end of the aisle, looking handsome in a coat of green velvet that must have been uncomfortable on such an oppressively hot day. At the sound of the trumpets, he turned to look for them. Olwynne saw how his expression changed when he saw Bronwen, and her heart constricted. She could only hope with all her might that they would be happy, these cousins who had been betrothed as children, knowing that their union was the only thing binding an uneasy peace treaty together.

She hoped Bronwen would be kind to him. Donncan had loved Bronwen wholeheartedly for years, and Olwynne knew how he had suffered from not knowing her feelings in return. No one could ever really be sure of what Bronwen felt. She was always so cool and enigmatic, so quick to turn away emotion with a clever, mocking jest. Perhaps she feared betrayal and disappointment and so tried to pretend she cared for nothing. Or perhaps she truly did not care. Olwynne had days when she was sure of it.

Certainly she was very beautiful. As the Ensorcellor's daughter walked slowly down the rose-lined path, the silk of her gown sliding over her slender form, there were little sighs from the courtiers crowding the formal garden. Olwynne tried not to feel jealous. *I am just weary*, she thought.

Olwynne was not sleeping well. Nightmares stalked her heels. She dreamed she was being pursued by a tall man in black, whose shadow strode ahead of him down a long corridor. She dreamed she was in a coffin and could not get out. She dreamed she had lost something very precious to her. She dreamed of weddings and funerals, till one seemed much like another, and it was no comfort to remind herself that all dreams go by contraries.

Olwynne had tried every trick she knew of in her search for sweet dreams, and if not sweet, then at least not bitter. She had hung her stockings over the end of her bed with a pin stuck through them and piled cold iron under her pillow, old skeelie remedies that had not, of course, worked. She had drugged herself with poppy syrup and valerian, she had tried meditating, she had tried not sleeping at all.

Nothing helped.

Olwynne knew her conscience was not easy. She tried very hard not to think of Rhiannon but instead thought of nothing else. She told herself many times that what she had done was for the best and listed the many reasons why, but it did not help. Olwynne was not finding the joy in Lewen that she had expected. Her love was twisted awry by her jealousy. If Lewen even sighed and looked pensive, she imagined he was thinking of Rhiannon and was eaten with a canker of pain and longing.

Once or twice she had even wished she had not cast the love spell on Lewen but had suffered alone in silence. It was too late now, though. She had to make the best of it. Soon Rhiannon would be dead, and in time Lewen would forget her and come to love Olwynne truly. She knew it.

The bridal procession reached the stone-paved circle at the center of the garden. Tall red candles stood at the four points of the compass, their sweet-scented flames flickering wildly in the hot, rough wind.

The Keybearer stood under a flower-hung arbor before a stone altar on which rested a beautifully carved statue of the god and goddess, naked and embracing. Spread out under the statue were two more red candles, anointed with rose and jasmine oil, a silver goblet of dark wine, a plate of new bread, a pot of honey, and a double-bladed knife with a handle of white bone. There was also a coil of red ribbon and a thick scroll of parchment from which dangled myriad red seals. The Pact of Peace.

Isabeau took the bell from Roden with a grave nod, and he stepped back with some thankfulness to stand beside his parents, who were gathered with the rest of the guests around the circle. The Keybearer rang the bell three times, then walked the circle, ringing the bell at the four cardinal points and calling upon the elemental powers to bless and protect them all this day.

The Rìgh and Banrìgh were sitting on tall thrones to one side, smiling with pleasure at the pretty sight the wedding party made. Seated behind them were Olwynne's grandparents, Ishbel and Khan'gharad of Tìrlethan, and her second cousin, Dughall MacBrann of Ravenshaw, with his adopted heir, Owen. There were many other friends and relatives too. Olwynne saw Nina and Iven, Finn and Jay, Gwilym the Ugly and Cailean of the Shadowswathe, Iain of Arran and his wife and son, and the round figure of Brun the cluricaun, bouncing up and down on his seat in excitement.

On the other side of the circle sat Bronwen's uncle Nila, the king of the Fairgean, and his wife, Fand. Beside them, dressed in a simple dark blue gown of rich satin, was Maya the Ensorcellor, with a long rope of exquisite pearls wound thrice about her throat, then dangling to her waist.

Olwynne could not help widening her eyes at the sight, for she had never seen Maya dressed in anything but her drab servant's gown and a grubby apron. The Ensorcellor was still a very beautiful woman, Olwynne admitted to herself. The midnight blue of her dress deepened the blue of her eyes, and emotion had brought color to her high cheekbones. The pearls wound about her throat hid the stark blackness of the nyx ribbon that bound her to silence. For the first time Olwynne could see how it was possible that Maya had once been called the most beautiful—and the most dangerous—woman in the world.

The Keybearer again rang the bell three times, then directed Bronwen and Donncan to walk around the circle from east to south to west to north, and then back to face the east once again. The sky was spitting with rain, even as the last long rays of the sun struck out from under the black-bellied clouds. Thunder growled, and many gathered in the garden looked to the sky, the women lifting their parasols to shield their hair from the rain.

The Keybearer looked weary as she intoned the midsummer rites, and Olwynne wondered what it meant for her, the failure of the summerbourne to run that morning. Normally the Keybearer seemed to blaze with a white aura of energy and vitality. Today all that was dimmed. The elongated rays of the blinkered sun haloed her with darkness so that Olwynne, watching her through a haze of tears that dimmed her sight, could barely see her, as if she was fading away.

Then Isabeau spoke the words that she herself had never vowed, so that the betrothed couple could repeat them after her.

"I, Donncan Feargus MacCuinn, have come here o' my own free will, in perfect love and perfect trust, to commit myself to Bronwen Mathilde NicCuinn, in joy and adversity, in wholeness and brokenness, in peace and turmoil, living with her faithfully all our days."

Donncan repeated the vows, stumbling once or twice and having to correct himself; then Bronwen repeated the words, as sure of herself as ever, her gaze downcast. They were like sunlight and shadow, Olwynne thought, her brother all warm and open with his golden eyes and hair and wings, and Bronwen so cool and remote, her black hair crowned with moonflowers, the long ropes of pearls about her throat hanging almost to the floor.

Isabeau gave them the cup of wine to share, and bread smeared with honey, to bless their union with sweetness. The bride and groom kissed, and the crowd clapped and smiled and threw rose petals over them. The kiss was brief and formal, and many in the crowd urged them on to a more passionate embrace. Color rose in Donncan's cheeks and he glanced at Bronwen, half shyly. She returned his look coolly and, although they kissed again, it lasted little longer than the first time.

The tower bells rang out, peal after joyous peal, to let the city know the wedding vows had been sworn. Donncan and Bronwen both had to sign their marriage documents, and then Lachlan and Nila came up to put their signatures together at the bottom of the peace agreement. The melting candle was dribbled onto the parchment, and the royal seals were pressed deep into the wax.

Isabeau then took up the remainder of the ribbon and bound together Donncan and Bronwen's wrists to show that their lives were now tied together for evermore. Then Donncan and Bronwen walked back together through the crowded garden, towards the palace square where the remains of the bonfire smoked sullenly in the gloom of the stormy dusk. A page in royal livery held a great black umbrella over it, trying to keep the spitting rain away. The court all followed close behind, talking and laughing, some of the women trying to hold their coiffures in place as the wind grew stronger. The bells rang the changes.

Together the newly wed couple ran and leaped over the low, flickering flames. Donncan kept his wings folded tightly down his sides and released his clasp on Bronwen's hand as soon as they had landed on the far side, holding up his wrist for Isabeau to unwind the ribbon. Glances and raised eyebrows among the guests expressed their surprise and disappointment at the couple's lack of enthusiasm, and Olwynne saw Lachlan and Iseult exchange troubled looks.

Bronwen's face was expressionless. She moved away as soon as she was free and went to speak to her mother, who was waiting close by, alone among the crowd. Maya embraced her affectionately, and then set her back, looking into her face intensely as if trying to communicate all she felt with that one glance. Olwynne looked at her brother. As polite and composed as ever, Donncan was receiving the compliments of his mother's parents with a graceful smile. Olwynne thought he looked pale and unhappy, and sighed.

In a year, Lewen and I will jump the fire too, but we will laugh and be joyful, Olwynne thought fiercely. *In a year he shall have forgotten her. . . .*

The feast began with a blast of trumpets. The newly married couple led the way to the banquet hall, bowing to all the well-wishers who crowded about them, throwing grain and flower petals before them. The rain had blown over, but thunder still rumbled intermittently and every now and again lightning stalked the horizon.

The musicians struck up a stately pavane, and together Donncan and Bronwen swept up the hall, then turned to bow to each other. Both smiled out at the crowd, without meeting each other's eyes.

Olwynne made an effort of her own and smiled as Lewen bowed before her, offering her his hand. They fell into place behind Owein, who was dancing with the eldest daughter of the NicThanach. In strict order of precedence, the lords and ladies of the court followed them, and the swish of the ladies' silken skirts and the tap of their high-heeled shoes was like another instrument in the minstrels' troupe.

The banquet hall was softly lit by candles on the long tables set up along the sides and in candelabras on either side of the high table at the far end. Flowers had been wreathed around the base of the candelabras, adding their heavy scent to the air.

The high table, where Lachlan and Iseult presided, was set under a massive shield depicting the crowned stag of the Mac-Cuinn arms. Tradition demanded that the bride's mother should sit at the high table with the groom's parents, but given the long enmity between Lachlan and Maya, she had been seated at the table to the right, with her brother Nila and his wife, Fand, and various other Fairgean nobility. She sat quietly, listening to her brother speak, and then wrote her response on the slate she carried at her waist, as always.

The next table, where the Celestines had been meant to sit with various other forest faeries and witches, was half-empty,

and Olwynne wondered with a sudden stab of anxiety whether
Thunderlily was dangerously ill, as none of her family were
here at the wedding. She hoped not, for Thunderlily was one of
only a few Celestines born since the days of the Burning, and it
would truly be a dreadful thing if she died while under the care
of the Coven. She could tell by her aunt's face that Isabeau was
worried too. Dide was trying to coax her to dance and the Keybearer was shaking her head, a little frown between her eyes.
Brun, who sat next to her, was patting her hand in comfort.

The minstrels played in a gallery set high above the doors
that led out to the garden. The gallery ran down both sides of
the hall, supported by tall wooden pillars, beautifully carved
at the top with merry faces wreathed with leaves and flowers.
The pillars were all joined into archways by curving fretwork
carved to look like writhing vines. Through each archway
was a shadowy recess. Doors standing open onto the terrace
alternated with small curtained chambers where guests could
retreat for a more confidential conversation, or play cards or
dice if they preferred. Each of the private chambers was illuminated by lanterns of red glass that created a soft, warm
glow that shone out through the fretwork. The whole effect
was very pretty, and the Master of Revels looked about him
with a look of great satisfaction before bending over as far as
his tight corsets would let him to straighten a candle an in-
finitesimal amount.

Once the stately pavane was over, most of the more elderly
guests settled themselves down to eat and drink and dissect the
day, while the younger set enjoyed jigs and reels, the canary
and the galliard. Bronwen unhooked her elaborate train and
danced blithely, laughing and smiling while Donncan looked
on. Occasionally he stepped in to request her hand, and at once
her brightness would dim and she would restrain her natural
grace to his more subdued step.

Neil MacFóghnan did not dance. He brooded over his goblet of wine, lifting it often to drain it to its dregs and then sig-
nal the page for more. Elfrida sat beside him, drinking little,
eating less, her heavy gold fan fluttering back and forth so fast
it was almost a blur. Certainly she must have been hot, for although she had not worn her customary black in deference to
the superstition that it was an unlucky color to wear to a wed-

ding, her grey silk was as dark as thunderclouds and made high
to the neck and wrists as usual. Only a narrow edging of lace at
her throat and cuffs and a double row of tiny mother-of-pearl
buttons relieved its severity. Olwynne, who was uncomfortably
sticky in her pale silk, wondered why she had not worn something lighter. Then she saw the black-clad pastor sitting at the
Banprionnsa's right hand, his whole body stiff with condemnation and distaste at the music and dancing and feasting going on
all around him, and felt sorry for Elfrida. It must have been hard
to have been raised in a society that disapproved of all that was
bright and free and beautiful.

Olwynne danced with her father, and then with Donncan,
and then took her twin's hand and promenaded down the length
of the hall with him. After that, her duty done, she could rest,
Olwynne told herself, feeling her heart slam in the cage of her
ribs, her temples thudding. *I am just tired*, she told herself
again. *It's the heat.*

Owein was unusually quiet, and Olwynne was glad of it.
They turned and he raised his arm so she could duck beneath it,
then he ducked under hers. Then they stood, arms held high, as
other couples ducked through the long archway, one by one.

When it was time to promenade again, Owein said abruptly,
"Mam says *Dai-dein* plans to pardon the satyricorn girl."

Olwynne stumbled. Only long years of rigorous training by
her dancing master enabled her to go on. "What?"

"He'll make the announcement tonight, when he toasts
Donn and Bronwen."

Olwynne's heart beat so hard and fast she could barely hear
the music. She could not speak.

"Mam says he has told Johanna and Dillon the news already.
Johanna is no' here tonight, so she must be angry indeed. It's
true what they say: ye canna keep everyone happy."

Olwynne's eyes filled with tears. She kept her head high, her
face turned away, but her twin brother knew. "It's better this
way," he said consolingly. "Lewen would always have felt bad
and guilty about her, but this way she can be sent somewhere
far away, to do service for the Crown somewhere else, in
Ravenshaw, perhaps."

Olwynne nodded but still could not speak. She wished she
could raise her hand to blot away her tears, but someone would

see and comment on it. Olwynne could never bear to be the subject of gossip.

"Lewen loves ye truly. Ye ken that," Owein said awkwardly. "It'll make no difference to ye, if she lives. Ye'll see."

Lewen loves ye truly. . . .

Olwynne wished with all her heart that this was so. But it was all a lie, a sham, a concoction of blood and ribbon and withered flowers. "I have a headache," she said. "Please, Owein, I want to sit down."

Owein had spent as many years suffering dancing lessons as Olwynne. He swung her out of the set without missing a beat and led her to her seat at the high table. Lachlan and Iseult were smiling at each other over the rims of their jeweled goblets. Olwynne saw her mother reach out a hand to stroke her father's cheek. It was their wedding anniversary, she knew, and felt tears of envy and longing prickle her eyes.

"I'll find Lewen for ye," Owein said.

Olwynne nodded and sat, fanning herself rapidly. It was hot and oppressive, and the blazing candles swam before her eyes. The swirling dresses, the joyous lilt of the music, the heavy scent of the flowers, none of it gave her any pleasure. She was finding it hard to breathe.

Lewen had been talking with the other royal squires, but he came at once to her side, sitting and holding her hand in both of his. Olwynne clung to his strong, calloused hand like a drowning man to a spar. She willed herself not to weep.

"What's wrong?" Lewen whispered.

She made a helpless gesture with her hand.

Lewen looked to the dance floor, where Bronwen was dancing a bold galliard with one of the Fairgean lords. Donncan had returned to the high table, where he too sat and nursed his wine cup, as dark-visaged as Lewen had ever seen him.

"Are ye upset that Prionnsa Donncan seems so unhappy? I would no' fret, dearling. As long as I have kent him, he has had no eyes for anyone but the Banprionnsa Bronwen. I am sure it is just a lovers' misunderstanding, and all will be well. True love canna be broken so easily."

Olwynne said nothing. She put up one hand and pressed it against her eyes.

The music twirled, the musicians red in the face as they

piped and fiddled and drummed away, the dancers panting as they paused at the head of the procession. The flowers were wilting. The mint sorbet was melting in the little silver bowls even as the lackeys carried it in from the kitchen.

"Do ye wish to go out for a breath o' fresh air?" Lewen asked her. "Ye look very pale."

She nodded.

Together they rose and made their way through the archway of entwining wooden vines. Lewen opened the glass doors for her and ushered her out onto the terrace, closing the door behind him. It was not much cooler, but at least there was less noise and light.

"I'll get ye something to drink," Lewen said solicitously and left her sitting on a stone bench on the terrace. Olwynne could not rest. She rose, pacing up and down the terrace. A new tune began. Olwynne was drawn to the tall glass door. Looking in, she saw the banquet hall bright with candles. People in vivid silks and velvets danced or clustered in groups, talking and eating. Donncan had got up and was nodding curtly to the Fairgean lord as he asked Bronwen for a dance. She smiled brilliantly and looked up into Donncan's face as he spun her around so that her moonlight-silver dress swung out and billowed about her.

Olwynne gasped aloud. She had seen this before. She had seen it more than once. The wreath of white flowers on the midnight-dark hair, the silver dress swirling. She looked desperately for her father. He bent his dark head over her mother's red one, then nodded and turned to beckon to the Master of Revels, preparing to stand up, to make the toast. Olwynne took a step forward, her hands pressed up hard against the glass. "No!" she cried, but the noise she made was slight, no more than a croak.

There was someone in the shadows. A woman in a dark-colored dress. Olwynne felt she should know her. If the candles were not so bright, the shadow beneath the pillars so dark, she would recognize her, she knew. The woman moved. Dread surged up Olwynne's throat like vomit. She banged her hands on the glass as the woman glanced quickly from side to side. No one heard her. No one saw her.

Then the woman lifted one hand to her mouth, as if hiding a

cough or spitting a piece of chewed gristle into her hand. There was a flash of gold. Then something dark flew out from her cupped hand.

Olwynne watched it dart across the floor, fast and fierce, straight into Lachlan's throat. Tears choked her. She did not even try to cry out. She knew no one would hear her.

Lachlan jerked and slapped at his skin, as if at a stinging fly. Color surged up his skin. He stood, his chair crashing over. Olwynne could see her mother leap to her feet in dismay and seize his arm. The Rìgh swayed and then he fell.

Olwynne watched him fall away down behind the table, disappearing from her view, and then she fell to her knees, her hands over her mouth. *"Dai-dein,"* she whispered. "Oh, Eà, no!"

One by One

R oden lay on his bed in his nightgown, moodily attacking the wooden soldier he held in one hand with the wooden soldier in the other. *No' fair*, he thought. *Why do I have to come home, just 'cause I'm a laddiekin? I never get to have any fun.* He rolled over and kicked at his headboard with one bare foot. He had spent much of the past week hanging around the kitchen, watching wide-eyed as the palace cooks had created one sumptuous, extravagant dish after another. There was one dish in particular that Roden would like to have seen wheeled into the banquet hall. The head cook had planned a roast bhanias bird, carefully posed upon a bed of sugared roses and candied violets, and all its magnificent feathers reattached so that it looked as though it was still alive. Into the great bird's belly he intended to place a roast swan, which would in turn be carved to reveal a roast pheasant, which held within a roast lark.

Apart from this subtlety, the menu had included roast venison with the antlered head still attached and a ripe pomegranate in its mouth, to reflect the honor of the MacCuinn clan; a salad of rose petals and sugared apricots, to symbolize love and fertility; a roasted lamb for each of the thirteen tables, as well as a vast array of roasted vegetables, fruit, and flower dishes for the witches; poached lobster, eel pie, six types of fish, a whole baked dolphin, and wild rys from Arran wrapped in parcels of seaweed and dipped in brine for their Fairgean guests; a castle made from spun toffee and meringue; and best of all, a great pie from which a young cluricaun was meant to leap and dance a jig before the wedded couple.

Despite being heir to the Earl of Caerlaverock and entitled to the lofty title of marquis, Roden was the son of a witch who had sworn an oath never to eat the flesh of another living creature. The only time Roden ever got to taste meat was when his uncle Dide bought him a sausage roll at the fair, or when his new friends in the kitchen let him sample a bit of burned meat cut off from the end of the roast. He was very curious indeed to know what dolphin tasted like and had itched to sample the rosewater-iced cakes, each topped with a sugared violet.

Besides the expected culinary delights, Roden had been looking forward to the entertainment. Apart from the usual dancers, jesters, jugglers, acrobats, minstrels, fire eaters, stilt walkers, and musicians, there was, he had heard, to be a special performance from a woman who put her head inside the jaws of a roaring snow lion. Although his mother frowned at such tricks, muttering that it was a poor use of one's familiar, Roden had been keen indeed to see them.

But Nina had sent him home to bed. The wedding feast would go on too late, she said, and he was too young for it. Roden was very displeased with his mother. It was not as if he was even tired. Here it was, almost midnight, and it was his nursemaid who was fast asleep in her chair, snoring gently. She was a skinny thing with anxious eyes who had made Roden cross by drinking all his milk after he had refused it, saying with his nose in the air that he was far too old for warm milk before bedtime. Later, of course, he had wanted it, but it was all gone and she was asleep, and Roden knew he would be in extra big trouble if he was caught trying to go down to the kitchen by himself at this time of night. Ever since he had been kidnapped in the spring, his mother had been very strict about him not wandering off by himself. Once Roden would have just waited till the adult set to mind him was distracted and then slipped off, ripe for any adventure, but his experiences at Fettercairn Castle had frightened him. He was still quite glad to stay close to his mother, away from the cold, lonely ghosts of murdered little boys and the clutches of mad old women.

He glanced at the fire, which was sinking low, sighed, yawned, and wriggled round in his bed, pulling up his bedclothes. *Might as well go to sleep*, he thought to himself, disgruntled. *Naught else to do.*

A creak from the door startled him. He sat up, grinning with delight, expecting to see his mother come to check on him, or perhaps his beloved uncle Dide, with a tray of goodies to share.

His happy smile faded, though. A tall man in a heavy traveling cloak stepped inside the door, shielding a lantern so that only a whisker of light preceded him. Roden had never seen him before, but something about his smooth, white, expressionless face frightened him.

"Who are ye?" he quavered, sinking back down into his bedclothes.

The young man regarded him with displeasure. "Still awake are ye, brat? Didna ye drink your milk?" He cast an unfavorable eye at the sleeping nursemaid, grunted, and closed the door behind him. "Well, she'll sleep for days, with a double dose," he muttered, putting down his lantern and advancing on Roden.

"Who are ye?" Roden demanded, edging to the far side of his bed. "What do ye want?"

"I'm Irving, the laird o' Fettercairn's seneschal," the man replied, with an ironic inclination of his head. "I believe ye were acquainted with my father?"

As Roden launched himself from his bed, bare feet flying under his long white nightgown, the seneschal caught him in midair and tucked him under one strong arm, his other hand clamped over the little boy's mouth. "And what I want, laddie, is ye."

Olwynne rocked back and forth, her arms crossed over her stomach. "Oh, Eà, no, oh, Eà, no," she moaned.

There was a light footstep behind her and then someone kneeled down beside her.

"Your Highness? Are ye unwell?"

"My *dai-dein* . . ." Olwynne managed to say.

"Come, put your head down between your knees," the woman said. In the light streaming out through the window Olwynne saw the green of a healer's robe. She obeyed and found it a little easier to breathe.

"Here, drink this," the woman said. "It will help."

Olwynne took the glass and swallowed a mouthful, almost choking at the taste. "What . . . ?" she tried to ask, but her tongue was thick and would not obey her. Her head swam, and her vision blurred. She tried to sit up in a sudden panic, but the woman seized the back of her neck in a viselike grip. Olwynne struggled, but the woman's other hand had the cup to her mouth, tilting her head back so the foul liquid flowed down her throat. Olwynne coughed and spluttered, trying to spit it out, but the woman had dropped the cup and clamped her hand over Olwynne's nose and mouth. Olwynne could not breathe. She choked and instinctively swallowed. At once the hand over her nose and mouth relaxed, and she was laid down gently on the stones.

"Good girl," the healer said and turned and beckoned.

As two men bent to seize her, Olwynne looked up past their shadowed forms and into the face of the healer who had so skillfully and efficiently drugged her. She recognized the round face with cheeks like withered apples at once. It was the woman who had given such damning testimony at Rhiannon's trial. The lord of Fettercairn's skeelie.

Owein smiled mechanically, as the girl he was dancing with giggled immoderately at the lame witticism he had just uttered. She was an accomplished dancer and knew how to manage her skirts and her fan most gracefully, but Owein had never felt so bored in his life. He mustered another smile and looked over the girl's shoulder to the doors that stood open onto the terrace.

Fireworks were shooting up from the garth of the Tower of Two Moons, showering green and crimson sparks into the sky. Owein gazed towards the tower, wondering what Fèlice was doing. He doubted she would be enjoying the midsummer festivities with the other students. Probably she was grieving quietly somewhere for her friend who she still thought was to be hanged.

She was not in her room. Owein knew that, for he had gone in search of her, to tell her the glad news of the royal pardon his father was issuing on Rhiannon's behalf. He wished he could have found her and told her, but there had been so little time. He had to get dressed for the wedding, and sit through all the interminable rites and rituals, and suffer the boredom of the feast. All the time feeling sick with anxiety, for he knew how upset Fèlice had been at the judges' verdict, and how much she had blamed him for not helping. All he had been able to do was leave her a message, begging her to meet him as soon as possible.

The dance came to an end. Owein bowed gracefully and led the giggling girl back to her mother. He would have liked to have made his escape, but the determined mama had no intention of allowing him to escape easily. He was suffering her very unsubtle hints about the suitability of her daughter as a possible wife when a servant approached and bowed formally.

"Excuse me, Your Highness," the lackey said.

Owein turned at once, trying not to show his relief and gratitude.

"Yes?" Owein asked.

The lackey drew him a little away. Owein did not recognize his face, but given the extra staff hired for the wedding, this was not surprising.

"Your Highness, I am sorry to disturb ye but there is a young lady who requested me to bring a message to ye," the servant said in a discreetly lowered voice.

"A young lady?"

"Aye, Your Highness. Lady Fèlice de Valonis. She says she wishes the honor o' a word with ye, sir. In private." The lackey's face was impassive.

"Really?" Owein's heart gave a little jump.

"Aye, Your Highness. She is in the rose arbor."

Owein grinned. "I'll go at once," he said, straightening up. "I do so hate to keep a lady waiting."

"Aye, sir."

Owein strode down the steps and on to the wide expanse of lawn lit by long oblongs of light from the banquet hall's windows. Thunder rumbled far away, and there was a flicker of lightning across the dark soft underbelly of cloud hanging so close over the trees. Rain splattered briefly on the leaves.

Bad omen, he thought, *having a storm on Midsummer . . .*

"Would ye bring me a bottle o' the sparkling honey rose wine?" Owein turned suddenly to the lackey, who was bowing low as the Prionnsa went past. "Very cold, please. Oh, and two glasses, properly chilled."

"Aye, sir. At once, sir."

Feeling much more cheerful, Owein strode out across the lawn, the wind whipping his unruly curls out of his neat, ribbon-bound ponytail, the cypress trees bending and creaking so their long shadows on the candlelit grass looked like fingers shaken in reproof. He spread his wings, just to feel the hot air ruffling his feathers, and gave a little bound. *How like Fèlice*, he thought. *Clandestine assignations in the rose arbor at midnight . . .*

Behind him, he heard a sudden cry of alarm, and the music jangled to a halt.

Oh, no, Owein thought. *No' again.*

He knew his brother was holding his temper on a very short leash. Donncan had been hurt, shocked, and humiliated by the whole terrible affair with Mathias Bright-Eyed. He had found it hard to forgive Bronwen for flirting with Mathias in the first place, for exposing him to such a sordid scandal on the very eve of their wedding, and for her refusal to admit she was in the wrong and apologize to him. All evening, watching Donncan's stiff face as Bronwen danced and flirted as much as ever, Owein had had a very bad feeling. He had not thought it would take much for Donncan to lose his temper, and by the sounds of distress rising from the banquet hall, he had done so explosively.

It did not occur to Owein to turn and see what had happened. All his thoughts were focused on Fèlice waiting for him in the rose arbor. *Let Donncan sort out his own mess*, he thought.

The tall golden windows fell out of sight behind stiff dark hedges. Owein conjured a little ball of witch-light so he could see his way. It bobbed and swayed in the breeze, and almost flickered out, Owein too busy wondering what to say to Fèlice to concentrate on holding it steady. He came through an archway into the rose arbor and looked about for her. The scent of the roses was heavy in the breeze, and crimson petals flew past him, torn free by the wind. All was dark. Owein walked slowly, feeling his silken sleeve snagged by thorns he could not see.

He saw a cloaked shape in the stone-flagged circle at the heart of the garden and smiled. "Fèlice?" he called.

The figure turned towards him. Owein intensified his witch-light, stepping forward eagerly. Then he recoiled in disappointment. It was not Fèlice who stood there but a tall, thin, stooped

man with a sensitive, apologetic face. He had the familiar
hunched shape of a piper, his bagpipes slung over one shoulder.

"I'm sorry," Owein said, stepping back and turning to go.

"Nay, Your Highness, it is I who am sorry," the man said
contritely.

Only then did Owein become aware of other men closing in
from behind, one of them the grey-clad lackey who had directed him here. Owein felt instinctively for his sword, but of
course he had not worn it to his brother's wedding. He glanced
around wildly, spread his wings, and sprang into the air, only to
be caught in a tight-meshed net that was thrown over him by
the three men.

Owein thrashed and fought, but they held him down.

"I really am so sorry," the lord of Fettercairn's piper said as
he kneeled beside him. He held a strong-smelling cloth over
Owein's mouth and nose until at last the Prionnsa's frantic
movements faltered and grew still. Then the piper stood up and
gestured to the other men, who wrapped Owein in the net and
heaved him up, carrying the limp bundle out of the rose arbor
and into the darkness of the wind-ruffled gardens.

Iseult cradled Lachlan in her arms. The Rìgh thrashed in agony,
his face a mottled purple, his mouth frothing.

"Eà's blood!" Iseult wept. "Someone help him!"

"We need a healer!" Donncan cried. He kneeled beside his
parents, white with shock and distress. "Look, Mam!" He
pointed at a black thorn protruding from his father's throat.

"Don't touch it!" Iseult commanded sharply. "It may make
it worse. Isabeau! Where is Isabeau!"

"I'm here." Isabeau pushed her way through the horrified
crowd and kneeled beside her brother-in-law. "What in Eà's
name happened?"

"It's a bogfaery dart," Donncan said.

"Who did this?" Captain Dillon demanded, his hand on his
sword. "Did anyone see anything? Guards! Search the room!
Find the man who did this!"

"It's a bogfaery dart," Donncan said again, more loudly.
"Whoever shot it would have a blowpipe."

Captain Dillon spun on his heel. "No Yeoman would do this," he said icily.

"I ken," Donncan said, meeting his gaze steadily. "Bog-faeries and Yeomen are no' the only ones to have blowpipes, though. Someone in this crowd has one!"

Captain Dillon nodded. "Search everyone here," he commanded. "No one is permitted to leave this room until we have found that blowpipe!"

The Rìgh cried out and arched his back. His arms flailed. His protruding eyes stared into Iseult's anguished face. He tried to speak, but his lips and throat were rigid. He could not frame the sound.

"What, *leannan*, what?" Iseult cried.

The Rìgh's tortured gaze moved slowly from her face to that of his son. He jerked one hand at him, and they heard him stammer, "Donn . . . Donn . . ."

"I'm here, *Dai-dein*," Donncan said, taking his father's palsied hand. Lachlan's lips were blue and flecked with foam. He jerkily tried to draw Donncan closer, and the winged Prionnsa bent his head and listened as his father whispered in his ear.

"No, no, *Dai-dein*," Donncan cried. "No, we will make ye well. Auntie Beau! Help him!"

Isabeau had pulled the thorn out and had her mouth pressed to the tiny scratch, trying to suck the poison out. Still Lachlan endeavored to speak, and Donncan gripped his hand and listened, tears glistening in his eyes.

"Aye, sir," he said. "O' course."

Lachlan's head fell back into Iseult's lap.

Isabeau lifted her head and spat out a mouthful of blood. "No good," she panted. "I need . . . a healer! Someone, get Johanna!"

"I'll fetch her!" Donncan cried and scrambled to his feet. "I can fly faster than anyone could run. Where is she?"

"In her rooms, I imagine . . . I ken she is angry and upset, but . . . surely she will come. . . . Tell her . . . need . . . antidote . . . Does she ken . . .?" Isabeau said, alternating thumping on Lachlan's chest with both her hands to breathing into his mouth. "Quick . . . his heart failing . . . Cloudshadow! Find Cloudshadow . . . She could heal him!"

Isabeau stopped her rhythmic pounding to breathe into Lachlan's mouth. Donncan spread his golden wings and soared high into the air, over everyone's heads and out the door of the banquet hall. Never had he flown so fast.

It was beginning to rain, huge heavy drops that splattered his skin. Donncan flew high over the gardens, his head down, his arms stretched long to make his passage as swift as possible. It was hard to breathe. He felt as if a vise had been clamped on his lungs. Tears burned his eyes, and he bent his arm to roughly wipe his nose.

Take the Lodestar, his father had whispered. *Rule well . . .*

Donncan saw the dark bulk of the Tower of Two Moons ahead of him. He came down, stumbling, before the light-strung building and began to run, ignoring the groups of laughing, wine-flushed students gathered on the steps, who all turned to stare after him. Once he was inside the great doors of the Royal College of Healers, he spread his wings again and took flight, soaring up the grand spiral staircase.

It was dark in the healers' tower, and quiet. Only the occasional lantern shed its lonely circle of light. He wondered momentarily where everyone was.

He reached the top of the stairs and hammered on the head healer's door. "Johanna! Johanna!"

The door opened. Johanna looked out. For once she was not dressed in her treasured green healer's robe but in a brown woolen traveling dress with sturdy boots and a waterproof cape. Donncan barely noticed.

Gasping for breath, he cried, "Johanna! My father . . . the Rìgh . . . he needs ye. . . ."

"Good," Johanna said, smiling. "It is done then."

Donncan fell back in dismayed confusion.

"But . . . what do ye mean? . . . Ye canna mean . . ."

Johanna unsheathed a long, cruelly sharp dagger from a leather scabbard hanging from her belt. "I do, I'm afraid."

He stumbled back. "Ye kent . . . ye kent my father . . ."

"He pardoned that murdering satyricorn bitch," Johanna said unevenly. "After all the years that Connor and I have served him, risking our necks again and again, and yet when Connor is killed, he doesna care enough even to make sure justice is done. I would no' have helped them if he had just let things be, no matter how they pleaded or argued. . . . He is my Rìgh, after all. But once he told me she would no' hang . . ."

Donncan stared at the dagger, which she held close to her body as she had been taught long ago by his own mother. He took a step back, and at once the knife darted forward like an adder, so that he stopped, hands raised.

"What do ye plan to do?"

"I must be the one to raise him," she whispered, looking past Donncan into the shadowy corridor so that he jerked around to see what she stared at, only to find nothing but air. "He swore he would live again; he swore he'd outwit Gearradh in the end. . . ."

"Who?" Donncan whispered, his skin prickling with horror.

Johanna glanced back at him and for a moment did not seem to know who he was. Then she stepped forward and rammed the dagger tip against Donncan's ribs so that he gasped in pain and surprise. "Inside," she said, and he had no choice but to step into her room, though his heart slammed in sick fear.

Surprise made him stop short on the threshold, and Johanna jabbed him viciously so that he stepped forward again, crying, "Thunderlily!"

The young Celestine was lying on the couch, dressed in her silver bridesmaid's dress, her head lolling down onto her chest. Her hands had been bound with heavy rope.

"But why?" Donncan asked, turning slowly to stare at Johanna.

"The laird o' Fettercairn wishes ye to die, as his little nephew died so long ago, and I need a living soul to sacrifice," she said in the same tone of voice that she might have used to discuss the weather. "I kent someone would come to get me. I was hoping it'd be ye or your good-for-naught little brother, seeing as how ye can fly faster than any lackey could run. Dedrie will be so pleased with me."

"Who?" Donncan asked again, edging away from the sharp tip of the dagger and hoping to distract her.

She moved with him, keeping her body turned so he could find no opening to strike at her. "Dedrie, the laird o' Fettercairn's skeelie. She has become a great friend to me, loyal and true. I ken *she* shall no' betray me, as Himself did with his royal pardon. . . . She stayed here, at great risk to herself, just to

make sure she could testify against that murdering bitch . . .
and then Himself goes and pardons her! It's true—he cares
naught for those who love and serve him. Look at the way he
used up all those poor laddies, Parlan and Artair and Anntoin
and Tòmas, all dead in his service, and now Connor too."

As she talked, she forced Donncan forward and bade him
sit. He obeyed reluctantly, and she took up a little bottle from
the table and poured herself a cup of some rich golden liquid
with brown dregs in it that she stirred with the tip of her knife,
her hands trembling with eagerness. Keeping her eyes fixed on
the Prionnsa, the knife held ready in her hand, she slowly drank
down the wine and a shudder ran over her. For a moment her
eyes closed in ecstasy, and Donncan lunged to his feet, hoping
to take her by surprise. Whatever it was she drank, it did not
dull her senses, though, for her eyes snapped open and the dagger swung up, so that he halted, hands up, and slowly retreated
back to his chair.

"Smart lad," she said approvingly. "I would hate to have to
kill ye ahead o' time."

She drank the last few drops of the liquid slowly, savoring
every golden drop, then hammered the cork back into the bottle with the hilt of her knife, lovingly wrapped it in a wad of
cloth, and tucked it away in a small backpack on the table. The
backpack was hung with a lantern, a tin kettle, and a coil of
rope, and it bulged with various packages that Donncan eyed in
increasing anxiety. Johanna slung it over her shoulder, then
pulled a tam-o'-shanter on over her neatly coiled brown hair.

"It could be cold; always best to be prepared," she said in a
conversational tone and wrapped a woolly plaid about her
shoulders. She looked Donncan up and down and smiled in
amusement. He glanced down at himself, remembering he was
still dressed in his wedding finery, a green velvet coat with
sleeves slashed with scarlet and white and a scarlet sash with a
gold fringe over the MacCuinn kilt. He wished he had a dagger
at his belt or in his long black boot, but one did not wear such
things to one's wedding.

"Where are ye taking us?" he demanded.

She did not answer, just took a small jar from her pocket and
unstoppered it, waving it under Thunderlily's nose. The Celestine jerked awake, a shrill buzz of terror rising from her throat.

Johanna held the knife where she could see it, and at once the drone stopped, the Celestine's eyes wide with fear.

While Johanna carefully cut through Thunderlily's bonds, Donncan surreptitiously undid the brooch that held his plaid together and dropped it under the table. It was not much of a clue, but it was all he could manage under the circumstances. As the rope fell away, the Celestine sobbed aloud in relief and rubbed at her wrists. Donncan felt a slow burn of anger. Celestines were the most gentle of faeries. They would never raise a hand to strike an enemy. They were gardeners, healers, and astronomers, not warriors. They felt a loving kinship with all creatures. It hurt him to see Thunderlily used so roughly.

Johanna dragged Thunderlily to her feet and jerked her head at Donncan, indicating he should rise also. The healer had her knife held to the Celestine's bare throat. Donncan, staring at Johanna in amazement and horror, saw how the pupils of her eyes had shrunk to pinpoints. It made her seem somehow inhuman.

Donncan could do nothing but obey.

"Walk now," she commanded. "I will keep my dagger to the Celestine's back. If either o' ye make a single move or noise I have no' commanded, I will kill ye both. Do ye understand?"

Thunderlily sent Donncan an agonized look. He tried to reassure her, muttering, "Aye," and keeping as close to her as he dared.

Johanna forced them down the stairs and through the building. The healers' wing was dark and deathly quiet, as if they all slept, but the Prionnsa could hear drunken singing and partying coming from the Theurgia as the students celebrated the end of the midsummer revelries. The garth was full of people dancing and talking, and someone had set off fireworks in the garden before the students' wing. Quite a few turned to stare at the little party hurrying past, but Donncan did not dare give any sign that something was wrong. He kept his eyes down and his hands still, and hoped that no one would accost him.

"Good even, Your Highness!" someone called. "Congratulations!"

Donncan smiled and nodded in response, but hurried on and felt the student's eyes follow him curiously.

"The maze," Johanna muttered. "Do ye ken the way through the maze?"

"What? Why would ye want—"

She flicked the knife his way, scoring him across his back. He stifled a yelp of pain. "Do ye ken the way through the maze?" she demanded.

"Aye, o' course I do," he replied.

"Excellent," she answered, and he exchanged a baffled look with Thunderlily.

Johanna took them into the long garden where the healers grew many of their medicinal herbs and trees. There was a whole grove of willows, their long leafy tendrils tossing wildly in the thundery wind as if they were dancing a bacchanal. Donncan felt the wind shivering against the skin of his face, like hot eager hands. He realized he was terribly afraid. He tripped over a tree root and almost fell, and Johanna dragged him up, warning him in a hiss that she would cut Thunderlily's throat if he tried anything stupid.

They stumbled on through the garden and out through a tall iron gate that swung back and forth in the wind. Beyond was the witches' wood, where narrow paths ran through groves and gardens, and where the maze was hidden within its walls of yew trees.

Suddenly the bells began to toll. The sound was very low and somber, for the bells' clappers had been fully muffled, something that was only done at the death of a monarch.

Donncan started, the blood draining away from his face. *"Dai-dein!"* he cried.

"The Rìgh is dead. Long live the Rìgh!" Johanna cried, then poked Donncan with her knife. "But no' for long!"

She sounded quite mad.

On and on the bells tolled.

"Why?" Donncan demanded, tears roughening his voice. "Why have ye killed my father!"

"I didna kill him," she said. "I've done naught." She smiled. "I mean, I may have drugged the house wine so there'd no' be a healer or a Celestine awake when they were needed." She smiled more widely. "And I may have given Princess Thunderlily a cup o' it to drink when I tricked her to coming to my room. But otherwise I've done naught at all."

"Ye knew someone was going to kill my father!" Donncan screamed, blood pounding in his head. "Why? Why?"

"He deserved it," Johanna replied bitterly. "After all the years I have served him faithfully . . . and my brother too . . . and it means naught to him. Naught."

"Who?" he demanded. "Who killed him?"

Johanna laughed. "Ye'll never guess," she answered.

She had been forcing them on through the wild tangle of the witches' forest, Donncan and Thunderlily stumbling over root and stone, clinging together, the Celestine humming high in warning or distress. Then Donncan saw the ornate iron gate of the maze emerge out of the whispering yew.

"Where are ye taking us?" he demanded.

"Back," Johanna whispered. "Back to the beginning. He has been dead a very long time. He wants to live again, and I shall be the one to raise him. But we must go back. Naught left o' him but grave dust."

"Back where?" Donncan demanded, feeling terror mount up to strangle him.

"Why, to the Tomb o' Ravens, o' course," she answered. "A thousand years ago."

Icicle

❦

Rhiannon lay on her prison bed, her hands clasped on her breast, feeling the rise and fall of her breath, the subtle pulse of her heartbeat. Each breath, each heartbeat, was one more moment of life. At the moment that was all she had to hold on to.

She had fought every step of the way from the courtroom back to her cell. It had taken six men to subdue her, and she still ached all over from their rough handling. Rhiannon's shock and grief had been profound. They had promised her, over and over again—they had promised her she would be freed—yet the judges had found her guilty and condemned her to hang. Rhiannon did not know how old she was, but she knew she was young and greedy for life. There was so much yet to see and learn, so much loving and adventuring to do. When at last she realized she could not fight her way free, when the door had been slammed on her and locked and she found herself once again in the vile little cell she knew so well, Rhiannon had fallen to her knees and wept. It was too late for shouting and arguing, too late for screaming and fighting, too late for begging. She could only weep, her face bent down into her hands, her whole body racked with pain.

Rhiannon could not cry forever. A time had come when she had no more tears, and she had to get up, and mop her face, and blow her nose, and drag herself to her bed. She felt oddly calm, now the force of her grief had spent itself, scoured clean as a shell by the sea.

She did not know how much time had passed. It must be at least three hours, for her candle was guttering in its cage of iron. Any moment it would sputter out, and she would be alone in the darkness again.

There was a grating sound as the key was turned in the lock. The door squealed open, and Corey put his head in the door.

"Game o' dice?" he said, rattling his leather cup. Although he did his best to sound normal, his lugubrious face showed that he knew this was Rhiannon's last night alive.

Tears stung Rhiannon's eyes again. She had to clear her throat before she could speak. "Havena ye lost enough money yet?" she said. Her voice was rough and scratchy.

"Naught else to do," he said. "I'm on my own tonight. The rest o' the lads have got the night free, to go celebrate midsummer. I got the short straw, as always."

"Well, I've got naught else to do," Rhiannon said, trying to achieve an insouciant tone and almost succeeding. "No' that I need the coins. Ye heard I willna be enjoying your kind hospitality anymore?"

"I was at the courthouse," Corey said abruptly, not looking at her. She did not need to ask if he had been booing or cheering. Over the months Rhiannon had been locked up in Sorrowgate Tower, she had gotten to know her guards well. She had bribed them for extra candles, and for bags of seed for her little bluebird, and for the occasional jug of hot water to wash in; and, once they realized she was as much of an avid gambler as they all were, they had spent many hours playing cards and dice. Rhiannon was careful not to win too often, for she wanted to stay on the guards' good side and still entertained fantasies of being able to escape or bribe her way free. Corey was the guard she gambled with most, for he was the closest to her in age and found the long hours cooped up inside stone walls as boring as she did.

The older night guard, Henry, disapproved mightily, but he quite liked to put his aching feet up on the stool and read the latest broadsheet without being bothered by his fellow guard's fidgets, so had learned to turn a blind eye. Though he would never have admitted it, the story of "Rhiannon's Ride," which had been distributed widely that summer, had predisposed him to turning a more lenient eye to his infamous prisoner, though never to the extent of relaxing his vigilance.

"Henry gone a-feasting tonight as well?" Rhiannon asked

after she had let Corey win quite a few of her few remaining coins. "That doesna sound like our Henry."

"His daughter's jumping the fire tonight, just like the Banprionnsa," Corey said. "He was given leave to go. Funny. I never kent he had a daughter, and I've been working with him for nigh on two years now."

Rhiannon threw her dice, shrugged as once again she lost, and got up. At once Corey tensed, but Rhiannon waved at him irritably. "Relax, laddie! I just thought ye'd like some goldensloe wine, for midsummer. Nina brought me some the other day. It's just here, under my bed. Throw! What have ye got?"

Corey threw the dice and groaned. "A three and a two! The Centaur's beard! My luck's out tonight."

"It certainly is," Rhiannon replied and brought the chamber pot crashing down on his head. It was unfortunately full, and Rhiannon felt a twinge of compassion for the hapless young guard. It did not stop her from wresting away his bunch of keys, her nose wrinkling at the smell, nor from locking him up in her cell with his own keys. Feeling she may as well be hanged for a thief as a murderer, she also relieved him of his purse and his winnings, spilled across the table. She wiped the coins on his jerkin first.

With her few belongings bundled into her pillowcase and the little bluebird riding on her shoulder, Rhiannon went searching through the dark, quiet halls of the prison. She found the guards' storeroom. A lantern stood on the table. By its light, Rhiannon unlocked the cupboard and found her saddlebags within, neatly packed with all her belongings. It gave Rhiannon a savage delight to strip off the ugly prison garb and dress herself once more in the soft white shirt and breeches that had belonged to Connor. She strapped his silver dagger at her waist, slung her bow and arrows over one shoulder, and hung the saddlebags over her arm. The bluebird gave a questioning trill, and she whispered, "It's back to the mountains for us, my pretty."

No one challenged her as she made her way towards the stairs, and her heart began to beat a little more steadily. She did not dare make her way to the lower reaches, where she knew many guards would still be on duty, despite the midsummer celebrations. Instead she turned upwards, climbing up to the battlements. She had a fine view up there, of the bonfires in every city square and stringing their way across the countryside beyond the river. She could hear shouting and singing, and somewhere someone was setting off firecrackers, which scared her at first, as she had never heard anything so loud.

When the noise had died, the boys running away to do mischief elsewhere, Rhiannon took a deep breath and leaned over the battlement, her eyes drinking in the wide expanse of starry sky. Behind her the city glared, even at this late hour, but to the east was only the river and the forest, almost invisible under the heavy swathe of clouds.

Blackthorn, she called silently. *Dearling! It's time. Come!*

Long minutes passed.

Blackthorn!

Rhiannon's heart was shrinking with bitter disappointment when she heard, faintly, a high shrill whinny. It rocked her from head to foot.

Blackthorn! Blackthorn!

Again the whinny came, and then Rhiannon could hear wingbeats.

Sssh! Softly, softly . . .

Then out of the darkness came her winged horse, shaking her head and neighing with frantic joy. Her hoof knocked the stone coping and sent a piece of paving whizzing down into the darkness. Rhiannon did not wait for Blackthorn to land but seized her mane and leaped up on her bare back, flinging the saddlebags over the mare's withers.

Blackthorn wheeled and began to fly away from the city, her wings beating steadily. Rhiannon allowed herself to lay her cheek down on the silky mane and sob with grief and relief. Behind her bells began to peal.

What, they have discovered me gone already? Rhiannon thought. *We had best fly far and fast, dearling, else they'll have us again!*

The bells tolled out.

Iseult kneeled on the floor, Lachlan lying slack and lifeless in her arms. "Find the murderer," she hissed, low and vicious. "I want him staked out for the White Gods. I want him hanged, drawn, and quartered, and his entrails fed to the city dogs. Do ye understand me?"

"Aye, Your Highness." Captain Dillon bowed low, his face set in harsh lines. "Do no' fear. We will find him, if I have to turn this city inside out."

As he spoke, his blue-clad soldiers continued with their thorough search and interrogation of the wedding guests and servants, taking them one by one to other rooms where each had to give an account of the evening's happenings. Their clothes were patted and flounced, their pockets and bags turned out, their jewelry and accessories examined. All were shocked, many were offended, quite a few had hysterics.

Iseult's and Isabeau's mother, Ishbel, had fainted and now floated a few feet off the floor, cocooned in the floating tendrils of her long pale hair. Their father, Khan'gharad, submitted angrily to being searched before taking Ishbel back to their rooms, propelling her through the air with a firm hand on her shoulder. It was clear he would prefer to have been out helping with the hunt for his son-in-law's murderer, but once again Ishbel's strange malady had confounded and confined him, and he was forced to tend her while she was lost in her enchanted sleep.

Meanwhile, King Nila and Queen Fand and their children were whisked away by the Fairgean ambassador Alta, all looking grim and worried indeed. The bodyguards of the other prionnsachan closed around those they protected, weapons at the ready. If the Rìgh of Eileanan and the Far Islands could be assassinated in his own banquet hall, then no one was safe.

"Finn, canna ye do something? Canna ye find this villain for me?" Iseult demanded.

Finn the Cat was holding the black dart in her hand, her eyes shut. After a long moment, she opened her eyes and shook her head unhappily. "Whoever it was didna touch the dart long enough to leave a strong impression. They may have picked it up while wearing gloves or handled it through a cloth. I'm sorry."

"There must be something ye can do!"

"If ye can find the blowpipe, I'll be able to tell ye who the murderer is, for they will have held it to their mouth and blown the air o' their lungs into it. That will be enough for me."

"But canna ye help find the blowpipe?"

Finn shook her head reluctantly. "The dart must've passed through the pipe in a matter o' seconds. Whoever did this must've been careful no' to have let it touch any longer than that. All I get from the dart is an impression o' darkness and closeness, like a pocket or a bag. Beyond that, I can tell ye only that it comes from the swamplands o' Arran, but ye could guess that for yourselves."

Iseult switched her fierce gaze from Finn to Iain. Sick and white with shock, he kneeled beside Lachlan's sprawling form. Elfrida stood beside him, gripping her fan tightly. She put one hand on his shoulder, and he straightened slowly. "Ye ken we s-s-sell the blowpipes and barbs to the Yeomen," Iain said, beginning to stammer as he always did in times of strong emotion. "They . . . they take a hundred or so every year. And the b-b-bogfaeries sometimes sell them too, on the black m-m-market. There is no way for me to tell who m-m-may have one. I'm s-s-sorry." He hid his face again in his hands.

Iseult bent her head over Lachlan's lifeless form, smoothing his hair away from his face. Isabeau wrapped her arm about her twin and rocked her wordlessly. Iseult's chest rose and fell sharply, and her breath shuddered.

Like everyone else in the crowd, Lewen had been painstakingly searched and questioned by the soldiers, but he had been allowed to stay in the banquet hall in case his mistress had need of him. All the other squires had been hustled away by their respective families, everyone fearful of what might happen next.

Although numb with shock and grief, Lewen saw that the Banrìgh was in danger of breaking down completely and so he found a pitcher of wine and brought her a glass of the rich red liquid, kneeling beside her to proffer it on a tray. Isabeau gave him a quick glance of commendation and took the glass, holding it to Iseult's mouth. She managed to swallow a mouthful.

"I beg your pardon, Your Highness . . ." Lewen said, his stomach twisting with anxiety.

Iseult looked up at him blankly.

"Your Highness, I'm sorry but . . . where are Olwynne and Owein?" Lewen said in a rush. "I canna see them anywhere."

Iseult stared at him for a moment, then got to her feet, looking about her wildly. She was white to the lips. "Where are they?" she whispered. "They were right here afore . . . afore . . ." A shudder ran over her.

Isabeau stood up abruptly. "Owein and Olwynne are missing?"

"No," Iseult whispered. "No, no, no."

"But that's ridiculous," Nina said sharply. "They were here, at the feast. . . ."

"I saw Owein dancing with one o' the NicThanach girls just moments afore it all happened," Dide said, staring around him, grim-faced.

"But did ye see him again afterwards?" Isabeau demanded.

"Nay . . . but there was so much happening. It was all such confusion . . ."

"Aye, exactly," Isabeau said grimly. She turned to Lewen. "When did ye last see Olwynne?"

"She was on the terrace, my lady. . . . I went to get her a cool drink . . . but then His Majesty . . . I didna see her again," he managed to say, though his throat was rigid with fear.

"Did anyone else see Owein and Olwynne after . . ." Isabeau's voice faded away.

All the onlookers shook their heads, a loud murmur of dissent rising.

"Eà's green blood," Iseult said and swayed where she stood.

The wind wailed a lamentation. Sleet drove against the windows. All the air in the room turned to ice, so that Lewen could scarcely breathe. White clouds hung before their mouths. The tear spilling over Iseult's red eyelid froze into one long, glittering icicle.

"Iseult! Stop it!" Isabeau cried. "Do ye think turning the world to snow will make our job any easier!"

Her sister had not been named Iseult of the Snows simply because she had been raised in the icy wastes of the Spine of the World. Always her talent had been with ice and snow. It had proved useful indeed during the long years of the Bright Wars, when she had used her powers against their enemies, but it had been a long time since she had done more than chill her wine by cupping her hand around her glass. Iseult had never spent long years studying the nature and extent of her powers, as her twin sister had done, and so her control over her abilities was variable. Like many untrained witches, her Talent could manifest itself without volition and could prove very hard to rein back in once it had been unleashed.

Isabeau seized her shoulders and shook her. She was crying herself, but the look of fierce determination on her face did not falter.

"Iseult! They are no' dead. I can sense them still. They have been stolen away. We must try to find them! Come, Iseult. Breathe!"

The Dowager Banrìgh took in one long, shuddering breath, then breathed out again. The icicle melted and turned again into a teardrop. Lewen found his lungs released from the vise of cold, and though his breath still puffed white, he was able to inhale and exhale without pain.

"My bairns," Iseult whispered. "Who could've taken them? Why?" She began to pace up and down the hall, snow swirling from her skirts. None of those left in the room could do anything but watch her. Everyone was gripped with a dreadful feeling of helplessness.

"I need something o' theirs to hold," Finn said. "A glass they've just drunk out o', or something they've made with their own hands is best. Or a lock o' hair, or a scrap o' fingernail, or some o' their blood."

"I do no' carry a vial o' my children's blood around wi' me," Iseult cried.

"No' a lock o' baby hair?"

"O' course, somewhere!"

"Anyone ken which glass was Owein's?" Dide asked. They all glanced at the high table and saw the servants had been quietly clearing away the refuse of the feast.

Lewen slid his hand inside his coat and touched the withered nosegay he carried there. It had, he remembered, some of Olwynne's hair caught in the binding. He did not want to show anyone the little token she had given him, but he hesitated only a second, pulling it out and giving it to Finn.

"This was hers," he said quietly, the blood rising in his cheeks.

Finn took it into her hand, and her eyebrows shot up. She looked at it closely, glanced at Lewen, and then exchanged a quick look with Isabeau, who was watching intently, her brows drawn close together.

"Can ye feel aught?" Iseult demanded.

"Indeed I can," Finn said with another considering glance at Lewen, who tried not to squirm with embarrassment. She held the nosegay close to her breast, breathing in deeply, her eyes shut.

"No' far away," she muttered. "Underground. Dark. Stinky. Makes her feel sick. Moving fast. Bumped. Almost dropped. She's being carried! Water sloshing . . . smells horrible . . ."

"The sewers!" Captain Dillon cried.

"Who has her?" Dide demanded. "Can ye tell, Finn?"

Finn's face screwed up in concentration as she cast wide her witch-senses. Then her eyes snapped open. "The laird o' Fettercairn!" she hissed. "I ken his smell well, after all those weeks handling his vile collection. But how? Why?"

"Laird Malvern!" Nina cried. "Eà, no! Och, Your Highness, ye must find them. He is an evil, evil man. He means naught but harm to them. I should've kent he'd be behind Lachlan's murder! He and that poisonous skeelie o' his. But how?" Suddenly she turned and flung out her hand to her husband. "Iven!" she cried. "He wouldna . . . he couldna . . . Roden!"

Iven was at her side in an instant, his arm about her waist. He looked shaken. Cursing under his breath, Dide looked at Finn. The sorceress bit her lip and shut her eyes. When she opened them again, it was to nod her head unhappily.

The blood drained away from Nina's face, leaving her a ghastly yellowish white, like old bone. "Nay," she whispered; then suddenly her legs gave way and she pitched forward onto her knees. Iven and Dide were beside her in a moment, lifting her up, both haggard with shock. Nina was weeping, trying to speak but unable to get the breath to force the words out.

"No' Roden, no' my wee Roden," Iven cried. "But how? He was . . ." His voice died away.

"Eà's green blood!" said Dide. "That villain! That vile snake. When? How?"

"Roden," Nina whispered. "My babe . . ."

There was a tumult among those in the room. Cries and exclamations rang out.

"The laird o' Fettercairn again!" Gwilym said. "We should've lain him by the heels days ago!"

"If it hadn't been for the extra soldiers we needed to guard the wedding . . ." Captain Dillon said.

"How did this happen?" Isabeau whispered. She had known the little boy from birth and loved him as dearly as Dide did.

"So was it the laird o' Fettercairn who murdered my husband?" Iseult demanded. "How? How could he have got anywhere near him?"

"He could no' have," Captain Dillon said firmly. "My men were watching closely. I had double the usual guard."

"Yet someone murdered Lachlan," Iseult said. She was shaking as if with a palsy.

Captain Dillon bowed his head. His hands gripped his sword hilt as if he was trying to prevent it from leaping out of its sheath and laying waste around him.

"Let us go," Finn said, giving the nosegay back to Lewen. "If we are swift enough, we'll catch him and then we can be finding out about the how and why. For now, let us get on his trail!"

"I will send some men with ye," Captain Dillon said and beckoned to his lieutenants.

"Make sure they are fast," Finn said. "I will need to be able to send them back with messages. I canna scry in this weather, and I doubt I will have the time to stop anyway."

As Finn spoke she had been swiftly stripping off her heavy silk gown, till she was standing in nothing but her camisole and drawers. "Ye, give me your breeches!" she demanded of the closest soldier. Blushing hotly, he began to undress and she dragged on his clothes and his cloak, the grey side turned out. At once her tiny elven cat, which she had put down on the table for a moment, leaped back up to her shoulder again, its tufted ears laid back, its fangs bared in a hiss. The soldier, shivering in his underclothes, gratefully received the cloak of one of his fellow Yeomen and wrapped it about him.

Finn lifted her hand in farewell, then broke into a run, throwing open the door into the garden and passing out into the stormy darkness. Snow blew in through the open door, sending the candle flames dancing and making the women shiver and rub their bare arms.

Jay followed as swiftly after, slinging his viola case over his back. "We'll find them," he said over his shoulder. "Do no' fear, Your Highness. We will have them soon."

"Oh, may it please the White Gods!" Iseult cried, her hands pressed together.

Then they were gone.

There was a moment's silence. Lewen tucked away the nosegay in his pocket, his throat tight. His bonny Olwynne, in the hands of Lord Malvern! The thought made him feel ill with anxiety. What could the lord of Fettercairn want with Owein and Olwynne and Roden? If it was just revenge he desired, he could have killed them as he had, somehow, killed Lachlan. Lewen remembered how Rhiannon had seen the ghost of a dead sorceress bargaining with Lord Malvern, promising him the secret of raising the dead from life in return for his promise to raise her first.

"We have to get Olwynne back," he whispered.

Iseult had her hands pressed against her mouth. Her skin looked grey, with shadows like bruises under her eyes. "Donncan," she whispered. "Oh, Eà, if they have taken him too . . ."

Hailstones as large as fists smashed into the windows, cracking the glass from side to side and imploding sharp slivers into the banquet hall. The soldiers standing guard by the door yelled and flinched away. Through the fissure, shaped like a broken star, sleet drove in, and a bitter wind that snuffed out the candles.

They were all plunged into an icy darkness. At once a giant ball of witch-light sprang up in the center of the room, casting an eerie blue light over them all. Isabeau leaped to Iseult's side, supporting her crumpling figure. Dide brought her a chair, and they lowered her into it and gave her wine to drink. As soon as Iseult's hands touched the glass, the liquid within froze solid and the glass cracked asunder.

"Donncan," Iseult whispered.

"Lewen, find him!" Isabeau commanded, bending to chafe Iseult's hands between her own. "Bring him back here. We must ken he is safe!"

"Aye, my lady," Lewen said, though he was so racked with cold and fear and horror he felt he could barely walk. He managed to weave his way towards the glass doors leading out into the garden, his legs wobbling underneath him as if he had been drinking clamber skull all night.

"Wait!" Isabeau cried.

He turned back.

"It is bitterly cold," she said. "Guard, give Lewen your cloak! He is no' dressed for running through the snow."

Lewen looked down at himself. He was dressed for midsummer, not midwinter. Like everyone else in the hall, he was shivering uncontrollably. The soldier obediently unfastened his long blue cloak and passed it to Lewen, who wrapped himself up in it gratefully before pushing open the doors and stepping out into the storm.

Slivers of ice needled the bare skin of his face, the wind wailing like a banshee. He dragged the hood of the cloak up over his head and began to run.

The palace and the witches' tower were connected by a long avenue bounded on one side by a towering wall and by the wood on the other. The trees were all bending and blowing in the wind, and broken twigs and leaves battered against him. Over the tumult of the storm, the bells' relentless tone sounded out. Lewen spared a thought for the bell ringers, hauling on the thick heavy ropes as the muffled bells clanged out their message of grief and shock and outrage.

The Rìgh is dead! From house to house, town to village, hall to croft to peddler's cart, the news would be running throughout the land. *Murdered in his own banquet hall, as he drank a toast to his son and new daughter. The Rìgh is dead!*

He found that he was weeping and put up his hand to rub away the snow and the tears together.

He could not believe his Rìgh was dead. He had to repeat the words to himself over and over before he could even begin to believe it was true. Lachlan the Winged had always been such a powerful presence, roaring and stamping through the palace, his retinue hurrying to keep up with him. It seemed impossible that all that vibrancy and passion could be snuffed out so easily. Even more shocking was the manner in which he had died, writhing in agony from the poison of a bogfaery dart spat at him from the shadows. And then to steal away his children, his heirs. If Donncan was gone also, the great MacCuinn clan would be broken, its only offspring a quarter-Fairgean girl who spent her days dancing and flirting and devising ever more outrageous costumes. It seemed impossible. The MacCuinns had ruled Eileanan for hundreds of years. Could it all be over so quickly, so finally?

Lewen was so numb with shock and bewilderment, his legs felt as if they were made of lead. He could scarcely force them to keep running.

It took him close on half an hour to reach the Tower of Two Moons. The students of the Theurgia were milling around on the front steps, shivering with cold and apprehension as the low, slow, somber tolling of the bells went on and on. At the sight of Lewen, they clustered around, demanding news. When they heard of Lachlan's murder, many cried aloud in horror. Lewen had no time to comfort them or give them details, however.

"The Prionnsa Donncan . . . have ye seen him?" he panted.

"Aye," one said. "We saw him and Mistress Johanna go into the witches' wood, along with the Celestine princess, just afore the bells began to ring."

"They were in a right hurry," one of his companions chirped up.

"Into the wood?" Lewen was startled. "Are ye sure?"

"Sure we're sure," they answered.

"Did anyone see him come out?" Lewen asked. But they all shook their heads.

Lewen turned and looked at the wood, biting his lip in indecision. It was black and wet and wild. Try as he might, he could think of no good reason for Donncan to go within on such a night. He remembered Johanna as he had last seen her, screaming for Rhiannon to be hanged, and felt a sharp stab of fear and suspicion.

"We need to find him," he said. "Rouse up the Tower! Form search parties! We must find the Prionnsa." Sudden realization smote him: "He is Rìgh now," he said. "We must find the Rìgh."

RINGING THE CHANGES

"Ring out, wild bells, to the wild sky,
The flying cloud, the frosty light:
The year is dying in the night;
Ring out, wild bells, and let him die.
Ring out the old, ring in the new,
Ring happy bells, across the snow:
The year is going, let him go,
Ring out the false, ring in the true."

—ALFRED, LORD TENNYSON,
In Memoriam A.H.H., canto 106 (1850)

The Summons

Iseult pressed her temples with trembling fingers. Hail hammered on the roof. The Rìgh had been lifted up on to the high table and covered with a tablecloth. The Master of Revels arranged freshly lit candles all around the Rìgh's body, pausing often to mop his eyes and blow his nose. One of the servants noticed the Lodestar lying where it had fallen from the Rìgh's hand and bent to pick it up.

"Do no' touch it!" Isabeau cried. "It's death for anyone no' of MacCuinn blood to touch it."

The lackey's hand flinched back as if the scepter was a venomous snake and not just a softly glowing white orb set upon a golden rod.

"It's Donncan's now," Iseult said, and gripped her shaking hands together.

"Why is he no' here to pick it up?" Nina whispered, and wiped her eyes. "Where can he be?" No one could answer her, though many exchanged glances and whispers. Where was the new Rìgh, who had inherited the throne and the Lodestar so brutally and unexpectedly on his wedding day? Where were his brother and sister? What did it mean for them all, to have the Inheritance of Aedan lying on the floor amid a litter of crumbs and fallen flower petals and half-chewed bones?

"I will mind it for my husband," Bronwen said coolly. She came forward and bent to pick up the Lodestar. A white flame sprang up in the Lodestar's heart at the touch of her fingers, and those who had the gift of clear-hearing could hear a symphonic burst of music.

Bronwen herself was unable to help gasping aloud. Touching the Lodestar was like seizing the tail of a doom-eel. Electricity surged up the nerve strings of her arm and into her brain. She was irradiated with white power, a choir of soaring voices ringing in her ears, a sea of joyous energy pounding through her blood. Her breath caught. Her pulse thundered. She held the Lodestar in both hands and fought to keep her face impassive. She knew she failed, feeling her mouth curving in a fierce grin of triumph and exultation. All she could do was turn away, taking refuge by her silent mother's side, trying to pretend nothing had changed.

Of course there were those among the court who noticed. The Dowager Duchess of Rammermuir and her cronies noticed everything. As the chambermaids hurriedly swept out the banquet hall, many of them wiping their eyes on their aprons, the court gossips put their heads together and whispered and wondered.

Iseult stared at Bronwen suspiciously, color surging up into her face, but Isabeau touched her arm, shaking her head almost imperceptibly. After a moment, Iseult turned away. She could not sit still but paced the room like a caged lioness, spindrifts of snow swirling up around her at every step. Every now and again she stopped to stare out into the storm, but there was nothing to be seen except the bobbing lights of the soldiers searching the terraces and gardens, and the whirling whiteness of the snow.

Bronwen sat quietly, the Lodestar cradled in her hands, her eyes lowered. It was impossible to tell what she thought or felt from her face, although she was very pale. Maya wrote something on her slate, and Bronwen shook her head and said something in a low voice. Maya replied, the screech of chalk on slate setting everyone's nerves on edge and causing Iseult to shoot the Ensorcellor an irritated glance. Suddenly both Maya and Bronwen turned their heads and looked towards the door. Then the others heard the sound of running footsteps too, and tensed.

The door swung open. A grey-clad guard came hurrying in and dropped to his knees before Iseult.

"Your Highness! I beg your leave . . . !" He was a thickset man with dark hair and a reddish beard and rough hands. Isabeau recognized him from the day she had caused the prison to be scoured from dungeon to tower top.

"What is it?" Iseult asked, her voice roughened with weeping.

"News from the prison," the guard said, his head lowered. "The satyricorn girl has escaped. The warden thought Her Highness should ken . . ."

Iseult's eyes had been blank and unfocused, but at the guard's words, her gaze at once sharpened. "Did ye say the satyricorn girl has escaped from Sorrowgate Tower?"

"Aye, Your Highness."

Color crept up Iseult's face. "The satyricorn girl," she repeated softly. Then she rapped out, "How? How did this happen?"

"She hit her guard over the head with the chamber pot," he replied unhappily.

"A chamber pot!"

"Aye, Your Highness."

"How could he have been so stupid?"

"She took him by surprise, my lady."

"Was it full or empty?" Dide asked. He could not have said why, but he had to bite down a hysterical urge to laugh.

The guard went red. "Full, my laird."

Dide snorted with laughter, and tried to turn it into a cough. Iseult glared at him and he stepped back, straightening his back and composing his face.

"Tell me what happened," Iseult demanded.

The guard obeyed unhappily, and a little murmur arose from all those who listened.

"Did she no' ken the Rìgh planned to pardon her?" Nina asked. "Och, the poor lass. I wish he had told her."

"And ye say she took her pack with her, with all inside it?" All Iseult's attention was focused on the prison guard.

"Aye, Your Highness."

Iseult paced back and forth, her face looking thin and haunted. "Correct me if I am wrong, but was there no' a blowpipe and bag o' barbs in that pack that had once belonged to Connor the Just?"

"There was, Your Highness."

"Aha!" Iseult cried.

"But Rhiannon would no' have murdered His Majesty!" Nina exclaimed. "Ye canna think such a thing o' her."

"I can and I do," Iseult answered in a cold voice.

Nina got to her feet, her hands clasped tightly at her breast. "She wouldna have done it, Your Highness. Truly, she would no'."

"Then who did?" Iseult demanded. "All along we have been wondering who, who, who? Now we ken."

"But Iseult . . ." Isabeau said.

Iseult whirled on her. "Ye think it coincidence she escapes the very night my Lachlan was murdered? With a blowpipe and barbs in her bag?"

"Coincidences do happen," Isabeau said.

"Rarely," Iseult answered. "Ye were the one who taught me that."

"But how could Rhiannon have done it?" Nina asked, her words tumbling over themselves. "There were guards everywhere. They would have seen her. All the soldiers know who Rhiannon was."

"She would have disguised herself. She had Connor's uniform."

"But how would she have hidden her hair? It is very long. . . ." Iven said, frowning.

"She'd have cut it," Iseult replied curtly.

"But why? Why would she kill His Majesty?" Nina cried.

"It must've been her plan all along," Iseult said. "That was why she killed Connor, to stop him from bringing news o' the plot to us."

She began to pace up and down. "She must be in cahoots with the laird o' Fettercairn. We ken he wanted Lachlan dead, in revenge for the death o' his brother and his brother's little boy. The laird o' Fettercairn has been plotting and planning for more than twenty years now. We ken how loyal his supporters are. This Rhiannon girl must be one o' them. Connor must've found out somehow, and she killed him to keep him quiet. Then she got in with Nina and Iven and was coming in their train to Lucescere, with them none the wiser. But the discovery o' Connor's body made them take the shortcut through the Fetterness Valley. How Rhiannon must've cursed the ill chance that saw his body washed up at Barbreck-by-the-Bridge just as Nina and Iven rode past! She must've decided to keep her head down, pretend no' to ken the laird o' Fettercairn, no' to like him even. But then Nina discovered the truth about the laird—"

"It was Rhiannon who first accused the laird," Nina broke in.

"That would've been some ploy, to deflect suspicion away from herself." Iseult swung around to face the sorceress, her eyes glittering with conviction. "But then the laird was arrested and brought here too. She would've had to keep pretending they were enemies."

"They *were* enemies!" Nina cried.

"So she said."

"But Rhiannon was going to stand witness against him. Without her, we would no' have kent about the necromancy."

"She did no' stand witness against him, though, did she?"

"Only because he escaped from prison."

"Yes. Lucky chance, that one."

"The laird tried to break her out o' prison too, remember, and she would no' go."

"Again, according to her. There were no other witnesses to it."

"What about the laird o' Fettercairn's skeelie, Your Highness?" Iven said. "She stood witness against Rhiannon. Why would she do that if they wanted Rhiannon free to kill Lachlan?"

"I do no' ken," Iseult admitted. "Perhaps to throw dust in our eyes. Perhaps to force the satyricorn girl to do as they bid. There could be any number o' reasons."

"But—" Iven protested.

"Do no' argue with me," Iseult cried. "I ken ye are fond o' this girl, despite her crimes. Yet I canna see how ye can still defend her! She escaped from her prison with a blowpipe and a bag o' poisoned barbs the very hour Lachlan was murdered with the same weapon! She has the uniform o' a Yeoman in her bag on a night when the Yeomen were almost as thick on the ground as wedding guests. And . . ." Iseult paused for effect. "And whoever killed Lachlan had a quick escape route, one that succeeded in evading all o' the above Yeomen. What better than a winged horse?"

Both Nina and Iven hurried into passionate speech, but

Iseult raised her hand imperiously and they both fell silent, though with obvious difficulty.

Iseult turned to Captain Dillon, who was standing guard over his dead Rìgh, scowling ferociously as he listened to the prison guard's report.

"Dillon, we must find her!" Iseult commanded.

"She'll be long gone on that horse o' hers," he answered.

"She murdered my husband!" Iseult hissed. "She helped that blaygird laird steal away my bairns! I want her found and I want her hanged."

"It would be my pleasure, Your Highness," Dillon replied, "if I had a winged horse at my disposal to hunt her down. But I do no'. There is naught I can do to catch her. She would be miles away by now."

Iseult stood very still, biting her lip until blood began to run down her chin. "I will hunt her down myself," she said, and the air about her turned so cold it seemed she was surrounded by a nimbus of frost. She lifted her eyes to the shadow-hung ceiling, raised both her hands, and began to intone in a deep, strange voice, "Caillec Asrohc Airi . . ."

"Iseult, no!" Isabeau cried.

Her twin sister did not respond. Her eyes were rolling up in her head, and she was shaking with the force of the magical summons she spoke.

". . . Telloch Cas," she finished. "Come to me! Once more I shall ride the dragon's back!"

The vast wood that lay between tower and palace had come alive with hundreds of bobbing balls of witch-light as search parties hurried through the innumerable paths through the trees. It was the only form of illumination that could withstand the gale-force winds blowing with snow. Gusts of hail pelted the heads of the searchers, and lightning cracked like a whip of white fire.

Lewen stamped his feet in their thin leather shoes and rubbed his icy hands together, wishing he could take the time to go to his room and change. He dared not, however. His fear had expanded in his chest until he found it hard to breathe. Fear for his beloved Olwynne, fear for his dearest friend Owein, fear for his Rìgh. He was torn by conflicting needs. On the one hand, he wished to stay and search for the young Rìgh until he was found, yet on the other hand all he wanted to do was rush back to the palace and find out what had happened to Owein and Olwynne. His duty must come first, though.

Lewen knew that Captain Dillon and the Dowager Banrìgh would expect him to have made every effort to find the young Rìgh and to gather information about what could have happened to him, so, after he was sure the search parties were being coordinated properly, he hurried to the healers' wing to see if he could find any clue as to where Johanna had been taking Donncan and Thunderlily.

The Royal College of Healers was eerily quiet. He came into the front hall and found the porter fast asleep in his chair, his chin on his chest. Lewen tried to rouse him, but he only fell off his chair and lay snoring on the cold floor. No matter how Lewen shook him, he could not wake him. Wishing he had a sword, Lewen drew his little eating dagger and went on into the tower.

Lights blazed from the dining room, though there was no sound of any life. Lewen pushed open the double doors but stopped so abruptly on the threshold that the doors hit him as they swung back into place.

Long tables lined the hall, laden with platters of roasted vegetables, and stuffed mushrooms, and little round pies of baked egg and herbs. Half-empty wineglasses and mugs of flat ale sat by every plate. The hall had been decorated with garlands of flowers and colored ribbon, and more flowers adorned the heads of many of the people who lay slumped over the table or fallen onto the floor. There were at least two hundred of them, men and women, dressed in the green robes of the healers.

It felt as if an icy fist had closed about Lewen's heart. He staggered forward and dropped to his knees by the closest person, a man who lay fallen from his chair, a puddle of red wine spreading across the flagstones like blood. Lewen's fingers fumbled for a pulse. The man's skin was cold, but a faint throbbing in his neck showed he was still alive. Lewen felt faint with relief. He checked another body, and then another. They all lived, but he could not rouse them.

Lewen got to his feet, hesitating, and then went blundering out into the hallway again, calling for help. There was no reply. Lewen went running through the tower, banging on doors and flinging them open. Most of the rooms were empty, for everyone had been at the feast. On the top floor of the tower, however, he threw open a door and found a pale figure collapsed on the floor. He saw the long pale hair and the simple straight lines of the robe, and his heart smote him. He went down on his knees beside her and gently turned her over. It was the Stargazer. Her pulse was so faint he could barely feel it, and when he bent his cheek to her mouth, he could not feel her breath at all.

Raised by his mother to revere the Celestines, rulers of the forest faeries, Lewen had to fight hard to keep panic from overwhelming him. He lifted Cloudshadow, who weighed no more than a small child despite her height, and laid her on the bed, covering her with the counterpane. The hearth was brushed clean and empty, for the weather had been hot until this unnatural winter had been conjured out of Iseult's grief. He chafed the Stargazer's cold hands between his own and looked for wine to dribble between her lips. He found some on a table near where she had been lying and had just lifted the glass to bring to her when he remembered the wine spilled like blood in the dining room. He stared at it in horror and saw heavy dregs of some undissolved powder still floating in the bottom of the glass.

Very carefully Lewen put the glass down again, and then, after making the Stargazer as warm and comfortable as he could, went slowly and methodically through the rest of the tower. He found the other Celestines drugged and unconscious also, and was unable to rouse any of them. Once he had covered them all up warmly, he went to Johanna's room, at the top of the tower. There he found signs that someone had been bound with rope and cut free with a knife. There were faint bloodstains on the rope, and a scrap of torn silver gauze. He also found Donncan's brooch, dropped under the table. He took it up in his hand, hardly able to breathe with fear. Holding the brooch tightly in his hand, he went running down the stairs and out into the garth, shouting hoarsely for help.

Outside, the storm shrieked and wailed with new intensity.

He put his arm over his face and leaned into the wind. Crossing the garth was like trying to cross a glacier. He could not believe how thick was the snow. He staggered into the main hallway of the Theurgia, where a command center had been set up to coordinate the search for the missing Rìgh. Huge fires had been kindled at either end, and Lewen could smell mulled wine and hot chestnuts. The change in temperature was such a shock to his system he almost fainted, but he pulled his swimming senses together and called out to Fat Drusa, the sorceress in charge.

"Lewen!" she cried and waddled towards him. "What is it? Ye're white as a sheet. Come, sit down. Drink some o' the wine. What have ye found? No' . . . no' . . ." Words failed her and she clasped her plump hands together before her in dismay.

"Healers' College . . ." Lewen gasped. "They're all drugged . . . unconscious . . . the Celestines . . ."

Someone passed him a cup of hot spiced wine and he gulped it down gratefully. Only then could he describe what he had found with any degree of coherency.

"We must go and tend them," Fat Drusa said. "Katrin, go and find as many blankets as ye can. Rouse up the chambermaids and bid them help ye. Cameron, we'll need firewood and plenty o' it! Take ye a party and see if there's any cut. If no', ye'll need to chop us some and right quickly! Edithe, run up to my bedchamber, will ye, and find my smelling salts. They're in the cupboard by my bed. Run, girl, run! Rafferty, do ye ken where Lewen's room is? Go and get him some warm, dry clothes, will ye? He'll catch his death in that thin shirt. Good girl, Fèlice, well done."

At the sound of his friends' names, Lewen looked up and only then saw that the room was crowded with young apprentices, all milling around and trying their best to do as Drusa commanded. It was Fèlice who had given him the cup of mulled wine. She was now kneeling before him, unlacing his sodden shoes and drawing them off his feet, which felt like blocks of ice. Gently she rubbed them dry with a warm towel. As feeling began to return, Lewen winced in pain.

"Fancy running around in the snow with naught on your feet but a thin pair of court shoes," Drusa scolded.

"I canna rest here," Lewen cried. "I must go and find His Highness! Give me back my shoes."

"Ye'll have frostbite if ye go out again without a proper pair o' boots on. Rafferty, go! Lewen wants some good stout boots, and a muffler and gloves too, if he's going out into that snowstorm again."

"No! Send someone else," Lewen cried. "I need Rafferty. He's the fastest."

Gladly Rafferty turned and came back, dropping down on his knees before Lewen. "Ye must take a message to the Dowager Banrìgh," Lewen said rapidly. "Tell her there's been foul play here as well. Tell her the Rìgh Donncan is missing too, and Thunderlily the Celestine. They've been taken by Mistress Johanna, I do no' ken where. Tell her we need soldiers to help us search the witches' wood—it's the last place they were seen. Tell her all the healers have been drugged or poisoned, I do no' ken which, and the Stargazer and her retinue too. Can ye remember all that?"

Rafferty nodded and rapidly recited the message, counting off the points on his fingers. When Lewen nodded in commendation, he was up and running out the door.

Fèlice seized Lewen's hand. "Ye said 'Donncan is missing too.' What did ye mean, Lewen? Who else is missing?"

Lewen's heart sank. He looked down at the pretty, frightened face turned up to his. "Olwynne and Owein have been taken," he said. "Roden too."

Fèlice's eyes widened, and her breath caught. "Taken? Taken where? By who?"

"The laird o' Fettercairn. We do no' ken where, or why."

Tears spilled down her face. "Oh Eà, oh Eà, oh Eà," she whispered. "No, no! No' Owein. He . . . I . . . I did no' ken . . . Oh, Lewen! He left me a message—he said he wanted to see me. I screwed it up and threw it away. Oh, if only I had answered it, if only I had gone to see him, maybe . . ."

"Their plans were very well laid," Lewen said, squeezing her fingers. "I think they would have found some way to kidnap him even if ye had answered his note. Do no' feel bad, Fèlice. It is no' your fault."

Fèlice hid her face in her hands. For a moment Lewen was afraid that she was going to dissolve into tears, when he had neither the time nor the energy to be comforting her, but she took a deep, shuddering breath and managed to control herself.

"What can I do to help?" she asked then, her voice trembling only a little.

"We must rouse the Celestines," Lewen said. "If anyone can help us find Rìgh Donncan, it is them."

Fèlice nodded. "I'll find Maisie," she said. "All Maisie wants is to be a healer. She's spent all her spare time studying and going to extra lectures. She'll ken the best way to wake them."

"Good," Lewen said. "Let me ken as soon as they wake. I'll be out in the woods searching for His Highness."

In only a few minutes, Fèlice, Maisie, and a large group of young female apprentice-witches were hurrying through the cold, dark halls of the Tower of Two Moons, taking the long way around to the healers' hall, rather than get their loads of blankets, warm cloaks, firewood, tinder, and kindling wet by cutting across the snowy courtyard. It had been difficult finding enough people to help. Most of the servants had been given leave to celebrate Midsummer's Day, and many of the witches and students had taken advantage of the holiday to go home to their families. Most of the Circle of Sorcerers had been at the wedding, leaving only Fat Drusa and Wise Tully behind to oversee the festivities at the witches' tower. Both were physically incapable of helping much with the desperate search through the snowy night or with setting up a hospital in the healers' great hall, one because of her immense size, the other because of her immense age. So it was left to those students not too inebriated after the day's partying to take on the responsibility.

Lewen was himself torn. All he wanted was to go sloshing through the sewers searching for his lost love, but he had been given his task and he was duty-bound and honor-bound to do as he was ordered. Find Donncan, the Keybearer had commanded, and so that was what he must do.

He gathered together a search party of young men, many of whom had spent the last hour fruitlessly tramping through the storm-tossed darkness and were not that keen to face the driving snow again.

"It's useless," one said angrily. "Any tracks the Prionnsa

may have left have been swept away by the storm. We've been searching for hours and found naught!"

"Everything's been covered with snow. All we found were our own tracks, going around and around in circles," said another.

"It's bitterly cold out there, Lewen," Cameron said. "Are ye sure . . . ?"

"Our Rìgh is missing," Lewen said tiredly. "If we canna find him, there will be no law, no order, no rule. We must try! Besides, I have an idea. . . ."

Lewen knew that the woods separating the witches' tower and the palace were sanctuary to thousands of faeries of all kinds, from the tiny bright-winged nisses to tree-changers to corrigans. Most would be sheltering from the storm whatever way they could, but Lewen hoped that some at least would answer his call and come to tell him what they knew. Having been raised near an ancient forest by his tree-shifter mother, Lewen knew most of the languages spoken by the forest faeries, and it was in these languages that he called.

He was lucky. It was not long before a nisse came swooping out of the darkness and swung off his finger, chattering away in high excitement.

"This way the star-girl went, glimmering and gleaming in her silver dress. I flew fleet following her and the two big ones of no account. Fast and far I flew, wondering why and where they went, but then the wind turned to ice, howling and hollering, and shivering shaking I flew fled back to my own safe snug tree. . . ."

"It is very cold," Lewen said gently. "If ye sheltered here under my scarf, could ye show me where they went?"

"Comfy and cozy," the little faery said approvingly, snuggling up under the soft wool. "I happy to settle stay here!"

With the arctic wind blasting him, needling his face with ice and blowing back his hair, Lewen tramped through the wildly tossing trees, his witch-light flickering above him. The nisse was not a reliable guide. She chattered away almost nonstop, and it was difficult to concentrate on her words when he was so very cold and tired and occupied by such an acute anxiety it felt as if someone was trying to drill their way out of his stomach.

Eventually, though, the nisse led Lewen and the search party to the very center of the forest, where lay the magical maze that protected the Pool of Two Moons. There, caught on the narrow iron gate that led into the maze, Lewen found the scarlet sash that Donncan had worn to his wedding.

Puzzled, Lewen stood, holding the sash in his hand and staring down the dark corridor of yews. Even with his witch-light bobbing just above his head, he could see only a short distance into the maze, with the frosty wind howling about his head and snow blowing into his eyes. He did not know the secret of the maze. It was a secret known only to those of the MacCuinn clan and the Circle of Sorcerers. It was impossible for him to go on. Already he was exhausted and so cold his hands and feet seemed to have disappeared. If he led his search party into the maze, they could all well die.

"We'll go back," he muttered. "We'll send a message to the palace. In the morning, perhaps, we can keep on searching."

His words were met with sighs of relief all around. Lewen, however, felt only misery and despair. If he could have found Donncan, it would have been worth not insisting on chasing after Olwynne. He would have been free to help in the search for Owein and Olwynne.

Then his heart lightened. Perhaps, back at the Tower of Two Moons, good news would be waiting for him as well as hot spiced wine and a warm bed. They said Finn the Cat always found what she sought.

Suddenly the nisse gave a high-pitched shriek and burrowed deep into his neck, drawing the scarf tight around her. Lewen felt her sharp nails scratching him. Even as he reached in and sought to drag her out, he heard, high overhead, the unmistakable trumpeting cry of a dragon.

It tore through the night like a rush of flame through paper. Lewen threw himself to the ground, his arms over his head, his face pressed into the snow, so overwhelmed with terror he felt his bowels loosen involuntarily. Sternly he clenched the muscles of his sphincter together, curling his knees to his chest. By the sudden odor, he knew some of his fellow searchers had failed to control their own bowels. Someone sobbed out loud.

High above their heads a volley of flame blasted the night sky. Glancing up, Lewen saw the sinuous shape of the dragon soaring through the darkness, the red glare of its breath lighting

up the massive heavy clouds, the wind-tossed trees, its great angular wings. For a moment all was white, black, red, like a
drawing of ink on paper; then the dragon passed over.

There was a rush of bitter-tasting air, then all was quiet and
dark again.

Winged Shadow

Rhiannon lay against the mare's warm side, Blackthorn's wing tucked over her, trying to stop shivering. The cold struck up from the snow-covered ground, penetrating the plaid she had wrapped around her and seeming to strike right into the very marrow of her bones.

Rhiannon had never seen a storm of such unnatural ferocity. It had seemed like a living creature with talons of ice, and fangs of lightning, that had harried her all the way from Sorrowgate Tower, across the river, and to the foothills. Rhiannon had hoped to fly much farther before resting, but their only hope of survival had been to land and seek shelter.

They must want to hang her very badly, Rhiannon thought to herself, to send such a storm after her. Here it was, midsummer, and icicles hung from all the trees. Drifts of hailstones lay everywhere. The copse of trees in which they sheltered bent and blew in the wind, their branches creaking. Rhiannon did not know what time it was. Surely dawn could not be too far away, but there was no sound of birdsong, no lightening of the howling darkness. It had been an endless night.

Rhiannon ached all over from their desperate ride through the hailstorm. Her head throbbed, and blood trickled down from a cut behind her ear. There was more blood on the arm she had raised to shield her face, and on Blackthorn's sweat-scudded hide.

Rhiannon would have liked to light a fire and melt some snow to make a hot drink, but she did not dare. She could still hear the faint sound of bells. She had never heard such a melancholy sound.

Blackthorn shivered and put back her ears.

Do no' fear, they willna catch us, Rhiannon thought. *Nothing can fly as fast as a winged horse. He named us well, my beauty. Rhiannon, the rider whom none can catch* . . .

Something pierced her heart, cut short her breath, brought a rush of tears to her eyes. The emotion she felt was far too strong, too fierce, to be called contentment, or even its brighter cousin, happiness. It was too dark, too sharp, to be called joy. She had no word in her vocabulary to describe it. *I am alive*, she thought, dumbfounded. *I am free.* All she could do was bend her head to the ground and rest her forehead there, her eyes shut, feeling the blood throbbing in her throat and her temples. *Alive* . . .

Suddenly Blackthorn scrambled to her feet, neighing in panic. Rhiannon was tumbled sideways. The bluebird trilled in terror and took wing. Rhiannon drew her knife, searching desperately for any sign of danger. Blackthorn reared above her, eyes rolling white.

Out of the darkness fell a darker shadow, immense and terrifying. A hot blast of wind whipped Rhiannon's hair about her face, smelling of fire and ashes. The air roared with the sound of vast wings. Sudden dread weakened her legs, so that she fell to her knees in the snow.

A blast of fire lit up the dark sky from horizon to horizon. The skin on her face was scorched. She threw up one hand to protect it and felt fire lick her fingers.

A dragon was hurtling down from the sky, trumpeting with rage. It was flame incarnate. Blazing eyes as big as suns, dreadful wings as wide as the world, a whipping tail that sliced the sky open. Rhiannon bent to the ground, her arms over her head.

Blackthorn took flight, screaming with terror. *No!* Rhiannon shrieked silently. She saw the dragon lash out with one terrible claw, and Blackthorn neighed in pain and swerved.

Looking up through the tangle of hair and fingers, Rhiannon saw her beloved winged horse fly free, eyes white-rimmed, wings straining. Then there was only terror, and despair, as the great golden beast plummeted down upon her.

Expecting to be crushed, or incinerated, or torn apart, Rhiannon lay still, waiting, feeling again the dark rapture she had experienced earlier, in even greater intensity for knowing it would soon end in agony and death. *Alive . . .*

But the dragon landed lightly beside her, in a gush of smoke and cinders, and clamped one immense talon over her prostrate body. Rhiannon's breath rushed out of her. She rested her face on the ground, her mouth and nostrils full of snow. Tears choked her.

Two boots landed with a thump near her head. They were long, black, and shiny. They were also far too small to belong to a man. Rhiannon's stomach clenched. She craned her head to see more, but it was no use. It was too dark.

A woman's voice said coolly, "Thank ye, Asrohc. Ye can let her go now."

Delicately the dragon raised its claw, and Rhiannon was able to lift her face from the snow and look.

The Banrìgh stood beside her, dressed in leather gaiters and breastplate, a close-fitting helmet on her head.

"Ye think ye can escape justice so easily?" she hissed.

Rhiannon could only stare at her. Never, in her wildest imaginings, could she have expected this. The last time she had seen the Banrìgh, it had been at the Court of Star Chamber, dressed in long ceremonial robes, with a crown on her head. She had looked grave and remote, her hands folded in her lap. Now she was livid with rage, her blue eyes blazing. She carried a naked dagger in her hand.

"Get up," Iseult said.

Rhiannon staggered to her feet.

Iseult took a step closer, her dagger held close and steady to her waist. "Throw down your weapons."

Rhiannon dropped her knife. Iseult searched her, quickly and efficiently, then stepped away and went through her pack, which lay half-open on the ground. She straightened, holding in her hand the blowpipe and bag of barbs that Connor had long ago used to defend himself against the wild satyricorn herd.

"Ye really thought ye'd get away with it?" she said furiously.

Rhiannon was puzzled. She did not know how to answer.

"Asrohc, seize her!" Iseult commanded. "Take us back to Lucescere!"

Swift as a striking snake, the dragon's immense claw flashed out and closed about Rhiannon. She had no time to even flinch. Then the dragon bent its great sinuous neck so that Iseult could mount up and sit astride it.

With a jerk that snapped Rhiannon's neck painfully and made her gasp, the dragon launched off into the dark sky. Her head whirled. Her vision swam with desperate tears.

She had heard the stories from Nina, of course. How the Khan'cohban warrior, Khan'gharad, had saved the baby dragon princess from death and so had been given the dragon's name as a reward, to call in time of desperate need. How both Iseult and Isabeau had inherited that privilege and the right to cross their leg over the dragon's back. How the seven sons of the queen dragon had come flaming out of the sky to help Lachlan MacCuinn win the final battle against the Fairgean at Bonnyblair. The tales of the dragons were among the favorites of the young apprentice-witches, and Rhiannon had heard them told many times on their long journey through Ravenshaw. She had just never, ever expected the dragons to be called upon to track her down. In all the tales the jongleurs told, it was emphasized what a rare privilege it was, the right to call the dragon's name. All Rhiannon could think, all through the swift, vertiginous journey back to Lucescere, was that the Rìgh and Banrìgh must have valued Connor the Just very highly to employ such awesome means to track her down.

Now Blackthorn was gone, who knew where, and Rhiannon had no way of knowing how badly she was hurt by that spiteful swipe of the dragon's claw. And her little bluebird gone, fled into the forest. All hope of escape gone too. No matter how quick or clever or strong Rhiannon was, she had no hope of ever escaping a dragon.

Far below her, the orange smoky glare of Lucescere swung through the darkness, blurred by Rhiannon's hopeless tears. Closer and closer it came, and then Rhiannon could smell it, the stench of two hundred thousand unwashed people and all their goats and pigs and chickens and children rising up in a great reek that made her cough and choke. Then she heard it, the clatter and whine and bang and groan that filled the city even in the dead of night. She heard the rush of the waterfall and felt its spray dampen her cheek; then the dragon was swinging low over the city, giving a little ironic spurt of flame so that Rhiannon could clearly see the few people in the streets running and cowering, and hear their shrieks of alarm.

"Asrohc," the Banrìgh said reprovingly, and the dragon snorted with what could only be dragonish laughter.

Then there was the palace below them, its windows all blazing with lights. The great square was lined with flaming torches, their smoke torn into rags by the wind raised by the dragon's strongly beating wings. Lines of soldiers with raised spears waited as the dragon came down with impossible lightness and grace and laid Rhiannon down lightly on the flagstone. It was not until the dragon had stretched its magnificent huge wings and soared away that the Captain of the Yeomen came forward and waited on bent knee for the Banrìgh's orders.

"Take her to the tower," Iseult commanded. "I found the evidence in her bag. I want her hanged at dawn, do ye understand me?"

Dizzy from her wildly swinging flight, dazed with misery and despair, Rhiannon could barely grasp her meaning.

"It will be my pleasure," Captain Dillon said grimly and jerked his head so the soldiers stepped forward to seize her.

"But, Iseult . . ."

Rhiannon turned her numb face towards the Keybearer, who came hurrying across the square, Dide close behind her. Isabeau looked white and exhausted.

"I found all the evidence I need," Iseult said defensively and brandished the blowpipe. "There's a bag o' barbs here, missing quite a few thorns, and a bottle o' poison too."

"But to hang her, out o' hand, without even an attempt at a trial. Iseult, it's wrong!"

"She's had her trial and she was found guilty. That's good enough for me."

"But that was for Connor's death and Lachlan was to pardon her. . . ."

"Lachlan is dead now and his soft heart with him."

"But, Iseult, ye canna be sure."

"Aye, I can."

"But—"

"Do no' argue with me!" Iseult cried.

There was a long silence. Iseult drew a ragged breath. When she exhaled, a white frosty plume filled the air before her mouth. She raised a hand and dashed it across her eyes. "Do as I say," she commanded the captain, who bowed his head. He gestured to two of the soldiers, who seized Rhiannon's elbows. Two more stood on either side with their spears at the ready. All were shivering in the cold.

"I will see justice done," Iseult said in an unsteady voice. "She is lucky I do no' have her strangled with her own intestines."

Then she turned and hurried away towards the palace, a gust of snowflakes blowing behind her.

Rhiannon could only stare.

Isabeau grasped Captain Dillon's arm. "She is half-mad with grief," the Keybearer said in a low, urgent voice.

"As are we all," the captain replied in heavy tones.

"Dillon, I beg ye, do no' be hasty."

"I must obey Her Highness."

"There is more to this than meets the eye. I must have time to find out the truth o' it."

"I have my orders, Keybearer."

"Give me until the morning. I will talk with her."

"The prisoner will hang at the ringing o' the dawn bell, unless I hear otherwise," Captain Dillon said, his mouth hard.

Isabeau let his arm go and turned to Rhiannon. "I am very sorry. I will do what I can."

Rhiannon reached out a hand to her, then gasped as the soldiers jerked her back painfully. "What am I meant to have done?" she asked. "This is something new, isn't it? This is no' just because I escaped?"

Isabeau stared at her. "Ye think my sister would call the dragon's name simply to chase after an escaped prisoner? Eà, no! Child, do ye no' ken? Did ye no' hear the bells toll? Rhiannon, the Rìgh was murdered tonight. With a poisoned barb spat through a blowpipe."

The night whirled around her. "They think I killed the Rìgh?"

Isabeau nodded.

"Dark walkers, spare me," Rhiannon whispered.

Whoever Holds the Lodestar

Iseult found it difficult to keep her feet. She walked slowly, keeping her back straight and her gait steady only with a great effort of will. For the last few hours she had been sustained by anger and the fierce hunger for revenge. Now that the satyricorn girl was captured and thrown back into prison, her death only a few hours away, Iseult found her savage strength gone. It was all she could do not to weep as she made her weary way back to the palace.

Lachlan dead; her youngest children stolen away; her eldest son, her beautiful winged Donncan, possibly in danger. Iseult could not bear it. In only a few hours, her whole world had been dismantled and laid in ruins. Iseult had been raised by the Khan'cohbans, though, raised to be strong and ruthless, to never submit to weak emotion. No matter how much Iseult wanted to crawl into a dark hole somewhere and howl her heart out, she could not. Someone had to take the reins and look after things till Donncan came back.

She heard hurrying footsteps behind her and turned, recognizing Isabeau's quick step. Her twin came stumbling through the snow, her cheeks as white as the ground, her red hair falling out of its pins to straggle wildly around her face. She looked fierce and wild and angry and haggard with grief all at the same time, and Iseult had a sudden insight into how she too must look. She put up a hand to her own hair and tried to smooth it back.

"Iseult, this is wrong—ye ken this is wrong," Isabeau said, gripping her arm. "Even if Rhiannon is involved with all this mess, ye shouldna be hanging her out o' hand. We need information! We need—"

"She killed the Rìgh," Iseult said icily. "Ye think I can hesitate over this? If I show the slightest weakness, anyone who hates the MacCuinns and plots against the Crown will gather around us like vultures around a corpse. She dies at dawn, and so too shall any other o' these vile plotters that we can lay by the heels."

"But if I can show ye, if I can prove to ye that she is innocent?"

"How?"

Isabeau hesitated.

"There is no way ye can prove so to me," Iseult said and walked on.

As she climbed the steps into the banquet hall, the light of the torches her lackeys carried went with her. Isabeau was left in the icy darkness. Snow drove steadily into her face. Dide stood beside the Keybearer, holding her close, as she shivered violently, her teeth chattering.

"What will ye do?" he asked.

For a long moment she did not answer; then Isabeau said slowly, "There may be a way. Ye remember the silver goblet Connor carried with him everywhere?"

"The one ye were so curious about?"

"Aye. If ye remember, I think it could be some kind o' cup o' truth. What if we gave it to Rhiannon to drink from?"

"Ye would have to convince Iseult first," Dide said dryly. "If she does no' believe it truly is a magical cup that forces truth telling, she will just say Rhiannon lies and naught is changed."

"Aye, I ken."

"So how . . . ?"

"If it is in *The Book o' Shadows*, Iseult will have to believe," Isabeau said.

"Did ye no' mean to look it up afore?"

Isabeau nodded.

"Then why . . . ?"

"I'm afraid," Isabeau replied, and she shuddered so violently Dide was startled and moved to grasp her closer.

"Afraid? Afraid o' what?"

"Afraid o' what *The Book o' Shadows* will show me," Isabeau said and looked past him into the black storm-ridden night.

Inside the banquet hall, the dead Rìgh lay on his bier, candles surrounding him.

The room was virtually empty now. The last of the wedding guests had found their beds, and only a few soldiers still stood guard on the doors. Gathered around the fire at the far end of the room were the privy councillors, drinking from steaming goblets, heavy velvet mantles thrown over their midsummer finery. Nina and Iven sat together, holding each other's hands. Brun the cluricaun sat beside them, his tail twisting anxiously behind him. Gwilym the Ugly sat with his wooden leg elevated, his face creased with pain. The other witches were gathered about the bier, their heads bent in silent prayer. There was Stormy Briant and his brother Cailean, his huge shadow-hound lying at his feet; Ghislaine Dream-Walker, looking very frail; and Jock Crofter, scowling as usual.

On the far side of the bier, Iain of Arran rested his head in his hands. Elfrida sat beside him, fiddling with the heavy knobs of her antique fan. Their son, Neil, was sitting some way away from them, his eyes fixed anxiously on Bronwen's face. She had withdrawn from the others, sitting with her mother on one of the trestles drawn up against the wall, the Lodestar cradled in her lap.

A scullery maid was on her hands and knees, sweeping up the last of the mess on the floor. She stopped every now and again to wipe her red eyes on her apron. Otherwise the only other people left were the Lord Steward and Lord Chamberlain, both sitting in vigil by the Rìgh.

As Iseult came in, everyone rose to their feet and bowed. Iseult felt a heavy despondency fall on her shoulders. She had not been gone long, no more than half an hour, but that time had been spent in swift, decisive action. She had flown high above the storm on dragon-back, felt the wind screaming in her face, and had the fierce satisfaction of seizing the satyricorn and wresting her back to justice. Here all was the same.

"Any news?" Iseult demanded, even though she knew there had scarcely been time. Neither Finn nor Lewen would send a message until they had something to report, and any messenger would have to bring the news on foot, since Finn was somewhere under the city in the labyrinthine sewers, while Lewen was at the Tower of Two Moons. It took at least half an hour to walk from palace to tower on a sunny afternoon; there was no doubt it would take longer on such an inclement night. Horses were not kept at the tower, for there were no stables or grazing land for them. Any sorcerer who desired to ride out into the city would use a mount from the palace stables, and the students were all expected to use their legs. She and Isabeau often communicated by scrying when they had not the time or the inclination to walk the distance, but no one could scry when the heavens were in such turbulence, except perhaps through Scrying Pools or crystal balls of great power. So they would have to wait for any messenger from the tower to run the gamut of the storm. Until then, all they could do was wait in patience.

The chancellor indicated as much with an expressive gesture of his hands and shoulders. He, like the rest of Lachlan's councillors, was at a loss as to the best course of action. They had been at peace for so many years now, and Lachlan had ruled the Privy Council with a firm hand. The events of this long, terrible night were quite outside their provenance.

"Did ye capture the escaped prisoner?" the chancellor asked.

"O' course," Iseult replied and came to warm her hands at the fire, stripping off her heavy leather gauntlets first.

"What have ye done to her?" Nina's voice rose high with distress.

Iseult found it hard to meet her gaze. "She'll hang at dawn."

Nina sobbed out loud.

"If dawn ever comes," Ghislaine said and pressed her fingers against her eyes. "I feel as if this night will never end."

"But why? Why?" Nina sobbed.

"We found all the evidence we needed in her saddlebags," Iseult said coldly.

"What evidence?" Nina demanded.

"It is late," Iseult said. "We have all been up all night. I ken how distressed ye are, Nina. Perhaps ye and Iven had better retire? Try to get some rest."

"I will wait for news," Nina said defiantly.

"Very well," Iseult said and accepted a goblet of wine from the Lord Steward. "Let us hope it comes soon."

"Finn will capture Laird Malvern and all his foul minions, and then ye will realize Rhiannon is innocent," Nina said, tears running down her face. "Oh Eà, please, let her catch up with them soon!"

Just then there was a knock on the door, and Dide came in, with a boy dressed in the black robe of an apprentice-witch. He was no more than seventeen, but tall and brown-skinned. He was blue, and shivering with cold, and panting so hard he could hardly speak.

"I found this lad running down the avenue," Dide said. "His name is Rafferty, he tells me. He comes from Lewen with news."

"Your Highness," Rafferty said, going down on one knee before Iseult. "I . . . I come from . . . the Tower o' Two Moons."

Bronwen made a sharp movement, instantly stilled.

"Ye have news o' my son?" Iseult demanded.

"Aye." He took a deep breath, his chest heaving. "It is no' good news, I'm afraid, Your Highness."

Iseult sat motionless, all the color ebbing from her face.

Bronwen's hand clenched tight upon the Lodestar. "What has happened to Donncan?" she demanded sharply. "Is he . . . is he dead?"

Rafferty turned to face her. "I dinna ken, Your Highness. I do no' think so. We are no' sure. . . . He has disappeared."

He held out his hand and unclenched his fingers. Within was Donncan's stag brooch.

"Disappeared too?" Iseult reached out a trembling hand and rested it upon the table. "Nay, nay, the White Gods could no' be so cruel!"

"How? What happened?" Bronwen said fiercely.

Rafferty told the news as clearly and concisely as he could, but met a barrage of questions from everyone that he had trouble answering. At last, though, the tale was told. Bronwen sat down and hid her face in her hands, and Maya bent over her, comforting her wordlessly.

"Donncan . . ." Iseult whispered. "Gone too!" Her legs could no longer hold her up. She sat down and then put her head between her knees, sick with horror.

"I must go to the tower," Gwilym cried. "Where is Isabeau? For the Celestines to be struck down like this when under our care . . . If the Stargazer dies, and her daughter missing . . .!"

The other witches were gathering up their belongings with frantic haste. "We need Isabeau," Cailean said. "She is the greatest healer o' us all. She will ken what to do."

"Where could she be?" Ghislaine asked.

"She had some mad idea o' proving to me this satyricorn girl's innocence," Iseult said, raising her head.

Dide said quietly, "She has gone to consult *The Book o' Shadows*. She believes the goblet Connor carried was a cup o' truth telling. If she can find it is so, she plans to ask Iseult to let Rhiannon drink from the cup and tell us the truth o' all she kens."

Iseult snorted in derision, and Nina pressed her hands together and said fervently, "Oh, Isabeau, thank ye!"

"She has gone to the Tower o' Two Moons? We will go and join her there," Gwilym said and drew up the hood of his cloak, preparing to go out into the snow, now driving against the windows harder than ever. "Dide, Nina, will ye come with us?"

"I must wait for news o' my son," Nina said quietly. Iseult hid her face again.

"I didna see the Keybearer on my way here, sir," Rafferty said diffidently. "Surely I should've passed her?"

"She would have flown," Gwilym said gruffly. "In the shape o' an owl, I imagine. It is her favorite form. That is one o' the many advantages o' being a shape-changer—one does no' need to slog through heavy snow on foot, like we must do. Come, lad, ye had best come back with us."

As the witches prepared to face the storm, the door opened once more, banging against the wall. Captain Dillon came in amidst a swirl of snow, his face graven with deep, unhappy lines, his hand on his sword hilt. He went down on one knee before Iseult.

"What is it?" she asked faintly.

"Finn couldna catch them," Captain Dillon said heavily. "They moved too fast."

"Finn couldna catch them?" Iseult repeated his words in absolute disbelief.

"No!" Nina cried and pressed her hands against her mouth. Iven put his arm about her, and she sagged against him.

Dillon shook his head reluctantly. "Whoever it was laid their plans well. They had a guide to show them the secret way out through the caves. It seems their guide was a thief who had been condemned to hang but was released by that prison warden who escaped last week, the one they call Octavia the Obese. The message Finn sent says she almost caught them in the Thieves' Way, but they had a boat waiting for them on Lucescere Loch."

"What o' the Queen o' the Thieves? Are ye trying to tell me the thieves' guild collaborated in my husband's murder?" Snow rose in an eddy around Iseult's head.

"The Queen o' the Thieves swears she kent naught about it, Your Highness."

"Surely she kens all that goes on in her tunnels?"

"There had been a feast. Much wine was drunk. It may have been drugged. Certainly I found them hard to rouse."

"More drugged wine," Iseult said. "Who is this poisoner?"

"The laird o' Fettercairn's skeelie," Nina said bleakly.

"She was there," Captain Dillon said. "Finn was close enough to see them all. She recognized the skeelie from her appearance in court. She saw the Prionnsa and Banprionnsa, Your Highness, and young Roden too. They were being carried over the men's shoulders. She thinks they were unconscious."

Nina gasped and hid her face. "My laddiekin," she whispered. "Oh, what do they want with him?"

"If she was close enough to see them, how could she let them escape!" Iseult demanded in despair.

"Finn says the laird o' Fettercairn has some ability with the weather. Despite the storm, he was able to harness the wind and bring it to fill their sails. Their boat took off across Lucescere Loch as if dragged by a sea serpent. There was naught she could do. By the time she found a boat and set off in pursuit, they were long gone. Finn is on the trail, though. Jay is with her, and some o' my men. They will catch them, never ye fear, Your Highness."

"Oh, please, oh, please," Nina said and broke down completely, sobbing in her husband's arms. Dide crouched beside her, stroking her disheveled chestnut hair, tears in his eyes.

"Come, dearling, let me take ye to bed," Iven said. "Ye're exhausted. Let us go and try to get some rest, and in the morning we may have some good news."

"Sleep? Sleep? Ye think I can sleep?" Nina cried, but Iven and Dide helped her to her feet and together led her away. Brun trotted after them, tears running down his hairy face.

"What o' Donncan?" Bronwen demanded as the door shut behind them. "We need to be searching for him too!"

Iseult got to her feet wearily. "Captain Dillon, will ye take some men and go to the witches' tower to search for Donncan yourself? Send me word as soon as ye can." She swayed with exhaustion and had to put her hand on the table to steady herself. "For now, a state o' emergency must be declared. Gentlemen, will ye come to the Privy Chamber with me? We must . . ."

Bronwen got suddenly to her feet. "I thank ye, my lady, but I think it is my place to be ordering the Privy Council now," she said, the Lodestar held stiffly in her hands. Maya stood up too, her pale eyes shining.

Iseult was completely taken aback.

"Am I no' Banrìgh now?" Bronwen asked. "Do I no' hold the Lodestar?"

There was a long, long moment of silence. Iseult could only gaze at her daughter-in-law in utter consternation and dismay.

"Am I not a NicCuinn by blood as well as marriage?" Bronwen went on steadily. "Is it no' my right to order the Council and the Yeomen?"

"Ye?" Iseult said incredulously. "Order the Council? What do ye ken o' such things?"

"The throne is no' yours, my lady," Bronwen said softly. "Ye do no' have the right. With Donncan missing, I am the Banrìgh now."

Although she spoke in a low voice and with an expression of great respect, there were exclamations of surprise from everyone around her, and then a quick murmur of conversation.

Iseult lost her temper. "Ye are naught but a lamb-brained lassie who cares more about the cut o' her gown than the state o' the nation," she said furiously. "How dare ye think to seize the throne?"

Heat rose in Bronwen's cheeks. She bit her lip, clenching the Lodestar tightly.

"Go to your room," Iseult said icily. "I will discuss this with ye later. For now, I have better things to do."

For a moment it looked as if Bronwen would obey, though her cheeks were hot with rage and humiliation.

"Ye are no' the Banrìgh anymore!" A woman's voice rang out strongly, filled with vicious joy. "Ye are naught but the Dowager now. How does it feel, Iseult?"

Everyone in the room, from the velvet-clad councillors to the cowering scullery maid with the scrubbing brush in her hand, turned and stared. Maya was standing close behind her daughter, her head thrown back, laughing. "Oh, Jor o' the seas, the delicious irony o' it," she said at last, when she could stop laughing. "How does it feel, *my lady*? Your husband is dead and ye are naught, just a poor auld dowager, with no power o' your own. *Ye* get to *your* room, Iseult, and wait upon the pleasure o' the new Banrìgh."

Bronwen took a faltering step towards her mother, whispering her name.

"Maya," Iseult hissed. Sudden color suffused her face. "Ye did this! It was ye!"

Maya shook her head. "If I had wanted to murder Lachlan, I could have done so any time these past twenty years."

"This is the first time ye've set foot in the palace since ye were thrown down," Iseult said furiously. "Ye could no' have got near Lachlan afore now!" She looked about her wildly. "Dillon! Guards! Seize her!"

"No!" Bronwen cried.

Captain Dillon shook his head. "My lady, do ye think I would have allowed the Ensorcellor to come within spitting distance o' His Majesty and no' had her watched? I had guards placed over her. She did no' move from her table, no' once. She was in clear view the whole time. I ken every mouthful she ate or drank, and every word that was spoken to her. She herself did no' speak, though I ken what she wrote on her slate. I didna ken she *could* speak."

"The nyx ribbon," Gwilym cried. "Ceit Anna's ribbon! It dissolved when she died?"

"Aye, o' course," Maya said, smiling. "But I dared no' let

anyone ken. Ye would've bound me again, would ye no'? Twenty years o' silence and servitude would no' have been enough. But my daughter is Banrìgh now! She holds the Lodestar! She willna let ye bind me again."

"No, I will no'!" Bronwen's voice rang out. She held the Lodestar before her like a sword. "Ye are right, Mama. I am Banrìgh now."

"How dare ye!" Iseult said. "My husband is no' yet cold—"

"Neither was mine, when ye seized power from me," Maya reminded her.

"Is that what this is about?" Iseult spat.

"This is about the right to rule," Bronwen said, her voice and face hard. "I am the Banrìgh, by blood and by marriage. I hold the Lodestar and I will hold the throne. If I allow ye to call the Privy Council and order the Yeomen, what would I be? Naught but a pretty puppet, just like ye and my uncle have always wanted me to be. Well, I won't be that puppet! I won't!"

"Ye expect me to just stand aside and—"

"While ye stand here arguing and clinging to your power like a greedy auld witch, my husband is missing and in all probability is in danger," Bronwen said passionately. She shook the Lodestar, and a searing white light sprang up in its heart, dazzling their eyes. "Must I raise the Lodestar to prove my right?" she cried. "I am the Banrìgh now! Ye are naught but my mother-in-law and dowager to the dead Rìgh. Stand aside, my lady."

"I will no'! How dare ye?" Iseult cried.

"I think ye forget who ye are addressing. Have some respect for your Banrìgh," Maya said. Her voice rang with vengeful glee.

Iseult stared at Bronwen in a white, icy rage that shook her from head to foot, but Bronwen stared back, not quailing. Iseult glanced at the Lord Chancellor, and he bowed very low, raising his shoulders in an eloquent shrug.

"I am sorry, my lady, but the law is clear. Whoever holds the Lodestar holds the land."

"Aye, I suppose it is," Iseult said at last. She then bowed her head and said with utter precision, "If ye will excuse me, then, Your Majesty. I would be alone with my husband."

"O' course," Bronwen said and gathered up her silvery skirt in her hand, sweeping towards the door to the palace.

There was a moment's indecision, no one else quite sure what to do. Bronwen turned. "Come, gentlemen," she said imperiously. "There is much to discuss."

Gwilym bowed. "If ye will excuse me, Your Majesty, I wish to attend upon the Celestines at once."

"Aye, please do," Bronwen said. "I will need to speak with them as soon as possible."

Gwilym bowed and led the witches out towards the garden. Captain Dillon made as if to follow them.

He was recalled by Bronwen's sharp voice. "Captain Dillon, I require ye in the Privy Chamber! Please attend upon me at once."

He hesitated, looking between her and Iseult.

"Go on then," Iseult said, arctic blasts of air swirling up from her skin and clothes. "Go! All o' ye! I would be alone."

"But, Your Highness . . . my lady . . ."

"Go," she said coldly and turned away.

One by one, everyone went out, all bowing to Iseult respectfully. She ignored them, sitting by the candlelit bier and taking up Lachlan's limp, grey hand in both of her own, bending to press her face against it.

There she stayed, alone, while hail clattered around the doors and windows of the palace, piling up in frosty swathes across the lawn where yesterday laughing couples had gathered to watch a procession of fantastical animals made of painted silk.

Isabeau crouched before the fire in her room. She could not get warm, no matter how many faggots of wood she threw on the fire or how many cloaks she wrapped about her. The world slipped in and out of focus. Her pulse thundered.

I will live again, a deep insistent voice whispered in her mind, *and ye shall be the one to raise me. Come to me now. I will live again, and ye shall be the one to raise me. Come to me now. . . .*

The voice had tormented her ever since she had read the words of the spell for raising the dead. All through the wedding

and the feast that followed, all through the dreadful events that
had followed Lachlan's murder, she had heard the voice in her
mind, commanding her, imposing his will upon hers, sapping
her strength and vitality until she had been giddy on her feet
with the effort of withstanding him. Never had she felt such a
strong compulsion. It was like a hunger, a lust in her, to give in,
to submit her will to his and do as he demanded.

Come to me now. I will *live again, and ye shall be the one
to raise me.*

She hardly dared glance at *The Book of Shadows*. She was
so afraid her pulse hammered in her ears. *I am the Keybearer,*
she told herself sternly and lifted her maimed hand to cup the
talisman hanging around her neck. Its familiar shape comforted
her and gave her courage. *I will no' be your puppet,* she told the
voice. *I can withstand ye. I* will *withstand ye.*

She lifted both hands and laid them on the worn red leather
of *The Book of Shadows*. She breathed in and out, in and out.

I will live again, and ye shall be the one to raise me.

"Stop it!" she cried out loud. "Leave me alone!"

*I will live again, and ye shall be the one to raise me. Come
to me now.*

Isabeau slammed her hands down. "I will no'," she said. "I
will no'!"

The blood sang in her ears. She closed her eyes and concentrated on her breathing. In, out. In, out. In, out.

In her mind, she pictured the goblet that had been found in
Rhiannon's pack. Plain silver. A crystal set in its graceful stem.
A goblet that made those who drank from it tell the truth. *Tell
me*, she commanded *The Book of Shadows. What is this cup?*

She opened the book and, fighting her dread, bent and read
the page. In red curlicues, the title read "The Cup of Confes-
sions."

"Also called the Goblet of Truth, this cup was first made by
Morgausa the Dark in 422 AC . . ."

Even as Isabeau absorbed the words, an unfelt breeze sprang
up and the pages began to riffle over.

"No!" Isabeau cried. She laid her hand on the book, trying
to hold her place, but it was too late, it was gone, and Isabeau
was staring at the page she had dreaded. As if written in fire,

words sprang up from the page and seared themselves once more into her brain.

"To Raise the Dead, one needs a living soul . . ."

"I will no'!" Isabeau cried and slammed the book shut. Her whole body shook as if she had an ague. Sweat sprang upon her skin. She found her legs had folded beneath her. She was sitting on the floor, *The Book of Shadows* clutched against her chest, and the words of the spell pounding out and into her skin like the needle of some tattooist, emblazoning the compulsion into her blood and bone and nerves.

I will live again, and ye shall be the one to raise me.

"Who? Who?" she cried, pressing the book ever closer. "Where are ye?"

Come to me, at the Tomb o' Ravens, on the day o' my death, one thousand years ago. Bring with ye a living soul, willing or not, and a very sharp knife . . .

"Who are ye?"

I am Brann, and I will live again.

A Wilted Crown

Bronwen sat on the tall throne at the head of the table in the Privy Chamber, clutching the Lodestar close to her body and trying to listen as everyone talked at once.

"All gone, all gone!" the Lord Chancellor cried. "What are we to do?"

"I would have thought that the first course o' action was obvious," Bronwen said, a faint trace of sarcasm darkening her words. "Find my husband!"

Hubbub broke out again. Bronwen found it hard to concentrate on what was said, for they all spoke at once at different volumes, and all the time her own tumultuous emotions surged up and filled her ears with a white roar so that for a moment she heard nothing at all.

"Eà rest Lachlan's poor murdered soul," Iain of Arran said unhappily. "He was a great Rìgh."

"What does this mean to the Pact o' Peace?" the Duke of Rammermuir asked.

"Surely it will stand," Bronwen said sharply.

"When the line o' inheritance is unclear . . ." cried the Master of Horse.

"Aye, but the Lodestar!" the Lord Chamberlain said.

"Happen we should look to Tìrsoilleir for our murderer," said the Lord High Admiral, who had been born in the Bright Land himself and had reason to be suspicious of the Fealde and her General Assembly.

"We would have kent if there was any plot against the Rìgh in Tìrsoilleir," Neil said angrily with a quick glance at his mother, who sat quietly, her pastor standing at her shoulder as usual. The pastor, who was one of the Fealde's closest advisers, only grew more stern-faced, his lips thinning in disdain.

"The Fealde may have philosophical differences with the Coven," Neil went on a little more moderately, "but she would no' stoop to regicide."

"Ah, philosophical differences. That's rich!" jeered the Master of Horse.

"What are we to do?" moaned the keeper of the privy seal.

"It's a scandal! Captain Dillon should be dismissed at the very least," said the captain of the general army, who had always been jealous of the influence the Captain of the Yeomen wielded.

"We need to get out the dogs and the bailiffs and turn that city inside out. Bloody thieves and murderers!" cried the Master of the Ordnance.

"It's a conspiracy," the Lord Steward whispered unhappily. "The MacCuinn clan, rooted out and destroyed in one dreadful night. Who did this! Who?"

Bronwen's head snapped round. "No' all the MacCuinn clan are gone," she reminded them angrily.

The Lord Steward had evidently forgotten how acute was the hearing of those of Fairgean blood, for he flushed and bit his lip in chagrin. He would not back down before Bronwen, however. "Nay, no' all," he said with heavy meaning.

"Are ye suggesting I had aught to do with this?" Bronwen demanded. "Careful what ye say, sir!" The Lodestar leaped with sudden cold fire, and the Lord Steward bowed his head at once, stammering an apology. Bronwen saw that it was insincere, however, and that others among the councillors silently agreed.

Donncan, Donncan, she thought, with a rush of grief.

Then, on a note of rising terror, *How did this happen? What do I do now?*

Then, *I am Banrìgh! I hold the Lodestar and I will hold the land!*

Her mother turned and smiled at her, her pale eyes shining.

Bronwen took a deep breath and rapped the table sharply with the end of her scepter. "That is enough!" she cried.

The tumult died down and they all turned to stare at her. She found her mouth was dry. She had to swallow convulsively be-

fore she could speak. "Well, gentlemen," she said, "I thank ye
for your service to my uncle the Rìgh. I know he found ye loyal
and steadfast. We are now in a state o' the direst emergency. I
therefore have no choice but to dissolve the Privy Council until
such a time that peace and security are returned to our land. I
ask that all o' ye stay at hand should your services be required
again."

An angry babble arose.

Bronwen raised her voice. "Captain Dillon, it has been suggested that ye should be dishonorably discharged for your failure to protect my uncle. I do no' believe now is the rightful
place or time to initiate such an inquiry. I trust that your loyalty
and diligence in the next few weeks will make such an inquiry
unnecessary. Will ye please arrange an escort for these noble
gentlemen back to their quarters? And then take your men and
search the woods yourself. I want my husband found!"

"Yes, Your Majesty," he said with a low bow. A jerk of his
head, and each of the flabbergasted councillors found a guard
behind his chair.

"Lord Chancellor, will ye stay, and ye too, Master o' the
Ordnance? I will have need o' ye. Neil, would ye stay too? I
would be grateful for your support."

A rush of blood to Neil's pale face brought him sudden
warmth and vitality. He smiled with pleasure and murmured,
"O' course, Your Majesty."

Bronwen smiled at him in gratitude. She became aware of
the avid gleam in Elfrida's eyes as she watched them, and
looked away, her smile fading. Elfrida curtsied as she went past
and murmured, "Good night, Your Majesty."

"Good night, Your Grace," Bronwen said, very properly, and
then acknowledged the obeisance of the pastor coolly.

Taking their lead from Elfrida, the other lords and councillors made their farewells formally, many no doubt hoping to in-
gratiate themselves with her when it came time for her to form
her new government. Although Bronwen was so weary and
heartsick she felt quite faint, she forced her brain to work faster
than it ever had before. If she was to hold the power in the land,
she must be seen to wield it well and wisely.

"Lord Constable, I bid ye stay also. I shall need your help in
tracking down these miscreants. We must have messages sent

posthaste down river, to stop the laird o' Fettercairn afore he reaches the sea. Let us have the infantry and cavalry on standby, in case o' need."

She saw by her mother's glittering eyes that Maya was pleased with her and exerted herself to greater efforts.

"We must find out as much as we can about this Laird Malvern. Will the clerks o' the council sift through the evidence brought back from Fettercairn and see if we can find some idea o' this madman's plans? Send a page to the MacBrann also, and ask him to attend on me later in the morn. I would ken what he knows o' this laird o' Fettercairn."

As she spoke, the councillors were all escorted from the Privy Chamber, and the door shut smartly behind them. The long room was now eerily quiet. Bronwen took a deep breath, racking her brains for more orders to give. As long as she seemed to be in command, Bronwen thought, the more likely it was others would believe her to be so.

It troubled her how heavily the Lodestar weighed on her lap. She straightened her back and did her best to let no one see it. Her head ached, and she put up one hand to find she still wore her wreath of flowers, now wilted. She dragged it off her head and flung it on the floor.

"I must have news o' the Celestines," she said. "If anyone can tell me what has happened to Donncan and Thunderlily, it is the Stargazer. I need to ken whether the healers have been able to rouse her, and whether she is well enough to attend me here. Perhaps I should have a carriage sent to the tower for her? It is too far to walk in this blaygird storm! Neil, will ye arrange it for me? Ye can be my new Master o' Horse, to replace that fool Dacey."

"Aye, Your Majesty. Thank ye, Your Majesty," he cried, his cheeks glowing.

As he rose and beckoned a page to him, Bronwen sighed. It had been a long, exhausting night, and it was not over yet. She had much to do and a need for a clear head. She laid both her hands on the Lodestar and felt fresh energy flow up her arms and into her heart and her brain. It was intoxicating, having all that power throbbing at her fingertips. It was frightening too.

"Let us all try to get some rest now," she said. "It has been a dreadful night, and dawn is no' far away. We will be no good

to anyone with our wits befuddled with exhaustion. Let us meet
again at noon, and hope for better news."

She rose, and at once they all rose too, and bowed. Bronwen
felt giddy. Who would have thought yesterday that today she
would be the Banrìgh?

As she made her weary way towards her boudoir, her
thoughts turning longingly towards a bath and her bed, Neil
hurried up behind her.

"Bronny . . . I mean, Your Majesty . . ."

Bronwen was so tired the ground seemed to move under her
feet like the deck of a ship, but she smiled and dismissed her
ladies-in-waiting with a nod. Neil held open the door of
her room for her, and she went in and sat down heavily on the
chaise longue drawn up close to the fire. She had to lay
the Lodestar down. It made her arms ache fiercely. She had
never realized how heavy it was. She wished only to put her
head down on her arms and cry, but Neil was waiting, and even
though he was one of her oldest and dearest friends, she still did
not wish him to see her weep.

"Tea, please," she said to Maura, who clucked her tongue
and went bustling out.

The room was dark and cold, the curtains drawn against the
storm. Bronwen could hear the wind rustling in the trees. It was
a desolate sound.

She turned to look up at Neil, but her words died on her lips
as he flung himself down on his knees before her. He seized her
hand and bent his head over it.

"I am so very sorry, Bronny," he said. "What a dreadful,
dreadful thing to happen. And on your wedding day!"

She said nothing. Her throat muscles moved convulsively.

"Ye were marvelous, though, Bronny," he said and raised
glowing eyes to her. "What a Banrìgh!"

"Ye think I did well?"

"So well! Ye confounded and baffled them, all those auld
goats! They didna ken what hit them. It was masterly."

Somehow his words of praise worked on her as sympathy
could not. Involuntary tears flooded down her face.

"I'm sorry," she gasped, drawing her hands away to cover
her face.

He sat next to her and put his arm about her shoulders and,

worn out as she was, Bronwen could not help resting her head on his shoulder and letting her tears flow. She vaguely heard him as he comforted and reassured her.

"Oh, darling Bronny," he said, "I ken, I ken. It's all right. Everything will be all right. I'm here, I'll always be here when ye need me. Don't cry. Please don't cry."

Bronwen could not stop.

"Ye'll ruin your complexion," he said, and that raised a watery laugh from her. She tried to sit up but he would not let her, and it was easier just to relax and let him mop up her face with his handkerchief.

"Still as bonny as ever," he said, looking down at her.

She heaved a great sigh and smiled at him ruefully. "For sure I am," she said caustically, "with my eyes all red, and my nose running, and my hair looking like a bird's nest."

"I'd find ye bonny in sackcloth and ashes," he said and bent his head and kissed her on the mouth.

Surprise held her still; then she leaped away from him, looking at once to make sure no one had seen.

"Neil," she said unsteadily. "What are ye doing? Have ye run mad?"

"I'm sorry," he said. "I couldna help myself."

"Ye must no' do it again, no' ever. I am married now, remember, and to your best friend."

"Captain Dillon is right, Bronwen. I think ye should prepare yourself for the worst."

"Am I to be a wife for only a few hours, as I was once Banrìgh? No! I refuse to be. Donncan is no' dead. I do no' ken what has happened to him, but I will no' believe he is dead until they lay his body afore me. He is my husband, we are sworn one to each other, and I will stand by that oath, I will!" The words poured from her in a torrent, as if the tears had washed away some barrier in her.

"But Bronny, darling . . ."

"Have ye forgotten that I am your Banrìgh now?" she asked icily. "Ye will speak to me with respect!"

He looked sad. "Nay, I have no' forgotten, Your Majesty. I apologize."

Bronwen bit her lip, sorry to have spoken so to someone she

had known since they were children together, someone she knew sincerely cared for her.

She would not say so. Bronwen had always found it difficult to admit herself at fault. Instead she seized Neil's hand and said with as much earnestness as she could muster, "If I am to hold the land together, Neil, I must be seen as being strong. I must command respect."

He nodded, the misery on his face easing. "Ye can count on me, Your Majesty. I am here to serve ye."

"I thank ye for it. I will need your help in the days to come, Neil. But now ye must go. We must no' be alone again. I want no gossip."

Neil nodded. She rose, and he rose with her, bowing his head. "Remember, though, what I said, Your Majesty. Whenever ye need me, I will be here, no matter what comes."

She nodded her head and waited by the chaise longue until he had gone. Then she dropped down upon the velvet seat, her shoulders drooping. The Lodestar glowed softly white. She cradled it in her hands, staring into its depths.

Donncan, where are ye?

There was only silence.

Iain felt like a very old man. He and Elfrida walked slowly through the empty corridors, not speaking. A lackey carried a branched candelabra for them, lighting their way. Although dawn could not be far away, the palace halls were as black as the inside of a mine.

At the door to their suite of rooms, the pastor bowed and silently left them. His rooms were right across the hall, so Elfrida could call him at any time of day or night for spiritual succor. Iain had given up wondering what so haunted his wife that she had turned to a minister of the church she had once hated to be her prop and guide. In recent months, he had been troubled and unhappy too, with his sleep disturbed by memories he had thought long buried.

The lackey opened the door for them and bowed as they passed in. Both Iain and Elfrida stopped short on the threshold, staring in sudden affront.

Soldiers were searching their room.

At the sound of the door, a lieutenant of the Blue Guards turned abruptly. It was clear from his face that he would have preferred not to have had the room's inhabitants come back before he had finished his task. He bowed and apologized politely. "Captain's orders," he explained. "If ye would please take a seat, we will soon be finished."

Iain lowered himself stiffly into an armchair by the fire, Elfrida choosing a hard-backed chair nearby. They watched in silence as the soldiers methodically and painstakingly turned his quarters inside out. They emptied vases of flowers, they raked through the coals on the hearth, they slit open pillows and counterpanes, they felt through every pocket of every article of clothing in every trunk he and Elfrida had brought with them.

Iain wanted to protest. He wanted to shout at them angrily, "Do ye no' ken he was my greatest friend?" But he said nothing. He knew it was to be expected. After all, until recently, the countries he and his wife ruled had been Eileanan's greatest enemies. His own mother had sworn to destroy the MacCuinn clan, root and branch. It did not matter that Iain had laid aside the centuries-long feud between Arran and the MacCuinns, or that his wife had signed the Pact of Peace and brought Tìrsoilleir, which had once been known as the Forbidden Land, to join the rest of Eileanan under the Rìgh's rule.

Lachlan the Winged had been murdered, and now all friends and allies were suspect.

Iain looked over at his wife. Her hands were clenched on her fan and reticule. Although her back was as straight as ever, her feet side by side as she had been taught by her jailers as a child, she looked sick and weary. There were violet smudges under her downcast eyes.

"Will ye be much longer?" Iain asked the guard in a sudden surge of irritation. "We are both exhausted. We wish to retire."

"I am sorry, my laird, it shall no' be much longer," the lieutenant said politely. "We must be thorough, ye ken. It is no' just ye who we search, but all at the palace."

Elfrida moistened her dry lips and gripped her hands more tightly together.

Iain gestured for some wine to be brought to her, worried she might faint.

Her brows drew together and she shook her head. Her pastor disapproved of alcohol, and so Elfrida no longer drank even a glass of wine with her meal. Iain was by no means a heavy imbiber, but he enjoyed the occasional glass and had no desire to drink alone. He gestured to the page now, though, and saw his wife frown in condemnation as he drank some of the rich sweet liquor.

"To keep my strength up," he said with a wan attempt at a joke, but she did not smile or answer, just dropped her eyes.

Iain did not speak again.

At last the soldiers abandoned their search and allowed the chambermaids in to straighten the room. Elfrida did not rise from her chair until the last maid had withdrawn, and then she moved so stiffly that Iain came to her side in alarm and took her arm. She allowed him to help her up, and then went to her dressing table and laid down her fan and reticule. Iain had changed out of his wedding finery into his nightshirt and dressing gown, but Elfrida was still dressed in her simple grey gown. She fumbled at the buttons, and Iain came to help her, saying irritably, "Why did ye dismiss your maid afore ye were changed, my dear? Ye ken I am all thumbs."

She did not answer. He undid the tight, plain cuffs and then laboriously unbuttoned the back. She stepped out of it, and he saw with distaste that she wore a hair shirt beneath it. It had rubbed her fine skin red and raw.

"Elfrida . . ." he protested, but she ignored him. He saw her blue eyes were shining strangely, as if with excitement or pleasure. She sat down and began to unpin her hair, which she wore coiled neatly at the base of her head.

Iain stood by her for a moment, trying to find a way to tell her he disliked her new pastor and thought him an evil influence upon her. But he could not find the courage. He turned to leave and accidentally knocked the fan and reticule to the floor. He bent to pick them up, but Elfrida was before him, stooping with a cry and snatching them up from the ground.

"Why, that is my mother's fan," Iain said in surprise.

"Is it?" Elfrida said. "I had no' realized. Does it matter?"

"No," he answered. "I suppose no'."

"I kent it would be hot," Elfrida said, "and I had heard that fans were all the rage again in Lucescere. This one is very pretty."

"I wouldna have thought it was in your style," Iain said. "It's so very heavy and ornate." He reached and took it from her, turning it over in his hand. It was very large, with a frame made of thick embossed sticks, and gilded pigskin painted with stylized purple thistles.

"Oh, ye think no'?" she said and took it back again. "Well, I shall no' carry it again then." She opened the drawer of her dressing table and dropped the fan within, shutting it away.

Feeling vaguely troubled, Iain went to the door that led to his room. He turned to say good night to his wife but stopped in surprise. Elfrida had quietly locked the drawer of the dressing table and was hiding the key inside the jet brooch she used to pin her collar. Iain had not even known the brooch had a concealed compartment. Elfrida tucked the brooch inside her jewelry case and began to brush out her long fair hair. She was smiling to herself.

Iain dropped his hand and went through to his own bedchamber without saying a word.

Bird in the Hand

Lewen sat in his cupboard of a room in the Theurgia, watching intently as his knife curled one shaving after another away from the wood he held in his hand. His knife was growing blunt. He stopped to whet it against his sharpening stone, and then resumed his whittling. He was not making anything. For once no shape was emerging from the wood as if it had always been imprisoned inside, waiting for him to release it. He was just whittling the wood away to nothing.

He did not know how much time had passed since he had returned from his search through the snowstorm. It had been at least an hour, maybe more. Lewen had made no attempt to undress or to sleep. It felt like he was in a kaleidoscope that had been turned upside down and shaken, all the known pattern of his life jumbled up and changed into a new and quite terrifying shape.

He heard a sharp rap on the glass of his window, and then a flurry of wingbeats. The rap came again. Lewen got up and went to the window. It was still dark outside. He could see nothing. He unlatched the clasp and opened the window.

A tiny bluebird flew in, its wings whirring desperately. It flitted about Lewen's head, uttering shrill cries of distress. Lewen put up his hand and caught it, and it lay quiescent in his palm. He could feel its heart pounding away.

"Rhiannon?" Lewen said. "What has happened to Rhiannon?"

The bird panted, its beak open. He bent over it, and suddenly, unexpectedly, it pecked him sharply just under the eye.

Lewen jerked back, then put the fingers of his other hand up to touch the bead of blood welling up from the tiny wound.

"But why?" Lewen asked aloud.

The bird spread its iridescent wings and gave a loud cry. Lewen found himself unexpectedly short of breath, his eyes smarting with grief.

Folding the fingers of both hands over the bird, he got up and blundered out of his room. The corridors were mostly dark and empty, with only the occasional knot of students standing about and discussing all that had happened that night. Lewen paid them no heed. He went clattering down the stairs with no clear idea of where he was going or why.

Joggled in his hands, the bird gave a little cry of distress. Lewen opened his jacket and went to tuck the bird inside his breast pocket. Olwynne's nosegay was inside it, withered and brown and smelling of rot. Lewen pulled it out and let it fall, tucking the bird inside the pocket instead and drawing the jacket protectively over it. His pace lengthened. He felt a rush of new energy, as if he had been climbing a ladder out of a dark hole and at last seen sunlight above him.

Nina, he thought. *Nina will ken what to do. . . .*

The sorceress was not with the other witches, working desperately to rouse the drugged healers and the Celestines. It was a scene of chaos. Apprentice-witches trudged up and down the hall with their shoulders under the armpits of drowsy men and women, forcing them to keep on walking. Many were so lethargic they could not take a step themselves, and the young exhausted apprentices had to slap their faces or shake them to keep them awake.

Others held basins and buckets for those forced to vomit up the drugged wine. More hurried about with steaming kettles, making restorative teas that had to be held to the slack mouths of those afflicted, forcing them to sip.

Gwilym came limping down the hall, scowling ferociously. "Has anyone seen the Keybearer? Where's that foolish lad I sent to find her? We need her! The Stargazer is ill indeed."

"H-h-h-here I am, sir," the boy piped up. "I c-c-canna find her, sir. Her room is all locked up, sir."

"Where can she be? Ghislaine! The healer we've managed to wake says boiling the root o' devil's bit in wine and honey may help. It'll bring on the sweats and help drive out the poison through the skin. Can ye send someone to the simples room to make us up some as soon as can be? Ye! Lass! I need more o' that tea!"

The sorcerer saw Lewen and said sternly, "I thought I told ye to get to bed, Lewen, and get some rest! The last thing I need is ye coming down with fever."

"Please, sir, have ye seen Nina?"

"Nina is still at the palace," Gwilym said. "She is utterly distraught. What a dreadful night this has been."

He did not pause to wonder why Lewen was asking for Nina but stumped away, calling for Ghislaine to come and help him at once. Then suddenly he turned. "Lewen, since ye're up, can ye run a message to the palace for me? Tell the Banrìgh the Stargazer is ill indeed, and she canna be seeing her tonight. There's a horse outside waiting."

"Aye, sir," Lewen said gladly and ran out the door and into the bitter dark. It had stopped snowing, but a black frost had set in, and the wind was cruel. Lewen grabbed the horse, which was being walked up and down by a shivering, miserable lad, and unbuckled its blanket. He did not wait for the saddle to be set on its back but leaped up and urged the horse into a gallop.

It was a mad ride through the darkness, the road slippery with ice. It was so cold the bones behind Lewen's ears ached, and each breath pierced his lungs. The wind was driving away the clouds, showing a black frosty sky overhead where the stars were beginning to pale along the eastern horizon.

Lewen passed on his message to the sentries at the gate, who at once sent a page running for the Banrìgh's bedchamber, and then he went in search of Nina. Her door was opened by a servant who scanned Lewen's face suspiciously and demanded his business.

"I need to see Nina," Lewen stammered.

"I am sorry, Lady Ninon is no' receiving visitors," the servant replied and went to shut the door.

"Wait!" Lewen cried. "She will want to see me, she will!"

"Lewen?" Iven's voice called. "Is that Lewen?"

"Aye," he said gladly, and pushed past the servant and into the chamber beyond.

The room was dim and very quiet. Iven was sitting at a table, his fair hair ruffled, his shirt unbuttoned and crumpled, writing letters by the light of a three-branched candelabra. He looked up as Lewen came in and greeted him in a low voice, indicating he could go through to the bedchamber beyond. As Lewen went past, he saw Brun the cluricaun was sitting disconsolately by the fire, a pot of ale before him. Dide sat with him, occupying his hands with six golden balls that he rolled over his knuckles or poured from one hand to another in a glittering stream. He looked tired and sad, but he made an effort to smile at Lewen, rising to accompany him into the bedchamber.

Nina was lying on the bed, dressed in a green satin dressing gown embroidered with huge pink roses. Her chestnut hair was loose and waved wildly over her shoulders. She turned at Dide's gentle touch and sat up, pushing back her disheveled hair with one hand. Her eyes were red-rimmed and swollen. At the sight of her Lewen's heart swelled with pity. He could not imagine how distressed she must be, to have her six-year-old son snatched away from her like that.

"I'm so sorry about Roden," Lewen said.

Tears welled up in Nina's eyes. "I should never have left him, never," she said. Her voice trembled. "I kent that evil laird had escaped. I should've kent he'd want to take Roden with him. I heard him say they would find him again when the time was right. With my own ears I heard him say it. I should've kent!"

"Don't distress yourself anymore," Dide said. He cast Lewen a reproachful look. "Please, have some wine, Nina. It'll make ye feel better."

"I don't want wine!" Nina said and pushed the glass away so violently it spilt. She did not notice, sitting up with both hands clasped at her breast, dark eyes fixed beseechingly on Lewen's face. "Oh, have ye come with news, Lewen? Any news at all?"

He shook his head. "No. I'm sorry," he managed to say.

She drooped with disappointment, turning back to lie on her pillow, her hand over her eyes.

"Then why have ye come?" Dide asked, not unkindly.

"The little bird . . ." he said and could say no more. From his breast came a soft cheep.

Nina looked up. "Ye have a bird there? What bird?"

"It's the bird I carved Rhiannon," Lewen said. "It came to me. . . . Something's wrong."

Nina sat up and held out her hand. "Give it to me," she said.

Gently Lewen took the bird out of his breast pocket and gave it to Nina. Its heart was not pounding away quite so violently, but it was still panting and its eye was dull.

Nina held it between her hands and whispered something to it. It opened its beak and gave a high, wild shriek, flapping its wings wildly. She whispered to it again and smoothed down its bright blue feathers, and the bird calmed.

"Dide, can I have some honey water for it?" Nina asked. When her brother had dropped some honey into warm water and brought it to her, she dipped her finger in it and trickled some drops down the bird's throat. It drank thirstily.

"The poor wee thing is terrified," Nina said. "It must've been there when the dragon came for Rhiannon."

Lewen had a most peculiar sensation, as if the world was receding away from him. "A dragon came for Rhiannon?" he repeated stupidly. "What dragon?"

Nina and Dide exchanged glances. "That's right. Ye were no' there when they brought the news."

"What news?"

"Rhiannon escaped from Sorrowgate Tower," Nina said.

"Rhiannon escaped!" Lewen's heart leaped.

"She hit the guard over the head with her chamber pot," Dide said and chuckled.

"Iseult was infuriated. She called the dragon's name. She flew after Rhiannon and brought her back."

"I saw the dragon fly over," Lewen said. "The Banrìgh was riding it? But why? Why would the Banrìgh call the dragon's name for such a little thing? What does she care whether Rhiannon escapes or not?"

"She's convinced Rhiannon murdered Lachlan. She has condemned her to hang at dawn, at the ringing o' the bell."

"But . . . but why?" Lewen suddenly found it hard to breathe.

"Iseult is utterly distraught," Dide said. "I have never seen her so angry, so wild. She walks in a cloud o' ice and snowflakes and turns the world to winter wherever she is."

"She has lost her husband and all her children," Nina said

softly. "I can understand her sorrow." She heaved a great sigh. "But no' her rage. She is quite mad with it. Luckily Isabeau thinks so too. She said she would convince Iseult to let Rhiannon drink from that goblet o' Connor's, to prove her innocence. She should've done so by now."

"When did she say this?" Lewen demanded, his heart thumping so hard he could barely hear his own voice. "For no one has seen the Keybearer for hours and hours. They were calling for her at the healers' hall. The Celestines were all drugged, we think by Johanna, and all the healers too. Whatever it was they swallowed hit them hard. We almost lost the Stargazer. It's been like a madhouse; they had to give them something to make them vomit and walk them up and down the corridors for hours to stop them falling asleep again. Isabeau was no' there then, and no one could find her."

Nina stared at him, wild-eyed. "Eà's eyes! Do ye mean to tell me Isabeau is missing too? And Rhiannon is still to hang? Oh, my goddess!"

She got up in frantic haste, stripping off her vivid dressing gown. Lewen averted his eyes, embarrassed. "We must find out what has happened to Isabeau, and we must convince Iseult to spare Rhiannon. Surely the first madness o' her grief is over, and she will see reason? I swear, if she will no' listen, I will knock her head against the wall until she does! No, Iven! Do no' try to stop me. Dide! Where is Isabeau?"

"She was going to consult *The Book o' Shadows*," Dide said. "She was . . . she was very afraid. I do no' ken why. I didna think . . . She is the Keybearer, for Eà's sake! Who could harm the Keybearer!"

"We must find her!" Nina cried. "What time is it? Eà, Eà! It is almost dawn now. We do no' have much time. Lewen, come with me!"

Lewen nodded. He took the bluebird back from Nina and tucked it into his inner pocket, as Nina dragged on a dress and cloak and pulled on her boots. Brun the cluricaun came and put one wrinkly paw on his arm.

"Remember this, lad," Brun said solemnly. "There is a body without a heart that has a tongue and yet no head. Buried it was afore it was made, and loud it does speak although it is dead."

Lewen stared at him in utter stupefaction.

"Think on it, laddie," the cluricaun said, nodding his head. "Still its tongue and it canna speak."

"All right," Lewen said, though he did not understand. The cluricaun sat back, satisfied. Lewen only had time to think that perhaps the old cluricaun was losing his wits with age before Nina imperiously beckoned him from the door. "Come on!" she cried.

Swept along on the wave of Nina's vehemence, Lewen did as he was told, though he was so topsy-turvy in all his emotions he could not have said why. Too much had happened in recent days. He had thought he hated Rhiannon and loved Olwynne, but the sight of the judges' red mantles had wrung his heart so powerfully that he had been afraid and pressed as close to Olwynne as he could. He had jumped the fire with her and promised to be true to her. Then Olwynne had disappeared. Lewen had been too shocked, and too overwhelmed by events, to know what to think or feel.

Then, hearing from Nina that Rhiannon had escaped, Lewen had been shaken by such joy and longing that he had been ashamed. *Olwynne is my true love. I am handfasted to her. Rhiannon means naught to me*, he had told himself, but it was not true, not true. He had realized this as he held the bluebird in his cupped hands, feeling its heart beating frantically against his palm, its throat pulsing with life and breath that Lewen had somehow given it. No matter if it had been ensorcelled or not, the love he had felt for Rhiannon had been the truest and deepest thing in his whole life. He could not stand by and let Rhiannon die.

Yet he did not know how to save her.

They found Iseult still sitting her lonely vigil by her husband's dead body. Though they pleaded with her, she sat as stiff and cold and white as if dead herself and said simply, "Why ask me? What power do I have over life and death now? I am naught but a dead Rìgh's widow. Ask the Banrìgh." Her last word was bitter and scornful.

Nina and Lewen did not understand her, and she would not explain. They went away, confounded and upset, only to learn of Bronwen's seizing of power by a serving girl come to stoke up the fires in the hall. So they ran to the Privy Chamber, which was dark and empty, and thence to Bronwen's chambers.

The ladies-in-waiting guarding her rooms would not wake

the new Banrìgh, no matter how much Nina and Lewen begged and pleaded. They were proud and contemptuous, reveling in their newfound power. Neither Nina nor Lewen had any influence with them. The court was still in such turmoil over the sudden shift in power that no one was at all willing to stick their neck out for a satyricorn girl found guilty of murdering a Yeoman, particularly one suspected of being involved in the Rìgh's murder. Nina argued until she was hoarse, to no avail.

So Nina and Lewen galloped together down the avenue to the witches' tower, Nina's hair streaming behind her like a banner. For once Lewen did not spare the horse, whipping it on with the reins. Breathless, their faces stinging, they ran into the great hall, demanding from everyone they met whether the Keybearer had been found. Anxious denials were all they got.

Fèlice was kneeling before the fire, stirring a great cauldron from which rose a ghastly bitter smell. She turned and rose to her feet, pushing back her disheveled hair with one hand.

"Nina! I heard about Roden. I'm so very, very sorry." It was clear Fèlice had been crying. Her nose was red and her eyes were swollen, and she was so pale she looked as if she might keel over at any moment.

Nina nodded. "All we can do is pray to Eà that Finn finds them," she said tersely. "Fèlice! We need the Keybearer at once. Have ye heard the news? Rhiannon is to hang at dawn. Iseult has commanded it, and we canna get in to beg the new Banrìgh to pardon her—they willna let us in. They will let Isabeau in, though. We must find her!"

"Rhiannon is to hang? At dawn?" Fèlice put out her hand and grasped Nina's arm. "No!"

"Aye! Unless we can stop it."

"No one's seen the Keybearer," Fèlice said rapidly. "Though someone said they saw an owl fly in her bedroom window some hours ago . . ."

Nina and Lewen exchanged a quick glance and then began to run up the stairs, taking two at a time. Behind them, Fèlice looked out at the paling sky and bit her lip, tears running down her face. Then she threw down her spoon, and ran out the front door, calling frantically, "Landon! Cameron! To me!"

Lewen reached the Keybearer's door first. He banged his fist upon it, shouting at the top of his voice. There was no an-

swer. Nina reached his side and added her voice to his. Again
and again they knocked, and called Isabeau's name, and rattled
the door handle, but there was no answer. Then Lewen heard a
faint moan.

They looked at each other, filled with a dreadful fear; then
Nina took a deep breath and began to sing. Higher and higher
her voice soared, until the pitch was so unbearable Lewen had
to press his hands over his ears. The bluebird lying against his
heart shrieked in terror.

There was a flash of blue fire as the wards on the Keybearer's door suddenly burst asunder, leaving a lingering sigil
burned upon Lewen's eyeballs. The door blew off its hinges,
crashing to the floor. Nina stepped in, holding her arm up over
her face to protect herself from the blue sparks hissing all round
the frame. Wordlessly, Lewen followed.

Isabeau was curled in a fetal position on the floor, her chin
pressed down into her chest, her hands held over her face as if
trying to hold off a blow. Every now and again she jerked, as if
stung by a doom-eel. *The Book of Shadows* lay facedown on the
floor, its pages bent beneath it as if it had been thrown or
dropped. There was an unpleasant smell in the air, like burned
leather. Glancing at the ancient tome, Lewen saw its red cover
was scorched with dark, smudged marks like handprints.

Calling Isabeau's name, Nina felt her forehead, and then her
pulse. One was clammy and cold, the other tumultuous. The
Keybearer did not respond to the sound of her name. When
Nina tried to pull Isabeau's hands away, she cried out and cowered away.

"Isabeau! What has happened!" Nina cried. "Oh Eà, help
me! What could have happened?"

Isabeau's pale lips moved. A croaking sound came out.
"Gwilym . . . Get Gwilym."

Nina bent over her. "But what has happened?" she asked.
"Are ye ill?"

"Ensorcelled," Isabeau whispered. "Very strong . . . I
canna . . . get Gwilym."

Nina turned to Lewen, and he rose from his knees, ready to
go and fetch the sorcerer as asked.

Just then, the bluebird stirred inside Lewen's jacket and
began to trill. Outside another bird answered, and then another.

"It is dawn," Nina said heavily. "We are too late. The bell will ring at any moment. Oh, poor Rhiannon!"

Lewen stared at her, his breath catching in his throat; then he turned and began to run.

A Body without a Heart

They had left Rhiannon a candle marked with lines that showed the passing of the hours. She had not wanted to be alone in the dark. She watched the flame slowly devour the candle until all that was left was a pale nub crouched in a pool of wax.

It was still dark when they came for her. They unlocked her chains and manacles and set a fine breakfast of baked ham and coddled eggs before her, which Rhiannon could not eat. She asked for the goldensloe wine Nina had brought her for midsummer, and they stood by and watched as she drank it. It helped ease the trembling of her hands. No one spoke much, which she thought was kind. Then they brought hot water and harsh soap for her to wash with, and another shapeless grey gown with seams that made her itch unbearably. *The Keybearer's fire did not get rid of all the lice*, Rhiannon thought.

She had an escort of six guards, all heavily armed, with black hoods and black armbands. They were not her usual guards but strangers to her, which saddened her. She had grown quite friendly with Corey and Henry, and hoped that the younger of the two had not been punished for her escape. She wished the chamber pot had not been full, or that she had been able to find another weapon with which to knock him out.

The guards obviously knew she had escaped once before. They snapped the manacles and chains back on and kept their spears at the ready, prodding her painfully if she lagged behind or looked about her too closely.

Still Rhiannon looked for chances to escape. She called to Blackthorn with all her strength, hoping for some sense that the winged horse was not badly hurt, that she had escaped the dragon's claw and would come and save her from the noose. Bound in iron and stone, she felt nothing.

The escort took her down through the prison and out onto the snow-covered battlement that spanned the gate. It was bitterly cold. They hung over the wall with torches in their hands and prodded her forward with their spears so she could see the row of skulls hanging above the lintel of the gate. On the far end were two freshly severed heads. She recognized the short grey hair of Shannley, the lord of Fettercairn's groom. He had been hanged the day before, they told her. His face was almost unrecognizable, for the birds and the rats had been enjoying a feast. His eyes were gone, and most of his cheek.

The other head was that of a young and pretty girl with long golden hair, now matted with blood. Rhiannon recognized her as the girl in the Murderers' Gallery who had killed her baby. The sight filled her with rage, though she could not have explained why. She stepped back, saying nothing, but she would have liked to strike out at her guards or shout at them. She did not. Somehow, Rhiannon was still hoping for deliverance.

"We'll hang your head there too, when we're done," one of the guards said.

"As an example to others," another said, grinning.

Rhiannon stared at them, saying nothing. She imagined her head stuck on a pike, the birds pecking at her sightless eyes, and felt a shudder rack her body. She tried not to let the prison guards see.

The sight of the skull-laden lintel of the gate had induced a jocular mood in her guards. They talked and joked as they marched her on down the ice-slick stairs and into the large courtyard below, where the gallows stood. Not many people had been hanged in Lachlan's time, they told her. They wondered whether the new Banrìgh would be more like her mother, Maya the Ensorcellor. In her day, the guards said, cartloads of people had been brought regularly to the gallows or, if they were witches or faeries, burned alive on a bonfire.

"No' that we want those days back again," the oldest of the guards said reprovingly and looked at Rhiannon apologetically.

The courtyard was lit with flaming torches. The stark shape of the gallows was silhouetted against their orange glare. Rhiannon stared in fascination. She had never seen such a contraption before, but it was clear what its function was. Then she looked to the sky, her pulse beginning to thump, both dreading and longing for the familiar shape of Blackthorn in the sky. But all she could see was the sky paling to grey. It was dawn.

A large crowd had gathered to watch. She was the latest sensation, her guards told her. They forced her up the steps to the gallows. Rhiannon resisted with all her strength, but they only laughed, pleased with her for putting on a good show for the crowd. It was a noisy mob. Some had come armed with old fruit and vegetables to lob at her, some shouted for her death with a frenzy that alarmed and sickened her, and others prayed for her with bent heads. Rhiannon scanned the crowd desperately, but there was no familiar face, no friend there to ease her last moments or to try one last reckless attempt to rescue her. Her eyes filled with tears despite herself. *Lewen*, her soul yearned. *Lewen*.

But he was not there.

A big man with a thick neck and arms was waiting for her by the gallows. His face was obscured with a black hood. They dragged Rhiannon the last few feet and secured her arms behind her back. A hood was dropped over her face. She struggled to choke back her tears, to breathe while she could. She felt the thick rope of the noose being fitted about her neck.

"At the first ring o' the tower bell, I'll pull this lever here and the boards beneath your feet will fall," a deep, wheezy voice said in her ear. "Do no' fear, lass. It'll be quick. Have ye friends in the crowd? They can pull on your feet to make it quicker if ye like."

Dumbly Rhiannon shook her head. *No friends*, she thought. *No friends anywhere*. The thought brought the tears gushing. She took a deep, shaky breath and felt the big man drop a comforting hand on her shoulder.

"Sorry, lass," he mumbled.

They waited. Rhiannon listened intently. She could hear

the hisses and catcalls of the crowd. She could hear the heavy breathing of the hangman. She could hear one of her guards shuffle his feet impatiently. Beyond the wall, the river rushed towards the cliff, flinging its great body of water over in a dull roar that filled the city every minute of every day. Birds were singing as blithely as ever, caring not a bit that today was the day Rhiannon would die. Somewhere a cart rattled over cobblestones. A dog barked. A shop sign squeaked in the freshening breeze. Rhiannon felt it flatten her coarse dress against her body. Someone called, "Ee-ee-eels, ee-ee-eels, ee-ee-els alive-oh!"

The muffled darkness pressing so close about Rhiannon's face began to lighten. The material had soaked up her tears, and it was damp against her face. Her skin itched.

"Where's that bell?" someone muttered.

"It's dawn. Why have ye no' hung her?" someone else called.

"Come on, hang her!" another voice screamed.

A chant began to rise from the crowd. "Hang her, hang her!"

"Why hasna that bell rung?" the hangman asked. "I got to wait for the bell."

The crowd had begun to stamp their feet, to clap, to bang wooden staves against the iron railing. "Hang her, hang her, hang her," they shrieked.

"It's a sign," someone else called.

Rhiannon's heart leaped. She recognized Fèlice's clear, sweet, aristocratic voice. "It's a sign from Eà! Eà has stilled the bell so it canna ring. Spare her!"

"It's a sign!" someone else repeated. Rhiannon could not be sure, but she thought it might be Rafferty. "A sign from Eà!"

"Hang her, hang her, hang her!"

"The bell has no' rung! It's a sign from Eà!"

"Hang her!"

"I canna hang her without the ring o' the bell. That's the law," the hangman muttered. Rhiannon heard him shift his weight anxiously, and the board below her feet creaked ominously. She could not help but curl her bare toes, dreading the sudden yawning of space below her feet.

"The Banrìgh must have pardoned her," Fèlice called again. "Eà bless the Banrìgh!"

"Hang her, hang her, hang her!"

"Nay, it's a sign, a sign from Eà. Rhiannon is innocent!" Landon called. Rhiannon knew his voice at once. Her heart warmed within her. She did have friends after all.

"She's innocent! Spare her!"

"Hang her, hang her!"

"The Banrìgh! The Blessed Banrìgh must've pardoned her!"

"Where's that bloody bell?" the hangman muttered.

The screams and calls echoed around the courtyard. The stamping and clapping grew frenzied. Rhiannon could feel her guards growing restive. She spread her feet on the boards, tense and ready for action.

"Havers, why have ye no' hung her yet?"

"Hang the bitch!"

"The bell has no' rung!" the hangman cried out loud, sounding ruffled and upset. "I canna hang her without the bloody bell ringing. I canna!"

Now the light was strong in her eyes. She felt the cloth about her face warming. The dawn singing of the birds had faded, but the sound of the wakening city was loud. Then she heard the sweet, high cry of a bluebird, and then the familiar light weight as her bird landed on her shoulder. Tears choked her.

"Just hang her, damn it," one of the guards said crossly. "I'm getting hungry!"

"I canna hang her without the ring o' the bell," the hangman said stubbornly. "That's what I've been told."

"Just do it, so we can get out o' here," another guard said.

"Nay, I will no'," the hangman said. "What if the Banrìgh has sent a pardon? It'd be my head then."

"Flaming dragon balls, we'll have a riot soon. Hang her, will ye!"

"I will no'," the hangman said. "Ye hang her, if ye're so anxious to see it done."

There was a pause, during which the competing screams of the crowd seemed to grow even louder. Rhiannon waited for the response with straining ears.

"Better no'," the guard muttered at last. "If they wanted her hung, they'd have rung the bell."

Rhiannon's head swam with utter relief. Her knees almost buckled, but with a great effort she locked them straight, not wanting to hang herself by fainting now that a reprieve of sorts had been won.

"Eà bless ye!" Fèlice called, her voice ringing over the noise of the crowd.

Just then Rhiannon heard the thunder of hooves approaching. Anxiety gripped her heart tight. She could barely breathe. She strained her ears to listen. She heard the rattle of wheels, the snap of a whip being cracked; then she heard Fèlice's joyous voice. "Nina!"

Nina's clear, strong voice rang out. "A reprieve! I have here a reprieve, signed by the Banrìgh Bronwen Mathilde NicCuinn. Rhiannon o' Dubhslain has been pardoned! Unchain her!"

There was a great scuffle. Rhiannon swayed on her feet. The hangman put his thick arm about her. "Hold up there, lassie," he whispered. "Just a minute more."

She heard the raucous crowd being pushed back by soldiers; then someone clattered about behind her. Her chains fell to the boards with a clunk. Rhiannon ripped her hood off. The light dazzled her eyes, but she shielded them with her arm, taking deep, panting breaths of air that suddenly seemed deliciously pure and clear. Nina sprang up onto the gibbet and embraced her fervently. Her hair was wild and disheveled, her clothes in disarray, but Rhiannon had never seen Nina look so beautiful. She hugged her back with all her strength.

Fèlice waved wildly, her face lit up with jubilation, from the other side of the iron railings. Cameron, Rafferty, Landon, and Maisie were with her, leaping up and down, laughing and screaming with excitement. Gwilym the Ugly was trying to control the rearing, lathered horses threatening to tip the little cart over, while beyond the line of soldiers the crowd seethed and shouted, some angry and disappointed, others sure they had seen a real live miracle.

"It was Gwilym who did it," Nina said, the words tumbling one over the other. "He's kent Bronwen since she was just a lass. Lachlan had told him about the pardon. He convinced Bronwen that we would never find the true culprits if we hanged ye. Ye are the only one . . . Ye ken the most o' anyone . . ." She had to stop to take a deep, panting breath. "I canna believe we got here

in time! I was sure we'd be too late. Too late!" She laughed
wildly and wiped her tears away.

"The bell," Rhiannon said. "The bell didna ring."

"It's a miracle!" Fèlice called. "That bloody bell has rung
nonstop all night, and yet it didna ring in the dawn! Eà was with
us. Eà was on our side!"

"The bell?" Nina asked. "They didna hang ye because o' the
bell?"

"Aye," Rhiannon said, wiping her eyes and nose with the
back of her hand. "The bell didna ring. I dinna ken why."

"There is a body without a heart that has a tongue. . . ." Nina
said slowly. "A bell, o' course! Still its tongue, and the bell
canna speak."

The old bell ringer hurried up the dark, cobwebby stairs, tense
with anxiety. As long as he had been tower captain, the bells in
the watchtower had rung out just when they ought to, with clear
true voices, to tell the people of the city that all was well, or not
well, within the bounds of their world. Never had he known one
to stay mute when he had called upon it to ring.

He reached the top of the bell tower. Six bells of varying
size hung below him, their sound bows gleaming faintly in the
gloom. He reached out and seized the rim of the largest of all
the bells, the tenor, whose great girth measured more than
forty-five inches across. She was named Aingeal, and around
her belly were inscribed the words, "I to Eà the living call, and
to the grave do summon all." It was her voice that rang out over
the city every dawn, to call the workers to their tasks, and then
again at sunset, to call the curfew, and the shutting of the city
gates, and the downing of tools. As tower captain, he had the
honor to ring her, and it was always her voice that was heard
last, after the ringing of the changes.

The bell ringer ran his hand over Aingeal's shining, volup-
tuous waist, and then seized the wheel with one hand and the
rope with the other, dragging the sound bow upwards so he
could examine the clapper. He himself had removed the double
muffler from the clapper after ringing Aingeal for six hours
straight. All had been sound then. Even if some fool had replaced the leather and horsehair device, the bell still should

have sounded its muted, portentous voice. Only removal of the clapper, which he knew by experience was no easy task, or complete immobilization, could prevent Aingeal from singing.

Slowly the bell swung upwards, till its rim was facing the arched ceiling and the old bell ringer could peer inside her hollow body.

He cried aloud in surprise.

A young man was clinging tightly to the clapper, his legs braced against the sound rim. He was white and sick-looking, as indeed he should be, having just been swung three hundred and sixty degrees over and over again. He had tied himself in place with a crumpled black apprentice-witch's robe but had evidently hit his head hard, for blood was trickling down the side of his face.

"Eà's eyes!" the bell ringer cried. "No wonder the bell wouldna ring. Ye're lucky ye didna kill yourself!"

The young man stirred, groaning. "Still its tongue," he muttered. "Do no' let it speak."

"Let's get ye off there afore ye fall," the bell ringer said, seizing the young man about the shoulders and drawing his knife to cut the robe that tied him in place. "Young fool! What was it? A wager?"

"Is she dead?" the young man demanded, opening dazed brown eyes. "Did I save her?"

"It's ye who should be dead, ye young fool," the bell ringer said gruffly. "Stopping my bell that way!"

"I stopped it?" he asked. "I stilled its tongue?"

"*Her* tongue," the bell ringer said. "A bell is always called 'she.'" He grinned, and said, as he sawed away at the knot of the twisted material, "Ye ken why? 'Cause they have big mouths and long tongues."

"I stopped her," the young man said contentedly, then fainted.

THE SNARE IS BROKEN

"Our soul has escaped even as a bird out of the snare of the fowler: the snare is broken and we are delivered."

—Psalm 124, verse 6,
The Book of Common Prayer

The Golden Fan

The Keybearer lay in her white bed. Although it was mounded high with eiderdowns and blankets, still she shivered as if sleeping under snow. In the firelight dancing over the walls, her eyes looked very big and very black, the pupil so dilated that the blue of her iris was almost completely swallowed.

"It is a very strong spell," she said. Her voice was low and husky. "I have never felt such a strong compulsion. If I had no' had such a spell laid on me afore, I do no' think I would recognize it now for what it is. I do no' ken how long I can resist it."

"But who could weave such a spell?" Gwilym the Ugly asked. He was sitting beside the bed, his saturnine face set in a ferocious scowl. Cailean of the Shadowswathe was there too, and his brother Stormy Briant, and Ghislaine Dream-Walker, and Jock Crofter, and Fat Drusa, and the wizened old sorceress Wise Tully, who was so old she rarely left her own quarters anymore. Nina the Nightingale sat on the far side of the bed with Dide, who was holding Isabeau's crippled hand in both of his.

"It was Brann the Raven," the Keybearer said and stopped for a moment, trying to control her breathing. "Do ye no' remember how he swore he would outwit Gearradh and live again? It was no' an idle boast. Somehow he learned the secret o' raising the dead and wrote it in *The Book o' Shadows*. Concealed within the words is another spell, a very strong and subtle spell. Whoever reads the spell is compelled to go to the Tomb o' Ravens and resurrect him from his grave. This is no easy task. . . ."

She stopped again, and Dide held a glass of water to her lips so she could drink. When she spoke again, her voice was stronger. "Brann died a thousand years or more ago. There is naught left o' him but grave dust. The Spell o' Resurrection is most potent when spoken as soon after the corpse's death as possible. The more that remains o' them, the more strongly the spirit lingers in the flesh. To raise him now would be impossible."

"Then how . . .?" Nina asked.

"Brann was clever, diabolically clever. He kent it might be a long time afore someone was foolish enough to seek to ken the Spell o' Resurrection. So the compulsion is a complex one. It is no' enough to go to the Tomb o' Ravens and disinter his grave. One must go back in time to the day o' his death first."

"The Heart o' Stars!" Ghislaine exclaimed. "That is why Thunderlily and Donncan . . ."

"And Johanna," Isabeau said heavily. "Do no' forget Johanna."

"*Johanna* forced Thunderlily and the Prionnsa?" Fat Drusa asked blankly. "It is hard to believe."

"I should have seen it coming," Isabeau said. "But I was so caught up in my own concerns . . ."

"It was Dedrie," Nina said, beginning to understand. "She wanted the Spell o' Resurrection for the laird o' Fettercairn, so he could raise his brother and the little dead boy, the one who looks like Roden."

"Aye, I think so," Isabeau said. "She wriggled her way into Johanna's confidence . . ."

"Convinced her to look up the spell in *The Book o' Shadows* . . ." Nina said.

"Aye, but Johanna was caught by Brann's compulsion like a fish on a hook. She wouldna have had a chance. If I'm not mistaken, the skeelie has been working on her will for a while. Many o' those village skeelies have no compunction in using their magic to bend the will o' others to their own. It's forbidden to those o' the Coven, o' course, but . . ." Her voice trailed away wearily, and she shrugged. "It is a hard temptation to resist, I ken."

"So if this skeelie had been molding Johanna to her will for some time . . ." Gwilym said slowly.

"And drugging her too, I bet!" Nina interjected. "Dedrie likes drugs and poisons."

"Then she would've been very susceptible to Brann's spell o' compulsion," Gwilym finished.

Isabeau nodded. "Aye. I do no' think Donncan and Thunderlily's disappearance had aught to do with the laird o' Fettercairn's plot. I think he just wanted the Spell o' Resurrection, and then three living souls, willing or unwilling. . . ." She shuddered.

"Why three?" Dide asked. "I understand Owein and Roden—one for his brother who died, and one for the little boy—but why Olwynne?"

"To raise Margrit o' Arran," Isabeau replied.

A gasp of surprise and horror ran around the room.

"Och, aye," she said, nodding. "I've suspected Margrit's hand in this for a while, even from beyond the grave. She is the one—or at least, it was her ghost—who told the laird o' Fettercairn where he could find the Spell o' Resurrection. It is just the sort o' thing she would've known o'. It must've been unbelievably frustrating for her, to ken where to find such a spell but to have no hands or feet or voice to work the spell. Twenty years she has been dead. It is a long time to cling to one's life, waiting for a tool to come along."

"So it was the ghost o' Margrit o' Arran that Laird Malvern and his necromancers raised at the Tower o' Ravens?" Nina said, beginning to understand. "But how did Johanna come to be involved?"

"Margrit may have told Laird Malvern where to find the Spell o' Resurrection, but he and his servants could never have come near *The Book o' Shadows* by themselves. They needed to find someone who was close enough to me to know how to get into my rooms, yet who was willing to betray me."

"I would never have thought it o' Johanna," Fat Drusa said in distress.

"I imagine they promised her they would raise Connor from the dead," Isabeau said. "Even so, she may no' have helped them, I think, if Lachlan had no' decided to pardon Rhiannon. Else Johanna would've looked up the spell afore now, surely. And in return for her finding them the spell, they killed Lachlan afore he could announce Rhiannon's pardon."

"He always said revenge was a dish best eaten cold," Nina said and pressed her hand against her mouth.

"It was Rhiannon who made me suspect Margrit o' Arran was involved," Isabeau said. "I am so glad ye were in time to save her, Nina! She is quick and clever, that lass, and has real power. I am so sorry that it should've been Iseult who gave the order for her to hang, but she is always the same, once her temper gets the better o' her. She does no' see clearly."

"She is half-mad with grief," Fat Drusa said pitifully. "It is all so sad!"

"But how can ye be so sure the ghost is Margrit?" Gwilym demanded. He had once been the Thistle's second-in-command and her lover. It was not a memory he was fond of.

"The ghost o' a powerful sorceress who had been poisoned to death? Someone whose grave was a long way away, somewhere across the sea? Someone powerful enough to cling to this world and seek another body to inhabit, the body o' a young and beautiful dark-haired girl, one with power . . ."

"Margrit o' Arran," Gwilym said grimly.

"Aye, I fear so," Isabeau said and heaved a great sigh. "If only I had realized earlier . . ." Her fretful fingers plucked at the sheets.

"If ifs and buts were pots and pans, there's be no need for tinkers' hands," Dide said, quoting a maxim of her old guardian, Meghan, that made Isabeau laugh and helped clear the air a little.

"So what are we to do?" Ghislaine said.

"It's a sorry tangle indeed," Isabeau said, and it was clear it cost her to keep speaking. Perspiration slicked her skin, and she was very pale. Her arms moved jerkily. "But Meghan, Eà bless her wise heart, always said a problem is like a tangle o' thread. If ye can just find the end o' the thread, ye can pull the tangle undone."

"So what is the end o' the thread?" Ghislaine asked.

"Two ends," Isabeau said. "One is Donncan and Thunderlily. We must go and get them back. That means traveling the Auld Ways and, perhaps, facing Brann the Raven."

"No easy task," Ghislaine said blankly.

"No," Isabeau said.

"We will need a Celestine to guide us," Gwilym said. "Cloudshadow would be best."

"Aye," Isabeau said. "She kens the Auld Ways better than anyone."

"But a thousand years!" Cailean marveled. "Is it possible?"

"Och, aye, it is possible." Isabeau's voice was husky with exhaustion, and she sounded dreamy and strange. Dide cast a quick glance at her. She did not meet his glance, her eyes fixed on the window that overlooked the gardens. Although it was past midday, it was gloomy outside, for the sky was dark with clouds, and occasionally sleet drove against the glass.

"If it must be done, it will be done," she said in the same low, dreamy voice. "All things are possible if ye desire it enough."

Dide frowned.

"We will need to be very sure o' our bearings," Gwilym said. "Do the Celestines no' navigate the Auld Ways by means o' the stars and planets? I will need to go and research the exact placement o' the constellations on the night Brann died. . . ."

"I suspect Johanna will already have done the research," Cailean said dryly. "Ask the librarians what books she has looked at recently. I'm sure we will find clues there."

"What else will we need?" Gwilym said. "We had best plan carefully. . . ."

Isabeau looked away from the window. "No' 'we,'" she said gently. "Ye must stay, Gwilym."

There was a moment's silence.

She indicated his wooden leg. "To travel the Auld Ways safely, ye must be able to run. Ye ken that. Besides, someone must stay here, to lead the Coven, in case I do no' come back."

The witches stirred in dismay.

"Brann is a very dangerous man," Isabeau said, "and the Auld Ways are always perilous to travel. We must no' pretend otherwise. Gwilym, ye are my second-in-command—ye must stay."

"But, Beau, ye are ill," Dide said.

"I am no' ill," she said. "I am fighting the strongest urge . . . a longing . . . a desperate desire. . . . If I could just give in . . ." She groaned and clenched her hands on her bedclothes. "Do no' speak o' it," she said harshly.

"But surely, by going, ye are doing just what Brann's spell commands?" Dide said. "How can we be sure that ye're no' doing exactly what he wants?"

She flashed him an angry glance. "I do no' go to raise him from the dead, I go to make sure he stays in the grave where he belongs," she said coldly. "Ye think I want Brann the Raven to live again? What would that mean for history? Perhaps the world we now know would no longer even exist. My mind boggles at the thought. And here's another for ye. What if he compelled Johanna and Thunderlily to bring him back to our time?"

There was a long silence.

"So I will go, with Cailean and Ghislaine and Cloudshadow," Isabeau said, sinking back wearily into her pillows. She turned her face from side to side, as if the texture of the pillow hurt her. "Dobhailen will be there to guard us. I ken he can run."

At the sound of his name the huge shadow-hound at Cailean's feet lifted its great head and looked at Isabeau with shining green eyes. Cailean fondled its silky ears, and it lay its head back down on its paws, growling softly.

"Why no' me?" Briant demanded, offended. He was a tall, handsome, swaggering man with a talent for thunderstorms, as different as could be from his thin, shy, subtle brother.

"Because ye will need to go in pursuit o' the laird o' Fettercairn," Isabeau said. Her voice was reedy and faint. "He'll be heading towards the Fair Isles. That is where Margrit o' Arran died, and where her bones will lie. He is some kind o' weather witch, this laird, and will raise a spell-wind to speed his passage. If Finn canna catch him afore he reaches the port, we will need ye to whistle up a wind for our ships to overtake him."

"Aha!" Briant said, his eyes coming alight. He loved summoning a good storm, and it was something he was rarely permitted to do.

"Surely Finn will catch him afore Dùn Gorm?" Fat Drusa cried. Usually happy and optimistic, she now looked wretched indeed. Clasping her plump hands together between her enormous bosoms, she glanced appealingly from Isabeau to Dide, whom she recognized as an unfailing source of information.

"Finn has no' been able to catch him so far," Dide said. "The laird has laid his plans well. They left the boat somewhere near

Alloway and went cross-country. Finn says they had horses waiting. She and Jay are crippled by no' kenning what he means to do next. Anyone else would've kept on sailing down the river, but Finn felt him moving off overland and pulled to shore herself. But it took them a couple o' hours to find some horses themselves, and by then the trail was growing cold. She'll catch him up, though, no fear. There's no stopping the wolf once it has its nose to a trail."

"But if we ken they're heading for Dùn Gorm . . ." Briant said.

"But we do no'," Dide replied. "They could have a ship waiting for them in any one o' a thousand coves on the coast o' Ravenshaw. If they head far enough west and manage to slip past the cordon we've set up around Dùn Gorm, well . . ."

"Things are no' made any easier by the damn weather," Gwilym said. "Iseult should've been sent to the Theurgia long ago, to learn to control her Talent. I canna approve o' the way the prionnsachan and banprionnsachan are allowed to go on wreaking havoc however they like without—"

"Ye ken as well as I do that the Crown needs to keep its autonomy from the Coven," Isabeau said tersely. "Iseult is no' the only one who would've benefitted from a few years at the Theurgia. But she is a banrìgh, no' a witch. Her control over her powers is incomplete. When she is grieved or angry, she brings snow, and ice, and storm. Do no' be so hasty in judging her. She has lost her husband and all her bairns this night. Just be glad she has no' buried us in snow."

"But o' all the Talents, weather working is the most dangerous, the most difficult to control," Gwilym argued. "Surely she—"

"She is the Banrìgh no longer," Briant cut in eagerly. "Happen she will join the Coven now?"

There was a long silence. Everyone looked anxiously to Isabeau, who often found Briant's tactlessness exasperating and was sometimes quick to depress his pretensions. But either Isabeau was too tired, or too sick, or too grieved to take umbrage, for she merely shrugged and sighed and laid her head back on her pillows, turning her cheek away from them.

"So is the weather very bad then?" Wise Tully asked. Everyone turned to her with a little stir of surprise, for she had been so quiet, with her head sunk on her chest, that they had thought her sleeping.

"Horrendous," Dide answered. "Hailstorms and snowstorms and freak strikes o' lightning all across southern Eileanan."

"The summer harvest is ruined. Ruined!" Jock Crofter said.

"The city sorceress of Dùn Gorm says the seas are running so high and wild, no one wants to set out from the safety o' the port. Bronwen . . . Her Majesty . . . has ordered the navy on standby, though, for we must stop Laird Malvern afore he reaches the Fair Isles. . . ." Nina said, her voice cracking with the strain.

"Which is where ye come in, Briant," Cailean said with an affectionate, mocking glance.

Briant did not see the mockery. "Sounds like fun," he said eagerly and got up, wanting to go and battle the stormy seas at once.

"And what o' me?" Dide asked softly.

Isabeau turned her great dilated black eyes on him.

"Ye must choose what ye will," she said. Her words came slowly, and she paused to fight for breath. "I thought Nina would want ye to go with her, to save Roden. He is your blood, your heir, the hope o' your house. I canna ask ye to come with me, as much as I want ye to, when I ken he has need o' ye."

Dide did not reply. He was clearly torn.

Nina put her hand on his arm. "Go with Beau," she said gently. "She needs ye more than I do. Her Majesty has pledged us a battalion o' soldiers to pursue the laird o' Fettercairn, and a fleet o' ships if we want them. Finn and Jay are already hot on his heels, and we leave in the morning with the best boatmen the river can offer. The laird will never make it to sea, and even if he does I'll have Iven there, and Finn and Jay too. . . ."

"And me!" Briant said gaily.

"And Stormy Briant as well. I would dearly love your support, but . . ."

"I will go with Beau," Dide said, clearly grateful. "Thank ye."

"We will go tomorrow, at dawn," Isabeau said. "It is best to open the doors at the change in the tide o' powers. Cailean, Ghislaine, will ye be ready? Try to get some sleep. The Auld Ways are perilous indeed. Ye will need all your wits about ye.

Gwilym, will ye seek audience with Her Majesty and tell her what we plan? She will want to ken."

They nodded and rose, Cailean helping Wise Tully to her feet with his usual grave courtesy. Isabeau was too overwrought to do more than murmur her thanks, but Gwilym drew them aside, issuing a series of directives and commands that the two sorcerers did their best to absorb.

Gradually the room emptied. Dide stayed where he was until the very end, but at last rose, his dark eyes concerned. "Ye look worn out, *leannan*," he said. "I'll go. Try to get some sleep."

Isabeau groaned and moved her hands fretfully. "I'll never sleep, Dide. Canna ye see? This spell . . . this compulsion . . . It's taking all my strength, all my concentration to fight it! Please . . ."

"What can I do?" Dide said at once, seizing one of her restless hands.

"Stay with me," she said. "Distract me! Oh, Dide. I feel my own mortality keenly. Help me . . . I want . . . I wish . . ."

"It'll be my pleasure," Dide said and bent to kiss the pulse beating so frantically in her throat.

Iain of Arran stood in his wife's bedchamber, staring at himself in the dressing table mirror. He looked thin and old and ineffectual. His hair, never thick, was now receding so that his face seemed all bony temples and pointy nose. His shoulders were stooped, and his neck was scrawny. His hands, protruding from the cuffs of his shirt, trembled slightly. He clenched them together, and then, reaching a decision, bent and put his finger to the lock of the dressing table drawer.

There was a faint click inside as the lock sprang open. Iain's mouth relaxed a little. He was, though few people realized it, a powerful sorcerer. Gently he drew the drawer open. His mother's fan lay inside, neatly folded.

Iain took the fan out and turned it over in his hands. His mother had carried it often, for the marshes of Arran were steamy hot most of the year round, and there was rarely any breeze to relieve the weight of humidity. He had not seen it since her death, though. He had no idea where it had been. Most of his mother's things had been packed away, for they were far too opulent for his wife's austere taste and besides, they carried unhappy memories for Iain, who had been deathly afraid of his mother.

Margrit of Arran had been a malevolent swarthyweb spider of a woman. She had plotted and conspired to help bring down the Coven of Witches, merely so that she would be the most powerful sorceress in the land. She had helped cast a curse on Lachlan that had struck him down into a living death, and she had kidnapped children with magical talent from all over the country to incarcerate them in her witch-school so that she, and only she, would control all the magic in the land. It was Margrit who had arranged Iain's marriage to Elfrida NicHilde of Tìrsoilleir. Elfrida had spent all of her life as a prisoner of the Fealde, taught to abhor all of the natural pleasures of the world as frivolous vanities that led inexorably to hell. She had not been allowed to sing, or dance, or hear music, or laugh, or talk idly, or play games, or eat sweets, or wear any color other than black or grey. She had to pray as many as six times a day and was taught to mortify the flesh to exalt the spirit. Many, many times she was forced to renounce her dead parents as devil worshippers and heretics, and spit upon their portraits.

Elfrida's childhood had been so bleak and cruel that Iain had been overwhelmed with sympathy for her. They had shared bitter tales of their upbringing and, in sharing them, drawn much of the sting out of them. Together they had found the strength to reject those who sought to use them as pawns in their games of power, and together had fled Arran and pledged their support to the newly crowned Rìgh, Lachlan.

That had been many years ago. Their twenty-four years of marriage had been years of contentment and tranquillity. Iain loved his wife and son wholeheartedly and had felt himself blessed indeed.

Yet slowly a shadow had darkened the small, quiet rhythm of their days. He had found his sleep haunted by memories of his mother and more than once had woken from sleep with a cry of fear in his throat, and tears scorching his eyes. He knew his restlessness disturbed Elfrida, for she too slept badly and woke most mornings heavy-eyed and listless. Iain had sought to spare his wife his hag-ridden nights and so had taken to sleeping in a separate room. Elfrida did not seem to sleep any better, though, and sometimes he was awoken by her crying out in the night. She complained of headaches and began to spend part of each day locked away in her room with the curtains drawn.

Once or twice a year, Iain and his wife went on a procession through Tìrsoilleir, so that Elfrida could keep in touch with her people and visit Bride, the city where she had been born. The people of Bride had always been glad to welcome her, and Iain and Elfrida would spend a few weeks being entertained by the great lords and merchants, and looking over guild agreements and new laws and the accounts of the Lord Treasurer.

The last time they had visited, there had been a noticeable difference in the way they were entertained. The people of Tìrsoilleir had always been suspicious of any kind of merrymaking, and so the feast and masques put on for them were always dour in comparison to those staged in Lucescere. This time, though, there was precious little entertaining at all. Grizelda, the new Fealde, disapproved of any sign of merriment, they were told, and sought to bring the people of Tìrsoilleir back to a godly way of life.

When Iain and Elfrida came home again to Arran, Father Maurice came with them, an appointment urged on them by Grizelda. He had been a cold, unpleasant presence ever since, as constantly behind Elfrida as her shadow. She had given up even such small pleasures that she had ever allowed herself and taken to wearing grey and black again. Iain had been sorry for it, but he loved his wife and knew that a childhood as filled with terrors as hers had been was hard to shake off.

Which was why it had been so odd to see her carrying a sumptuous gold fan on the night of the wedding. Elfrida never wore gold, and she had never carried a fan in her life, not even in the very midst of an oppressive Arran summer. She did not care for the vagaries of fashion, thinking it all vanity and frivolity. To see his mother's fan in Elfrida's hand had given Iain's heart a very queer jolt, and he had been upset and troubled ever since.

He furled and unfurled the fan a few times, and then sat down on his wife's stool so he could examine it more closely. Many of his mother's things had a trick to them. Rings that twisted open so poison could be slipped into a guest's cup, or dresses made from material that had been soaked in some toxic liquid so that the wearer died horribly, and mysteriously, far away from the giver. One pair of Margrit's shoes had a hidden blade concealed in the heel that could cut a man's hamstrings with a backward flick, and the arms of her throne had daggers concealed within that could be thrown forward with a press of one's thumb on a secret button.

It took him only a few seconds to discover the trick of the fan. He twisted one of the embossed golden sticks that framed the fan, and the knob came off in his hand. He was able to draw out a slender golden tube. Very carefully, Iain tipped the tube up and out fell three of the black barbs the bogfaeries used to kill their enemies. Handling one with great caution, Iain lifted it to his nose and sniffed. He could smell the unmistakable odor of the poison the bogfaeries distilled from one of the marsh plants.

Iain's pulse beat rapidly in his throat. He had difficulty swallowing. He carefully put the barbs back inside the golden tube and slid it back in place within the fan's frame. He furled the fan closed and held it there on his lap, his mind a blank.

The door opened, and Elfrida and Neil came in together.

"I am so glad, darling!" Elfrida cried. "Well done!"

"It is a very great honor," Neil said. "I just hope I do no' let Her Majesty down."

"Iain!" Elfrida called, but then came to a halt just inside the door, her eyes on her husband, who sat on her stool, the golden fan in his hands. The color drained away from her cheeks, leaving her a pasty white.

Neil did not notice. He came on in a great burst of excitement, his cheeks glowing with color. "*Dai-dein*! Ye'll never guess! Bronwen . . . Her Majesty has appointed me Master o' Horse. Me! I'm to ride behind her everywhere she goes, and have quarters in her wing, and everything."

"That is a very great honor," Iain said. His voice came out oddly.

Neil noticed some of his father's strain. "I ken it means I will be away from Arran for some time," he said and came to stoop over his father and kiss the bald top of his head. "But I have lived half my life in Lucescere, anyway, and I'll still come home to visit . . . though no' until wintertime!"

Iain tried to smile.

Neil rambled on. "I am to wear the Banrìgh's livery—she

has designed it herself. It is to have the MacCuinn stag quartered with the sea serpent o' the Fairgean royalty and be all in blue and white. She says I must find her a white palfrey to ride on. And Mama says she will stay a while, here in Lucescere, just until all is settled, to help me and advise me on how to go on, for indeed, it is a great leap from being a mere squire to one of the three greatest officers o' the household. Will ye stay too, *Dai-dein*?"

Iain looked at his wife, then down at the fan in his hand. He carefully laid it back in the half-open drawer and closed the drawer.

"No," he said, "I shall go home to Arran."

The Courtiers of the Court

Rhiannon came quietly in to Lewen's room, closing the door behind her. It was late afternoon, but the room was dim for the shutters had been drawn over the windows. Lewen slept, but the healer had told Rhiannon that he had woken and eaten some soup at noon and drunk some of the strengthening tea she had brewed him, and she was satisfied that he would soon recover.

The healer had spoken with great warmth and kindness to Rhiannon, for the story of how Lewen had saved her from hanging had already raced all around the Tower of Two Moons. It was considered a great romance, and Landon was already hard at work writing another ballad which he hoped would be as enormously popular as "Rhiannon's Ride."

Rhiannon had spent most of the morning with her friends, celebrating her unexpected salvation at the Nisse and Nixie with the best meal she had eaten in months, laid on for her by the ogre proprietor. She had been too shaken to eat much, though Cameron and Rafferty made up for her abstinence by gorging themselves on the roasted meats, a luxury denied to them at the Theurgia.

The Nisse and Nixie had been crowded with friends and well-wishers, with such a hubbub that Rhiannon had been overwhelmed after her months of solitude. She had sat with a glass of goldensloe wine in her hand, searching the crowd for any sign of Lewen, and then, when it was clear he was not there, trying hard not to succumb to black depression.

Nina and Gwilym had drunk a glass of wine with her, but then excused themselves, being eager to get back to Isabeau at the Tower of Two Moons. Of all those present, Nina seemed to understand best how Rhiannon felt, for she drew her close and kissed her, saying in a gentle undertone, "He was with me all night, trying to find some way o' freeing ye, Rhiannon. He didna abandon ye."

"Then where is he now?" Rhiannon said gruffly.

"I will see if I can find him for ye. He was distraught, Rhiannon, when he heard."

Rhiannon nodded and tried to smile, but it seemed to her that if Lewen had cared so much, he would have been there at the gallows with her other friends, shouting themselves hoarse in an attempt to save her. Nina kissed her and smoothed back her hair, saying, "Come to me at the palace, Rhiannon, when ye are ready. Her Majesty will wish to have audience with ye, so that ye may thank her and hear what plans she has for ye."

"Plans? She'll have plans?"

Nina nodded. "Royal pardons are rarely given without some strings attached. The Banrìgh is only young still and new to this game, so she may no' think to demand service from ye, but if so, I would be surprised. She is the Ensorcellor's daughter, after all."

"So I am no' free," Rhiannon said in heavy disappointment.

"Ye are alive," Nina said, and with that, left her.

So Rhiannon had picked at her food and drunk her wine and tried to smile, while her friends grew hilarious with relief and too much free wine, and then she had come back to the palace in company with Fèlice and Landon and Edithe, the latter being suddenly very friendly with her and wanting to walk arm in arm with Rhiannon.

"What will ye wear to see the Banrìgh?" she asked.

Rhiannon shrugged her off. "I dinna ken," she said blankly.

Edithe laughed, a silvery, tinkling sound. "Ye canna go in your prison gown, ye silly! Let me lend ye some clothes. I am considered tall, though o' course, no' as tall as ye. I am sure I'll have something that will fit. There is no time to have aught made, o' course. . . ."

"Why ye want to lend me clothes?" Rhiannon demanded.

"I just want to help," Edithe said, offended.

Rhiannon regarded her suspiciously but had no desire to

stay in her rough, itchy, lice-ridden gown anymore. "Maybe," she said. "Bath first."

"She just wants to get the notice o' the Banrìgh through ye," Fèlice whispered later as she washed Rhiannon's hair for her. "She thinks the Banrìgh will have a soft spot for ye, having saved your life, and will most likely take ye into service. Edithe would very much like to be one o' the Banrìgh's ladies-in-waiting too."

"What do ladies-in-waiting do?" Rhiannon leaned back against the rim of the hip bath, luxuriating in the hot soapy water.

"Read to the Banrìgh, and walk with her, and write her private letters for her, and sit with her in her chambers and sew," Fèlice answered.

Rhiannon screwed up her face. "Sounds boring."

"A lady-in-waiting has a lot o' power at court," Fèlice answered. "People will flatter ye, and give ye gifts, and try to persuade ye to speak on their behalf to Her Majesty, and men who wish to advance at court will woo ye."

"What woo?"

Fèlice giggled. "Ye sound like Buba, the Keybearer's owl! Woo means to court ye." At Rhiannon's look of bafflement, she giggled again. "To seek your hand in marriage."

"Men at court will court me," Rhiannon said, shaking her head in disbelief. "What a stupid language ye speak!"

"The courtiers o' the court will court ye in the courtyard most courteously," Fèlice said, laughing out loud.

"Stupid," Rhiannon repeated.

When Nina came to find her, Rhiannon was ready and waiting. Having no desire to become a lady-in-waiting, she had spurned Edithe's offer of a gown and was dressed in the rough brown breeches and white shirt that Lewen's mother, Lilanthe, had given her so long ago. In a concession to the formality of the court, she wore Lilanthe's beautiful embroidered shawl over the top, with the rowan charm Lewen had whittled her back in its accustomed spot around her neck.

Nina looked as if she had been crying again, but she smiled at Rhiannon and kissed her.

"What news o' Roden?" Rhiannon asked, and Nina sighed and shook her head.

"Laird Malvern's slipped the net again. I do no' ken how. Finn is on his trail, though, and she never fails to find what she hunts for. I just hope she finds him in time. . . ." Her voice trailed away, and Rhiannon grimaced. They both knew how ruthless was the lord of Fettercairn.

"I found Lewen," Nina said, and she smiled broadly as she told Rhiannon what Lewen had done. Once Rhiannon understood, she was transfigured. She would have gone to him at once, but Nina shook her head, saying that she must not keep the Banrìgh waiting.

"Lewen is sleeping. Ye can see him later. Come now, Rhiannon, come and make your curtsy to the Banrìgh."

She led Rhiannon through the crowded palace halls. Rhiannon had never seen so many grandly dressed people, or such rich and opulent surroundings. Her face turned from side to side as she endeavored to absorb it all.

They entered a long hall crowded with people sitting or standing, some looking bored or angry. Nina explained that these were all the people waiting to have an audience with the Banrìgh. The men in the rich doublets being mobbed at the far end of the hall were the gentlemen ushers, and they controlled who was allowed in or not. This made them very powerful, Nina explained in an undertone, and so they were much courted by those who wished to secure their favor.

"Courted?" Rhiannon said blankly. "Ye mean, their hands are sought in marriage?"

"No, no," Nina said. "People try to make friends with them, or do them favors."

"Such a stupid language," Rhiannon muttered.

Her entry caused a minor sensation. Everyone stared and murmured to each other, and a few smiled and bowed their heads or called out a friendly greeting. Rhiannon gripped her hands together and jerked her head in response, mindful of what Fèlice had said. She was grateful when the gentleman usher swung open the double doors at the end of the hall for her straightaway, as she would not have to sit and wait with all those eyes on her.

The room beyond was almost as crowded. Groups of men stood around, some with sheaves of papers in their hands. The Banrìgh sat in a high-backed chair near the window. To

Rhiannon's disappointment, she was wearing a dress much like any other woman at the court. Rhiannon had been expecting something scandalous. Sitting on low stools or on the floor were a number of women in full-skirted dresses. Some were sewing, one was reading from a book, and another was playing a clàrsach. The Banrìgh was frowning over a pile of papers on a table drawn up at her elbow. A young man with an eager face and straight brown hair that flopped into his eyes was sitting beside her, conversing with her in a low voice.

The Banrìgh was only young, but she looked pale and weary. Rhiannon had been very curious to see her, for she was always the topic of so much conversation. Rhiannon did not find her beautiful at all. Her mouth turned downwards, like a fish, and Rhiannon found the shimmering texture of her skin and her green-blue frilly fins rather repulsive. Her hair was very black and lustrous, though, and when she looked up and smiled, her whole face warmed, and Rhiannon was able to see that her eyes were a most striking silvery-blue color and very large.

Nina curtsied gracefully, and Rhiannon did her awkward best to copy her.

"Ye are Rhiannon o' Dubhslain? The lass who rides the winged horse?"

"Aye, Your Majesty."

"And where is your pretty mare?"

"I dinna ken, Your Majesty. The dragon scared her away."

"That's a shame."

"I will call her, and she will come again."

"Will she just?" The Banrìgh's interest quickened, and she looked Rhiannon over.

"Aye, she will."

"Well, I hope so. A lass that rides a winged horse! That is something new indeed. It would've been a shame to lose ye."

"Aye, Your Majesty. I mean, thank ye, Your Majesty," Rhiannon stammered and flushed, then gritted her jaw, hating to be made to look foolish.

The Banrìgh said, "I hope ye will stay close, Rhiannon. I can see a thigearn being o' great use to me in days to come."

"Aye, Your Majesty. It would be an honor to serve ye." Rhiannon spoke the words Nina had taught her, even though she did not believe them.

The Banrìgh regarded her a moment longer, her gaze thoughtful. "Call your horse to ye," she said, then abruptly, "and have a message sent to me. I would like to see ye ride her."

Rhiannon nodded and agreed, even though she had no desire to bring Blackthorn anywhere near men armed with ropes and bows and arrows. As if reading her thoughts, the Banrìgh said sweetly, "But do be careful no' to fly too far away just yet, Rhiannon. It would be a shame to have to fetch ye back again."

"Aye, Your Majesty," Rhiannon said, and then the interview was over. The Banrìgh turned back to her papers, and Nina led her out of the room.

"Ye had best call Blackthorn straightaway," Nina said. "One thing we have learned about our new Banrìgh is that she is very impatient."

Rhiannon nodded, though she seethed with rebelliousness. They were taken out to the stableyards by the young man with the floppy brown hair, whom Nina called Neil. He was the new Master of Horse, he told Nina proudly, and it was his job to overlook the work of the grooms and stablehands and to ride out with the Banrìgh each morning.

There was a big field behind the stables where a curious crowd gathered as soon as it was realized Rhiannon meant to call her flying horse. Rhiannon was angry and told Neil to tell them to all go away. After a moment's hesitation, he retreated a little but did not leave.

Rhiannon gripped her hands into fists and called to Blackthorn silently. She was anxious indeed about her horse, for the last time she had seen the winged mare, Blackthorn had been reeling from the spiteful swipe of the dragon's claw. She had fretted and worried about her ever since but had had no chance to do more than fling out a silent plea, or query, and hope that all was well.

Long minutes passed, and the crowd grew restive. Still Rhiannon called, her eyes searching the sky. Her eyesight was much keener than everyone else's. She saw the far-distant shape of the flying horse long before anyone else, and her shoulders sagged with relief. Then someone in the crowd spotted the mare, and a roar went up.

Rhiannon turned on Neil. "Tell them to shut up," she hissed, "else they'll scare her away!"

Neil looked rather taken aback at her lack of respect but did as she asked, then turned to a page to send a message to the Banrìgh.

Blackthorn came circling down, looking as delicate and unearthly as ever, with her great blue-tipped wings spread wide. She landed daintily on the grass and bowed her head to nudge Rhiannon on the shoulder before dancing away nervously, her ears back, her eyes showing a rim of white. There was a long cut on her flank, crusted with dried blood. Rhiannon examined it anxiously, but thankfully it was shallow. The dragon had judged its swipe precisely.

Rhiannon soothed and petted the mare lovingly, reassuring her and bringing her to eat at a trough Neil had ordered filled with warm oat mash. Blackthorn fed greedily and drank some water, then allowed Rhiannon to tend the scratch. Then, and only then, did Rhiannon mount her winged beast and fly around the field, much to the delight of the watching courtiers. Blackthorn flew easily, not at all troubled by her sore flank, and Rhiannon felt a warm tide of happiness rise up through her. She was free, she was alive, Lewen loved her, and the Banrìgh had called her a thigearn. A thigearn would not be expected to stay at court and sew a fine seam and listen to gossip. Perhaps the Banrìgh had other, more exciting plans for her.

Rhiannon's face was glowing when she made her way back to the Banrìgh, who was watching intently from the sidelines.

Bronwen nodded at the sight of her. "A bonny creature," she said. "Tell me, how far can she fly?"

"A long way," Rhiannon said. "I do' ken how far. When I first captured her, she flew many, many miles, all the way down from Dubhslain to Lewen's parents' farm."

"Two hundred miles or more, Your Majesty," Nina said.

"And how fast can she fly?" Bronwen asked.

"Very fast," Rhiannon replied and added belatedly, at Nina's frown, "Your Majesty." Rhiannon thought it was a stupid thing to call a woman who was only a few years older than she, but then, many, many things these humans did seemed stupid.

"Excellent," Bronwen said. "Let me think on this. I will call ye when I want ye."

Rhiannon nodded, and then, as Nina nudged her sharply with her elbow, said woodenly, "Aye, Your Majesty. It would be an honor to serve ye."

Bronwen's face relaxed into a spontaneous smile, which made Rhiannon understand, for the first time, why she was considered so beautiful. Then the Banrìgh walked away with a beautiful liquid movement that Rhiannon found fascinating. Looking around her, she saw she was not the only one.

Rhiannon spent another happy half hour with Blackthorn in the stable, grooming her and feeding her carrots. Then, wiping her slobbery hand on her breeches, she had gone in search of Lewen.

Now she stood, watching him sleep. His lashes made two dark crescents on his cheeks, and he breathed shallowly, occasionally turning his head against the pillow. Once he muttered her name, and Rhiannon's pulse leaped.

There was a warm, painful glow about her heart. Lewen had saved her. He could have died, everyone said so, and yet he had risked his life and limbs to stop the bell from ringing. He must love her. No matter what spell that witch Olwynne had cast upon him, somehow Lewen had remembered her, the girl he had named Rhiannon.

She took his hand and pressed it to her cheek. He sighed and stirred and turned his head on the pillow. She laid down his hand, stripped off her clothes and, naked except for the wooden charm around her neck, slipped into bed beside him.

At the feel of her bare skin, he roused sleepily. She pressed every inch of her long body against him, wrapping her arm about his chest and kissing the side of his neck. He turned towards her, still half-asleep, and she kissed his ear, and then his cheek, and then his mouth. The kiss was all sweetness, a long, slow, languorous kiss that made her shiver with longing and grief.

She lifted her mouth away and dropped a kiss on his chest, laying down her head so her black hair flowed over him.

"Rhiannon," he whispered.

She could not look at him. "Aye," she whispered back.

"What are ye doing here? Ye should no' . . ."

She did not want to hear him, so she burrowed her head under the bedclothes, kissing and licking and biting her way

down his body. There was a great bruise on one side, and she
kissed it gently and eased her weight away from it, tangling his
thick dark pubic hair with her fingers. He moaned. With her
mouth and her hand, she pleasured him, and his response was
fierce and immediate. When he was so close to climax that his
back was arching, she mounted him and took him within her,
feeling her own urgent desire flowering. For a few fast, frantic
moments, they coupled, each panting and crying aloud, and
then together they subsided, still glued together.

Lewen ran his hands down her back to her buttocks, and
then up again. "Rhiannon."

"Aye."

They were silent. His hands repeated their slow caress. She
felt his chest heave beneath her. She sighed herself and eased
herself away from him, curling up against his side.

He tangled his fingers in her hair. "Rhiannon, ye should
no' . . . *I* should no' . . ."

"Ye saved me," she said fiercely.

"Aye," he answered and smoothed her hair down.

"They had the noose about my neck. They were yelling to
him to hang me, but he wouldna, for the bell had no' rung. He
said he had to wait for the bell to ring. But ye stopped it, ye
stopped it!"

"That's good," he said, and put one hand up to gingerly feel
the great bruise marring his temple.

She bent her head and kissed his hand. When she glanced up
again, there was a long look between them, charged with emotion that was impossible to read.

"That's good," he said again and sighed.

"Why did ye do it?" she demanded. "I thought ye hated me."

"The bluebird came to me," he answered, lifting his other
hand and letting it fall. "I . . ."

He stopped, unable to frame the words.

"I could no' let ye die," he said at last, simply.

"I'm glad," she said in that same fierce, exultant voice. "Me
yours, ye mine."

He bit his lip and looked away. "Olwynne . . ."

"That's all a lie and a sham," she said. "She ensorcelled ye!
She's a witch and a cursehag, and I will never, ever forgive
her."

"She's been taken," he said and felt tears flood into his eyes. "Owein and Roden too. Laird Malvern has them. He means to kill them—I ken it!"

"I imagine so," she agreed.

Lewen could not speak.

She frowned. "Ye're mine," she reminded him. "No' hers! Why do ye look so?"

"She was always my friend, my dearest friend, and Owein too," he managed to say. "And . . . I still love her, Rhiannon! We are handfasted!"

She jerked a shoulder. "So what? Anyone can jump a fire together. It is what's in here that matters!" She pounded her heart.

He shut his eyes. "I ken. I ken. Oh, but Rhiannon . . ."

She lay silently for a moment. "Ye say ye love her still," she said at last. "Do ye mean ye do no' love me?"

"I dinna ken," he said miserably. "I mean, I do, I do, Eà damn it, I do! When ye are with me, when I think o' ye being hanged . . ." He shuddered. "But there is something . . . that ties me still to her. I canna understand it. I never thought this could happen to me. I've always believed, I've always thought . . . but . . . still there is something . . ."

She got up.

"Where are ye going?" he asked. There was despair in his voice.

"I am going to get her," she said.

Whatever Lewen had been expecting, it was not this. He gaped at her in surprise, then rose up on one elbow as she began to drag on her clothes.

"Rhiannon! What do ye mean? Where are ye going?"

"I will call Blackthorn, and I will go and save her from that blaygird laird," she said matter-of-factly. "And Owein and Roden too. I dinna want him to kill Roden."

"But . . . but . . . why?" was all Lewen managed to say.

"Ye're mine," she said passionately. "I will go and save her, and then I'll get her by the neck and I'll squeeze and squeeze until she swears to let ye go again. If a spell can be spun, it can be undone, and she's the only one who can do it."

"What if it is no spell?" Lewen asked.

She looked at him in surprise and scorn. "O' course it's a spell. She's a witch, isn't she? A witch who wanted my man.

Well, she's no' going to have ye. Ye're mine! And I'll make her admit it if I have to kill her to do it."

Lewen could not help but laugh. "Oh, Rhiannon."

"What?"

"I'm sorry," he said awkwardly. "Everything is all such a mess. I dinna ken. . . ."

"I do," she said. "Ye saved me. Ye mine and me yours. What else is there to ken?"

He lay back down, watching with regret as she covered up her nakedness.

"Naught," he said. "Naught at all."

Black into Black

Thunder growled as deep and menacing as a shadow-hound. Lightning stalked the horizon, and all the horses in the stable shifted uneasily, their hooves clattering on the cobblestones.

"Are ye sure ye wish to do this?" Nina said, clasping her hands together. "It'll be so dangerous. Are ye sure, Rhiannon?"

Rhiannon looked up from the girth she was tightening. "Sure I'm sure."

"Oh, thank ye, Rhiannon, thank ye! We will no' be far behind ye. We'll be following just as fast as we can. And Finn and Jay are close on their heels too. Ye will no' need to face them alone. Just find them for us, and . . . and . . ." She faltered, not wanting to say *and save my little boy for me*, but meaning it nonetheless.

Rhiannon nodded and gathered the reins together, swinging into the soft saddle she used to pad Blackthorn's bony back.

"Just send me the wee bluebird if ye have news," Nina gabbled. Tears were streaming down her face, and she wiped them away impatiently. "It'll ken how to find me. Birds always do."

Rhiannon lifted her hand to the bluebird perched on her shoulder. It trilled gaily in response, and flitted down to the pommel of the saddle, and then across to Nina's shoulder. She caressed it, then handed it back to Rhiannon, who tucked it away in the breast pocket of her coat. Rain began to pound down into the stableyard, turning the ground to mud, and Rhiannon drew her cloak more firmly about her.

Once again Rhiannon was wearing the thick blue cloak and tam-o'-shanter that had once belonged to Connor, but this time she wore them honorably, with the permission and blessing of

the Banrìgh Bronwen Mathilde NicCuinn. It seemed that she
and Bronwen had had the same idea, for when Rhiannon had
gone to the gentlemen ushers and demanded an audience with
the Banrìgh, it was to find a page had just been sent to summon
her.

Apart from the natural affection with which Bronwen regarded her cousins, it was clear to the Banrìgh that she must be
seen to be making strenuous attempts to rescue them from the
lord of Fettercairn if she was ever going to be free of malicious
gossip concerning their disappearance. She had done everything she could think of to waylay the evil lord and his minions,
but again and again he had somehow managed to evade capture. It was clear his plans had been extremely well laid, and he
had spent a great deal of money in ensuring nothing could go
wrong.

Having escaped Lucescere by boat, he had ditched the yacht
at the first village and had fine horses ready and waiting. Riding hell-for-leather, they had cut across country and been met
by two light traveling carriages, each pulled by four strong
horses. Bronwen had arranged for the roads to be blockaded,
but he had galloped through the first barricade and disappeared
somewhere before the second.

Finn had found the tracks of the carriages leading into the
forest, her latest message had said. Their own horses were
foundering, however, and she thought it would take some time
to find more as every hack in the area had been mysteriously
bought the previous week.

Bronwen was seriously disturbed by this news. The lord of
Fettercairn must be found and stopped, yet his lead on his pur-
suers was growing with every hour. It was clear to her that their
best chance of finding Owein and Olwynne and Roden was to
send Rhiannon and Blackthorn after them. It was a perilous mis-
sion, to send one young woman after a gang of desperate kid-
nappers and murderers who had already shown their utter
ruthlessness, but Bronwen considered Rhiannon's life hers, since
she had saved her from the gallows at the very last moment, and
she was prepared to say so quite strongly, if Rhiannon was to
balk at the job.

Bronwen had been most pleased then, when, having
explained all this to Rhiannon with the utmost care and tact,

Rhiannon had agreed readily, saying, "Och, aye, but o' course. That is why I am here. I go now."

Bronwen had smiled. "First, let me make it official. If ye ride on my business, ye must be made one o' my own guards. I canna call ye a Yeoman—can we say Yeo-woman?"

"I dinna think so!" Captain Dillon had protested, white-lipped with horror. "Your Majesty, I must protest!"

"What, at the word, or the entire concept?" Bronwen's mouth had hardened.

Captain Dillon took a deep breath, ready to speak angrily, but she had held up her hand. "No' now, Captain Dillon! I have no' the time nor the patience to listen. Our only concern now must be getting back my cousins. I hereby name thee, Rhiannon o' Dubhslain, the Banrìgh's own guard. When ye are safely returned to us, I will have a new livery made for ye. In white, I think. But for now, ye can wear the blue o' the Yeomen. Very well?"

"Aye!" Rhiannon had cried, filled with fierce gladness. And so she wore the cloak and hat that had once belonged to Connor, with a white shield hastily tacked on to the breast, showing Bronwen's new arms, the MacCuinn stag quartered with a white sea serpent.

Her saddlebags hung on Blackthorn's withers, loaded once again with supplies and weapons, as well as a signed and sealed contract from Bronwen giving her the freedom to demand help in the Banrìgh's name. Bronwen had felt no need to warn Rhiannon not to abuse this privilege, but Captain Dillon had, in no uncertain terms. Rhiannon had only smiled.

"I must be off," she said now to Nina. "I'll do my best to get him back for ye."

"I ken how good your best is," Nina said, weeping again. "Thank ye!"

Rhiannon nodded, gave her an awkward salute, and wheeled Blackthorn about, trotting out of the stable and into the yard. A stableboy opened the gate for her, and she urged Blackthorn forward, bending her head against the icy sleet lashing her face.

A dark figure lurched at her out of the darkness. Blackthorn whinnied and reared in fright. Rhiannon brought her down with an iron hand on the reins, and drew her dagger, wheeling the mare about.

Lightning flashed, frighteningly close. It hit the top of a nearby oak tree with a great whizz and bang and a sudden leap of silver fire. Blackthorn screamed and reared again, almost throwing Rhiannon. The dark figure put up a hand and seized Blackthorn's bridle and, at the familiar touch of the hand and the familiar smell and murmur, the winged horse quietened and came back down to earth.

"Lewen!" Rhiannon cried.

His wet hair was plastered to his head, and water streamed down his face. "Rhiannon! I could no' let ye go without—"

His words faltered. He seized her arm. She bent and they kissed passionately, their skin wet and cold, the rain pounding on their backs. It was so cold, their breath blew in white plumes when at last they drew reluctantly apart.

"Rhiannon, Rhiannon!" he cried. "Have a care for yourself!"

"I will."

His breath heaved. "Come back to me," he managed to say.

"I will."

He stepped back, and Rhiannon dug her heels into Blackthorn's sides. The winged horse sprang up and away and disappeared into the storm, black into black.

Glossary

acolytes: students of witchcraft who have not yet passed their Second Test of Powers; usually aged between eight and sixteen
ahdayeh: a series of exercises used as meditation in motion. Derived from the Khan'cohban art of fighting
apprentice-witch: a student of witchcraft who has passed the Second Test of Powers, usually undertaken at the age of sixteen
arak: a small, monkeylike creature
Arran: southeast land of Eileanan, ruled by the MacFóghnan clan
Aslinn: deeply forested land ruled by the MacAislin clan

banprionnsa: princess or duchess
banrìgh: queen
Beltane: May Day; the first day of summer
Ben Eyrie: third highest mountain in Eileanan; part of the Broken Ring of Dubhslain
blaygird: evil, awful
Blèssem: rich farmland south of Rionnagan, ruled by the MacThanach clan
Blue Guards: the Yeomen of the Guard, the Rìgh's own elite company of soldiers. They act as his personal bodyguard, both on the battlefield and in peacetime
Brann the Raven: one of the First Coven of Witches. Known for probing the darker mysteries of magic and for fascination with machinery and technology
Broken Ring of Dubhslain: mountains that curve in a crescent around the highlands of Ravenshaw
Bronwen NicCuinn: daughter of former Rìgh Jaspar MacCuinn

and Maya the Ensorcellor; she was named Banrìgh of Eileanan by her father on his deathbed but ruled for just six hours as a newborn baby, before Lachlan the Winged wrested the throne from her.

Candlemas: the end of winter and beginning of spring

Carraig: land of the sea-witches; the northernmost land of Eileanan, ruled by the MacSeinn clan

Celestines: race of faery creatures renowned for empathic abilities and knowledge of stars and prophecy

Clachan: the southernmost land of Eileanan, a province of Rionnagan ruled by the MacCuinn clan

claymore: a heavy, two-edged sword, often as tall as a man

cluricaun: a small woodland faery

Connor: a Yeoman of the Guard. Was once a beggar boy in Lucescere and member of the League of the Healing Hand

corrigan: a mountain faery with the power of assuming the look of a boulder. The most powerful can cast other illusions

Coven of Witches: the central ruling body for witches in Eileanan, led by the Keybearer and a council of twelve other sorcerers and sorceresses called the Circle. The Coven administers all rites and rituals in the worship of the universal life force witches call Eà, runs schools and hospitals, and advises the Crown.

Craft: applications of the One Power through spells, incantations and magical objects

Cripple, The: the leader of the rebellion against the rule of Jaspar and Maya

Cuinn Lionheart: the leader of the First Coven of Witches; his descendants are called MacCuinn.

Cunning: applications of the One Power through will and desire

cunning man: a village wise man or warlock

cursehags: a wicked faery race, prone to curses and evil spells. Known for their filthy personal habits

dai-dein: father

Day of Betrayal: the day Jaspar the Ensorcelled turned on the witches, exiling or executing them and burning the Witch Towers

Dedrie: a healer at Fettercairn Castle; was formerly nursemaid to Rory, the young son of Lord Falkner MacFerris

Dide the Juggler: a jongleur who was rewarded for his part in Lachlan the Winged's successful rebellion by being made Didier Laverock, Earl of Caerlaverock. Is often called the Rìgh's minstrel.

Dillon of the Joyous Sword: Captain of the Yeomen of the Guard. Was once a beggar boy and Captain of the League of the Healing Hand

Donncan Feargus MacCuinn: eldest son of Lachlan MacCuinn and Iseult NicFaghan. Has wings like a bird and can fly. Was named for Lachlan's two brothers, who were transformed into blackbirds by Maya the Ensorcellor

Dughall MacBrann: the Prionnsa of Ravenshaw and cousin to the Rìgh

Eà: the Great Life Spirit, mother and father of all

Eileanan: largest island in the archipelago called the Far Islands

Elemental Powers: the forces of air, earth, fire, water, and spirit that together make up the One Power

Enit Silverthroat: grandmother of Dide and Nina; died at the Battle of Bonnyblair

equinox: a time when day and night are of equal length, occurring twice a year

Fairge; Fairgean: faery creatures who need both sea and land to live

Falkner MacFerris: former lord of Fettercairn Castle

Fettercairn Castle: a fortress guarding the pass into the highlands of Ravenshaw and the Tower of Ravens. Owned by the MacFerris clan

Finn the Cat: nickname of Fionnghal NicRuraich

Fionnghal NicRuraich: eldest daughter of Anghus MacRuraich of Rurach; was once a beggar girl in Lucescere and Lieutenant of the League of the Healing Hand.

First Coven of Witches: thirteen witches who fled persecution in their own land, invoking an ancient spell that folded the fabric of the universe and brought them and all their followers to Eileanan in a journey called the Great Crossing. The eleven great clans of

Eileanan are all descended from the First Coven, with the MacCuinn clan being the greatest of the eleven. The thirteen witches were Cuinn Lionheart, his son Owein of the Longbow, Ahearn Horse-laird, Aislinna the Dreamer, Berhtilde the Bright Warrior-Maid, Fóghnan the Thistle, Rùraich the Searcher, Seinneadair the Singer, Sian the Storm-Rider, Tuathanach the Farmer, Brann the Raven, Faodhagan the Red, and his twin sister Sorcha the Bright (now called the Murderess).

Gearradh: goddess of death; of the Three Spinners, Gearradh is she who cuts the thread.
gillie: personal servant
gillie-coise: bodyguard
Gladrielle the Blue: the smaller of the two moons, lavender-blue in color
gravenings: ravenous creatures that nest and swarm together, steal lambs and chickens from farmers, and have been known to steal babies and young children. Will eat anything they can carry away in their claws. Collective noun is "screech."
Greycloaks: the Rìgh's army, so called because of their camouflaging cloaks

Hogmanay: New Year's Eve; an important celebration in the culture of Eileanan
Horned Ones: another name for the satyricorns, a race of fierce horned faeries

Irving: seneschal at Fettercairn Castle
Isabeau the Shapechanger: Keybearer of the Coven; twin sister of the Banrìgh Iseult NicFaghan
Iseult of the Snows: twin sister of Isabeau NicFaghan; Banrìgh of Eileanan by marriage to Lachlan the Winged
Iven Yellowbeard: a jongleur and courier in the service of Lachlan the Winged; was formerly a Yeoman of the Guard; married to Nina the Nightingale and father to Roden.

Jaspar MacCuinn: former Rìgh of Eileanan, often called Jaspar the Ensorcelled. Was married to Maya the Ensorcellor
Jay the Fiddler: a minstrel in the service of Lachlan the

Winged. Was once a beggar boy in Lucescere and member of the League of the Healing Hand

Johanna: a healer. Was once a beggar girl in Lucescere and member of the League of the Healing Hand

jongleur: a traveling minstrel, juggler, conjurer

journeywitch: a traveling witch who performs rites for villages that do not have a witch and seeks out children with magical powers who can be taken on as acolytes

Keybearer: the leader of the Coven of Witches

Khan'cohbans: a faery race of warlike, snow-skimming nomads who live on the high mountains of the Spine of the World

Lachlan the Winged: Rìgh of Eileanan

League of the Healing Hand: a band of beggar children who were instrumental in helping Lachlan the Winged win his throne

leannan: sweetheart

Lewen: an apprentice-witch and squire to Lachlan; son of Lilanthe of the Forest and Niall the Bear

Lilanthe of the Forest: a tree-shifter; married to Niall the Bear, and mother to Lewen and Meriel

loch; lochan (pl): lake

Lucescere: ancient city built on an island above the Shining Waters; the traditional home of the MacCuinns and the Tower of Two Moons

Mac: son of

MacAhern: one of the eleven great clans; descendants of Ahearn Horse-laird

MacBrann: one of the eleven great clans; descendants of Brann the Raven

MacCuinn: one of the eleven great clans, descendants of Cuinn Lionheart

Magnysson the Red: the larger of the two moons, crimson red in color, commonly thought of as a symbol of war and conflict. Old tales describe him as a thwarted lover, chasing his lost love, Gladrielle, across the sky.

Malvern MacFerris: lord of Fettercairn Castle; brother of former lord Falkner MacFerris

Maya the Ensorcellor: former Banrìgh of Eileanan, wife of Jaspar and mother of Bronwen; now known as Maya the Mute
moonbane: a hallucinogenic drug distilled from the moonflower plant

necromancy: the forbidden art of resurrecting the dead
Niall the Bear: formerly a Yeoman of the Guard; now married to Lilanthe of the Forest, and father to Lewen and Meriel
Nic: daughter of
Nila: king of the Fairgean; half brother of Maya the Ensorcellor
Nina the Nightingale: jongleur and sorceress of the Coven; sister to Didier Laverock, earl of Caerlaverock, and granddaughter of Enit Silverthroat
nisse: a small woodland faery

Olwynne NicCuinn: daughter of Lachlan MacCuinn and Iseult NicFaghan; twin sister of Owein
One Power: the life-energy that is contained in all things. Witches draw upon the One Power to perform their acts of magic. The One Power contains all the elemental forces of air, earth, water, fire and spirit, and witches are usually more powerful in one force than others.
Owein MacCuinn: second son of Lachlan MacCuinn and Iseult NicFaghan; twin brother of Olwynne. Has wings like a bird

prionnsa; prionnsachan (pl): prince, duke.

Ravenscraig: estate of the MacBrann clan. Once their hunting castle, but they moved their home there after Rhyssmadill fell into ruin
Ravenshaw: the deeply forested land west of Rionnagan, ruled by the MacBrann clan, descendants of Brann, one of the First Coven of Witches
Razor's Edge: a dangerous path through the mountains of the Broken Ring of Dubhslain, only used in times of great need
Red Guards: soldiers in service to Maya the Ensorcellor during her reign as Banrìgh
Rhiannon: a half-satyricorn; daughter of One-Horn and a captured human

Rhyssmadill: the Rìgh's castle by the sea, once owned by the MacBrann clan

rìgh; rìghrean (pl): king

Rionnagan: together with Clachan and Blèssem, the richest lands in Eileanan. Ruled by MacCuinns, descendants of Cuinn Lionheart, leader of the First Coven of Witches

Roden: son of Nina the Nightingale and Iven Yellow-beard; Viscount Laverock of Caerlaverock

Rory: deceased son of Lord Falkner MacFerris of Fettercairn and Lady Evaline NicKinney

Rurach: wild mountainous land lying between Tìreich and Siantan, and ruled by the MacRuraich clan

sabre leopard: a savage feline with curved fangs that lives in the remote mountain areas

sacred woods: ash, hazel, oak, rowan, fir, hawthorn, and yew

Samhain: the first day of winter; festival for the souls of the dead. Best time of year to see the future

satyricorn: a race of fierce horned faeries

scrying: to perceive through crystal gazing or other focus. Most witches can scry if the object to be perceived is well known to them.

Seekers: a force created by former Rìgh Jaspar the Ensorcelled to find those with magical abilities so they could be tried and executed

seelie: a tall, shy race of faeries known for their physical beauty and magical skills

seneschal: steward

sennachie: the genealogist and record-keeper of the clan chief's house

sgian dubh: a small knife worn in the boot

Siantan: northwest land of Eileanan, famous for its weather witches. Ruled by the MacSian clan

skeelie: a village witch or wise woman

Skill: a common application of magic, such as lighting a candle or dowsing for water

Spinners: goddesses of fate. Include the spinner Sniomhar, the goddess of birth; the weaver Breabadair, goddess of life; and she who cuts the thread, Gearradh, goddess of death

Talent: the combination of a witch's strengths in the different forces often manifest as a particularly powerful Talent; for example, Lewen's Talent is in working with wood and Nina's is in singing.

Test of Elements: once witches are fully accepted into the Coven at the age of twenty-four, they learn Skills in the element in which they are strongest, i.e. air, earth, fire, water, or spirit. The First Test of any element wins them a ring that is worn on the right hand. If they pass the Third Test in any one element, the witch is called a sorcerer or sorceress and wears a ring on his or her left hand. It is very rare for any witch to win a sorceress ring in more than one element.

Test of Powers: a witch is first tested on his or her eighth birthday, and if any magical powers are detected, he or she becomes an acolyte. On their sixteenth birthday, witches undertake the Second Test of Powers, in which they must make a moonstone ring and witch's dagger. If they pass, they are permitted to become apprentices. On their twenty-fourth birthday, witches undertake the Third Test of Powers, in which they must remake their dagger and cut and polish a staff. If successfully completed, the apprentice is admitted into the Coven of Witches. Apprentices wear black robes; witches wear white robes.

Theurgia: a school for acolytes and apprentice-witches at the Tower of Two Moons in Lucescere

thigearn: horse-lairds who ride flying horses

Tìreich: land of the horse-lairds. Most westerly country of Eileanan, ruled by the MacAhern clan

Tìrlethan: land of the Twins; ruled by the MacFaghan clan

Tìrsoilleir: the Bright Land or the Forbidden Land. Northeast land of Eileanan, ruled by the MacHilde clan

Tòmas the Healer: a boy with healing powers who saved the lives of thousands of soldiers during the Bright Wars; died saving Lachlan's life at the Battle of Bonnyblair

The Towers of the Witches: thirteen towers built as centers of learning and witchcraft in the twelve lands of Eileanan. Most are now ruined, but the Tower of Two Moons in Lucescere has been restored as the home of the Coven of Witches and its school, the Theurgia. The Coven hope to rebuild the thirteen

High Towers but also to encourage towns and regions to build their own towers.

tree-changer: a woodland faery that can shift shape from tree to humanlike creature. A half-breed is called a *tree-shifter* and can sometimes look almost human.

trictrac: a form of backgammon

uile-bheist; uile-bheistean (pl): monster

Yedda: sea-witches

Yeomen of the Guard: Also known as the Blue Guards. The Rìgh's own personal bodyguard, responsible for his safety

Kate Forsyth lives in Sydney, Australia, with her husband, Greg; their three children, Benjamin, Timothy and Eleanor; a little black cat called Shadow; and thousands of books. She has wanted to be a writer for as long as she can remember and has certainly been writing stories from the time she learned to hold a pen. Being allowed to read, write, and daydream as much as she likes and call it working is the most wonderful life imaginable and so she thanks you all for making it possible.

You can read more about Kate on her Web site at http://www.ozemail.com.au/~kforsyth or send a message to her at kforsyth@ozemail.com.au.